NEVADA BARR

ILLWIND

AVON BOOKS NEW YORK

For Deb and Ed, without whom...
Well, frankly, I shudder to think.

AVON BOOKS, INC.
1350 Avenue of the Americas
New York, New York 10019

Copyright © 1995 by Nevada Barr
Published by arrangement with The Putnam Publishing Group
Visit our website at www.AvonBooks.com
Library of Congress Catalog Card Number: 94-33370
ISBN: 0-380-72363-8

First Avon Books Printing: April 1996
First Avon Books Special Printing: November 1995

AVON TRADEMARK REG. U.S. PAT. OFF. AND IN OTHER COUNTRIES, MARCA REGISTRADA, HECHO EN U.S.A.

Printed in the U.S.A.

WCD 10 9 8 7

ILL WIND

1

NO GRAVEYARDS; that bothered Anna. People died. Unless you ate them, burned them, or mailed them to a friend, the bodies had to go somewhere. In any event, there would at least be bones. A civilization that lived and died for six hundred years should leave a mountain of bones.

No graveyards and then no people. Inhabitants cooking, weaving, farming one day, then, the next, gone. Pots still on cold ashes, doormats rotting in doorways, tools lying beside half-finished jobs.

So: an invading army swooped down and massacred everybody. Then where were the bashed-in skulls? Chipped bone fragments? Teeth sown like corn?

A plague: the American version of the Black Death, an antiquated form of Captain Tripps, killing two out of every three people. The survivors abandoning a desolated community, carting thousands and thousands of dead bodies with them? Not bloody likely. Not in a society without benefit of the wheel.

Once people got factored into an equation all bets were off; still, there ought to be corpses. Anna couldn't think of any civilization that couldn't be counted on to leave corpses and garbage for the next generation.

*　　*　　*

A hand smacked down on the Formica and Anna started in her chair.

"Where were you?" hissed Alberta Stinson, head of Interpretation for Chapin Mesa.

"Anywhere but here, Al," Anna whispered back. She dragged a hand down her face to clear it of dreams and looked surreptitiously at her watch. The staff meeting had been dragging on for two hours. The coffee was gone and there never had been any doughnuts.

Stinson poked Anna in the ribs with a blunt forefinger. "Stay awake. The Boys are on a rampage." Al always referred to Mesa Verde's administration rather disdainfully as "The Boys." Stinson was fifteen pounds over what the glossy magazines recommended, with salt-and-pepper hair that looked as if it had been cut with pinking shears. Leading tours, giving programs, wandering the myriad ruins on the mesas, she had a face creased by the weather from forehead to chin, and the skin around her eyes was crinkled from squinting against the sun's glare. Near as Anna could tell, the woman had but two passions in life: discovering why the Old Ones had vanished and seeing to it that any despoilers of their relics did likewise.

Anna pulled Stinson's yellow pad toward her. Beneath Al's sketches of nooses, guillotines, and other means of mayhem, she scribbled: "No help here. I'm a lowly GS-7. No teeth."

Al snorted.

Thirty minutes had elapsed since Anna had mentally checked out and still the debate raged. Money had come down from Congress, scads of the stuff, allocated for the digging up and replacing of the antiquated waterline serving the homes and public buildings of Mesa Verde National Park. Since May heavy machinery and heated arguments had roared over the ancient land. Meetings had been called and called off on a weekly basis.

The resultant acrimony clogged the high desert air like dust from the ditcher. As always in small towns, toxins trickled down. When the powers that be waged war, the peasants took sides. Even the seasonals gathered in tight groups, biting assorted backs and sipping righteous indignation with beer chasers.

New to the mesa, Anna'd not been drafted into either army, but the constant dissension wore at her nerves and aggravated her hermit tendencies.

Around a table of metal and Formica—the kind usually reserved for the serving of bad chicken at awards banquets—sat the leading players: a lean and hungry-looking administrative officer with a head for figures and an eye for progress; the chief ranger, a wary whip of a man determined to drag the park out of the dark ages of plumbing and into the more impressive visitation statistics additional water would allow; Ted Greeley, the contractor hired to pull off this feat in a timely manner; and Al Stinson: historian, archaeologist, and defender of the dead. Or at least the sanctity of science's claim on the dead.

When the Anasazi had vanished from the mesa, their twelfth-century secrets had vanished with them. Stinson was determined to stop twentieth-century machinery from destroying any clue before it was studied. Since the entire landscape of Chapin Mesa was a treasure trove of artifacts, the digging of so much as a post hole gave the archaeologist nightmares. The contractor had been brought on board to trench seventeen miles of land six feet deep.

Theodore Roosevelt Greeley of Greeley Construction had a job to do and was being paid handsomely to do it.

Though Greeley had a veneer of bonhomie, he struck Anna as a hard-core capitalist. She suspected that to his modern Manifest Destiny mentality, the only good Indian was a profitable Indian.

Fingers ever-tensed on the purse strings, the chief ranger and the administrative officer leaned toward Greeley's camp.

Anna and Hills Dutton, the district ranger, were the only noncombatants present. Dutton's impressive form was slouched in a folding chair near the end of the table. He'd removed the ammunition from the magazine of his Sig Sauer nine-millimeter and appeared to be inventorying it bullet by bullet.

"Anna?"

As was his want, the chief ranger was mumbling and it took her a second to recognize her name.

"What?"

"Any input?" The chief was just shifting the heat from himself. None of this august body gave two hoots about what she thought. She and Hills were there only because the secretary refused to go for coffee.

"Well, if all nonessential personnel were required to live out of the park the problem would be alleviated considerably." Nonessential included not only seasonal interpreters, but also archaeologists, department heads, the administrative officer, the chief ranger, and the superintendent himself. Anna's suggestion was met with annoyed silence. Satisfied she'd offended everyone at the table and it would be a good long time before they again bothered her for her "input," Anna retreated back into her own world.

When visitors left for the day and evening light replaced noon's scientific glare, she escaped the hubbub.

It soothed her to be where the people weren't. After working backcountry in wilderness parks—Guadalupe Mountains in Texas and Isle Royale in Lake Superior—Mesa Verde, with its quarter million–plus visitors each year, struck her as urban. During the day, when the ruins were open to the public, she couldn't walk far enough to escape the hum of traffic and the sullen growl of buses idling as they disgorged tour groups.

After closing time, on the pretext of a patrol, she would slip down into the new quiet of Cliff Palace, one of the largest of the Anasazi villages ever discovered. Climbing as high as was allowed, she would sit with her back to the still-warm stone of the ancient walls, around her rooms and turrets and towers, sunken chambers connected by tunnels, plazas with stone depressions for grinding.

The pueblo hung above a world that fell away for a hundred miles, mesas, buttes, and green valleys fading to the blue of the distant mountain ranges that drifted into the blue of the sky. The air was crisp and thin. Without moisture to laden it with perfumes, it carried only the sharp scent baked from piñon and ponderosa.

From her perch high in the ruin she would gaze down Cliff Canyon. Dwellings appeared singly, first one, then two, then half a dozen, like the hidden pictures in a child's puzzle.

Tiny jewel cities tucked in natural alcoves beneath the mesa stood sentinel over the twisting valleys. Nearly all faced west or southwest, catching the heat of the winters' sun, providing shade through the summers. The towns were built with fine craftsmanship, the work of practiced masons evident in the hand-chipped and fitted stones. Walls were whitewashed and painted, and decorations of stars and handprints enlivened the sandstone. Doorways were made in the shape of keyholes. Ladders, constructed of juniper and hide, reached rooms built on shelves forty and fifty feet above the slate of the alcove's floor.

These were not tents for folding and slipping away silently into the night. These were edifices, art, architecture. Homes built to last the centuries. If the builders had been driven out, surely the marauders would have taken up residence, enjoyed their spoils?

If the Old Ones had not died and they'd not left of their own volition and they'd not been driven out . . .

Then what? Anna thought.

Food for thought.

Plots for Von Daniken.

Anna's radio crackled to life and everyone at the table, including Al, looked at her as if she'd made a rude noise.

"Excuse me," she murmured.

As she left the room she found herself hoping for something dire: a brawl at the concession dorm, another medical at Cliff Palace, a bus wreck—anything to keep her out of the staff meeting.

"Seven hundred, three-one-two," she answered the call.

"Could you come by the CRO?" the dispatcher asked. Frieda, the chief ranger's secretary and the park dispatcher, was always even-toned and professional. From her voice one could never tell whether a bloody nose or grand-theft auto awaited at the chief ranger's office.

"I'm on my way. And thank you."

"KFC seven hundred, fourteen-eighteen."

The chief ranger's office was built from blocks of native stone and beamed-in logs darkened by time. Like the museum and the upper-echelon permanent employees' houses, the CRO was a historic structure built in the nineteen thirties by the Civilian Conservation Corps when "another day, another dollar" was the literal truth.

Anna banged through the screen door and leaned on the glass-topped counter. In true bureaucratic fashion, the inside of the graceful little building had been cobbled into cramped "work areas" and further vandalized by the addition of indoor-outdoor carpeting and cheap metal desks.

Frieda Dierkz looked up from her computer. In her thirties, with short reddish-brown hair cut in an ear-length wedge, more hips than shoulders and more brains than just about anybody else in the Visitor Protection and Fire Management Division, Frieda was the heart of the office. Or, more correctly, as the computer-generated sign on the bulletin board above her desk announced, Queen of the Office. Anna guessed there'd been a time, maybe not yet quite past, when Frieda had hoped to be Queen of a more intimate realm. But a plain face and, more damaging to matrimonial prospects, an air of absolute competence, had made her a career woman.

Though Frieda might have seen that as a bad thing, Anna didn't. It was always the breadwinner, she'd noticed, who had the adventures. Support staff—whether at work or in the kitchen—seemed ever relegated to keeping the tedious home fires burning.

"So . . ." Anna said for openers.

"Patsy called. Tom's in the park." As ever, Frieda was economical with words.

Patsy Silva was the superintendent's secretary; Tom the estranged husband. Ex-husband. "What this time? Bad guitar music at three A.M.?"

"Suicide notes and chocolates. The chocolates were put through her mail slot. The dog opened them. Half melted on May's bank statement. The dog threw up the other half on a four-hundred-dollar Indian rug." Frieda laughed. In his capacity as two parts joke, one part pathos, Tom Silva had been a thorn in law enforcement's side since Patsy had been hired the previous winter. Had they lived outside the park they would have been the problem of the Colorado police. Inside park boundaries the task fell to the rangers.

Anna hated domestic disputes. The good guys and the bad guys kept switching roles; an outsider didn't stand a chance. "Where's Stacy?" Anna hoped to drag another ranger along for moral support.

"Occupado. Another medical at Cliff Palace. Elderly lady."

"Damn. What does Patsy want us to do about it?"

"Just go talk to her, I guess. She wasn't too specific. 'Do something but don't say I said.' "

Anna nodded. "On my way." Halfway out the door she stopped and turned back. "Frieda, can I come visit Piedmont tonight?"

"Anytime," the dispatcher returned, already back at her computer. "If I'm not there, let yourself in. Door's never locked."

The tower house was the most picturesque, if not the most convenient, of the historical homes. Named for the round tower that housed the master bedroom, the staircase, and a small round living room, it sat on a gentle hill just west of the museum behind the more conventional homes. For one person it would have been perfect. For a woman with two teenage daughters it had proved a nightmare of bathroom scheduling and closet-space allotment.

Rumor had it, because of the girls, Patsy would be moved as soon as a two-bedroom became available, leaving the tower house up for grabs. Due to the housing shortage, when Anna entered on duty eight weeks before, the district ranger had parked her in the seasonal women's dormitory till more suitable quarters could be found, so it was with a more than slightly proprietary eye that she allowed herself to be ushered in.

Patsy Silva was compact, with the voluptuous curves of a woman who has borne children. Her hair was close-cropped and honey-blond, her eyes made impossibly blue by tinted contact lenses. Teeth as straight as an orthodontist's slide rule were shown off by hot-pink lipstick drawn on slightly fuller than her natural lip line.

Patsy smiled and waved distractedly toward the living room with its mess of clothes and magazines littering every flat surface. "Missy and Mindy are over at Frieda's watching the VCR," she said, as if the temptation of video explained a hasty and untidy departure. "She's got quite a movie collection and lets the girls watch almost anytime. It helps."

Anna nodded. Bucolic park living was fine for adults and children but could weigh heavily on adolescents with a long summer on their hands.

"Sit down. Sit." Patsy shooed Anna toward the kitchen. "Coffee or anything?" With the offer, as with most of Patsy's communications, came a tight bright smile. More a habit of placating, Anna suspected, than a genuine show of happiness.

"Coffee'd be fine."

The kitchen, the only square room in the house, was small but efficiently made, with wood cabinets and a restaurant-style booth under one of the two windows. Anna slid into the booth. Patsy busied herself at the counter. Anna wasn't particularly fond of reheated coffee, but people seemed more comfortable after their hospitality had been accepted. Maybe some ancient instinct about breaking bread together. Or maybe it was just the comfort of having something to keep their hands and eyes occupied.

Patsy put the cups on the table along with a sugar bowl and creamer in the shape of ceramic ducks wearing blue calico bonnets.

"Thanks." Anna pulled the cup to her and poured pale bluish milk out of the duck's bill. Patsy's smile clicked on then faded slowly, the effort for once proving too great.

"It's Tom," she said, as if admitting a tiresome fact.

"Chocolates."

"And a note. It's awful. How can you protect yourself from that? The police act like I'm lucky to have such an attentive husband."

"Ex-husband."

"Yes. Thank you. He makes me forget. Ex-husband. Ex, ex, ex as in exit, finito, gone. Except that he's not." She put her fingers to her temples, looking as if she would have run them distractedly through her hair had not each wave been expertly coaxed into place.

"What makes him more than a nuisance?" Anna asked. At a guess, she might have added "other than guilt?" How could a woman not feel guilty for walking out on flowers, candy, and serenades?

"I was afraid you were going to ask that," Patsy replied with an explosive sigh. She slumped back in the booth. "I don't know. I mean, he doesn't really do anything. It's just kind of an increasing sense of weird. Know what I mean? As if my not folding like I always did with the flowery courtship business is pushing him near some edge. This last note seemed, well . . . edgy." Patsy apologized with a particularly bright smile.

Anna would have laid odds that Patsy Silva had apologized a lot in her thirty-seven years; sorries and smiles poured like oil on life's troubled waters. "Can I see the note?"

"Yes. I kept it. At least I've learned that since the divorce. Anything edgy, I keep. You can't imagine how silly this all sounds, even to me, when I try to tell it to some big burly policeman who thinks his wife would die and go straight to pig heaven if he ever paid her this kind of attention. Here it is."

While she talked, Patsy rummaged through a doll-sized bureau complete with miniature vanity mirror. Decals of ducks matching the creamer were centered on each tiny drawer. From the bottom drawer she pinched up a scrap of paper. Holding it by the edge as if she didn't want to smudge incriminating prints, she laid it on the table.

In a childish but legible scrawl, more printing than script, was written: "What do you want, Pats? I've give you everything. A car, nice close, everything. What do you want? Maybe you want me to do like that guy you told me sent somebody his ear. I'll go him one better. I'm not living without you, Pats. I'm not."

"And you think it's a suicide note," Anna said. To her it read more like a threat but she was not privy to the inner workings of Tom Silva's mind. Being the new kid on the block, Anna'd not yet caught up on the gossip.

"I wish it was a suicide note!" Patsy snapped.

Anna liked the anger better than the shiny smiles. At least it rang true.

Patsy, who'd been rereading the note over Anna's shoulder, slid onto the bench beside her. Such proximity made Anna uncomfortable. Before her husband, Zachary, had been killed, when she'd lived in the confines of New York

City, Anna'd fought for personal space on elevators and in subway cars. Since joining the Park Service and moving to less constricting climes, the need had increased, rather than the opposite. An acre per person and bullhorns for communication struck her as about right for socializing.

She turned as if to give Patsy her full attention and put some space between them.

"I told Frieda it was a suicide note because it seemed easiest—you know, made sense for me to be calling." Patsy picked up her coffee but just stared into it without drinking. "It was that ear thing he said—like van Gogh. Besides the chocolates there was an envelope. One of those little square ones that come with florists' arrangements."

Anna waited, sipping coffee made gray and tepid by skim milk. Patsy didn't go on with her story. "And the envelope?" Anna prompted.

"I burned it."

Since silences didn't draw Patsy out the way they did most people—too many years of being a good girl and not speaking till spoken to, Anna guessed—she asked her what was in the envelope.

"A little piece of brown material, soft, like expensive crepe. Tom isn't circumcised. I think it was foreskin."

Anna winced. It seemed a little "edgy" to her as well.

For maybe a minute neither spoke. Whether Patsy sensed Anna's discomfort with her proximity or, once her information was told, no longer needed the closeness, she moved to the sink to dump her untouched coffee. When she returned she resumed her place on the bench opposite.

"What do you want me to do?" Anna asked.

Patsy burst into tears.

While Patsy Silva cried, Anna thought.

"I don't suppose Tom has any outstanding wants or warrants against him?" she asked hopefully.

Patsy shook her head. "I'm sorry."

Anna didn't know if she was apologizing because she still cried or because her ex-husband wasn't a known felon. "I'll run him anyway. You never know." After a moment she said: "Maybe a court restraining order; keep the guy away from you. I'll look into it; see if you have to prove harassment, what it will take to keep him out of Mesa Verde."

"It's too late. He's here," Patsy wailed, sounding like the little girl who saw poltergeists. "He's got a job with the contractor putting in the new pipeline."

The waterline. It was getting so Anna was tempted to blast the thing herself. Perhaps Mesa Verde's staff had been on the outs for decades—living in isolation where dead people were the main natural resource had to have an impact—but since she'd entered on duty the pipeline had been the lightning rod.

"Are you dating anybody?" Anna asked abruptly.

Patsy looked pained. "Not exactly," she said, not meeting Anna's eye.

She was dating somebody. A tidy old-fashioned triangle in the making. "Does Tom know?"

"No! I don't even know for sure." Patsy smiled a shy smile. Inwardly Anna groaned.

"Talk to him," Patsy pleaded.

"Sure," Anna promised.

"Talk to his boss. Mr. Ted something. He seems reasonable."

"Ted Greeley. I can do that."

"But don't get him fired. With Missy and Mindy both in high school next year we're counting on the child support."

Anna repressed a sigh. Domestic stuff. "Gotta go," she said, glancing at the clock over the sink. "Quittin' time."

Patsy laughed for the first time in a while. "Hills blew his overtime money on an all-terrain vehicle. I'm kind of glad he did—he's so cute at budget meetings when he begs."

"Take care," Anna said, setting her Smokey Bear hat squarely on her head and taking a last look around quarters she hoped soon would be hers.

"I'll keep anything else . . . personal . . . Tom sends and give it to you," Patsy promised as she held open the door.

"I can't wait."

Summer was off and running.

2

NO REST for the weary—or was it the wicked? Anna couldn't remember. There was definitely no rest for those fated to share dormitory quarters.

Her briefcase, used for carrying citation notices, maps, and brochures, banged against the screen door, jarring her elbow. Simultaneously her ears and nose were assaulted. The first by the Grateful Dead and the second by a kitchen that would daunt even the most hardened health inspector.

Early on in this allegedly temporary housing arrangement Anna realized she had two choices: bite the bullet or play Mom. As she had neither the taste nor the inclination for the latter, she had spent the four and a half weeks since the seasonals entered on duty knee-deep in unwashed dishes and empty beer cans. The mess wasn't as hard to take as the noise. After some sparks had flown she'd been given a room of her own but the walls of the flimsy, prefab structure were so thin, at times she swore they served better to conduct than deflect sound waves.

Clad in a homemade ankle-length sarong of double knit, Jamie Burke was draped across one sofa. Jennifer

Short, the other woman with whom she shared the two-bedroom house, was sprawled in a pajama-party attitude. They were intelligent, funny, interesting women. Left ignorant of their domestic habits, Anna would undoubtedly have found them delightful.

As she tried to slip unnoticed into her bedroom the imperious call of "Stop there!" arrested her progress.

The order came from Jamie, one of the army of seasonal interpreters hired on each summer to lead tours of the cliff dwellings and, for a short time—or so Hills repeatedly promised—Anna's housemate at Far View.

Dutifully, Anna waited, briefcase in hand.

In her late twenties, Jamie had the look of someone who has been athletic all her life. Muscular hips and legs gave her a stocky silhouette that was accentuated by the flat-brimmed hat and cloddy shoes of the NPS uniform she wore on duty.

In contrast to her juggernaut physique, her face was a perfect oval, the skin flawless, setting off pale blue eyes and a sensuous mouth. Jamie's hair, fine and smooth and blue-black, fell to her knees in a single braid thickened by red yarn woven through and bound around, Apache style, at the tail.

Jamie boasted that she inherited the black tresses from a half-blood Cherokee mother but Anna strongly suspected that she dyed it. In a women's dorm there were few secrets. All of Jamie's body hair was not of the same raven hue.

"What's up?" Anna asked, trying to keep the weariness from her voice.

"Stacy had to walk an old lady out of Cliff this morning. Where were you?"

Anna ignored the accusatory tone. "What was the problem?"

"Some kind of pulmonary thing. Wasn't breathing right. There was that old guy last week."

"Yup." Again Anna waited.

"They're pissed. I'm not surprised, either."

Now Anna was lost. The previous week's carry-out had gone well. The man's wife had even sent a glowing thank-you letter. "The man's family is pissed?"

"No-o." Jamie drew out the syllable slightly, as if Anna was too obtuse for words. "The Old Ones. The Anasazi. They should close this park to everybody but native peoples. It's not Frontierland, it's a sacred place. We shouldn't be here."

Jamie Burke leaped from one drama to the next. In the few short weeks Anna had known her she'd been through exposure to AIDS, been engaged to a nameless state senator in Florida, and been involved in an affair with a married man so discreet it had to be imaginary. The pipeline was a bandwagon made for jumping on.

"Ah. Chindi." Anna used the Navajo word for spirit or—she was never quite sure—evil spirit. "Could be. Listen, I've got to slip into something less deadly." She grimaced at her gun and escaped down the hall.

Once divested of the dead weight of her gun and the airtight shoes required by NPS class "A" uniform standards, Anna felt less hostile. By the time she'd poured herself a generous dollop of Mirassou Pinot Blanc, she was civilized enough to join the party in the front room.

The television was on with the volume turned down and Jamie was verbally abusing Vanna White as she turned the letters on "Wheel of Fortune." It was a nightly ritual that seldom failed to amuse.

"Arms like toothpicks! Look at that," Jamie was exclaiming. "I don't think she's pretty. Do you think she's pretty? Who in God's name thinks she's pretty? Little

Miss Toothpick Arms. Little Miss White Bread."

Anna curled her feet under her on the nubby fabric of an armchair. The boxy room was furnished in Early Dentist's Office but it was serviceable. Anna, barefoot, in pink sweatpants and an oversized man's shirt, surrounded by girls with Budweisers—or women that looked like girls from a vantage point of forty—had a sense of being an uncomfortable traveler in time. Even the cheap southwestern print of Jamie's sarong put her in mind of the India-print bedspreads she'd found so many uses for in her college days. In a gush of self-pity she felt her world as dead as that of the Anasazi. She missed Christina and Alison, the woman and her daughter with whom she'd shared a house in Houghton, Michigan, when she worked on Isle Royale.

Chris was a rock: gentle and soft and stronger than Anna ever hoped to be. Alison, at six, was like a kitten with brains—irresistible and a little scary.

Anna'd left on the pretense Mesa Verde was a promotion as well as a return to her beloved southwest. In reality she'd cleared out because she knew Chris was in love but wouldn't move in with her sweetheart if it meant abandoning Anna. So Anna'd abandoned her.

I'm a fucking saint, she thought sourly, watching Vanna turn E's on "Wheel of Fortune."

The job wasn't too bad. Though at times Anna felt more like a nurse than a ranger.

Mesa Verde was an old and staid national park. As early as 1906 it was clear that the ancient cliff dwellings, though already largely looted of artifacts, were a part of America's heritage that must be preserved.

Visitors to Mesa Verde went out of their way to get there and had the money to do so. Consequently, the clientele tended to be older, with gold cards and expensive RVs. Retired folks with bad hearts and tired lungs from San Diego, Florida, and the south coast of Texas found themselves up at altitude for the first time in thirty years. If drug dogs were called in Anna suspected they'd sniff out more nitroglycerin tablets than anything else.

There'd been two fatalities—both elderly visitors with cardiopulmonary problems—and eleven ambulance runs, five of them out of Cliff Palace. And it was only early June.

Swallowing the last of her wine, Anna leaned back and let the alcohol uncoil her mental springs.

Jennifer wandered back to the TV with a fresh beer.

Short was a round-faced woman with good hair, bad skin, and too much makeup. Fresh out of Tennessee State's one-semester course, she was the new law enforcement seasonal in her first national park job. Jennifer was a Memphis belle in what Anna had thought was a bygone tradition: all magnolia blossoms, little-ol'-me's-led-a-sheltered-life, and eek-a-mouse. Proven tactics, guaranteed to turn the boys to putty.

Anna hadn't yet decided whether she was more irritated or intrigued with the femme fatale routine. On the one hand it would be interesting to watch. On the other, given the job, it could get a person killed.

"Jamie, I saw that poor little thing you were talking about," Jennifer was saying. Or, to be more accurate: "Ah saw thet pore lil' thang yew were tawkin' abaht."

"She had the cutest face, but her little body! I just couldn't live like that. High school is going to be pure hell. It'd be a mercy to drown people like that at birth. I don't want to sound mean, I mean for their own sakes. I wouldn't want to live like that. I just wouldn't."

A natural silence fell and they all stared at Vanna. Jennifer had been talking about Stacy and Rose Meyers' daughter, Bella. A sadness threatened Anna and she was glad when loud knocking interrupted her thoughts. She made no move to uncoil herself. Jennifer sprang up, "I'll get it" out of her mouth almost before the knocking ceased. The first week on the mesa she had announced one of her prime motives for choosing law enforcement: a way to meet straight men.

A moment later two seasonal firefighters from the helitack crew followed Jennifer back in. Because of the wealth of ruins and artifacts on the mesa all wildfires were put out in their infancy by a crew of wildland firefighters flown in by helicopter. Dozers and other heavy equipment customarily used to cut fireline would be so destructive to the cultural aspects of the park that fire was never allowed to spread if it could be helped. When nothing was burning, helitack performed the high- and low-angle rescues often needed to evacuate sick and injured people from the less accessible ruins.

Jimmy Russell and Paul Summers had the youth and build of most seasonal firefighters and the living room fairly crackled with sexual energy. Russell's heavily muscled arms and back were shown off in a tight T-shirt emblazoned with a flying insect wearing a yellow shirt of fire-resistant Nomex. A budding good ol' boy from Kentucky, Jimmy chewed his words like tobacco. Summers was a striking blond with a born-again surfer haircut and finely chiseled features. Somehow managing to look sophisticated in worn Levi's and a baggy, wrinkled, oxford shirt, he carried the libations: a six-pack of Coors Light dangled from each hand.

"Hiya, Anna." Paul smiled at her and she was annoyed to find herself flattered.

Popping a Coors, Russell settled cross-legged on the carpet. Jamie pulled herself around on the couch and began kneading the muscles of his neck and shoulders.

Let the mating rituals begin, Anna thought sourly. Unfolding her legs, she levered herself up: time to go visit Piedmont.

On the way through the kitchen she grabbed up what was left of the Mirassou Blanc.

Frieda Dierkz had a house in what was called the Utility Loop. It was near the maintenance yard, about a mile from the Headquarters/Museum Loop. The houses were small, white one- and two-bedroom homes with the charm and inconveniences of 1940s construction. These homes were for lower-level permanents, the GS-4s and -5s and -7s. Higher-ups claimed the beautiful historic homes in the Headquarters Loop. The fire dorm, where helitack was housed, was also on the loop, as were a couple of aging trailers rented out to seasonal interpreters each summer.

Frieda lived in number thirty-four. Most of the front yards were overgrown with weeds and native grasses. Her marigold border and tended lawn looked out of place in piñon-juniper country.

A sad-eyed black lab was resting on some newly dug up and soon to be dead marigolds. He thumped his tail half-heartedly as Anna came up the walk.

"Hi, Taco." She stopped to pat him on the head. The dog yawned widely to show his appreciation. "Where's Piedmont?" Anna demanded, cradling the animal's jowly face between her hands. "Don't tell me you've eaten him?"

"Alive and well." Frieda had come to the door and stood behind the screen. A large yellow tiger cat, so limp it looked dead, was draped across her arm. With her free hand she pushed open the door and let Anna in.

Anna traded the wine bottle for the cat, buried her face in the soft fur of his neck, and breathed deeply. "Ahh. Thanks. I needed that."

"For me?" Frieda eyed the already opened bottle.

"Park Service social motto: Bring something to share."

As Frieda went into the kitchen to get glasses, Anna sat down on a couch identical to the one in the Far View dormitory and spread the cat across her knees.

Seasonals in the Park Service were not allowed the solace of pets. As long as Anna was stuck in the seasonal housing dorm, her cat had to board with a permanent employee fortunate enough to get "real" housing.

Frieda returned with two Kmart wineglasses and poured them each a healthy slug.

"If you're in the middle of something, Piedmont and I can go out in the yard," Anna offered. "I just needed a medicinal cat this evening."

"Don't know what I'd do without Taco," Frieda said by way of agreement. She propped her feet up on the scarred coffee table and took a long drink.

"But Taco is only a *dawg*," Anna confided to the cat in a stage whisper.

The dispatcher laughed. It was a rare sound and surprisingly pleasant, close to what Anna and her sister, Molly, had called "the Princess Laugh" when they were children. A sound that put one in mind of tinkling bells. She and Molly had even spent time practicing it but had never graduated from girlish "tee hee hees." Bells were for princesses. And, evidently, the Mesa Verde dispatcher.

"When I see you with that cat I can hardly believe

you're the same hard-ass who tickets little old ladies in wheelchairs for parking their cars in the handicapped spaces without a permit," Frieda said.

Frieda was just making conversation but still Anna was stung. "I don't," she insisted but felt compelled to add: "How am I to know they're handicapped? For all I know it could be Joe Namath parked there."

"Namath's handicapped," Frieda returned. "Bad knees."

"Gotta have a permit."

Again the dispatcher laughed her silvery laugh and they drank in silence. Tired of being adored, Piedmont leaped off Anna's lap. Moments later they heard feline lappings from the direction of the bathroom bowl.

"What do you know about Tom Silva?" Anna asked, her mind inevitably returning to NPS chores.

Frieda thought for a moment. "Patsy was divorced when the superintendent hired her—last fall, November, I think. She brought the girls up to live with her when school ended in May, so Tom hasn't been around much socially—not where you'd get to know the guy. I've seen him up here. He's good-looking. Younger than Patsy, is my guess, but not by much—maybe thirty-five or so. Maybe just looks young. He's got that kind of perfect olive skin that's practically indestructible."

"Does he come up to visit the girls?"

"More than Patsy would like. She thinks it's just a ruse. I guess his lack of interest in his kids was part of the reason she left him. From hints she's dropped, I gather Tom's thirty-five going on seventeen. She once said she couldn't handle being a single parent to three teenagers. Luckily he's been doing roofing or framing or something for an outfit in Grand Junction. The two-hour commute keeps him down to a dull roar."

"The contractor putting in the new waterline just hired him," Anna said.

"Oops."

"Yeah. Oops." Piedmont came back and settled down on the couch just out of Anna's reach. She contented herself with holding the tip of his tail. Occasionally he twitched it to show his displeasure.

"Sulking," Frieda noted, and Anna nodded. They sat for a while without speaking. It wasn't a comfortable silence, at least not for Anna. She hadn't known Frieda long enough for that.

"Do you think Silva's dangerous?" Anna asked.

"Maybe. No—I don't think so. He seems like a guy more into gestures." Cutting off one's foreskin was a hell of a gesture, Anna thought, but she didn't interrupt. In park society a person's private life seldom was, but as far as she knew Silva's penis had not yet made it into the public domain.

"The one time I met him he did strike me as a bit of an opportunist, though."

"Like a magpie? Won't kill it but doesn't mind eating it if someone else does?"

"Exactly like that. You hit it. He even looks kind of like a magpie, dresses too well, talks too loud, struts."

Silence fell again. It was a little easier this time but after a minute or so the strain began to get to Anna. "I better go," she said, giving Piedmont's tail a last gentle tug. "I want to call my sister tonight and it's already nine-twenty New York time. Thanks for the visit."

"Thanks for the wine," Frieda replied as she followed Anna to the door.

On the four-mile drive back to the dorm Anna found herself once again lonely for Christina and her daughter, missing Molly, missing silences that didn't chafe.

Fending off self-pity, she forced herself to concentrate on the delicate scent of juniper blowing in the Rambler's window, the piles of cumulonimbus the setting sun was painting in glorious shades of peach, the glistening peaks of the La Plata mountains, still wearing a veil of winter snow.

From many places the view was unchanged from when the ancients had inhabited the mesa. A time Anna liked to believe was simpler. Along Chapin Mesa Road were villages, skeletons now, but still imbued with an unmistakable human spirit. If she squinted, let her mind play, Anna could almost see women with bundles on their backs watching thunderheads build as she did, wondering if the rains would come in time for the corn.

The considerable benefit of this environmental therapy was blasted away the moment the Rambler pulled into the dorm parking lot. The nucleus of people she had left had spontaneously combusted into a flaming beer party.

Something that, to rock-and-roll-trained ears, sounded like 33⅓ Muzak played at 78 was audible through the open windows. Half a dozen cars were parked in the lot and at least that many bodies were standing around in the living room. Theatrically, Anna rested her head against the steering wheel and groaned.

With ill-concealed bad grace, she slammed the car into reverse and drove back down the Chapin Mesa Road.

A mile shy of the Museum Loop she turned onto a spur road, parked, and let herself into the Resource Management building. It was small and square, built of the same pink stone blocks as the chief ranger's office. The single room was filled to capacity by two desks, filing cabinets, dead lizards, bones, rocks, and what had to be at least fourteen years' worth of accumulated paperwork.

For those lucky enough to have keys—the people who really needed them and law enforcement—Resource Management had the after-hours attraction of a private phone.

Anna cleared off a chair and, still standing, punched in the twenty-four numbers of her sister's home phone and her AT&T calling card. She suspected if she could clear her brain of all memorized numbers there would be space enough created for housing all of Shakespeare and some of Johnson.

As Molly's smoke-roughened voice growled a characteristic "Dr. Pigeon," Anna dumped herself into the swivel chair.

"I'm too old for this," she said in lieu of a greeting.

"Damn old," Molly agreed.

"Too damned old. If it wasn't politically incorrect, I'd get my eyes done."

"On an NPS salary you could only afford to do one."

"Some psychiatrist you are. Whatever happened to 'You're as young as you feel' and 'Age is just a state of mind'?"

Molly laughed, a chuckle that sounded evil to the uninitiated. "That's what young psychiatrists tell their middle-aged clients. I'm pushing fifty. Take it from me: damn, yes, it's a bitch. Gird up the sagging loins and get on with it. Come to New York. I'll buy you a day at Elizabeth Arden's. 'Behind the Red Door': not quite an erotic fantasy but one that sells just as well. Youth! Men want to buy back the dreams they once had of themselves. Us old bats like the dreams of our middling years, it's our faces we want to buy back.

"So, one foot in the grave, the other on a banana peel. How's the rest of your life?"

Anna laughed. Her face could fall, her hands gnarl, her hair acquire another streak of gray. The camaraderie of women on the wrong side of *Mademoiselle*'s hit list was a joy she'd never been taught to expect.

"Dorm living is a drag. I'm leaning hard on the district ranger."

"Hills Dutton."

"I was trying to avoid the name."

"Got to be an alias."

"Nope. Too imaginative. Forced to think up an alias, I expect Hills would ponder a good long time, read all the Standard Operating Procedures, then settle on John Doe."

"Is he going to get you a house?"

"I don't know. To give the devil his due, he's up against it. They're redoing a waterline laid down a zillion years ago. A whole passel of archaeologists have been brought on board to analyze every foot of the digging. No housing left, everybody's hair in a knot, heavy equipment roaring around."

The waterline put Anna in mind of the afternoon's drama and she was glad to unfold the story of Patsy's Tom and the piece of foreskin.

After she'd finished there was a silence broken by a sighing sound. Molly was lighting up. Camel straights: Anna had heard them sucked into her sister's lungs for twenty years. Molly was an MD, she knew what the cigarettes were doing. She was a psychiatrist, she knew why she smoked them. And Anna was in law enforcement, she knew drugs had a logic of their own. So she said nothing.

"Sounds like the man's in trouble," Molly said finally, and Anna imagined thick smoke coming out with the words. "A construction worker?"

"That's what I gathered."

"Not a likely candidate for voluntary therapy. Any alcohol problems, drugs, things of that sort?"

"Probably," Anna replied, then thought better of her prejudice and added: "I don't know, really. I've heard he goes on a drunk now and then."

"People who cut themselves—hurt themselves—usually have a problem with self-esteem. A healthier attitude is 'Damned if I'm going to hurt anymore over you.' He may be harmless. I'm talking physically here; emotionally he could be devastating to anybody who gets tangled up with him. But now and again it goes beyond self-injury. In extreme cases I've seen the murder/suicide pattern. Shoot the wife then shoot yourself. That's rare but not so rare it doesn't crop up in the case history books and on the front page of the *Post* fairly regularly.

"I'd tell her to watch him, Anna. Watch him and watch herself. Whoops. Got to go," Molly finished in the abrupt manner Anna'd grown accustomed to over the years. "I've got an article due tomorrow for the *Times* on co-dependency. An are-you-or-aren't-you kind of thing. Of course it turns out everybody is. Keep me posted." She rang off, leaving Anna still holding the phone to her ear.

Shoot the wife then shoot yourself. Anna hung up the phone. Before she wrote Mr. Silva off as a magpie she'd do a little digging. It hadn't escaped her notice that more than a third of the women who came to hospital emergency rooms for treatment had been damaged by husbands or boyfriends.

Full darkness had come and she drove slowly back up to Far View. Cottontail bunnies, scarcely bigger than kittens, tried to find their way into the next world under her tires, but she successfully avoided them.

At the dorm, the parking lot was still full, the noise still blaring, and the bodies still in evidence. Anna slumped down in the Rambler's seat, wondering not for the first time if she should have taken the promotion that, along with Chris' defection, had tempted her back to the southwest, whether the seductive sense of smug selflessness and the warm dry climate had been worth the trade-offs.

3

BEFORE SHE'D properly gotten to sleep, Anna's alarm was buzzing like a hornet. She swatted it into silence and lay for a minute staring at the acoustical-tile ceiling above her single bed. The beer party had clanged on well past midnight.

Now that she had to get up the house was finally quiet. Rolling up on one elbow, she looked out into the new day. A breeze blew cold on her naked skin. At eighty-two hundred feet, summer never got a firm foothold. Chapin Mesa, a thousand feet lower than Far View, was often as much as ten degrees warmer.

A family of chipmunks had taken up residence under a scrap of black plastic Maintenance left behind when they finished the rear deck. With much flipping of tails, chattering, and scurrying, they were maintaining their cute Disneyesque image. Anna'd been so inculcated with Chip and Dale that she'd felt betrayed when she'd first seen a chipmunk breakfasting on a luckless brother squashed in the road. Roadkill provided food for a lot of animals. Anna sometimes speculated as to whether or not scavengers looked upon highways as a sort of endless buffet catered by Chrysler.

Squeaks, flusters, and the chipmunks vanished under the plastic. A lone red-tailed hawk spun careful circles over the serviceberry bushes.

A toilet flushed. The dorm was stirring earlier than anticipated. Leaving the chipmunks to their fate, Anna pulled on her robe. This morning she intended not only to get a shower, but also a hot one.

Jennifer shuffled past in the hall. Her eyes were puffy and her cheeks dragged down. " 'Morning," Anna said.

"Unhh."

As Anna lifted the coffeepot down from her kitchen cupboard she heard the thump of a wished-she-were-dead weight falling back into bed.

"Three-one-two in service." Anna made the call around her second cup of coffee. Once the initial insult of regaining consciousness was over, she enjoyed early shifts. Since neither the cliff dwellings nor the museum opened for visitors until nine, the park was quiet.

In the clear morning air a comforting illusion of isolation crept over Anna. Law enforcement at Mesa Verde taxed her energies in a way the hard physical work in the backcountry never had. People's needs were immediate and complex, their wants changing with the hour. Anna suspected mankind descended not from the ape but from the mosquito. In swarms they could bleed one dry.

With morning's peace came the animals: those just coming on diurnal duty, those going off nocturnal shift, and the crepuscular crew with a split shift framing the day. Two does and a fawn still in spots grazed between the white-flowering serviceberry bushes; from a fallen log an Abert squirrel showed off its perfect bushy tail.

At Far View Lodge, a black bear lumbered down from

the direction of the cafeteria, where it had undoubtedly been raiding garbage cans. Anna hit her siren and the bear bolted across the two-lane road into the underbrush below the Visitors' Center.

This year several "problem" bears had been knocking over trash cans. The bureaucratic machinery was beginning to grind at its usual snail's pace, but Anna doubted a solution would be found, agreed upon, funded, and implemented before these particular bears died of old age. Or were shot in the name of visitor protection.

She gave one more blast on the siren for good measure, then headed down toward Chapin Mesa, opening gates to ruins that Stacy Meyers had closed seven hours before. Coyote Village was first. Just a mile south of Far View, it was one of the highest pueblos on Mesa Verde, and Anna's favorite. Though it lacked the drama of the cliff dwellings with their aeries and towers, she loved the maze of intimate rooms and the patterns the ruined walls made against the dun of the earth. Perhaps since it was less alien she could better identify with the people who had once dwelt there, and so wonder at what prosaic magic had caused them to vanish.

Archaeologists hated the word "vanished," with its implication they'd not done their homework. Visitors loved it. In it was carried the mystery they felt walking through the ancient towns, peering in windows dark for seven centuries.

Theories of where the Anasazi had gone proliferated: war, draught, famine, loss of topsoil, overpopulation. No one concept carried the burden of proof. Theories changed with the political weather.

More than once it crossed Anna's mind that the best thing about the Anasazi was that they were gone. Their ruined homes forged chalices into which a jaded modern people could pour their fantasies. Never in dreams were there noisy neighbors in the dwelling next door, the reek of raw sewage, chilblains, or rotting teeth. In memory, especially one so magnificently vague as the lives of the Old Ones, the sun always shone and children didn't talk back.

In a tiny room, not more than five feet square, a cottontail nibbled at grasses prying up through the smooth flooring. Not wishing to disturb the new resident, Anna left quietly.

At Cedar Tree Tower Ruin Anna stopped to watch the sun clear the treetops and pour its liquid gold into the centuries-old kivas. These circular underground rooms, roofless now, were centers for worship or clan gatherings or places of work: the interpretation changed over the years as fads came and went and the science of archaeology grew more exact—or thought it had.

For Anna it was the symmetry and sophisticated simplicity of function that spoke to her of the Old Ones. Air shafts to ventilate fire pits, complex masonry, fitted stones handcrafted by a people who had no metal for tools.

In Europe King Arthur was dreaming his round table. Peasants lived in huts, the Black Plague waited just around the century's turning, and war and starvation were a way of life. Here where Colorado, Utah, New Mexico, and Arizona would one day meet, a people had farmed, traded, worshiped, and worked in peace and prosperity for six hundred years.

Park interpreters stressed the terrible hardships the Anasazi must have faced, the daily battle to wring a livelihood from an ungiving land. To Anna the kivas, the tunnels, the towers, the plaster and paint and pottery, suggested a people with an eye for beauty and at least enough wealth and leisure to pursue it.

The sun higher and the shadow play over, Anna continued to the last gate on her rounds, the one located at the four-way intersection near the museum. It blocked off the roads leading to the mesa top ruins, Cliff Palace and Balcony House. As she had every Tuesday for the last six weeks, she made a mental note to tell Stacy not to twist the chain into a figure eight before latching the padlock on his late shift. Placing the butt of the lock up as it did made the key easier to insert, but the chain was pulled so tight it took a wrestling match to get the lock arm pulled free of the links.

As she was securing the gate, Meyers called into service. Due to a paucity of vehicles, he would patrol with her.

Stacy and his family lived in a one-bedroom bungalow several houses down from Frieda's. With his daughter, Bella, it had to be cramped, but he was lucky to get it. A temporary appointment didn't carry much more in the way of perks than a seasonal.

Anna pulled up in the shade of an apple tree that grew near the wall shoring up an elevated yard. A picnic table sat under the branches. Two plastic milk bottles with the sides cut away lay tipped over near it. Presumably at some point Mrs. Meyers had intended to hang them for bird feeders. The bottles had been in the same place since Anna entered on duty. The lawn was ill kept and, for a home where a child dwelt, surprisingly untrammeled. No one used this yard as a playground.

Anna had seen Bella Meyers only a couple of times. From the waist up she had developed normally. There was no distortion of her facial features or upper body, but her lower limbs were stunted, half the size they should have been. Bella suffered from dwarfism.

Stacy and his wife, Rose, never brought her to any of the endless potlucks Mesa Verde was so fond of. There were two schools of thought in the park about this obvious cloistering. One was that the Meyerses were ashamed of Bella's deformity. The other was that the child suffered from delicate health.

Though the latter was the more charitable of the two rumors, it struck a deep chord of sympathy in Anna. Stacy wasn't a permanent employee. He was what was called a temporary one-to-four-year appointment: no medical, no dental, no retirement. A GS-5's eighteen thousand–plus a year wouldn't go far to purchase comforts or specialty needs for a delicate child with a physical disability.

The sound of the screen door banging announced Stacy. A tall, slender man, six-foot-two or -three, he had dark hair and eyes, and a neatly trimmed beard. On his narrow hips the gunbelt looked out of place and the long sensitive fingers clasping his briefcase more suited to a surgeon or pianist than an officer of the law.

Rose Meyers followed him out.

Mrs. Meyers kept to herself. Jamie and Jennifer were convinced she felt government employees beneath her socially. Anna'd never spoken to the woman. She'd called Stacy at home on business once or twice but always got the phone machine with Rose's over-sweet message: "Hi! I'm so *glad* you called!"

Mrs. Meyers didn't look glad this morning. Her face was twisted into a mask of contempt. Short dark hair was molded in sleepy spikes. Rose carried quite a bit of excess weight. The pounds didn't form voluptuous curves or wide generous expanses as on more fortunate women, but sagged in lumps like sodden cotton batting in a ruined quilt.

" 'Bye, darling," Stacy said, and Anna smiled. No one

but Cary Grant could call somebody "darling" and not sound stilted. Stacy leaned down to kiss his wife but Rose stiffened as if the kiss had a foul taste. Anna looked away to give Stacy the illusion of privacy.

Moments later he threw his briefcase and hat into the rear seat and slid in beside her.

" 'Morning," she said. Stacy didn't respond. Anna was unoffended. She clicked on the radio for company.

"Where to this morning?" he asked after a while. Wherever his preoccupation had taken him, he was back with her now, the light in his brown eyes lost its inward shadows. His were compelling eyes, as liquid as a doe's, and framed with long lashes that showed black against clear skin. He put Anna in mind of the young dandies from the turn of the century who'd purposely exposed themselves to tuberculosis to attain the pale burning look lent by a fire within.

"We're going out to Wetherill Mesa," she told him. "Patsy's ex-husband Tom's been hired on by the pipeline contractor. He'll be surveying line near mile two. We need to talk with him."

"Has he been bothering Patsy again?"

"More or less. Sending her candy and notes that sound threatening or suicidal, depending on how you look at it. This time he sent her a bit of something that Patsy thinks was foreskin."

"Holy moly," Stacy said, and, "God I hate law enforcement."

Stacy had chosen law enforcement not as an avocation, but as a way in. With crime pouring out of the cities onto the nation's highways, more law enforcers than naturalists were hired in the national parks, more citations given than nature walks.

"You're a born tree hugger," Anna remarked amiably. "I could do without the domestic stuff. One way or another the ranger always comes out with a sore thumb. Matrimony is a dangerous game to referee."

"Were you ever married?"

"Widowed." She could say it now without feeling a hollowness in her chest.

"Lucky."

Anna laughed. "Troubles at home?"

Realizing what he had said, Stacy apologized. And blushed. Anna had never seen a forty-five-year-old man blush before. It charmed her.

"Not Rose. Rose's good to me. I just wish I could do more for her. She's used to better. You should have seen her in high school. God was she beautiful! She didn't even know I was alive. I was just this pencil-necked geek who played trombone in the marching band. She even modeled for *Glamour* magazine once."

Anna knew that. Stacy had dropped it into their first conversation. Evidently he dropped it into most conversations about his wife. One evening after she'd sharpened her tongue on Vanna, Jamie had ranted on about it. "*Glamour!* Give me a break! Maybe for the *Glamour* Don'ts! And a quarter of a century and sixty pounds ago."

Stacy noticed the smile. "She did, you know."

"She's a good-looking woman," Anna agreed politely. "So what did a pencil-necked geek have to do to get a fashion model's heart and keep it?"

Stacy laughed. "Are you kidding? In high school Rose wouldn't give me the time of day. No, we met again about three years ago. I was out on the west coast visiting old friends and there she was."

"Love at first sight?"

"Let's say interest at first sight. I was going through a divorce. Rose saved my life," Stacy added simply. "I'll always owe her for that."

"Your ex the one that made widowerhood seem so desirable?"

"She wasn't a bad woman. There were just too many people she had to meet—without her clothes." Stacy paraphrased Leonard Cohen.

"Ah." Anna wasn't going to touch that remark with the proverbial ten-foot pole.

Past the Far View cafeteria, she turned left onto the Wetherill Mesa. Wetherill was just one of the five mesas, spread out like the fingers of an open hand, that made up the park. The road wound down the mesa's edge for twelve miles. Along the way there were overlooks, most on the west side. The views changed with the hour of the day and with the weather. Sleeping Ute Mountain nearby kept watch over the town of Cortez in the valley. The solitary white mysticism of Lone Cone pierced the horizon to the northwest. The Bears' Ears peeked coyly from behind a distant mountain range. To the south glimpses of Ship Rock in New Mexico tantalized. The craggy volcano neck bore a startling resemblance to a ship in full sail gliding through a sea of haze created by the power plant near Farmington. Farmington, Cortez, and Shiprock were home to most of the nontourist-related industries in the four-corners area; smelting the silver for the jewelry trade, the machinery for the farmers.

"Rose would never leave me," Stacy said quietly.

Since the silence between them had been so long, and he seemed to be speaking only to himself, Anna pretended she hadn't heard. She pulled the patrol car off onto the overlook where Greeley's company pickup was parked and switched off the ignition. "You want to do the talking or shall I?" she asked.

"You do it. Silva's supposed to be quite the ladies' man. Maybe we'll get lucky and he'll underestimate you."

Anna laughed. "I like you, Meyers."

Following the pink plastic tape marking the section of line already surveyed, they started down into the ravine. Mesa Verde's oakbrush grew to the size of small trees—some reaching twenty feet or more—but retained the many branches of a lesser shrub. In places the bushes were virtually impenetrable and provided habitat for quail, rabbits, and other creatures who lived longer if they went unnoticed.

The survey crew had cut a swath through the brush with loppers and chain saws. Suckers, severed just above ground level, stuck up sharp as pungi sticks. Intent on where she put her feet, Anna nearly ran into a man working his way up the hill.

"Whoa there, honey!" He spoke with a slight lisp and he put his arms around her as if she were going to fall. "I do love hugging women packing heat."

Anna extricated herself from his grasp. The man was Ted Greeley. He was not much taller than Anna, maybe five-foot-eight. In his early fifties, he had startlingly blue eyes and snow-white hair that hugged his round head in tight curls. He'd kept himself in good shape. Anna couldn't help but notice the muscular arms when he'd grabbed her. Beginnings of a potbelly attested to the fact that physical fitness was an ongoing struggle.

"Checking up on me, eh?" He reached down and pulled up a blade of grass to chew on.

"Good morning, Ted," Stacy said.

"Ted," Anna echoed the greeting. "We need to talk with Tom Silva. Is he working this stretch of line?"

"You girl rangers really make a difference." Greeley winked at Anna. "In the construction business all I ever see are men's ugly pusses. Say, how's that wife of yours, Stacy? Still eating your cooking?"

Stacy just smiled.

"And how's my little Bella?"

"Bella's fine." Stacy's tone was icy and Anna sensed a sudden hostility. "Dispatch said Tom Silva was working this section. Do you know where we can find him?" Stacy dragged the conversation back to business.

Greeley's smile broadened. "Tom in some kind of trouble? Let me know if any of my boys get out of line. You know what they say: you get in bed with somebody, it pays to stay friendly."

"No trouble," Stacy said stiffly. "We just need to talk with him."

"Help yourself." Greeley gestured down the hill. "He's holding the dumb end of the tape for an overpaid surveyor, so don't keep him too long. Anna." He tipped an imaginary hat as he brushed by her.

The surveyor was at the bottom of the ravine setting up his tripod. "Silva?" Anna asked as they approached.

"Keep walking," the man replied without taking his eyes from his instruments. Ahead, down a fresh-cut line, a second man sat on a boulder smoking a cigarette.

"Tom Silva?" Anna asked when they were close enough to be heard.

"You're looking at him." Silva blew smoke out in a thin stream and looked Anna up and down. The half smile on his lips suggested she should feel complimented.

She didn't.

"I'm Anna Pigeon. This is Stacy Meyers. Can you take a break for a minute? We'd like to talk to you."

"Taking five, Bobby," Silva shouted past them. "Somebody set the law dogs on me." He smiled up at Anna. "Pull up a rock and sit down."

Anna crouched, rocking back on her heels, her forearms resting on her knees. Stacy remained standing, seeming tall as a willow from her new vantage point.

For a moment Silva studied them, and Anna him. The morning's heat was beginning to collect in the canyon, held close by the oakbrush thickets. Shirtless, rivulets of sweat traced trails through the dust on Silva's smooth chest. Stick-straight black hair stuck out from beneath a battered, straw cowboy hat. With his unlined olive skin and dark eyes, he was pretty rather than handsome.

Meeting Anna's eyes, he crushed out his cigarette and pointedly tucked the butt into the rolled cuff of his jeans. "No litter here," he said. "This is a national fucking park."

A challenge: Anna chose to ignore it.

"Patsy asked us to talk with you, Tom," she said evenly.

"What's old Pats up to now?" He shook another Marlboro from the pack that rested beside him on the rock, then made a show of offering one to Anna and Stacy.

Anna declined. Stacy just shook his head.

"Suit yourself. Mind if I do?" The question was rhetorical and neither bothered to reply. Silva didn't light the cigarette but played with it between his fingers. The gesture was so classically phallic that Anna felt tired.

"Patsy's concerned that some of the presents you've been giving her might have more than one meaning," she began. "This latest—attention—has her fairly upset."

"So she screamed for the rangers? God, Pats loves a good scene."

"Your ex-wife—"

"My wife," Tom interrupted.

"—would be more comfortable if you stayed away from her."

"Hey, a man's got a right to work. She's always hollering I don't pay enough goddamn child support, now she's trying to lose me my job. Christ!"

"Patsy's not trying to get you fired, Tom. She mentioned specifically that she didn't want that to happen. She just wants you to stay away from her."

"What grounds, man? She's got my kids, for Christ's sake." Tom quit playing with the cigarette and lit it, striking a wooden match with an expert—and probably much rehearsed—flick of his thumbnail. "There ain't no way she can keep me from going over there. I've never done a damn thing, not one damn thing she can hold up in a court of law to say I can't. Hell, I never even hit her."

"I believe you, Tom," Anna said soothingly. "But there's a thing called harassment. Patsy has pretty strong feelings about some of your gifts."

Tom shook his head. Smoke poured from his nostrils. His eyes were fixed on a point beyond Anna's left shoulder. Behind her she could hear Stacy shifting his weight.

"She's got a scrap of skin in an envelope, Tom. She said it was foreskin. That's a pretty loaded thing to send somebody." Anna was uncomfortably aware of the unintentional humor. She heard Stacy clearing his throat, a small cough that could have been thwarted laughter.

Fortunately Tom seemed not to pick up on it. For a moment he sat smoking and Anna waited, letting the silence soak in, work for her.

"Christ! It was a joke," he finally burst out.

Stacy spoke for the first time. "A joke? It must've hurt like crazy. Where's the funny part?"

Tom looked up at him, his mouth twisted with irritation. "I didn't take a fucking knife to myself, if that's what you mean. The doc did it. Pats had been after me for years. I thought she'd like it."

"You got circumcised in your thirties?" Stacy asked. Anna bit back a laugh at the "oh ouch!" she could hear under the words.

"That's right." Tom smiled; his teeth were square and white. "Barnum and Bailey got a new tent."

Inwardly, Anna sighed. "Here's where we stand, Tom. You, Patsy, me—we've all got to live together on this mesa top. At least for a while. I'd suggest that you steer clear of Patsy. If you've got visiting rights to your kids, you two work that out. I'll ask Patsy to file whatever agreement you reach at the chief ranger's office. You stick to that and you won't have to deal with us, okay?"

"Fuck!" Tom flicked his cigarette butt into the brush. Anna didn't even follow it with her eyes. "Why don't you rangers do your job instead of hassling people that work for a living? You get a fucking free ride from the government and can't even keep the fucking roads safe. Monday night a big goddamn truck nearly ran me off the road. Where the hell were you then? Christ!"

"We'll look into that." Pushing herself to her feet, Anna heard both ankles crack in protest.

"Will that be all, *ranger*?"

"Almost," Anna returned. "Just find that cigarette you tossed and put it out and we'll be out of your hair. Fire danger's bad this year. Manning Class four yesterday."

"Find it yourself," Silva muttered.

"I got it." Stacy had crushed the life from the butt and now tucked the filter into his pocket.

"Good enough for me," Anna said. "Take it easy, Tom."

"Yeah."

*   *   *

When they'd passed the surveyor and were climbing out of the ravine, Stacy said: "Foreskin is a loaded gift," and the laughter Anna had swallowed came bubbling out.

"The way he was playing with the cigarette . . ." Anna's laughter took over and she had to stop climbing just to breathe. "You'd think he was auditioning for the role of Johnny Wad in *Debbie Does Dallas*."

"You mean that didn't toss your confetti? I kind of thought I might give it a shot. Run it up the flagpole, see if the cat licks it up."

Stacy stopped beside her. Pressed close by the brambles, Anna was aware of the smell of him: freshly laundered cotton and soap. Heat radiated from her, and it wasn't only from the sun and the climb. Anna stifled her basic instincts and shook herself like a dog ridding its fur of water drops.

Abruptly, she turned and pushed up the side of the ravine. In places it was so steep she pulled herself along using the low branches. Her laughter had evaporated.

"You drive," she said as they reached the patrol car. "These seats break my back."

"You're too short. This is a man's machine. A car for Johnny Wad." Stacy slipped behind the wheel and slid the seat back as far as it would go.

"Thanks for picking up that cigarette butt. What was I going to do? Shoot the guy? Never try to out-macho a construction worker."

"Believe it or not, picking up litter is why I went into this business. I don't work for the Park Service. I work for the parks."

Anna settled back into the seat. "The NPS could use a few more fern feelers. I, for one, hope you get on permanent."

"So do I," Stacy said. "So do I."

His tone was so grim, so determined, Anna dropped the subject. Everybody had to contend with their own demons. Some of hers were such old familiars she considered naming them and renting them closet space.

Leaning her head back against the vinyl headrest, she closed her eyes. Zachary was dead eight years come August. She could no longer consistently call his face to mind. Without his memory clear and present, her fortieth might turn out to be a damn lonely year.

4

HOUSEMATES OUT, television off, Anna had been sleeping with glorious abandon. Deep sleep, REM sleep, sleep without nightmares. Of late a good night's sleep had become such a rarity her fantasies about it bordered on the erotic.

Hence the cursing reluctance with which she relinquished it to answer the phone.

"Anna, Frieda. Sorry about this."

Anna turned on her bedside light and snatched up the alarm clock: 2:02 A.M.

"Nobody else to home," Frieda said. All law enforcement on MEVE shared an emergency party line called the '69 line because of the last two digits of the number. Every call rang in quarters on Chapin and at Far View. Anna'd been the unlucky ranger who picked up first.

"What's up—other than me?" Anna was already threading her legs into yesterday's underpants.

"Got a report of lights in the maintenance yard. Somebody needs to check it out."

"I'm headed in that direction." Maintenance was scarcely a hundred yards from the housing loop on Chapin. Stacy would have been the logical one to respond but he never answered the '69. Scuttlebutt was he unplugged it nights. Some said for Bella, others said Rose did the unplugging.

Loss of sleep was a trade-off for money. Every call, short or long, earned two hours' overtime. As she buckled on her duty belt, Anna totaled it up. Two hours at time and a half was close to thirty bucks. She'd've paid nearly that for an uninterrupted night's sleep.

From the patrol car, she called in service. Frieda responded—not because she had to, she wasn't officially on duty. There would be no overtime or base pay for her. Frieda monitored because she took her job more seriously than her employers did. She didn't like rangers out without at least rudimentary backup.

The air was cool and fresh. Anna rolled down the Ford's windows and let the darkness blow in around her. On her first late shifts she'd had a new experience—or if not new, one she hadn't felt for a long time, not since leaving New York City. Anna'd found herself afraid of the dark.

Walking trail in Texas, skirting islands around Isle Royale, she'd worn the night like a star-studded cloak. But Mesa Verde was all about dead people. In the mind—or the collective unconscious—there was a feeling they'd not all left in the twelve hundreds. Or if they had, perhaps whatever it was that drove them out had taken up residence in the abandoned cities. Everywhere there were reminders of another time, another world.

Given the propensity of Jamie and some of the other interpreters to capitalize on New Age voodoo, Anna never admitted her fear but she patrolled with an ear open for voices long gone, footsteps not clothed in mortal flesh.

A half-moon threw bars of silver across the road, enough to see by, and as she turned onto the spur leading to Maintenance, she clicked off her headlights. The Maintenance yard, a paved area with a gas pump in the center, was surrounded by two-story buildings: offices, garages, a carpenter's shop, storage barns. Built in the 1940s, the buildings were of dark wood with small many-paned windows. One remnant remained from the thirties: the fire cache, where helitack stored the gear needed to fight wildland fire. It was of stone with juniper beams supporting a flat roof. Behind the cache a twelve-foot cyclone fence topped with barbed wire enclosed the construction company's equipment behind padlocked gates.

In the inky shadow of a storage barn, the car rolled to a stop. Anna called on scene and received Frieda's reassuring reply. Setting the brake, she listened. Pre-dawn silence, fragile and absolute, settled around her. The pop of her tires as they cooled, the clicking of insects flying against the intruder lights, pattered like dry rain.

Trickling out of the quiet, it came to her why Mesa Verde nights pricked some nerve deep in her psyche. Like New York City, the mesa was comprised of peopled dark, dark that collected in the corners of buildings and under eaves, choked alleys, and narrow streets. A darkness permeated with the baggage of humanity. Dreams and desires haunted the mesa the way they haunted the rooms in old houses. Traces of unfinished lives caught in the ether.

Anna felt her skin begin to creep. "Why don't you just rent a video of *Hill House* and be done with it?" she mocked herself.

Another minute whispered by. Apparently nothing was going to manifest itself in her windshield. She loosed the six-cell flashlight from its charger beneath the dash.

Metal clanked on metal as she opened the car door and she froze. It wasn't the familiar click of door mechanisms, it was what she'd been waiting for: something not right, a sound where silence ought to be.

Noise gave her direction. Leaving the car door open rather than risk a racket, she moved quietly toward the fenced construction yard. Between her car and the fence were three board-and-batten shacks used to store hand tools and pesticides. In the colorless light the short road looked like a scene from Old Tucson's back lot.

Anna followed the line of buildings till she ran out of shadow. Two junipers framed a picnic table where the hazardous-fuel-removal crew cleaned their saws. She slipped into the protective darkness. Closer now, she could see the gates to the yard. A chain hung loose, its padlock broken or unlocked.

Within the confines of the cyclone fence, equipment clustered like prehistoric creatures at a watering hole. Bones of metal linked with hydraulic cable in place of tendons thrust into the night: the skeletal neck of a crane, the scorpion's claw of a backhoe, the rounded back of a water truck—one she'd never seen in use though dust from construction was a constant irritation. Easily a million dollars' worth of machinery brought in to do the work needed for the waterline.

Again came the clank, softer this time and followed by a faint scraping sound. Moving quickly, Anna crossed the tarmac and slipped through the gates. Moonlight caught her, then she was again in shadow, her back against a wheel half again as tall as she.

When heart and breath quit clamoring in her ears, she listened. Concentration revealed sounds always present but seldom noted: the minute scratch of insect feet crossing sand, a whispered avian discussion high in the trees. Nothing unnatural, nothing human. Odd, Anna thought, that "man-made" and "natural" should be considered antithetical.

Time crawled by; the slight adrenaline rush brought on by the act of sneaking faded and she began feeling a bit silly crouched in the darkness chasing what was undoubtedly a wild goose—or at worst a chipmunk who'd decided to build her nest in one of Greeley's engines.

Probably the last guy out had forgotten to lock the gate. Monday nights Stacy had late shift. He should have checked it but something may have distracted him.

Realizing she'd been taking shallow nervous breaths, Anna filled her lungs. Muscles she hadn't known she was clenching relaxed and she felt her shoulders drop. Expelling a sigh to blow away the last of the chindi-borne cobwebs, she switched on her flashlight and stepped out of the shadows.

Weaving through the parked machines, she played the light over each piece of equipment. Nothing stirred, scuttled, or slithered. A backhoe at the end of the enclosure finished the group. Anna shone the light over the yellow paint, up an awkward angle, and into the mud-crusted bucket. Nothing.

The goose could consider itself chased. Anna was going back to bed. Turning to leave, her beam crawled along the oversized tires and across the toe of a boot, a cowboy boot, scuffed and brown like a hundred thousand others in the southwest.

Like a dog chasing cars, she thought. Now what? Indecision passed with a spurt of fear. She stepped into the shadows and moved the flashlight out from her body lest it become a target.

"Come on out and talk to me," she said. "No sense hiding at this point."

There was only one way out of the yard that didn't involve scaling the fence, and Anna waited for the intruder to show himself or bolt for the gate.

The toe twitched. "Come on out," Anna said reasonably. "You're not in too much trouble yet."

Slowly, with a feeble skritching sound, the toe pulled back into darkness. A peculiar shushing followed and Anna realized whoever it was was pulling off the boots.

Little hairs on the back of her neck began to prickle. "Enough's enough, come out of there." She walked toward the backhoe's rear tire, unsnapping the keeper on her .357 as she went.

The intruder was quick. On silent sock feet, he'd retreated into the jungle of blades, tires, and engines. Anna had no intention of following. Backing slowly out of the alley between the metal monoliths, she ducked clear of the moonlight and took her King radio from her belt.

Frieda, bless her, was still monitoring. "We've got an intruder in the construction yard," Anna said clearly. "Get me some backup."

The radio call stirred the stockinged feet. Distinct rustling from a careless move riveted Anna's attention on a ditcher parked one space nearer the open gate. Staying well back in the shadow, she waited. Silence grated on her nerves and she listened as much for the approach of help as she did for the movements of the person she tracked.

Scuffling: the tiny sound made her flinch as if a cannon had gone off near her ear. Behind her now, beyond the backhoe; loath to leave the dark for the glaring moonlight, Anna knelt and turned her light between the wheels. A flick of gray; a tail disappearing through the fence. She turned the flashlight off. Time to move. The rodent had tricked her into giving away her position.

Easing to her feet, she tried for quiet but knees and ankles popped like firecrackers in the stillness.

A foot scrape on concrete and a singing of air: a black line with a hook windmilled out from the rear of the ditcher. Moonbeams were sliced, air whistled through the iron. Someone was swinging a heavy chain with an eight-inch tow hook attached to the end.

Reflexively Anna dropped to her belly and rolled under the backhoe as the weighted chain cut through the air, striking the tire where she'd been standing. Iron links whipped around the hard rubber and struck the back of her neck, the links cracking against her temple. Shock registered but not pain.

Wriggling on elbows and knees, Anna worked her way deeper under the belly of the machine.

Footsteps, soft and running, followed the cacophony of chain falling. Whoever it was ran for the gate. Courage returned and Anna scrambled into the open. She was on her feet in time to hear the gate clang shut. Sprinting the twisted path across the pavement, she caught a glimpse of a figure flitting through the shadows of the utility buildings beyond.

When she reached the gate she stopped. The chain had been strung back through and the lock snapped shut.

"Damn it!" Greeley had his own locks and the rangers had not been given access keys. With a jump she reached halfway up the fence and hung there. A double line of barbed wire slanted away from the fence top. She could probably thread her way through with only a modicum of damage but not in time to catch whoever had locked her in.

Smothering an obscenity, she dropped back to earth and unsheathed her radio. Not even Frieda heard her call this time. Leaning against the wire, she caught her breath and let the nervous energy drain away. Fatigue welled up in its place and her legs began to shake. Where the chain had lashed ached and her head felt full of hot sand.

She crossed the asphalt and rested her back against the tread of a D-14 Cat. Her insides shook and her breath was uneven. What scared her wasn't so much the attack but her lack of readiness to meet it. Like a rookie—or a complacent old-timer—she'd wandered happily into the middle of a crime in progress. And nearly been killed for her stupidity. She'd gotten sloppy, let down her guard.

Mesa Verde was old and slow and visited by the old and slow. Situated on a mesa in the remote southwestern corner of Colorado, approachable only by twenty miles of winding two-lane mountain road, it didn't get the through traffic of a park on a major highway. No accidental tourists on their way from Soledad to Sing Sing.

Mesa Verde's dangers had struck Anna more akin to the pitfalls of Peyton Place. Societies, like other living organisms, sometimes fell ill. But she hadn't expected violence. She had let herself be lulled into a false sense of security.

Scrapes from the chain throbbed and she brought her mind back to the machinery yard. What had the intruder been after? The stuff was too obvious to fence, too big to steal. Something important enough to risk imprisonment. Assault on a federal officer was a felony offense.

The fog in her head was clearing and only a dull ache behind her eyes remained. Anna pushed herself to her feet. Somewhere beneath the backhoe was her flashlight. Before morning's business stomped over the whole place, she would use it to see if Mr. Brown Boots had left anything behind.

Cigarette butts were scattered beneath the ditcher. Sherlock Holmes might have made hay with such an abundance of clues but Anna didn't bother. Half the construction workers smoked and, near as she could tell, all of the maintenance men. Marlboro, Camel Lights, Winston, she noted the brands for the sake of feeling useful but they were too common to draw any conclusions.

In the cab of the Caterpillar she found some battered hand tools. Behind the seat of the water truck were a pair of welding gloves and what looked like a gas mask left over from World War II. Unless they were some brand of rare antiques they didn't look worth stealing.

The D-14 Cat yielded up the answers. Beneath the iron tread Anna found a plastic bag with a trace of white powder in it. She didn't taste it. She didn't have to. It was sugar.

Monkeywrenching was the only thing that made any sense. Someone waging guerrilla warfare against the new waterline. There was no telling how much time the intruder had had before Anna interrupted, how much damage had been done. As soon as she was let out of her pen she'd have to call Greeley. The contractor would not be pleased.

Monkeywrenching—sabotage—was an ancient form of combat. Anna respected it in its purest form: David Environmentalist against Goliath Industries. Whether or not this was the case with the waterline, she'd not decided.

Rogelio, her lover in Texas, had thrived on such night action. She'd met many of the ecotage experts he ran with. They didn't tend to violence against persons. No swinging of chains, crushing of skulls. Brown Boots had a good deal to lose, it would seem. Or a good deal to gain.

Al Stinson cared enough to throw a wrench in the works, a sabot in the machine, but it seemed absurd to risk a twenty-year career when she had legal avenues at her disposal.

Jamie maybe. She had nothing to lose materially and might still be naive enough to believe she wouldn't be thrown in jail if she were caught.

Somehow Anna couldn't see either Al or Jamie swinging a tow chain, but then she'd been wrong about people before. Brown boots: Tom Silva was the consummate drugstore cowboy. He probably had a whole closet full of boots. It wasn't too hard to picture him with a chain. Did he have a grudge against his employer, access to a key?

Again she tried Frieda.

This time there was an answer. "Sorry. I've been trying to raise somebody for you," the dispatcher apologized unnecessarily. "I finally went over to Stacy's. He'll be there shortly."

"Thanks." Anna called 316, Stacy's number. "Wake up Maintenance," she told him. "Find somebody entrusted with Greeley's master key."

Minutes ticked by. Anna didn't mind the wait. The night was dry and not too cold. A slight breeze whispered through the pine trees and she wasn't lonely. Closing her eyes she tried to recall everything she could about the intruder. One boot toe, brown, and a retreating form in dark clothing. She couldn't even say for sure if it was male or female, tall or short.

Outfoxed, outmaneuvered, and left penned up for everyone to see, Anna was beginning to get testy about the whole affair.

Boots ringing on pavement brought her head around. Stacy, in uniform, defensive gear, and flat hat, ran across the maintenance yard following the beam of a flashlight.

"Got the key?" she called.

"Got it."

Anna pushed herself to her feet and waited impatiently while he fumbled with the lock. "Whoever it was had a key," she remarked.

Stacy didn't say anything.

"Did you check it before you went off shift?"

"I honestly can't remember." Stacy was sullen, it was unlike him. The "honestly" bothered Anna.

The lock came open and he pulled the chain from the gates. Once freed, Anna demanded: "Why didn't you answer the six-nine line?"

Stacy turned his back to her and locked the gate. "The phone plug got knocked out somehow," he said flatly.

Rose. Anna didn't pursue it.

Stacy declined a ride home but Anna swung through the housing loop anyway. As she'd hoped, Frieda's light was on.

"Dropped by to say thanks," Anna said when the dispatcher answered the door.

"Likely story. Piedmont thinks you're here to see him."

It gladdened Anna's heart to see the yellow streak that ran to the screen at the sound of her voice. Scooping him up she kissed him between the ears. "Coming home sucks without a cat to meet you at the food dish."

Because all good dispatchers are mind readers, Frieda brought Anna a glass of wine. Out of deference to regulations, Anna removed her gun before taking the first draught. Piedmont spread himself down the length of her lap, his orange-and-white chin draped over her knees.

Anna related the night's tale to the dispatcher. Frieda was genuinely interested and Anna too keyed up to shut up and go home.

"Greeley hasn't made a lot of friends up here," Frieda said. "The interps are making quite a stink about the disturbance of the mesa. Al eggs them on—not on purpose, but most of them are of an age when passion's contagious."

"I'd like to think she'd draw the line at offing a ranger," Anna grumbled.

Frieda laughed. "Hard to picture. Maybe it's not ecotage at all. Just pure meanness. Greeley's own guys aren't that crazy about him either. He's a little on the oily side."

Anna took a long drink of wine and tried to call the construction workers to mind. They all ran together: big men in hard hats. The ache at the base of her skull suggested she pay a little more attention in the future.

"Sorry about the backup screwup. I'm glad you're not dead. Would I ever have felt a fool," Frieda said.

"Did you have trouble prying Stacy out of bed?"

"He was up watching television. I tried everyone else before it dawned on me he might have turned his phone off."

"Got 'accidentally' unplugged," Anna said cattily.

Frieda nodded. This was clearly not a surprise.

It crossed Anna's mind that had Stacy been the saboteur, he would have had time to run from Maintenance to the housing loop in the ten minutes it had taken Frieda to come knocking on his door. Meyers had the right temperament for a monkeywrencher—passion and a sense of his own importance in the scheme of things. Had he found the lock open when he made his last rounds and felt an opportunist urge to strike a blow for conservation?

Anna didn't like to think Stacy would swing an iron hook at her head.

Before she left she presumed on Frieda's hospitality one more time and borrowed her phone. If Greeley was home he wasn't answering.

"I'll try him again first thing in the morning," Frieda promised.

When Anna got back to the dorm it was after three and all the lights were blazing. Laughter and the rattle of voices met her at the door. "You were there, did it happen or not?" Jamie was shouting.

On Mesa Verde, it would seem, no one but Anna had any interest in sleep.

"Jimmy, you saw it—" A thud followed by laughter interrupted.

"Jimmy's had so much he couldn't see past his own nose." Jennifer Short's Memphis drawl.

"The spirit veil, oooooooh." Another voice, probably Jimmy Russell's, wailed like the ghosts in the Saturday morning cartoons. Then laughter shouted down by Jamie's: "Funny, real funny, you guys—"

Anna banged through the kitchen door. Moaning like Casper the Friendly Ghost, Jimmy Russell was traipsing around the living room in a drunken parody of a wraith. His face was flushed and his eyes bright but he was steady on his feet. Anna had known he was a drinker. Noting how well he'd learned to cope, she couldn't but wonder if, at twenty, he was an habitual drunk.

A study in superiority, Jamie was leaning in the entrance to the hall. "Laugh away," she was saying. "They're here. I've seen them before. Are you going to pretend you didn't, Jennifer? You were practically peeing your pants tonight."

"My, my, Jamie. Such a ladylike phrase," Jennifer drawled.

Rolling his eyes and fluttering his hands, Jimmy wailed.

"Keep it up. Keep it up," Jamie said with exaggerated patience.

Sprawled in one of the armchairs, her body limp, Jennifer percolated giggles in support of Jimmy's antics. "Aw, come on, Jamie. He's only teasin' yew."

"It's not me he needs to worry about." Jamie had taken on an air of secret knowledge.

"Excuse me," Anna cut in. "Could you guys take the party elsewhere? I've got to be up at six."

"We're sorry, Anna," Russell said contritely. Head slightly lowered, he looked at her from under thick blond lashes.

Undoubtedly it had been irresistible when he was six.

"Jamie saw the third world or whatever coming through that thing . . . a see-poo-poo—" Dissolving into giggles, Jennifer couldn't go on.

"Sipapu. See. Pah. Pooh." Jamie pronounced the word with the care one might employ when conversing with an imbecilic and not much loved child. "It's too bad law enforcement doesn't require their rangers to learn about the places they are supposedly protecting."

The merriment went out of Jennifer's face and a hardness came into it that Anna had never seen before. "Y'all can piss and moan the rest of the night if you want to. I'm going to bed. 'Night Anna."

The magnolia blossom apparently had a core of good Southern steel.

" 'Night," Anna returned automatically.

"Jamie really did see something. She's got a weird sense like that—you know, ghosts and shit," Jimmy Russell said somberly.

The boy was so transparent, if she'd not been tired and cranky, Anna might have found him amusing. Jennifer gone, Russell was trying to re-ingratiate himself with Jamie. *Somebody wants to get laid tonight,* she thought without charity but with undoubted accuracy.

Russell fell back on the sofa, his feet splayed out in front of him. Brown cowboy boots. Anna had no trouble picturing him with an implement of destruction. Environmental concerns didn't seem to be the Kentucky boy's mainstay but drunken pranks might be. After a six-pack or two Jamie could probably talk him into almost anything.

Anna began to wonder if all the ghostly theatrics were designed as a cover story for more practical measures taken to protect the Anasazi heritage.

Jamie interrupted Anna's train of thought. Stalking to one of the two refrigerators in the kitchen, she took out a Tupperware container and kicked the refrigerator door shut. "Bonegrinder!" As she spat out the word, she jerked open a drawer. In one continuous motion she fished out a serving spoon and popped the plastic lid off the food container.

"If somebody took one of those huge ditchers and started chewing a trench through Forest Lawn you can bet there'd be an outcry. It just wouldn't happen." Ladling a bite of some pasta concoction into her mouth as if to calm her nerves, Jamie went on. "You can't go around digging up white people's cemeteries. Oh no. Big sacrilege. They won't get away with it." Jamie inhaled another servingspoonful of pasta. "The whole mesa is sacred ground."

Though it had been in vogue at one time, there wasn't any archaeological evidence to support that theory, but Anna didn't say anything. She dumped her hat and gun on the dinette table and collapsed in one of the straightbacked chairs.

"They're not going to get away with grinding our bones up. Not this time."

Anna noted the "our." She also noted that Jamie's brown roots were just beginning to show at the base of her part. Raising her eyebrows politely, she invited Jamie to continue ranting.

"Solstice is coming," the interpreter said with finality.

June twenty-first; perhaps that was the proposed date of some planned event. Anna let the idea filter through her mind. Why would Jamie divulge that bit of information in the presence of a law enforcement ranger? Unless, as was often the case in publicity stunts, the law was necessary to provide the drama required to lure out the press. It was illegal for government employees to "tattle" to the press on touchy issues. But bringing down the wrath of the six o'clock news was almost the only way to effect any real change. Like any other entrenched bureaucracy, the Park Service was filled with people passing the buck and covering the hindmost parts of their anatomy.

"What happens on solstice?" Anna asked.

"It's a sacred day to the Old Ones," Jamie replied, with the air of an insider who only hands out information in pre-approved sound bites.

"Are they going to hold those Indian dances or something?" Jimmy Russell wanted to know.

"Not likely. 'They' have been dead for seven hundred years," Anna told him.

"They might," Jamie said cryptically.

"Ah. Chindi." Anna was suddenly too tired to play along.

"The spirit veil, ooooo—" Jimmy's wail ended abruptly at the look on her face.

"Are you driving, Jimmy?"

"Yes, ma'am." He dangled his car keys.

Anna took them and slipped them into her pocket. If Russell was her chain-swinging eco-terrorist, he was too far gone to do much damage till morning.

"You're drunk. Sleep on the couch. I'll leave your keys on the table when I go to work. Good night."

A few minutes of murmuring came through the wall as Jamie dragged out bedding for the inebriated helitacker, then the house was blessedly quiet. Anna took two aspirins for her head. For her nerves she recited the only prayer she knew all the way through: "From ghoulies and ghosties and long-leggety beasties/And things that go bump in the night, Good Lord, deliver us!"

5

At eight a.m., when Stacy pulled up in the patrol car, Jimmy Russell was still curled up on the couch. He didn't even twitch when Anna walked through. Without so much as a twinge of guilt, she let the door bang shut behind her.

Usually Stacy's aesthetic countenance was a welcome sight, but lack of sleep had left Anna surly. Evidently the night's festivities had left their mark on him as well. In lieu of "good morning" he said: "Mind if we stop by my house? Rose's going to Farmington and Bella needs a ride to Maintenance. Drew said he'd keep an eye on her till six."

Anna wanted to ask why Rose didn't take the kid along, but she minded her own business. The radio was tuned to a Navajo station and a language that sounded like Chinese sawed at her nerves. With an abrupt movement, she switched it off.

"Wrong side of the bed?" Stacy asked.

"Tired. My housemates kept me up after our rendezvous in Maintenance. Jamie said she'd seen a veil or some damn thing. Chindi passing from the underworld to this one. They were out at Cliff Palace, drinking and scaring each other is my guess."

"I checked the book." Stacy sounded alarmed. "There were no permits for Cliff Palace last night."

Any employee going anywhere—or anytime—the public was not allowed had to have a backcountry permit signed by the chief ranger. Cliff Palace after hours fell under that restriction.

Anna wondered if Stacy entertained the same suspicions she did about possible monkeywrenching business. "If that's really where they were then I doubt much harm was done."

"When I made my sweep at eleven I didn't see any cars," he said stubbornly.

"Maybe they were on bicycles." Leaning her head back against the seat, she closed her eyes and let the subject drop.

At the housing loop, she fiddled with the radio while Stacy went in to fetch Bella. A little mental arithmetic told Anna that Bella was his stepdaughter. She was a first- or second-grader and he'd met his wife three years ago. Taking on the responsibility, not only of someone else's child, but a child with a disability, spoke of powerful love—or powerful need.

"Hello, my little pine nut," she heard Stacy call when he was halfway up the walk. He disappeared into the house to reappear moments later with Bella. The child's face was a testament to her mother's youthful good looks. A rounded heart set off by a crop of carefully tended curls. Brown hair, several shades lighter than Rose's, caught the morning sun and glinted with blond highlights. Wide-spaced eyes sparkled above a small straight nose. This loveliness made more pathetic the rolling gait and bowed legs, far too short for her upper body.

Hand in hand with Stacy, Bella chattered up at him. For

every glitter of hero worship in her eyes, there was an answering glow of adoration in his. Stacy's slender frame shaped itself into a question mark as he curbed his steps, leaning down to hear her.

What Anna had seen as a burden clearly lightened the load Stacy professed to have carried after his first wife left him.

"You're Anna Pigeon," the child announced when they reached the car.

"You got me there." Anna leaned over the seat-back to shove briefcases and hats out of Bella's way. Fleetingly, she wondered if Stacy had been talking about her.

"I read your name tag," the child explained as she swung herself into the rear seat. "That's in case you thought I might be a psycho or something."

Stacy laughed. "Psychic, pine nut. Psycho is crazy."

"I'm not old enough to be crazy," she said confidently. "Do you have children, Mrs. Pigeon?"

"None to speak of."

"Oh." Bella sounded disappointed.

"I have a cat." Anna tried to exonerate herself.

"Don't you like children?"

"Some of my best friends are children." Anna was thinking of Alison, her Michigan housemate's daughter.

The truth must have rung through the words. Bella brightened immediately. "That's okay then. If the cat has kittens, can I play with them?"

"Your mom's allergic, pine nut," Stacy reminded gently.

"Not have, Stacy. Play with. I'd wash after."

"Piedmont's a boy cat," Anna said. "So no kittens. But he might like it if you'd come play with him. Sometimes I suspect he misses the little girl we used to live with."

"Does he try to hide it?" Bella asked, and Anna sensed she was already adept at hiding hurt and loneliness.

"Yes. Sometimes he goes out and kills mice. Then I think he feels better."

"I like mice."

"So does Piedmont." Anna was losing ground in this conversation. A smile played on Stacy's lips. She was willing to bet it was at her expense.

The maintenance yard was loud with heavy equipment. Stacy pulled up in front of the fire cache. "Stay in the car, honey. Too much traffic. I'll find Drew."

"Are you married?" Bella resumed the interrogation as Stacy disappeared into the cache.

"Used to be," Anna replied.

"Did he divorce you?"

"He died." Anna wished Stacy would come back. "Maybe I'd better go and see what's keeping your dad."

Her cowardly exit was thwarted. "No. Stay. Stacy'll be right back. He never forgets. My first dad divorced us because I wasn't born normal," Bella stated matter-of-factly. "Momma said."

Anna didn't know what to say to that. She was saved by Stacy's reappearance, Drew beside him. Drew Kinder was as close to a "mountain of a man" as Anna'd ever met, made of a core of stone-hard muscle covered with a layer of baby fat a couple of inches deep. Unruly eyebrows and a moth-eaten mustache grew like lichen on his round face.

Next to the helitacker, Stacy's six-foot-two looked average, short even, and his slenderness was accentuated. Seeing the two men together, an image of a bass fiddle and bow flashed through her mind.

"Hiya, Drew," Bella called.

"Hiya, beautiful." Drew leaned down, hands on the door frame. His head filled the window. "I gotta fuel the truck, then we hit the road."

"Hit the road," Bella repeated, as if the phrase had struck a harmonious chord within her.

"I'll help you with the truck," Anna volunteered. She didn't want to be left alone with Bella again. The child's unrelenting forthrightness was unsettling.

"Can't hack it?" Stacy asked over the roof of the patrol car as she climbed out.

Anna just laughed.

While Drew filled the fire truck with diesel, she leaned against the fender. In his huge hands the nozzle looked like a child's water pistol.

"Bella's quite a girl," he said.

"Seems smart enough. Too bad she's . . ." Aware she was giving pity where none was asked, Anna left the sentence unfinished.

Drew straightened up. The sun was behind his head. In silhouette he loomed as solid as the proverbial brick outhouse. "Maybe that's what makes her so strong, so smart. She sees right through people. Maybe she got that from being the way she is. Ever think of that?"

"I will now," Anna promised.

"Her mom wants her to get all these operations on her legs. Pretty painful stuff. Make her more 'normal.' Maybe it's a good idea, maybe it's not. All I know is it's got to hurt. I don't like seeing kids hurt."

"Nobody does," Anna said mildly.

Drew shot her a look that startled her with its venom. "Don't kid yourself," he said, and went back to pumping diesel. "Her folks ought to leave her alone. I'm a giant. She's a dwarf. We're the variety that adds spice."

A blue Ford six-pac carrying five men in orange hard hats pulled up behind them in line for fuel. Ted Greeley was driving.

"Well, if it isn't my own personal ranger," Greeley greeted Anna. "How am I doing? Running afoul of the law?"

"Not yet," she returned.

He looked at his watch. "It's early."

"Did Frieda get ahold of you about last night?"

"She did. Damn near too late. You guessed it. The son of a bitch dumped sugar in the gas tank of my ditcher. If anybody'd fired it up I'd've been proud owner of a piece of shit retailing at close to a hundred grand. I'm none too happy one of my boys left the gate unlocked and I'm none too happy one of your boys didn't catch it. I'd hate to think all my tax dollars are paying for are cute uniforms for pretty little rangers." He winked and Anna managed not to spit in his open eye.

Silva got out of the truck. He had his shirt on this time—a western cut with pearl snaps—but the tails were out, the cuffs not snapped, the collar open. He looked just tumbled out of a woman's bed or ready to tumble into one.

" 'Morning, Ranger Pigeon," he said lazily as he looked Anna up and down. Again she wasn't flattered.

"That ever work for you?" she asked.

He didn't even play coy. "More often than not. Is it going to work on you?" Silva removed his hard hat and ran a hand through his shock of black hair. "Or are rangers' sex drives too low?"

"IQs are too high," Anna retorted.

Everybody laughed but Silva. Anna guessed she'd struck a nerve. A smile broke slowly on Tom's face but it never reached his eyes. She braced herself. She had the sinking feeling the repartee was about to take an ugly turn.

All he said was: "Better watch it. I'm getting more and more eligible every day. By August I ought to be Bachelor of the Year. Ain't that right, Ted?"

Greeley didn't return Silva's smile.

"Got to hop to it," Silva said. "The boss wants to leave early to get in a round of golf. Me, I can't play golf. I'm not over the hill yet."

"Come on," Greeley growled. "I don't pay you to chase—"

Anna was sure he intended to say "pussy" but he saved himself at the last second.

"—your tail," he finished.

"See you around," Silva said to Anna as he put his hard hat back on.

"By the way, I never did find out anything about that truck that ran you off the road," Anna told him.

"Was no truck," Tom said as he turned away. "I was just jerking your chain."

He was wearing brown cowboy boots. But then so were Greeley and two of the others. So was Anna, for that matter.

Drew finished fueling the truck and Stacy brought Bella to the gas shed. As he lifted her onto the high front seat their radios rasped to life.

"Seven hundred, this is Beavens at Cliff Palace."

As one, Drew, Anna, and Stacy turned up the volume on their portables. The interpreters in the ruins seldom called in unless there was a problem.

"Lockout," Drew offered.

"Let's hope," Stacy said.

"Shhh."

"Cliff Palace, this is seven hundred. Go ahead," Frieda's voice came over the air.

"We've got a litle girl here having trouble breathing. She doesn't look too good."

Anna and Stacy began to run for the patrol car. Anna flipped on the vehicle's lights and siren. "Nothing like starting the day off right."

"Jesus. Not another one."

The anguish in Stacy's voice startled a laugh from Anna. "Hey, it's something to do."

The two-way road to Cliff was narrow and twisting with no shoulders. Despite lights and sirens, tourists plodded ahead, refusing to give right-of-way.

Trapped behind an RV, Anna and Stacy crawled along at twenty-three miles an hour. Anna grabbed the public address mike and turned up the volume. "Pull to the right, please. Pull to the right. Pull to the right, please." She repeated the command until the RV's driver came out of his comatose state and began to slow, squeezing the oversized vehicle to the side of the road.

"Damn. Just once I'd like to ride shotgun with a shotgun and permission to use it."

Stacy said nothing. His eyes were fixed on the road as he hunched over the wheel. Above the dark line of beard, his cheek was pale. Tension pulled his shoulders almost to ear level.

Cliff Palace lot was full. They parked in a handicapped space near where the trail started down to the ruin and Anna called in: "Seven hundred, three-one-two, we've arrived on the scene."

Having taken the red trauma pack and an oxygen bottle from the trunk, she led the way down the crowded trail using "excuse me" the way a frustrated motorist uses the horn.

As soon as they climbed the eight-foot ladder that brought them within the cliff dwelling, they saw the knot of people surrounding the sick child.

On the periphery was Jamie Burke. The moment she noticed Anna and Stacy she marched toward them. They met halfway through the alcove and the interpreter started in: "It's not like you weren't warned, for God's sake. Nobody listened. This time it's a child. Solstice—"

"Hold that thought, Jamie," Anna cut her off. "I'll get back with you this evening." Dodging past the other woman, she plowed through the tourists at a fast walk.

Mesa Verde's most famous cliff dwelling, Cliff Palace filled an alcove several hundred feet long. The dwelling itself was composed of two hundred and seventeen rooms, twenty-one kivas, and, at the far end, a four-story tower, the inside room of which boasted intact plaster with discernible paintings. The entrance to the tower was reachable only by ladder that led to a narrow path around yet another roofless kiva.

In this congested part of the ruin was a frail-looking child. She strained for air with the rounded chest of those suffering chronic pulmonary disorders. Dark hair fell forward over her face, and stick-thin arms and legs poked out from beneath an oversized T-shirt. The child was propped in a sitting position against a stone wall built seven centuries before she was born. A man—probably her father—sat on the wall, one leg on either side, supporting her. A hand-lettered sign reading PLEASE DO NOT SIT OR CLIMB ON THE WALLS had tumbled to the path at the foot of the wooden ladder.

The girl braced her hands on her knees and leaned forward. Tendons in her neck pulled like ropes with the effort of breathing, yet only squeaks of air were pushed out.

Anna eased through the crowd and put down her gear. "Hi, I'm Anna," she introduced herself as she removed a nasal cannula from the oxygen kit and fitted it to the cylinder. "What's your name?" The girl hadn't enough breath to spare for an answer.

"Her name's Stephanie," the man seated on the wall answered for her. "Stephanie McFarland. She's got asthma."

An ominous blue tint colored the skin around Stephanie's lips and in her fingernail beds.

"She was doing fine a bit ago, then she started feeling like she might throw up," a thin-faced woman in her early thirties told Anna. "She's been at altitude before and we've never had trouble like this. We're from Denver. It's nearly this high. Steph should be used to it. I'm her mom," the woman finished in a whisper.

"Well, Stephanie, we're going to get you down to a doctor so you can breathe better, okay?" The girl nodded slightly, all her concentration taken by the effort of drawing and expelling air.

"Meyers, hand me the—" Anna broke off as she looked over at Stacy.

Clutching the red trauma bag to his chest as a frightened woman might clutch her baby, he stood at the edge of the circle of concerned onlookers. The blood had drained from his face and he was so pale Anna was afraid he was going to pass out.

"Meyers!" she said sharply.

The brown eyes turned toward her. They were clouded with fear—or shock.

"Hand me the bag. Then give Frieda a call and see if we can't get helitack down here with a litter. We're going to need the ambulance as well."

For a moment it seemed as if he didn't understand, then his eyes focused. Anna watched him for a few seconds more but he began making the calls. She turned down her radio so she could talk with Stephanie and her parents.

Seven minutes and Drew called on scene at Cliff Palace parking. In that time Stephanie had begun to go downhill. By the time Drew arrived with the Stokes, she had lost consciousness.

Keeping up a running commentary to calm the parents and Stephanie if she wasn't beyond hearing, Anna had taken the IV kit from the trauma bag and prepped the child's thin arm. "This is just to get some fluids in her; it may help to break up the congestion. And, too, if she needs medication at the hospital, they can just put it right in."

She swabbed the skin with alcohol and readied a number-sixteen needle. To Drew she said: "We're not wasting time with this. One try; if I don't get in, we're out of here."

"Do it," Drew said.

"Damn," Anna whispered. "This kid has no veins."

"What? Have you got it?" Drew asked.

"No. Load and go. Wait. I'm getting a flashback."

"Too many drugs in college," Drew muttered under his breath.

Anna noted the red of blood in the flashback chamber of the IV catheter with satisfaction. She was in. Carefully, she pulled the catheter off the needle, sliding it into the vein. "Pop the tourniquet." She taped the catheter in place. "Go."

Anna addressed herself to the little girl strapped into the evacuation litter. "Stephanie, we're carrying you out. You're in good hands." Maybe the child's eyelids twitched in response. Maybe it was just the play of the sun.

Drew had taken his place at the head of the litter.

Crouched down, elbows on thighs, he looked solid, like a rock. When he began to rise Anna was put in mind of the unfolding of the stony peak of Bald Mountain in Disney's *Fantasia*.

Stacy knelt at the foot of the Stokes. His lips were pressed in a thin line and his eyes turned inward, unreadable.

"Ready?" Drew asked.

Meyers didn't respond. "Stacy!" Drew raised his voice. Like a man in a trance, Stacy slowly began to lift. "Atta boy," said the helitacker.

The Stokes was of orange plastic hard enough to haul up inclines and drag over rough terrain. Encasing the fragile form of the child, it resembled a medieval instrument of torture rather than the secure embrace of modern emergency evacuation equipment, and Anna felt bad for the parents, already frightened half out of their wits.

Four ladders of juniper wood, polished to a dark gloss by the palms of countless tourists, led up twenty-five feet through the crack in the cliff's face to the mesa.

Stephanie McFarland would not be roped up this incline, but carried back out the entrance trail. The distance was greater but the ascent not so precipitous.

"Coming through," Drew boomed. Curious onlookers parted reluctantly. Drew going first, the procession began to move down the path fronting the cliff dwellings. Tourists shifted, pressing back against stone walls. Bright-hued clothing, cameras, sunglasses, all combined to create a jarring kaleidoscope of color against the serene peach and buff of the ancient village.

Over the centuries roofs had fallen in, paint chipped away, and fiber mats rotted from doorways; the clangor of life leeched away until the structures had taken on the timeless purity of Greek statuary. But, like the ancient Greeks who had painted their pale marble figures vivid colors, the Anasazi had plastered the warm neutrality of their sandstone exteriors, then decorated them in red and black patterns.

Mesa Verde's Old Ones might have been as much at home with the cacophony of neon and spandex as the moderns.

The pathway clear, Drew picked up the pace. Holding the IV bag above shoulder level, Anna walked beside the litter. Stephanie's chest movement was barely perceptible and the tissue-thin eyelids blue and delicately veined. Some of the pallor was probably natural but the faint bluish at lips and fingernails was not.

Anna stroked back the dark hair. The child's skin was cool to the touch, clammy.

"Seven hundred, three-one-four."

"Seven hundred," Anna and Drew's radios bleated as Dispatch responded. Anna turned hers down.

"The ambulance has arrived at Cliff Palace. We're at the entrance. Repeat: the entrance."

"Seven hundred copies. Did you get that, three-one-two?"

Anna pulled her radio from her duty belt. "I got it. We'll be up in ten minutes or so. Two helitacks are standing by at the stairs. There's a narrow spot there. Send somebody down from the overlook to clear the visitors out of it."

"Ten-four. I'll send Claude Beavens." The dispatcher named the seasonal interpreter, who had radioed in the incident.

Anna put her radio back on her belt and watched her footing as she trod the uneven pavement. Like all the park's ruins accessible to tourists, Cliff Palace had a paved path leading to it from the parking lot on the mesa top. When the ruins were first opened there'd been primitive trails that ladies in long dresses and picture hats had picked their way down, carefully placing each buttoned-up boot. In the thirties the Civilian Conservation Corps had come in and earned their Depression dollars with the back-breaking chore of carving staircases from native rock and shoring up trails with stone.

Beauty and grace had gone the way of cheap labor. Now the paths were a hodgepodge of asphalt and rock, patched and repatched.

The trail switched back several times then narrowed to hand-hewn steps leading into a crevice between two boulders. After more than half a century the workmanship of the CCC still held fine. Only the lips of the steps had been fortified with pale scabs of modern concrete.

The stairway, just wide enough to admit people single file, was choked with tourists who'd started down before Claude Beavens had been sent to stop traffic.

"Gonna have to ask you folks to go on back up," Drew called over the low-grade chatter. The hips of the better endowed scraped a patter of sand from the soft rock as they shifted in the confining space. Faces displayed the sheeplike vacancy of vacationers who've come upon the unexpected.

"Ask the guy behind you to turn around," the helitack foreman suggested patiently. He spoke over his shoulder, his thick arms showing no strain at holding Stephanie's little weight.

Attuned to the vital signs of her patient, Anna caught a faint sigh. She laid the palm of her hand on the girl's diaphragm. Through the knit T-shirt, she could feel the bones of the rib cage but not the gentle rise of lungs filling with air.

"What?" Drew pressed.

Anna shook her head, waited. With a sucking sound, like the hiss of a new kitten, the child drew a sudden breath.

"Thanks," Anna said to no one in particular. To Drew she said: "We're in a hurry." Edging past him, she stood at the foot of the stairs.

"Got to move you out. This girl needs medical attention. Up you go. Thanks. Thanks." Anna spoke pleasantly, but she was prodding rounded backs and pudgy shoulders, herding people up the stairway.

As they began retreating, she turned back to Drew. His head was sunk between his massive shoulders. The little braided pigtail he affected poked out incongruously as he stared down into the litter.

Adrenaline spurted into Anna's system. "What? What've you got?"

"Breathing, but way too slow. Assholes," Anna heard him mutter. "Bringing a sick little kid way out here."

Paul Summers, looking as close to a GQ model as anyone could in the ill-fitting Nomex, thrust his head over the rock above Anna's head.

"You gonna need ropes?"

Drew shook his head. "It'd take too long. Here, Anna, you hold the front." Stacy's arms had grown slack, his end of the litter close to slipping from his grasp. "Stacy, pay attention," Drew snapped as he handed Anna the litter and eased butt first under the loaded Stokes. "Put the weight on my back."

Taking the head of the litter, Anna looked down at her patient. Even with the oxygen canister, lashed for security between her knees, turned to fifteen liters per minute on a non-rebreather face mask, the blue tinge around Stephanie's mouth remained.

Crouched down, Drew was in place underneath the Stokes. He straightened up, and like a rowboat on the crest of a wave, the litter with its fragile burden was lifted into the air.

Anna's arms were fully extended when he stopped. "Let's do it," she said.

One step at a time, she backed up the stairs. The orange plastic scraped along the sandstone but, balanced on Drew's back, the Stokes was high enough to clear the narrowest part of the crevice. "Keep coming," Anna said. "We'll make it but just barely."

"Barely's good enough," Drew grunted through a kinked esophagus.

Tossed as if on stormy seas, the orange litter wobbled through the crack in the rock. The GQ helitacker peered anxiously down, his blond head bobbing in sympathy as he worked his way along the top of the boulders they crept through.

Arms at full reach, Anna was out of eye contact with Stephanie McFarland. As the seconds ticked by, she could feel her anxiety rising.

"Paul," she called up. "What's she look like?"

"Not good."

"Breathing?"

"Can't tell."

"Get the bag valve." Anna kept her voice calm both for her patient and for the audience of tourists she could hear Claude Beavens organizing twenty feet up the trail behind her.

At last Drew's head and shoulders emerged from between the walls of stone. Humped over, he carried the litter onto the landing at the foot of a long metal staircase leading up to a viewing platform cut from the mesa top.

Over her shoulder Anna glimpsed a gauntlet of visitors yet to be run. Instead of stopping them on the spacious platform, the interpreter had arranged them all on one side of the stairs, where they stood like a Busby Berkeley musical kick line waiting to go into their eleven o'clock number.

Beavens, all bony elbows and wrists, with a neck so long and skinny his flat brimmed hat took on the aspect of a plate balanced on a broom handle, was waving his arms like an officious dance master. "People, people," he shouted. "Give them room. Emergency evac. Give the rangers room."

"Down," Drew said. Slowly he knelt, Anna and Stacy keeping the litter stable.

Stephanie McFarland came into view. Her face was gray and her hypoxia had grown more pronounced. Again Anna laid a hand on the child's diaphragm. Drew and Stacy repositioned themselves around the Stokes.

"Ten," Anna announced, timing the child's respirations. "Let's bag her. Paul!"

There was a scuffling sound as he slid down the sandstone to land lightly on his feet. "Okay!" he called back up the face of the boulder. An unseen person pushed a green airway kit over the edge and it fell neatly into his waiting hands. Within seconds he had the Ambu bag—a soft plastic barrel about the size of a football with a face mask on one end and a length of plastic tubing trailing from the other—out of the satchel. With an economy of movement that in one so young and so pretty always took Anna by surprise, he hooked the length of tubing to the green oxygen cylinder, then handed Anna the bag so she could fit the mask over Stephanie's mouth and nose.

"Take the IV, Paul. Ventilating her at twenty-five breaths a minute," she informed them, as she began pumping air into the child. "Go."

Keeping in step with Anna as best they could, they carried the Stokes up the metal stairs. Drew had taken the foot and used his height to keep the litter level.

"In and out and in and out and," Anna chanted under her breath, keeping time as she forced oxygen into the failing lungs. Behind her she could feel the gentle battering of camera cases and shoulder bags as she pushed past the line of people along the stair rail. Occasionally she felt something softer than steel mesh beneath her boots and heard a squawk of pain but she was only dimly aware of these things. Her eyes and mind were fixed on the now deep and regular rise of the little girl's chest.

"Looking good," Drew was saying. "She's pinking up."

Anna glanced at Stephanie's face. The deathlike pallor had abated somewhat. "Paul," she said quietly. "Radio for a patrol car escort. We'll be running hot. I want the road clear."

The firefighter keyed his mike with one hand. Keeping the IV drip high with the other, he began a series of radio calls.

The stairs were behind them. "Clear sailing," Drew said cheerfully.

Anna secured the Stokes to the gurney with webbed belting. Stacy'd gone catatonic and without his help, she banged it ungracefully into the back of the waiting ambulance. Not for the first time, she cursed the antiquated equipment a poverty-stricken Park Service was forced to make do with year after year.

Anna and Stacy rode down in the ambulance. Paul Summers drove, Mrs. McFarland rode in the passenger seat. Anna changed Stephanie to humidified oxygen and rechecked the girl's vital signs. Strapped into the seat near the gurney's head, Stacy held the run sheet on his lap, but it didn't look as if he was writing the numbers as she called them out. He'd not said a word since he'd completed his radio requests half an hour before.

Anna patted the little girl's arm. "You're doing real good, Steph. Hang in there." The child had not regained consciousness and Anna had no way of knowing if she heard. To Stacy she said: "Are you okay?"

Stacy just shook his head.

Two emergency room nurses met them in the ambulance bay at Southwest Memorial. Stacy stayed in the ambulance while Anna replaced the inventory they'd used on the run from the hospital's stock room. Anna then took a couple of minutes to talk with Bill McFarland. Stephanie had had a severe attack once before. Ridiculous as it was, the information comforted Anna, as if the park had been somehow exonerated.

Anna drove the ambulance on the return trip. Paul Summers threw himself on the cot. "These carry-outs are getting to be a bore," he complained. "How many now? One last Tuesday, one the week before that."

"Maybe it's a conspiracy," Anna returned. "Hills gets a healthy chunk of the five hundred dollars paid for each run for his budget."

"Hills'd do it, too," Paul said with a laugh. "Mr. Tightwad. How about you, Stacy, are you getting a cut?"

Stacy's silence remained unbroken. Paul abandoned light conversation with a "G'night."

Meyers had panicked, frozen. Anna wasn't so much angry with him as sympathetic. Everybody had a panic button. The heroes just managed to stumble through life without it being pushed. Two hundred feet beneath the icy waters of Lake Superior Anna had met up with her own cowardice.

But she could avoid deep cold water. If Stacy wanted to be a ranger he'd have to get used to handling sick and injured people. In most national parks the only doctors available were there on vacation.

Writing the report on the McFarland medical fell to Anna. In the crowded back of the CRO, where three desks were crammed into a space where only one should have been, she sat in front of an old IBM Selectric and stared down at the 10-343 threaded around the platen. The form was five thicknesses. Hitting a wrong key meant Wite-Out in quintuplicate.

Putting off the inevitable, she turned to the district ranger. Hills Dutton was a large square-faced man with thinning sandy hair that curled at his collar. From somewhere in the mare's nest that was his desk top, he'd retrieved a pair of calipers. Shirttail in hand, he was measuring the thickness of the excess flesh on his belly.

"Hills, what did you think of the medical today?"

"Nine percent body fat," he announced with satisfaction, and carefully wrote in the numbers on a physical training graph he'd colored with felt-tipped pens. "Bet you can't top that, Anna. You're a woman more or less, right? Maybe eighteen percent? Women can be up to twenty-eight percent before they're considered fat. Men pork out at seventeen. You got it easy."

Unzipping his pants, he tucked the shirt in and gave his flat belly an affectionate pat before putting his gunbelt back on. "Not bad for an old man."

"Seems like there've been an awful lot of carry-outs at Cliff this summer," Anna persisted. "What's usual for June?"

"It happens," Hills admitted vaguely. "Lots of senior citizens up here."

"Today we carried out a third-grader."

"Asthma." Hills fished a tool catalogue off the top of the pile.

Anna gave up and went back to staring at the 10-343, trying to screw her courage to the sticking place and make that first typo.

"Frieda," Hills called over the partition to the front desk. "Call Maintenance and see if they've got any old ratchet sets they can spare. I've got to get some for the vehicles."

"Your credit's no good with Maintenance," Frieda returned. "So tight he squeaks," she muttered.

"I heard that," Hills said. "Maybe I'll order some. Got any DI-ones?" He named the purchase order form.

"Sure you will," came the murmur. Then: "All out." There was no forthcoming offer to run over to Administration and get them. Frieda's territory as the chief ranger's secretary and dispatcher was carefully defined. It didn't include running errands for the lesser rangers.

"I'll get them," Anna offered, glad of an excuse to postpone writing the report a bit longer. "I need to talk to Patsy anyway."

She poked along the twenty feet of path between the buildings, stopping to watch a tarantula make its majestic way across the asphalt. After the tarantulas she'd met in the backcountry of Guadalupe Mountains National Park in Texas, these northern creatures were decidedly non-threatening. Beside their teacup-sized Trans Pecos cousins they seemed almost cute. Still, Anna didn't get too close.

No one had yet dispelled to her satisfaction the myth that they could jump long distances.

"Don't you just love them?"

Anna looked up from her bug to find Al Stinson, hands on knees, studying the tarantula with a look akin to true love. Off duty, Stinson dressed in classic archaeologist style: khaki shorts and a white oxford shirt. Gray hair poked out around her lined face. Chapped knuckles and clipped nails made her hands as ageless and practical-looking as any working man's. "Just beautiful," Stinson said of the spider.

"Maybe to a lady tarantula," Anna hedged.

"This is a female. Lookie." The interpreter reached down and touched the creature gently on one of its legs. "See? No hair. I don't know about European girls, but ours don't have leg hair. Only the males."

"You're kidding."

"No." Stinson laid her hand flat on the asphalt and the tarantula tested it gingerly with a hairless foreleg. Something was evidently amiss. The creature backed away and took another route.

"Too bad," Stinson said. She straightened and rested her hands on prominent pelvic bones. "It feels neat when they walk on you. Little elfin feet."

"It'd take four elves to make that many tracks," Anna returned, not envying Al the experience.

Stinson sniffed the air with a round, slightly squashed nose. "God! I love it."

Politely, Anna sniffed too. Mixed with the smell of bus exhaust and hot tar was a delicate perfume, warmed off the tiny yellow blooms of a bush near the walk. "The bitterbrush?"

"The silence. It was after three-thirty. Construction had stopped for the day. No roaring bonegrinder. Some bones were uncovered. May mean a burial. Wouldn't that be great? We'll get Greeley shut down yet." Al laughed, a nasal but infectious whinny. "The Boys will not be pleased."

One of the many mysteries of Mesa Verde was that so few Anasazi burial sites were found. Some remains had been uncovered in sealed and abandoned rooms in the dwellings and some in the midden heaps below the cliff dwellings, but no burial ground had been discovered and surprisingly few individual sites for a society of near ten thousand souls that had flourished for more than five centuries.

Talk of the pipeline put Anna in mind of her housemate. "Al, Jamie was on duty in Cliff Palace when we had that medical this morning. Lately she's been dropping heavy-handed hints that something's going down on solstice. Is there anything I ought to know?"

Stinson threw back her head like Barbara Stanwyck in *Maverick Queen* and snorted a laugh. "The less law enforcement knows, the better I sleep nights."

Anna laughed with her, partly at the sentiment and partly at a mental image of Al Stinson as Queen of the Cattle Thieves. Amid the merriment she found herself wondering if the maverick queen could swing a chain as well as a lariat.

"If you hear anything that sounds like it could get somebody hurt or fired, let me know and I'll see if I can't fulfill my role as Professional Party Pooper."

"Better you than The Boys."

By the time Anna wandered into Administration it was after four P.M. and people were stirring to leave for the day. The receptionist's desk was tidied and, engrossed in a phone conversation, she barely gave Anna a nod.

Anna fetched the procurement forms from the storage

room in the basement. On her way back she stopped in the doorway of Patsy Silva's office.

The superintendent's secretary kept her office in a state of impressive order. Plants in macramé hangers, pictures, and a stained-glass image of Kokopelli, the flute player, in the window kept the orderliness from being oppressive.

"Hills could use your decorating service," Anna said as she leaned against the door frame.

"Hills could use a bulldozer," Patsy replied with a smile.

"How's it going? I didn't get a list of times and places for paternal visits so I just assumed you and Tom worked it out."

Patsy turned away briefly, fussed with some papers. Anna tried to read the expression on her face but it was too fleeting.

"We're doing okay," Patsy said.

"Any more gifts of the weird persuasion?"

"Only this." Patsy produced an extra bright smile as she held up her left wrist for inspection.

Anna whistled long and low. The watch Patsy wore was—or looked to be—fourteen-carat gold with at least a carat's worth of diamonds sparkling around the face. Even with the union doing its fiscal magic, the watch must have cost Silva a month's wages.

"Tom?"

Patsy nodded and Anna caught the expression again. This time she pegged it: embarrassment. Evidently it wasn't all gifts Patsy took offense to. Only cheap ones.

"Good for you." Anna glanced at her own Wal-Mart special. She'd managed to kill enough time. In six minutes she was off duty. The 10-343 had been effectively avoided for one day.

She called Stacy on the radio and he brought the patrol

car to give her a lift to Far View. He still wore a haunted look and drove through the empty parking lot with the same hunched intensity as when weaving down a narrow road with lights and siren blaring.

"What happened to Bella?" Anna asked to make conversation.

"What do you mean?" Alarmed, Stacy lost his inward look. "Did something happen to Bella?"

"Drew was on the carry-out. Wasn't he baby-sitting today? I just wondered where he'd stashed her."

Visibly, he relaxed. "Bella stayed at the fire dorm watching cartoons with Jimmy. He called in sick. That's all I need, for Bella to catch a dose of something."

"Don't worry. Unless she comes down with a case of Coors, Bella won't get what Jimmy's got."

They rode without speaking till Stacy turned off Chapin Mesa Road toward the Far View dormitories. There was something familiar in the drawn face, the tight voice. Putting it together with the medical, Anna realized where she'd seen it before. He carried himself like a man in pain.

"Take off your gun and I'll buy you a beer," she offered on impulse.

For a moment she was sure he was going to turn her down. "I'll get you home before six," she added, remembering Bella and Drew's baby-sitting schedule.

"A beer would taste good tonight."

The lounge at the Far View Lodge was on the second floor and boasted an open-air veranda to the east side. The view, though somewhat curtailed by an expanse of tarred roof studded with air-conditioning ducts, justified the name of Far View. Mesas receded into mists that melded seamlessly into mountain ranges. In the afternoon light, strong at midsummer, the muted blues and grays were given an iridescence that at some times made the mesas appear as unreal as an artist's conception, and, at others, the only reality worth living.

When Anna arrived Stacy was not there. She took a table that backed on a low adobe wall. The plaster radiated heat collected during the day and deflected a cold wind that had sprung up.

Anna's nerves jangled. She couldn't shake an unwelcome First Date feeling. Possibly because she'd taken the time to comb her hair out of its braids and dab perfume between her breasts. A Carta Blanca took the edge off. By the time she was halfway down it, Stacy arrived.

The edge came back.

He looked as awkward as she felt, and wordlessly she cursed herself for moving their relationship out of the secure arena of work.

Stacy ordered a Moosehead and folded himself into one of the wire garden chairs.

"I hardly recognized you with your clothes on," Anna said.

"Ah. Out of uniform."

"You clean up nice."

"Thanks."

Small talk died. Anna sipped her beer and resisted the urge to glance at her watch. "I thought the medical went well this morning," she said to get the conversation into neutral territory.

"God." Stacy shook his head. Pain was clear in his eyes.

Anna forgot her discomfort. Leaning across the table, she took hold of his arm.

A familiar laugh brought her head up. Ted Greeley had taken a table across the veranda. As he caught her eye, he raised his highball in a salute. Anna smiled automatically then returned to Stacy. "What is getting to you?"

"Stephanie McFarland died. I called the ER before I came."

Anna felt as if he'd slapped her. "That's not right," she said. "Stephanie was just a kid with asthma. They got the name wrong."

Stacy shook his head. "The name wasn't wrong. She died."

"Fuck." Anna took a long pull on the beer. It didn't help. "Third grade. What the hell happened? She didn't have to die."

"Yes she did."

Stacy sounded sure of himself, like a man quoting scripture or baseball scores.

"Why?" Anna demanded.

"Figure it out," Stacy snapped. "You saw me. I couldn't do a thing, not one damn thing."

Anna looked at him for a long moment. Self-pity in the face of the child's death struck her as blind arrogance. "Give it a rest. We did what we did. You were useless, not deadly. Don't make yourself so important."

Stacy stared at his hands. Clearly this was a cross he was determined to bear. Maybe he was Catholic.

"I'm sorry," Anna said.

"Yeah. Me too. Sorrier than you know."

Stacy made circles on the glass tabletop with the beer bottle.

Anna finished her beer and ordered another.

"Bella can get bone grafts in her legs," he said, as if this were part of an ongoing conversation instead of a non sequitur. "She could dance, fall in love, marry, save the world—whatever she wanted."

"Does Bella want the operations?" Anna asked, remembering Drew's sour appraisal of the treatment.

"She's scared. But Rose wants them for her. Rose was so beautiful. She once—"

Anna nodded.

"I've probably told you. But she was, and it meant a lot to her and she wants that for Bella."

"What do you want for Bella?"

"I want her to have a chance at the brass ring, whatever that means." Stacy took a long drink of his beer and let his eyes wander over the panorama that was northern New Mexico. "It's not cheap."

Anna's eyes followed his over the soft blue distance. The beers were taking effect. Words were no longer as necessary.

"Rose's used to better," Stacy said after a while.

"So you've said. Old Number One was rich?"

"A lawyer. Megabucks."

"The vultures always eat better than anyone else on the food chain," Anna said. Meyers barely smiled.

"Rose left him. She says she had a problem with commitment." Stacy made it sound like a compliment.

Remembering Bella's remark about her dad leaving because of her deformity, Anna said nothing.

Stacy folded his hands around his Moosehead in a prayerful attitude and looked across the table at her. She smiled and he smiled back. Something sparked, ignited the rushes of emotion the medical had left strewn about their psyches.

Nature's narcotic: more addicting than crack, harder to find than unadulterated Colombian, and, in the long run, more expensive than cocaine. But, God! did it get you there. Anna's breath gusted out at sudden, unbidden memories of love.

"I've got to go." She stood so abruptly her chair over-turned.

"Yes." Both of them pulled out wallets and tossed bills on the table. The waiter would get one hell of a tip, Anna thought as she walked out of the lounge.

"Can I give you a ride?" Stacy called after her. Anna just waved.

Unwilling to return to the cacophony that was home, she walked down the Wetherill Mesa Road till she was out of sight of the lodge, then sat under the protective drapery of a serviceberry bush. She felt like crying but was too long out of practice.

6

ANNA GROPED her way to the kitchen to start her morning coffee. Clad in striped men's pajamas, Jennifer sat at the dining room table eating cereal. Already in uniform, Jamie played with an unlit cigarette.

She held it up as Anna passed. "Trying to decide whether or not to have breakfast," she volunteered.

"Better light up," Jennifer said. "It's going to be a long day."

"The longest." Jamie pulled herself out of the straight-backed chair and took her morning drugs out onto the rear deck.

"Long day," Jennifer repeated.

Since it was obviously expected of her and because early in the morning Anna actually found Jennifer's refined version of the Southern drawl soothing, she asked, "Why long?"

"Longest day of the year. June twenty-first."

"Right: solstice. If something doesn't happen, I'm going to be miffed." Anna spooned coffee into the drip filter.

"Oh, nothin' will. You know Jamie. There's always got to be something. A bunch of the interps got a backcountry permit to go down into Balcony House to watch the moon rise. That's about it."

"I'd think they'd want to watch the sun rise." Coffee was dripping through the filter but too slowly. Balancing the cone to one side, Anna managed to pour what was in the pot into her cup without making too much of a mess. "That's when all the magic is supposed to happen: spears of light through scientifically placed chinks—that sort of thing."

Leaning in the doorway, she sipped and watched Jennifer eating cereal.

She and Jennifer had such disparate schedules they seldom had the opportunity to work together. But bit by bit Anna was getting glimpses that this hair-sprayed and lipsticked magnolia blossom had a penchant for heavy drinking, late nights, and speaking up for herself. Anna found herself warming up to the woman.

"Jamie mentioned something about Old Ones and solstice again last week when we were carrying Stephanie McFarland out of Cliff Palace." Anna threw out the line, not sure what she was fishing for.

"Who knows what Jamie's up to," Jennifer said impatiently. "She says she hears Indian flute music coming out of the ruins at night; she's always seeing some big thing— ghosts and mountain lions and big-horned sheep and cute boys. I never see anything except illegally parked cars."

Jennifer sounded so disgusted that Anna laughed. "What about Paul Summers? He's as cute as they come."

"He's got a girlfriend back home."

"Back home is back home. Going to let it get in your way?"

"No, but it's sure gettin' in his. I just hate fidelity."

"Jimmy Russell?"

"He's ten years younger than I am." Jennifer pronounced "ten" as "tin." She shrugged philosophically. "If things don't start looking up soon, I'm going to have to start poachin'."

Anna's coffee was done. She walked back into the kitchen.

"Stacy's kinda cute," Jennifer mused.

Anna didn't want to get into that.

Running late, she called into service from the shower. At quarter after seven, hair confined in a braid and her teeth brushed, she pulled out of the Far View lot.

Hills was in Durango attending a wildland fire seminar, so Anna had the small four-wheel-drive truck. It was newer than the patrol car and had been built by Mitsubishi. Anna attributed the commercial success of Japanese cars to the fact that they were designed and built by a small people, hence they tended to fit American women far better than the wide-open spaces Buick and Dodge incorporated into their vehicles. At any rate, the seat didn't hurt her back.

Late June marked the peak of the tourist season and there were cars waiting at the locked gates to Far View Ruin and Cedar Tree Tower. The four-way intersection was backed up four cars deep. Anna liked to play hero with the simple act of letting folks go where they wanted to. This morning the kindly ranger routine was turned into a comic interlude while she wrestled with one of Stacy's signature twisted chain locks. Eventually she succeeded and was embarrassed by a round of applause.

Leaving the Four-Way, she drove slowly around the Museum Loop, stopping to check the picnic grounds for illegal campers. It was blessedly empty and she was spared the unsavory task of rousting out people in their night-gowns.

As Anna was passing the Administration Building, Patsy Silva flagged her down. The clerical staff wasn't required to wear uniforms and Patsy was in a flame-orange blouse and close-fitting gray trousers. Her lipstick echoed the color of her top.

Though immaculately dressed and every hair character-istically in place, Patsy looked somehow disheveled, as if she'd had a bad night or bad news.

"What's up?" Anna asked as she rolled down the pickup's window.

"Can you believe it, I lost my keys!" Patsy smiled apolo-getically. "Would you radio one of the Maintenance guys to let me in?"

Anna made the call.

Patsy didn't look relieved. "Are you all right?" Anna asked.

"I need to talk to you."

A slight gray-haired man with a dowager's hump came from the direction of the museum. When he saw them, he jangled a ring of keys.

"The superintendent's having a breakfast meeting. I've got to set it up. Can you come over to the house around twelve?" Patsy pleaded.

"Will do."

Patsy clicked on her smile and started thanking the jani-tor before she'd closed the distance between them.

Anna managed to kill twenty minutes cruising the ruins road. Cliff Palace was about halfway around a six-mile loop. Just before the parking lot the two-lane road became one way. Beyond the ruin a mile or so, at Soda Point, it crossed onto the Ute Indian Reservation. When the road had first been designed it had been incorrectly surveyed and a quarter-mile stretch crossed the park's boundary onto the reservation. A dirt track, never used anymore, ran for several miles into the piñon/juniper forest owned by the Utes. Brush had been piled across it to deter wandering visitors. A plan to barricade it had been in the works for years but nothing had ever been done.

Where the dirt road started into the woods, on a wide graveled turnout, was a curio shop and a trailer selling Navajo tacos and Sno-Kones. Short of rerouting the existing road, Mesa Verde's superintendent had little recourse but to accept this unauthorized invasion of commercialism. Authorized park concessionaires had jacked food prices so high the little stand did a booming business, especially among the rangers.

Past Soda Point, back on park lands, the one-way road widened into a parking lot at the Balcony House ruin. A mile or so farther on, the loop completed, traffic rejoined the two-lane road.

On Isle Royale Anna had patrolled in a boat, in Guadalupe Mountains on horseback. Both were preferable to the automobile. Anna wondered what it was that was so alienating about cars. Somehow, more than any other machine, they seemed to create a world of their own, a mobile pack-rat midden full of personal artifacts that utterly separated man from the natural environment he hurtled through. Maybe, she thought as she crept along in the line of cars trolling for parking spaces at Balcony House, that was why Americans were so enamored of them: power without connection, movement without real direction.

At nine, she returned to Far View, picked up Jennifer, and took her to Maintenance, where the patrol car was parked. As the seasonal dragged her briefcase from behind the seat, she volunteered to pick up Stacy when he came on duty. Anna remembered the poaching threat but forbore comment. If the Catholics were right and the thought was as bad as the deed, she was in no position to cast any stones.

With two rangers on duty and nothing happening, Anna felt lazy. She parked the truck and wandered over to the fire cache to find someone to amuse her. Helitack was gone. Physical training, she recalled. Every morning for PT Drew ran his firefighters two miles down the Spruce Canyon trail, then back up the steep pathway to the mesa top.

As she turned to leave, a clattering arrested her attention. Moments later a child's bicycle with pink training wheels came into view around the corner of the cache. It wasn't one of the modern plastic monstrosities, but a classic, old-fashioned, metal bicycle. Extensions had been welded onto the pedals so Bella Meyers could ride.

She rolled to a stop in the shade beside Anna. "Drew's not here, Mrs. Pigeon. He's supposed to be back by nine but he's always late. He says it takes him longer to shower because there's so much of him. I'm always early."

"That's good to know. Does your dad know you're here?" Anna was thinking of Stacy's concern about traffic the only other time she'd seen Bella in Maintenance.

"Stacy'd already gone to work. Me and Momma only got back from Albaturkey this morning."

Stacy didn't come on duty till later and it crossed Anna's mind that the child was lying. But Bella didn't seem the type. Life, for her, had to be full of personal triumphs and grown-up dramas. She had no need to fabricate.

"I thought Stacy was on project shift," Anna probed

gently. Project days were scheduled from nine-thirty till six.

"Sometimes he goes early. He likes to go off by himself and look at birds and things. Sometimes he takes me. I like being by myself with Stacy."

Anna leaned back against a workbench set up outside the cache.

"That's where they clean their chain saws," Bella warned. "You'll get grease on your behind."

"Too late now."

"Glad I'm not your mom."

"Doesn't your mom approve of greasy behinds?"

"Hates 'em," Bella returned. "You know why Stacy always looks so good?"

Anna shook her head.

"Momma dresses him. Stacy'd just put on whatever was laying closest on the floor. Never iron it or anything. When we got him he was a mess."

Anna smiled. "Like a stray dog brought home from the pound?"

"Not that bad," Bella answered seriously. "He didn't have fleas or anything. But he was pretty scruffy."

Anna glanced at her watch more out of habit than anything. There was no place she had to be, nothing she had to do. In parks with backcountry her days had been spent walking, looking for people in—or causing—trouble. In the automobile-oriented front country of Mesa Verde the days were spent waiting for Dispatch to send her on an emergency or visitor assist.

"You're too old to have anyone dress you," Bella said, giving Anna a frank appraisal. "You do pretty good."

"Not as good as your mom?"

"No," the child answered honestly. "Mom's going to

buy her and me all new stuff when she gets thin again and I get my legs fixed."

Bella seemed disinterested and Anna suspected the new clothes promised a greater delight to Mrs. Meyers than to her daughter.

"I got to go," Bella announced. "Drew comes walking over now." Having carefully looked both ways, she rode across the maintenance yard toward the asphalt path that wound down to the housing loop several hundred yards away and invisible behind a fragrant curtain of evergreens.

No one left to play with, Anna decided to head for the chief ranger's office to fill out a few forms and pester Frieda. As she crossed the tarmac to where she'd parked, Greeley's six-pac rolled in. The contractor wasn't in evidence and a man she recognized but had never met was driving. Tom Silva rode shotgun. The pickup pulled in close to her truck. Since there wasn't room for both vehicle doors to open at once, Anna waited while they got out.

Silva was completely dressed; everything buttoned, belted, and tucked in. "'Morning," he said as he slammed the door. He didn't meet her eye and, for once, there was nothing bantering in the way he spoke.

"Good morning, Tom. Have you gotten any closer to Bachelor of the Year?"

His head jerked up as if she poked him with a cattle prod. There was something different about his face as well as his demeanor. He struck Anna as older, less alive.

"I was just messing around," he said sullenly. "I didn't mean anything by that. 'Scuse me." He pushed by her and disappeared into the shop where the soda-pop machine was housed.

Anna speculated as to whether this new subdued Tom

had anything to do with Patsy's lunch invitation. The day was definitely getting more interesting.

Anna reached the tower house before Patsy and sat in the sun on a stone wall by the front door fantasizing about how she'd arrange the furniture if she inherited the house. She'd just gotten around to hanging curtains when Patsy hurried up the walk.

"Sorry I'm late," she panted. "You could have let yourself in!"

"I've only been here a minute," Anna assured her. "I was early."

"You didn't have to sit out here all that time."

Anna gave up and let herself be apologized to.

Patsy bustled around the kitchen making bologna sandwiches and small talk. Anna kept up her end of the conversation. Perhaps they were to follow formal rules of dining: no business discussed until brandy and cigars were served.

After every condiment and chip had been taken out of cupboards and put on the table, Patsy sat down. Anna noticed she no longer wore the expensive wristwatch. A Timex with Pluto's face on the dial had taken its place.

Anna bit into her sandwich. Patsy pushed her untouched plate away as if she'd already eaten. "It's about Tom," she said.

Anna nodded encouragement.

"He's been so full of himself lately. He was bragging and giving the girls school money. You saw the watch he gave me. I guess he thought he'd bought his way back in. When I said no, he got sore."

Anna waited but Patsy showed no inclination to finish the story unprompted. "What happened to the watch?" she asked to get the wheels turning again.

"I threw it in his face. He made a lot of noise about the money having nothing to do with anything, but I noticed he took it with him when he left."

Anna washed the sandwich down with Diet Pepsi. "I saw Tom this morning. He didn't seem like his old self."

"He's not." Patsy picked up a potato chip and began breaking it into small pieces. "Or else he's so much more like his old self it's scary. He gave me a gun."

"Did he say what the gun was for?"

Patsy shook her head. "I didn't see him. He left it sometime last night. A couple of times I woke up thinking I heard something—the girls are in Gunnison with their grandma. When I'm alone I don't sleep well. I hear things—you know: branches scraping and the wind. I scare myself silly thinking it's an escaped murderer or a crazy person."

"With a hook instead of a hand?"

Patsy laughed. "You know him?"

"I first heard of him at a pajama party at Mercy High School. When I moved to Manhattan I swear he had a sublet under my bed."

"Campfire Girls," Patsy explained her arcane knowledge.

"Anyway . . ." Anna brought the subject back to Tom and his gun.

"Anyway last night I woke up a couple of times but I never came downstairs. I scare myself more if I start peeking in closets and under beds. For once it wasn't all my imagination. This morning there was a gun in the middle of the kitchen table."

Patsy got up and opened a cupboard door. Bundled onto a high shelf was a blue apron with white eyelet ruffling. She took it down and unwrapped the apron from around the gun.

"It's a derringer," Anna told her. "A twenty-two." The

flashy little gun seemed in keeping with Tom Silva. "Do you know for sure it was Tom who left it?"

"I recognize it. He won it in a stock-car race. And there was a note." Patsy had tucked the note in the pocket of the apron. She unfolded it and handed it to Anna.

"'Pats, see how easy it is to get into this place? Get yourself new locks,'" Anna read aloud. "Definitely edgy."

"I thought so."

"I'll look into it," Anna promised. "Meanwhile I'd do what he suggests: get new locks. Give Maintenance a call, okay?"

Patsy said she would. As Anna was leaving, she stopped her. "Do you want to take the gun?"

Anna thought about it for a moment, thought of Tom, of the girls. "Do you know how to use it?" she asked. Patsy nodded. "Then why don't you keep it for a while."

Anna went off duty at three-thirty. Ninety minutes before tradition allowed cocktails. She peeled off her uniform and, sitting on her bed, opened the top drawer of the dresser. Expensive lace underwear, a legacy of more intimate times, mingled with cordovan-colored uniform socks, hollow-point bullets, and half a dozen ragged handkerchiefs.

In the back, lying on its side, was a metal container. With its fitted lid and wire handle, it was much like a paint can sans label.

Jamie Burke professed singular discomfort living in a house tainted by the presence of a firearm. Anna wondered what the interpreter would think if she knew that the remains of Anna's husband rested amid her underwear.

"You were always happiest when you were in my pants, Zach." Anna smiled as she closed the drawer.

The clock on the dresser read 3:47.

The hell with tradition. Anna went into the kitchen to pour herself a drink. Glass in hand, she wandered out onto the rear deck. Four miles away, on Chapin, it was warm enough for shorts. At Far View, a thousand feet higher, Anna was slightly chilled in long pants and a sweatshirt.

The serviceberry bushes were in full bloom and the valley between Far View and Wetherill Mesa looked as if it had been decorated for a wedding. Glittering emerald-green hummingbirds with ruby-colored throats were busy at the blossoms. Mating, showing off, or just celebrating the day, they flew up thirty or forty feet then dove down in a buzz of wings.

Leaning against the wall of the dormitory, Anna let her legs rest on the sun-warmed planking and closed her eyes.

Tom Silva wasn't the only one who wasn't acting like his old self. Till she'd left Michigan for the southwest, Anna hadn't realized how big a part of her life Christina and Alison had become. The gentle, clear-thinking woman and her spirited daughter had kept her on an even keel. Kept her looking ahead instead of back.

Banging of the kitchen door announced the end of solitude. Jennifer was off shift. Anna took a long drink and held it in her mouth, savoring the rich bite of the alcohol and trying to shut out the muffled thumps from within as the seasonal law enforcement ranger noisily divested herself of briefcase and gunbelt.

Moments later the sanctity of the rear deck was invaded. Wearing a T-shirt and faded jeans, Jennifer came out to share the last of the afternoon's warmth. She folded down, crossing her legs tailor-fashion, then popped the top of a Bud Light.

"You devil, you!" She shook an admonitory finger at Anna. "You snatched old Stacy right out from under my nose."

For a brief instant Anna wondered if Stacy had stated some preference for patrolling with her. She couldn't decide whether she was more flattered or alarmed.

Jennifer laughed. "Still waters and all that. When I went to pick him up, his wife said he'd already left."

"Not with me he didn't," Anna defended herself.

As if in counterpoint to their conversation, Anna's radio, clearly audible through the open bedroom window, crackled to life.

Three times, seven hundred called Meyers' number. Finally came Frieda's voice saying: "No contact. Seven hundred clear. Sixteen-forty-five."

This was followed by three attempts to reach "Any Chapin Mesa patrol ranger" and "No contact."

"I thought Stacy was on till six," Jennifer said.

"He is." Anna waited for an uneasy feeling to pass but it didn't. "I guess I'd better make a few calls." She looked longingly at the wine in her glass, righteously considering pouring it over the deck railing. Instead, she took it all in one gulp. Something told her she might need it.

7

STACY DIDN'T turn up that night or the next or the night after that. Though Hills Dutton, in his capacity as district ranger and resident scrooge, had grumbled about paying her overtime for working on her lieu days, Anna had been on duty. She was needed to cover Meyers' shifts. And to search.

Investigation indicated that at the end of Stacy's late shift on Monday night, all the ruins' gates had been locked, and the patrol car he'd been driving was parked in the maintenance yard. Apparently, somewhere on the hundred yards of paved path between Maintenance and the housing loop, he had simply disappeared.

Tuesday Hills spoke with Mrs. Meyers. Coming home late from Albuquerque, she and her daughter had chosen to spend Monday night in Farmington where they could take in a movie and do some shopping rather than continue the two hours on to the park. Around seven—the time Stacy customarily took his meal break when he was on late shift—Rose phoned him from the motel. He had answered and they spoke for several minutes. Rose said Stacy had seemed calm and cheerful.

AT&T long distance corroborated the call.

Just after eight Monday night, while she was taking her evening walk, Al Stinson said she saw Stacy locking the Cedar Tree Tower Ruin gate. After that Stacy had been neither seen nor spoken to by anyone. At least not anyone willing to come forward.

On arriving back in the park Tuesday morning, Mrs. Meyers found the bed made and the sink free of dishes. As her husband was a man of tidy domestic habits, she couldn't say if this indicated whether or not he had slept at home.

Wednesday Anna saw Bella on her bike riding back from Maintenance. Nine-thirty A.M.: Anna guessed she'd been escorting Drew to work after his physical training.

Pulling the car to the side of the narrow lane, Anna called the girl's name. For a moment the green eyes looked at her without recognition. When a spark did dawn it was feeble and suddenly gone as if very little held the child's interest anymore.

Bella rode up to the Ford and Anna climbed from behind the wheel. Wordlessly the girl looked up. Anna could read the question as clearly as if it had been written in felt marker across the unlined brow. "No," she said gently. "We haven't found Stacy yet."

Bella didn't change expression but it was as if her soft cheeks froze. Anna ached to see so adult a reaction on a six-year-old's face.

"We're looking real hard everywhere," Anna told her.

Sadly, Bella shook her head. The curls, as carefully tended as always, glimmered in the sunlight. "Not everywhere. Not where he's at."

"No," Anna conceded. "Not there."

"I wish Aunt Hattie would come," Bella said, and propped her chin in her hands, her elbows resting on the handlebar. "She knows things."

"How to find things?" Anna asked.

"No. Just things."

"Like what?" Anna leaned against the fender of the patrol car, enjoying the warmth of the metal through her trousers.

Bella screwed up her face with the effort of thought and Anna was glad to see, for a moment at least, she was distracted from her worry over Stacy.

"Not *knowing* knowing exactly. But Hattie plays with you. Not like she's a grown-up who's playing with a little kid. Like she's *there*. Sometimes we'll be witches. We turned Timmy Johnson into a toad."

Bella looked pleased. Anna was careful not to look anything.

"Why a toad? So you could kiss him back to handsome princehood?"

"Yuck-oh!" Bella stuck out her tongue as if she were gagging on something foul. "He said mean things about me."

Anna could guess what.

"We didn't exactly turn him into a real toad," Bella said after a moment's thought. "I mean to other people he still looked like a piggy little boy. But Hattie said he'd turn his own self into a toad if he kept doing toady things so we just helped a little. I could see the toad parts though, after that. He'd say stuff and I'd squint and laugh at the greeny warts just ready to pop out on his pig face. But that was a long time ago when I was little."

Anna laughed. "Do you think the transformation's done by now? Is he all toad?"

"Maybe not," Bella said kindly. "He stopped being so toady after a while. He may have saved himself. Aunt Hattie thinks so."

Bella laid her chin on the handlebars of her bike and pushed back and forth, rocking herself absently. "Aunt Hattie's like those big colored balloons, the ones with the little baskets for the people to ride in. She just lifts you up, zoop, zoop, zoop."

Bella accompanied the words with floating gestures, small white hands like leaves blowing upward.

"We could all use some of that," Anna said.

"Maybe she'll come. Sometimes she does," Bella said hopefully. "I have to go." She stood up on the pedals of the bike and wobbled past Anna.

"'Bye." Anna felt slightly abandoned. "I have to go too," she added childishly.

Bella pedaled faster and never looked back. Worry was back in the hunch of the little shoulders.

That evening Anna spent an hour with Rose going over Stacy's routines and the times of the phone call and her return to the park. Rose mixed vicious snipes at Hills, Ted Greeley, Drew Kinder, the superintendent, and the National Park Service with seemingly heartfelt pleas that no stone be left unturned in the search for her husband.

Bella crept about like a tortured spirit. White-faced and silent, she hid herself behind coloring books that she didn't color in, dolls that she didn't enliven with imagination. Twice the child curled up at her mother's feet the way a dog might, her knees pulled up, her chin on hands fisted like paws. The only time Anna saw her play was when Bella dressed up in Stacy's class "A" uniform jacket and winter hat. On the child's stunted frame the jacket brushed the floor.

Anna had to look away, aware for the first time how terribly costly Stacy's abdication would be. His wife had an edge; she would cut her way through life regardless. Bella truly loved.

In the end it was the interpreter Claude Beavens who found Stacy. Or, more accurately, a family of canyon wrens that had made their home high in the ancient ramparts of Cliff Palace.

Early the Thursday morning after Stacy's disappearance, Beavens was down in the ruins. He climbed into the back reaches of the dwelling in hopes of finding a vantage point from which he might see the wrens' nest. Clambering around the fragile site was forbidden to all but officially permitted archaeologists and NPS brass. But, finding himself with a quarter of an hour till visitors would be allowed down, Beavens had decided to take a few liberties.

Given the nature of his discovery, admitting his transgression seemed the lesser of two evils.

Anna was at Navajo Overlook on the Ruins Road Loop with binoculars pressed to her eyes. Jennifer Short, back to the canyon, stood at her elbow.

"It's not like every damn inch of those trails you keep lookin' at haven't been looked at before," Jennifer was saying. She leaned against the chest-high cyclone fence. Endless civil suits designed to dig money out of Uncle Sam's "deep pocket" had forced the government to mar every precipitous view with safety devices. Jennifer's flat-brimmed hat was pushed back to protect her hairdo. It gave her a Rebecca-of-Sunnybrook-Farm look that Anna found annoying.

"If y'all ask me, he just took a powder," the seasonal drawled, rehashing a theory that had been voiced by a number of people in the park as the search wore on. "Found himself a woman who hasn't let herself go, kept her figure. Can't blame him. If they ever strayed from the missionary position he'd be squashed flatter'n a bug. Uh-uhg-lee!"

"Reubens wouldn't agree with you," Anna said mildly. "I doubt Stacy would either." Again she traced the fragment of trail visible in the canyon below. Worn bare of vegetation over the centuries by feet and paws and hooves, it showed white, a ribbon in the canyon bottom. Brush and scrub grew to either side, becoming taller toward the cliffs. Finally, at the base, where walls sheered up toward the mesa and the strata of sandstone met a strata of slate, natural seep springs nourished the grander ponderosa pines.

Anna didn't expect to see the straggling—or fallen—form of Stacy Meyers. It had not escaped her notice, nor Hills', that Meyers had vanished in full defensive gear with his radio. If he wanted to be found or still had strength and voice, he would have called for help. Looking was just something to do. And Anna needed something to do.

Had anyone dared to suggest she was falling in love with Rose Meyers' husband, Anna would have denied it. When she chose to consider her loss, she could not but see the wraithlike face of Bella and know that the vague emptiness she felt was of no importance. Still, the days of seeking without finding, of work and worry and waiting, had worn her down in a way that was more than professional frustration or budding friendship.

"And that poor little thing!" Jennifer sighed gustily. "What man'd want to deal with that when it wasn't even his?"

"Bella," Anna corrected, finding "it" offensive. In saying the child's name something she had sensed from the onset became crystal clear: "Stacy wouldn't leave Bella. No way. No how."

"I don't know—" Jennifer began again.

"I do," Anna said flatly. Maybe Rose, maybe. But never Bella, never his pine nut. With that realization came another: Stacy Meyers was dead or close enough it wouldn't matter unless they found him soon.

Anna lowered her binoculars. "You drive," she said. "My back is killing me."

That was when Claude Beavens made his call.

The transmission was garbled. In the patrol car, Anna fiddled with the radio's volume as Frieda said: "Unit calling seven hundred, you are broken." Scratches and crackles came over the air a second time.

"Head toward Cliff Palace Loop," Anna told Jennifer. From within the Cliff Palace and Balcony House ruins radio transmissions were frequently too broken to understand.

Frieda repeated Anna's thought over the air: "Unit calling seven hundred, you are still unreadable. Try again from higher ground."

Silence followed. "Pick up the pace," Anna said. The patrol car smoothly picked up speed, Jennifer conning the boxy vehicle neatly around the meandering RVs and rental cars.

" 'Nother carry-out?" she asked.

"Maybe," Anna said.

"Good. I keep missin' out. Everything seems to happen on Tuesdays, when I'm off."

They were heading up the straightaway toward the intersection with Cliff Palace Road when the radio crackled to life again.

"Seven hundred, can you hear me now?" was bleated out in breathy tones.

"Loud and clear."

"This is Beavens at Cliff Palace. You better send somebody down here right away."

There was a short silence. The entire park waited for particulars. "What's the nature of the incident?" Seven hundred asked evenly.

"I—uh—I found Stacy Meyers. He's up in one of the back kivas." Another silence followed, longer than the first. Then in a sudden blurt of sound Beavens said: "I think he's dead. There were flies."

"Holy shit!" Jennifer whispered. She flipped on the lights and siren.

Anna thought to switch them off again. No sense going code three to a body recovery. Speed meant nothing to the dead, and the commotion could startle the living into having accidents. In the end she let Jennifer call the shots. Somehow the outward shrieking was in keeping with the small cries trapped in her skull.

And, she told herself, there was a slim chance Beavens was mistaken and Meyers was alive. Slim.

Hills' 4X4 was already there when Anna and Jennifer screamed into the Cliff Palace lot. The district ranger was fumbling with the lock on the tool box in the bed of the truck.

He handed Anna the green oxygen kit. "Might as well," he said, echoing her pessimism. Shouldering the trauma bag, he started down the path at a fast walk. Anna and Jennifer had to run to keep up with his long-legged stride. In an unconscious parody of Scarlet O'Hara, Short was clutching the top of her flat hat to keep it from flying off.

Tourists drew aside as they passed, curiosity enlivening their stares. Revolver hammering one thigh and the O_2 bottle the other, it crossed Anna's mind that they—or she and Jennifer at any rate—looked like idiots. With his trim bulk and square face, Hills was protected by the inviolate image of John Wayne To The Rescue. Guilt followed: guilt that she could harbor such petty thoughts en route to what was most likely the death of a fellow ranger.

Armed with cameras, visitors were already fanned out along the low wall that surrounded the overlook platform. Dimly, Anna was aware of the clicking of shutters as photographers tried to capture the ruin below.

At the foot of the long metal staircase leading from the platform, Jamie Burke had just finished unlocking the barred gate, opening Cliff Palace for the day.

"Lock it behind us," Hills said as he brushed past.

Burke pulled the gate closed so abruptly that Anna had to turn sideways to fit through. As she pressed by, she noticed Jamie's pale eyes narrow as she muttered: "Claude saw."

Still holding on to her hat, Jennifer clattered after and Anna was pushed into the stone stairway that formed the first part of the descent to the ruin.

Claude Beavens was waiting for them at the top of the ladder where the alcove began. A green NPS windbreaker was zipped up tightly under his Adam's apple. Bony wrists protruded from sleeves an inch too short. Long knobby fingers danced an uncomfortable jig on his thighs. "It's about time," he snapped, and his Adam's apple vanished momentarily behind the windbreaker's collar.

Beavens was a skinny, busy man, not well liked by Anna's housemates. He tended to officiousness and factual-sounding declarations that had little basis. Jamie had once grumbled that he seemed incapable of uttering the one true answer to many of the questions about the Anasazi: "We don't know."

"Show us what you've got." Hills could have been asking to see baseball cards or a skinned knee. In the face of his unflappable calm, hysteria was almost impossible.

Beavens settled down perceptibly. His fingers still fidgeted, but now they plucked at the fabric of his trousers instead of simply twitching.

"Yeah. Okay." He turned and began leading the way down the asphalt path in front of the ruin. At a small wooden sign bearing the number three, he leaped up onto a retaining wall that served both to reinforce the ancient structures and to keep tourists from climbing on the ruins.

"Watch where you step," he said, panic gone and officiousness returned. "These dwellings are fragile."

Hills grunted. Behind her, Anna heard Jennifer mutter: "Crimeny, we're not from Mars."

With sureness bred of familiarity, the interpreter guided them up the slope above the public pathway. Claude was quick and light on his feet. For all his size and strength, Hills had trouble keeping up with him. To their left the alcove dug deep into the side of the mesa. To the right was Cliff Canyon, filling now with early sunlight. They passed a terrace, then a crumbling wall pierced by a single high window.

Beavens turned into an alleyway formed by two buildings, roofless now but still more than a story tall. To keep her mind from their mission and because the magic of these suddenly deserted and long-empty villages never palled for her, Anna took note of this, her first venture into the closed part of Cliff Palace.

Much of the masonry was intact even after seven hundred desert winters. The stones still bore the signature of their architects in the many fine chips where harder stones had sculpted them to fit. Rubble, fallen between the walls, harbored dozens of pot sherds: pieces of white pottery, some the size of half dollars, marked with black geometric shapes.

The short alley dead-ended at another masonry wall. With a bit of scrambling, Beavens was on top of it. Catlike he walked along the stonework. Hills followed, then Anna. Last, Jennifer handed up the O_2 kit then climbed. Her boots dislodged a stone. When the sound reached Beavens' ear, he turned as if he'd been stung.

"Careful!" he hissed.

The whisper bothered Anna. People whisper in secret, in church, and around the dead.

The wall Claude led them down widened out into an abbreviated terrace. A sheer, circular wall dropped off to the right forming a kiva, one of the round subterranean rooms favored by the ancient people.

"Not this one," Beavens said, and stopped. "There." He pointed. At the end of the flat area where they stood was a low wall, a moon-shaped shadow suggesting another kiva, then a tower of stone with a high window.

Rapunzel, Rapunzel, let down your hair, Anna thought idiotically.

Ever pragmatic, Hills stepped past Beavens then over the parapet. "Let's get to it."

Anna didn't move.

Hills looked down into the kiva gaping at his feet, then turned back. His square face was devoid of expression. "Yup. This is it," he said.

8

AN INVISIBLE switch was thrown in Anna's head. She ceased being a shocked spectator and again became a ranger. Stepping over the wall, she stood next to Dutton. A miniature hail of gravel dislodged by her boots pattered into the kiva below. The skittery sound thickened the silence, fixed it hard in her ears.

At their feet stone and mortar walls curved away then became one again, forming a circle twenty-five feet in diameter. Approximately four feet down, halfway to the floor, the wall widened abruptly into a bench called a "banquette" by the archaeologists. Built up from the bench were six stone pilasters. When the kiva was still in use, the pilasters had supported a roof. Like many others, this kiva roof had long since been destroyed by fire. When Cliff Palace had been excavated the debris had been cleared away, leaving an open pit.

On the south side of the circle, at banquette level, was a recessed stagelike area that graced most of the Mesa Verde kivas. A hundred theories and ten times that many guesses had been put forth as to its use, but none had ever been validated by archaeological data.

Below the recess a rectangular opening large enough for

a small child to crawl through led back into the masonry to connect with a ventilator shaft that kept air flowing into the underground room to feed the fire and the occupants. Directly in front of the shaft was a section of wall several feet long and a couple of feet high. This deflector wall was a yard or so from a shallow depression ringed with blackened stone: the fire pit. Forming a south-to-north line with the fire ring and deflector wall was a pottery-lined opening the size of a coffee cup. Taken from the Navajo language, it was called a "sipapu" and was assumed to be symbolic of the opening through which the ancients had been said to move from the destroyed underworld to this one.

Within the kiva only two things were out of place. A flat-brimmed NPS hat had been placed carefully in the center of the deflector wall and, curled into the fetal position, face tucked against his knees, Stacy Meyers lay on his side within the tight circle of stones around the fire pit. His right arm was stretched over his head, partially concealing his face. His fingers were spread. It looked as if he was reaching for—or attempting to ward off—something that had come out of the sipapu.

Protected by the deep alcove, the kiva was perennially in shadow. Even in December the sun did not sink low enough to touch the back wall of Cliff Palace. The temperature remained relatively constant throughout the year. Consequently the deterioration of Stacy's body had progressed in a stately fashion, leaving out none of the classic steps of decomposition.

From where Anna stood, ten feet above and fifteen feet away from the remains, she could smell the sickly sweet odor of decay. Flesh had made the inexorable change from living tissue to inert matter. From the cuff of Stacy's summer uniform shirt to the tips of his patrician fingers, the skin was deathly pale and dimpled. Blood, stopped from flowing when the muscle of the heart could no longer function, had settled to its lowest point. A shadow of postmortem lividity showed on the underside of the arm where it stretched toward the sipapu.

Curled on his side, only Stacy's left eye was visible. It was open, the brown iris partly obscured by the upper eyelid, as if Meyers' last glance had been in the direction of the fabled underworld.

A black fly dug at the tear duct, searching for any trace of moisture. Flies clustered around the nares of the nose. In death Stacy's mouth had fallen open, or was frozen in a final cry. His beard and mustache camouflaged the flies and maggots around his lips but the tiny all-encompassing movement was more repellent than obvious incursions.

Two days. Stacy had been missing since Tuesday morning. Two and a half, if he had died on Monday night. By now his every orifice would be infested with flies and, therefore, maggots.

The bitter sting of bile backed up in Anna's throat and her vision tunneled. She had been expecting a corpse—expecting Stacy Meyers' corpse. She had steeled herself for it. But in her desert-trained mind, she had seen a desert corpse. A person dead seventy-two hours under the relentless sun of the Trans Pecos. A body jerked like prime beef, baked red then brown, then black; peeling, seared, dehumanized. Purified by the arid desert winds. The bulk of the human body that was water purloined by the sun. Moisture, blood, the stuff of life, sucked away, a mummy created. A thing so elemental soul and memory had no handhold where grief could cling.

This was immediate demanding death. Death not yet

turned back to the earth. This corpse would be hard to make peace with. There was no indication the soul had found its way free.

And it was the death of a friend.

Shaking her head clear of ghosts, Anna schooled her mind. "Want me to call for the Polaroid?" she asked Hills. Her voice had a quaver she didn't like.

"Somebody better." The district ranger turned and stared out across the sun-drenched canyon. A wren called its characteristic dying fall of song. "Yeah. The Polaroid, chalk—ah, Jesus!" he interrupted himself. "If we chalk the outline of the body on the floor of this kiva we'll have every archaeologist in the southwest jumping down our throats. Hell. Where was I?"

Glad to rest her eyes on the living, Anna glanced up at him. Something had kept her from following his example and turning her back on Stacy. A perverse puritanical lust to punish herself? A desire to bid Meyers good-bye? She made a mental note to ask her sister. "You were at chalk," she answered Dutton's question.

Hills ran his tongue along his upper teeth as if clearing them of spinach particles. "Yeah. Hell. Get chalk, a body bag. Bring down an accident kit from one of the vehicles—it's got chalk, tape. You got that, Jennifer?"

As was his habit, Hills had been talking in a low monotone. Its usual effect was to dissipate panic and reduce trauma. This time he seemed to have outdone himself. Both Jennifer and the interpreter looked as if they had fallen into a trance.

Hills snapped his fingers. "Jennifer, got that?"

Short came awake with a comic, "Huh?"

"Here, let me." Anna pulled a notebook from her hip pocket and hastily scribbled down a list of the items Hills had asked for. Adding a couple of requests of her own, she spoke aloud to clear them with Dutton. "Get helitack over here for a carry-out. Tell Jamie to keep the ruin closed till we're out of here, and get the ambulance up top."

"Ambulance? Then he's not—" Jennifer began. She'd kept close to Beavens, the crumbling wall blocking her view down into the kiva.

"He is," Hills said shortly.

"It's the ambulance or we toss him in the back of the four-by-four," Anna said.

"Logistics," Jennifer said firmly, as if that one word explained away the messy business of transporting the dead. In a way it did.

Anna stepped over the wall and handed Jennifer the list.

"What do you want me to do?" Claude Beavens sounded alarmingly eager, and there was an avidity in his face that made Anna uncomfortable.

"Uh . . ." Hills looked to Anna but she gave him no help. Making the hard decisions was what he was paid the big bucks for. "You go with Jennifer, I guess. You can fill out a witness statement. Frieda'll explain."

Beavens shrugged—a definite pearls-before-swine shrug—then hurried past Jennifer so that he would be the one leading the way out.

"Watch your big feet," Anna heard him say as he dropped down the wall into the blind alleyway.

"Yew watch yer big mouth," Jennifer snapped back.

Hills laughed, a high-pitched giggle. Hysteria would have been Anna's guess had she not known the big block of a man always laughed that way.

"Guy gives me the heebie-jeebies." Dutton shuddered. On so large an individual the gesture seemed out of place.

"Kind of like a Jim Jones wannabe?" Anna asked.

"I guess." Hills had turned his attention back to the kiva and its contents. "Shee-it." His East Texas heritage showed briefly. "Everybody ever died on me was fresh. Did CPR all the way to the hospital and let 'em die for sure there. What the hell do we do now?"

Anna didn't know. Three times in her career there'd been bodies to deal with, but the crime scenes had been so unstable, they'd needed to be moved. "Secure the scene, collect evidence, maintain the chain of evidence," she said, parroting a list from her federal law enforcement training.

"Right," Hills said. "We'll stay out of the kiva and call the feds. Stay here," he ordered. "I got to make some calls."

He scrambled down the wall into the alley and headed for a place open enough he could radio Dispatch. Anna felt abandoned. "Shee-it," she echoed.

For a moment she just stared out through the junipers, watching a scrub jay scolding an invisible companion. Scenes from old movies and books came to mind: wives, mothers, grandmothers, dressed in widows' weeds, sitting in darkened rooms knitting or crying with no company but one another and death personified in the body of the man they'd bathed and dressed and powdered, lying in state on the bier. Unbidden a picture from Dickens' *Great Expectations* took over: the moldering wedding feast, mice and maggots the only partakers.

"Not your bridegroom," Anna said aloud, narrowed her mind to the task at hand, and turned to face the deceased.

There were a few tracks and scuffs on the stones around the kiva: hers, Hills', probably Claude Beavens' or the stabilization crew's. The surface was too hard to make any inferences. No buttons, threads, dropped wallets, white powder, semen, or anything readily identifiable as a bona-fide *clue* was in evidence.

Keeping to the stones topping the kiva wall, she walked around till she stood over the ventilator hole, looking down into the southern recess, then to the deflector wall, then the fire ring with its cold tinder.

No obvious signs of violence were apparent, at least not on the side of the body that was exposed. The soft layers of dust that had accumulated on the floor of the kiva were freshly raked.

It was customary for interpreters to rake out human tracks made in closed areas. Both so the footprints wouldn't entice others to trespass and to retain an illusion of freshness, of the first time, for those who would come next.

One line of footprints crossed the raked dirt. It led from below the banquette on the west side of the kiva to the fire pit.

Stacy reached away from her with one long bony arm that was looking more spectral every moment she was left alone with it. With him, she corrected herself. The flesh was pale, life's blood pooled on the underside of his arm. Near his sleeve, on the upper side, was an old bruise, a reminder that once this flesh could feel.

"Wait," Anna whispered. Stacy's shoes were off, lying untied very near where his feet were tucked up by his hip pockets as if he'd kicked them off to get more comfortable. Something about the stockinged feet was so vulnerable, so human, Anna felt an unaccustomed pricking behind her eyes.

She forced herself to continue the study. Except for the shoes and the hat on the deflector wall, Stacy was immaculately dressed. If, as Bella said, Rose dressed him, she would find nothing to be ashamed of. His shirt was crisply ironed, his trousers neatly creased, his duty belt firmly buckled on with gun and speedloader visible.

Anna continued her circuit, viewing the scene from every angle. Nothing more of interest turned up. She was relieved when Hills finally hauled himself out of the alleyway and crossed to join her.

"Frieda got the federal marshal out of Durango on the line. They'll send somebody up. This won't keep." He waved a hand toward what had once been a man. "We got to get what we can, bag it, and take it down to the morgue. I've got Drew's boys coming."

Hills crossed his arms and stared down into the kiva. "What'd he do? Just walk in, curl up in the fireplace, make hisself comfy, and die?"

"Looks that way."

"Jesus." The district ranger blew a sigh out through loose lips. "This is a hell of a note. Solstice. Some of the seasonal interps are going to make hay with this."

Remembering the strange spark in Jamie's eyes as they passed her by the gate, Anna didn't doubt it one bit.

9

THE GLASS had started getting in the way so she'd left it behind and drank straight from the bottle. Never had the Rambler driven so smoothly. Green eyes of a deer or a coyote flickered in Anna's peripheral vision as the headlights picked them out of the night. A vague and uninteresting idea that she was driving too fast crossed her mind. The proof of it, the squealing of tires as she made the ninety-degree turn into the Resource Management area, made her laugh out loud.

When she'd recovered control of the car, she felt between her legs. The wine bottle was still upright, its contents unspilled.

"All present and accounted for, officer," she said. "No casualties." The Rambler rolled to a stop in front of the square stone building. "Car in gear, brake set," Anna said. Then: "Whoops. Key *off*. Too late!" As she took her foot off the clutch, the car hopped and the engine died.

For a time she leaned back against the seat, glad to be still. "Nights in White Satin" played on the oldies station out of Durango. Through the open window the air blew cool, smelling of juniper and dust. Overhead, without the pollution of the glaring intruder lights that had become epidemic even in remote areas during the last decade, the stars were fixed in an utterly black sky. Small night sounds kept the dark from being lonely. Anna could hear scufflings of some nocturnal creature digging in the pine needles, the sigh of a breeze approaching through the forest's crown, clicking and snapping as tiny twigs or bones were broken.

Only humans, cursed with the knowledge of their own mortality and that of those whom they loved, were truly alone; each trapped in an ivory tower of skull and bone peeking out through the windows of the soul.

The body recovery, as sanitized language would phrase it, had gone on till afternoon. The packaging of the meat that had once called itself Stacy Meyers had taken only a few minutes, but the attendant crime-scene recording and preservation had worn on so long even Hills' deep-seated nerve endings had become frayed.

Hills had even less experience than Anna with foul play in the form of park corpses, and his plodding methodicalness took a definite turn toward the anal retentive. Pictures were taken and retaken from every angle.

"Don't know when somebody's going to pop up out of the woodwork saying how you should've done it," he explained. "So by God we're going to do it all. Hell of a note. Where are the feds when you need 'em? We forget something and our tit's in the wringer."

This and more of the same was muttered in an ongoing monotone as he directed the investigation. After the photographs, stones around the kiva were examined, swept, and the leavings collected in a plastic bag that Anna dutifully marked KIVA DUST with the date and her initials.

"Maintain the chain of evidence," Hills said.

"It's dirt," Anna returned.

"You never know . . ."

The kiva floor was photographed, re-raked, all items bagged and marked. Then, finally, Stacy was photographed and zipped into the body bag. His hat and shoes wouldn't fit in the narrow plastic shroud. Anna threw them in the trunk of her car to return to Rose.

The entire "dog and pony show," as Hills termed it, had taken several hours. During most of it Stacy lay curled absurdly in the fire pit, reaching toward something the living couldn't see, his beard growing ever blacker with flies.

It was odd how the human mind switched off an unpleasant reality. Moose slept seconds at a time, their brains clicking on and off like binary computers, allowing them to rest yet never be long out of a dangerous world in need of watching. Anna, Jimmy, Drew, Paul, Jennifer, they'd all clicked in and out of the reality of death in the kiva. Jokes were told, people laughed, measurements were taken, even mild flirting between Jennifer and Paul.

Interspersed with this flow of life were chalky looks, strained silences, and equally strained conversations as someone saw again Stacy's face, remembered his wife, his child, recalled him as he had been in life, and woke to the realization that this fly-blown corpse was all that remained.

The schizophrenia wore Anna down. She had already needed a drink in the worst way when Hills dragged her to Meyers' house to give condolences to the widow.

Blessedly he had foisted off the chore of informing Rose onto Frieda. Their visit was mere formality—courtesy, the East Texan said. "Leave any questions to the feds."

"The feds" Hills relied on so heavily was a federal investigator the superintendent had called in. Mesa Verde was under exclusive jurisdiction, which placed it off local law enforcement's turf.

The Meyerses' house was shut up. Windows closed, blinds drawn like a Victorian house of mourning.

Hills knocked tentatively then stepped back, leaving Anna marooned on the welcome mat as Rose opened the door. She was neatly dressed in dark blue polyester pants and a white blouse with a Peter Pan collar. Her short dark hair was combed and she wore pearl earrings, but her face was in disarray; dry eyes rimmed with red, her cheeks drawn and pale.

Anna looked to Hills but he was studying a crack in the sidewalk. "We just stopped by to tell you how terribly sorry we are, Mrs. Meyers," Anna managed. "Your husband's body is being taken to Durango."

Rose waited. When Anna could find no more words, Rose closed the door. In the curtailed view of the living room there'd been no sign of Bella. For that Anna was grateful. The child would have been hard to face. She turned to Hills.

He shrugged. "That about does it," he said, and: "You're off the clock."

"Overtime. You're a real sensitive guy," Anna groused as they walked back to the patrol car.

"Gotta be thinking of something," he said philosophically.

Anna raised the bottle from between her thighs and peered at it, measuring the level against the dull glow of the dashboard lights. One third left. Of how many bottles? she wondered. Surely this was only the second. Maybe the third.

She took a mouthful and speculated on any possible

New Age numerological significance that one third of the third might have. "Got to ask Jamie," she said. "Warthog." This last descriptive was triggered at the memory of her housemate.

Jamie had been hovering at the dormitory door when Hills dropped Anna off. Burke was decked out in the sarong, her hair, free of its braid, fanned into a crimped black curtain that fell past her butt. Kohl—or some modern equivalent—ringed her eyes and she wore a single gold earring beaten into the stylized shape of a lizard. Her face was somber but excitement radiated from her in tangible waves.

"Like a bitch in heat," Anna told the wine bottle.

"We've got to talk," Jamie had said grimly.

"Not now." Anna had tried to squeeze by but Jamie'd laid hold of her briefcase.

"Now."

Anna dropped her hat and gunbelt on the nearest chair. "So talk."

Jamie ignored her rudeness, or was too caught up in her own drama to notice it. With a sigh, she spread herself on the sofa. "Stacy and I were very close. Very."

Anna doubted that, but the declaration in no way surprised her. The dead had more friends than the living. Especially those meeting an untimely end. It was as if knowing a murder victim invested one with some sort of celebrity. Jamie had wanted something to happen on solstice. Murder must've been beyond her wildest dreams.

Murder: Anna hadn't said it to herself so bluntly. Suicide, accident, incident, those were the words Hills had resolutely stuck with all day. In thinking it, Anna believed it to be true. Stacy was too much a conservationist to defile the ruins with his twentieth-century corpse.

"We all know dead people, Jamie," Anna said unkindly. Then: "Sorry. I'm beat." She picked up her duty belt and turned to go. Again the interpreter stopped her.

"Claude saw," she repeated her cryptic phrase of the morning, playing it like a trump card in her bid for attention.

Anna was almost too tired to ante up but she managed a mild show of interest. "Saw what?"

"The night Stacy was taken. He saw it."

The spark of interest flickered and died. Anna was too tired to play. "Get him to write 'it' up on his witness report." She dragged herself to the questionable sanctuary of her room.

The evening continued to unravel from there. Through the thin walls of the Far View dorm, Jamie could be heard holding court. Once—or maybe twice—Anna slunk from her lair to return with reinforcements in the form of alcohol. Finally, needing air, but unable to again run the gauntlet of avid faces greedy for details, she opened her window, popped off the screen, and climbed out, taking the last undead soldier with her.

She poured wine into her mouth and a bit on her chin. "Quick," she said as she closed her eyes and rested her head on the Rambler's seat. "Red or white?" Could've been either. "Some palate." She pushed open the car door. For a moment it was impossible to make any headway. Then she remembered to undo her seatbelt and tumbled out.

Molly picked up on the seventh ring. "What? What is it?" she demanded.

"It's just me." Anna was mildly offended.

"Where are you? What's going on? Talk to me." Molly rattled out the words.

"Can't," Anna replied. "Can't get a word in edgewise. Just called to chat."

There was a long silence devoid, for once, of the poisonous note of tobacco smoke sliding into dying lungs. Then Molly spoke very deliberately. "I don't know what time zone you're in, but here in the civilized world it's three twenty-seven in the morning. If you're okay, you'd better lie to me. Tell me something dire enough to warrant this rude awakening."

Three twenty-seven. Anna pushed the tiny silver button on her watch and squinted at the lighted dial. It was hopeless. The numbers were small and furry. "That can't be right," she said.

"Trust me on this one." A sigh: the cigarette. "Begin at the beginning, Anna. Before your first drink."

Anna started to cry, great whooping sobs that hurt her throat. Tears poured down her face, dripped from her jaw. "Zach's dead," she barked when she was able. Her sister said nothing, choosing not to try and override the storm of grief.

When finally she quieted, Molly said, "That's right, Zach's dead. Been dead a long time. Kids born the day he died are old enough to rob liquor stores. What's going on, Anna?"

"Zach?" Anna was confused.

"You said Zach was dead."

Anna digested that for a moment, taking a little wine and letting it burn under her tongue. "No I didn't," she said at last. "Stacy's dead. Stacy Meyers."

"Who is Stacy Meyers?"

"Goddamn it, listen to me!" Anna screamed.

"You're drunk, Anna," her sister said reasonably. "I love you—Lord knows why—and I want to help you. But you're beyond me. I'll call you tomorrow."

The line went dead. Anna laid her head on the desk and wept.

10

Consciousness dawned like a foggy day. Anna opened her eyes. She was facedown on a rough brown surface, her cheek wet from drool, and she was terribly cold. Thin gray light filtered from somewhere. Through the static in her head she could hear the fussy chatter of scrub jays.

Without moving, as though to do so might prove dangerous, she took stock of the situation. She was lying on the front seat of the Rambler, her clothes rumpled and damp. Pins and needles prickled through her right arm and leg where they were pinned under her. Graying hair, clumped and sticky-looking on the vinyl, fell around her face.

Slowly she raised her head. Her first instinct had been right: to move was dangerous. Even her eyeballs ached. Her mouth was so dry her tongue rattled between her teeth like the clapper in a bell.

She pushed herself to a sitting position. The sun was not yet up. The Rambler was still parked in front of the Resource Management Office. The car and her hair reeked of stale wine. Anna checked her wristwatch: five thirty-five.

She shoved her stinking locks back with both hands. "What the fuck happened to me?"

The keys were in the ignition. She slid over behind the wheel and tried the starter. There wasn't even a whimper of life. When she'd stumbled out the night before, she had left the ignition on as well as the radio and the lights. "Lucky for me and God knows who else." Her head dropped back against the seat and she grunted with the ache of it.

The last thing she remembered was dialing Molly's number in New York. She wondered what she had said.

Tires humming on the pavement brought her back into the present. Soon the park would begin to stir, archaeologists on their way to the lab, the tree kids toting chain saws into the woods to remove hazardous fuels, helitack jogging by on physical training, maintenance men, trail crew, tourists.

Panic tore the fog of alcohol clouding her mind. This was no way to greet the public. Balancing her head carefully on her shoulders, she retraced her steps to the Resource Management Office. The door was unlocked and open. Inside, on one of the desks, was a bottle with half an inch of red wine in the bottom. Mercifully it was upright and the resource management specialist's nest of papers unbesmirched by her night's debauchery. The bookcase had not fared so well. It was overturned and the books hurled around the room. Memory, like a snapshot, flashed in Anna's mind: her hands pulling the shelves toward her, books and periodicals cascading down over her feet.

Why she had done it, what she'd been looking for or trying to prove, remained a mystery.

She dropped to her knees, righted the bookcase, then crawled after its contents and restored them in what she hoped was relative order. Having finger-combed her matted hair and braided it off her face, she tied it with a piece of pink plastic surveyor's tape she'd found in the office.

Putting on the best face—and the best lie on it—she could, she walked the mile through the woods to the heli-tack dorm. Paul Summers drove her back in the fire truck and jump-started the Rambler.

Driving back to Far View, Anna felt weak-kneed and queasy. A strong sense of God not being in Her heaven and all's wrong with the world pervaded every cell of her body. Not only the hangover shook her, but the hours in blackout. A chunk of time she'd been active, talking, walking, evidently hurling research manuals, was utterly alien to her. A black hole she'd fallen into and, but for a dead battery, might never have crawled out of.

A hot shower steamed the booze from her pores and rinsed it from her hair but not even hot coffee could burn the fumes from her brain. As she pulled on her uniform, she hoped no great feats of kindness, courage, or intellect would be required of her for a few days. She longed to call Molly, but embarrassment combined with the need to sort things out on her own stayed her hand.

Purposely avoiding the Museum Loop, the chief rang-er's office, and most of the visitors, Anna patrolled the tra-ditionally uneventful four and a half miles from Far View Lodge to Park Point, the highest place in the park at 8,571 feet. The twisting road to the mesa cut through the flanks of mountains in two places, Bravo Cut and Delta Cut. Rocks falling from the unstable hillsides littered the road-way and were a constant headache. After rains the rocks were numerous and sizable enough to present a hazard to motorists. Delta Cut, the higher of the two, presented a slashed hillside to the town of Cortez far below. Held in by a metal railing, the road ran along a ragged drop edged with thickets of oakbrush. Today Anna found nothing but pebbles, none even as big as a woman's fist. Still she parked the car and meticulously began kicking each little rock off the asphalt.

It felt good to be quiet and alone and in the sunlight.

Bit by bit her mind cleared and she thought of Stacy Meyers. Not of Stacy Meyers the man, with his intellectual charm and heartfelt commitment to the land—that would have led her back to those lost hours in the Resource Management building. Anna thought of the "Meyers Incident," reducing it to a puzzle, a mystery that, unlike mysteries of the heart, might prove solvable.

On the grounds of woman's intuition she'd been quick to discount suicide but it was a real possibility and one that would have to be explored. Stephanie McFarland came to mind and Anna remembered Stacy's anguish at panicking. Could he have decided he no longer deserved to live? To a sane mind, it seemed excessive, but Anna knew from experience depression could breathe an insane logic into the most bizarre courses of action.

Anna knew very little of Stacy's inner life, or, as Molly would say, his real life. It was clear that he had financial problems. Short of a generous trust fund, any temporary GS-5 with grown-up responsibilities would have money problems. Stacy's were exacerbated by Bella's needs and Rose's wants.

Would he fake his own murder to provide for them? Anna took out the yellow notebook she carried in her hip pocket and wrote "Life Insurance?" on the first clean page. She had worked a couple of suicide investigations in the past and dreaded them. In many ways they were more destructive to those left living than homicide. Always, with unnatural death, came anger. Homicides had a healthy target, a suitable bad guy, a foe worthy of hatred. Suicide carried the same furious baggage but it fed on the bearer. As widowhood was said to be easier than divorce, so murder was easier than suicide. At least no one chose to leave.

The other possibilities were accident, natural causes, murder, and, if Jamie had her way, vengeful intervention of spirits. Hills was overwhelmingly in favor of the first idea but even he, faced with the neatly placed hat and doffed shoes, had to admit that: "If it was an accident it sure was a lulu."

Anna harbored a secret preference for the Revenge of the Anasazi. Paranormal foul play would be a nice diversion from man's daily inhumanity to man.

Foul Play: Anna smiled at the phrase and flicked a stone off the roadway with the side of her foot. It sounded so English, so Old School, implying subtle distaste for something not quite cricket, not entirely sporting. Homicide had an American feel, a businesslike violence-as-usual ring to it. Anna preferred Foul Play. She said it once aloud. In the gentle silence of a summer's day spoken words grated and she didn't try it again.

The sun was warm on her back, and a breeze, blowing across from the snow-covered peaks of the Abajos a hundred miles away in Utah, smelled gloriously of nothing. Up high there was only air in the air and Anna took a moment to fill her lungs to capacity.

If one must think of murder, this was the kind of day to do it: a pure day, one without guile.

Murder, then; the motives were usually predictable. Somebody got mad, got greedy, or got even. The pathologically neat arrangement of the scene seemed to rule out a crime of passion. Those killed in sudden heat were customarily found sprawled and bloody in bedrooms, barrooms, on kitchen floors, and in parking lots.

Getting even seemed a possibility. By leaving the corpse in such an odd place perhaps the avenger had hoped to pay back not only the dead but, in some way, the living—the widow, a friend, or even the National Park Service. Again Anna pulled out the notebook. "Enemies?" went under "Life Insurance."

Greed was Anna's favorite. Greed seemed to motivate a goodly number of human behaviors, murder among them. But, if greed were the motivating factor, the grandstand play of laying the corpse in the fire ring of a kiva struck her as out of place.

Why wouldn't the body be buried, hidden, disposed of somehow? Only the very naive would think Stacy's remains would go undiscovered in Cliff Palace. Even if the archaeologists or the stabilization crew didn't stumble across it, eventually the odor or the vultures would have given the location away.

Stacy was meant to be found. To prove something? To frighten someone? To stop the search before too many noses were poked into too many places? Beneath "Enemies" Anna scribbled "Where Else Should We Have Looked?" and "Greed/Rose" with an arrow drawn back up to "Life Insurance."

She'd run out of stones. The stretch of road through the cut was clean. Disappointed to have completed so pleasantly mindless a task, she began to walk back along the highway to where she'd left her patrol car.

A gold Honda Accord was stopped fifty yards or so from her vehicle. The hood was up in the international symbol for motorist in distress. Anna perked up, walked a little faster. Citizen assists were good clean ranger work, the equivalent of firemen rescuing kittens from trees.

A generous behind covered in rich plum fabric was

swaying rhythmically to the left of the front fender. Anna approached the far side of the vehicle and looked under the hood. An exceedingly round woman with a froth of chestnut curls shot with gray and held off her face by a yellow plastic banana was chanting "drat, drat, drat" and shaking small dimpled fists at an unresponsive engine. Her face was as round as the rest of her and showed no signs of age. Earrings of green-and-yellow parrots dangled to her shoulders, the birds looking at home against the print of a Hawaiian shirt.

"Trouble?" Anna said by way of greeting.

The woman looked up, bright blue eyes sharp-focused behind glasses nearly half an inch thick. "Oh, hello. Do you know anything about these horrid things?"

Her voice was high and had a singsong quality about it that was exquisitely comforting. Anna, who usually disliked voices in the upper registers, placed it instantly. In her mind she heard Billie Burke in *The Wizard of Oz* asking Dorothy, "Are you a good witch or a bad witch?" The resemblance didn't end there. This woman was big, two hundred pounds or so, but seemingly as light and translucent as the bubble in which the Good Witch of the North traveled.

She shook her fists again and Anna half expected her to float with the effort.

"I only know about six things to poke," Anna apologized. "If that doesn't work, I call a tow truck."

"Ooooh." The woman sounded wickedly delighted. "Let's poke."

Anna laughed and took a hard look at her companion. The familiarity wasn't born just of fairy tales. "You're Aunt Hattie!" she declared. Bella hadn't described her aunt in physical terms but she had painted such a clear picture of her spirit, Anna was certain. Hattie bore a slight resemblance to her sister, Rose, but her features were more refined and looked to have been sculpted by laughter where Rose's were etched by discontent. Rose carried less weight, but she seemed cursed by gravity. The pounds dragged her down. Hattie was buoyant, uplifting.

While Bella's aunt tried the starter, Anna pushed butterfly valves and rattled air filters. Finally, noting a depressing lack of fuel squirting into the carburetor, she gave it up as a lost cause and radioed Dispatch to call a tow truck from Cortez.

The Honda disposed of, Anna gave Hattie a lift to the mesa top. Hattie appeared completely at her ease, simply sitting, riding, watching the scenery. Hattie had seemed at ease shaking her fists over a dead engine and Anna was surprised to find herself at an unaccustomed comfort level as well.

"You came because of Stacy?" Anna asked.

"For Bella."

"Rose call you?"

"Bella," Hattie said again, and laughed. "This is a bit of a surprise visit, I'm afraid. But I don't think Rose'll mind. She'll have so much on her mind. And I do think she will have a hard time of it without Stacy. He was a good man and Rose isn't used to that."

"Her first husband?" Anna prodded.

"A pig face. Rose was besotted." Hattie shrugged soft graceful shoulders. "Where's the fun? I liked Stacy. And Bella liked Stacy."

This last was clearly the most heavily weighted factor in the equation and Anna let it sit without comment for a while. Remembering the conversation she'd had with Bella about her aunt and how she "lifts you up, zoop, zoop, zoop," Anna said: "Bella will be glad you've come."

"Bella's a magical spirit," Hattie said. "Till I got to

know her I'd pretty much forgotten how the world looks when you're new."

Not new anymore. After a murder the newness got lost. Even at six—perhaps especially at six. This would rob Bella's world of a lot of magic.

Hattie scrunched down in the passenger seat and leaned her head back. The breeze through the open window ruffled her hair, teasing it into a froth around the banana clip. The parrots danced gaily. Life cloaked Bella's aunt so vibrantly; coupled with the scent of pine and the warmth of the sun, made it infinitely precious. Anna could remember a time, the years after Zach died, when it was a tremendous burden. One she might have shucked if it hadn't been for Molly and a good healthy dose of cowardice.

"Do you think Stacy could have committed suicide?" she asked impulsively.

Hattie straightened up, the languor gone, the blue eyes sharp. "Rose said he was killed."

Anna sensed a question behind the statement and waited, hoping the silence would draw it out. On the radio a country-western artist began singing "When I say no I mean maybe." Anna switched it off.

Conning the car around the last in a series of hairpin curves, she started up the last climb to the mesa top where Far View Lodge looked down over the southwest. An oversized RV plodded ahead at twenty-six miles an hour. Anna was glad of the delay. Once the buildings came in sight, tour-guide questions would distract them both.

"That would be the worst possible thing for Bella," Hattie said at last. "The worst kind of abandonment. The most awful rejection. God, I hope not."

"But maybe . . . ?"

"Bella, in a little kid's way, thinks maybe. She never said

so much but Rose and Stacy had a shouting match on the phone the night he disappeared. Bella thinks about that. Rose wouldn't've bothered to hide it from her. Rose is a tad self-centered. She believes anything she says or thinks is worthy of publication. God forbid one of her emotions should go unvented."

The acid touch cut through what Anna had perceived as an almost too-sweet soul and she delighted in it. A few snakes and snails made the sugar and spice more interesting.

"What was the fight about? Did Bella say?"

"She thinks it was about her. A six-year-old's view of the world is limited. My guess is it was about money. Rose always argued about money—even when she had it."

Rose hadn't mentioned a fight. That didn't surprise Anna. Couples were often embarrassed they quarreled, never quite believing it was as common as dandruff in most marriages. If the fight had been over money, Rose might have had more than one reason for not mentioning it. Insurance companies didn't pay off on suicides.

They crested the hill and the mesa spread south; a green tabletop. The RV turned on its blinker and lumbered off the road into the Visitors' Center parking lot. Talk turned to other things.

By the time they reached the housing loop it was midday and the place was deserted. Anna let the patrol car roll to a stop under the tree in the Meyerses' yard, then got out to retrieve Hattie's luggage from the trunk.

The screen door banged open and Rose cried, "Hattie!"

As the women embraced in the middle of the walk, Anna dragged the heavy bags from the back of the car. On Hattie's side the hug appeared to be heartfelt, but Rose was kissing air. "What a surprise," she said. And: "I hope you packed a lunch. Stacy left us with nothing to live on. Nothing."

Anna slammed the trunk a bit harder than necessary.

"Are those yours?" Rose eyed the size of the suitcases.

"All mine," Hattie said cheerfully.

"You can put them in the front room," Rose directed Anna.

As her younger sister turned to reenter the house, Hattie put her fists on her ample hips and cocked one eyebrow at Anna in a perfect parody of a disapproving schoolmarm. Anna laughed and hefted the bags. Bella had been right. Zoop, zoop, zoop.

As she dumped the luggage and turned to go, Rose issued a last directive.

"Bella took her sandwich over to eat with that Drew. Tell her her aunt's paying us a visit."

Anna resisted the urge to pull a forelock and back humbly out the door.

Irritation short-circuited her brain till she'd driven out of the housing loop. As she was turning right at the stop sign to backtrack around the island of piñons separating the houses from the maintenance yard, the short exchange between the sisters sprang back into her thoughts with sudden clarity.

"Stacy left us with nothing to live on. Nothing."

No insurance; no insurance, no suicide-dressed-as-murder. At least not for monetary reasons. That was one item Anna could cross off her list.

Bella was just leaving the fire cache. She walked her bike, laboriously pushing it ahead of her as if the machine were as heavy as her heart.

Anna pulled up beside her, letting the Ford creep along at idle, keeping pace with the child. "I've got some good news for you," she said.

Bella didn't even look up. There was no more good news to be had in the world.

"Your aunt Hattie's here," Anna said quickly.

"Aunt Hattie?" Something, maybe two parts relief and three parts joy, enlivened Bella's face. "That's okay then." She pulled herself astride the bike and began pedaling.

"Wait," Anna called as she cruised up beside the girl again. "What did your mama and Stacy fight about on the telephone?"

Bella stopped, shot Anna a cold look.

Anna couldn't back down. "It might be important," she said.

Whatever Bella weighed in her mind evidently came out in Anna's favor. "Some man," she said, and rode down the path into the trees.

Suicide was back. Because Rose, like the infamous ex, had "too many people she just had to meet"? Or murder by the jealous boyfriend? Both solutions were too mundane and melodramatic for Anna's taste. But if people died only for good reasons, a lot of mortuaries would go begging.

11

Aɴɴᴀ ʜᴀᴅ barricaded herself in her room.
Etta James singing "Stop the Wedding" on
the boom box served to block the tinny sounds of "Wheel
of Fortune" coming from the other room. Anna wasn't in
the mood for Jamie, even if she was abusing Vanna White.
A glass of chardonnay waited on the dresser by the bed.
Anna sat cross-legged in the middle of a Mexican blanket
bought when she'd worked in Texas. The phone was in
her lap.

As the wine worked its way down into the muscles of
her neck, she let her head rest against the wall. Tonight
she would go easy. There must be no more black holes.

Molly answered on the third ring. "Yes?" she said per-
emptorily.

For an instant Anna felt like slamming down the receiver, hiding in silence. The prospect was too lonely. "It's
just me," she said, sounding unnecessarily cheerful.

"How are you feeling?" Molly asked, and Anna knew
she would not be allowed to pretend last night had never
happened.

"Better than I was," she admitted.

"A little hair of the dog?"

"No," Anna lied. "Anyway, that's not what I called to talk about."

"Better me now than the entire staff at Hazelden in a couple of years. You've got a problem, Anna."

Anna took a long sip of the chardonnay in a lame gesture of rebellion. "No. I've got a solution."

There was a sucking silence, then Molly mumbling: "Ten, fifteen, twenty, twenty-five . . ."

"What're you doing?"

"Trying to count up how many times in my umpteen years' practice I've heard that one. It's no go, Anna. Normal people—at least people over the age of seventeen—don't drink until they black out."

"I didn't black out." Second lie in as many minutes. Anna was beginning to worry herself.

"What did we talk about the third time you called me?" Molly demanded.

"Oh shit." Anna vaguely remembered the one call. "Okay. I blacked out."

"Hah."

"'Hah'? Is that substance-abuse parlance? One blackout does not an alcoholic make."

"What's the magic number? Three? Ten?"

Anna chose not to answer.

"Okay, talk about Stacy Meyers."

"Maybe I don't want to." Anna felt peevish.

"That's not the idea I got during call number three at four-ten A.M. this morning."

Anna sighed, fortified herself with another draught of wine. "How many times did I call?"

"I don't have the foggiest. After number three I unplugged my phone."

Depression settled like coal dust across Anna's mind. "Tough love? Or are you just in a very bad mood?"

"I want you to take this seriously, not to weasel, charm, or rationalize your way out of it."

"It won't happen again," Anna snapped.

"It happened."

"A friend of mine was murdered."

"Stacy Meyers."

The conversation had come full circle. Anna told Molly about Stacy, his wit and intense brown eyes, his undeserving wife and high ideals.

When she had finished, Molly said: "You kept calling him Zach last night."

"Caught the girl in the Freudian slip?" Anna teased.

"Freud was a deeply troubled man," Molly returned.

"In vino veritas, then?"

"Hardly. Maybe in mucho vino mega confusion. You had the two men mixed up in your mind last night. There was a physical resemblance?"

"Slight."

"A similar intensity?"

Anna said nothing.

"Confusion, Anna. That's what I heard. Lots of it. Psychological wounds are like soft-tissue injuries. You get hurt in the same place twice and they may never heal. You need clarity right now, not oblivion. The time for that, if there ever was one, is long past. No sense playing that scene out again. This time you might not survive, and boy would I be pissed.

"Gotta go," Molly finished. "Stay alert."

"What's a 'lert'?" Anna whispered the childhood joke into a dead phone line.

She finished the glass of wine but didn't pour herself a second. Clarity: she thought about that for a while. There were times reality didn't have all that much to recommend it. "Like now," she said to the face in the mirror, then, thinking of Bella, was shamed out of her self-pity. "Clarity," she repeated aloud, and slipped on her moccasins. At least she could do what she was good at: aggravating people into telling her more than they wanted to.

Down on Chapin it was significantly warmer. The difference between summer and fall, shorts and long pants.

Anna slowed the Rambler to an idle and crept past the houses trying to organize her thoughts. Day's end; it was warm and the light would last till nine o'clock or later. People were out walking dogs, sitting at picnic tables gossiping while dinners cooked on outdoor grills. Several members of the helitack crew sat on the steps of the fire dorm drinking beer. Drew waved her over, pointing at the bottle of Colt 45 in his hand.

"The devil is at mine elbow," Anna muttered. She pulled the Rambler in and parked in front of the dorm. Drew, Jimmy, and Paul sat on the steps looking for all the world like fraternity boys on a Saturday afternoon.

"How goes the hunt?" Drew asked.

"An arrest is imminent," Anna said, and declined another offer of a beer.

"It won't help Bella," Drew said. "She's breaking my heart, poor little kid. Who'd've thought she'd take it so hard? Stacy wasn't even her real dad. With all that threat of cutting her legs up, I'd've thought she might be relieved. She hid it pretty good, but it scared her a lot. What a waste." Drew sucked down half a Colt at one gulp and crushed the can into a wad of tinfoil.

"Sure you won't have a brewski?" Jimmy asked as he popped another for Drew and one for himself. Anna wasn't at all sure she wouldn't so she took her leave.

By the time she parked under the tree in front of the

Meyerses' bungalow, her plan still hadn't taken on any real form. She toyed with the idea of returning to Far View but the need to keep busy forced her out of the car.

The door was open. She peered through the screen. The front room was a mess of magazines and newspapers. The couch, desk, and much of the floor were littered with them. No toys, she noted. A television, a *TV Guide* open on top of it, stared with a blank eye from a small table in the corner. Familiar sounds of an evening game show came from elsewhere in the house.

A TV in the kitchen or bedroom, Anna guessed. "Hello, anybody home?" She rapped lightly on the door frame.

Clattering from the kitchen answered her query. A moment later Rose Meyers appeared on the other side of the screen. "Yes?" she said when she saw Anna on the doorstep.

"In the neighborhood," Anna said. "Just thought I'd drop by."

"No one is here. Hattie and Bella went for a walk."

"That's okay."

Rose looked nonplussed. Several seconds ticked by during which she evidently remembered her manners. "Would you like to come in for a minute?" she offered.

"Thanks. That would be nice."

Rose stood aside, holding the door, while Anna slunk by. "I hope I'm not interrupting anything. . . ." Anna began, and waited for the usual reassurances but none were offered.

Shoving aside several days' worth of coupons in the midst of the clipping and sorting process, Anna settled on the couch. "I've always liked these little houses," she said, looking around the room with its wooden floor and wood-burning stove. She'd seen the homes redone for permanent employees. They had wall-to-wall carpeting and more recent paint jobs—more comfortable but less picturesque.

"It's cramped," Rose said.

"After dorm living, a doghouse would look like a mansion to me if I had it all to myself."

Rose gave up her post at the door and went so far as to perch on the edge of a chair but she didn't get comfortable. That this was not to be a long visit was made abundantly clear.

"I can't stay long," Anna said to put her at her ease. "Only an hour or two," she added, just for the fun of watching Rose flinch.

Mrs. Meyers looked as if she were ill and Anna, remembering widowhood, softened. "How are you doing?" she asked. "That's really all I came by for. This is a hard time."

"Yes." The rigid cast of Rose's features trembled and for a moment it looked as if her control might crack but she recovered herself. "Hard."

"Was Stacy depressed over anything?" Anna ventured. "Poor health, family problems, finances—anything like that?"

Rose's head jerked up, her face so full of anger Anna was half surprised her hair didn't catch on fire. "Stacy was in perfect health," Rose said coldly. "And, not that it's any of your business, but, no, there were no 'family problems,' as you put it. If you're implying my husband killed himself, you can put a stop to that line of thinking right now. This minute. Stacy wouldn't do that to me."

Anna waited a minute, letting Rose cool off. She searched her mind for a way of connecting with the woman, breaking through the wall of fury. "My husband was killed,"

Anna told her. "I had a real bad time for a while." Still have, she thought, but didn't say it.

"How was he killed?" Rose asked without interest.

Anna hated this part. More than once she wished Zach had had the good taste to die rescuing a child from a burning building, or skiing in avalanche country. "Crossing Ninth Avenue against the light, he was hit by a cab."

Another silence began. Anna watched Rose's drawn face and downcast eyes. Her need for information seemed petty in the face of this grief and she made up her mind to quit badgering. "Are you going to be all right?" she asked impulsively.

"All right?" Rose laughed. "Now that's relative, isn't it? I have no job, no income, a child with special needs. All right?" Rose's voice was becoming shrill. The dam was breaking and Anna wasn't altogether sure she wanted to be there when it gave way. "No, I'm not going to be all right. Maybe if the Park Service would stop piddling around and find out who did this, I could be all right. You can bet your cozy little government job I'm going to sue for everything I have coming to me. No health insurance, no retirement, no death benefits. Like Stacy was a migrant worker, no better than a strawberry picker. Temporary appointment!" She spat out the words. "We can't even stay here much longer. Not that that's a big loss but it is a roof over our heads.

"Oh, yes," she continued, as if Anna had argued. "I'm going to sue all right. Tell that to Mr. Hills Dutton. And tell him to stop writing parking tickets and talk to Ted Greeley."

"Ted Greeley?" Anna probed.

"Money can buy anything, anybody," Rose said, then snapped her mouth shut so hard her jowls quivered. Anna doubted she would get another word out of Rose with anything short of a crowbar.

"Well . . ." She levered herself up out of the nest of papers. "I'll sure tell him. We can use any help you can give us. Let me know if you need anything." With that and other platitudes, Anna paved her way to the front door and escaped down the walk.

She'd gotten what she wanted, a flood of unedited words. Out of which "Ted Greeley" and "Money can buy anything, anybody" merited consideration. Rose seemed to be suggesting Greeley had bought off Hills, paid him to steer the investigation away from him or his. If he had, Greeley was a fool. Hills wasn't the head of this incident, the Federal Bureau of Investigation was. Their man was due in in the morning.

That left the possibility that Rose believed the contractor had something to do with her husband's murder. Coupling Rose's finger-pointing with Bella's admission that the fight on the phone between her mom and Stacy was over some man made for interesting hypotheses. Was "some man" Greeley? Was Greeley jealous of Stacy, in love with his wife?

Anna made a mental note to mention this interview when she met with the federal investigator.

She dropped the Rambler in gear and pulled around Rose's Oldsmobile. Her mind flashed back to the day she and Stacy had confronted Tom Silva about the foreskin note. Greeley had said something that chilled or angered Stacy. Anna remembered: "How's my little Bella?"

Could Greeley be Rose's rich first husband? No, Anna remembered, Number One was a lawyer. Greeley as Rose's lover? Worth pondering. Uncharitable as it was, Anna thought it unlikely any man would kill for the pleasure of Mrs. Meyers' company but she knew that was pure prejudice on her part. On like occasions her father used to say: "Perhaps she has talents we are not privy to." The human heart, though often predictable, remained unfathomable. People loved who they loved and killed who they killed. Rhyme and reason, when they entered in, were often so skewed as to be meaningless to an outside observer.

Anna shoved these new ingredients to the back burner of her mind to stew awhile.

Killing time, she drove down to the Museum Loop and through the picnic grounds. Snuggled down in the evergreens, the picnic area seemed common, if charming, but a few steps carried one to the lip of Spruce Canyon. There the mesa fell away in staggered steps of fawn-colored sandstone, before a sheer drop to the wooded ground below. Like many canyons cut into the mesa, Spruce was small. For Anna there was always a sense of Shangri-la about these hidden places. Each had its own dwellings, long since abandoned by their owners and bleached back to the color of the earth.

Since Mesa Verde's cliffs had first been inhabited the Anasazi, the Utes, the Navajo, cowboys, hunters, and tourists had all tramped the trails. Yet there remained a tremendous sense of discovery. In that lay much of the park's allure.

Anna parked the Rambler and walked out toward the canyon rim. The sun was just setting, casting golden light that made the trees greener and the sandstone seem to glow from within. Blue-and-black-winged butterflies settled on the milkweed as if trapped in the amber light.

Since there was no camping on the mesa top, the picnic grounds were gloriously deserted in the evenings. Anna breathed in the solitude.

Not wanting to break the peace, she made her way through the band of junipers between the picnic area and the canyon with great care, placing each moccasined foot on bare ground to avoid snapping needles and twigs.

Such stealth had paid off several times since she'd moved to Colorado. Once she had seen a mother lion with two speckled cubs behind Coyote Village and once a bull elk looking fat and fine and full of himself at Park Point.

This evening she crept up on a much stranger game.

Out on the canyon's lip the sandstone had been worn into a shallow trough sixty feet wide. Over the centuries summer rains had scoured it smooth. In the middle of the pour-over a stone block the size of a sofa and relatively the same shape had come to rest. Lying on the rock, dyed red by the setting sun, was the body of Bella Meyers. Her hands were crossed on her breast in the classic pose of the deceased. Aunt Hattie, her hair a frizz of sun-drenched brown, bent over the child. The woman's small, perfect hands were doubled under her chin. She was murmuring or singing.

Anna stopped at the edge of the trees. The little scene played on; the child motionless, Hattie moving occasionally as if exclaiming or weaving spells. After a time, Anna ventured out into the dying light, her footfalls soundless on the stone.

When she was eight or ten feet away she heard Hattie asking in her high, pleasant voice: "Shall I kiss you awake now?" and was relieved to see a small shake of Bella's head. The child had not been slaughtered in some bizarre ritual.

"Oh my, but she was such a beautiful girl, beloved of all in the kingdom." Hattie sighed over the little body.

Hattie glanced up then and saw Anna. "Someone else has come to pay their last respects to the lovely Bella," she said in her storybook voice. To Anna she whispered: "We're playing Dead Princess."

Anna cocked an eyebrow.

"It's a game Bella made up when she was little," Hattie explained in a whisper, careful not to break the spell. "The princess lies in state and is admired by all and sundry until she is awakened by the magic kiss."

"Sounds like my kind of game," Anna returned.

"The princess has been dead a very long time today," Hattie said sadly. "She doesn't seem to want to be kissed back to life."

"Aunt Hattie!" came a remonstrance from the side of Bella's mouth. Her eyes were still squeezed shut.

"Yes, Royal One?"

"Okay. Now."

Hattie leaned down and placed a gentle kiss in the middle of the child's forehead. Slowly Bella opened one eye, then the other, and looked around as if she were in a strange place.

"Welcome back, little one," Hattie said. "The crowds are cheering your return to the world of the living. You have been sorely missed."

Bella smiled a little. "Okay. I'm done." She sat up abruptly and swung her short legs over the side of the boulder.

Hattie sat beside her and both of them looked at Anna. "We're done," the aunt said.

Anna squatted on her heels. The sun threw their shadows a dozen feet, shading her eyes. "I didn't mean to interrupt your game," she apologized.

"That's all right," Bella assured her. "I was about to come to life anyway. My behind was getting tired of the rock. Being dead isn't as easy as it looks."

"I guess not."

"Do you want to play?" Bella offered. "My behind's waking up some."

"I don't know how," Anna told her, and Bella looked disappointed. "Maybe your aunt Hattie could teach me," Anna relented, and won one of Bella's smiles.

"It's a good game," Bella promised as she lay back down and folded her hands over her chest.

Anna stood and looked down at the little girl with her angel's face and stunted legs, so peaceful in her pretended and admired state of suspended animation. Anna was glad Hattie had come. Everybody needed someone to kiss her back to life.

"Does the kiss always work?" Anna teased the other woman.

"It does if you do it right."

12

Fᴵʀsᴛ ᴛʜɪɴɢ the following morning, Anna received a secondhand message by way of Jennifer Short that she was to meet Hills at the CRO. Unable to sleep, she came down early and sat on the bench opposite the office door, enjoying the freshness of the day. Soon buses and cars would begin puffing the park full of carbon monoxide and noise. The first hours after sunrise were new made, hinting of wilderness, of what the world was once and, in dreams, might be again.

Across the walkway, amid the knife-point leaves of the agave, a yellow-and-black bull snake uncoiled himself into the warmth of the sun. The snake lived in a hole in the stonework of the superintendent's porch. At least that's where Anna'd seen him flee other mornings when the first foot traffic of the day began.

She stretched her shirt against her shoulder blades and took primal pleasure in the sun's rays. "I think I'm an exotherm," she said. The snake didn't even blink.

An unnatural sound, high heels clacking on paved ground, got a better response. Anna looked in the direction of the racket and when she turned back her narrow fellow had gone.

"You scared away my snake," she complained as Patsy Silva came down the walk.

"Good. Nasty things." Patsy was dressed in a colorful Mexican skirt with a turquoise blouse and sandals. She looked chipper. But she always looked chipper so Anna deduced nothing from that.

"You look chipper," she said to see if it were so.

"Found my keys." Patsy dangled a ring with a neon-pink rabbit's foot on it. "Good omen."

" 'Bout time. What with chindis and"—she almost said "dead guys" but realized to those not in law enforcement it might seem unnecessarily cavalier—"what not," she finished safely. "Find them in the last place you looked?"

Patsy laughed. "Usually. Not this time. They were in my purse all along. They'd fallen down among the used Kleenex and dead lipsticks—the bottom-feeders."

"Speaking of: how goes it with Tom? Since I haven't heard, I've assumed no news is good news."

"I suppose so." Patsy sat down beside Anna, deciding to take time for a proper chat. "He's not around. I mean he's here and I see him and the girls see him, but it's like he's sneaking. Lurking, sort of."

"Spying?"

"Not spying, I don't think. I'd've reported that for sure. No, it's sort of like a storm cloud always on the horizon. Not really threatening you, but you know it's raining on somebody somewhere."

Anna shook her head. "I'm still not getting the picture. Does he come over and moon at you or leave notes or what?"

"No. I'd've called you for that too, I think. He's just around, in our peripheral vision, sort of. Like the girls'll be waiting for the bus and he'll drive by at a time he should be working. Or I'll come home after dark from somewhere and he'll just be walking by my house. Mindy and Missy and I came out of the movies in Cortez and he was across the street having coffee at that little lunch place."

"Following you?"

"Maybe—but from a big distance."

"Does it scare you or the girls?"

Patsy laughed again. "I suppose it should but it doesn't. It's sort of comforting, like that old song 'Someone to Watch Over Me.'"

Tom's behavior struck Anna more in the stalker than the guardian-angel mode. "He doesn't talk to you or the girls, he just sort of skulks?"

"Doesn't talk. In fact he seems to be avoiding us. A couple of times we've responded, you know—like friends— and Tom acted like he wanted to get away."

"Well, holler if he starts scaring you," Anna said, because she could think of nothing else to say. She looked at her watch: seven fifty-seven.

Adept at taking hints of dismissal, Patsy stood and arranged her purse on her shoulder. "Waiting for Hills," Anna explained. "I've been summoned for God knows what."

"Oh." Patsy brightened. "I bet it's to go to Durango. The FBI man is arriving on the ten-eleven from Albuquerque. The superintendent had me book it."

"That's it then. Pigeon's taxi service."

Patsy picked up on her annoyance. "Hills thought you'd want to go. It turns out the investigator is an old friend of yours, a Frederick Stanton."

"You're kidding! Frederick the Fed? I'll be damned."

"He's not an old friend?" Patsy had such a practiced look of concern Anna would've pegged her as a mom even if she hadn't known of the girls.

"We worked together once," Anna said. "We're more like old acquaintances."

Hills strode up looking lean and marvelously rangerlike with his blond bulk and tight pants. Her assignment was, indeed, to fetch Frederick Stanton from the Durango airport ninety miles to the east.

The drive between the park and Durango wound down off the mesa and through the Mancos Valley nestled between the snow-topped La Plata mountains to the north and the red mesas to the south. Fields were carpeted with dandelions, and blue irises lined the streams. Several hundred sheep, herded by men and boys on horseback, stopped traffic for twenty minutes, making Anna late to the airport. Fortunately, the flight was even later.

Abandoning the terminal for the out of doors, she sat on the concrete with her back against the warm brick of the building and passed the time remembering Frederick the Fed.

Isle Royale had been a while ago but she still remembered the gory details. The FBI agent was a tall gangling man with well-cut features a size too large for his face. Anna estimated his age at thirty-five. Dark hair, cut in the inimitable style of a third-grader, class of fifty-eight, flopped over his forehead; skin showed white around the ears where the clippers had cut too close.

Stanton had a vague and bumbling manner but was usually a step or two ahead at the end of every heat. Too much Columbo, too much Lord Peter Wimsey, Anna thought. Or, perhaps, *Revenge of the Nerds* and "Saturday Night Live." Stanton didn't fit the mold. It made him hard to type and impossible to predict. Which was, Anna guessed, exactly why he did it.

He used people. He'd used Anna and he'd done it effortlessly; that was the part that rankled.

A twin-engine prop plane, the commuter out of Albuquerque, roared in from the taxiway and came to a stop on the ramp beyond the chain-link fence.

Anna eased herself up.

The fourth passenger off was Stanton. Anna laughed at how like himself he looked. Same haircut, even the same clothes. He wore a short-sleeved madras shirt he must have unearthed from a vintage clothing store, rumpled khaki shorts, white socks, and brown lace-up shoes. As he came down the metal steps that folded out from the fuselage, he kept looking behind him, swatting at his posterior.

Absorbed in this activity, he ambled across the ramp. When he reached the fence he looked up. If he was surprised to see Anna, he didn't show it. "I think I sat in something ooky," he said, wrinkling his long nose. "Anything there?" He turned to give her an unobscured view of his backside.

There was perhaps a speck of something on his right hip pocket but Anna wasn't in the mood to enter into a discussion of it. "Looks fine to me."

Stanton craned his neck and looked down over his shoulder. "Okay then," he said. "I'll have to trust you on this one. Sure felt sticky for a minute."

"Luggage?" Anna said to get things moving.

"Got it." He shook the strap of an oversized leather shoulder bag he carried.

"You must be planning on wrapping this one up in record time."

"I heard you were on the case so I only brought one change of underdrawers."

There wasn't much to say to that so Anna merely nodded.

With what seemed a maximum of fuss and fiddling

around, she got the federal agent buckled into the passenger seat of the patrol car and started the trip back to the park.

As they drove to the main highway, Stanton waved graciously at passing traffic. "Boy, I love riding in cars with lights and sirens," he said. "Everybody waves back. They think they did something and you're not stopping them for it. Kind of makes you pals."

Anna laughed. "I wondered what it was."

Stanton made idle conversation, the kind she'd grown used to working with him on the island. During the weeks of that investigation she'd come to look upon it as his personal music, the kind designed to soothe the savage beasts; charming in its whimsy, disarmingly inane. When one became complacent, convinced he was a complete boob, he'd pounce.

"Okay," he said as she pulled out onto highway 160. "Tell me the good-parts version."

Anna switched off the radio and pulled her thoughts together. As succinctly as possible, she recounted the disappearance, the discovery of the body, the widow's whereabouts the night of the murder, and Rose's casting blame in the general direction of the pipeline contractor.

Stanton sat for a while humming "I Heard It Through the Grapevine" under his breath. The patrol car crawled up the long slope out of Durango. Anna unfettered her mind and let it wander over the now-green ski slopes of Hesperus and the fresh new-leaved poplar trees skirting the mountain ravines. The sky was an impossible blue, a blue seen only on hot midwestern summer days and high in the mountains. Cornflower blue—the phrase flickered through her mind, though she'd never seen a cornflower.

"That's no fun," Frederick said finally. He twisted

around in his seat till the shoulder strap pushed his collar up under his right ear and his bony knees pointed in Anna's direction. "Tell me the gossip, innuendo, lies, suppositions, weird happenstance. Dead guys are pretty dull without some good dirt. Do dish me."

"The dead guy was a friend of mine," Anna replied irritably.

"Oops." Stanton looked genuinely contrite and she was sorry for such a cheap shot. She'd thought of Stacy as the dead guy not three hours earlier. She's almost made up her mind to apologize when Stanton spoke again.

"Callous, that's me all over. How about this: Deceased individuals, however meritorious in life, lack the essential spontaneity to generate interest. So those left living must keep their spirits alive through the practice of the oral tradition."

Anna snorted. "Callous is right. The dirt." Out of spite—or self-defense—she told Stanton everything she could think of that occurred in the park, or in anyone's imagination in the park, around the time of the murder: Jamie's chindi, the pipeline, medicals, evacuations, the superintendent's secretary's marital problems, the monkey-wrenching, the dorm, Piedmont's foster home, Bella's dwarfism. She got bored before he did, running out of words as they passed through the tiny town of Mancos.

"And the meritorious deceased?" Stanton pushed.

Anna was torn between a desire to snub the fed for his flippancy and a need to talk of Stacy. The need to talk won. She'd used that need a dozen times to pull information from people. Mildly, she cursed herself for giving in to it now. To retain some vestige of self-respect, she culled all emotion from her tone. Dispassionately, she recounted Stacy's sensitivity, love of the parks, his attachment to Bella and addiction to Rose.

At the word "addiction," Anna realized she was being catty. Hoping it had slipped by Stanton, she made a mental note to talk to Molly about it.

"Rats," he summed up when she'd done. "Sounds messy and domestic. Widows and orphans and who's divorced and who's dead. Any drug dealings, you think?"

He sounded so hopeful Anna laughed as she shook her head. "Doesn't seem like it."

"Too bad." Stanton screwed himself around in the seat, draping one long arm over the back and looking down into the valley as the car climbed the winding road cut in the side of the mesa. "Drug dealers make such satisfying bad guys. Not so good as Nazis or Hell's Angels, but then who is? Hate doing the widows, especially when they're all fresh and weepy."

Hills Dutton was waiting for them in the CRO. In the past Anna had often found rangers loath to turn an investigation over to an outside agency. Some hated surrendering the power, others suffered a natural discomfort at letting anyone not a member of the family paw through the dirty laundry. Lord knew what they might choose to air.

Dutton was the exception; he couldn't wait to dump this one in somebody else's lap. Statements, paperwork, the photographs, and the autopsy—unopened and dated two days previously, Anna noted—had been stuffed into a manila envelope. Hills thrust it into Stanton's hands the instant the introductions were over. Lest the abdication appear incomplete, he added: "This is our busy season and I've got a park to run so I'm giving you Anna for whatever while you're here."

"My very own ranger," Stanton gloated as he and Anna walked back to her patrol car. "Just what I always wanted . . . well, next to a pony."

Anna grumbled because it was expected of her but she was pleased with the assignment. Parking tickets and medical evacuations had begun to pall, replaced by an undoubtedly unhealthy obsession with Stacy Meyers, living and now dead.

She took Stanton, the envelope still clamped under his arm, to Cliff Palace and played tour guide as she led him down the steep path into the alcove where the village was built. During the descent a metamorphosis took place. By the time they stood before the ruin, Stanton had lost his puppyish ways. Even his physical appearance was altered. The angles of his bones had sharpened, his stride was no longer gangling but purposeful, and his step had softened till the leather soles fell with scarcely a sound. Anna was put in mind of the time they had sat on a rock overlooking Lake Richie on Isle Royale waiting for a murder suspect; the sense she'd gotten then of the wolf shedding its sheep's clothing.

The ruin was packed with tourists moving through the ancient pueblo in a sluggish stream. At the base of the tower where Anna and Stacy had found the asthmatic child, people were backed up twenty deep waiting to stick their heads through the window to see the paintings.

"Like the Matterhorn at Disneyland," a voice from above and behind Anna sneered.

Jamie Burke was seated high on a boulder in the shade. A silver counter rested in her right hand and she clicked off tourists as they came by. The usual questions: when? who? how? and where did they go? were all answered in the same way: "It's in the brochure."

Anna was not impressed. Unlike the wilderness parks, which she staunchly believed were for the animals and plants dwelling therein, Mesa Verde was for the visitors.

Humans paying tribute with curiosity and awe to human ancestry. On Isle Royale and in Guadalupe, law enforcement was there to protect and preserve. The main function of rangers on the mesa was to keep the flow of traffic orderly so the interpreters could bring this history to life.

"Hi, Jamie," Anna said neutrally.

Ignoring her, Jamie slid down from the rock to land on legs strong as shock absorbers. "Are you the FBI guy?" she demanded of Stanton.

The agent stuck out his hand. The unhinged, bumbling look had returned, donned like a disguise. "Yes indeedy."

Jamie didn't shake his hand. Putting fists on hips, she squinted up at the walls filling niches high above the dwelling. "You're too late. Too bad Stacy had to die. He was my closest friend," Jamie said. "Maybe he'd still be alive if you'd listened to me."

"You" was generic, as in "they," and Anna didn't bother to challenge it.

"How so?" Stanton asked politely.

"Al said this strip-mining was killing the sacred land. They've got to be given their home, their peace. Are you going up into the ruin?" she asked suddenly.

"That's what us FBI guys do."

"It's a sacred place. Fragile. People aren't allowed to go stomping around up there and for good reason."

Annoyance was nibbling away at Anna's already strained patience. She drew breath to speak. Stanton heard and shot her a look that shut her up.

"What's the good reason?" he asked.

"Death."

He didn't react to the melodrama. "Wow," he said with seeming sincerity. "Whose?"

"Stacy was not the first. You want him to be the last, then stop intruding."

Stanton was mystified. Jamie was enjoying her part in this homemade theatrical and would play it out as long as she could.

Anna jumped in with the punch line. "Old Ones, Anasazi, chindi, ghosts, spirits," she told Stanton. "Jamie believes—"

"Along with a lot of other people," the interpreter stuck in.

"—that the ghosts or spirits of the original inhabitants of the mesa are popping up out of the underworld now and then, showing their displeasure at the modern tourism industry by striking down a select handful of the hundreds of thousands of people who pass through here every year."

"Not exactly!" Jamie snapped.

"Girls, girls," Frederick chided, and Anna quelled an impulse to bite him.

"We'd best get moving," she said, glancing at her watch as if time was of the essence.

Jamie puffed out an exaggerated sigh. "I'd better go with you. That's an easily impacted area."

"Stay," Anna ordered.

Jamie bristled but stayed. Anna didn't add "Sit!" but she thought about it.

"Will you be here for a while?" Stanton asked the interpreter. "I'd like to talk with somebody who really has a feel for this place."

Jamie's bristles lay back down. She tossed her braid over her shoulder and almost smiled. "I'll be here."

"More flies with honey, Anna. Got to get them flies," Stanton said as they walked down the path.

The kiva had not been disturbed since the body was carried out. Yellow tape marked POLICE LINE DO NOT CROSS and held down with stones was placed in an "X" over the top of the kiva. Once Stanton had examined the scene the tape would be removed and the floor raked smooth.

The FBI agent sat down on the edge where the roof had once been and dangled his legs over the side. "Other folks find bodies in dumpsters, storm drains, vacant lots. Yours turn up in bizarre places. Your karma must be very strange," he said to Anna.

"Out in the sticks you've got to take what you can get." She sat down next to him.

He took the envelope he'd been carrying under his arm for the last forty minutes and pulled out the photographs of the crime scene. Pictures of the body had been blown up into 8x10 color prints.

Looking at the photos, Anna knew memories of Stacy in life would be hard to come by. This was how she would remember him: a banquet for flies. She'd never viewed Zach's body really, just the barest of glimpses to ID it. Studying pictures of Stacy, the value of open-casket funerals, the laying out of the body, night watches—rituals that cut across religious and cultural lines—became clear. To let the living see the dead were most certainly dead and so to let them go. Ghosts were not the spirits of the dead returning but the memories of the living not yet laid to rest.

"The man is dead." Frederick startled her with an echo of her thoughts. "He's curled himself up—"

"Or been curled up by somebody."

"In a what . . . a fire pit?"

"Yes."

"Gun on, radio on, no marks of violence, no tracks but his, the ground all raked neatly and his little hat tidy on that wall thing."

"And his shoes off. See." Anna pointed to the cordovan shoes tucked up near the brown-stockinged feet.

"You know what I like? I like big old bullet holes and somebody standing a few feet away with a smoking gun screaming, 'My God, I killed him! I killed him!'"

"That happen often?"

"All the time. How do you think we catch as many as we do?"

Anna stared down at the trampled kiva floor. "At least this gives us job security."

Stanton laughed and she realized how rare that occurrence was. Too bad, it was a good wholesome sound.

He put the photographs back and took out the autopsy report. "The envelope, please," he said as he ripped it open. "And the winners are . . ." His voice trailed off as he looked over the three single-spaced typed pages.

Anna couldn't read the small type without all but sitting in his lap so she possessed her soul in patience, passing the time by imagining how the village would have looked with cook fires burning, people hauling water, weaving cloth, children playing on the kiva roofs.

"Time of death."

Her attention snapped back to the twentieth century.

"Somewhere between eight P.M. and three A.M. Monday night, the twenty-first of June. Had rice and chicken for dinner and red licorice for dessert. Cause of death, heart failure."

"Can't be!"

"Right there." Stanton pointed a big-knuckled finger at the bottom of the second page.

Anna took the report and read the offending sentence. "Natural causes?" she ventured, then read on. "Doesn't say."

"Could be a lot of things. Did he have a history of heart disease?"

"His wife said he was in perfect health. Perfect. And that's a quote."

Stanton pondered the underground room. "Shock, fear, drug overdose, respiratory failure, what causes the heart muscle to stop?"

"Electrical current, lightning, blunt trauma." Anna couldn't think of anything else.

"I opt for one of those," Stanton said. "Even if he had a bad heart, I can't see a guy with chest pain, nausea, having trouble breathing, climbing up, crawling down, kicking his shoes off and the bucket."

"Callous."

"Sorry."

"Neither can I."

"Read me that third paragraph on page two—after all the chemical breakdown gobbledygook," Stanton said.

"There was no sign of drug or alcohol in the blood or muscle tissue."

"There goes drug overdose," Stanton said sadly.

"No bruising of the soft tissue."

"There goes blunt trauma."

"No sign of ingested poison. No entrance or exit wounds. No occluded arteries or symptoms of arteriosclerosis."

"Damn. So much for natural causes. That pretty much leaves us with your Miss Burke's spirits. Fear and shock. Guy lays down for a nap in the fireplace, up pops a sipapu and *wham!* scares him to death. Case closed."

"A sipapu's a place, not a thing." Anna pointed to the crockery-lined hole. "Your bogeyman had to come out of there. Pretty tight squeeze for a truly terrifying critter."

"Bad things come in small packages."

Anna went back to the autopsy report. "'Oval burn marks approximately one inch by an inch and a half, first degree, on the right arm between the elbow and the shoulder. Similar mark on the left upper arm two inches above the antecubital space.'"

"I saw that. That mark. I thought it was a bruise. I get bruises there sometimes from the butt of my gun banging my arm."

Stanton pulled a pair of half glasses out of the breast pocket of his madras shirt and shoved them up onto his nose. They were the kind with heavy black frames sold by drugstores. A children's show host Anna had watched as a child wore those same glasses. Uncle Happy, she remembered.

The agent held the photo they'd been discussing under his chin and stared down at it through the magnifying lenses. "Oval burn marks. That smells clue-y to me. What did they look like?"

Anna took her eyes from the picture, rested them on the stone of the kiva floor, and let Stacy's corpse rematerialize. "I didn't inspect them closely at the time. Like I said, maybe bruises from the gun or being grabbed too hard. Thinking back, they were brownish—no purples, greens, blues, or yellows you might find with a healing bruise. And scaly. I touched one and it felt the way sunburned skin does when it's just beginning to peel."

Stanton whistled "An Actor's Life for Me," from *Pinocchio.* Lost in thought, he waggled his feet over the open air. "Leaning against something hot," he suggested. "Like a motorcycle manifold."

"Both arms and both on the inside? Odd."

"True. He'd have to be hugging the Harley. Pretty silly he'd look too, if you ask me. Sorry," he apologized automatically.

They thought awhile longer. "Something dripped?" Anna ventured. "Hot wax. He was reaching up to take a candle off the mantel or something."

"Could be. Kinky sex stuff? I've seen wax used in S and M movies—strictly Bureau research, of course."

"Of course."

"Stacy didn't seem the type."

"Still waters?"

"Maybe." But Anna didn't think so.

They fell into silence again. The steady hum of the tourists below provided white noise, the occasional call of a canyon bird a pleasing counterpoint.

Grating sounds cut through and Anna pulled her thoughts up out of Stacy's grave. Jamie Burke marched toward them along the wall that accessed the kiva where they sat, her heavy tread designed more to garner attention than to protect an "easily impacted area." Claude Beavens was behind her. There was no tow rope visible but he moved with the reluctant hitching motion of a vehicle not under its own power.

"That's him." Jamie pointed an accusatory finger at Frederick Stanton. "The FBI guy."

Stanton scrambled to his feet and stuck out his hand. "How do you do?" he asked formally.

Beavens looked around for someplace else to be. Not finding one, he took the proffered hand and mumbled, "Pleased to meet you," the way children are taught to in grade school.

"Look," Beavens began. "This isn't my idea. I just—"

"Tell him," Jamie insisted.

Looking annoyed but beaten, he shrugged. Beavens had been so anxious to be a part of the murder investigation the day the body had been found, Anna wondered what held him back now.

"Claude was here the night Stacy died," Jamie said for him, and Anna understood. Few people wanted to participate quite that intimately in the investigative process.

"Not *here* here," Beavens defended himself.

"But here," Jamie said. "Tell him."

Frederick folded himself back down onto the lip of the kiva and stared expectantly up at the interpreter.

"I was out on the loop Monday night—that's when Jamie says Stacy was . . . was here. That's all. No big deal."

Stanton seemed less interested in Beavens than in Jamie. She stood with her profile to them, her long black hair trailing down her back. Her arms were crossed and her feet were planted wide apart in what, for good taste's sake, Anna hoped was an unconscious parody of Hiawatha.

"Monday night. You hit it right on the nose, Ms. Burke." Stanton flapped the papers from the autopsy. "The coroner says that's the date."

Not willing to break the pose, Jamie shot him a scornful look from the sides of her eyes. "Summer solstice."

Stanton waited. Beavens fidgeted and Anna watched. Claude was clearly uncomfortable about something but there was no way of telling what sort of ants were inhabiting his mental trousers. Guilt, embarrassment at being dragged into Jamie's little drama, nervousness at being questioned by the FBI—all were possible, as were a dozen things that didn't come readily to mind.

Jamie was basking in the limelight, dragging the interview out with cryptic sentences and pregnant pauses.

Anna was sorely tempted to spoil the show, but Stanton was satisfied to let the scene play out.

"It's when things tend to happen," Jamie said after a

moment. "Some people have a feel for these things. A kinship. I felt it. Ask Anna. Something was coming down on the twenty-first."

"Or up," Anna said, pointing at the sipapu.

"Go ahead. Investigate me, Mr. FBI." If one could judge by the glint in Jamie's pale eyes, the prospect wasn't unwelcome. "You'll have to look in your paranormal films for this one," she finished.

"The X Files," Stanton said gravely.

Jamie liked that. She turned on Beavens, now with hands deep in pockets, poking at a dung beetle with the toe of his shoe. "Tell him," she ordered.

"Better tell me," Stanton said. "Just the facts, like Joe Friday says. Nobody'll interrupt you." He didn't glance at Jamie when he said it. Somehow he didn't need to.

"Doggone it, Jamie!" Beavens exploded, then took a deep breath. "It really is no big deal. I was out here that night—Monday. I didn't go to Balcony House with everybody. That New Age stuff—crystals and mantra-ing at the moon—is crud." His hand went to his throat and he nervously fingered a tiny gold cross Anna hadn't noticed before. "I just rode my bike out here. Sat on the rocks over the canyon till the moon was up. Later I guess, two or two-thirty, maybe. Then I rode home. No big deal. I didn't see Stacy or anything." He stopped, waited a moment, then shrugged. "That's it. No biggie."

"God, I hate invertebrates masquerading as men," Jamie sighed. Turning her back on Claude, she said to Stanton: "Claude saw."

Anna remembered the phrase; the words she had used the morning the body was discovered. She'd hissed it as Anna squeezed through the gate above Cliff Palace.

"Just spit it out," Anna growled.

Stanton deadpanned in her direction. "You're such a people person, Anna."

"Claude saw what?" she pressed.

"Where they come through, the veil," Jamie said triumphantly. "He told me Tuesday morning, before anybody'd even thought to look for Stacy. He said he'd seen the shimmer in the light of the solstice moon as if the spirits were passing through."

"Not exactly," Claude complained.

"Exactly," Jamie countered.

"Exactly in your own words." Stanton stopped the argument.

"What's the time?" Beavens asked.

All three of them glanced at their watches. "One-ten," Anna said before anyone else could.

"Gotta go. Balcony House tour in twenty minutes."

"The veil?" Anna asked again.

Beavens pulled his hands out of his pockets. Again the shrug Anna was beginning to think was a nervous habit. "I was just kidding around. Jamie's always on about this spirit garbage. I was kidding. Ask the other interps. I heard some of them leaving the loop in their truck later than I did."

They watched Beavens trot off, surefooted, down the balcony to disappear into the ancient alleyway.

"He is a lying little weasel," Jamie stated.

It was the first thing she'd said all day that had the ring of truth.

13

ANNA AND Stanton followed Jamie out of the closed part of the ruin and left her at the entrance clicking visitor statistics into the metal counter.

Rather than go against the flow of traffic, they climbed the four ladders at the western end of the alcove and regained the mesa top. The climb always winded Anna but she forced herself to breathe silently through her nose, enjoying the sound of Stanton's puffing. "Want to rest?" she asked solicitously as they walked back toward the parking lot.

"Yes, please," he said humbly, and threw himself down on half a log round smoothed to make a bench. Gratefully, Anna sat beside him and refilled her hungry lungs with the thin air. Her childishness made her laugh.

"I hope you're duly impressed," she said. "It's damn hard to hold your breath after that climb."

"Tell me about it. I do it to impress the young agents. Nearly did myself in last training session. Gets harder every year."

They sat for a while just breathing and feeling the sun on their faces. Anna made small talk with the visitors who came panting up from the ruin. The uniform made it mandatory and it was a part of the job she took pleasure in. Sharing beauty with total strangers made the world seem a friendlier place. In a culture dominated, if not by violence, then certainly by the overheated reports of it dished out by a ratings-starved news media, it reassured her that the love of peace and natural order was still extant in the human soul.

"Let's do lists," Stanton suggested after a while. "Pretend we're organized."

Anna reached in her hip pocket and fished out the yellow notebook. She'd already written "Life Insurance," "Enemies," "Where Else Should We Have Looked," and "Greed/Rose." "Life Insurance" was crossed out since she'd overheard Rose telling Hattie that Stacy had left her and Bella with nothing.

"I'll be the secretary." Stanton lifted the notebook from Anna's hands and the government-issue ballpoint from her shirt pocket.

"No life insurance?" he asked.

"Apparently not."

He wrote "Check" beside the crossed-out words. "Greed, always good. Was there an inheritance? That's a good one for Greed."

"No. Stacy wasn't rich."

"'Where Else Should We Have Looked'?"

"It's my guess we were meant to find the body and be mystified by it. Too coy, too precious, to be an accident. The only reasons not to hide the corpse are to prove death to get insurance or something or to stop people from looking for it in embarrassing places."

"Good point." Frederick underlined it. Beneath he wrote, speaking the words aloud as he did so: "'C. Beavens on scene. Interpreters in truck. J. Burke knew date. Spirit Veil.' Anything else?"

"Put down Greeley. The widow wants us to talk to him. It's worth finding out why."

Dutifully he wrote the name at the bottom of the list, then tapped the pen against his teeth. The top row was white and even but his bottom teeth were crowded, one pushed forward. As he tapped he hummed a tune Anna didn't recognize.

"So," he said finally. "We've got the wife because—who knows? Because there's always a good reason to kill your husband. Beavens because he was in the neighborhood. Burke because she knew the time of death and hates the white man's depredation of sacred grounds. Stacy was a white guy?"

Anna nodded.

"I remember." Stanton shook the autopsy envelope. "Said so. And we've got Greeley because the wife says he might know something. What else?"

"There's always us," Anna stated the obvious. "A ranger. We've all got what it takes."

"Oooh." Stanton looked impressed. Anna chose not to be amused.

"Keys to the ruin, to the Four-Way, knowledge of the upper kiva. Stacy would trust one of us. We could get him up here. All we'd have to say is we'd found some archaeological crime—graffiti, digging, theft, whatever."

"Any ranger got a motive?"

Other than her own story of unrequited bullshit, Anna couldn't think of any. She shook her head. "He was a temporary employee so he wasn't a threat to anybody promotion- or job-wise. He should have been—he was one of the best rangers we had. But without permanent status he couldn't get promoted. He wasn't even eligible for pay raises, and I don't think he had anything worth stealing. Unless you count his wife, and I'd question that one. Sorry," she apologized for the nasty remark. "Personal taste. Count her. Nobody seemed to hate him, and if he was blackmailing anyone or selling drugs he was good at it. No rumors."

"Somebody offed a nice, poor, unthreatening park ranger. Not promising."

"Nope."

Stanton closed the notebook and pocketed it along with Anna's pen. "Let's do Greeley first since nothing else makes a whole lot of sense.

"Want to have lunch first?" he asked as they drove past the Navajo taco stand.

"Not hungry."

Stanton looked pitiful but Anna didn't notice.

Ted Greeley was sitting at the break table in the maintenance shop along with Tom Silva and several other construction workers. Tom and two of the others were smoking. Ashtrays, already full, and soda pop cans cluttered the scarred Formica.

Greeley's feet, crossed at the ankles, were propped up amid the debris. Even in heavy Red Wing boots his feet looked small. His white curls were stuck to his forehead with sweat and he sucked on a Diet 7-Up.

"Hey, Ted," Anna announced herself. "Don't you guys have to work for a living?"

"Not much longer if *Ms.* Stinson has her way. We can sit right here in the shade drinking sodie pops and whistle for our paychecks. The old witch—spelled with a 'b'—is still trying to get the pipeline shut down till they dig up some beads and bones. A shitload of money to keep a handful of eggheads employed, if you ask me."

"Ain't nobody ever asks you, Ted," one of the men said.

"Boy, you got that right."

Anna would have expected the smart remark to come from Tom Silva but he sat a little apart from the others quietly smoking his Marlboros. He showed no interest in the banter. To Anna he looked thinner than when she'd last seen him, and paler—not as if he'd been out of the sun for a while—it wasn't so much a lack of color as a lack of energy, vividness. Somehow he'd turned in on himself, faded.

She remembered Patsy talking of his haunting her and the girls and hoped he wasn't winding up to a psychotic break of some kind.

"Howdy, fellas, Tom," Anna said to check his social reflexes. There were none. The others nodded or grunted, said "hi" or cracked jokes. Absorbed in his own thoughts, Silva gave no sign he'd even heard her.

"What's with him?" she asked Greeley.

"Time of month."

The men laughed and Anna knew there was no use pursuing that line of questioning.

"This is Special Agent Stanton of the FBI. Agent Stanton's here to investigate the death of Stacy Meyers. I'd appreciate it if you could give him all the help you can." Her little speech given, Anna was happy to step out of the spotlight. As Stanton shook hands all around, she slipped back to the refrigerator, put a dollar in the coffee can, and took out two Cokes. One she put in front of Stanton, the other she kept. Not only was she thirsty, but the role of waitress rendered her comfortably invisible.

The construction workers, with the exception of Silva,

were taken by the romance of the FBI. They clustered as happily as scouts in a den.

Opening her Coke, Anna leaned back against the tool bench and watched.

For a few minutes they chatted about the shutting down of work on the pipeline. Ted held forth on the financial burden of running a construction company. Stanton got an unedited earful about Al Stinson. The nicest thing she was called was a fruitcake. Occasionally, when the language grew rough, one of the men would remember Anna and mumble "Excuse my French, but it's true" or "I'm no sexist, but . . ." and then, conscience salved, dive back into the conversational fray.

Stanton listened, made all the right noises, and looked as solemnly interested as a priest taking confession. Once the political landscape had been colorfully painted, he moved the talk around to the investigation.

To Anna's surprise, the construction workers didn't hold her high opinion of Stacy. "Full of himself," "A little light in his loafers" were some of their comments.

Greeley summed it up. "Meyers was a nineties kind of guy. Sensitive, caring, proud of his feminine side."

"Yeah, what's that cologne he used?" a man still wearing his hard hat asked.

"Jasmine Dick," a short block of muscle replied, and spit tobacco juice in an empty Pepsi can.

By the practiced laughter, Anna knew it was an old joke and no doubt what they called Stacy behind his back.

Buoyed along on the Old Boy laughter, Stanton managed to get the whereabouts at the time of the murder of everybody but Greeley and Tom before they caught on.

"Alibis?" Ted asked finally, and raised his eyebrows. "Hey, we're suspects!" This amused them nearly as much as Jasmine Dick. Still, the men who'd cleared themselves looked relieved. "How 'bout it, Tom," Greeley took over for Frederick. "Where were you the night Stacy was tagged?"

"Nowhere," Silva snapped.

"I guess that lets Tom off the hook," Greeley laughed. "Me too. At least nowhere I can say and keep in the lady's good graces."

"Better to keep in mine," Stanton said with a half smile that sobered Ted instantly.

"When I gotta say, I'll say. Not till then," Ted returned sharply. "Break's over." Greeley fixed Anna with a cold look. "You want to make yourself useful? Catch the s.o.b. who's been screwing with my equipment." The men gathered up their cigarettes and left Anna and Frederick in possession of the battered lunch table.

"Well, that was certainly productive," Stanton said. "All non-suspects were in jail with seven nuns at the time of the murder; the two suspects were 'nowhere' and 'nowhere with a lady.'"

"Is Silva a suspect? I don't think he even knew Stacy to say hello to."

"It may end up being a choice between Silva and the chindi," Stanton cautioned.

"Now that you mention it, Silva looked guilty as hell," Anna said.

"If you ever quit rangering, you might try the FBI. I think you've got a flair for this sort of work."

Anna glanced at her watch. "It's three-thirty. Do you want to drop by the Widow Meyers before we quit for the day?"

"Is she all sad-eyed and teary?"

"Nope."

"Looks guilty as hell?"

"I don't think she was in the park that night."

"Too bad."

"She could have made it," Anna said hopefully. "There's a phone call placing her in Farmington at seven P.M. That's only two hours from here. She could have driven up and back in one night easily."

"Well, that is good news," Stanton mocked her amiably.

"Beats chindi."

"Could we have something to eat first?" he asked plaintively. "I'm faint."

"Sorry. I forget."

"Probably how you keep your boyish figure."

Rose was at home. When not shopping in Durango or Farmington, Rose was usually at home. Nature apparently held little allure. The front windows of the bungalow were closed and the shades drawn to shut it firmly out of doors. All the interior lights were ablaze. Rose was on the sofa opposite the wood stove. Magazines—*Self, Money, House Beautiful*—littered the floor. The remains of an iced tea and a plate covered in crumbs held down a pile of like literature on the coffee table.

A single bed, the kind on wheels that folds in half to be rolled into storage, was made up in one corner beneath the window. It was the brightest spot in the room. A cotton coverlet in rich red, green, and blue paisley covered the mattress. Throw pillows in similar colors—some prints, some solids—were tumbled in organized chaos, giving the bed the look of a gay and welcoming nest.

The window above was the only one in the room open, the shade up. Hattie sat cross-legged amid the kaleidoscope of color, holding a sketch pad. Bella had a pad of newsprint propped up against her aunt's thigh. She lay on her belly with her legs bent at the knee, little bare feet in the air. They stopped their work long enough to be introduced to Frederick Stanton.

Rose fussed with the magazines, moving them from one place to another without creating any real order. She was more on edge than Anna had seen her in the past week or so. Though the death was tragic, Anna would have thought the wait would have been worse on the nerves and the conclusion harder on the heart. Short, controlled movements as she stabbed at the clutter and tight muscles around her mouth spoke of something more than anxiety or irritation. Rose was furious.

There was bound to be some anger at Stacy for having had the bad judgment to die—if Rose had not profited by the death—but it was more specific than that. It was directed at Anna.

Frederick was offered a chair and a glass of tea. Anna was snubbed. She was not even invited to sit. Indeed there was no place left to do so. But for Hattie's bed and the couch, Stanton had been given the only chair in the room, an office swivel tucked in the kneehole of an old wooden desk.

Sensing this production of "good cop, bad cop" had already been cast, Anna left the federal agent to question Rose and wandered over to the sunlit bed.

Obligingly, Bella scooted over and Anna sat down, happy in the cheerful disarray. "What are you guys drawing?" she asked to make conversation.

"We're doing landscapes," Bella told her. "Here." She tore off a sheet of newsprint and handed it to Anna. "You can do it too. Put a coloring book under it so you can write on it. You can share my pens."

Obediently, Anna put the paper on the hard cardboard cover of a *Birds of the Southwest* coloring book and selected a pink felt-tipped pen from the pile. "Aren't we supposed to have a landscape to draw from? Or are we just drawing the living room?"

"We're doing *inner* landscapes," Bella said importantly. "Tell her, Aunt Hattie." The little girl dropped the black pen she was drawing with, picked up a dark purple one, and promptly forgot them in her concentration.

Anna looked expectantly at Hattie. The woman stopped sketching and thought for a second. Her hair was pulled up in a knot, curled wisps escaping in all directions from where she'd stored and plucked colored pencils. Seven or eight still resided in her bun, poking out like the spines of a rainbow porcupine.

"We-ell," Hattie said, dragging the word out. "You close your eyes."

Anna waited.

Hattie waited.

Anna realized this was for real and closed her eyes.

"You go down your esophagus."

"That's your throat," Bella volunteered helpfully.

"Turn left at your breastbone."

Anna snuck a peek. Hattie's face was serious.

"Go into your heart."

"Cree-aa-eek." Bella provided the sound of a heavy door opening on rusted hinges.

Maybe because I haven't opened it in a while, Anna thought, caught up in the game.

"Look around you," Hattie continued. "What do you see? Don't tell it, draw it."

Anna wasn't about to tell it. Or draw it. In her mind's heart she'd seen a lot of furniture covered with drop cloths. Molly would have a field day with that one.

To keep her credit good, she drew a picture that was supposed to be of Piedmont. A great orange blob with four legs and a tail. The eyes she made emerald green because Bella didn't have a bronze pen.

Hattie stopped drawing, a frown creasing her otherwise smooth brow. She was looking down at Bella's picture.

The child had made black-and-purple concentric circles filling the page. It looked like the top view of a tornado or a giant whirlpool. In comparison, shrouded furniture seemed perfectly okay for decorating a heart.

"What is that, Bella?" Hattie asked easily, but the worry was still on her face.

"Just colors," Bella replied. "Like in a flower."

More like a bruise, Anna thought.

Stanton and Rose emerged from the kitchen where they'd vanished a while before. Stanton was just finishing a tall iced drink and Anna realized with some annoyance how thirsty she was. After her time on a damp island in Lake Superior, she had forgotten how the arid climate of the southwest could suck the moisture from the human body.

Stanton looked at her lumpy pumpkin-colored drawing. "Are you done?" he asked politely.

"All done."

"Can I see?" Bella asked.

Anna showed the child. "You forgot his whiskers," Bella told her. "If you don't draw him whiskers, he'll run into things. That's how cats know how big the world is. They feel it with their whiskers."

Anna picked up a black pen and began to fill in the missing items. "I'm making them extra long," she said. "In case Piedmont wants to explore the galaxy."

"Good idea," Bella agreed.

"Honey, come here," Rose said to her daughter as Anna

and Frederick let themselves out. "Momma needs to talk to you."

The sun was still high but the angle had changed. Light streamed between the trees in long fingers filled with golden dust. The cicadas had hushed and the bulk of tourists gone from the mesa top.

Loath to confine themselves inside the patrol car after the claustrophobia of Rose Meyers' living room, Anna and Frederick leaned against the Ford, their backs to the bungalow. In front of them a fringe of trees separated the houses and Spruce Canyon. From where they stood the piñon-juniper forest, not a hundred yards wide, seemed to stretch on forever.

"I had fun," Anna said.

"Bully for you. I didn't. The good news is I did get some iced tea."

"Rub it in."

"What's she got against you?" Stanton asked. "The claws were definitely unsheathed whenever your name came up."

"Beats me. Today's hostility is a new development."

"The bad news is we're back to Silva and chindi as far as suspects go—unless Burke or Beavens show some spunk."

"How so?"

"Rose was in Farmington with Ted Greeley."

Anna thought about that for a moment. It fit none of her preconceived notions. "I thought Rose hated Greeley."

"She does. Not only did she say she'd had no inter-course—her word, not mine—with that 'little, little man' since Farmington, but she alibied him through clenched teeth. I got the feeling she'd've rather put him in the gas chamber than admit she'd been with him in Farmington. But she swore to it."

"All night?"

"Most of it."

"Go figure." Anna shook her head, remembering Bella saying the argument her mom had had on the phone with Stacy that Monday night had been over some man. "Maybe we're back to suicide, maybe Stacy couldn't hack another wife cheating on him."

"It's been known to happen." Stanton didn't sound convinced. "No gunshot wound, no knife cuts, no pills, no poison—'it is a good day to die'? Meyers just lay down and willed his life away?"

"Not likely." After Zach died Anna'd tried it enough times to know it didn't work.

"Frederick!" Rose was calling from the front steps. "Do you have Stacy's things? Hills said Anna had taken them."

She made it sound like petty theft. It took Anna a minute to realize what she was referring to.

"His shoes and hat," she said. "I'd forgotten. They're in the trunk," she hollered to Rose as she walked around to the rear of the Ford.

They were still where she'd tossed them the day of the body recovery. The hat was a little the worse for wear, crushed by the toolbox. Anna pushed the dent out. She had to dig under traffic cones, shotgun, and shovel for the shoes.

"Got 'em," she called, and pulled them out. As the clear afternoon light hit them, she sucked in her breath. "Hey, Frederick, come here for a minute."

Reacting to something in her voice, the FBI agent was beside her in seconds.

"Look familiar?" Anna showed him the low-cut cordovan shoes. On the heel of the right and the instep of the left shoe were the same oval burn marks the coroner had described on Stacy's arms.

*   *   *

Sipping the Beaujolais, Anna was careful not to let the wineglass clink against the telephone receiver. She was in no mood for another lecture from her sister on the evils of worshiping Bacchus.

She'd just finished an acerbic account of the interview with Mrs. Meyers. "The green-eyed monster," she said. "One of us is acting like a jealous woman."

"Gee, yah think?" Molly returned sarcastically. "Obviously you had a proprietary interest in her husband, for whatever reasons. Maybe because he had some of the same characteristics as Zach?"

"Maybe because he had a brain. Rare in these backwoods."

Molly laughed. "Your jealousy is obviously rooted deep in childhood trauma and will require umpteen thousand dollars' worth of therapy to root out. What's more interesting is why she's jealous of you—if the anger was inspired by jealousy."

"I sure don't know. Maybe Stacy said something."

"It started before the murder?"

Anna thought about that. "No. After. Way after. I mean she was never My Friend Flicka but the outright hatred is new."

"Something since? She could have found a torrid entry in his diary or an unmailed love letter."

The idea thrilled Anna in a morbid sort of way. She sighed deeply and sucked down some of the red wine.

"Somebody telling tales out of school?" Molly suggested.

"Stacy and I were never together except professionally," Anna said. "It could be all in her head, a way to justify a less than ideal marriage. Looking at it from the outside, it didn't seem to be based on the principles of wellness.

More mutual need than mutual respect and admiration, if you know what I mean."

Molly chortled her evil-sounding chortle. "Why do you think I never married? Nothing like an internship in family counseling to put the fear of matrimony in one's soul."

"I hate feeling jealous!" Anna said with sudden vehemence. She pulled in another draught of wine and felt comforted. "It makes me feel like such a *girl*."

"Ah, yes. Such helpless, emotional creatures. Given to anorexia and fainting fits. Run like a girl, throw like a girl, whistle like a girl."

"My point exactly."

"Stacy's gone on two counts," Molly reasoned. "He's dead and he wasn't yours. I'd recommend you grieve like a girl. Let it run its course. It's not cancer or frostbite, it's just pain."

"Like the phantom pain in an amputated limb?"

"Very like. Not much you can do with a feeling till you give in and feel the damn thing. As long as you mask emotions, anesthetize yourself, the confusion will only get worse."

Anna had the irritating sense that Molly wasn't talking only about jealousy.

"You know, Anna, you don't have to do everything alone. Even out there in the back of beyond there are bound to be support groups." Molly cut the inevitable argument short: "Just think about it. It works. Lord knows why. It's not profitable to us honest shrinks. If there weren't plenty of nuts around to keep me in pin money, I'd keep mum about it."

After that Molly let Anna change the subject and they talked on for a while but it failed to eradicate the hollow feeling behind Anna's breastbone.

When she'd hung up, she sat awhile on her twin bed playing with the fringe of the Mexican blanket that served as a spread.

To the lamp, she said: "I could sure use a good game of Dead Princess long about now."

14

WINTER WAS never far from the high country, and Anna woke into a day cold and dreary enough to remind her how fragile the warmth of summer could be.

Thunderheads pressed low on the mesa but didn't obscure the view. Beneath the lowering gray, black piles of cumulonimbus rolled like billiard balls from the mountains of Arizona to the Colorado buttes. Through the thin walls of the dormitory, Anna heard the grind of thunder.

Helitack crew would be delighted; good fire weather. Lightning could bury itself deep in a juniper and smolder for days. When the weather let up and the fuels dried there might be hazard pay all around.

Throwing back the covers, Anna leaped out of bed. In the lowlands around Lake Superior weather fronts, with their attendant changes in pressure, gave her headaches. Not so the mountain storms. Cracking thunder and flashing lightning filled the air with ozone till it tingled in the lungs, rejuvenating body and spirit much the same as the air at the seaside or near waterfalls.

Having braided her hair off her face, she jammed herself into uniform and, catlike to avoid getting wet, ran from the dorm to her patrol car. Thunderstorms made for good thinking weather: the tourists were chased safely indoors and the brass wouldn't venture out and so catch one cogitating.

Anna drove the short distance to the Far View cafeteria parking lot and pointed the nose of the Ford toward the panorama of northern New Mexico. Many-tined forks of lightning in the grand tradition of Frankenstein movies shattered a slate sky. Virga fell in curtains, now obscuring, now lifting to reveal a distant butte or valley. Colors were muted, the greens almost black, the reds of the earth somber.

The car radio was tuned to National Public Radio and something vaguely high-toned was being played on a harpsichord. The ordered gentility of the music and the wild vagaries of the weather suited Anna, and she rolled down the window to better enjoy the concert.

Special Agent Stanton had taken Stacy's shoes with their odd marks to Durango so they could be sent to the lab in Hobbs, New Mexico, for analysis. Since she'd been assigned to him for the duration, she wasn't on Hills' schedule. The day was pretty much hers to do with as she pleased.

She took the lid off her plastic coffee mug and took a sip. Once she'd had a severe coffee habit but luxury had cured it. After she'd begun fresh-grinding beans and using heavy whipping cream, the brew with nondairy powders found in most offices didn't tempt her in the least. However, two cups of the good stuff each morning was a ritual she never missed.

Anna unbuckled her seat belt, rearranged the .357 and cuffs, and settled in for some serious thinking. Humanity, thus examined, struck her as sordid. Rose and Ted Greeley having their affair—or whatever it was they were having—in a motel in Farmington with little Bella . . . where? Left in the car? Packed off to a movie? Anger and disrespect—at least from Rose's side—the hallmark of the encounter.

Drew's love of Bella seemed a bright spot in this dreary landscape but it too was tinged with anger. For reasons of his own he was tilting at what Anna hoped was a windmill: the abuse of that lovely child. To Anna's way of thinking the operations might cause less pain in the long run than fighting the good fight against prejudice.

Tom and Patsy Silva held together even after divorce by greed on Patsy's side and some as yet inexplicable obsession on Tom's. A fixation that had gone from an alarming but active harassment phase to an even more alarming but passive stalker phase.

Jamie and her posthumous affair with Stacy—in the past two days it had gone from "dear friend" to "dearest friend." A bizarre form of psychological necrophilia, rare but, according to Anna's sister, not unheard of. Molly lamented the loss of the melodrama that had been such a part of American life before the turn of the century. A time when people took themselves more seriously, were less bored, less sophisticated. A time when widows wore black veils, the occasional duel was fought, and, though there were no documented incidents of it, people were believed to die of shame and of love.

The human animal needed its dramas, the psychiatrist believed. Denied, it sought them in unhealthy ways. Like imagined romances with dead married men. This last thought struck too close to home. Made physically uncomfortable by the parallel between her and Burke, Anna literally squirmed in her seat.

An affair with a dead married man. "That's got to be it," she exclaimed. Taken back to her nonexistent romance with Stacy, she flashed on their one rendezvous: the curtailed cocktail hour at Far View Lounge. Ted Greeley had been there. Anna remembered him making a mock toast as she grabbed Stacy's arm, remembered the leer he was passing off as a smile.

That's why Rose was so hostile. In the last couple of days Greeley must have told her, or led her to believe, Anna had been having an affair with her husband.

"Damn!" Anna struck the steering wheel with an open palm. Everything seemed so sordid. Everything.

Lightning struck through the looping black clouds, the wide fork straddling the valley between Chapin and Park mesas. Automatically Anna began to count "one Mississippi, two—" Thunder drowned out the thought. The strike had been less than a mile away.

She took another sip of excellent coffee and leaned back, letting past conversations with and about Rose drift through her mind. Why hadn't Rose said right off the bat that she was with Greeley in Farmington? It certainly got her off the hook more effectively than one seventeen-minute phone call several hours before the murder. Embarrassment over being caught in a compromising position? Possibly, but had she been up front about it, no one need have known. It was the nineties. No one believed dinner—even a late dinner—with a member of the opposite sex doomed a woman to wear the scarlet "A."

Earlier in the investigation Rose had been pointing the finger at Greeley. A lovers' quarrel now patched up? Love me or go to the gas chamber? Anna shook her head. The facts, if such a hodgepodge of information and instincts could be labeled that, didn't support the theory. Stanton said Rose was loath to let the contractor off the hook, said she hadn't seen or spoken to "that little, little man" since Farmington.

Rain came down more heavily, blowing in sheets against the windshield, and Anna was forced to roll up her window or drown.

Rose's hostility had sprung full blown less than an hour after Stanton had questioned Greeley in the maintenance shop. Ergo, whatever had turned Rose against Anna had occurred recently, within the last couple of days. If Anna was right, and Rose's ire stemmed from jealousy, and that jealousy was ignited by Greeley, then Rose had lied. She had "had intercourse" with that "little, little man" since Farmington.

Did Greeley invent Stacy's infidelity so Rose would be less reticent to expose hers, thus giving them both an alibi?

Surely Greeley was aware it also gave them both a motive.

Sharp rapping at the window startled Anna out of her reverie. She yelped in a decidedly unrangerlike fashion and slopped coffee on her knee. Adding insult to injury, a kindly-looking elderly woman under an enormous black-and-white umbrella said, "Sorry to wake you up," as Anna rolled down the window. "Could you tell me how far it is to the cliff dwellings?"

After the information was disseminated, Anna opted to move her brown study to a less accessible locale. More because it was secluded than for its ghoulish ambience, she chose the closed section of Cliff Palace. In her exalted capacity as the FBI guy's chauffeur, the ruin was still open to her.

Weather had driven the tourists from the lesser-known

sites but Cliff was doing a booming, if soggy, business. It was one of the most famous cliff dwellings in the world. Visitors, some on the mesa for only a day, had traveled from as far away as Japan, Germany, Australia. Come hell or high water, they would see Cliff Palace.

Tucked up in the ruin, out of sight lest she stir envy in lesser beings, Anna felt her privilege. Deep within the alcove she was completely dry and out of the wind, yet privy to the wondrous perfume the rain struck from a desert land. One hundred feet below the mesa top, Cliff Palace was still several hundred feet above the bottom of Cliff Canyon. Anna had a lovely view out past ruined walls and turrets. Along the canyon rims rainwater had begun to pour over the sandstone, cascading down in thin ribbons of silver.

Near Jug House, a closed ruin on Wetherill Mesa, there was a stone reservoir built at the bottom of such a pour-over. The archaeologists surmised it could have been a tank to save the water. Anna was surprised there wasn't one at every ruin, but then the Anasazi were such accomplished potters, perhaps they had caught and stored rainwater in earthenware vessels.

Impromptu waterfalls delighted the tourists as much as they did Anna. From her hiding place she could hear the occasional squeal of pleasure. Leaning back on her hands, Anna let the sounds wash over her. She couldn't identify with Jamie's need to invent supernatural phenomena. As far as Anna was concerned these were the spirit veils. Common miracles that never lost their power to stir the human soul.

Just for the hell of it, she said a vague, nondenominational prayer for the spirit of Stacy Meyers.

Feet dangling into the abandoned kiva, the white noise

of running water and muted voices to still her mind, she let the world settle around her. Details came sharply into focus: a small handprint in black on the alcove overhead, the stark slash of a vulture's feather fallen in the center of an ancient building block, concentric circles marking the butt of a centuries-dead juniper hacked down by stone axes.

Half an hour melted away. No earth-shaking realizations came to her, no revelations as to why Greeley might have told Rose she and Stacy were having an affair. No guesses as to why Rose lied about having communicated with Greeley after the night of the murder; whether Beavens lied to Jamie when he said he saw the veil or lied to Anna when he said he didn't.

Hunger and cold overcame pastoral beauty and her thoughts began to turn materialistic. She stood and slapped some life into her rear end, then surreptitiously made her way back to the populated areas of the ruin.

A tall gray-haired interpreter, a retired philosophy professor from San Francisco State, was talking to a group of people near the tower. His long arms, encased in NPS green, semaphored information and enthusiasm.

Claude Beavens held down the post at the mouth of the alcove. Not only was he not speaking to the visitors but he also didn't seem interested in them even as statistics. Anna could see the silver counter dangling from an elastic band around his wrist. Binoculars obscured the upper half of his face. Because of the rain, birds were roosting, deer tucked up somewhere dry, and Anna wondered what he stared at so intently. She followed the direction of his gaze down Cliff Canyon toward Ute reservation lands. Without the assistance of field glasses, she couldn't see anything out of the ordinary.

"What've you got?" she asked. Beavens jumped as if she'd goosed him with a cattle prod.

"Nothing!" he snapped, pulling the binoculars from around his neck as if they could testify against him.

"No law against looking," Anna reassured him.

A visitor stopped beside them and asked what the Anasazi used for bathrooms. Beavens escaped into an earnest discussion of waste disposal in thirteen hundred A.D.

Anna stepped up to the rock where he'd been holding his vigil and looked down the canyon. All seemed to be as it always was. Then it came to her. "Somewhere out there Jamie's spirit veil does its elusive thing, doesn't it?" she asked as the visitor moved on.

"Who knows?" he said with his signature shrug. Whatever it was, it had ceased to interest him and, so, to be of much interest to Anna.

She was not sorry to reach her patrol car. Not only was it warm, dry, and upholstered, but a moving vehicle was one of the few places in the modern world a person had some semblance of privacy. Cellular phones were an abomination. Along with bullet-proof vests and panty hose, it was a piece of equipment she'd never submit to. The radio was intrusion enough.

Driving back to the chief ranger's office, she went as slowly as the traffic would allow. There was something about rain that opened the doors to dreaming. The steady beat, a softening of the edges of things, promoted a meditative state that unraveled the threads of linear thought. The drift was restful and Anna found herself glad to be freed from Stanton's sharp mind for the day.

Through the CRO's windows she saw enough gray and green to color a medium-sized swamp. The office was clogged with rangers holing up till the rain stopped. Not quite ready to rejoin the real world, she ducked around the building to the balcony in back. Set as it was into the side of Spruce Canyon, the front of the chief's office was only one story high, its door opening directly onto the walk to the museum. The rear of the building was comprised of two stories. A heavy wooden balcony framed in the blocky saw-cut gingerbread of the southwest provided a picture-perfect view down into the canyon. On the far rim three silvery ribbons fell from pour-overs smoothed into troughs edging the cliff top. Through a screen of huge pine trees, black now with turkey vultures sitting out the storm, was Spruce Tree House; one hundred and fourteen rooms and eight kivas tucked neatly into a natural alcove.

The timbers framing the balcony were dark with water. A sand-filled standing ashtray and a bench built in the same massive style as the framing were the only furnishings.

To Anna's relief there was only one visitor seeking sanctuary there. A woman in an ankle-length cranberry slicker and a canary yellow nor'easter hat stood near the far corner looking at the sky where the storm was darkest. Clouds hung down in bruised mammalia. Lightning was generated not only between heaven and earth but from cloud to cloud, as if the gods fought among themselves.

The woman turned slightly and bent her head. Anna amended her earlier census: there were two seekers of sanctuary. A child sat on the wide railing, enfolded securely in an ample cranberry embrace.

It was Hattie and Bella. Somehow they didn't qualify as destroyers of solitude and Anna was surprised to find she was glad to see them. Lest she be the one to shatter the peace, she slipped quietly onto the bench and watched the lightning play against curtains of rain.

Thunder's grumbling was foreshadowed and echoed by faint feral sounds closer to home. Soon Anna lost interest in the meteorological show and watched Bella and her aunt with rapt attention.

They were growling.

Because of the innocence that blessed both faces, the sight was not frightening but it was disturbing. Bella Meyers' perfect little mouth was pulled back into a square, exposing small white teeth. Her cheeks pushed up till they made slits of her eyes, and her hands—at least the one Anna could see clutching the sleeve of Hattie's raincoat—were curled into a caricature of a claw.

The growls, nearly soft as purrs, were not amusing. There was too much anger for that. Bella snarled and clawed at something very real—at least to her. What kept the scene from being alarming or, worse, pathetic, was the power. A definite force, even in so small a girl, commanded respect. It was not the desperate anger of helplessness. It had focus. And, too, the child was safe in the loving arms of her aunt.

Growling at the universe isn't half scary when you know you're loved, Anna thought.

Hattie was snapping and snarling too, but her fury was diluted. Maturity and understanding had undermined the purity of her attack. Hers was more of a supportive growl, giving Bella's anger confirmation.

The minutes passed. The storm moved to the south. Bella's growls and snarls grew less ferocious. Hattie rested her chin on top of the child's head and hugged her tightly. Finally the last little "grrr" was squeezed out and they stood still as statues. The rain stopped.

"Well. I guess that's that," Hattie said.

"Sure is," Bella returned with satisfaction. Using her

bottom as a fulcrum and her aunt's arms as a brace, the little girl levered her legs over the rail and slid to the balcony floor.

"Hi, Anna," she said, apparently unsurprised. "Aunt Hattie and me were making it storm. But mostly me because I'm the maddest."

"You sure cooked up a doozy," Anna said. "I practically got drowned."

"Everybody did," Bella said, unrepentant. "Even the vultures."

"How did you make it storm?"

Bella pulled herself up on the bench beside Anna and patted the seat, inviting her aunt to join them. "Aunt Hattie taught me. First you have to be really, really, *really* mad. Then you screw it all up into a ball and put it right here." She reached up and tapped the middle of Anna's brow where the Hindus often drew the mystical third eye. "Then you just point it at some clouds and order them to do it."

"Ah," Anna said.

"It helps if they're the black piley-up ones."

The three of them were quiet for a minute, just sitting in a row listening to the pine needles drip. "Do you say something like 'Rain, rain, don't go away, come and stay today'?" Anna asked after a while.

"No." Bella sounded as if that was an exceedingly stupid question and Anna felt as if she'd asked Willard Scott what he meant by partly cloudy. "You talk cloud language," Bella explained, and growled for Anna—but not too loudly lest it unleash another deluge.

"You must have been really, really, *really* mad," Anna said. "That was one of the best storms I've ever seen."

"I was pretty mad," Bella conceded.

"What were you mad at?"

Bella looked at her aunt.

"You can be mad at anybody you want to, honey. It's okay. Sometimes I even get mad at your uncle Edwin."

"Really, *really* mad?"

"Yup. Sometimes I get really mad at God."

Bella looked impressed.

"She doesn't mind one bit," Hattie said. "She probably gets mad at the angels sometimes."

"When would anybody get mad at an angel?" Bella asked skeptically.

"Maybe when they're molting," Anna offered. "Dropping feathers all over heaven."

That seemed to make sense. "Okay." Bella dropped her voice to a whisper. "I'm really, really mad at Momma." She waited. No stray lightning bolt struck. With greater confidence, she added: "Rose is a thorny, thorny, morny, dorny, thorny old Rose."

Anna laughed and Bella was offended. "What're you mad at your mom about," Anna asked to win the child back but it was too late.

"Can't tell you," Bella said, and jumped down from the bench.

"Why not?" Now Anna was offended.

"Because Momma said blood's sicker than water."

"I can't argue with that."

"Nope."

The sun was beginning to peek through. Hattie and Bella left. Anna waited a few more minutes to allow the newly clement weather time to lure the crowd out of the office, then walked around to the front door. Jennifer Short sat on the table behind the counter swinging her legs and eating candy out of a jar Frieda kept stocked. Her hair was squashed flat against her head from crown to ears, then stuck out at right angles.

"Idn't it awful," she was complaining to Frieda. "Ah feel like something out of a horror flick. The one that goes crazy and hacks everybody up at the slumber party."

"Terminal Hat Head," Frieda contributed. "Occupational hazard." The dispatcher sat behind her desk, her computer for once dark, the radio mike near her right hand.

"Hey," Jennifer greeted Anna.

"Howdy." Anna leaned her elbows on the counter. Beneath the sheet of glass that topped it were maps of the park and surrounding areas. "Talked to Patsy lately?" she asked Frieda when it became obvious she'd killed the conversation in progress.

"Matter of fact." Frieda laughed her delicious laugh. "She's doing okay but Tom's got her and the girls all atwitter."

"She'd better be careful," Anna said. "Stalking is stalking, not flattery. This guardian-angel-in-a-Chevy-truck routine strikes me as a bubble or two off plumb. I think Tom is one weird guy."

"I think Tom Silva's cute," Jennifer said. "Kee-ee-yoot."

"Better watch out," Anna kidded her. "Remember what happened to the last guy you thought was cute."

"Serves Stacy right for bein' married," Jennifer retorted. "All the good ones are married."

"All the good ones are dead," Anna said before she thought.

She was rewarded with an awkward silence and averted eyes.

"Guess I better look like I'm doing something constructive." Jennifer smashed her hat down over the ruined hairdo and swaggered toward the door. It wasn't braggadocio, Anna knew from experience. For a short woman there was no place left for the arms once the gunbelt was strapped in place.

"I should too," Anna said. Grabbing a handful of Frieda's butterscotch candies, she made her way back to the eight-by-six-foot cubbyhole that served as an office for Hills, the fire management officer, Anna, half a dozen seasonals, and the Xerox machine.

Her desk was nearly as bad a rat's nest as Hills', and most of the rubble wasn't of her making. Space shared—shared with Homo sapiens who'd not yet attained their thirtieth birthdays—was reduced to chaos. Anna preferred order and knew herself to have entered upon that stage of the game Molly dubbed the Pre-Curmudgeon Warm-ups.

Everything that wasn't hers she scraped into an accordion envelope, marked it "The Poltergeist File," and stowed it in the kneehole under Hills' desk. Before anyone dared to dig that deep the stuff would be transmogrified into historical artifacts by the sheer passage of time.

To impose some semblance of organization, she unearthed all the 10-343 Case Incident and 10-344 Criminal Incident reports that had been turned in since the beginning of the tourist season in April. Thanks to Frieda, they had all been neatly filed in chronological order. Hills hadn't yet found the time to stir them into his ongoing stew of papers.

Anna separated out all the incidents that had occurred in or around Cliff Palace and ordered them again according to date. The last was the report she had written on the discovery and evacuation of Stacy Meyers' body.

Reading through it, the day was re-created in her mind but no new details or connections were generated.

Slouching down in the chair, she put her feet up. More blood to the brain. Again she read the report. Words on a page: no leaps of logic, no sparks of genius.

Putting the 344 aside, she picked up the sheaf of 343s and thumbed through them. Most were medicals: broken wrist, respiratory failure, anxiety attack, tachycardia w/confusion, asthma, fractured C-spine from a kiva diver— the local parlance for tourists who tumbled into the underground rooms.

Anna selected out all the evacuations. But for the wrist and the C-spine, each carry-out was in some way, shape, or form a heart, brain, or breathing difficulty. Not unusual at seven thousand feet with a high percentage of elderly visitors. She set the two fractures aside and looked through the remaining reports.

Pretty standard stuff; the only thing peculiar was the number of them. Anna carried the file into an ex–coat closet now pressed into service as a computer room and called up all the 343s for six summers past. Even accounting for the steady increase in tourism, medical evacuations had quadrupled at Cliff Palace this season. She checked reports for Balcony House and Spruce Tree House. They had remained more or less constant.

"Frieda, are you busy?" she hollered.

"Always."

"Too busy?"

"What do you want?"

"Computer-nerd stuff."

"Come here then, I can't leave the front desk."

With Anna breathing down her neck, Frieda used D-Base to cross-reference all the evacuations by the patients' point of origin, age, sex, race, and primary complaint. "Looks like a normal group," Frieda said. "Old people and sick people. You were expecting somebody else?"

"I don't know what I was expecting." Anna sat down on Frieda's desk and looked through the reports again: ten-thirty, eleven o'clock, eleven-eighteen, April twelfth, twenty-sixth, May third, twenty-fourth, and thirty-first, June seventh, June fourteenth. "Try by time."

Frieda complied. "All but two were in the morning."

That was something. The usual time for rescue excitement was midafternoon, when the day's heat was setting in. "Try by date."

"Hey ho." Frieda clicked the keys. "Well, lookie there!"

"What?" Anna demanded.

"All but two—the afternoon ones—fell on Tuesday. And I thought Mondays were tough . . . Coincidence?"

"Got to be," Anna said. "Thanks, Frieda."

Back at her own desk Anna fanned out the reports now reduced by two, the two neither in the morning nor on a Tuesday. "What do I know now?" she whispered to herself.

"What?" Frieda called.

"Nothing," Anna answered both her own question and the dispatcher's. She pored over the paltry bits of information she had gathered. Rose lied about when and where she'd seen Greeley both the night of the murder and since.

Greeley was still grousing about the sugar in his D-14 Cat's fuel tank. The murder had so overshadowed it there'd been no further investigation to speak of.

"Hey, Frieda," Anna interrupted herself. "Do private vendors like Greeley have to show proof of insurance before they're hired?"

"Yes. Too much liability otherwise. Why?"

"Just wondering." Even if Stacy had been the sugar-slinging chain swinger, his ecotage had been aborted. Had he succeeded, all Greeley would have suffered was a fat check from the insurance company—not even much in the way of inconvenience or delay. Greeley killing Meyers to avenge the Caterpillar was absurd.

Tom Silva was sullen and scared or angry—Anna couldn't tell which. Beavens was lying to somebody, either to her or to Jamie about his veil sighting. His report of leaving before the other interpreters had yet to be checked out. Jamie was claiming a closer kinship with the deceased than Anna believed existed and riding the revenge of the Anasazi theory pretty hard. She had even filed a back-country permit to hold a vigil all night in the fatal kiva. The request had been denied.

How any of that tied in with seven evacuations from Cliff, all cardiopulmonary or central nervous system problems, all early in the day on a Tuesday, Anna couldn't fathom.

An unpleasant thought wandered through her tired mind. "No," she breathed as she dragged a calendar from the middle of a pile. On it she marked all the days of the evacuations with a tiny, faint "X" in pencil. Forgetting her gun and radio, she took the calendar over to the museum.

Jamie Burke was working the front desk. Several visitors clustered around a single brochure arguing over the drawing of Mesa Verde's road system. Jamie stood behind the counter, her elbows resting on the glass, reading Louis L'Amour's *Haunted Mesa*.

"Got a minute?" Anna asked.

Jamie raised her head with a practiced look of long-suffering patience. When she saw it was Anna, she relaxed. "I'm stuck here till five-thirty."

Anna pushed the calendar over the glass. "Could you mark the veil sightings for me, if you remember when they were?"

Jamie studied the calendar for a minute, then borrowed Anna's pen. "April the eleventh, May twenty-third, the thirteenth of June, and, no matter what he says now, Claude saw one on the twenty-first." As she counted each day she made a big black check mark on the page.

"Thanks." Anna gathered up the calendar without looking at it and tucked her pen back in her shirt pocket.

"Aren't you going to tell me what this is all about?" Jamie asked.

"When it gels," Anna lied easily.

Back at her desk in the CRO, she took out the calendar and studied it. All alleged veil sightings were on Monday nights before the Tuesday morning medical evacuations.

"Damn."

"What?" Frieda hollered.

"I said I'm calling it a day, giving up the ghost, so to speak."

Chindi.

"Pshaw!" Anna used her sister's word for "expletive deleted."

15

"**Y**OU SHOW me yours, I'll show you mine," Stanton said.

"No dice. Yours first."

Stanton hummed the first few bars of "Getting to Know You" from *The King and I* and Anna laughed. There'd been too many times on Isle Royale when he'd gotten her to share more than she intended, then failed to return the favor.

"I got the marks on the shoes analyzed," he said. "You know what amazed me the most?"

Anna waited.

"That the NPS actually makes you wear them. They're symptomatic of a severe fashion disorder."

"The marks . . ." Anna prompted.

"Yes. The marks. They were spaced right for fingerprints." She and Stanton were sitting on the ledge above the Cliff Palace ruin, a wide chunk of sandstone tucked up in the shadows under the trees. In front of them stone fanned out in an apron to the cliff's edge, then there was darkness; the gulf of Cliff Canyon. Beyond the black was another pale ribbon where the far side of the canyon cut down through reservation lands. Even without a moon the sandstone picked up illumination from the night sky, reflecting back the dim glow of starlight. The soft down-canyon wind brought on by cooling air settling had died and the air was absolutely still.

Stanton scrunched his legs up more tightly, hugging his knees to his chest, and sucked air through an architecturally generous nose.

"Sitting on a cold rock in the dark is so much more fun than crawling into bed after a long day. Wish I'd thought of this years ago."

"You were showing me yours."

"You've no romance in your soul, Anna. Too many years hobnobbing with Mother Nature. Too pragmatic a lady for my money. In south Chicago we know what moonlight's all about."

"Moon's not up."

"In Chicago we have glorious streetlights and we can turn them on whenever we want. But have it your way. Showing you mine." He dropped a long arm down and snatched off his shoe without untying it. The white sock was pulled partway off and dangled trunklike over the rock. "The marks were here, here, and here on the right shoe." He placed his thumb and two fingers so the thumb was on the inside of the shoe and the index and middle fingers on the outside, his palm cupping the heel, as if the shoe walked on his hand.

"They weren't smudges so much as burns. Something reacted with the leather and caused the discolorations."

"Funny I never noticed them till the other day," Anna said.

"They may not have shown up right away."

"Any idea what made them?"

"Acid—what kind he didn't know." Stanton studied the

shoe. "But looky." He held it up at eye level, still grasping it with his palm beneath the heel. "We can figure Meyers didn't pull it off himself. It wouldn't be impossible to take your own shoe off with your hand in this position, but highly unlikely."

"So something with caustic digits removed his shoes after he was dead?" Anna teased.

"That seems to about sum it up."

"That fits hand in glove with what I've come up with."

"Goody." He stretched his legs out in front of him and waggled his feet. His bare shins gleamed in the starlight. "Now do I get to find out why I'm sitting on a rock in the middle of the night instead of curled snug in my little bed?"

"We're on chindi patrol."

Stanton groaned.

"I'm getting overtime," Anna added helpfully.

"I'm exempt."

"Too bad. This promises to be a long one." Anna told him her story of carry-outs and spirit veil sightings, Monday nights and Tuesday mornings, and left him to flounder with cause and effect.

He continued wagging his feet as if transfixed by the metronomic motion. "Ms. Burke lying?" he suggested after a minute or two. "Putting her paranormal next to the normal to lend it credence?"

"I wouldn't put it past her, but I didn't tell her when the medicals were or why I wanted the sighting dates."

"Could she have gotten the dates of the medicals out of the files?"

"I suppose. She doesn't have a key to the CRO and it would cause comment if she came in and looked through the files. They're no guarded secret or anything, interps just never look at them, so it'd be something to gossip about when who's sleeping with whom grew thin."

"Could she get into the office at night, when no gossips were about?"

"Sure. Somebody'd probably let her in if she asked. Security—except for the administration building—is pretty lax. It seems a stretch though. Why bother? She never bothers to substantiate any of her other stories. Anyway, at least one Monday night I heard her talking about the veil and then the next day we had that medical. There's no way she could've planned to have all the cardiopulmonary and central nervous system problems occur on Tuesday mornings."

"Was she on duty each time there was a carry-out?"

Anna thought about it. Near as she could remember, she was.

"Jamie Burke, Medicine Woman." Stanton bounced his eyebrows suggestively. Light and shadow dappled his fair skin, and Anna realized the moon had risen.

"Wouldn't Jamie love that," she said. "She's an opportunistic actor. Takes every chance to dash out on stage. But I doubt she has the tenacity to write the script to that extent."

"If she didn't set it up and she's not lying, then we really are out here waiting for the dead to walk."

"When you've ruled out the impossible, whatever's left . . ."

They sat awhile without speaking. Anna was enjoying herself. A smear of lights over Farmington, fifty miles distant, was the only flaw in a perfect sky. Deep in the canyon an owl called and was answered.

"So write me your autobiography and we'll get this life-long friendship rolling," Stanton dropped into the stillness.

Anna would have laughed but, remembering how sound carried in these natural amphitheaters, settled for a smile.

"Aw, come on," Stanton pleaded. "Since we can't have cheeseburgers and coffee out of paper cups, that's the next best thing for making this feel like a real stakeout."

If an expectant stare indicated anything, he was serious. Suddenly Anna felt shy.

"Just start any old where," he encouraged.

"Well, I was born naked—"

"Not the ishy parts! I don't want to know you that well."

"I thought you should know the worst if we're to be lifelong friends."

"Okay then. Ever married?"

"You consider that the worst?"

"My ex-wives did."

It was Anna's turn for raised eyebrows, metaphorically if not literally. *"Wives?"*

"Two."

"Children?"

"Several."

"Ages?"

"Oooh, that's a toughie. Thirteen going on fourteen—second marriage. Nineteen and twenty-three—introductory marriage. Girl, girl, boy, respectively."

Anna revised her estimate of Stanton's age from late thirties to mid forties. She didn't ask what had happened. Once or twice in the past, when she was feeling excessively polite or nosy, she'd asked that question. Nothing new happened under the sun and certainly not before the altar.

"You ever married?" Stanton asked again.

"Yes."

"Died?"

"How'd you guess?"

"A lady who finds corpses on sunken ships and in kivas wouldn't be so bourgeois as to be divorced. No glamour, no drama."

A pang of embarrassment let Anna know he was right. Like other widows, especially young widows, she was prone to wearing her weeds like a badge of honor. Widowhood conferred a mystery and status divorce lacked. The difference between returning World War II and Vietnam veterans. Both had been through a war, but a judgmental public conferred glory only on those who had been victimized in a socially acceptable manner. In divorce, as in a police action, nobody truly won and everybody got wounded.

"You know the only reason Romeo and Juliet didn't get a divorce is because they died first," Stanton said.

A rustling stirred the pine needles behind them. "Are there snakes?" he demanded abruptly.

"Snakes don't tend to be nocturnal. They're too cold-blooded."

"Most of the cold-blooded creatures in Chicago are exclusively nocturnal."

"Our tarantulas come out at night," Anna offered.

"Stop that!" He pulled his legs up again. "Don't tell me that. You're such a bully.

"So tell me about the dead guy," he said after he'd gotten himself arranged in a defensive posture.

"I already told you all I know and then some."

"Not the kiva dead guy, the dead guy you're married to."

Anna noticed he didn't use the past tense and wondered if he'd tapped into her idiosyncrasies. "Neurosis," she heard her sister's voice in her mind. "Spade for spade." All at once she felt terribly tired. A middle-aged lady up past her bedtime sitting on a rock in the dark.

Stanton was still looking at her, his face open and interested. Briefly, Anna thought of what she might tell him, wondered if it would have the cathartic effect of confession. Or if she'd merely paint the old pattern of the perfect marriage. Romeo and Juliet Go To New York.

"Nothing's perfect," she said finally. "It was a long time ago."

Stanton laid a hand on her arm. At first she resented his pity, then realized that wasn't inherent in the gesture. He was shutting her up, pointing to the west where a quarter mile distant the walls of an ancient ruin appeared in a flicker of light then vanished again into darkness. The effect was unsettling, as if, like Brigadoon, the pueblo had appeared momentarily in the twentieth century.

"Headlights," Anna shattered the illusion. "That's Sun Temple. It's on another part of the mesa but your headlights rake across it when you come around the bend before the Cliff Palace parking lot."

"The last ranger sweeping out leftover tourists?" Stanton ventured.

Anna shook her head. "Too late. Jennifer went out of service at midnight." She squeezed the tiny button on the left side of her watch and squinted at the barely illuminated numbers. "It's after one. Probably interps. Maybe Jennifer gave them the key. They may be out for the same reason we are." Levering herself up, she stomped some blood back into her feet. "Might as well go after them. We're legal; they're not: in a closed area without a permit."

"A firing offense?"

"Definitely a calling-on-the-carpet offense."

The roar of an engine followed after the lights. "Sounds like a truck." Following the deer trail they'd taken to the mesa's edge, Anna began threading her way quickly through the junipers.

"You must have eyes like a cat," Stanton complained.

She stopped, took the mag light off her duty belt, and shone it back down the trail for him. He wasn't far behind. When he chose he could move quietly.

The sound of an engine being gunned stopped them both. "Saw the patrol car," Anna said. She began to run and heard Stanton follow. In less than three minutes they reached the parking lot but the truck was gone. "Rats."

"No lights and sirens?" he asked as she backed the patrol car out.

"They have no place to go," Anna reminded him. "We'll catch them at the gate unless they left it open." Still, she drove as fast as the winding road permitted. Partly to catch the offending vehicle and partly for the sheer fun of it.

"Whee!" Stanton said, and pulled his lap belt tighter.

"Three-one-two, three-zero-one." The radio commanded their attention.

"That's you," Stanton said. "Boy, you've got an exciting job. Wish I were a park ranger."

"Stick with me. You may get to see a dog off leash." Anna picked up the mike and responded with her call number. Three-zero-one was Frieda's personal number.

"Are you still on duty, Anna?"

"Yes. I'm on Cliff Palace loop with Agent Stanton. We've a vehicle in a closed area."

"You may have to leave it. There's a disturbance at Patsy Silva's residence. It sounds serious. Al called. She said she's heard shouting and what she thinks might be gunshots."

"I'm headed that direction. See if you can't get somebody else out of bed to lend me moral support."

"Ten-four. Three-zero-one, zero-one-thirty-four."

Anna made an educated guess that the instigator of this particular melee was Tom Silva and refreshed Stanton on the Silvas' post-matrimonial relationship.

"Bet you're glad I'm along," he said smugly.

"And why would that be?"

"You'll need somebody to calm the hysterical wife while you're disarming and subduing the enraged husband."

Anna laughed. "You've got the more dangerous of the two jobs."

"I wish you were kidding."

She took the turn at the Three-Way too fast and scared herself into taking her foot out of the carburetor. By the time they reached the four-way intersection she'd slowed to a safer speed.

The gate was closed and the chain in place.

"We couldn't have been far behind. Where's the truck?" Stanton demanded.

"They hid out somewhere along the way. Looped back around or ducked up a fire road. We won't catch them tonight."

In the headlights she could see the padlock's arm was through the chain links but not clicked closed. "The gate is false-locked," she told Stanton. "Get it for me, would you?"

Stanton complied, relocking the chain behind him. "Maybe we'll get lucky, lock 'em in."

Anna's thoughts had moved ahead to the upcoming festivities. Shortly before reaching the tower house, she told Frieda she had arrived on scene, then opened the car window and turned off the headlights. Moonlight was enough to see by.

"Stealth ranger?" Stanton whispered as the car crept up the short drive.

"The dark is my friend," Anna quoted a self-defense instructor from the Federal Law Enforcement Training Center in Georgia.

The Silvas' residence was dark and, at the moment, quiet. Anna grabbed her flashlight from the recharger and pushed open the car door. Stanton folded himself out his side. "This is the creepy part," he whispered.

For a moment they stood in silence not softened even by the hum of night insects or the rustling of predators and prey. Just when they'd come to count on it, the stillness was destroyed by the sound of shattering glass and shouting. "Goddamn you, Pats! Let me in. Jesus, Mary, an' Joseph, listen to me, for Crissake!" Fierce pounding followed.

"Ahh. Better," Stanton said. "Now we know where he is and his church of choice."

"It's Tom." Quietly, Anna led the way up the flagstone walk curling around the building. Behind the jut of the square kitchen, set into the curved wall of the tower, was the front and only door. It and the small porch protecting it were wooden. The rest of the dwelling was stone.

"You're a dead woman if you don't let me in!" came a cry so slurred it hardly sounded like Silva.

Anna switched on the flashlight. In her peripheral vision she saw Stanton melt out of the moonlight into the shadows as the beam spotlighted the man on the doorstep.

Looking like a refugee from the movie set of *Bus Stop*, Tom Silva, in Levi's, boots, an open white shirt, and battered straw cowboy hat, leaned on the front door. Both arms were raised, fists balled, propping him up. He rested his forehead against the wood. The hat was pushed to the back of his head.

"Tom," Anna said softly.

"Gun," Stanton said just as quietly, his voice penetrating from the shadows.

Almost swallowed up in Silva's right fist was a derringer. Anna took her .357 from its holster and trained it on him.

"Tom," she said again. "Put the gun down. It's Anna."

Silva turned. The act unbalanced him and he stumbled backward, his shoulders crashing into the planks. The derringer sparked in the light as his arm swung up. Anna's stomach lurched and her finger tensed on the trigger but he was only shading his eyes with the weapon, squinting to see past the glare.

"Fucking idiot." Shaken by the anger adrenaline leaves behind, Anna said: "You just nearly scared me into shooting you, you know that? Put that gun down. Slow! Don't you dare scare me like that again."

"Anna?" Tom staggered half a step forward then fell back once more against the support of the door. "*Ranger* Anna? No shit?"

"The gun," Anna reminded him. "Put it down."

Tom brought the derringer in front of his face and studied it. Anna's breath caught at the movement. She was becoming uncomfortably aware of the strain of holding the revolver at arm's length in one hand and the six-cell flashlight in the other.

"This is my door knocker," Tom said. It looked a match to the one he'd given Patsy.

"Drop the damn thing," Anna snapped.

"Jeez-Louise," he mumbled. "Keep your pants on."

"Now," Anna ordered, trying to cut through the alcohol shrouding his mind.

"I'm not dropping it," he said petulantly. "It's got a pearl handle. How 'bout I set it down real nice like? Okay?"

"Okay. Just do it."

Silva bent down to lay the little pistol on the cement, lost equilibrium, and fell against a post supporting the porch roof. The derringer clattered to the concrete. "Fuck," Silva growled. "If you've busted it . . ." He reached for the pistol but a hand shot out of the shadows and snatched it away.

"I'll go ahead and take care of this for you, Mr. Silva," Anna heard Stanton saying politely.

Flashing blue lights and a screaming siren made Anna jump. She squeaked as well but fortunately the clangor drowned her out. Silva screamed outright. "Sheesh!" He collapsed on the welcome mat, his back to the door, and hid his face in his hands. "Pats is a dead woman. Missy and Mindy: dead. Fuck." In slow motion, he rolled to his side and vomited into the petunias.

Anna holstered her weapon and took a deep breath to steady her nerves. Stanton materialized out of the shadows and began patting the incapacitated Silva down for weapons. "Now you've done it, Anna," Stanton said.

"Don't I know it. I took 'it' out," Anna said, referring to her revolver.

"Gonna be paperwork to atone for that."

Loud bootfalls on the flagstone announced Jennifer Short's arrival. "The pitter-patter of little feet," Anna muttered unkindly. "Hey ya, Jennifer," she said as the other woman came up beside her. "You might want to call 'in service' when you go out and 'on scene' when you arrive. It's okay to spoil the surprise."

"Sorry. Damnation. I'm always forgettin' that."

The porch light came on, giving Stanton light to work by, and Anna switched off her flashlight.

Jennifer's face was flushed and her eyes bright. Clearly she was scared, but excited too. Maybe she'd arrived a bit like Wyatt Earp into Dodge but she'd made a quick response from Far View and she hadn't hung back. "Good to see you. Come to join the fun?" Anna asked.

"Looks like it's all been had. Ol' Tom the only perpetrator?" Jennifer asked, disappointed. "Frieda made it sound like a riot."

"He had a gun," Anna tried to sweeten the pot. Jennifer perked up a little. "Why don't you go work with Special Agent Stanton," Anna suggested. "I need to check on Patsy and the girls."

Tom Silva was still retching, Agent Stanton standing beside him looking mildly ill. Jennifer strode up, jammed her hat more tightly down on her head, then fumbled out her handcuffs. "You have the right . . . Oh shit." She pulled her Stetson off and tugged a bit of paper from inside the hatband. "Hold this." She handed the hat unceremoniously to Stanton and finished reading Tom his rights from the paper. When she'd done, she turned to Anna. "What now? Cuff him?"

Anna nodded. "There's a belt in the trunk of my car. A leather one with some metal rings on it. Put it around his waist and cuff his hands in front of him and to the belt. Frederick will assist. You're looking good."

"It's my first," Jennifer said, and grinned. "Y'all be gentle with me," she said to Silva. He threw up again.

Anna waited till Jennifer and Stanton had helped Tom to his feet and led him away, then she knocked on the tower house door. "Patsy, it's me, Anna. Tom's gone. Are you okay?" There was a scraping sound from within, as if something heavy was being dragged away, then the door opened a crack. Looking terribly young with her short hair and pink pajamas, Patsy stuck her head out and looked around to discern the truth of Anna's statement.

"Are you all right?" Anna repeated her question.

"I guess. Mindy! Missy!" The girls came up from the living area and stood on the landing looking wide awake and confused. "Yes, we're okay," Patsy said, comforted by having her girls around her. "He never got in or anything."

"He wouldn't have hurt us," Mindy complained. At thirteen or fourteen, she was the younger of the two daughters. "You don't have to take him anywhere. He was drunk," she added, as if this exonerated him.

"Maybe you could make me a cup of coffee," Anna said to Patsy. "Instant would be fine."

The girls settled in the little booth in the kitchen. The domesticity of Mother putting the kettle on seemed to soothe all of them. Patsy poured the water over the coffee crystals when it was barely warm and handed Anna skim milk from the refrigerator.

Anna leaned against the counter and forced down a swallow. "What happened?" she asked now that a semblance of normalcy had been restored.

"It was Tom," Patsy said unnecessarily. "He came over earlier. I could tell he'd been drinking and I wouldn't see him. He went away again but came back about half an hour ago. He was pretty drunk."

"Blotto," Missy said.

"Not blotto," Mindy contradicted her.

"Blotto."

The girls were so close in age and so alike in blond good

looks, Anna often got them confused, which didn't endear her to either one of them. Both wore their hair long and straight, framing round scrubbed faces marked with a scattering of pimples. Mindy wore a nightshirt with Bart Simpson's likeness on it, and Missy an oversized T-shirt and boxer shorts, both the worse for wear.

"Go on," Anna said to their mother.

"That's about it. He was drunk. Blotto," she added, giving Mindy a yes-he-was-too look. "He tried to get in. That's when I locked the door."

"What did he want?"

"I don't know." Patsy started to cry.

"He kept yelling he was going to kill us," Missy said.

"He did not!" Mindy punched her sister in the arm.

"He did too, you little creep."

"Girls, that's enough!" Patsy slapped the tabletop with the flat of her hand and the girls were quiet.

"He didn't say he was going to kill us," Patsy said. "He just said things like 'You're dead if you don't listen to me' and 'You're a dead woman, Pats.' Things like that. He did not threaten to kill us, Missy. Don't you go saying things like that."

"Like that's not a threat." Missy tossed her hair and started French-braiding it back off her face.

The comments struck Anna as threatening as well, but Patsy and her daughters, even Missy, didn't seem particularly terrified by the incident, so maybe they weren't. Maybe it was a fairly standard family interaction. "Is that all you can remember?" she asked Patsy.

"That's about it. I think he maybe shot that little gun off once or twice. He was mad that I gave it back to him. I left it in his pickup the other day. With the girls, I didn't want it around the house."

Anna waited a moment but no more information was forthcoming. "Okay. We're going to arrest him and take him down to Cortez. What do you want to charge him with?"

"Arrest him?" Patsy looked alarmed. "You don't have to do that. Can't you just take him somewhere till he sobers up? You don't have to arrest him."

"I already did."

Now she looked aggrieved. "I won't press charges."

"I will." Anna rinsed her cup and put it in the sink. "Drunk and disorderly, disturbing the peace, unlawful possession of a firearm in a national park, refusing to obey a lawful order, obstructing a federal officer in the execution of her duty, public intoxication, DUI if he drove here, noise after quiet hours, and brain off leash. If I were you, I'd think it over before I let him off the hook. His behavior is unacceptable, illegal, and unsafe. You let me know if you change your mind."

Anna left the three of them sitting at the table giving her and each other dirty looks.

Tom was cuffed and belted into the back of the patrol car. Jennifer and Frederick stood by the open door, waiting without talking. As Anna walked up, Frederick stepped away from the vehicle and addressed her in hushed tones. "Can you and Ranger Short take Mr. Silva in by yourselves?"

"I think we can manage that," Anna said dryly.

"Oh whew. You don't have to give me a ride home even. I can walk back to my quarters from here easy."

"Tired of my company?" Anna asked as he turned to go.

Stanton looked over his shoulder. "He's going to throw up in your car. All the way down the hill. Ish."

"Coward."

"Hypersensitive gag reflex," he called back cheerily.

Blue lights still blazing, Jennifer had parked the 4X4 truck behind the patrol car. She was leaning against the fender, apparently enjoying the evening.

"Agent Stanton opted out," Anna told her. "Follow me to Maintenance. You can leave your vehicle there and ride down to Cortez with me."

"Guess I gotta turn out the overheads," Jennifer sighed. "Too bad. They're kinda pretty."

As Anna pulled into Maintenance, the patrol car's headlights shone on the gate to the locked yard where the pipeline contractor kept his equipment. In the beams Anna could see the red water truck and the ubiquitous yellow of heavy machinery. A man in dark clothes, welding gloves stuck in his hip pocket, was fiddling with the lock to the enclosed area. Anna flipped on her high beams and drove up to him. Shielding his eyes, he turned. It was Ted Greeley. She glanced at the dashboard clock: two-nineteen. Greeley didn't stay on the mesa top nights; he rented a place in Mancos.

" 'Morning, Ted." She stepped from her vehicle and stood behind the open door. "You're up early."

"So're you. But I knew that. Running my little buddy out of town?"

"Something like that. What're you doing up here at this hour?" It was late, and she was too tired for prolonged pleasantries.

"Why, Anna, I didn't know you cared. As it happens, I was visiting a sick friend. I heard on the radio that my boy Thomas was on the rampage and I got to wondering if he'd borrowed a cup of sugar from any of the neighbor ladies. That boy's one butt short of a pack and he's got a key to the yard. His kind of help I don't need."

"I didn't know you had a radio."

"I don't." Greeley winked and said good night.

For a moment Anna was nonplussed. Then she remembered: neither she nor Hills had gotten Stacy's personal protective gear from the widow. Rose still had his revolver and his radio. But a lot of people had radios: Drew, Jimmy, Paul, Jennifer, Al, Frieda. Though most of the seasonal interpreters didn't carry them, they all had access to those kept in the museum for use in the ruins.

Anna let the thought go. Something else had been triggered by Greeley but she was at a loss as to what it was. She let her brain empty and the thought floated up: Tom Silva had a key to the equipment yard. Had his sudden increase in cash flow that washed Patsy's new watch into the picture come from pilfering parts? Tools?

Stanton was right, of course. Silva vomited half a dozen times on the way down. Jennifer, riding beside him in the backseat, swore every time he threw up. "These're my Class A's, damn you," she snarled at one point. Anna rolled down her window and turned the air-conditioning on to clear the air. By the time they reached the Cortez sheriff's office Silva was nearly comatose. During the car trip he'd been too far gone to question; now it would have to wait till morning.

Anna turned him over to the booking officer and wrote him up for drunk and disorderly and illegal possession of a firearm, knowing without Patsy's corroboration not much else would stick.

She and Jennifer took the car over to an all-night Shell station on Main Street and swamped out the backseat.

It was after four A.M. when they started the long drive

back up to Far View. Anna'd never been comfortable in the cold predawn hours, that waiting time from after midnight till sunrise. As a child she could remember standing shivering watching her parents load suitcases into the trunk of the old Thunderbird. On their rare vacations, the importance of getting an early start was paramount. Upon reaching adulthood she'd expanded the concept of "vacation" to include sleeping in, and seldom booked a flight before noon if she could help it.

Now those unholy hours were allocated for pacing the floor on bad nights.

At Anna's request, Jennifer was driving. The late hour and the abandoned road had awakened the Indy 500 driver lurking just under the surface of every American, and Short was taking the curves with expert and nauseating speed. The two swallows of instant coffee Anna'd choked down in Patsy's kitchen felt like they'd lodged behind her breastbone and were trying to burn their way out.

"Slow down," she griped, "or we'll be mopping out the front seat."

"Sorry." Jennifer didn't sound it.

Events of the night had pushed the truck Anna and Stanton had heard on the loop out of her mind. In her irritation it resurfaced.

"You had late shift?" she asked, knowing the answer.

"I got two lates now Stacy's kaput."

"What time did you lock Cliff Palace loop?"

Jennifer thought a moment. "Maybe ten or thereabouts."

"Did you have to go back out later? Get a call or anything?"

"No. Why?" Jennifer's voice changed slightly, that touch of wariness that signaled the end of conversation and the beginning of interrogation.

"Around one-thirty a truck of some sort drove through

the Cliff Palace parking lot," Anna told her. "About then I got the call to come rescue Patsy. We were right behind the truck—not close enough to see it, but we had to be close. Somehow they hid out. Nobody was at the Four-Way when we got there. The gate was false-locked, so whoever was in there had access to a key. I wondered if Jamie'd talked you out of yours so she could go play with her little dead friends."

"That's against the rules," Jennifer said piously.

"Everybody bends the rules once in a while," Anna tempted confession.

"Not everybody." Jennifer put her in her place.

"Did anybody have a backcountry permit for tonight?"

"No. I checked. I always check."

"Who of the interps owns a good-sized truck?"

Jennifer was more comfortable with this line of questioning. It didn't cast aspersions on her merits as a ranger. "Nobody I know of," she said after a minute. "Interps have subcompact minds—you know; no extra irreplaceable fossil fuels and shit."

Claude Beavens had said the "interp's truck" left after he did the night of the murder. Offhand Anna couldn't remember if he'd seen or only heard of it. She made a mental note to ask.

"Jimmy Russell's got a truck," Jennifer volunteered. "He'd've took 'em. Jimmy's always looking to get his horns clipped or at least a couple of free beers. If it was a party, he'd've been there."

"Have you been locking the Four-Way funny? Like Stacy used to, all twisted and tight and hard to undo?" Anna asked abruptly.

Jennifer hooted. "Ranger Pigeon, what is the matter with you? You're as fussy as a cat with new kittens. You on the rag?"

"Past my bedtime," Anna grumbled. "Have you?"

"My locks aren't twisty and tight," Jennifer said primly, and turned on the radio to drown out any further assaults on her character.

Anna didn't push it, but promised herself she would do some serious checking of stories when the world opened for business: Jamie, Beavens, Jennifer, Russell. She had a feeling if rangers were puppets, the mesa would have more long noses than trees.

16

"I'M NOT LOOKING forward to this." Anna switched off the ignition. She and Frederick sat in the patrol car under the shade tree in Rose Meyers' front yard. "What I'm looking forward to is a nap." By the time she and Jennifer had returned to the mesa it had been close to five. She'd had less than two hours' sleep before she went on duty at seven A.M.

"Getting old?" Stanton teased.

"I'm too tired even to yawn."

"Want me to do it?"

For a second Anna thought he was offering to yawn for her. Then she focused on the task at hand. "It's bound to be tedious, personal, and unpleasant. Of course I want you to do it."

"Generous to a fault."

Anna twisted in her seat till the bones in her lower back popped. "I'll do it, but you'd better come with me in your capacity as Hysterical Wife Sedative."

Hattie answered the door in her nightgown, a knee-length poet's shirt in burgundy with the sheen of satin and the wrinkle-free texture of good polyester. Graying hair was wild around her face. She looked the embodiment of an elemental force. Whether of earth or sky, for good or evil, Anna couldn't hazard a guess. Greek mythology had never been big in Catholic school.

"You're just in time for a cup of tea," Hattie said. Much of her usual spark was banked beneath fatigue or worry, though still she sounded genuinely welcoming. "C'mon in, Anna. Agent Stanton."

"Fred," Stanton said, and Anna shot him a startled look. In the years she'd been acquainted with him "Frederick" was the only accepted form of address. She looked back at Hattie. The elemental force: the quintessential aunt with all the rights and privileges conferred therein. One's aunt would scarcely call one "Frederick" unless some formal trouble were in the air.

"Fred," Hattie said warmly. "I've never known a weak or dishonest Fred."

"Or a pretty one, I bet," Stanton said.

Hattie laughed as she opened the screen and waved them in. "Maybe to a Fredericka."

"The only one who finds a papa moose handsome is a momma moose."

The banter carried them indoors, where they pooled in front of the archway leading to a small built-in eating nook that separated the living area from the kitchen. Rose and her daughter sat in their nightgowns over breakfast. Rose had two plastic curlers clipped on the crown of her head, just enough to give her coif that rounded pouf short hairdos seem to require. A definite chill radiated from the woman as she looked at Anna.

Bella, in a sleeveless white nightie covered with little blue sailboats, huddled on the bench opposite her mother. Knees tucked up and arms pulled inside the armholes, she hid her face in the open neck of the gown; a personal fallout shelter.

Anna guessed discussion over this morning's bananas and Grape-Nuts had been somewhat strained.

"Yes?" Rose said in lieu of a greeting. She opened her hands to encompass the food-littered table. "As you can see, it is a bit early for receiving callers."

It was after ten o'clock. Anna resisted the urge to glance at her watch. In true coward's fashion, she stepped aside and drew Stanton into the line of fire.

"Agent Stanton and I are just tying up a few loose ends," she said. "Did Hills happen to collect Stacy's duty belt?"

Rose looked blank but she knew exactly what was referred to, Anna would have laid money on it.

"C'mon, punkin," Hattie said. "Let's get dressed and go for a walk."

Eyes full of alarm, Bella glanced at Stanton.

"We'll change in your mom's room," Hattie assured her. Modesty met, Bella climbed from the bench.

"Hiya, Bella," Anna said.

"Hello." Bella was merely being polite, she didn't meet Anna's eyes.

While Bella slid to the floor, Rose managed to pluck the rollers from her hair and secret them away somewhere. "Would you care for a cup of coffee?" She was talking to Stanton.

"No thanks," Anna replied just as he said: "That'd really hit the spot."

Accordingly, Rose went to the kitchen and returned with a mug of coffee for the FBI agent. Anna wondered if she would have gotten one even if she'd said yes.

"Any progress finding Stacy's murderer?" Rose asked as she regained her seat.

Stanton sat down across from her. "Not as much as we'd like. But Ranger Pigeon and I are still chipping away at it."

Rose didn't look up at Anna leaning coffeeless in the archway.

Amid the breakfast debris on the table were papers that had an official fill-in-the-boxes look to them. "Looks like we've caught you at a bad time," Stanton said apologetically.

"Yes, rather." This time Rose did look at Anna.

Disrespect, verbal and sometimes physical abuse was often directed at the uniform, the badge. Anna'd become practiced at not letting it get under her skin. But this was personal and it felt personal. She found herself becoming irked and began to count to ten in Spanish.

"Death and taxes?" Stanton asked solicitously.

"Medical forms for Bella," Rose said.

Anna'd just gotten to *cinco, seis*. She quit counting. The conversation was getting interesting. "Is Bella sick?" she asked.

Rose ignored her. "Bella's getting an operation," she told Stanton. Excitement was clear in her voice. "It's been something I've been wanting for a long time. She can't have it yet, but in a few years. They think they can fix her legs, make her normal."

"That's wonderful," Stanton said.

Anna was undecided. "We're the variety that adds spice," she remembered Drew saying.

"Stacy's insurance left us with enough money to cover medical expenses." Rose volunteered the information and Anna wondered why.

"Stacy had a life insurance policy?" she asked.

Rose took a second to respond. In that second the silence shouted "Not that it's any of your business but— yes, he did, Miss Pigeon. Stacy was a good husband."

Good was emphasized, and logically or not, Anna found herself wanting to defend Zach for dying broke and unprepared. She chose not to rise to the bait—real or imagined.

"You're welcome to see the policy, if you want, Miss Pigeon."

"Sure, why not."

Rose rolled her eyes for Stanton's benefit and left the table to get the form.

There was a murmured exchange in the bedroom, then Hattie and Bella emerged and slipped out the back door with exaggerated sneakiness. Anna suspected some Hattie-led game was afoot.

Rose returned. Her hair was combed and Anna's female eye detected a discreet layer of blush brushed on the high cheekbones.

"Miss Pigeon?" Rose held out the insurance policy then, dismissing Anna with a look, sat again. "All that's of no interest to the Federal Bureau of Investigation, I imagine," she said sweetly to Stanton. "Is there anything I can help you with this morning, Agent Stanton?"

"Coffee's all I need," he said. "Anna?"

She laid the two-hundred-thousand-dollar life insurance policy on the table. "Just Stacy's duty belt—gun, radio, leather gear."

"I have no idea where I put it," Rose said disinterestedly. "I'll drop it by the CRO later this afternoon if it turns up."

In a house the size of a postage stamp, inhabited by a six-year-old child, it was unlikely she'd mislaid her recently deceased spouse's gunbelt. Whether she lied to hide something or just for spite, Anna hadn't a clue. Admitting defeat she said: "Thanks, Mrs. Meyers. That'd be a big help. We won't take up any more of your time."

"Thanks for the coffee," Stanton chimed in.

"Anytime, Fred. It was so sweet of you to come by." Rose blessed him with a Pepsodent-perfect smile.

"Watch out," Anna said ungraciously as they climbed back into the patrol car. "You've got Husband Number Three written all over you.

"First there's insurance, then there isn't, then there is. There's chindi, then they're gone, then they're back. Gates are locked, unlocked, locked. Silva's a thug, a guardian angel, then presto chango, a thug," she ranted.

Stanton rolled up the windows of the car and cranked up the air conditioner.

"Everybody's got a radio, then there's not a radio to be found. Interps have trucks, then they have subcompacts. The truth is getting to be such a variable. New realities to be announced as needed." Anna turned the air conditioner off and rolled down her window. "What now? You're choreographing this show."

"Gee, thanks." The radio cut off anything further. Jamie Burke at Cliff Palace was reporting a medical. Unceremoniously, Anna shushed Stanton and turned up the radio. A boy, fourteen, was complaining of faintness and shortness of breath. He insisted he could walk out, his parents demanded he have medical attention.

"Do you need to go?" Stanton asked.

Anna shook her head. "Hills and Jennifer are both on today. They can do it." For a second she stared at the radio thinking. "Damn," she said finally. "Let's go anyway. I've got some questions to ask."

Cliff Palace parking lot was full and a line of cars extending a hundred yards back up the one-way road followed those creeping slowly through the lot looking for nonexistent parking places. Anna turned on her blue lights and, driving on the shoulder, nudged past the sluggish stream. She parked with two wheels in the dirt and two in the "motorcycles only" zone.

The sun burned through the thin atmosphere, touching the skin ungently. Anna loved its rough kiss and had the wrinkles and age spots to prove it. Red-faced tourists queued up at the drinking fountains.

Down in the Palace the heat and the crowding would be exacerbated. To keep from adding to the congestion, Anna and Stanton stayed on the mesa top monitoring events over the radio.

In the fifteen minutes it had taken them to get to Cliff, the boy's condition had deteriorated sufficiently. Burke's voice had gone from self-important to mildly panicky. Hills had called in on scene. From the two patrol vehicles parked in the lot, Anna guessed in all the excitement Jennifer had forgotten again.

Stanton found a bench in the shade at the trail head. Two German women, both in their seventies or early eighties, wearing print dresses and straw hats, moved over to make room for him.

Anna leaned on the split-rail fence behind the bench and tilted her head back to catch the sun on her face. The heat drew wind up the canyons and she reveled in its touch.

"Some questions to ask, you said. Let me in on your secret?" Stanton asked.

"I wish I had a secret. It'd make me feel superior. This doesn't even qualify as a hunch." Since she didn't choose to add to that, Stanton made small talk with his bench companions in German and Anna was duly impressed. She would have been more so had the ladies not laughed so much as they tried to puzzle out what he was saying.

The ambulance arrived, Drew driving, Jimmy riding shotgun. They came to wait with Anna.

"They're walking him out," Drew said. "A kid again. Asthma, up at seven thousand feet. His parents ought to be shot."

Hills' voice, phlegmatic as ever, came into the conversation via the airwaves. "Seven hundred, three-eleven. We're going to need some help. Fella's collapsed on us. If the Stokes isn't already up top, don't wait on it. We're to the metal stairs. Send me some big boys 'n' we'll hand-carry the kid out."

"Lifting heavy objects, that's you, Drew," Anna said. The helitack foreman and Agent Stanton followed her toward the overlook at a trot.

Looking disgustingly heroic, Hills was halfway up the metal stairs, in his arms a pale young man in khaki shorts and a blue T-shirt. Oversized unlaced sneakers—the fashion that summer—made the boy's legs look even skinnier than they were.

Walking beside and behind, Jennifer carried an oxygen bottle, the mask affixed to the patient's face, plastic tubing connecting him to the cylinder. Following so closely they trod on Short's heels were the boy's parents.

A panting woman with permed reddish hair and an overheated complexion held on to one of her son's feet to comfort him or herself. The father was lost in testosterone hysterics. Fear masquerading as anger, he berated the stolid Dutton even as Hills carried his boy. Behind them walked an older couple, grandparents, Anna guessed.

Drew came alongside Hills. They propped the young man, still conscious but barely so, against Anna and interlaced their arms. The boy's breathing was labored, the wheezing audible without a stethoscope. His lips pursed with effort and he sipped at the air, sucking it into his lungs a bit at a time, working to push it through shrunken bronchial tubes. Anna eased him into the chair the men had made of their arms. "You're almost there," she said encouragingly. He nodded and made a valiant attempt to smile.

Her part in the process completed, Anna stepped back, letting Hills and Drew carry their patient to the waiting ambulance. She fell into step with the elderly couple. They seemed the sanest of the group. Both wore wide-brimmed hats, baggy shorts, and the comfortable walking shoes of experienced tourists.

"Grandson?" Anna asked.

"Our first," the woman said.

"And probably last," the man snarled. Obviously this was an old bone of contention in the family.

"Not now, Harold. He has had asthma ever since he was a baby," the grandmother told Anna.

"It's usually not bad," Harold argued. "I told Eli not to bring him up this high."

"Okay, Harold. I don't think it's the altitude," she whispered conspiratorially, though her husband could easily hear. "Dane has been up to seven thousand feet half a dozen times and been just fine. It's radon. Like in caves. Last time Dane was taken this bad it was something like that."

"Irma! Leave the lady alone. It wasn't radon. He was sniffing that glue like the kids all got crazy about."

"Nonsense."

The party reached the parking lot and the grandparents were lost in an organizational shuffle.

As the ambulance drove away, Stanton came to stand by Anna.

"All your questions answered?" he asked.

"Oh, yeah. The pattern's crystal clear. I have no idea what it's of, but it's clear." She twisted the watchband around on her wrist and showed the face to Frederick. "Tuesday, eleven twenty-eight A.M. Another collapse, another carry-out, right on schedule."

"Whose?" Stanton asked.

"You tell me."

17

A PRETTY LITTLE mouse with ears Disneyesque in their cuteness and whiskers Gus-Gus would have been proud of poked her nose out of the kitchen and contemplated crossing the risky expanse of carpet in the living area.

"You're getting fat," Anna warned. "One day you won't be able to squeeze under the door."

The mouse looked up at the sound of her voice but was otherwise unmoved. When Anna had first arrived at Far View there'd been no mice. With the largesse left on countertops and on dirty dishes by her roommates, the little creatures had come to stay. This one was so plump Anna was put in mind of an ink drawing in her childhood copy of *Charlotte's Web;* a very round Templeton the rat lying on his back at the country fair saying: "What a gorge!"

Early on Jennifer and Jamie had set out d-CON. Dying mice had staggered out with such regularity the living room began to resemble the stage after the final act of *Hamlet.* Disgusted, Anna'd thrown the poison out. "Not cricket," she told her housemates. "You can feed them or kill them. Not both."

Since then they'd all come to terms with one another

and the dorm no longer had pests but, as Jennifer had dubbed them, politically correct pets.

Anna's wristwatch beeped. The mouse squeaked on the same frequency and ran behind the refrigerator. Three A.M. on the nose: Anna tried a combination of invisible-to-the-naked-eye buttons on the watch to turn off the hourly alarm. The beeping stopped but she had no idea whether it was of natural causes or if she'd won. "Man against Nature: Woman against Technology," she mumbled.

Half a glass of burgundy sat before her on the table. Her third, but since the first two were downed six hours earlier, she figured they didn't count. Hopefully, this one would help her to sleep and without the usual cost: waking with the jitters just before dawn.

Jack of diamonds: she put it on a black queen in the solitaire game she'd been playing since one-thirty. A space was freed up and two more moves revealed a second ace. She enjoyed a vague sense of triumph. Her mind wasn't on the game, merely in free-fall, unloosed by solitaire's mantra of boredom. This game had many of the earmarks of the one she and Stanton had spent the day pursuing. One by one they'd peeled away lies in hopes of uncovering a truth they could play, one that would start the game moving again.

Another of Frederick the Fed's infernal lists cluttered up her notebook. While Jennifer and Hills attended to the medical at Cliff Palace, the two of them had divided up all the stories in need of checking. "The lie detector part," Stanton had called it. A line cut down the middle of the yellow notepaper. On Anna's side was "Policy, Truck, Rose/Radio" and "Beavens/Veil." In her own handwriting was added "Stephanie/Dane." On Stanton's side was "Silva/Gun/Threats."

Stanton's day had been a complete washout. Before he could question him, Silva had been let out on bail, paid not by Patsy but by Ted Greeley. Neither Greeley nor Silva could be found.

Anna's half of the investigation had gone well. One phone call proved Rose Meyers a member of the liars' club. The two-hundred-thousand-dollar life insurance policy she'd shown Anna had been canceled six months previously for lack of payment.

Knowing the truth without knowing the rationale behind it was fairly useless. Maybe Rose was not yet aware the policy had been canceled—or knew but wasn't ready to admit it to herself or anyone else. Maybe she'd been trying to impress Stanton. An underpaid public servant might find a lady a wee bit more enticing if she had two hundred grand. Money was a proven aphrodisiac.

Whatever the reason, Mutual Casualty and Life told Anna there was no policy, no payoff. Rose had said Stacy'd left them with nothing, then changed her tune when the truth was nothing.

Red seven on black eight; nothing revealed. She turned over another three cards.

It seemed unlikely Rose would be lying to Bella and Hattie about the operation. That would be cruel, and despite her dislike of the woman, Anna believed that in her own way Rose loved her daughter. Therefore logic would suggest Rose did have money. Fact indicated it did not come from where she'd claimed.

Anna was too old to believe that people always lied for a reason. Mostly they lied because it was easy, felt good, or was habit. However, this particular lie was complex, suggesting a more focused motive. If Rose wanted to hide the source of the money, it was probably illegal or embarrassing.

Greeley as a potential new stepdaddy might have that kind of capital. Would Rose want to admit she and Ted were that intimate? Sharing a bed meant nothing but sharing a checkbook was a real commitment. And money was a stronger motive for murder than love.

Anna put a red four on a red five, woke up to her game, and took it back. Things just weren't adding up: murdering one's spouse was passé. Stacy had no inheritance, no insurance, and though in a divorce he might sue for custody of Bella, he had the proverbial snowball's chance in hell of winning. Rose could be intimate with whomever's checkbook she pleased without much in the way of adverse consequences.

If there was a good reason for Rose to kill her husband, Anna was missing it. A woman scorned crossed her mind but she dismissed it. Her own presumed affair with Stacy might possibly foment a woman miffed, but hardly scorned.

Twenty-four-carat motive or not, Rose had a lot of money and was lying about where she'd gotten it. That qualified her as a suspect.

"Truck," the next item on Stanton's hit list, referred to the elusive truck Beavens reported hearing and Anna and Stanton had chased. A tour of the housing areas revealed the whereabouts of thirteen trucks. Trucks were in vogue even for suburbanites. In parks they were de rigueur. Without exception they were teensy little Toyotas, Ford Rangers—toy trucks. Only Tom Silva owned a good old-fashioned bubba truck complete with shovel and gun rack. But even Silva's Chevy couldn't grind out the kind of racket that had pulled Anna and Stanton from their chindi vigil.

The thought of Silva jogged something in the back of Anna's tired mind. She set down the playing cards and stared into her wine as if waiting for a vision. Trucks and Tom and noise and trucks and Tom . . . It was coming to her. Back in June, before all the fuss, Tom had complained a "big goddamn truck" almost ran him off the road. Anna remembered following up on his complaint just to prove she was fair-minded and finding nothing. She'd even written a case incident report to keep her credit good. Later Silva'd said he was just "jerking her chain."

Tom drove a real pickup and wore cowboy shirts with the sleeves ripped out. What would he consider big? Surely not a snubby-nosed little Mitsubishi. To a construction worker, "big truck" would mean a Kenmore, a Peterbilt, a Mac.

First a truck, then no truck, now a truck. Another lie. Anna swallowed the medium through which the oracle had revealed this truth.

Next on the list was "Rose/Radio." That had been a worthless line of inquiry. Rose had returned belt, gun, and radio to the CRO around two o'clock. When Anna'd dared ask if she'd lent or used the radio, Rose had climbed into an uncommunicative huff and departed.

Feeling spiteful, Anna had taken the radio out of its leather holster and dusted the hard plastic case for fingerprints. There wasn't a print on it. Either Rose was an anal-retentive housekeeper or it had been wiped clean so the last user could go undetected.

"Beavens/Veil" had proved a bit easier. At least Beavens was still speaking to Anna, that was a start. She'd found him down in Spruce Tree House just as he was being relieved for a meal break. He'd brought a bag lunch and they sat together in the cool of the alcove at the rear of the ancient pueblo amid the prosaic needs of a modern-day Park Service: oxygen bottle, backboard, first-aid kit, and white helium-filled balloons. The last interpreter out of the ruin in the evening affixed these to the upper ramparts. Al Stinson's brainchild, the balloons kept the vultures from roosting and whitewashing the national historic treasure with bird droppings.

Beavens had been his usual self: shrugging, replying to everything with "no big deal." Halfway through his bag of Doritos—that and a ruin-temperature Dr Pepper constituted lunch—Anna noticed he was nervously fingering a gold chain around his neck. At an earlier meeting she remembered him holding on to a small gold cross suspended from it as Stanton had questioned him about the veil.

On a hunch, she turned the conversation along more spiritual lines. After a moment's silence, she said, "One thing I don't like about living in the park is it's so far to church."

Beavens' face, pasty despite the best efforts of the high desert sun, lit up for the first time in Anna's short acquaintance with him. Animation lent him youth and even a certain charm. "Have you accepted Jesus as your personal savior?" he asked.

Such was the hope in his voice, Anna might have felt guilty had she not been fairly sure she'd stumbled on the key that would unlock his confidence. "Washed in the blood of the lamb a year ago next month," she said.

A boyish smile curved up the corners of his mouth and transformed his face. "You!" he exclaimed. "I never would have guessed."

"The Lord works in mysterious ways."

"Amen. Which church do you go to?" He was leaning forward, defenses down. Anna didn't want to lose him with a wrong answer.

"I've only been here a couple months. So far I haven't

found anything that really works for me," she equivocated.

Beavens nodded sympathetically. "I can't find anything either. This New Age stuff is like a cancer. It's eaten away a lot of real belief. Maybe we could get together a Bible study group up on the mesa?"

Anna had a sinking feeling she was going to pay dearly for this particular deception. "The park is kind of a magnet for the New Agers," she said. "What with crystals and the American Indian thing that's caught on."

Beavens' face continued to look receptive, so she pressed on. "All this sitting around in kivas waiting for spirits, I don't know . . ." She trailed off, hoping he would fill in with his own ideas. She wasn't disappointed.

"It's just an invitation to Satan, that's all it amounts to," he said eagerly. "The Bible warns us that there'll be stumbling blocks on the road to heaven. These people are just providing the Devil with tools—or maybe I should say fools—to do his work. It's like holding séances or messing with Ouija boards. You can't go calling up this kind of stuff. You've got to turn away from it, turn to the Bible."

"Prayer," Anna said.

"Yes!" Beavens looked relieved beyond measure; someone understood him.

Anna ignored a mild pang of remorse. "What with all that's been happening, I kind of think the demons have been called up already."

In the middle of a sip of Dr Pepper, Beavens nodded his agreement and nearly choked himself to death. When he'd recovered somewhat, he managed to squeak out: "Burke, the spirit veil."

Now Anna leaned forward. "Summer solstice—the night you saw the interp's truck—"

"Heard it."

"Heard it, then. Did you really see the veil?" she asked as one conspirator might ask another.

"I saw something," Beavens replied in the same tone. "But we can't give it credence, can't spread the bad word. I say get thee behind me, Satan!" He laughed, but Anna could see he was serious, nervous and serious. He was fiddling with the cross again.

An instinct to pounce welled up strongly. Forcing it down, she leaned back and crossed her ankles. "That kind of thing spreads like wildfire," she agreed. "People want to believe in signs and portents."

"Original sin," Beavens said.

Anna didn't know where that fit in or exactly what it was. Sister Mary Judette had explained it in religion class but that was close to thirty years before. To say something, she threw in a cliché from her own formative years and hoped it was general enough to fit any conversational requirement: "If you're not part of the solution, you're part of the problem."

"Exactly."

"What was it like, the something you saw?"

"Weird," Beavens confided. "'Spirit veil' is a pretty good description. It's Jamie Burke, she'd better cut it out, too. She's got no idea who she's messing with."

Anna looked interested.

"She's got half the interps in the park watching and thinking and waiting. So it shows up. You call up the Devil, he comes."

Anna nodded sagely. "Was it like a kind of curtain?" She brought the conversation back to where she wanted it.

"Kind of. An iridescent shimmer. Maybe a hundred feet long. It was really neat-looking," he said, then thinking better of it added, "But then it would be, wouldn't it?"

Another interpreter, a frosted blonde art teacher from

Oklahoma, came into the shade of the alcove. "They're all yours, Claude," she said as she took a Flintstones lunch box out of the first-aid cabinet and sat down cross-legged on the smooth stone floor.

Anna walked Beavens out into the sunlight. "You didn't want to admit seeing the veil because it'd just give the Devil his due? Recruiting for him, sort of?"

"No sense being Lucifer's patsy."

As Anna turned to go, he followed her a couple of steps. "Let's do that Bible study, okay?"

"Anytime." Anna escaped into a knot of visitors.

So there had been something—a spirit veil or the Devil's shirttail, but definitely something.

Anna stared at the cards on the table. Nothing left to play. Miss Mouse was back, poking her little gray nose around the door frame from the direction of the kitchen. "I've got a cat," Anna threatened. The mouse twitched her whiskers but didn't run away.

Eyes down at the tabletop with its scattered playing cards, Anna rested her head in her hands. Three choices: finish her wine and try to get some sleep, deal another hand of solitaire, or cheat. Cheating seemed the most profitable course.

Shuffling the remaining cards into what she hoped would prove a more cooperative order, she eyed the last item on the list, the one she had written: "Stephanie/Dane."

Hills would have a few choice words to say about the phone bill she'd run up tracking them down. Stephanie McFarland was the asthmatic girl she and Stacy had carried out of Cliff Palace. The child who had died. Dane was the boy helitack had evacuated earlier in the day. Both were young and, other than asthma, in good condition. Both sets of parents had insisted the children had been up at seven thousand feet before without ill effects.

Fourteen long-distance calls had gathered the information Anna'd been looking for. Both children had had previous attacks of like severity. Stephanie's had been triggered by fumes when as a child she'd locked herself in a broom closet and shattered a bottle of cleaning solution in her attempts to dislodge the door. By the time her mother had found her she was suffering statis asthmaticus and she very nearly lost her life.

After a bit of cajoling, the ER nurse at Southwest Memorial in Cortez told Anna Dane's parents, Eli and Dina Bjornson, were staying at the Aneth Lodge. Immediate danger to their son past, they'd been fairly communicative. Dane had had one serious attack before, brought on not by radon or sniffing glue but by exposure to chemical Mace some boys at his junior high school had been playing with.

One explanation of the Cliff Palace incidents was that the ruin was exhaling poisonous vapors, perhaps the dying breath of the fabled underworld blowing through the sipapus. Stacy had been reaching toward the entrance to that world with his last dying gasp. Or so the corpse had appeared. Anna put no credence in the underworld as a mythical entity but there had been cases of poisonous gas, naturally generated, escaping to the detriment of humankind. Could that be the rationale behind the sudden and complete departure of the Old Ones? A phenomenon that for some geological reason was just now reasserting itself?

Another solution was coincidence. Two asthmatic kids with similar medical histories collapse within a few weeks of one another on a Tuesday morning. Not really much of a coincidence. It wouldn't have raised an eyebrow with Anna had it not been for Stacy and the rest of the Tuesday Morning Club.

Anna was stuck with the facts: something or someone was causing people to collapse in Cliff Palace on Tuesday mornings. Not random, not coincidental, not paranormal, but cause and effect. Anna figured the culprit or culprits were individuals with greater material desires than your average ghost.

She turned her mind back to her solitaire game. Reshuffling hadn't broken a single space loose. She gathered up the playing cards and reboxed them. Miss Mouse had gone to bed. Anna would follow suit.

She'd just swallowed the last of the dry red sleeping draught when the phone rang. In the dead of night it was always a sickening sound, though at Mesa Verde nine times out of ten it was a false alarm from the concessions facility. The new motion detectors were so sensitive, the least vibration set them off, sometimes two or three times in a night. Anna often wondered how much money the hapless taxpayers had forked out in overtime so fully armed rangers could shoo mice out of the Hostess Twinkies. With the monies concessions pulled in they could easily afford Pinkertons.

Again the phone rang. Anna threw herself on it as if it were a hand grenade. Half the night she'd been up, and if there was any overtime to be had she was damned if she'd let anyone else get it.

"Mesa Verde."

A short silence followed, punctuated by a sharp intake of breath. "What?" came a faltering voice.

"Mesa Verde National Park," Anna elaborated. "You've reached our emergency number."

"This is an emergency?" the voice said uncertainly. It was either a very timid woman or a small child.

"What can I help you with?"

"A car's gone off the road down here. I think some-body's still inside."

Anna felt her stomach tighten and her mind clear. "Where are you calling from?"

"A phone by the road."

There were only two, one at Delta Cut and one at Bravo Cut, two places where the road to the mesa top sliced through the side of a hill. "Are you closer to the bottom of the mesa or the top?"

"The top, I think."

"Are you hurt?"

"I don't think so, I mean no, I'm not. We . . . I was out on the point looking at the lights when we . . . I saw the headlights go over. They're way down. Somebody drove off. That's all I know." There was a click and the interview was over. Whoever had called had been out frolicking under the stars, Anna guessed, with an inappropriate "we" and, now that the altruism brought on by shock had worn thin, had thought better of involvement.

Delta Cut was sheer on one side, a dirt-and-stone bank rising vertically from the roadbed. The other side dropped off precipitously in a jungle of serviceberry and oakbrush. Unless traveling at impossible speeds, a passenger car wouldn't have the clout to break through the iron and concrete. A vehicle over the edge would've had to run past the railing on one end or the other.

Anna changed phones and put in a call to Frieda from the bedroom as she pulled on her uniform trousers. Frieda would wake up someone to bring the ambulance and call out helitack in case a low-angle rescue was needed.

The call completed, Anna banged on Jennifer Short's bedroom door. No one grunted. Jennifer slept like the dead. Anna pushed open the door but the room was empty. Either Jennifer was partying late or had gotten lucky and found a more entertaining bed for the night.

Stars hung close to the mesa, not dulled by moisture or atmosphere. A half-moon spilled enough light to see by. Garbage was strewn over the walk, and as she walked to the car Anna saw a big brown rump vanishing into the underbrush. When she returned she'd clean up the mess and not mention the marauder to the brass. At Mesa Verde the solution to problem bears might be to shoot first and justify later.

As she backed the patrol car out of the lot and started down the main road the three miles to Delta Cut, she ran through her EMS checklist. Rehearsing emergency medical procedures and inventorying available equipment calmed and centered her.

With no traffic to slow her, she reached Delta Cut before she'd played out more than a few possible scenarios. Not surprisingly, no car waited at the pull-out. The phone box hung open as if deserted in haste. Anna pulled the Ford into the left lane, switched on her spot light, and cruised slowly along the guardrail.

Serviceberry grew thickly down the bank, camouflaging drops and ravines. Late blooms glowed white. Beyond, the thickets were impenetrable in their darkness. Anna rolled down the car's windows and listened but nothing was audible over the hum of the engine.

A crank call? It hadn't sounded it. Crank calls were usually accompanied by a background of party-animal noises. A trap? The thought made the little hairs on the back of her neck crawl. Could someone have lured her out in the dead of night for sinister purposes? Highly unlikely, she soothed herself. For one thing, there was no guarantee she'd be the one to answer the '69 line, for another, who could've guessed she'd come alone other than Jennifer and whomever she was with? The only reason for making her a target was the Meyers investigation and she hadn't exactly been burning up the turf in that department.

Reassured by her own sense of inadequacy, she left the patrol car to walk the same ground. Free from the distraction of machinery, she found what she was looking for. Eighty or a hundred feet down the bank, almost hidden by the thick foliage, was the yellow glow of automobile headlights. To the left of the lights she could just make out the pale shape of a vehicle's body and adjusted her thoughts: not a car, a pickup truck, white or yellow in color.

Having radioed in the exact location of the wreck, she collected the jump kit and a flashlight, backtracked to the end of the barricade, and shone the light into the brush. A barely discernible trail of broken branches and scarred earth showed where the truck had left the pavement. There were no skid marks, no deep cuts in the sod indicating the brakes had been applied.

Hunching up like a woman in a windstorm, she forced her way through the brush, following the broken trail. Four or five yards down the steep bank the ground fell away. A cliff, maybe thirty feet high, was cut into the hillside where the undergrowth had let go of unstable soil during the previous winter's snows. Dirt and scree dropped down to a rubble of boulders scattered on a shoulder of land. Past that was a sheer drop to the valley floor, where the lights of Cortez twinkled invitingly.

The pickup had cut through the brush at the point where she stood, then hurtled over the embankment. Boulders stopped its fall. The nose of the truck was crushed, the windshield and both side windows smashed. Either time was of the essence or all the time in the world would not be enough. Whoever was inside would be lucky to be alive.

Anna'd been carrying the orange jump kit in front of her like a shield. Now she strapped it on her back. Eroded soil made the bank soft enough she could work her way down crablike, heels and butt breaking the descent. Prickly pear sank disinterested fangs into the palm of her right hand and she swore softly. Tomorrow, without adrenaline for an anesthetic, the barbs would itch and burn.

From above, she heard the whooping cry of the ambulance approaching and was glad of the company.

At the bottom of the broken bank, the ground leveled out in a litter of rocks from fist- to house-size. Anna leaped from one to another, her balance made uncertain by the moving flashlight beam.

The truck was wedged between two rocks. One beneath the front axle, the other crumpling back the hood and holding the vehicle at an angle almost on its right side. Both rear wheels and the front left tire were free of the ground. The front tire still turned slowly. The crash had been recent and Anna felt a spark of hope that she was not too late.

"Anna!" It was Hills on her radio.

"Down here," she responded, flashing her light up to the road till she got an answering flash.

"What've we got?" Hills asked.

"Stand by."

Between her and the cab were two boulders roughly the size of Volkswagens and woven together by a tangle of oak brush. For lack of a better place, Anna shoved the flashlight down the front of her shirt, then, hands free, scrambled to the top of the first boulder and jumped the crevice to the second.

The tilted cab was on a level with the rock, the driver's door parallel with the top of the stone where she stood. Heat radiated from beneath the hood; the engine was still running. Anna rescued her flash and surveyed the scene. Broken and hanging in fragments, the safety glass of the side window fell in ragged sheets. Isolated pieces sparkled in the beam. From the interior came strains of country-western music. A faint green glow emanated from the dashboard lights. All else was lost in a darkness fractured by moonlight through fragmented glass.

Anna unstrapped the jump kit. Cursing her slick-soled Wellington boots, she inched down the boulder where it sloped to within eighteen inches of the truck. Spinning gently, the pickup's front tire, along with the broken angles of metal and stone, gave her an unsettling sense of vertigo, as if she might topple into the window as into a bottomless well.

At the boulder's edge she stopped, recovered her equilibrium, and peered inside. From her new vantage point, the cab and a small slice of the passenger door were visible. On the far window, where it had been forced inward, drops of ruby mixed with the glittering diamonds of glass.

Fresh blood was startlingly red—too red for paintings or movies. Comic-book red; believable only in fantasy and real life.

Gingerly, Anna pushed at the truck's exposed undercarriage with a foot. It held steady. Apparently the truck was wedged firmly between the rocks. How firmly, she was about to find out.

Getting down on her knees, she restored the flashlight to its bruising hammock between buttons and breasts and crawled her hands out onto the door. Bit by bit she transferred her weight from the rock. The truck remained stable. Emboldened, she brought one knee onto the door. catching hold of the handle to keep herself steady.

Moonlight reflected off the white paint. Details, overwhelmed by the hard light of day, were surrealistically clear: a pencil-thin scratch beneath the side mirror, a square patch where a sticker had been inexpertly removed, fading black stenciled lettering, once showy flourishes almost obliterated by time, spelling the initials T. S.

Tom Silva, Anna realized. It was his truck. Better a stranger; no psychological buttons pushed interfering with efficiency.

Pulling herself up to her knees on the slanting metal, she braced butt on heels and took the flashlight from inside her shirt. Silva was crushed down on the far side of the cab, his back to her. One leg trailed behind him, wedged beneath the driver's pedals. His left arm, the palm turned up, rested on the hump between the seats. She couldn't see his face. "Tom," she called clearly. "Can you hear me?" No response.

Having wrested the King from her duty belt she made her assessment out loud, sharing it with Hills. "One individual, white male," she began, avoiding Silva's name lest Patsy or the girls should hear in such a manner. "About thirty-five. Unconscious, no seat belt. He's half on the floor at the far side of the cab nearest the ground. He submarined," she added, taking note of where the operator's pedals had bent and the floor mat ripped when Silva's unrestrained body was hurled beneath the steering wheel. "His right leg's broken. The foot caught beneath the clutch and twisted a hundred and eighty degrees from anatomical position. I can't see his face but there's a lot of blood on the dash and windows."

In the minute the climb and assessment had taken, the

rubies had pooled into a puddle of crimson. As she spoke it spread, a bright beautiful stream dripping from dash to windshield. "Bring the Stokes, backboard, oxygen, and jaws of life. I'm off radio now, I'm going to try and get to him." She heard the ubiquitous "ten-four" as she doffed her gunbelt and tossed it back onto the boulder. The radio she kept, using its heavy leather case to knock the remaining glass from the window frame.

"Sorry about that," she muttered as fragments rained down on Silva's back, caught shining in his hair.

One hand on either side of the window, she lowered her legs into the cab until she straddled the body of the man inside. Her left foot was on top of the passenger door above the shattered glass. Her right foot she wedged in the angle made by the windshield and the dash inches from where Silva's head rested.

Hanging on tightly to the outside door handle lest her precarious perch give way, she stretched down and switched off the ignition. Blessedly, the tinny sounds of country pop were silenced and the bizarre party feeling quenched. A click of the headlight button turned on the interior light and she freed up the hand she used to hold the flashlight.

Edging down till her knees rested along the upper edge of the passenger door, she slipped two fingers between Silva's jaw and shoulder, seeking by touch his carotid artery. Blood, warm and slippery, reminded her she'd forgotten to put on rubber gloves. Rangers with emergency response duties were required to be given hepatitis B vaccinations, but at a hundred and fifty bucks for each ranger, Hills couldn't bring himself to comply. AIDS, there was no shot for.

"You better be clean, Tom," Anna said as she pressed down. No pulse. Holding on to the rearview mirror for support, she crouched lower and repositioned her fingers in the hollow of Silva's neck beside his trachea.

"Bingo," she breathed as she felt the faint and thrilling thread of life. Given the mechanism of injury—a headlong flight off a cliff—and the absence of a seat belt, there was a good chance Silva had suffered damage to his spine and she was loath to move him without at least a short backboard. "Hills," she barked into the radio. "Where are you guys?"

"Just starting down."

"Jesus," she whispered. Since she'd dropped into the truck it seemed as if half an hour must have passed but she knew in reality it had been minutes. "It's bad," she said. "Bring a short spineboard. He's all crunched down on the passenger side and the truck's tipped. We'll have to haul him straight up through the driver's door."

Hills undoubtedly responded but Anna'd quit listening. Silva had made a sound. She crouched as low as she could, the man's dark head between her knees. Cupping his chin in her left hand, she supported his head and neck in the position she'd found it. "Tom, Tom, it's Anna."

A gurgle, half felt through her fingers, half heard, came from the injured man. Liquid trickled over her fingers where they curled around his chin. "Hang in there, Tom, help's here. Stay with me. We'll get you out."

"No," came out with more blood. "Killed Pats."

The adrenaline rush in Anna turned to cold horror. With her free hand she fumbled the radio from where it rested on the drunken tilt of the dash and held it to her mouth. Her right leg had begun to shake uncontrollably. "Hills, send somebody to check on Patsy Silva."

He asked something but Anna'd dropped her radio. The fragile beat of life beneath her fingers had stopped. "Fuck."

Silva was wearing a denim jacket, the collar turned up. Grasping collar and shoulder seams in her fists, she pulled the dead weight upward, straightening her legs to take some of the strain off her back. Silva's head fell against her forearm. In the uncompromising light of the dome she could see the gash in his forehead. White bone gleamed through the torn flesh.

Grunting with the effort, she pulled him chest high and wedged her right knee under his rump. Locking him in her arms, she looked up at the driver's window a couple of inches above her head. Impossibly far. Silva was a slight man, not more than one hundred and thirty-five or forty pounds, but she doubted she could push that much weight over her head.

"Come on, Tom, don't wimp out on me, damn you, come on," she murmured in his ear. Blood dropped onto her neck. "On three, ready, Tom. Jesus!" Anna coiled the strength she had into her legs and back. "One, two, three!" With all the power she could muster she pushed Tom up toward the night sky. Her back creaked in protest and she felt the muscles burn and grow watery in her shoulders.

Eyes squeezed shut, she tried to force him beyond her strength, but the soft weight of him was slipping from her.

Then, miraculously, he went, his body light as air. Anna's eyes sprang open and the air exploded from her lungs. Her hands fell away and still Silva rose like Christ on Easter. As his feet drew level with her face, Anna heard voices. For an instant, Drew's face was visible in the glare of someone's light. He held Silva by the shirtfront, supporting him with one arm.

"Get him flat," Anna shouted. With shaking arms, she tried to lever herself out of the cab. Drew grabbed her wrists, lifted her clear of the truck, and set her on the rock near Tom. "Get me an airway," Anna said. "He had breath and pulse not a minute ago."

Crawling, she positioned herself over Silva's chest, placed two fingers on his carotid and her ear an inch from his mouth. "Damn."

"Nothing?" Drew asked.

"Nothing. Airway," she snapped. Behind her she could hear Hills pawing through the jump kit. She tilted Silva's jaw, pinched his nose, and blew two slow breaths into his lungs. "Compressions, Drew."

The big man leaned over Silva and, elbows locked, depressed the man's chest for five counts, forcing blood through the now quiet heart and into the dying organs. Anna breathed for Silva. Five more compressions and another breath.

Sour vomit from Silva's stomach filled Anna's mouth and she spat it out, refusing to let her own bile rise in its wake. "Airway," she barked as Drew compressed the chest.

A curved plastic oropharyngeal airway was pressed into her palm and she took a second to work the plastic into Silva's throat to keep his airway patent.

Drew compressed and Anna performed rescue breathing while the backboard was moved into place. The time for delicacy was past. Emergency personnel often referred to the Golden Hour, those first sixty minutes in which quick transport to a medical facility can still save a life. Time for Silva was running out, if, indeed, not already gone.

Unceremoniously, Silva was slid onto the board and strapped in the Stokes. Paul Summers took one end, Hills the other and lifted. Anna breathed, Drew compressed.

"Can't do it," Paul cried, shame and anger hot in his voice. The downward pressure of the compressions were too strong for him to support.

"Switch," Anna called.

Drew moved to the head of the Stokes and Paul took over compressions. "Breathe," she said, and blew into Silva's lungs.

"And one, and two . . ." Paul counted off as they crabbed awkwardly along the two boulders.

"Stop," Drew ordered when they reached the edge of the second rock. Anna and Paul stepped back. Drew set the litter down, Hills knelt still holding his end. The helitack foreman jumped from the rock then took up the Stokes again.

Hills scrambled down and they moved with startling speed over the river of boulders. Paul and Anna ran after. The big men, the litter, the moonlight, the rocking and rocky passage, gave the scene a jerky, keystone-cops look and Anna felt inappropriate laughter pushing up in her throat.

It came out in gasps as they reached the foot of the steep incline.

"Now," Drew said.

Anna felt for pulse, listened for breathing. Nothing. Again she gave two slow rescue breaths, then Paul began compressions. Bones broke—Silva's ribs—another rescue breath, five compressions.

Jimmy appeared from somewhere with ropes. Stanton's voice behind Anna said, "Can I spell you?" Anna blew oxygen into Silva's lungs, then shook her head. Five more compressions, more ribs snapping.

"Stop," Drew commanded.

Gratefully, Anna stepped back and wiped her mouth on

the back of her hand. The Stokes was roped up. Jimmy and Stanton had regained the top of the dirt slope and on a three count began to haul Silva upward.

CPR couldn't be interrupted for more than a minute. Without bothering to catch her breath, Anna began to claw her way up the incline. On the other side of the Stokes, she could see Paul bounding up the hill and envied him his youth.

The Stokes bumped to a halt on the cliff top. Anna was there waiting. "Now," Drew ordered. No breath, no pulse: Anna blew into the lungs. Paul did compressions. Bile spewed up, the acid burning Anna's lips. She spit it out and heard gagging. For a second she thought it was Silva breathing on his own, but it was Stanton.

The agent pushed ahead, trying to keep the oakbrush from scraping the rescuers away from their patient. Branches scratched Anna's face and hands but she was aware of them only peripherally, she didn't feel the sting or cut.

Finally they broke free of the brush. In minutes the Stokes was loaded into the ambulance. "Jimmy drives. Me, Drew, Paul, here in back. You guys see if you can figure out what happened." Hills slammed the door on the last of his words and the ambulance drove off, leaving Anna and Frederick standing in the middle of the road.

Darkness and stillness returned. The moon, temporarily eclipsed by the ambulance lights, reasserted its dominion. Shadows softened. Night creatures began timid explorations. Anna noticed she was cold and her back hurt like the dickens.

Pressing her hands into the small of her sacrum, she stretched in an attempt to ease it. "I've lost my strength of ten men," she said to Stanton.

The FBI agent was looking at her oddly and pawing at the side of his mouth. Moonlight gave his face a ghoulish cast. Primitive fear of the dark pricked Anna's sensitized nerves.

"What?" she demanded. "What is it?"

"You've . . . um . . . got something . . ." Tentatively he reached toward her but pulled back short of actually touching her. "It's . . . ah . . . vomit."

Anna wiped her mouth. Sour-smelling chunks came off in her hand. "I hate CPR. They're dead. If they don't sit up and take notice in the first sixty seconds, they're going to stay dead. But we've got to pound and poke and blow just like it made sense. Got a hankie?"

Stanton fished an enormous white handkerchief from his hip pocket and handed it to her. She scrubbed her mouth and cheeks, then pocketed it out of deference to his hypersensitive gag reflex.

"So, what happened?" Stanton turned and looked down the hill. Oakbrush and serviceberry had closed ranks, creating a wall impervious to the moonlight. Beyond, down the sharp slope, the pickup's carcass showed as a paler boulder in the boulder field.

"Drunk, I would guess. The cab reeked of alcohol, among other things." Anna, too, stared down the slope. The excitement over, fatigue weighed heavily and the thought of climbing back down the hill wasn't pleasant.

"Got a flashlight?" Stanton asked.

"It's down there. You?"

"Not me. Got a spare in your car?"

"Of course. Doesn't work though." The dark grew darker. Prickly pear spines lodged in Anna's hand were making themselves felt.

"The blind leading the blind?" Stanton asked.

"I'll go first."

"Good. Snakes and things, you know."

"First person just wakes them up and makes them mad. They always bite the second person. That's a proven statistic."

"Where'd you read it?" Stanton demanded as he hurried after her into the arms of the oakbrush.

"*U.S. News and World Report.*" Anna gave him the standard comeback of the 1968 Mercy High School debate team.

Without lights, music, and Silva, the wreck looked old, all life gone, metal bleached like bones. Anna appreciated its peacefulness. Lowering herself back down into the cab, she felt a kinship with Tom. It had less to do with ghosts than with the now all-pervasive odor of alcohol.

"Here but for the grace of God" crossed her mind like a prayer as she remembered the night she'd lost to booze and self-pity.

By the dome light, she retrieved her flashlight from where it had fallen down next to the door and passed it up to Agent Stanton.

Searching the cab was a job for a contortionist. Anna squatted over the broken passenger window and poked through the debris that had been shaken from under the seat and floor mats. A pack of Marlboros, two cigarettes remaining that would go unsmoked; five empty cans of Budweiser and one full, still cold to the touch; a McDonald's bag, the contents so old they no longer smelled; bits of paper, maps, and registration from the glove box; a pencil with a chewed eraser and broken lead; and a golf ball completed the inventory. But for the golf ball, it was more or less what she had expected to find. Silva didn't strike her as a golf sort of guy. A bowling ball or squirrel rifle would have been more in keeping with the image she had of him.

Hoisting herself out of the cab, she sat on the door with her feet still inside. The effort cost her a wrenching pain in her lower back, muscles protesting the lifting of one hundred and forty pounds.

"Ooof!" Stanton dragged himself up on the boulder nearby. "Find anything?"

"Just what you'd expect: beer, cigarettes, fast food. The detritus of a misspent youth."

"I didn't find anything revelatory outside the truck," Stanton said. "We ought to come back by the light of day but it looks like what it is: DUI with fatality. Back on the hill the truck left the ground and was airborne till it struck here. What I want to know is where Silva was between getting bailed out of jail and getting killed."

"Killed. Patsy!" Anna remembered with a fresh sense of horror. "Tom said he'd killed her."

18

PATSY WAS fine, at least until they told her about Tom. "Seriously injured" was how Anna put it. One of the great contributions of cardiopulmonary resuscitation was that nobody ever died on a carry-out, or in an ambulance, for that matter. Through the vomit and the cracking bones and the blood, the body was kept pumped up with oxygen, the organs pantomiming life till a doctor pronounced it officially dead.

Patsy wept like a shattered bride. Regardless of divorce, this had apparently been a till-death-do-you-part kind of relationship. "There's always hope, Mom," Missy said, holding her mother's shoulders in an odd moment of role reversal.

Anna had ambivalent feelings about hope. Just because artists depicting the last refugee from Pandora's box always dressed the horrid little bugger like Tinkerbell, people tended to think hope was a good thing. Often it was the worst of the evils let loose to plague humankind.

"Is there hope?" Patsy pleaded.

"It was pretty bad," Anna told her. "He was still talking when I got to him. He said your name."

Patsy cried harder but it was different and Anna was glad she'd kept the context of Tom's remark to herself.

The sun was rising when she and Agent Stanton left the tower house. Too tired to sleep, Anna sat for a moment behind the wheel of the patrol car, staring stupidly in front of her. "My back is killing me," she said to no one in particular though Frederick was in the seat next to her.

"Want me to drive?"

The offer sounded so halfhearted, Anna realized she'd never seen Stanton behind the wheel of a car. "Have you got a license?" she asked abruptly.

He laughed, a sound that soothed her frayed nerves. "Almost like new, only use it on Sundays."

"Don't like to drive?"

"I'd rather look out the window."

"It's not far." Anna referred to the tent frame Frederick was bivouacked in. "I'll drive."

"Goody. I'll give you a back rub. My first wife—or was it my second? Anyway, I come highly recommended in the back rub department."

Leaving the tower house, Anna turned right and drove three hundred yards the wrong way on the one-way to the tent colony where VIPs and stabilization crew were housed.

Like the other service areas in Mesa Verde, this was on a loop. Communal showers, toilets, washer/dryer, and pay phone occupied the island created by the gravel drive.

Some of the dwellings were charming. Of native stone, they were built in the round style of Navajo hogans, but the majority were single-room plywood shacks called tent frames. Sixteen by sixteen feet square, they had just room for a bed, stove, and refrigerator. There was no running water. At one time they'd been wooden platforms with canvas forming the walls and roof. When housing became short, they'd been walled in and wood-burning stoves added to give them a longer season of use.

Though cramped and primitive, Anna saw in them

blessed privacy and a home for Piedmont. When Stanton left, she would lean on Hills to give her his tent frame till permanent housing became available.

She pulled the Ford into the graveled spot in front of number seventeen. A picnic table under the junipers provided a platform for two scrub jays squabbling over a bit of orange peel. A fire pit with grill was near the table. "I could live here," Anna said.

"Come in. I'll give you the fifty-cent tour. Make some decaf."

Not ready yet to go home, Anna accepted. The tour consisted of "Honey, I'm home," called to imaginary scorpions. Anna sat on the single bed. It was made up so neatly it worried her. What kind of man made his bed when called out on a motor vehicle accident at three A.M.?

Apparently reading her mind, Stanton said: "Not anal retentive." He pointed to the long wooden table that occupied the wall between the wood stove and the foot of the bed. It was covered with papers and sketches, some in tidy piles, some scattered about where he'd been working into the wee hours.

Anna got up and looked to keep herself occupied while Stanton busied himself with coffee, drawing the water from a five-gallon plastic container with a spigot.

Photos of Stacy in the kiva, of the shoes with burn marks, were laid out neatly. Drawings of the kiva, of Cliff Palace—quite good drawings—with entrance and exits marked, were placed like maps above the autopsy and 10-344 report. Lists were everywhere; lists of clues and suspects, lists of things done and things left to do, lists of lists.

"Not anal retentive, you say?"

"Well, not about housework anyway. Although my second ex-wife—or was it my first—thought I should be."

"You don't think much of marriage, I take it?"

"Are you kidding? It's my favorite hobby. Spend every spare penny on it. I'm completely in favor of it, wish both ladies would remarry today."

Anna laughed. "No doubt about it, widowhood has its upside." She took the coffee he offered and sat in the straight-backed wooden chair. There being no others, Stanton perched on the foot of his bed.

"Come up with any bright ideas?" Anna indicated the desk. The hasty report she'd written on her previous day's findings was lying above a legal pad where yet another list was forming. A pair of half glasses served as a paperweight.

"Nothing brilliant. I'm getting slow," he said. "Can't solve them in record time anymore. I used to do it with one victim. 'One-corpse Stanton' they called me. Now it takes two or three before I catch on."

He was poking fun at himself but Anna understood. There was no solving a crime till it happened. By then the damage was done. What kept the chase worth the effort was the hope a second could be prevented.

"Pushing forty-five," Stanton said. "Headed over the proverbial hill."

"Over the hill," Anna echoed.

"You aren't supposed to agree with me," he complained. "For a park ranger you sure don't know anything about fishing."

"No," Anna said absently. She put down her coffee and took the golf ball from her shirt pocket. "This was in Silva's truck."

"And?" Stanton looked at the little ball with interest. His instant attention was gratifying. She trusted Anna not to waste his time.

"Over the hill," Anna repeated. "In a conversation once,

Tom said he couldn't play golf because he wasn't over the hill yet."

"Not his ball."

"What do you figure would happen if you wedged a golf ball in the linkage over a gas pedal?"

"When the car crashed the ball would roll out."

"When the pickup crashed." Anna swiveled in her seat to set the ball down amidst Stanton's case work. Twisting tore the damaged muscles and she groaned.

"Ready for that back rub?" Stanton asked.

"No thanks." Anna had been given a goodly number of back rubs over the years. They'd been anything but relaxing and healthful. Most had degenerated fairly quickly into wrestling matches. She was too tired to defend her virtue.

"You'll like it. It'll be good for you. Really." Stanton was bustling: setting down coffee, grabbing up pillows and blankets. "I've been to school. I'm certified and everything." He carried the bedding out through the screen door.

He was shaking an army blanket out on the picnic table. The jays had fled to the branches of a nearby juniper and watched with interest. "Soft is no good," he was saying as Anna came up behind him. "You can't really do much with soft. Padded is best but this'll do." He plumped a pillow down on one end of the table. "Climb on up," he said. "Office hours have commenced."

More out of curiosity than anything else, Anna complied, lying belly-down on the tabletop.

"I'm a Rolfer," Stanton said, climbing up and straddling her. "A proponent and practitioner of the art of Rolfing." With that he pushed his knuckles into her back.

What followed was the least sexual and most healing

experience Anna had ever had. His strong fingers seemed to knead and pry the pain from between her muscles and realign her much maligned vertebrae.

When he'd finished, she lay quiet for another minute or so, enjoying the heat radiating through her back. "That's the first honest-to-God back rub I've ever had," she said truthfully.

By mutual agreement she and Stanton put the investigation on hold till they'd rested. Anna suffered from the pleasant but frustrating sense that things were just about to come clear, words on the tip of the tongue, connections about to be made. She doubted she'd be able to sleep but natural fatigue and the continuing warmth Stanton's fingers had worked into her back conspired to shut down her brain and she slept without dreaming.

Around two-thirty that afternoon she awoke. Even that late in the day she was doomed to a cold shower. "Sorry," Jennifer said when she stalked into the kitchen to make coffee. "I didn't figure anybody else'd be showering so late. I was steaming me out a hangover. A doozy. Alcohol poisoning of the worst kind. Have some of my coffee as a peace offerin' whilst yours does its thing."

Anna accepted a mugful and dressed it with a dollop of heavy whipping cream.

"How do you stay so skinny?" Jennifer demanded. "I get fat on NutraSweet and water."

"Are you on late today?" Anna asked.

"Yes ma'am. Till forever. I can't wait till you stop messin' with that FBI guy. With both you'n Stacy off the schedule, seems all I do is work night shifts."

Anna tried to look sympathetic out of gratitude for the coffee. "Where'd you get your hangover?"

Jennifer laughed, then clutched her head. "Jamie and I

did Durango. She's still in bed. You should've seen her. She got to arm-wrestling boys for drinks. She's just too strong for her own good. We like to drowned."

"Sounds like fun," Anna fed the conversation. Not yet through her first cup of coffee and already prying suspiciously into other people's lives; she'd be glad when the investigation was over and she could resume the life of a disinterested third party. "Who drove you home?"

"The bartender at Flannigan's took Jamie's car keys. We had to crash in her station wagon till he opened up around ten this morning."

Jennifer buckled on her gun and left Anna to finish the coffee.

By four-thirty Stanton still hadn't called. Anna left word with Dispatch to radio her if he checked in, and drove down to the CRO. The events of the previous night were settling in her mind and she needed to sort them out. Laying out facts in the no-nonsense format demanded by government form 10-343 seemed to help. As senior person on the scene, Hills should have written the report but Anna had no worries that he'd beaten her to the punch. Like a lot of district rangers, Hills had joined the NPS because of a love of hiking, canoeing, shooting, backpacking, climbing—challenging himself physically. When he climbed up into management he was forced to confront his worst fear: paperwork. Brawling drunks he could handle. The sight of a computer lit up the yellow streak down his broad back.

As she banged into the CRO, she asked Frieda, "Has Stanton called?"

"Not yet."

"Silva?"

"DOA. Massive cerebral hemorrhage."

"Too bad."

"Yes indeed. You, Hills, and the guys are scheduled to

do a fatality debriefing with Dr. Whitcomb Friday morning. Write it down."

Successfully resisting the urge to unload the night's pressures on Frieda, Anna slipped around the partition to her desk. As usual it was piled with clutter not of her making. Evidently Hills had dumped Stacy's personal defensive equipment there after inventorying it. Anna scooped it up to dump back on the district ranger's desk. The radio's leather case tumbled out of her clutches. "Whoa!"

"What?" Frieda called over the room divider.

"Nothing." Anna dropped the gunbelt back where she'd found it and pinched up the radio case between thumb and forefinger. Burnt into the leather were two prints, etched marks such as had manifested on Stacy's shoes. The prints on the case hadn't been there when Rose had returned it. Anna was sure of that. In her fingerprinting frenzy she would have noticed.

The prints on Stacy's shoes had taken between one and three days to appear. Lost as they'd been in her trunk, Anna couldn't be more precise.

If these marks came from the same hand, and it was hard to imagine they hadn't, they'd been made not more than one to three days previously, considerably after Stacy had died and before Rose had returned the radio.

Anna closed her eyes and ears and marshaled her thoughts. Whoever removed Stacy's shoes had used the radio. Whoever used the radio had access to Rose's house. Did Stacy's murder have anything to do with Silva's death? Probably. Two murders in one sleepy park were highly unlikely. Rose might have killed Stacy for some matrimonial crime as yet unpublished, but why Tom? Greeley killing Silva for pilfering, monkeywrenching? Overkill to say the least. *Strangers on a Train?* You kill mine, I'll kill yours.

There weren't enough players for a really good game of

detection, Anna thought. Drew was in and out of the picture. Clearly he felt Stacy and Rose were making the wrong choices for Bella. Did his protectiveness over children extend to Silva's? Did he believe Tom was abusing Missy and Mindy in some way? Anna thought back to the wreck. Drew's efforts to salvage Silva's life seemed genuine enough.

Rousing herself, Anna called over the wall. "Frieda, Stanton call yet?"

"You're sitting on the phone back there. Did it ring?"

"I guess not," Anna conceded. Taking the radio case, she again gave Frieda the message to let her know when Stanton woke up. Frieda rolled her eyes but Anna was wrapped up in her own thoughts and missed it.

There was one last thing to check, then she would go stir Stanton up whether he was rested or not.

The maintenance yard was empty when she drove in. Maintenance and Construction worked seven A.M. to three-thirty Monday through Friday. By three thirty-one there was never any sign of them.

As she'd expected, the chain-link gate to the fenced-off area where Ted Greeley kept his heavy equipment was locked, the chain and padlock as she had thought they would be.

Frieda called then and Anna abandoned her train of thought. Stanton was awake. She found him sitting on the picnic table with his feet on the bench nursing a cup of coffee.

"Good morning." She sat down beside him, adjusting her gun so the butt wouldn't pry against her ribs. "Get a good nap?"

"Yes indeedy. Is it still Monday?"

"All day."

Anna told Stanton about chains and locks and their connection with Stacy Meyers, Monday nights, and the Cliff Palace loop. "What I can't figure out is why and how. Without those, 'who' is pretty worthless."

Stanton took another sip of coffee. Anna wished he'd offer her some. Not because it looked particularly good, but because it was something to do with her hands. In lieu of the coffee, she picked up a twig and began methodically snapping it in small pieces.

They sat in silence for a time. The sun was low in the sky and bathed them in amber light. To the west, Anna could just see the tops of thunderheads. It was probably raining in Dove Creek. A small doe wandered out from behind the tent frame. The air was so still they could hear the tearing sound as she cropped the grass.

Stanton seemed transfixed by the nearness of the graceful animal.

"Missing Chicago?" Anna ribbed him.

"In Chicago we have rats bigger than that."

"Her."

"How can you tell?"

"No antlers."

"I thought they fell off."

"They grow back."

"No kidding!"

Anna felt her leg being gently pulled and laughed. "You're such a rube, Frederick."

The doe's head came up at the sound of laughter but the deer was looking not at them but down the footpath leading along the canyon's edge to the housing loop. Frederick and Anna watched with her. Moments later Bella and her aunt came into view. Bella was in the lead. In her arms she carried a basket woven of pastel strips, a relic of a previous Easter. If the care she took not to let the basket bump or tip was any indication of contents, Anna would've guessed nitroglycerin or at least goldfish. Hattie followed with a plastic spatula, the kind cooks use to scrape the last of the cake batter from the bowl.

"Howdy, Bella, Hattie," Frederick called.

"Fred and Anna!" To Bella, Hattie said: "I told you this was going to be a good walk. So far we've seen three deer, a chipmunk, a park ranger, and an FBI agent."

"An' a Abert squirrel," Bella added, clearly more impressed with the long-eared rodent than the last two sightings on her aunt's list.

Hattie left the footpath and forged through the high grass toward the picnic table. Ryegrass was beginning to plume and bright yellow mustard flowers dipped gracefully in her wake. Bella followed a few steps then stopped, hanging back.

"There's no snakes," Frederick assured her. "I made Ranger Pigeon check."

"Only babies are afraid of snakes," Bella returned. Anna forbore comment but bumped Stanton's knee with her own. "I don't want to get any stuff on you." Bella held the party-colored basket up like a dangerous offering.

"Is it full of nitroglycerin?" Anna asked.

"I don't know," Bella replied. "But probably not."

"Nitro's a liquid but it explodes like dynamite," Anna told her.

Clearly Bella didn't believe a word. "That'd be silly."

"You're right," Anna conceded.

"Battery acid," Frederick guessed.

"This is a basket," Bella said with a touch of impatience. "It'd leak out."

"Spiders," Anna tried.

Bella looked like that wasn't a bad idea but she shook her head. "It's sad thoughts. *Really* sad thoughts. Me and Aunt Hattie thought up all the saddest thoughts and we put them in the basket and we're going to dump 'em in the canyon when the winds go down."

"The winds aren't up," Anna remarked, noting the stillness of the evening.

"They are. Drew said. The winds go up in the morning and down at night."

Anna grabbed Frederick's arm. "Bella's right. You're right," she said to the child.

Slightly mollified, "Up at day, down at night," Bella reiterated. "We gotta go," she told her aunt.

"Gotta go," Hattie echoed, and, "Take care."

"Out of the mouths of babes," Anna said to Frederick as they watched the woman and girl pass out of sight behind a stand of piñons. "Firefighters always watch the winds. When the sun warms the air in the mornings it begins to rise and a wind blows up canyon. In the evening, as the cool air settles the wind shifts, blows down canyon. In the still of night it settles in the low areas. That's pounded into your head with a Pulaski in every fire class.

"You dump the sad thoughts at night, they blow down canyon, away, out to the wide valleys, and are dispersed. You dump them in the morning, when the sun rises, they blow up canyon, into the alcoves, settle into the ruins."

"Holy smoke," Stanton said. "A blinding flash of the obvious."

19

CLIFF PALACE loop was closed; the gate at the Four-Way closed the road and the starless night closed down the world. Clouds obscured a fledgling moon. Trees, crowding close to the road, seemed impervious even to headlights. Shadows were sudden, long, and unnatural.

"This whole place is one big graveyard. Doesn't that give you the willies?" Stanton asked.

"Only when I think about it." The Ford's beams were on low. If Anna'd had her druthers she'd've driven without lights but the night was too dark for that.

When the road widened into Cliff Palace parking lot, she switched them off.

"Yikes! What have we here?"

From the dim glow of the dashboard Anna could see where Stanton pointed. Along the split-rail fence separating the parking area from the trees were dozens of tiny glowing eyes, as if a herd of rats or other small night predators waited for the unwary.

"Glowworms," she told him. "Want to catch one?"

"No thanks. Wow. As in 'Glow, little glowworm, glow'? I'm disappointed. Not a 'glimmer glimmer' in the lot."

"Poetic license."

Again the road was enclosed by darkness. Anna slowed but didn't switch the headlights back on. From here to the Ute reservation the road ran along the canyon's rim. Though in most places there was a fringe of trees between the road and the canyon, any stray light could give them away.

At the Navajo taco stand on the tiny piece of reservation land accidently surveyed into the park, Anna pulled off.

Around the souvenir and taco stand the land had been leveled and graveled in. Beyond, a dirt road led back into the brush and trees. There'd once been a barrier across it to keep out adventuresome tourists but it had long since fallen into disrepair. For several years no one had been caught camping back there so there had been no impetus to get it fixed. Brush made a quick and dirty barrier, a solution often employed to make a track or trail less desirable.

Anna loosed her flashlight from beneath the dash and climbed out of the car. Hands deep in pockets, Stanton followed. "The mesa runs out there in a big finger of land with cliffs on all sides.

"You can see where the brush has been dragged back and forth." Anna shone the light on the bottom of the makeshift barricade. Twigs were snapped and dusty. "Not much in the way of tracks but we've not had rain for a while. Dry, this soil's like concrete."

"Here." Stanton had walked around the pile and poked a toe into the spill of her light. "Truck track. Old but still pretty clear."

Together they moved the brush aside. It took only a minute; the barricade had been culled down to three good-sized bitterbrush bushes so dry they weighed next to nothing.

"A real deterrent," Anna said dryly. "I'm surprised we haven't had wild packs of Bluebirds and Brownies rampaging around back here."

She drove the patrol car through, then they carefully replaced the brush the way they had found it.

The one-lane dirt road was rutted and, though she drove at a footpace, the car jounced from side to side. Without headlights, the trip put Anna in mind of Mr. Toad's Wild Ride in Disneyland. Three quarters of a mile and it ended in a wide turnaround where dirt and rock had been scraped away to help build roads in the park. On the far side of the tree-shrouded clearing was a pile of slash fifteen or twenty feet high.

Anna eased the Ford around behind it, forcing the car over the rubble of limbs. "I feel like a cat hiding behind a blade of grass, like there's bits of me sticking out," she said as she turned off the ignition.

Stanton laughed. He was at the same time more relaxed and more alive than she'd ever seen him. "You love this, don't you," she said.

"So do you, Anna, admit it. Cops and robbers."

Anna wasn't admitting anything.

Stanton tapped the long-lensed camera on the seat between them. "The Colorado Highway Patrol is on standby. We watch, we take pictures for the judge. We call Frieda. Frieda alerts the Highway Patrol. They nab our perpetrator at the entrance station. We're heroes. What's not to like?"

Anna thought of Stacy with his warm brown eyes and passionate love of the natural world. "I'd rather beat a confession out with a rubber hose," she said.

"You may get your chance. Odds are our sniffing around has set the alarm off and we won't get a thing. So far our evidence is pretty thin."

"It's Monday. For whatever reasons the veil was always on Mondays," she insisted. "If it was worth killing for twice, it'll be worth a last run or two. My guess is this particular chindi doesn't scare off easily." She turned off both her belt and the car radios. "It's got to happen because basically we've got zip."

"We know zip but we can't prove zip," Stanton corrected. "I hate these last-minute assignations."

"It's Monday night," Anna defended herself. "Maybe the last Monday night load." Clicking free of her seat belt, she let herself out of the car, taking the flashlight with her. A yellow circle of light joined hers as Stanton walked around the back of the vehicle. Familiarizing themselves with the area, they played their lights over the slash heap and around the car. The slash pile was comprised of the limbs and rounds of trees cleared from near the buildings by the hazardous fuel removal crew. The idea was that, should a wildfire break out on the mesa—a common occurrence during the thunderstorm season—there wouldn't be enough dead and down wood to carry it to any of the historic structures, a theory as yet not tested and not inspiring of much faith among firefighters. But it kept the stoves supplied all winter and a crew of high school and college students busy all summer.

Anna walked one way and Stanton the other till they'd circumnavigated the pile and satisfied themselves that the settled weave of pine and juniper branches was dense enough to hide the patrol car. Then Anna turned her attention to the clearing. Red soil, garish in the flashlight beam, was torn up by the tracks of heavy equipment.

Most were run over so many times the tread was indecipherable.

"There's enough for some good casts," Stanton said. He was down on hands and knees examining the dried mud.

"I'll take your word for it."

"Flunked plaster casts?"

"I don't remember being taught that. I thought it was a Sherlock Holmes kind of thing."

"*Au contraire.* We still do it. It's getting to be a lost art, though. Crime has come out of the closet. They do it right out in the open, then we just arrest 'em. Don't have to finesse much these days. Or else they do it all with computers and mirrors and we never know what hit us until we read about in the *Tribune.*"

Anna traced the mishmash of tracks toward the mesa's edge. They formed a broken fan narrowing to a drop-off point where an opening about forty feet wide made the canyon accessible. To either side trees and sandstone slabs closed in.

Careful not to walk on any salvageable tracks, she made her way to the cliff. Blackness swallowed the feeble beam of her six-cell. Instead of vertigo, it gave her a false sense of security, as if the drop wasn't there at all, as if it were solid and soft: black velvet.

"Don't stand so near the edge." Stanton's voice at her elbow made her flinch.

"Don't creep," she retorted.

"Don't shout."

"Don't snap."

"Nerves shot?"

"Yours too?"

He laughed easily. "A little moonlight would help. Stars. Streetlights. Neon signs. Anything. It is way too dark out here."

"The dark is my friend." Anna flipped off her light. "The invisible woman."

Stanton turned his off as well and they stood in the darkness and the silence. As her eyes adjusted, Anna began to see the faint light that lives in all but deep caves: a blush of peach on the underside of the clouds to the south over the town of Shiprock, a trailing edge of silver where a thunderhead thinned near the moon, a barely discernible difference in the quality of dark between earth and sky, cliff and treeline.

A cold breath of air, just enough to tickle the hair on her arms, was inhaled into the depths of the canyon; air settling as it cooled. Anna closed her eyes and breathed deeply.

"Almonds," she said.

Stanton sniffed, seeming to taste the air in nasal sips. "Could be." He turned on his flash and, in contrast, the night became impossibly dark again. The finger of light stirred in the dirt at their feet. Here the soil was more black than red and the truck tracks amorphous, as if made in soft mud. "Whatever it is, we're standing in it." With the light, he traced the discolored soil to where the canyon claimed it. "Whatever is being dumped goes over right here."

Anna took a plastic evidence bag from her hip pocket and scraped a sample of the dirt into it with the blade of her pocketknife. Not anxious to get a snootful of anything unfriendly, she sniffed it delicately, then offered it to Stanton. "Almonds," he confirmed.

Having rolled the dirt into a package reminiscent of a lid of marijuana, Anna stowed it in her shirt pocket. "Tomorrow we'll get down into the canyon bottom. Cliff Palace is up there at the head of the canyon. From the top of it this spot's clearly visible. If every veil sighting was in reality a Monday night drop, that'd be at least four dumps. At least—on a night like this nobody would see a thing."

"Upcanyon winds when the sun begins to warm and whatever gases this muck gives off drift to the Palace and pool in the alcove. Them what's got weak hearts and lungs fall by the wayside," Stanton said. "If the stuff's heavy it'd settle in the lowest spots. Maybe it filled the kiva Stacy was in, overcame him. That'd account for the single set of tracks."

"Burning prints from the flaming digits on Stacy's arms," Anna reminded him. "Marks like we found on his shoes and appeared on the radio case. I doubt Stacy's murder was quite so second degree."

For a minute longer they stood on the lip of the canyon, Anna feeling there was something more she ought to be doing but uncertain of just what.

"All we're going to do tonight is mess up what evidence there is," Stanton said finally. "Let's find a front-row seat and wait for the curtain to go up."

On the eastern edge of the clearing, they found a flat slab of sandstone partially screened by a thicket of juniper. Their rock was several yards above where the dirt road entered the clearing. Headlights of approaching vehicles wouldn't find them.

For a while Frederick tried to keep the conversation afloat. When he'd exhausted stories about his kids, Anna's pets, and ascertained that she had seen none of the recent movies, he fell silent.

Anna enjoyed the quiet. In complete darkness there was no awkwardness. Alone but not lonely; Stanton was there but invisible and, now, inaudible. Small stirrings as he shifted position, the crack of a joint as he straightened a knee, were comfortable, comforting. Sounds a man made in the bed as he slept beside you, Anna realized. It had been a while since those living human sounds had been there to lull her back to sleep when the nightmares woke her.

Within a couple of hours the meager heat the stone had collected during the day was gone. Beside her, Frederick's deep, even breathing suggested he'd fallen asleep. She didn't begrudge him a nap. Could she have slept, she would've had no qualms about waking him to watch while she caught forty winks.

Cold was settling into the low places and Anna's spirits settled with it. In the wee small hours of the morning, as the song went, was when she missed him most of all. The long and most thoroughly dead Zachary, the husband of her heart—or as Molly caustically put it when Anna waxed maudlin—the husband of her youth, back when all things were possible, all dreams unfolding.

Stacy's haunting brown eyes had a ghost of Zachary's intensity, a shadow of his remembered wit. Unfortunate as Meyers' death was, Anna knew it saved her from making a complete ass of herself. Had the affair become full blown, her life would have disintegrated into that morass of guilt, deceit, and recrimination even the most carefully orchestrated adultery engenders.

Despite Stacy's avowals of dedication to Rose, Anna had little doubt that the affair would have blossomed. Lust leveraged by memory was a powerful force. Ultimately it must have disappointed them both. The Hindus preached that there were three thousand six hundred gates into heaven. Anna doubted adultery was one of them. Like alcohol, it was just a short vacation from life-as-we-know-it.

Stanton's long fingers closed around her knee and Anna was startled into thinking a short vacation might be just what the doctor ordered.

"Listen," he whispered.

She strained her ears but heard nothing. "Sorry, too much loud rock-and-roll music in my youth."

"Shhh. Listen."

An engine growled in the distance. "I hear it now." They fell quiet again, tracking the sound. Anna frisked herself, loosened the baton in its holster, unclipped her keys from her belt, and put them in her shirt pocket where they wouldn't jingle when she moved.

"If the tracks are any indication, the truck will pull in, headlights on the slash pile, turn perpendicular to the canyon, headlights pointed somewhere south of us, then back as close to the rim as possible to make the dump." Stanton went over ground they'd covered in earlier discussions. "I'll stay here. Maybe work my way further around where I can get some clear pictures of the truck, the license plate, and, if we're lucky, the driver actually unstoppering the tank."

"Nothing like a smoking gun," Anna said. Then, because it was safer than assuming, she spoke her part: "I go behind the car, get the shotgun, stay put, shut up, and hope your career as a photographer is long and uneventful."

"Let's do it."

Anna felt Stanton squeeze her knee, then he was gone without a sound, like the mythical Indian scouts in children's books. Moving as quietly as she could, Anna was still aware of the crack and scuffle of her footfalls. She comforted herself with the thought that it was like chewing carrots, more audible to the doer of the deed than any accidental audience members.

In less than two minutes, she'd popped the trunk, unsheathed the shotgun, and was in place by the left rear fender of the car, trying to regain the night vision the trunk light had robbed her of. "Damn," she cursed herself. It was those details that got one killed. If the flash of light from the trunk had been seen, they'd either be in for a fight or the truck would simply keep going, taking all the good, hard courtroom proof of malfeasance with it.

Prying her mind from this treadmill of extraneous thought, Anna slowed her breathing and opened her senses. A feeling of clean emptiness filled her, body and mind receptive to the physical world: the earth firm beneath her feet, the smooth wood of the shotgun stock against her palms, the breeze on her right cheek, the weight of her duty belt, the smell of pine, the sounds of the night and the engine.

Fragments of light began filtering through the trees. She closed her eyes and turned her head away as the truck grew close. Spots of orange danced across her eyelids. The drone became a roar and she felt a moment's panic that she would be run down.

Lights moved, the roar grew louder. She opened her eyes. Headlights stabbed into the woods on the east side of the clearing. Confident the din would cover any sound, she moved to the end of the slash pile and took a stand behind a dead pine branch.

Racket and exhaust filled the clearing, then the sound of clanging as a big red water truck backed toward the canyon. When it was less than a yard from the cliff edge, the roar settled to an idle and the clanging stopped. Placing her feet as much from memory as sight, Anna moved to the rim of the canyon. Twin sandstone blocks, each the size of a small room, were at her back. To the left, between her and the cliff, were three stunted piñon trees.

They were scarcely taller than she but, on this harsh mesa, could've been a hundred years old or more. A bitterbrush bush eight or ten feet tall screened her from the water truck with spiny brown arms.

Headlights were switched off. The night drew close. Far to the west heat lightning flickered from cloud to cloud. If there was distant thunder the truck drowned it out. Engine noise filled all available space, creating confusion where stillness and clarity had reigned.

Tingling in her fingers let Anna know she'd tensed, her grip was too tight. Again she opened her mind, rocked on the balls of her feet, and moved her hands slightly on the shotgun. Over the idle of the engine she heard the slamming of a door. In her mind she heard the click of the camera shutter as Stanton captured the driver on film, the door, the truck, the license plate.

A shadow came around the back of the water truck, bent down, and began pulling or pushing at something. Envying Stanton his infrared scope, she strained her eyes, opening them so wide tears started, but there was no more ambient light to be gathered and she could see nothing more.

Metal clanked on metal and a liquid hiss followed as something cascaded onto the packed earth. Anna smelled almonds. Memories from old movies and Agatha Christie novels flooded sickeningly through her mind. Cyanide gas was said to smell of almonds. She stopped breathing—a temporary solution at best and one not conducive to clear thinking. Shrinking back toward the slash pile, she hoped the down-canyon winds would carry the fumes in the opposite direction. From all reports these night dumps lasted only minutes.

Sudden light flooded the clearing. The figure was spotlighted and Anna sucked in a lungful of almond scent. Not a man but a creature with a human body, the head of an insect, and one long, clawed arm hunkered there.

In an instant her mind recoiled from appearance to reality: a human wearing the self-contained breathing apparatus found on fire trucks stood in the spill of light brandishing a pipe wrench. Liquid, rainbow bright in the headlights, gushed from a line of sprinklers on the rear of the water truck in a fine, even rain. It would take only a beam of moonlight to turn it into a spirit veil.

Like an afterthought, blue overheads and the ululating wail of a siren added to the confusion. Someone shouted. A door banged.

"Goddamn it!" Anna whispered as Jennifer Short, fumbling her .357 from its holster, ran into the light. Once again the woman had neglected to call into service or Frieda would have headed her off.

"Freeze! Freeze!" Short was shouting like a cop in a TV movie. The insect head turned slowly, the pipe wrench fell from sight, hidden behind a trousered leg.

Anna stepped clear of the sheltering brush and chambered a round of double-ought buck. The unmistakable sound cut through the low-grade rumble of the engine and the siren's whine. Insect eyes swiveled toward her. She shouldered the gun. "Drop the wrench," she shouted. "Drop the wrench."

The pipe wrench was moved away, held out to the side, the eye plates of the mask black, unreadable.

"Drop it." Anna leaned forward, flexing her knee, ready to take the recoil if she had to pull the trigger. A cold vibrating in her stomach and the feel of the butt of the shotgun against her shoulder were all she was aware of. The world had shrunk, her vision tunneled till all that existed was the creature with the pipe wrench, clear and contained as a figure viewed through the wrong end of binoculars.

Movement pried open her field of vision. Jennifer, her pistol worked free of the holster, circled to the west, putting the insect directly between herself and Anna's shotgun.

"Jennifer, stop!" Anna cried. Either deaf from noise or adrenaline, Short ran the last yard, completing the line. Now she and Anna stood less than forty feet apart, guns pointing at one another.

The insect realized it as Anna did. Glittering eyes turned from her to Jennifer. The wrench disappeared behind a leg. Slowly, mesmerizing, with the gauntleted hands and inhuman head, it walked toward Short. Jennifer was shifting her weight, her feet dancing in the dirt. Even from a distance Anna could see her hands shaking. "Stop where you are," Anna shouted. Nausea churned in her stomach and she wondered if it was nerves or whatever she was breathing.

Aware that if she pulled the trigger, when the smoke cleared Jennifer might be dead as well, the insect ignored her.

To Anna's left was the canyon. If she shifted right the water truck would block her target. "Jennifer, move!" she yelled. "Move, damn you."

"Stop. Stop now. Don't come any closer," Jennifer was shouting. Shrieking like a banshee, the masked figure dodged right and charged. Anna saw the flash from the barrel of Short's .357 and hurled herself to the ground. High-pitched and ringing, a bullet struck stone. Sparks flew and Anna felt the sting of rock splinters hitting the back of her leg. Two more wild shots rang out, then a scream. Anna looked up to see Jennifer clubbed to the ground by the pipe wrench. The monster-headed figure leaped from sight behind the far side of the truck.

Head and torso behind the right rear wheel, Short lay without moving.

Another fracture of sound and a muzzle flash came from the boulder beyond where Jennifer lay. Stanton. Like Anna, he'd ended up their fools' chorus line.

Flickering blue lights lent his body the fast-forward movement of early films as he ran.

Anna was on her feet running, the shotgun clutched to her chest. Siren and engine roar clouded her brain, clogged her thoughts. Cacophony or cyanide was eroding her synapses. A car door slammed. The ground was uneven and becoming slippery. A stabbing pain, muscles outraged by sudden movement, nearly tripped her.

Stanton was shouting. Then a loud regular clanging cut through the engine's throb. The water truck had been thrown into reverse, the warning bell ringing the intention to back up. Through the shimmering curtain of toxic waste, Anna saw the rear wheels begin to tear free of the mud, crush the strip of ground between themselves and Jennifer Short.

No time to think. Anna threw the shotgun from her, guaranteeing the canyon would be the first to claim it, and hurled herself backward, clear of the moving vehicle.

The tire, silhouetted by garish blue light, filled her field of vision. A couple feet away, in its path, Short lay on her side, an arm thrown above her head reaching toward Anna. A glistening line of blood ran down her temple, over her closed eyelid and onto the bridge of her nose.

In a heartbeat the water truck would roll over her, cut her in two. Scrambling till her butt was on the ground and her feet splayed to either side of the unconscious ranger, Anna grasped Short under the arms and dragged her back, pulling her up like a blanket. Digging heels into the ground Anna shoved both of them back. Something gouged deep into her side, raking the flesh from her ribs: a stick from the slash pile. Ignoring the pain, Anna pushed hard with her feet. The broken end of a branch had caught where the butt of her .357 hooked up and back, and push as she might, she could go no farther.

The gap between the tire and Jennifer's legs was gone. No time: Anna unsnapped the leather keeper that held her gun in the holster. Again she dug heels into earth and shoved back with all the strength in her legs. A tearing at her hip slowed her, then the gun broke free of the breakfront holster and with it the stick. Loosed like an arrow from a bow, Anna shot back several feet, dragging Jennifer with her.

Light was eclipsed, noise crushed down. The truck with its burden of poison rolled toward the cliff's edge. Trees snapped like gunshots as the rear axle crashed over the lip of sandstone. Blue lights scratched across Anna's vision. She was seeing them from beneath the chassis of the truck. Tons of metal levered into the air, headlights stabbing wildly into the sky to rake the bottom of the low clouds.

Screeching wrenched the night and the underbelly of the truck scraped down, pulled backward by the weight of the load. A moment of shocked silence followed, broken only by the oddly peaceful sound of small rocks pattering after. Then a rending crash and stillness so absolute the faint oscillating whine of the patrol car's overheads was clearly audible.

Jennifer's head was on Anna's shoulder, her weight pinning her to the ground. "Hope I got your feet out in time," Anna whispered into the stiff web of sprayed hair that fell over her mouth and nose. She worked her right arm from beneath Jennifer's and found the seasonal's throat with her fingers. A pulse beat reassuringly in the hollow of the woman's neck.

"Hallelujah." Anna's voice rang loud in the new-made quiet and she wished she'd not spoken. As gently as possible, she eased herself from under Short and pushed up to her knees.

"Anna!" Stanton's voice.

"Here."

"Anna!"

Stanton was beginning to annoy her. "What the fuck . . ."

"Behind you!"

Anna dropped and rolled as a metal bar crashed into the ground where she'd been kneeling. White light flashed off the sightless eyes of the insect head. A heavily gloved hand raised again, the pipe wrench swung in a deadly arc.

Anna scuttled backward, fell to her left shoulder, and rolled again, grappling for her revolver.

The branch had torn it free of the holster. It lay somewhere in the dirt between her and her attacker.

Crouched, pipe wrench on shoulder like a ball player at bat, the insect ran toward her. Bent low and pressed close to the slash heap, the gamble was Stanton wouldn't shoot for fear of hitting one of the women.

Apparently it was going to pay off. "Shoot," Anna screamed, and kept rolling. Iron glanced off her upper arm followed by numbing pain, then smashed into the ground with such force she felt it through the earth.

Then Anna's collapsible baton was in her hands. In one desperate motion she rolled to her feet and whipped the weighted rod out to its full length.

The pipe wrench struck her shoulder. For a sickening instant she felt her fingers loosen on the baton but no bones had been broken and strength flooded back.

"Shoot!" she yelled as she lunged at her attacker swinging the baton. It connected somewhere between the gauntleted elbow and shoulder with a bone-cracking jar that pleased Anna to her toes.

The insect grunted but didn't fall down or back. The wrench was tossed from right to left hand and slashed at Anna's face.

Jerking the baton up, she braced the tip across her left palm and blocked the blow. The force shot angry pains down her wrists and left her hands tingling. Before her attacker recovered balance she kicked out, hoping to connect with a kneecap. Her boot cut along the inside of the assailant's ankle.

A scream was ripped loose. The wrench chopped down. Again Anna blocked it but this time her baton was forced to within an inch of her face. Her assailant was stronger and more heavily armed.

"Shoot!" she screamed.

"Get out of the way!"

"Jesus." Anna jerked the baton back. Overbalancing, the insect stumbled forward a step. She stepped into the opening and rammed the tip of the baton into the exposed gut with all her strength and weight.

Her attacker bent double. Both hands on the baton, she swung the butt down toward the back of the canvas-covered neck. The pipe wrench caught her across the shins. Her blow fell wild, glancing off the breathing apparatus.

A shoulder slammed into her chest and she fell back. Mud softened the landing but breath was knocked from her and her head snapped back, splashing muck into her hair and face. Curling up like a spring, Anna held the baton perpendicular to her body to ward blows from her face and upper body. With her feet she kicked out, keeping the pipe wrench at a distance.

"Shoot, goddamn it!"

The wrench arced up. Anna kicked but the cloying mud hampered her, adding to the nightmare feeling. Bracing her arms to absorb another strike, she yelled, "Look out!" in the slim hope of unsettling her assailant.

The insect should have heeded her unwitting advice. A gun's report hit Anna's ears at the same time the bullet struck. The force of the shot pushed her attacker upright.

For a bizarre moment the insect head hung over her, the wrench halfway down its arc, as if deciding whether to complete the strike or not. A second shot rang out and the fingers gripped so tightly around the wrench sprang open. The wrench fell, cracking Anna's knuckles against the baton, then slithered heavily into the mud at her side.

The masked figure stepped back stiff-legged, then crumpled, muscles and ligaments no longer receiving orders from the central nervous system. The strings that moved the puppet had been cut.

Anna felt as if the second shot had cut her strings as well. Her head dropped into the sludge, the baton fell from her hands, her legs were rubbery, useless. Confusion clouded her mind, her heart pounded, and she felt as if she were going to vomit.

Sirens and sucking sounds took over but she had little interest. A face formed over hers and she yelled.

"Take it easy," Stanton said. "Are you okay?" Taking her hand, he pulled her to her feet. Disoriented, nauseated, Anna shook her head to clear it. Nothing cleared. She tried to remember if she'd taken a blow to the head and couldn't. Cyanide gas: she remembered the almond smell.

Sirens closed in and the clearing was filled with chaos. "I called the cavalry," Stanton said.

Anna dragged her hand across her eyes trying to gather her wits. Her eyes began to burn viciously. Tears blinded her and she couldn't force her eyes open. Wherever the sludge had come in contact, her skin burned.

"My eyes," Anna said. "My eyes . . ."

"Holy smoke," Stanton said softly as she reached blindly for him. "Let's get you out of here."

Anna held tight to his arm and stumbled over the uneven ground. "Did you kill him?" she shouted over the sound of the sirens.

"I'm afraid so."

"Was it Greeley?"

"Yes."

"Good. What a son of a bitch."

"You're going to be all right," Stanton said.

"DOES IT HAVE to be so fucking cold?" Anna barked.

"'Flush with copious amounts of cool water,'" Stanton quoted sententiously.

"Cool, damn it, not cold."

Anna heard the protest of antique plumbing as Frederick turned the shower knob. "That better?"

"No."

"Well, think about something else, like July in Georgia."

"Shit. My eyes!" Water cascading down from her hair washed more acid into her eyes. The burning made her whimper. It felt as if the jelly of her eye was being eaten away.

"Keep flushing," Stanton said. "Tilt your head back." Anna felt his hand on the back of her head and tried to do as he said. "Try and open your eyes so clean water gets in them."

"Can't. Hurts." Anna heard the whine in her voice and shut up. She was shivering and not only with the cold. Blindness: now there was a bogeyman to put the fear of God into one. Blindness, paralysis, and small closed spaces.

"You'll see. We got it in time," Frederick reassured her. "I drove like the wind. You would've been proud. A regular Parnelli Andretti. Open now. Come on. A teensyweensy little peek," he coaxed, and Anna was able to laugh away a bit of her terror.

His fingers were plucking at the buttons of her uniform shirt, peeling it off her back as gently as if he feared he might peel the skin off with it. His very care scared her and she tried to help, jerking blindly at her shirttail.

He pulled it free for her. "Yowch! You've got an ugly gouge down your ribs. Greeley get you with the wrench?"

For a moment Anna couldn't remember. Her brain was fogged and that, too, scared her. The answer came in flashback. "Stick took my gun," she said. "Scraped me."

"You're burnt," Stanton said.

"What does it look like?" Anna strove for a conversational tone but missed.

"Not bad. Not bad at all. Looks like a sunburn but not blistering or anything. Here."

Cold water was deflected to stream down her back. Keeping her face tilted so the dirty water would run away from her eyes, Anna gathered her hair and held it out from her body.

"Let me get your shoes off," Stanton said. "We don't want this pooling in 'em and dissolving your toes."

"That's a soothing picture," Anna mumbled. She kicked off one shoe and felt him pull the other off as she lifted her foot.

"I'm going to cut your trousers off, okay?"

"Cut. And warm up the water. I'm getting hypothermic."

"Just a tad." The aged metal creaked in protest and the edge went off the cold.

Anna pushed her face into the stream and pried her eyes open with her fingers. She must have cried out because Stanton was asking what was the matter and she could feel the warmth of his hand on her bare shoulder.

"Don't touch me," she said. "You'll get this shit on you."

"Right. Are you okay?"

Anna shook her head. She couldn't hold her eyelids open for even a second. The fact that she could see light beyond her eyelids seemed a good sign, but the fluorescent light over the stall in the women's communal shower at the tent frames where Stanton had brought her was so bright even a blind woman could see it. The thought sent another stab of fear into her and Anna tried harder to get fresh water under her lids.

Stanton slit her pantlegs and Anna gasped with the cold and the relief. Her skin burned and itched where the acid-drenched mud had soaked through. As he cut away her underpants he said, "Oooh. Black lace. A collector's item. I shall have them stuffed."

Anna was grateful for the banter. Pain and panic had destroyed any vestige of modesty but she appreciated the thought. "As I recall, you never wanted to know me this well."

He didn't reply.

"How much more time have I got?"

"Thirteen minutes. 'Flush with copious amounts for twenty minutes,' the doctor said. You've done seven."

During the wild and, for Anna, sightless ride from the cliff's edge, Stanton had radioed Frieda to call the emergency room in Cortez. The doctor on call had given instructions for treatment. Stanton was carrying them out with kindness and precision. For the first time in more years than she cared to count, Anna felt taken care of. It made her weak and she was afraid she would cry.

Hoping Stanton would attribute the gesture to modesty, she turned her back on him. "Distract me," she said when she could trust her voice. "What do you figure? What happened?"

"The obvious: Greeley had the water truck rigged to smuggle toxic waste into the park to dump it. It shouldn't be too hard to trace where the stuff was from."

"Cyanide gas," Anna said. "Almonds, remember? And acid. Some kind of acid wash used in industrial manufacturing, maybe. Stacy stumbles onto the scheme. Greeley kills Stacy."

"Maybe."

The doubt in his voice irritated her. She ignored it. At present the topic held little interest for her, but it was the only thing she could think of besides her eyes and she didn't care to think about that. "Greeley must've made Stacy breathe the fumes," she went on. Fleeting sadness darkened her mind. "The prints on his arms and shoes were etched with whatever it is I've been rolling in."

"Think Greeley dumped him in the kiva just to be mysterious?" Stanton asked.

"We'll never know, but probably. Jamie'd been babbling on to everybody about the solstice and angry spirits. He might have been taking advantage of Jamie's ghostly brouhaha."

"So he carries him into the kiva, folds him up in the fire pit, rakes it all smooth, puts on Meyers' shoes, backs out, and tosses the shoes back where he got 'em."

"Mysteries are like magic," Anna said. "Once you know how the trick is done, it's obvious to the point of stupidity. I'll bet dollars to doughnuts Silva was blackmailing Greeley," Anna said, suddenly remembering the short-lived spate of expensive gifts he'd poured into Patsy's lap. "He reported seeing a truck at night once. He was out at all hours harassing Patsy. Maybe he saw something else. Put two and two together." Anna pressed her face near the shower head, hoping the water pressure would force it beneath her lids.

"Tom must have gotten greedy," Stanton said. "Ted probably started threatening the wife and kids to shut him up."

So Tom had been guardian angel and not stalker after all, looking after his girls the only way he knew how. "Killed Pats" wasn't a confession of firsthand homicide but guilt at putting her in danger. "Threats against his family would shut him up all right," Anna said. "Tom was obsessed with his ex."

"But you can't trust a drunk."

"Nope. And nothing easier than getting a drunk to take a drink. Point the truck in the right direction and wedge a golf ball in the linkage. Greeley was a golfer. Tom mentioned it one day."

Silence. "Are you still there?" she demanded. Panic rose in her chest and a sour taste poured into the back of her throat.

Something heavy slammed into the tile near her head. Covering her face and neck, Anna collapsed to the floor of the shower. "I can't see, goddamn it! I can't see!" she was screaming.

"Sorry, sorry, sorry, I'm so sorry. It was me, Frederick the idiot." Stanton's voice was in her ear, his hands on her shoulders. "A spider. A black widow. No kidding. As big as a Ping-Pong ball. Huge. It looked ready to pounce. I hit it with your shoe. Sorry."

"Fuck you. Fuck you." Anna began to cry. Stanton crouched down in the shower and held her. The slick fabric of his windbreaker stuck to her cheek and his arms were warm around her. Water dripped from his hair to her face. He held her as she would hold a frightened kitten, tightly, carefully so it wouldn't hurt and couldn't fall.

When she could finally stop, he helped her to her feet.

"Four more minutes," he said.

"Thanks," was all she could manage.

When Anna had only a minute left to go, Frieda took over. She and Frederick discussed Anna's disposal in hushed tones till she couldn't stand it anymore and shouted at them.

Frieda shut the shower off and wrapped a shivering Anna in clean towels. "Can you see?" she asked.

Anna forced her eyes open a slit. "I guess. No. Sort of." The pain was there but not so intense and she could make out shapes, light and dark.

"Keep your eyes shut," Frederick said, and Anna felt him winding soft gauze around her head. "I'm going to bandage them both closed. You know the routine. Don't want you looking hither and yon scratching things about." The bandaging done, he kissed her on top of the head and left to return to the crime scene.

As Frieda wrapped Anna's hair in dry terry cloth, she said: "I'm going to drive you to Cortez. Hills is out at the scene. Paul and Drew took Jennifer down soon as they got there. She'd come around. She got a hell of a wallop on the head, but it looks like a concussion and a good story's all she's going to come away with. Short's lucky."

"If I weren't so glad she weren't dead, I'd kill her."

"C'mon, you were young once," Frieda chided.

"No, I wasn't." With her aching muscles and acid-etched body, Anna felt as if it were true.

*　　*　　*

Dr. Dooley kept Anna overnight for observation but released her the next morning with eye salve and a cheap pair of sunglasses. The world was still a little fuzzy around the edges but it looked good to Anna.

She pulled on a pair of mechanic's overalls and rubber shower thongs Frieda'd dug out of her trunk and left for her. Her own clothes were ruined. Hopefully the duty nurse hadn't thrown them away. They were evidence.

On the way out, she stopped by Jennifer Short's room. Jennifer's head was swathed in bandages and both her eyes were swollen shut. She was so contrite Anna's anger, never heartfelt, evaporated entirely. It had taken a good deal of courage to go up against Greeley all alone in the dead of night. Tombstone courage that needed leavening with common sense, but courage all the same, and Anna respected that.

To her surprise, Short was determined to keep on being a ranger. "I'm going to get on permanent," the woman lisped through swollen lips. "Get me some trainin' and get damn good."

"I'll hire you," Anna said, and was pretty sure she meant it.

Hills was waiting near the emergency room desk when Anna walked out. "Where's Frederick?" she asked.

"Glad to see you too," he returned. "Get your stuff. We're gonna have paperwork up the wazoo over this thing."

"I'm wearing my stuff. And I'm on sick leave for a week. Doctor's orders."

"Doggone it. You gotta be more careful."

"You're glad I'm alive, admit it."

Hills grunted. Anna took it for an affirmative. The

depths of his feeling were revealed on the drive back up to the mesa top. He'd found Patsy and the girls lodging. The tower house was hers.

"When?" The question was so abrupt, Anna laughed at herself.

"If you was a tomcat I do believe you'd be up there peein' in every corner," Hills retorted. "It's yours today, I guess, if you want. Patsy had the movers there this morning. I'd think you'd want to let the sheets cool off before you went hopping in."

"Nope."

"Need help?"

"Nope. Thanks though," Anna added belatedly. What she had was in storage in Cortez. Her estate consisted of little more than a futon and frame, a rocking chair, and a few good Indian rugs.

The movers were late, and as it turned out Anna had to spend one more night in the dormitory. A little after eight the next morning she had her belongings stuffed into boxes and paper sacks and piled into the Rambler.

Zach's ashes were last to be loaded. As she carried the tin out through the living room she took a last look around.

"Find anything to miss?" Jamie asked.

"Not much. The company," Anna lied.

"Hah!" Jamie was unoffended. "You forgot your wine cellar."

Anna paused for a second in the kitchen and looked at the five bottles lined up on the counter beneath the shelves she'd claimed as her own. "Share it with Jennifer," Anna said. "Sort of a good-bye toast."

"My, my." Jamie clucked her tongue. "And they told me it was Jennifer who got hit on the head."

On her way down to Chapin, Anna stopped by Frieda's and gathered Piedmont into the canvas satchel that served as his travel carrier.

By two o'clock she'd brought all of her worldly goods up from storage. Her boom box had pride of place on the mantel and Louis Armstrong poured out "It's a Wonderful World" like honey-laced bourbon. Anna amused herself dragging rugs and pictures from place to place, then standing back to discuss the effect with a disinterested cat.

The only furniture she'd arranged so far was a rocking chair and, beside it, a small marble-topped table where the phone sat in solitary splendor. Soon she'd call her sister. Anna'd been promising herself that for three hours but had yet to drum up the nerve. There were things needing to be said, confessions to be made.

Rapping at the front door interrupted both her nesting and her dithering. With less than good humor, she went to the door.

Stanton waved at her through the screen. Despite a flash of awkwardness engendered by their unscheduled intimacy in the shower, Anna was glad to see him. Because it seemed less stilted than leaving him on the doorstep, she invited him into the kitchen and sat down in the booth. The little vinyl benches and polished tongue of Formica were too small to accommodate his lanky frame.

"Kitchens are made for girls," he complained, turning sideways to stretch his long legs. "Just to reach the sink without bending double I've got to stand with my feet so far apart I'm almost doing the splits."

"Sounds like an excuse to get out of doing the dishes to me."

"How're you doing?" he asked when he'd gotten himself arranged.

"Fine. Can't offer you anything. The cupboard is bare."

"I've been tying up loose ends," he said. "Rose is willing to turn state's evidence in return for clemency."

"For the false alibi?"

Stanton nodded. Anna shoved three carpet tacks the movers had managed to leave on the kitchen table into a pinwheel shape. "The woman's husband gives his life to stop the dumping, Greeley kills him, and Rose is still willing to alibi him. Go figure."

Stanton looked uncomfortable—miserable, in fact. He looked like Anna's dad when he had bad news about Fluffy or Bootsie or Pinky-winky—whichever of their multitude of pets had succumbed to the inevitable.

Anna waited. Everyone she knew was safe. Still, there was a hollow place in her belly.

"Stacy was on the take," Frederick said apologetically. "Greeley paid him to unlock the Four-Way and make sure the coast was clear. That's why Greeley did it Monday nights; Stacy was on the late shift. Greeley'd lock up when he was done.

"That funky twisty way with the chain," Anna said, remembering how the same lock configuration at the maintenance yard had tipped her off.

Stanton went on: "After he was killed Rose gave Greeley Stacy's radio so he could keep tabs on the rangers. Without Stacy's keys, Rose says she doesn't know how he unlocked the Four-Way. Presumably at some point Stacy made him a copy."

Anna looked at the table, her mind playing with something as her fingers played with the tacks. Patsy'd said the night Tom broke in and left the derringer, she'd been awakened twice. The next day she mentioned she'd "lost" her keys. "Greeley stole Patsy Silva's keys, copied them, then put them back," Anna said. "I can't prove it, but that's what happened."

Stanton nodded. "Rose said Stacy'd decided to turn Greeley and himself in after a little girl you carried out of Cliff Palace died."

"Stephanie McFarland."

"He and Rose argued about it over the phone the night she was in Farmington, the night Stacy was killed. Up till then he was in collaboration with Greeley to dump the toxic waste." The FBI agent seemed to be repeating the news in case Anna hadn't quite been able to grasp it first time around.

Anna had understood just fine. The devil buys on the installment plan. People are always shocked when he shows up to collect his merchandise.

"Everybody's got their price," Frederick said.

"Stacy's wasn't money."

"But money could buy it."

"And money bought Rose's alibi."

Stanton shook his head. "Matrimony. She hated Ted but he said he'd marry her and put Bella on his health insurance plan. Strictly business. He told her you and Stacy were having an affair to lower any sentimental inhibitions she might have had."

Anna pushed the carpet tacks around till they formed a jagged line, like a bolt of lightning, and she remembered the storm Bella had made with Hattie because her mad was so big. Rose had made her lie, say Greeley was in Farmington. At six telling a lie is still a great burden.

"What was Greeley dumping?" Anna changed the subject.

"There's electroplating plants in the area. One in Cortez, one near Shiprock, and a couple around Farmington. They use an acid for the wash and cyanide in the brass plating process. Greeley was contracted to dump it. I haven't got the particulars yet but evidently Greeley Construction was in financial trouble. Greeley couldn't finish the pipeline, he'd already spent the money. By dumping illegally he hoped to fix his cash flow problems long enough to avoid the penalties."

"Worth killing for?"

"One hundred thousand dollars a day for every day over schedule. Greeley didn't do his homework—or didn't care. He dumped the acid and cyanide in the same place. Mixed, it creates cyanide gas. Sometimes it mixed, sometimes it missed. But the gas was what was drifting up the canyon. Nausea, palpitations, confusion, tachycardia, hyperventilation, hypoxia."

"A smorgasbord of ills."

"Unless it was suspected for some reason, no doctor would even think to test for it."

For several minutes they sat without speaking. Piedmont, alerted by the silence, came and jumped onto the table between them. "Remember the monkeywrenching I told you about? Brown boots, insurance, key to the yard: my bet it was Greeley. A little self-sabotage to claim the insurance money, keep himself afloat awhile longer."

Stanton nodded.

"Case closed?" Anna asked.

"Fun part's over. The lawyer part will drag on till neither one of us can remember who did it." Stanton tweaked up Piedmont's long yellow tail and absently tickled his cheek with the tip of it. Murder might make for strange bedfellows but that wasn't always such a bad thing.

"We're not co-workers anymore, Anna. Want to go out to dinner? Maybe a movie?"

"A date?" Anna sounded appalled and Stanton laughed.

"A date. I come pick you up at the door at seven sharp. You wear lipstick, can't touch the check, and have to call the women's toilet the 'powder room.' How about it?"

"I have to make a phone call," Anna hedged.

Stanton glanced at his watch. "Okay, you've got just under five hours. Then the date."

"I guess. Sure."

Anna would have felt awkward but he didn't give her time. With startling grace he sprang from the cramped booth. "Got to figure out what to wear," he said, and: "Seven."

He was gone, the screen door banging behind him.

Anna stood up. Then sat down. All at once she didn't know what to do with herself. Scooping up Piedmont for support, she went into the living room and to the phone.

It was Wednesday. Maybe her sister wouldn't be at the office.

Molly picked up on the fourth ring. "Dr. Pigeon," she snapped.

"Hi," Anna said. "My name's Anna and I'm an alcoholic."

"Hi, Anna," Molly droned in parody of the group response, but her voice was warmer than Anna'd heard it in a while.

Explore Uncharted Terrains of Mystery
with *Anna Pigeon, Parks Ranger* by

NEVADA BARR

TRACK OF THE CAT
72164-3/$6.50 US/$8.50 Can

National parks ranger Anna Pigeon must hunt down the killer of a fellow ranger in the Southwestern wilderness—and it looks as if the trail might lead her to a two-legged beast.

A SUPERIOR DEATH
72362-X/$6.99 US/$8.99 Can

Anna must leave the serene backcountry to investigate a fresh corpse found on a submerged shipwreck at the bottom of Lake Superior.

ILL WIND
72363-8/$6.99 US/$8.99Can

FIRE STORM
72528-7/$6.50 US/$8.50 Can

ENDANGERED SPECIES
72583-5/$6.99 US/$8.99Can

Nationally Bestselling Author

J·A·JANCE

The J.P. Beaumont Mysteries

UNTIL PROVEN GUILTY	89638-9/$6.50 US/$8.50 CAN
INJUSTICE FOR ALL	89641-9/$6.50 US/$8.50 CAN
TRIAL BY FURY	75138-0/$6.99 US/$8.99 CAN
TAKING THE FIFTH	75139-9/$6.50 US/$8.50 CAN
IMPROBABLE CAUSE	75412-6/$6.50 US/$8.50 CAN
A MORE PERFECT UNION	75413-4/$6.50 US/$8.50 CAN
DISMISSED WITH PREJUDICE	
	75547-5/$6.50 US/$8.50 CAN
MINOR IN POSSESSION	75546-7/$6.50 US/$8.50 CAN
PAYMENT IN KIND	75836-9/$6.50 US/$8.50 CAN
WITHOUT DUE PROCESS	75837-7/$6.50 US/$8.50 CAN
FAILURE TO APPEAR	75839-3/$6.50 US/$8.50 CAN
LYING IN WAIT	71841-3/$6.99 US/$8.99 CAN
NAME WITHHELD	71842-1/$6.99 US/$8.99 CAN

The
Dinosaur
Princess

VICTOR MILÁN

TOR®
fantasy

A TOM DOHERTY ASSOCIATES BOOK | NEW YORK

This is a work of fiction. All of the characters, organizations, and events portrayed in this novel are either products of the author's imagination or are used fictitiously.

THE DINOSAUR PRINCESS

Copyright © 2017 by Victor Milán

All rights reserved.

Interior illustrations by Richard Anderson

Map by Rhys Davies

A Tor Book
Published by Tom Doherty Associates
175 Fifth Avenue
New York, NY 10010

www.tor-forge.com

Tor® is a registered trademark of Macmillan Publishing Group, LLC.

ISBN 978-0-7653-8213-9

Our books may be purchased in bulk for promotional, educational, or business use. Please contact your local bookseller or the Macmillan Corporate and Premium Sales Department at 1-800-221-7945, extension 5442, or by email at MacmillanSpecialMarkets@macmillan.com.

First Edition: August 2017
First Mass Market Edition: July 2018

Printed in the United States of America

0 9 8 7 6 5 4 3 2 1

To Melinda Snodgrass, for saving my life, for helping me improve my craft, and for being my friend for longer than would be kind to either of us to mention.

ACKNOWLEDGMENTS

The usual suspects proved invaluable in the writing of this book.

Thanks to all my friends for being my friends, and helping keep me alive. I love you all.

Thank you to the fine folks in the Albuquerque Science Fiction Society and at Archon in St. Louis for your love and support.

Thank you, again, to my current fellow writers of Critical Mass: John Jos. Miller, Matt Reiten, Jan Stirling, Steve Stirling, Lauren Teffeau, Emily Mah Tippetts, and Sarena Ulibarri, as well to all the past members who helped the project at every step of the way.

Thank you to my agent, Kay McCauley; my editor, Claire Eddy, and her indefatigable assistant, Bess Cozby; and to Richard Anderson, for what might be an even *better* cover than the one Walter Jon Williams called "the greatest cover in the history of the Universe." And to Irene Gallo for getting Richard to do it again.

Thanks to David Sidebottom, Lenore Gallegos, and the Jean Cocteau Cinema in Santa Fe for your support.

Thanks to Ron Miles, Webmaster Supreme, for resurrecting my website from the dead, again. And to Theresa Hulongbayan and Gwen Whiting for continuing to wrangle the Facebook Dinosaur Lords group!

Thanks to Diane Duane and Thomas Holtz for invaluable advice and information.

A heartfelt thank you to George R. R. Martin, for so many things.

Thank you to my Dinosaur Army for keeping the faith.

Thanks to Wanda Day for being there.

And as always—thank you for reading.

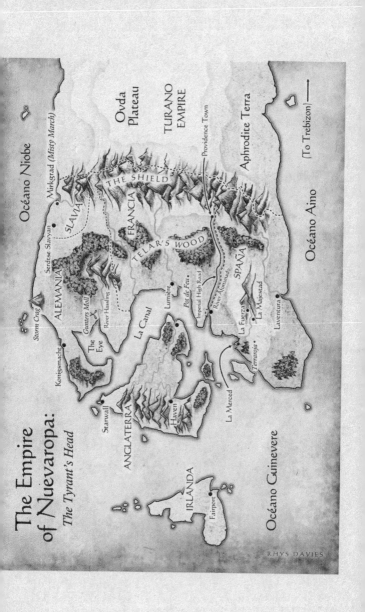

Leon Battista Alberti answers the question in *Della Famiglia*, written in the 1430s. Since the family is the social unit par excellence, Alberti says, any attitude or treatment that benefits your family or serves to increase its honor is acceptable, for this is the defining purpose of life.

—TIM PARKS,
MEDICI MONEY: BANKING, METAPHYSICS, AND ART IN FIFTEENTH-CENTURY FLORENCE,
ATLAS/NORTON 2005, P. 26

Part One

Intrusion

Prologue

El Mundo Debajo, **The World Below.** . . . —The fabulous
realm, claimed by legend to lie beneath the very soil of
Paradise, in which the Creators' servitors, the seven Grey
Angels, make Their home. Mortal humans cannot reach
there, but only supernatural beings. Some stories claim that
the *hada,* the Fae, dwell there as well. But those are probably only fables made up to frighten bad children, not like
you or me.

—A PRIMER TO PARADISE FOR THE IMPROVEMENT
OF YOUNG MINDS

THE GREY ANGEL RAGUEL'S DREAM,
THE WORLD BELOW

"Face facts," said Uriel to his host. "You had your
chance. And you blew it."

Raguel sighed dramatically. He sat with knees
crossed and hands around the upper one on a jut of ice
like a small pressure-ridge. His dream-armor was plate
made of ice. Uriel knew he was particularly vain about
the effect of the fluting he'd made in its breastplate and
limb-armor this time.

"Also, why do you insist on keeping it so blasted cold?" Uriel asked.

"You're Fire, I'm Ice," Raguel said. "What do you expect? I find your own Dream beastly hot, you know. Anyway, why are you complaining? Now you get to try your soft Fundamentalist hand at dealing with the human pestilence while I have to rusticate here in exile."

"You can go fight the Uncreated."

"To what end? We've been doing that for trillions of cycles and aren't any closer to winning that I can see."

Uriel was lean, though not gaunt like his Instrumentality or Raguel's. His own plate armor was green; the cloth-mimicking cape that fluttered from his shoulder-guarding pauldrons, red like flame. He currently favored a clean-shaven appearance, skin rather pallid to contrast with a thatch of black hair, and eyes of green—the prime color of his Patron Creator, Telar, the Oldest Daughter.

"Defeatism?" he asked softly. "Be careful whom you let hear you talking that way, my friend."

Raguel shot him a glare. When an Angel intended, such glares could wound. Even another Grey Angel. Especially here in Raguel's own dream, which he had constructed for himself Below.

But Uriel felt no fear. Such acts had consequences. No Angel had ever actually Ended another. But they knew to fear it. Especially given that, in their endless war, they were few, and the Fae, innumerable. And Uriel was a friend.

"Let me back into the fray Above, and I'll show you how 'defeatist' I am," Raguel said.

"Rules are rules, Ice," Uriel said. "You failed. Now you wait your turn again. Unless you care to take the matter up with Michael?"

"No need to bother Him," Raguel said. "And who is like Him? But it just wasn't fair, how it ended. It hurt the dignity of all Angels, to have that damned overgrown lapdog bite my Instrumentality in half."

"Then perhaps you should have been more cautious about taking it out and waving it around in order to impress the apes," Uriel said. "In any event—"

His words ran down. He was aware that Raguel was staring at him. Then his host turned to follow his gaze toward his personal horizon.

Across the ice-sheet walked a naked woman. The winds that howled here, except in the vicinity of Raguel and his invited guest, whipped her long blond hair around her body. She seemed to enjoy the simulated feel, though it must cut her pale skin like flaying-knives.

"Look who's here," Uriel murmured.

"Shit," Raguel said. He snapped to his feet. "Now this really pisses me off to no end. What do you think you're playing at, Aphrodite, invading my space like this?"

"I am the World, Ice Angel," she said, approaching, "and I walk where I please."

"I wish you wouldn't do it this way," Uriel said. "I find it . . . disconcerting."

She raised a brow at him. "You find the humans' form disturbing? Look at yourself. Or is it something else?"

"*I* resent that form," Raguel said. "Especially when it comes walking in here uninvited. You love the humans so much you actually *enjoy* appearing in their likeness."

Like his friend, Uriel found it an exasperating irony that he had by nature the mannerisms as well as the semblance of the humans who infected the Above like a malignant mycelium. But that was his nature—the nature of all his kind. The Creators had made the Grey Angels as their special servitors. And as with the world Paradise itself and everything on it, They had made the Angels as it pleased them to.

"I do," Aphrodite said. "I love all things of Paradise

and on it. Even you, Raguel, even when you act like a sulky human child."

Raguel sat down on his ice-jut, crossed his arms, and frowned. "How do you know how a human child acts?"

"Because I watch them," she said. "You might consider it. Rather than exceeding the Creators' mandate."

She had stepped within the charmed circle of calm that Raguel, for his own convenience, kept about himself and Uriel. Now her hair rose in a crackle of electricity, and her blue eyes glared.

"Wait, now," Uriel said. "I'm not the one here who was actively trying to exterminate the humans."

She spun on him. "No, you are merely trying to kill most of them."

"You're a fine one to talk, meddling in their affairs to help them. Perhaps we're not the only ones walking the knife edge of what our own Creation permits."

"I do no such thing. I was made to preserve Paradise—Creation itself. As you were made to maintain Holy Equilibrium within it. I do not 'help' the humans. I try to counteract your insane desire to unmake what the Creators made!"

"Fancy words," their host told her bitterly. "You helped that human pet of yours Karyl put an ignominious end to my Crusade. Even if that does fit your own built-in restrictions enough that you didn't destroy yourself, it's still infringing on our prerogative. You do not rule the Angels, World-Spirit!"

In response, she spread her arms. Around Uriel and his friend sprang up Paradise. The icy wasteland—so rare Above—turned to the lush and riotous green and tiny explosions of red and purple and white and gold of some flower-filled clearing in a forest of cycads and lordly conifers. Raguel cried out—whether in surprise or in pain from the touch of warm, humid Tropical air, Uriel didn't know.

"What are you doing?" Raguel shouted, jumping up again and waving his arms. "My Dream!"

"Indeed I do not rule you," Aphrodite said, "but I am the Caretaker of the World. From the outer air clear down to the core. And I have the power needed to carry out my mission."

Raguel held up his hands. To Uriel he looked as if he felt really sick. Uriel thought he understood; he himself was feeling vulnerable in a way none of the Seven had since—well, since the end of the great surface War against the Fae and their blasphemous human allies. And its fearful aftermath.

"Please, Caretaker," Raguel said. "Please—heal my Dream. You have made your point."

"But not sufficiently that either of you will desist," she said.

Raguel hung his simulacrum head.

"I won't either," Uriel said. "Though I will echo my friend's request. You won't win by kicking apart his ice castle."

"Very well." She held out her arms again. The ice and snow and wind whirled in again to supplant the riotous green growth, until all was as before.

"I'm sorry we find ourselves at cross-purposes," Uriel said, trying to play the peacemaker. Not even he was sure what might happen if for some reason Aphrodite simply decided to erase his friend's Dream, with them still inside. "Truly. We know that without you we wouldn't have a world in which to maintain Equilibrium. But you know we operate under the same constraints as you. Since none of us, neither Fundamentalist nor even Purificationist, has involuntarily destroyed himself or herself, our actions must arguably conform to the Creators' intentions."

"Through a long and twisted chain of reasoning," she said.

"Nevertheless."

A terrible, brilliant noise split the sky overhead.

Literally. Uriel saw rage twist Raguel's face as he looked up in alarm.

Have the Fae found a way in? Uriel thought in near panic. *Not just through our defenses, but into Raguel's own sanctum?* That would mean either some individual Faerie or some unprecedented demon coalition had gotten powerful enough to threaten the Angels with extinction. And thus Paradise. It was every Angel's ultimate nightmare.

But what poured through the rift in the dense cloud cover Uriel's host maintained above his Dream in emulation of the World Above's perpetual daytime overcast was glorious golden light in a shape that reminded Uriel suspiciously of a vagina. A resemblance only strengthened by the winged figure descending through it.

The intruder blew another blast of her golden posthorn. Uriel winced at the sound. And the arrogance that propelled it in lieu of physical breath.

"Say what you will about her," he murmured, "but Gabriel does know how to make an entrance."

"You just say that because she's one of yours," Raguel said. "Bitch."

"You know I can hear you, God-Friend," the Angel called, moving her horn from her lips. She was laughing. Uriel knew that was by no means an unequivocally reassuring sign.

The sky rift closed up again, leaving the clouds the same unbroken sea seethe they had been before. Uriel knew it wasn't by his friend's volition. Raguel looked as angry and unsettled by the act of repair as he had by the affront of opening it in the first place.

"You're not supposed to be here, Gabriel," Raguel said as she touched down before him on wings as wide as a Long-crested Dragon's. Which instantly disappeared. "Damn it."

Uriel knew he didn't mean that in terms of etiquette alone: an Angel's Dream was supposed to be inviolable in fact as well as courtesy among peers. That Aphrodite had invaded, annoying though it was, shouldn't be unexpected: she, after all, was the stuff their Dreams were made of.

But the very nature of Raguel's personal bubble-realm, within the shared and greater Dream that was the World Below, should have made it inaccessible to any other sprite, Faerie or Grey Angel.

"You didn't really think you could keep me out, did you, Raggy, dear?" Gabriel asked. Up close she had fine cream-colored features, a straight nose, blue eyes, and wavy red-gold hair that hung about the shoulders of the breast-and-back she wore over her yellow smock and brown leggings—the latter the colors of her Patroness, Mother Maia, the Creators' Queen. She was strikingly beautiful to Uriel's eyes—it was another point of resentment among the Seven that their own standards of beauty reflected those of the apes Above.

And under the circumstances, Uriel guessed that it especially rankled Raguel's semidivine ass that Gabriel, alone of all the Grey Angels, could maintain her beautiful semblance indefinitely while walking about on the surface. Whereas when Raguel mustered and led his abortive Grey Angel Crusade, the beautiful flesh he encased his Instrumentality in had inevitably decayed into a base form that was . . . something else entirely. Though it had impressed the mortals.

"Aphrodite isn't the only one who can walk where she pleases," Gabriel said.

"Even into Dissonance?" Raguel asked.

Uriel winced at his friend's gaffe. Gabriel's eyes began to glow blue-white in fury. Literally, like vents to a supergiant star.

The rest could do that trick too, of course. But all Grey

Angels were not Created equal. Gabriel's power was second only to that of the King's Angel, Michael. And that was before the thing Raguel had tactlessly and foolishly brought up: her captivity in the Venusberg, the hateful realm of Fae. As well as the things she did then, ostensibly under their enchantments.

"I—I," Raguel said. He stopped and looked wild-eyed, as if some Creators' geas had stuck his tongue to the back of his teeth. Apology did not come easy to an Angel.

Between them stepped a smaller figure. "Easy, children," Aphrodite said with maternal good humor—and firmness.

"Out of my way, divine janitor," Gabriel snapped. Blue lightning bolts crackled through her kinky hair, which began to lift up from the shoulders of her cuirass.

"Go ahead and blast me, Gabi, dear, if it'll make you feel better," Aphrodite said, smiling.

Gabriel showed her teeth. But the glow faded, the lightning died, and her hair settled back into place.

Uriel flicked his eyes toward Raguel, who shook his head in relief. None of them, possibly not even the World Witch Herself, knew what would happen if an Angel used her full destructive power on Aphrodite. Most likely nothing—but that was also the best possible scenario. The others were unthinkable—if all too imaginable to him.

"Let's all try calming down," Aphrodite said. She turned to confront Gabriel directly. "Now, God Friend, what were you thinking, barging in here like that? You Angels value your protocols so much. Surely you didn't treat your poor brother so rudely just to stage an entrance?"

"Don't underestimate her vanity," murmured Uriel.

Gabriel laughed. That laughter made Uriel nervous; it was still a danger sign. Then again, since her return to the fold, most things were. All taken with all, it worried him less than the lightning and the hell glow.

"Protocols are fine," she said. "They give the boys something to occupy their cycles. But I intended to give notice that just because Raguel here failed in his precious scheme doesn't mean Zerachiel and I failed with him. We know what we must do for the good of Paradise and Sacred Equilibrium. And we will do it—despite your meddling and the hand-wringing concerns of Uriel, Remiel, and Raphael."

"Shouldn't you take that up with Michael?" Uriel asked. "He agrees: it's my turn."

Gabriel only laughed again. Then turning to Aphrodite, who had stepped back to reopen the circle of discussion, she said, "As for you, my dear, my answer's simple: if our Creators don't want us exterminating the humans, they have but to tell us so."

"How do you dare take it on yourself to unmake what the Creators made?" Aphrodite said. She was frowning fiercely now herself, albeit without the pyrotechnics Gabriel affected.

Gabriel tossed back flame-colored hair. "And who made you ruler over us? You're a maintenance worker. Your job is to keep the sun from burning the land and boiling the sea. *We* are the Creators' appointed servants. Perhaps it's time someone taught you to keep your place."

Thoroughly alarmed, Uriel stepped between them. "Here, now," he said, in what he hoped was a soothing tone. "You know we don't dare harm Aphrodite, for fear of upsetting Sacred Equilibrium. If not returning the world to Hell."

There was more he might have said, of course. It tickled the tip of his virtual tongue. Beasts who came from chaos and lived to spread it without love or allegiance for one another or any other thing, the Fae still almost all shared exactly that aim: to return the whole world to the state from which the Creators had remade it.

But I'm supposed to be the diplomatic one, Uriel thought. *And I'm not about to repeat Raguel's screw-up by bringing up Gabriel's tormentors again.*

"As you so kindly remind us," Aphrodite told Gabriel, "we all have tasks we were created for. Mine is to preserve and maintain Paradise and all its creatures; I have no wish to see anyone destroyed."

For a moment, eyes glared into one another, sea-green and the brilliant unforgiving blue of sky momentarily left bare by a rip in the world's daytime raiment, clouds.

"Do you grieve for an ant crushed by a Thunder-titan, then?" Gabriel asked with a sneer. But her tone was quieter than before. If not notably softened.

"Yes."

"Well," Gabriel said. "I've done what I came to do: serve notice that I don't intend to placidly wait my turn to set things right in the world we guard."

"And I give notice," Aphrodite said, quite genially, "that I will stop you."

"Wait," said Uriel plaintively. "What about me? We all agreed on it in advance. You Purificationists had your shot. Now we Fundamentalists get to do it our way. *My* way. It's the work I've focused on for billions of cycles! You can't just trample on that!"

Again, Gabriel smiled.

"Just watch me, Fire of God."

"Your Highness, may we have a word with you?" the man in the tall black hat said in a voice like warm olive oil. And a dense *Griego* accent.

Montserrat Angelina Proserpina Telar de los Ángeles Delgao Llobregat stopped in the middle of the corridor.

It was dim, lit by nothing more than palm-oil lamps in periodic niches along the stone wall.

Are you talking to me? she wondered. While she was technically a Princess, she was the Imperial Infanta, meaning not scion of her father's line. *Alteza* was an honorific more commonly addressed to her older sister, Melodía. At least by nobles, which Montse reckoned these emissaries from the Basileus Nikephoros of Trebizon must be.

Silver Mistral, Montse's pet ferret, hopped sideways as if to block the progress of the trio of outlanders who had appeared in the door that led from the passage to an ancillary dining hall in the Firefly Palace's sprawling keep. She bristled her silver coat and black tail, beeping a warning at them not to come any closer. They ignored her, though the woman gave her a brief, uneasy flick of her heavily kohl-rimmed black eyes.

"May I help you, Señoras y Señoras?" asked Claudia. The tall woman with the grey skeins in her long dark hair was a senior Palace servant and Montse's friend. Montse had slipped her handlers to trail after her as she went about her morning duties, as she liked to do. "These are servant hallways. No places for noble folk such as yourselves."

The shorter of the two men was the first to speak. Unlike the rest of the male Trebs, his face was clean-shaven. His jaw was as square as a door. He looked to Montse as if he ground his teeth a lot.

"Her Highness is here," he observed in a reasonable tone. His Spañol was good, despite the accent.

"The Infanta lives in the Palace, my lord, and goes where she will."

As if by chance, Claudia had placed herself between Montse and the interlopers. Though more puzzled by their appearance than anything else, Montse hurried to scoop up Mistral and huddle the creature against the front of her linen smock—white that morning, grubby already. Making sure to support her long-backed friend's hindquarters with one cupped hand, of course. She didn't want to injure the ferret.

"We have resided here for months as we pressed the Emperor for answers to our suit," the noblewoman among the three said, with haughtiness unusual even for a *grandeza*. Montse decided she didn't like her. "Thus we live here, too. And as noble priests of Trebizon and emissaries of the Basileus, we go where we want as well."

"Not in El Palacio de las Luciérnagas," Claudia said, putting a touch of steel in her voice. "Here, allow me to call the Prince's guards. They can escort you to more . . . congenial surroundings."

"Please," the clean-shaven man said. "Our business is with the child."

"No," Claudia said.

Things got terrible with a speed that almost choked Montserrat.

The Trebizon lady slapped Claudia across the face. She was almost as tall, even leaving out the hat, and, as far as Montse could tell from her elaborate layers of robes, as slender as her friend. The unexpected blow snapped Claudia's head around.

Without hesitation Claudia spun back and punched the noblewoman in the face. She was strong from a lifetime of hard work, and, having grown up on the waterfront of La Merced, the great La Canal seaport sprawled at the foot of the promontory on which the Palace stood, she knew how to hit. The Trebizonesa reeled back against the wall.

She recovered instantly. From somewhere in her outlandish swaddling she snatched out a stiletto and stabbed Claudia beneath the right breast through her white cotton blouse. The servingwoman froze for a moment, then stepped back. But instead of locking up or moaning in pain, much less collapsing from the wound, as a horrified Montse expected her to, Claudia tried to launch another punch at the priestess's face.

The bearded man grabbed her arm from behind, stopping her swing. He clutched for a hold on her left arm as well.

From the hornface-leather belt she wore to cinch up her long brown skirt and to carry such items as her duties might require, Claudia drew a butcher knife with her free left hand. She plunged it down and back. The bearded man gasped and then squealed as it sank to the handle into his stomach.

He bent over, groaning. But he didn't let go of Claudia's wrist. The noblewoman stepped in to stab Claudia again and again like a bird pecking—so fast Montse lost count of the thrusts.

She became aware that she was screaming at them to stop hurting her friend. She had backed against the wall opposite the mouth of the side passage through which the three intruders had entered.

Claudia's blouse was a sodden red mass. She caught Montse's eye and mouthed, "Run!" Her teeth were individually outlined in red; Montse knew she'd dream about the sight as long as she managed to stay alive.

Montse saw the life leave her friend's eyes. Claudia's head lolled to the side. She sagged. The bearded man, still mewling in agony, released her suddenly dead weight to puddle on the floor in blood and sadness.

The clean-shaven man approached Montse. He held out a big, square hand. "Come with us now, little girl. We won't hurt you."

"Like the way you didn't hurt my friend?" Montse shouted, more in rage than grief. She turned to bolt for a secret passage—the Palace was honeycombed with them—to her left.

Instead, she turned straight into a tall man wearing a slashed-velvet doublet and short pantaloons over leggings, all in black. He gathered her against him, turned her, and pinned her against leanly muscular legs.

From the corner of her eye she saw that the entry to the secret passage, which was disguised as a lamp alcove, stood open. *Some servant sold us out!* she thought, sickened. *One of my friends.*

She opened her mouth to scream for help—not a natural action for her, or she'd have started earlier. Her captor clapped a hand over her mouth.

"What have you idiots done?" he demanded "Everything depends on avoiding violence."

The woman, whose dark robes were almost as blood-soaked as Claudia's blouse but showed it less, brandished the slim dagger and spat something in her native tongue.

"She's a valued servant and friend to the little princess, here," Dragos responded in Spañol. "Her employer, Prince Heriberto, will resent her murder here in his own palace."

"They were going to resent the girl's abduction, anyway," the beardless man said. "And she was impudent to Lady Paraskeve."

Montse had witnessed violence before. She'd attended tournaments, never by her own choice. She'd seen men and women injured, even watched an elderly knight die by accident during a recent tourney. But she'd never seen a friend die before. Nor had she experienced violence directed against her.

Being grabbed by a stranger shocked her. It felt like a violation. For a brief spell, it caused her to freeze in panic.

But she recovered fast and bit the muffling hand. Hard.

"Ow," her captor said, but mildly. "I deserved that, for not expecting it."

He shifted his hand to keep her quiet but removing her chance to chomp him again. Turning, he shoved her toward one of a pair of human nosehorns, locals by their look and dress, who had emerged from the not-so-secret passage.

"Mind her teeth, Diego. They're sharp. And she's fast and feisty."

Diego's hand was big enough that Montse's mouth could get no purchase. She kicked back furiously with a bare heel.

"Ow! My shin!"

The murderous Lady Paraskeve had put away her stiletto. Now she pointed toward Mistral, whose fur bristled and who was hissing furiously and writhing in Montse's hands. "Take that filthy animal away from her and kill it."

"No!" Montse tried to yell. But of course she only produced a muffled squeal of outrage.

Helplessness, she found, made her all the madder. But it did no good against Diego's strength and apparently durable shins.

"No," the man who had seized Montse said. He was tall, perhaps poor Claudia's height, slender as the Taliano rapier he wore at his fashionably clad waist, with neatly trimmed grey hair and beard. Montse had seen him at court the last week or so; several women and a couple of men, not all servants, had commented on what a fine figure he cut.

He continued in Griego. Which Montse couldn't understand a word of.

"You dare to contradict me?" Paraskeve snapped back in Spañol. "Who do you think you are, Dragos?"

"I think I am a specialist hired by your masters to keep you from making a total botch of this," Dragos said, his voice still level. "At which I've failed—which means you need me all the more just to get out of this Palace alive, much less out of the Empire, with your skins still attached. And I think I'm a man who has taken measures—including certain compacts with your masters—to safeguard against treachery on your part."

"Leave be, Paraskeve," the clean-shaven man said. "Can you walk, friend Stamatios?"

"I'm fine." Stamatios gave the lie to his words by the way he sobbed them, hunched over to one side with a hand pressed to his blood-pouring belly. "I can walk."

Blood drooled from his lips and matted his beard when he spoke. Montse found she didn't find that horrifying. She wanted him to die.

He took a step. His knees promptly folded. He only kept himself from going to the floor by falling against the dank stone wall.

"We have to leave him," Dragos said. "You—kill yourself. You'll slow us down, and we can't afford that. If we're caught, not only is Prince Heri likely to forget the Creators' Law against torture but, worse, our masters will be very vexed with us. And they seldom remember that Law to start with."

"You can't—" bearded Stamatios began. Seeing the set of Dragos's face, he looked to his male comrade. "Please, Akakios. Tell him he can't—"

Dragos stepped purposefully up to Stamatios as the wounded man pulled himself more or less upright. He brought the heel of his right palm savagely up against the underside of a bearded chin. Stamatios's jaws clacked together with a sound that made Montse wince despite herself.

The priest jerked. His black eyes shot wide open. Dragos pinned Stamatios against the wall by both arms as his mouth worked frantically, as if trying to take bites of the air. His body shuddered as if trying to shake itself to pieces.

His face turned a shade of forge-heated-iron red Montse had never seen on human skin before. His body shook in a spasm so fierce Montse expected bones to snap, then went as limp as Claudia had.

Dragos let go his arms and stood back. Stamatios plopped onto his face on the stone.

He's dead, Montse thought. For some reason it shocked her almost more than seeing her friend die. *I wanted him that way. I'm* glad. *Why does it feel so bad?*

Nausea welled up from her stomach. She willed herself to puke. *It'll serve this lout right for putting his dirty hand over my mouth!* But she sadly failed to vomit.

Dragos turned away from the corpse and straightened the discreetly frilled cuffs of his black silk blouse.

"Those poison teeth your masters insisted you all be tricked out with do have their uses," he purred to the two surviving emissaries. "Come on. We've wasted enough time."

He nodded to Diego and his companion, who was out of Montse's line of sight but whose presence she sensed looming nearby.

"Don't be more afraid than you can help, little princess," Dragos told her as the hand was removed from her mouth. She sucked in a deep breath to scream—and her vision was obscured by enveloping blackness.

Her heart almost burst from her chest in terror. *I'm blind! I can't breathe!* But then she realized a heavy bag had been pulled over her head by the feel of its coarse cloth on her nose.

"We need to deliver you alive and well," she heard Dragos's smooth baritone, "if we want to stay that way ourselves. Remember that, as the herbs in that bag help you to peacefully sleep."

Herbs? she thought. She found it hard to remember what the word meant. Her head spun.

Blackness swallowed her whole.

"Young woman, your father is damned!"

Air, forest swells, evening light, and emotions flooded Montserrat's world as the hood was yanked from her head. She was racked in turns by rage, grief, fear, confusion, and rage again. All battled furiously for the privilege of propelling the first word from her mouth when she at last confronted her captors.

But what popped out was, "What?"

"The Emperor is damned!" the woman who had murdered Claudia shouted, her face mere centimeters from Montse's. Her face was painted almost white, with rouge spots on the cheeks. They made her pores look huge. "He's condemned himself! Not only by the unpardonable insult he's offered our Basileus by refusing to even answer our suit for your sister to wed our Crown Prince, but now he's thwarted the will of the Creators themselves!"

"What are you on about?" Montse said. She asked the question in Spañol, which was what the woman asked it in. But despite the circumstances, she felt pride in translating an Anglysh phrase she'd read on the fly. She'd read a lot of books and treatises in Anglysh. She loved everything to do with the island Kingdom almost as much as did Prince Heriberto, ruler of the Principality of the Tyrant's Jaw and landlord of the Firefly Palace.

"She means we've just learned that your father's army has met and defeated the Grey Angel Crusade in western Francia, near County Providence," the man called Dragos said. "He saw Raguel off quite smartly, it seems, and with the Grey Angel's passing, the Horde broke apart like a melon dropped on flagstones."

The murderer turned her white rage-twisted face aside to screech at him, "Blasphemer! To make light of the death of one of the Creator's own servants!"

"Which of us is the blasphemer, Paraskeve," Dragos murmured, quite unfazed. "Me, or you for imagining a Grey Angel could be killed so readily?"

Producing a silken kerchief from his sleeve, he dabbed her spittle from his grey beard and the sun-browned skin of his cheek.

Montse had her bearings now. She had been hauled up and unmasked in a clearing in the forest that covered the hills inland from Firefly Palace and the great Channel port of La Merced. Insects buzzed and trilled in the trees around and above and in the fragrant ferns underfoot. A flying squirrel glided from limb to limb beyond the madwoman's right shoulder to take a nosehorn-fly the size of a big man's thumb in flight.

It's either the one where we took Melodía and Pilar when Claudia helped me break my sister out of the Palace, she thought, *or one a lot like it. Must be a popular stop for people running away from there*. A pair of carriages with curtained windows and a gaggle of horses stood at the base of a stand of tall pine trees whose slim yellow boles rose ten meters before branching out.

Then the memory of seeing Claudia brutally killed right in front of her twisted her stomach and clouded her eyes with tears.

"You monsters!" she shrieked. "Prince Harry will have all your heads for this! *You killed my friend.*"

"Did we?" asked a woman with wild hair and haunted eyes. Montse had seen her with the others in the Palace once or twice. Apparently her kidnappers had rendezvoused with the rest of the Trebizon emissaries.

Montse studied her face. It was less clownishly painted than Paraskeve's. *I have to remember everything*, she told herself firmly. *It will help me get away. I don't know how or when it'll help, but I know I need to do that.*

"A nobody, Tasoula," Paraskeve said. "A servant."

"She did kill Stamatios," the leader—Akakios, Montse remembered—said in his deep, rich voice.

"No, that greybeard with you did! And good riddance!"

"Please," Dragos said. "You make me sound so old. Consider my vanity."

"And where's Misti?" Montse yelped, suddenly remembering her other friend who had been with her.

"Safe," said Dragos. He held up a hemp sack that was squirming and kicking. "She bites, so we had to bag her, too. Like you, she has very sharp teeth."

Montse reached out, surprised to discover her hands weren't bound. She took the bag carefully, near the top. She could hear Silver Mistral chittering in muffled rage. She opened the drawstring, reached in carefully, and, as luck had it, found the soft-furred nape of Misti's neck before the ferret sank those teeth into her. She pinched loose skin, gently yet firmly, and lifted her friend out of the bag. Misti's struggles stopped at once and she relaxed, as ferrets did when you picked them up that way.

"I'm here, sweetheart," Montse told her. "I won't let the bad people hurt you."

"As to that," Dragos said, "I had to remind the others we'd agreed to keep her unharmed for you, Princess. When the Prince of Tyrant's Jaw takes my head, you will remember to ask him to make sure the headsman's axe is keen, I trust."

On being reunited with her beloved human, Mistral quickly calmed down. Scooping a hand beneath her fuzzy butt to support her, Montse curled the long, slender body and clutched the ferret to her chest.

She glared at her captors. All the ones she was used to seeing lurking about the Palace were there, minus the dead one, of course. The two survivors—three, if you counted Dragos, who didn't seem to be Trebizonés himself, or five if you included the two local bravos—had been joined by three men and the unkempt woman. The Trebizon emissaries all had dark skin—Montse could tell from Paraskeve's hands—as well as black eyes and hair. None of which made them stand out in Spaña, though to

Montse's eye they looked somehow different from her paisanos, even the highborn ones.

"You're evil," she said, with as much contempt as she could muster. She wasn't used to mustering much, really. She knew the adults around her—especially those her father put in charge of caring for her and keeping her under a modicum of control—were mostly stupider than she was. But that didn't really merit contempt, as far as she was concerned. Pity, more, when she thought about it. But now she made shift—as the Anglysh romances she loved would put it—as best she could. "Also, you're all crazy if you think I'm going to be all sad to learn my daddy won a battle!"

"Not *all* of us think that," Dragos said. "If it makes you feel better, we've also learned your sister Melodía apparently survived and has reconciled with your father."

That brought Montse up short. It did make her feel better. Of course! She'd been desperately worried since Melodía had been arrested on phony charges of plotting against her father. They'd redoubled when word came that the feared but improbable Grey Angel Crusade had actually broken out in Providence, where she had gone. It was wonderful news.

But it didn't stop Montse from being madder than she'd ever been in her life.

She pondered. She didn't often use bad words, believing that doing so was just sloppy and lazy. She didn't like sloppiness or laziness. She admired people who *did* things.

But sometimes . . . she told herself. And drawing in a deep breath, yelled, "*Fuck you!*" And turned and ran for the woods as fast as she could.

One of the Spañol hirelings caught her within a dozen paces, of course. He tucked her under one arm and carried her—kicking and squalling, waving Mistral in one hand and trying determinedly to bite—to one of the waiting carriages.

She still felt good for trying. *I didn't make it this time*, she thought. *But I won't give up.*

She decided the more her captors dismissed her as a hysterical child, the better. So she burst into tears.

It distressed her, though, how easy she found that.

And in a few sobbing breaths, it was no longer an act.

PART TWO

Aftershocks

ChapteR 1

Hada, the Fae—Also *demonio,* demon. An individual is called a **Faerie**. A race of wicked supernatural creatures, who defy the Creators' will and seek to tempt humanity into ruin. Fighting together, humankind, the Grey Angels, and the Creators Themselves defeated their attempt to conquer all Paradise during the dreadful Demon War. Notorious for their pranks, which can be cruel, and their fondness for driving bargains with mortal men and women. Which they keep, but seldom as expected.

> —A PRIMER TO PARADISE FOR THE IMPROVEMENT
> OF YOUNG MINDS

THE EMPIRE OF NUEVAROPA, FRANCIA, ARCHIDUCHÉ DU HAUT-PAYS:

"Lord Karyl, I'm your death."

Quickly though the sibilant crackle had snapped Karyl Bogomirskiy to wakefulness, thought caught his body already in motion, rolling out of the simple pallet in the sumptuous tent.

He hit the fine Ovdan carpet spread across the tent's canvas floor. Without need for conscious intent, he dropped his shoulder, rolled, and snapped to his feet, facing back at his bed. A spurt of yellow fire blazed up in a twist of stinking smoke—but briefly, since both the baggy linen mattress and the vexer feathers it was stuffed with were hard to kindle.

Beyond it, *something* floated in midair. All he could make out was a random seethe of lights and shadows, angles and forms, shapes and void. Now it looked like a beautiful nude woman with purple skin; now a miniature Three-horns; now a thorn-bush; now a black whirlwind; now a man with the head of the mythical Home beast called the ram, with two huge horns curling from it; now jags of primary-colored triangles like shatters of a pane of glass; now a flame. Chimes and grinding noises and gurgles like a Thunder-titan digesting its day's graze chased each other through Karyl's ears. He smelled jasmine, fresh dew, candles, shit.

In his hand he felt the cool, hard reassurance of a dagger hilt. He hadn't needed thought to grab that as he escaped the bed, either.

At the evening's great feast, to celebrate the day's great victory, Karyl had drunk sparingly of wine, and no ale at all. He preferred water. In the weeks after he had awakened from what he thought was sure death, he had sought shelter from the head pains and night terrors in a bottle. Even now, confronting horror, he felt a shudder of fear at the thought of what he had found instead. Sanctuary wasn't it.

Clear though his mind was, it took him a full, steady breath to come to grips with what he was confronting. Or perhaps merely to accept it.

"A Faerie?" He laughed savagely. "Why not? Everything I thought was impossible is the only thing that happens to me now."

Thought-quick, the thing struck at him. Pivoting out of its path, he slashed at it with the dagger. He felt impact.

Sparks flew. Dark smoke puffed and stank. "Iron!" the Faerie shrieked. "It stings."

"Good," Karyl said warily. But he saw his cut had done the creature no harm. The blade, though, was scored and still smoking, as if by strong acid.

He lunged toward the bed—and away from another stab of a thorned/flaming/frothing protrusion. His black-wood staff lay beside the pallet. Kneeling on the staff to hold it down, he whipped out the meter-long blade concealed inside. Then he grabbed the thin blanket off his pallet and threw it over the apparition.

The blanket thrashed. Squeals and sparkles came from underneath. Light glowed hellish yellow and blue through holes that appeared and rapidly grew in the goat-felt fabric.

The Faerie's reaction to Karyl's dagger stroke had taught him that, whatever else, it was palpable. As expected, the blanket disconcerted the thing as it would a mortal foe. Also as expected, it wouldn't for long.

As the blanket was consumed into glowing fragments and scraps that appeared to be being eaten up by some black growth and a frightful stench not just of burning goat-felt arose, Karyl leapt over the bed and thrust the tip of the single-edged straight sword through the center of the thing.

The shriek that battered his brain did not seem to enter through his ears. A terrific shock up his arm threw him back on his ass on the bed.

Now the crackles and gleams and fast-spreading blights seemed to be consuming the Faerie itself.

"I die!" it screamed. "But why?"

It seemed to be sucked in on itself. And out of the world.

For a moment Karyl simply stood, eyes wide, breathing hard. Though not from physical exertion.

"You saw the whole thing," he said without turning.

"Yes," came from behind.

Turning, he saw what appeared to be a small woman, features and form completely hidden by cloak and cowl. He weighed the sword briefly in his hand. But he already knew, from trying to strike her in despair and fury earlier that evening, that Aphrodite was not physically present; what he saw and heard was a projection, an illusion. Reassured nonetheless by the weapon's feel, he stooped to pick up the staff-scabbard and return the blade.

"You don't need to be seen to see, do you?" he said, tucking the dagger back into its sheath beneath his bed.

"No."

"And, of course, you didn't help."

"You know my nature, Lord Karyl. I cannot interfere in human affairs."

"What's stopping you? You've got absurd and mystic powers: To walk the world without substance. To grow back my hand. What can possibly restrict you?"

"What you might call a geas," she said. "One which will destroy me if I disobey."

"What could lay that kind of . . . enchantment on you?"

"The Creators," she said. "They made me that way."

He pushed out a sound that was half grunt, half sigh. "Very well. It seems I must accept that. Disbelief has long since played me false, and left me no solid ground to stand on."

He pointed the straight blade toward where the Faerie had hovered. The carpet was scorched beneath, and discolored, as if something had pissed on it.

"They made that too?"

"No," she said. "At least—not deliberately."

"It was a Faerie."

"Yes."

He shook his head. Which hurt. It wasn't one of the horrific headaches, like big iron spikes being driven through his brain, that often snatched him screaming from sleep or helped to sink his waking self into black despair. But it seemed to herald one.

"I notice the guards haven't exactly swarmed to my aid."

"It never occurred to you to call for them, did it? Practical though you are in so many things."

He raised a brow. "No. I'm used to fighting my own battles. Too used, perhaps. But the commotion should've caught somebody's attention."

"The Faerie spoke quietly—and as much in your mind as aloud, as you may have realized. Nor were the shines and flashes particularly visible through the walls of the tent. In any event, with the great threat gone, the few guards on duty tonight are fuddled by fatigue and wine themselves."

He nodded. "People always lose spirit and energy after a battle, even a victory."

"So I have seen, over centuries of observation as the Witness."

He picked up the staff, sheathed his sword, and tossed it on the bed. "I don't really know much about human feelings. And thinking processes, such as they are. Less than you, I don't doubt."

She pulled back her cowl. Her face was that of a pretty young woman, not even fifty, with green eyes and short red-gold hair.

"I have had more practice," she said.

Not for the first time, he wondered what she was. Or what she really looked like. He suspected she could take any semblance she chose, especially given that all he had seen of her was illusion.

She approached him, seeming to glide without moving her feet. She reached out a hand as if to stroke his hair. He flinched. Just because he couldn't touch her did not mean she could not touch *him*. He did not welcome such contact.

Her brow furrowed. The outsides of her eyes compressed as if in pain. She dropped her hand.

"Yet your words can rally women and men to serve your ends as few others."

"A mere sleight," he said, "like any common mountebank's."

Stepping back, she waved at his left hand. "Perhaps you should be less dismissive of conjuring sleights."

He scowled. When Rob Korrigan had taken Karyl to meet her in an inn in the Francés village of Pot de Feu, she had gestured mysteriously and shone light on the stump of his left hand, bitten off by a Horror on the brink of the Cliffs of the Eye. He had taken that as fraud—and as cruel mockery. Then his hand grew back.

Which in some ways was crueler.

"Why did the thing speak to me?" he asked. "I was sound asleep." *For once.* "If it had just struck, it would have killed me."

"The Fae are insane," Aphrodite said in her earnest childlike way. "It probably did not believe you could harm it. Humans seldom can."

"How *did* I harm it?" Karyl said. "And did I harm it badly enough that it won't soon come back?"

"You heard it. You killed it."

Karyl asked a question with his brow.

"Your sword is special. You must have surmised that, since when you woke again after your fall you found yourself a homeless beggar dressed in shabby robe and sandals—yet carrying a weapon of a quality only a rich *grande* could afford. And of a kind seldom seen in Nuevaropa: a single-edged sword with a straight blade, concealed in a staff."

"Indeed. Though I've seen swords just like it in Zipangu. They call it *shikomizue*."

"Have you noticed anything unusual about the sword?"

"I take it that you mean, other than that I have it at all."

"Yes."

"It's uncommonly sharp, and never needs sharpening. That's fairly strange, but I quickly came to take it for granted. I was not at my best mentally when I returned to myself. From wherever I'd been. Acceptance was easiest, so it was what I did. And later—" He shrugged. "There were more urgent things to think about."

She nodded. "It is as I thought. Certain . . . artifacts . . . exist which are imbued with the power of harming creatures from the World Below. Clearly, your staff-sword is one."

"Shiraa's bite was enough to make an end of Raguel."

"As I told you: Raguel is not dead. Though surely discomfited. And angry."

"But the Faerie's really dead."

"Yes. They lie. This one happened not to. They are unpredictable even in prevarication. They are mad."

"Could my staff-sword have killed Raguel?"

Her features, which even the anti-aesthete Karyl recognized as flawless, creased with concern.

"I do not know. That is truth. Some such artifacts might. Very powerful beings of the sort that you would regard as 'supernatural' have been truly destroyed before."

"Which begs the question of how I, a homeless beggar, came into possession of a mystic weapon of a degree of power too preposterous for even a romance."

She smiled sadly.

"You won't tell me," he said.

"When you are ready."

He made a disgusted sound and waved a disgusted hand.

"I'm thinking of declining the dukedom the Emperor announced for me at the banquet," he said, turning away. "I hate nobles. They're shit."

Of course, Karyl Bogomirskiy, once heir to the throne

of the Misty March, and years later its Voyvod or Warrior-Count, was noble himself. Aphrodite refrained from pointing out the obvious.

"Do you think you can do more to counter the evil they do as a bourgeois, or a peasant? A penniless outcast? Or as one of them, and powerful and well-respected even among them?"

"Am I to be spared nothing?" he said, hearing and hating the whine in his voice.

She shook her head. "I thought you never asked rhetorical questions, dear Karyl."

"That wasn't necessarily one," he said. "Sometimes I still dare to hope." *If doubt forsakes me, sarcasm still serves. Or anyway answers my summons.*

"You should," she said. "Indeed, you have to. But you must do more than hope, Lord Karyl, my dear. Because now the Grey Angels are angry. And, more, they are coming."

He walked. The crushed bone that metaled the road crunched beneath the sandals on his feet. He smelled warm soil and ripe growth, the vagrant hints of flowers growing wild in the ditch. The sun stung his bare and beardless face through a particularly thin scrim of overcast.

I need to get a hat, he thought.

He looked around at his surroundings. He was walking through a gently rolling land, fields of brown grain stretching left and right, dotted with scrub-topped hills and stands of evergreen broadleaf trees. Ditches whose spoil had gone to build up the roadway ran along both sides to drain it. Fifty meters to his left, three peasants, two men and a woman, naked or wearing only loincloths along with their inevitable conical straw hats, loaded sheaves into a wagon. A single nosehorn, dark green mottled over grey, munched contentedly in its harness at the contents of a feed bucket looped over its single big horn.

Wheat grew near enough to the road to provide cover for a quick strike from ambush, he realized. A tautness ran up the underside of his penis, knotted the base of his scrotum, coiled in his stomach. Was that fear? His left hand tried to clench but felt peculiar; his right hand clenched on something hard.

He looked down. Almost absently, he noted that his body was clad in a rough, almost sack-like robe or smock of greyish brown hemp. With a jolt he realized that his left hand wasn't there. His left arm, swinging into view at the rhythm of his pace, ended in a pink, puckered stub.

The apprehension in his belly turned to nausea. A spasm dropped him to his knees. Some reflex of propriety made him turn toward the ditch before he vomited.

All he could produce was dry heaves anyway.

When the convulsions passed, he got back to his feet with the aid of the blackwood staff he now noticed he was carrying in his right hand. Knowing nothing better to do, he walked on.

The nausea reaction to discovering the loss of his sword hand left him keenly aware of a growling emptiness in his belly. He was carrying something, by feel a pack or sack, over his shoulder by a strap of nosehorn leather, stained dark by sweat and weather-cracked, that ran across his chest. Perhaps he carried something to eat there? And also drink.

Before he could begin to rummage, memory snatched him like a Tyrant's Jaw—

He floats, he floats.
  Something sears his left arm. He screams. Yet no sound enters his mind.

He opens his eyes to nothing. To grey Void, speck-swarming.

Then faces. Inhumanly beautiful—shifting subtly to merely, monstrously inhuman. And back again. He feels as if he is being twisted—torn inside out. He longs for escape, for respite, for relief from the sudden lust that somehow threatens to explode his groin.

Then: Laughter! Laughter!

And—

He falls. He falls. He feels and sees the blood of his life pumping from the stump of his left arm, like a red rope unreeling from the cliff from which he fell, pulling out his life. Feels the fevered heat through the feathers of the narrow-keeled chest of the Horror he clutches to him with his right hand. Smells its fetid rotting-meat breath as the toothy snout snaps at his face, spattering droplets of his own blood hot on the face he still struggles desperately to keep from being bitten off. The dinosaur struggles furiously to rake his sides with the great killing-claws on either foot. But he grips it too tightly.

He is dead, and multiply so: from loss of blood, and from the surface of the great gulf called the Tyrant's Eye rushing up to smash him like a granite wall. But he fights on. That is what he does.

As for hope, he long since lost that.

Still, his balls and gut tighten in anticipation of the pain of impact: imminent, releasing.

He falls and falls.

And then—

His scream woke him before the guards, stumbling with weariness and drink but willing nonetheless, it brought into his tent could do so.

Chapter 2

Tricornio, **Three-horn**, Trike. . . . —*Triceratops horridus*. Largest of the widespread hornface (Ceratopsian) family of herbivorous, four-legged dinosaurs with horns, bony neck-frills, and toothed beaks; 10 tonnes, 10 meters long, 3 meters at shoulder. Non-native to Nuevaropa. Feared for the lethality of their long brow-horns as well as for their belligerent eagerness to use them.

—THE BOOK OF TRUE NAMES

T he closed-fist blow rocked Rob Korrigan's head to the right.

He reeled on his knees. *Quite the punch he packs*, he managed to think inside a brain that felt as if it were spinning in his skull like a child's top, *for such a swag-bellied old reaper.*

"Let that be the last blow you suffer from another without taking retribution!" declared the man who stood over him, the ginger fur of his paunch practically tickling Rob's nose in the shade of the silken pavilion atop the loaf-shaped hill.

Ah, but that clout struck me long ago, your Emp-ship, Rob thought. *When I parted ways at last with my original*

Master Morrison, that vile, drunken, one-eyed old Scot bastard.

"Arise, Montador Robrey Korrigan," Felipe said, "and assume the duties and privileges of a Knight and Baron of the Empire of Nuevaropa." Rob winced to hear his full first name—for the first time in many years. *Where on Paradise did the man go and dredge it up?*

I must've babbled it in my cups. Aye—I certainly babbled it in my cups; isn't that me to the life? Possibly to that vexer Melodía.

Felipe reached down a hand wound in bandages to cover the burst blisters. For all the presumed softness that had led to them, his Imperial Majesty latched a substantial grip on Rob's forearm when he accepted. Gratefully, since he was still woozy. And, for a wonder, not because of a drink.

The day's young, he thought.

The sun was high and hot and the clouds were thin, a sort of watered-milk white. A brisk wind from the ridges to the north snapped the bright banners and boomed the gold and scarlet silken canopy overhead. Rob wished he had a hat to shield his face. Sweat streamed down his forehead, stinging at his eyes and making his beard itch abominably. At that the *grandes—my fellow grandees*, he reminded himself, though most considerably *grander*—suffered considerably more. The courtiers crowded onto the hilltop wore little but fripperies of gold and glittering jewels, green and red and blue flashing darts of reflection in every direction, but if nothing else the headbands of their grand feather headdresses had to chafe, and the showy great plumes of bird and dinosaur offered little protection from the sun. And they were the lucky ones.

From behind him Rob heard a snort. That would be one of the famous war-Triceratops of his commander—and friend—Karyl Bogomirskiy. They were arrayed at the base of the hill next to the glorious but sadly few remaining hadrosaurs of the Companions of Our Lady of the Mirror—also glorious and sadly few after riding at least twice through the whole Horde during yesterday's slaughter.

That was an uneasy pairing, and not just because Three-horns' terrible long brow-horns were the bane of the dinosaur knights' showily crested sackbut and morion mounts. Around and beside the two blocs were arrayed the rest of the two armies, previously hunter and hunted, who had come together yesterday to defend the Empire and people of the Tyrant's Head from Raguel's mad Crusade.

Rob became uncomfortably aware that thousands of eyes were on him right now. *You should've got away whilst the getting was good, me boyo,* he thought glumly. *It's well and truly stuck you are now.*

The fact that the Emperor had strong hands despite their softness needn't have surprised him. In his youth Felipe had famously pushed a pike as a simple soldier for his uncle the King of Alemania. The hand that hadn't helped Rob up held still the longsword used to knight Rob moments before, its tip now stuck in the turf of the round hill called *Le Boule*, whose blade showed numerous notches that had not, by all accounts, been there yesterday. Despite the self-sacrificing efforts of his elite bodyguard, the Scarlet Tyrants, and their commander, the huge Alemán Duke Falk, on his albino Tyrant Snowflake, Felipe had struck hard blows in his own defense.

A young man and woman in the crimson and scarlet tabards of Heraldos Imperiales flanked Rob and, with respectful firmness, marched him off the top of the round hill and away from the Imperial presence and party. A murmur of commentary rippled through the onlookers: the courtiers and *grandes* crowded atop Le Boule and the thousands of surviving knights and common soldiers ranged on the battleground to watch the hilltop ceremony. Which, having dragged on for over an hour, was finally closing in on its climax.

Then at last the real question struck Rob. But there was no way to ask it, because the next to receive elevation was already being led before Emperor Felipe.

The unquestioned hero of the final confrontation with Raguel: Rob's commander and best friend, Karyl Bogomirskiy.

"Arise, Mor Karyl, Duque Imperial de la Marca!"

At Felipe's exuberant call—and Melodía did rejoice to see her father enjoying himself so hugely, as he always did a spectacle—the slight man rose from the yellow bare-scuffed dirt before him. It struck the Princess that she wore almost the same garb he did. Except that he wore a straight-bladed arming-sword instead of a curved Ovdan *talwar,* slung to the right hip rather than the left.

Naturally enough, she thought. *After all, he rides to the fights armored like a light rider, too.*

Despite the sneers of certain courtiers, most or all of whom had managed to turn up soon after the desperate battle against Raguel and his Horde had ended, she was proud of her garb and of the nickname that went with it, *the Short-Haired Horse Captain.* She had earned them. Unlike her titles or family name.

Even though I guess I'll be growing my hair out again, now that I seem to be becoming a Princesa Imperial *again.*

Karyl stood up into a storm of cheers, in which the assembled thousands seemed to participate more eagerly than the courtiers gathered around the Emperor, even though the majority couldn't hear a thing. They knew the man who had saved them from Raguel, though. If not by sight, then by having him excitedly pointed out by those who had been so placed as to see him on the battlefield in person.

She let her gaze slide down the slope, which had been trod almost bare of cover. A man was walking up from the base of the cone-shaped hill. He was tall, and the breeze whipped his long, fine orange hair over sharp, fine features like a banner. He moved easily, despite his twenty kilograms of steel plate armor. The harness was so gouged and battered it was hard to make out the large orange Lady's Mirror emblazoned on a once gleaming-white breastplate. A longsword hung from his waist.

Warmth beyond the day's heat filled her. He was the Imperial Champion, Constable of all the Empire's armies and navies, Knight Commander of the Military Order of Our Lady of the Mirror, Jaume dels Flors. He was also her betrothed all but officially—and the lover she had driven from her over his refusal to resign command of an army ordered to a war they both agreed was unjust.

I was right, too, she thought. *Somehow that doesn't fill the hollowness his absence has left in me over these last months.*

The two apprentice heralds were escorting Karyl out of the Imperial presence, keenly aware of the moment and working their dignity hard. But he stopped, resisting their gentle but insistent hand-pressing to get him moving again. Like the torn-up remnant of the Scarlet Tyrants standing guard around her father, heralds had nearly unlimited license in the course of their duties to lay hands on persons regardless of rank.

Melodía's heart almost stopped. Her former commander was staring at the man who was climbing Le Boule toward him. Karyl's features were handsome enough, she supposed, for a man of his years and their hardness, though they were more gaunt than anything else. But his gaze was sharp and merciless as an Allosaurus's.

Karyl, she knew, believed the man approaching him so boldly had stabbed him in the back and destroyed his famous White River Legion in the River Hassling, when the Battle of Gunters Moll ended in an unexpected truce with the rebellious Princes' Party instead of the victory Karyl and his walking-fortress Triceratops were helping the Imperial forces win. And by the man's own regretful admission to Melodía, he was right.

They were the two most storied swordsmen in the Empire of the Fangèd Throne. Not even Melodía was sure the orange-haired knight would win. And she worshipped him.

I do Karyl too, I suppose. In a very different way, of course.

Jaume stopped a pace away from Karyl. The two stood facing each other for a moment that seemed to stretch out as if a hank of Melodía's nerves were being reeled off her on a spindle. Long turquoise eyes stared into intense eyes so dark they were almost black.

Karyl thrust out his left hand—his sword hand. Bare, wiry fingers closed on steel vambrace; steel gauntlets closed on linen-clad forearm, and the two heroes shook hands.

The applause from the massed soldiers was thunderous.

As Karyl walked on away from Jaume to join the other recently elevated nobles, one of them stepped haltingly forward and raised a hand.

Oh, no, Melodía thought.

"Pardon me all to pieces, Your Majesty," Rob Baron Korrigan said, "but I need to ask a question."

"Begging your pardon," Rob said to Felipe, "but you called me Baron. What might you have meant by that, if you please?"

Felipe's courtiers looked shocked at the question's impertinence, gathered with the Emperor beneath the gold-and-red silk canopy and spilling down the sides of the hill. Some were his buckethead captains, others the Eight Creators, though they were got up in enough feathers, and gilt to choke Falk's Tyrannosaurus, who was tethered well behind Le Boule, where his scent wouldn't upset the plant-eating dinosaurs commonly used in war. But the slim young woman who stood on Felipe's left wore not the scant yet gaudy garments of a noblewoman on such a momentous occasion, on such a warm day, but the nosehorn-leather jerkin and jackboots of a *jinete*. She caught Rob's eye and gave him a slow wink.

But the Emperor smiled indulgently. "I've decided your service demands not just knighthood but a true patent of nobility."

Well, there's your mistake, Rob thought. Though, somewhat to his own amazement, he didn't blurt that too.

He did blurt, "Baron? Of what?"

"That's up to your liege, the Imperial Duke Karyl, to decide. We decided it in council."

His "we" included a nod to the tall young woman by his side, her brush of dark-red hair ruffled by the fingers of a rising wind. She was plainly dressed in such a glittering gaggle, but anything but plain.

Rob's former Horse-Captain gave him a grin that made her look like a child of fourteen—the same age as her adored baby sister, Montserrat.

"I don't have to tell you the devastation the . . . recent events left behind," Felipe said. Rob got the sense the Emperor was speaking for the benefit of far more ears than his alone. "Many lords of the affected provinces were killed, and often their entire families as well. Their fiefs stand empty. Other knights and nobles willingly joined the Crusade. Their domains are vacated too."

His avuncular tone took on an edge for that last bit.

Though it seemed *treason* and *attainder* ran too contrary to the occasion's spirit. Which struck Rob as a sort of desperate festivity. Not unjustifiably, given that the Grey Angels were the personal servitors of the gods of this world, the Eight Creators, and that one of their Crusades was nothing less than the direct manifestation on Paradise of their awful justice. The Emp's having fought back against Raguel's Crusade left him and his Empire in decidedly dicey circumstances, theologically speaking.

"So I've decided to create or assign your Karyl a passel of loose lords," Felipe said. "And as a *Duque Imperial* he naturally enjoys privilege to create 'em on his own. So you'll accompany your new liege back to Providence, and he'll find the proper seat for you. Not doubt it'll be a fine one, since by all accounts you served as his strong right hand."

Rather the left, being his spymaster and chief skull-dugger, Rob thought. Then he felt the awful weight of Felipe's words land on him like a lightning-struck titan.

"But what am I to *do* with the job?" he all but wailed. "I'm a peasant rogue of a minstrel and dinosaur master, not a bucket—a *grande*. I don't know how to be a Baron!"

"Provided for as well," said Felipe, whose patience seemed as boundless as his cheer today.

Rob could see how surviving the certain destruction, not just of one's own personal arse but of family and Empire as well, could do that to a body. Especially the day after, when His Majesty and most of them had a chance to rest away most of the awful depression that followed battle.

"An important nobleman has kindly agreed to lend you a trusted, capable servant to serve as your seneschal. He'll take the burden of managing castle and estates, wherever they may be, off your shoulders. And I believe you can trust Duke Karyl to make sure you're not given more than you can handle at first, eh?"

Uncertainty still tied Rob's stomach in a knot. *Best to cut your losses and escape while you can, lad*, he told himself, and allowed the apprentice heralds to squire him to the side with the other glittering riffraff.

Count Jaume was presented to the Emperor, his uncle and liege, and a herald began to recite his many and mighty deeds, with emphasis on the ones performed just yesterday. Rob listened with half an ear, because Baron or not—and he still couldn't believe he was a Baron—he remained what he always was: a minstrel and a dinosaur master. Along with something of a scoundrel; but his experience suggested that was a career asset for a buckethead. He had written and sung many songs of the heroism of Jaume, as of his hero Karyl, and they had brought him silver.

And as fast as Maris's Wheel had turned to bring him these blessings, dubious as they were, he knew it could turn back again and dump him penniless in a ditch. He might *need* more songs.

Meanwhile, his eye wandered out across the mingled armies. They made a brave if battered spectacle: with pride of place in the front line going to Jaume's remnant Companions on their hadrosaurs, the surviving Tercio of Brown Nodosaurs, and Karyl's bloc of Triceratops with tall wicker-and-lath fighting castles strapped to their backs. All were sadly reduced by yesterday's unequal fight.

Flanking them were the other dinosaur knights of both armies, Karyl's Fugitive Legion and Felipe's Imperial one—which until midmorning yesterday had been hunting Karyl and his lot. And behind them the rest: chivalry, even more defiantly colorful in their display of heraldic banners and caparisons, as if to outshine their more massively mounted kindred; professional House-soldiers in their mail and peaked helmets; Imperial peasant levies, looking less slack and disgruntled than normal, since for once they'd had some stake in fighting; Karyl's ragtag light troops, infantry archers and Rob's own *jinetes*, less irreverent than usual and for the most part paying attention.

Beyond them, he could see scores of men and women canvassing the battlefield, seeing to the wounded, animal and human. Rob's own dinosaur grooms from Karyl's army were among them, as well as their erstwhile opposite numbers from the Imperial camp. His boys and girls had volunteered with an alacrity that might surprise an outsider. While most of the exceedingly valuable wardinosaurs who had any hope of recovering had been moved off the field last night, some remained who were beyond healing. Any true aspirant to Dinosaur Mastery—and Rob himself, who would've been out there if not for an engagement he couldn't escape, much as he wished to—would want to ease the great beasts' suffering in the only manner possible. Equerries performed the same final mercy for untreatably wounded horses, of which there were a good many more than dinosaurs.

Meanwhile, robed sectaries of Maia and Spada, the Creators most associated with healing and with war, searched among the most numerous casualties of all: their own kind. Hundreds had already been moved to hospital tents, improvised shelters, borrowed farmhouses nearby, and even as far as the village of Canterville several kilometers southwest, whose name had already been attached to the fight. Rob could see some being carried to ambulance wagons on makeshift stretchers.

Those who couldn't be helped received the same grace as the injured dinosaurs and horses, delivered with lead maces and the misericordia, or mercy-dagger.

War's a terrible mistress, Rob thought. *Yet somehow we can't quit her.*

Still the Imperial Herald droned on. She was up to Jaume's exploits in yesterday's battle, anyway. Rob began to hope he might soon find the shelter of proper shade and ale. *It's not as if my body and soul've fully recovered from yesterday,* he thought. *Not to mention the days and weeks preceding.*

The wind veered to blow from the east across the former battlefield, bringing the smell of tens of thousands of corpses, from those of children hag-ridden by the frightful Raguel to the three-ton morions of dinosaur knights, full in the faces of the nobles on their hill.

Rob blinked. His stomach gurgled unhappily but kept its place. The Emperor's smile as he looked upon his appointed Champion never faltered. The herald kept declaiming, showing her stomach was made of the same tough leather as her lungs. But the mercantile magnate who stood three places upslope turned, the sixty-centimeter green-and-white Ridiculous Reaper plumes sticking up from his silver bonnet wavering like yarrow shoots and his brown skin gone a sickly ashen-green, and gagged, spilling pale chunky vomit down the silver-and-feathered gorget he wore and across the garnet-bossed target strapped to his bare chest. Others joined him as he fell to his knees to offer his own special sacrifice to the soil of Paradise.

The smell of death wasn't uncommon. Even the glittering courtiers now either surrendering to sudden nausea or fighting valiant rearguard actions against it had encountered it before, surely. But a stench on *this* scale was anything but common. It seemed to coat your tongue and suffuse your whole body with uncleanness.

No one Rob knew of ever got used to it. You just learned to deal with it. He felt a certain stab of admiration at the Emperor's aplomb.

Rob kept his face stiff with the reflex of a peasant who knew too well that the mere hint of a smile at his betters' discomfiture could earn him at best a buffet, and at worst a noose. Then he remembered, *Wait, I'm one of these hada now!* And let himself guffaw.

And of all things, that broke him.

Thought of the Fae inevitably brought their archenemies the Grey Angels to mind. The reminder that the rudely ejected Raguel had mates shot a memory into him like a stinger-bolt in the stomach.

It was last night. Sure, he'd been thoroughly ossified—drunk enough to find himself not just pissing on the backside of the Emperor's own tent but daring to peep inside through a small slit, which he may or may not have improved with his dagger for the purpose. But Rob had never drunk enough to make him hallucinate.

Which meant he had really seen raw horror.

He now knew a thing apparently unknown to Felipe, or anyone else in the Empire: that the Emperor's confessor and closest confidant, the mysterious Fray Jerónimo, was himself the same terrible thing as Raguel.

A Grey Angel. Who likely enough, even now, sat in his screened cell in that selfsame pavilion not fifty yards from where Rob stood.

And thus he dropped to his knees and added the gruel, flatbread, and fatty-bacon he'd had for breakfast to the offerings he'd just been mocking from his fellow lords and ladies of Nuevaropa.

Chapter 3

Matador, Slayer. . . . —*Allosaurus fragilis.* Large, bipedal carnivorous dinosaur. Grows to 10 meters long, 1.8 meters at shoulder, 2.3 tonnes. Nuevaropa's largest and most feared native predator. Famed for its often incredible stealth.

—THE BOOK OF TRUE NAMES

When the wind changed, Shiraa raised her head. And growled.

The several small, skinny, tailless two-legs her mother had left to care for her grew agitated. One of them tossed a slab of meat from a long-crested two-leg plant-eater into her pen of palings driven into the hard dirt.

She scooped it up in her long, strong jaws, tossed up her head, swallowed it. It pleased her, of course. It was meat! But it didn't take her mind off that smell.

The strongest smell was the delicious aroma of dead flesh ripening in the daytime heat. Though she was well fed—of course, now that she was back together with her mother!—and little driven by hunger, the smells themselves were like a feast. Normally she would've simply lain down and slept in sheer pleasure, the decaying meat filling her nostrils with joy and her dreams with plenty.

But another odor rode that wind. It was faint. Beside the aroma of so much food becoming tender and more tasty, anything would have been, except perhaps the smoke of a wildfire. Yet it stung like a thorn driven deep in her flank by brushing against a nosehorn bush.

It was *him*. Her enemy. Raising her head, she looked furiously around for the hated white Tyrannosaurus.

I will *kill him!*

As the pyroclastic-flow of stench rolled over her, Melodía Estrella Delgao Llobregat, heir to the Archiduché de Los Almendros and Princesa Imperial, ground her jaw defiantly.

I'm damned if I'm going to lose control and my break-fast like some of these perfumed and pampered hangers-on around me. Especially since the Imperial Herald kept right on singing her long-lost lover's praises in stupefying detail without so much as blinking at the stench.

She'd smelled that smell before. If not, admittedly, at that intensity. She was a veteran of many battles. And by Maia and Bella and all the Creators, she was going to act like one.

Which wasn't easy. *Does anyone ever get used to the stink of death?* she wondered. Even Karyl's famous and fabulously rare matadora war-mount, Shiraa, responded with a roar to the wind shift.

From her vantage point atop the conical Boule, Melodía could see work gangs gathering the tens of thousands of human dead into piles. Armed patrols circled the slaughter grounds, keeping all but the most intrepid—or small, or winged—of scavengers at bay.

It wasn't for the sake of the dead. The waiting slayers and raptor-packs would get their feast. There was no practical way to dispose of all that carrion other than to leave it to nature's ravenous appetite. The watchful sentinels, many of whom were her own light riders, were guarding the mercy-parties and the corpse-handlers from the deadlier meat-eaters—unseen, but unquestionably lurking nearby.

At least there are no settlements near enough to risk a disease outbreak from all the decay, she thought. Disease was rare and thus terrifying; plagues were dreaded as greatly as Grey Angel Crusades. And the army would soon have to shift camp toward Canterville to keep itself safe from an epidemic.

But the reason nobody dwelled nearby was as awful as the stink: the Imperial command had already begun getting reports that hardly any survivors could be found in the villages or farmsteads east of here, probably all the way to the Shield Range. The few people reconnaissance parties spotted were wary as wild mother vexers.

The Grey Angel Horde had acted like a swarm of soldier ants—up to and including a self-sacrificing lack of concern for personal safety, or even hunger or thirst. Everything human in its path had either joined it or been eaten, or just gruesomely killed. Even Canterville and its surrounding farms lay empty, its residents having prudently fled west at word of Raguel's approach.

Not all the survivors were victims who had managed to hide, either. Most of the men and women clearing the battlefield were former Hordelings. Deprived by Shiraa's heroic and conveniently timed jaws of the terrible Grey Angel glamour that had compelled them to commit atrocities with suicidal abandon, they found themselves exhausted, scabby, and sickly from personal neglect and deprivation, befuddled, demoralized, and far from home.

Felipe's declaration, right after the battle, of blanket amnesty to commoners who had belonged to Raguel's Horde had outraged many in her father's camp. Melodía knew it was the only sensible thing to do. Tens of thousands of them had survived. Trying to punish them all would be a crime to match the ones Raguel had driven them to.

And Melodía knew something the protesting *grandes* could not: the awful power to compel that a Grey Angel has. She herself had been victimized by Raguel's power, though she had been compelled to forget, not serve. The memory made her skin crawl still. It was the second greatest violation of her life.

Of course, what really outraged the *grandes* about Felipe's amnesty was his decision to exempt the knights and nobles who had fought for Raguel. He had promptly placed them under attainder, declaring them outlaws to be hunted down and killed without hesitation, warning, or mercy.

Melodía agreed wholeheartedly with her father—as had Jaume and most of the nobles who had actually been present for the battle. The majority of dinosaur knights and chivalry who'd served the Angel as the leaders and elite striking arm of his Crusade had done so willingly. For once she approved of the fact that Felipe, though easily influenced before he made a decision, tended to drop his hindquarters and dig in like a balky dray-nosehorn once he did decide.

The wind continued to blow from the east. Courtiers continued to be overcome by vomiting fits. Shiraa continued to roar from her pen behind La Boule. And Melodía had to keep part of her mind on keeping her stomach in check.

It was still easier to resist the nausea the stink caused than the nausea of having to bear the nearness of the man who had falsely accused and then raped her.

Though her father had won Election on the basis of appearing to be the most unassuming and unambitious eligible member of Torre Delgao—from which Emperors of Nuevaropa were always Elected—Felipe's flair for showmanship was only one of many ways he'd surprised his supporters. He had shown it by choosing to launch today's elevation ceremonies with one of the three most conspicuous heroes of yesterday's battle and to end with the other two.

That first one was Falk, Duke von Hornberg, made an Imperial Duke in recognition of his saving the Emperor's life from the Horde.

She knew it was true, too. The Imperial bodyguards, the Scarlet Tyrants, had suffered incredible casualties guarding the Imperial body from waves of reeking and shrieking flesh. Even at that, Melodía's father had had to swing a sword in his defense. And Falk and the albino Tyrant Snowflake had fought in the forefront against the mad Crusaders. *Everyone had seen it.* Including her beloved Jaume.

So his courage and prowess are equal to his evil, she thought bitterly. *I will not forget. I will not forgive. Least of all will I condone.*

And yet he saved my father's life against unimaginable odds. How can I accuse him of falsely arresting and then raping me?

But then she heard her father order Jaume to approach, and all thoughts of vileness—the stench of tens of thousands of decaying corpses, the stench of Falk's nearness, far worse—fell out of her mind. She would not let them spoil her enjoyment of her friend and lover's receiving the honor he had so richly earned.

I'll even pretend that annoying meat-eating dinosaur bellowing behind the hill is celebrating what is to come for my Jaume.

"What's wrong with that beast?" said a female knight standing near Rob amid the Imperial retinue somewhat down the side of La Boule from Felipe and his shade. Though she wore plate enameled in intricate patterns of silver on blue, the very fact the paint job was pristine showed she was one of the late arrivals.

The man she questioned in response to the roars, which he recognized as Shiraa's, was a Baron So-and-So whose name Rob hadn't caught and didn't care to learn. He laughed.

"It smells the feast laid out for it and its kind."

And isn't that a buckethead to the life? Rob thought. *Your life depends on your war-hadrosaur, and yet you know nothing of dinosaurs.*

True enough it was that meat-eaters, including Nueva-ropa's largest native predators, matadores like Karyl's mount, were waiting in cover to share the carcass bounty when armed guards quit blocking them from joining the winged scavengers, the Eye-takers and Corpse-tearers and toothed crows already feeding.

But his master's beloved lifelong companion was well fed, certainly, and she so recently rejoined to Karyl. And fortuitously—enough so to prickle the back of Rob's neck with suspicions of supernatural interference.

Though Rob knew little of the art of tending to big meat-eating dinosaurs—the rarest beasts on the battle-field, for reasons obvious and other—he knew his dino-saur roars. He wasn't hearing a hungry slayer.

He was hearing an angry one.

And unless Rob missed his guess, as he knew he didn't, it wasn't the scent of any notional rival matado-res lurking in wood or scrub who had so righteously en-raged her. It was the Tyrannosaurus who had attacked her from behind at Gunters Moll, as his rider had Karyl, and treacherously torn a strip from her shoulder.

Creators, please see the palisade we made to hold her stands, if this goes on much longer, he silently prayed. *And that the Fae don't work their tricks.*

At which he felt the superstitious shiver he got whenever he mentioned the Faerie Folk. Even inside his own head.

And then he heard the sound he feared even more than the Fae.

Falk's heart still hammered his rib cage from inside. *Now I'm a* Duque Imperial, *and not just* Graf von Hornberg!

His new rank, being mostly symbolic, brought little by way of additional power and a stipend he didn't care much about. But it was an enormous boost in precedence. That was what made him giddy with triumph.

Not bad for a man who, merely two years before, had been the most successful field commander of the Alemán Princes' Party rebellion against the very Emperor whose body he had protected with his own.

For his elevation he wore his own royal-blue plate he had brought with him from the tiny north-coast Duchy of Hornberg, rather than the gilt and scarlet panoply of the Scarlet Tyrant commander. It was the armor he'd worn to battle yesterday, and its dents and gouges bore testimony that he and Snowflake—his one true friend in all the world—had fought the Horde as well as any. Indeed, better than most.

His manservant, Bergdahl, told him that bards were already composing songs to praise his exploits alongside those two great darlings of ballad and romance, Jaume and Karyl. Not even his servant's sneers had been able to quell his elation at that.

I wonder if that's enough to make my Mother think well of me at last?

His stomach turned over. He knew the answer to that.

But still. He had done what she had told him to—and so much more. He had risen high.

And I will rise higher still. On my honor, I shall!

After endless heraldic blather, Jaume was finally kneeling to receive his own reward from the Emperor. Falk's smile felt as if it fit strangely on his mouth. *I wonder how he'd feel if he knew I fucked his beloved little Princess in the ass?*

Yet he was glad the Imperial Champion didn't know. Not because he feared him—although the time they faced each other on the tourney field Jaume had beaten him fair and square, regardless of the lies to the contrary that Bergdahl spread as a matter of policy—or because if the fact were known it would cost him all his rank and repute (and, if he were very lucky indeed, just his head). But because even a man as famously devout as Felipe might violate Creators' law for such a crime against his own child.

In the end, what made Falk most glad that Jaume didn't know was . . . Jaume. Yes, he was a rival for Imperial favor. And for all the work Falk had done, the pain he had given, Jaume still stood higher than he in Felipe's eyes.

Yet Jaume was a hero. A real, genuine, honest-to-Lanza hero. Falk knew that as surely as he knew his own name.

Falk had been raised to revere strength. For all his wispy manner and languid grace, Count Jaume of the Flowers was the strongest man Falk had ever met. Falk had come south to do his best to make sure the Empire had the strongest possible hand gripping the hilt of Rule. Through the rightful Emperor, of course—especially since Felipe had shown Falk his own brand of strength.

Falk was no longer sure that the strongest hand belonged to him.

With feelings that warred against one another like the black-and-white halves of the *taijitu* symbol of Holy Equilibrium, Falk watched Jaume step up to receive the last and highest honor of the day.

At least I'll soon be relieved of Bergdahl's presence, he thought. *My servant. My master. My mother's spy.*

And that was a triumph sweeter than any.

Melodía's heart almost exploded with joy as she watched her love rise up from her father's feet, as a newly created Prince of the Empire.

Karyl's new title brought with it a fief: the counties of Crève Coeur, Providence, and Castaña—Melodía was concerned that her former commander might get trouble along with it, since her father had punished Duke Eric of Haut-Pays for refusing to join the Imperial Army facing Raguel by stripping him of the first two counties, on the grounds that he had abandoned them to the Horde. Duke Eric was not known as an accommodating man. Although he could not act directly in defiance of Imperial decree, especially after hanging back from the Battle of Canterville.

Unlike Karyl's earlier grant of Imperial Dukedom, but like that of her enemy's, Jaume's shiny new title was mostly ornamental. As was her own designation as Imperial Princess, for that matter, since of course she couldn't inherit the Fangèd Throne. And Jaume remained behind her in courtly precedence, though that didn't matter to her.

What did matter was that at last he had noble rank to befit his true position. Though the Emperor called him his Imperial Champion, that wasn't an official title. Neither his rank of Marshal in command of the Army nor as Constable over all the Imperial armed forces, including the Sea Dragons and the Nodosaurs, gave him any more standing among the nobility than his hereditary title of mere Conde dels Flors. Although as Captain-General of the Orden Militar he was a de facto Cardinal, which conferred Imperial rank as a Duke, that didn't really count among the arrogant *grandes* of Nuevaropa, either.

Now her beloved stood not just tall and beautiful in his hero's armor but higher in rank than any except her sister, herself, the Pope-Metropolitan, and her own father. Even a full King of one of the Cinco Gentes had to acknowledge him as peer.

And, coldly, she knew that also meant he at last had unequivocal preference over the rapist bastard from Alemania.

Felipe took his nephew into a hearty *abrazo* and lightly kissed both his cheeks. Then, beaming so wide it seemed his moon face might split, he stepped back.

Jaume raised his eyes to Melodía's. His blue-green gaze struck through her like a spear.

But she hesitated.

"Go on, girl," her father said. "What are you waiting for? Step up and kiss your man."

So she did.

Behind her, cheering turned to screams.

Shiraa raised her muzzle from the haunch of freshly slaughtered springer that the tailless two-legs who cared for her in her mother's absence had tossed to mollify her. She smelled their fear: it was her due.

The wind had changed again. The smell that had set her to angry roaring was stronger now. The smell of *him*. Her enemy, who had attacked from behind and hurt her and robbed her of her mother for so long.

Now she also smelled the running water.

Now she knew where the white monster was.

Rage! Rage red/black like fire-mountain! Shiraa destroy!

She barely felt her keelbone shatter the wooden palings as she charged through them.

Chapter 4

Tirán Rey, **King Tyrant**, Tyrant . . . .—*Tyrannosaurus rex.*
Large, bipedal meat-eating dinosaur; 13 meters long, 7
tonnes. Aphrodite Terra's largest known and most feared
predator; notorious even in Nuevaropa, to which it is not
native. Sturdier than Allosaurus. Like the matador, encountered rarely as a war-mount.

—THE BOOK OF TRUE NAMES

The shrill screams of his dinosaur grooms alerted
Rob even before the rising volume of the Allosaurus's roars made clear what had happened.

The wind was blowing from the Río Afortunado now.
Which meant it also blew directly from Duke Falk's albino King Tyrant war-dinosaur Snowflake. Whom Rob
had personally seen strip a chunk of meat as big as his
own thigh from the shoulder of Shiraa, in the middle of
the Hassling. Just an eyeblink before Falk's axe dented
in Karyl's helmet—and seemingly his skull.

"Oh fuck me," he groaned, and started to run.

Between the hill and the drawn-up armies. Directly
into the monster's path.

"The monster's loose!" Melodía heard someone scream.

At once Jaume thrust her behind him. She felt first relief, then guilt for it.

I've proved myself in battle! But going up against a nine-meter matadora in full howling rage was a prospect that all but dissolved her bones.

She wasn't alone in that fear. From the way courtiers—even some wearing battle-worn armor—bolted screaming down the slope of the hill, Melodía first thought Shiraa was heading for her father—and for her. But then she saw the creature bounding forward on her two mighty hind legs past the base of Le Boule, between the round hill and its loaf-shaped companion to the south, La Miche, lean its black-on-tawny-striped body horizontal to the ground. She turned right, between La Miche and Karyl's phalanx of Triceratops. Who began to toss their signature three-horned heads and bellow belligerently.

Shiraa ignored them. She raced straight for the river. Where Melodía realized Falk's war-mount, Snowflake, was likewise penned. The albino Tyrannosaurus was roaring back defiance.

Directly into the charging monster's path stepped a single, slight figure: Karyl.

And another, burlier and bandy-legged, came running up right behind.

Even before Rob reached him, he heard Karyl say, "Enough. You don't need to be here."

Rob stopped. He slumped. Even the sight of the tonne and a half of rage and teeth bearing down at the gallop didn't hit him as hard as the rejection he heard in those words.

But he held his ground. *I'll yield to neither dinosaur nor noble. A dinosaur master doesn't!*

Jaume started forward. Without even glancing his way, the Emperor held out a hand to stop him.

"Stand your ground," Felipe said. Jaume frowned but obeyed.

"Arbalests!" Falk was shouting. "Bring crossbows and shoot the monster down!"

"Are you crazy?" Felipe yelled. "The Angel's Bane? She's the greatest hero of all!"

"Wait, my friend," Jaume told the Alemán.

Though it hit her like a horse's kick to hear her lover call her rapist *friend*, what Melodía felt was mostly fear on Karyl's behalf. Yes, the matadora was his pet—bonded permanently to him when he was the first living being Shiraa saw when she hatched, though he was drenched in the blood of her mother, whom he had just slaughtered. Yes, the creature had crossed most of the continent to rescue him—and the Empire—at the literal last second by snapping the Grey Angel Raguel in half in her giant jaws.

But she was still a monster, and furious. And Karyl just a man—not even a large one, who stood, unflinching, facing the avalanche of flesh and fangs.

"No!" he called when she came within ten meters. He raised a peremptory hand. "Stop."

Shiraa rocked back, put her tail down, and plowed a furrow in the hard-tramped soil, trying to halt her 1,500 kilograms' mass from a full killing charge. She came to a stop, centimeters away from crushing the puny lone human. And no doubt the only slightly less puny one behind him.

"Bad Shiraa!"

The Allosaurus emitted a call between a groan and a chirp. To Melodía's amazement, it sounded plaintive.

The slayer pressed the tip of the dinosaur's lethal meter-long muzzle into the turf at Karyl's feet. And she whimpered.

Karyl stood a moment gazing sternly down at her. Melodía saw the monster roll her scarlet eye to look up at him beneath the short horn-like flange in front of it.

Shaking his head, Karyl knelt. He scratched a sensitive nostril, murmuring to her in unfamiliar liquid syllables Melodía took for Parso, the language of his mother's people, with whom he'd spent a great deal of time during his exile from the Misty March. Shiraa raised her head slightly. He reached to scratch beneath one browhorn.

Shiraa trilled and nuzzled him lovingly.

"Aww," Melodía said.

The armies of the Empire erupted in the day's loudest applause.

"Highness."

Melodía snapped awake. Her tent was dark except for the yellow-orange quavering of an oil lamp.

A young oval face peered in the flap of her simple canvas tent, lit orange by the lantern the woman held in front of her.

"Emilia," she said. Slowly, she laid her *talwar* in its sheath back on the hemp rug beside her pallet.

A longtime light rider, Emilia was a short, skinny Spañola who rode a bay mare. Like many of the scouts, not just *jinetes* but woods-runners as well, she had chosen to stay with the Short-Haired Horse Captain—not so short-haired anymore—helping her father and his commanders sort out the horrendous disaster left behind by Raguel's Crusade. Even with the mostly highly capable help of a slew of newly struck or promoted nobles, like Karyl, it was proving to be a surprisingly brutal job. Melodía wasn't sure when enough of the job would be done that her father could return to turn the Imperial Army home and release the army back into its component formations.

Keeping it orderly was likewise proving a demanding task. But Jaume and his Companions, the pitiful handful remaining, formed of a couple of new aspirants who had distinguished themselves among their Ordinary heavy-cavalry auxiliaries, were performing wonders in that role. So, too, was her enemy. *I have to admit it,* she thought. *If Karyl taught me one thing—if he taught me anything—it's that underestimating your enemy can be fatal.*

She reflected how much she'd miss the life she'd led with the Army of Providence and then the Fugitive Legion. For all its brutal and horrifying moments, she belonged, and had an importance she'd actually earned by merit and actions. But reconciliation to her father, and the legal clearing of her name, meant she had to go back and serve as Princess once again.

Duty to family overrode all.

Belatedly, she registered the concern on the young woman's face. "What is it?" she asked, feeling alarm spread within her like flames on spilled oil.

Emilia's eyebrows came together, and her mouth quivered briefly, as if she were fighting back tears. "Your father wants to see you, Captain. It's urgent."

The night air slipping in around the *jinete*'s sturdy form along with the sounds of crickets was cool but didn't raise plucked-scratcher bumps on her bare skin. Since time counted, Melodía was answering her father's summons naked, the way she slept.

Slipping her feet into light sandals, she followed Emilia's small beacon out and across the few steps to the full-size silken pavilion her father's servants insisted on pitching for him every night, despite his insistence that a common soldier's tent such as the one his daughter occupied was good enough for him. Ferny ground cover crunched softly beneath nosehorn leather soles, raising a piney scent. The Imperial Army had shifted camp a kilometer west, halfway to the actual village of Canterville. Whose inhabitants had largely returned.

She didn't really need the illumination. The night sky was clear, and a waning Eris shone blue-white and large above the eastern wooded hills toward which it sank. *It's not as if I haven't gotten used to finding my way in darker nights than this, over trickier terrain*, she thought.

A paltry handful of oil lamps lit the sitting-chamber into which Emilia, bowing, led Melodía. The bow itself alarmed her. The light riders were an informal bunch, who accepted her guidance not because of rank, and far less because of her exalted birth, but because she was good at her job and cared about them.

Jaume was already pacing, naked as well. He held Beauty's Mirror by its sheath. Felipe sat half in shadow, his bearded chin sunk to his chest, his ginger-furred belly overhanging his thighs.

Jaume stepped to Melodía and embraced her with his left arm. "*Querida.*" She was too concerned to feel arousal at the touch of his bare skin on hers.

"What's going on?" she asked.

Her father didn't raise his head. But he lifted the right hand that hung futilely beside his camp stool. It clutched a piece of parchment.

"The most terrible thing has happened, *mi amor,*" he said. "A rider from La Merced brings news that your sister Montserrat has been kidnapped by the emissaries from Trebizon."

Chapter 5

Compito. . . . —*Compsognathus longipes.* A small, fuzzy-feathered, meat-eating dinosaur; 1 kilogram, 1 meter long. Native to Alemania but common throughout the Empire, and indeed on many continents of Paradise, apparently introduced by traders and travelers as pets or simply stow-aways. Sly and shy, it feeds on tiny animals such as lizards, frogs, and mice.

—THE BOOK OF TRUE NAMES

THE EMPIRE OF NUEVAROPA, FRANCIA, DUCHY OF THE BORDERLANDS, BARONY OF TERTRE HERBEUX

"Well, at least they wiped," Rob said, detouring at the last possible moment around a torn-out page of a book, which was smudged with an unfortunately recognizable brown stain. "At least some of them, some of the time. Not a thing a body would expect from Hordelings."

Other debris, moister and less identifiable, squelched beneath his thick hornface-hide boot soles.

"I hope my new baronial salary's enough to pay for a new pair of boots, then," he said sourly. "I'm burning these the moment we get out of here."

"I'd burn the whole damn thing down and start over," said the woman knight with the longsword at her hip who accompanied them.

The room was well lit with morning sun pouring in from the west and—fortunately—airy from high, narrow windows. It was a study of sorts in the west-wing annex built onto the original stone keep. It had been the seat of the barony belonging to the man Rob and Karyl knew as Town Lord Melchor. Who, having joined and served Raguel, apparently of his own free will, had become a hunted outlaw.

And this is the reward his semidivine master dealt him, Rob thought. His lips pulled back at the ends and compressed up under his nose in a grimace resembling a smile. *Can't say the Grey Angels lack all sense of justice. They're wanting proportion, though.*

Rob Korrigan had seen the sort of vandalism inflicted on dwellings by hostile occupiers before, usually fueled by herb and alcohol. He also suspected the sprees of seemingly capricious destruction reflected the resentment the lesser, who made up the bulk of any army, felt against the greater, who of course were the ones who lived in manse and castle, squatting on the masses' necks. Not that bucketheads ever held back from bad behavior against their own kind, or their property, when the pretext offered.

But I've never seen the like of this. With his aesthete's sense, housed in a somewhat brutish body—though the lasses sometimes claimed to find him fair of face, not always for pecuniary reasons, or so his vanity told him—Rob thought what he saw here was an expression of mindless destructiveness. Albeit guided by malignant purpose.

And what better description of a Grey Angel Crusade could you compose, then, he thought, *even if you had Bella's own gift of a silver pen like the pretty Prince*

Jaume, rather than a nib carved from a bouncer's ass-plume and dipped in ale-mud, like Rob Korrigan, Baron of Nowhere Yet by the Grace of Emperor Felipe and his iron whim.

"He knew how to do all right by himself, did our erstwhile Baron Melchor," he said. "For a plausible and treacherous little oiled toad of a man." He had surrounded himself with beauty: art, some evidently ancient, in painted canvas, murals, silken screens, and woven-feather hangings; stained glass; excellently wrought furniture; and, to Rob's surprise, an abundance of books and scrolls.

And now it was all gone to wreck. Smashed, slashed, splintered, strewn, and, by the smell lingering after several weeks since the Horde had moved on West, thoroughly bepissed.

Even the ceiling had been vandalized: blunt stalactites of flung shit spattered the painting that adorned its dome of a white-robed fat woman, her grey complexion suggesting she'd passed to the wrong side of the border between life and death, being hoisted by a squadron of bizarre naked winged pink babies—surely no part of the Creators' Canon—up a starry black sky toward a stylized blank-black circle at the apex representing the Creators' legendary abode, the Moon Invisible. At least Raguel's malice, or anyway His gift of organization, hadn't been up to the task of mustering ladders or scaffolds to do a proper job of effacing all human-caused beauty. Though Rob had to credit the Hordelings for zeal.

Neither that nor the occasional piles of human shit on the once-fine floor, mostly now ant-eaten to oddly architectural slumped ruins, was what most disturbed Rob. Or, it seemed, the others.

"Look at this," said young Tristan, the new captain of the light riders, now that the Princess had taken her hacked-off wine-red hair and cinnamon skin back off with her daddy, where she doubtless belonged. The brown-haired young man stood with his right hand hovering tentatively by a painted wall and his left firmly gripping the pommel of his arming-sword.

The mural had been—something. Hints of naked men and women gamboling amid stylized greenery remained, a glimpse of water with an abnormally large galley bird taking up most of it, and no one showing the least distress or even awareness that, in the background, a Long-crested Dragon grounded on short back legs and wing-knuckles was skewering a screaming man with its long beak. It could be smut, or allegory, or both; none were uncommon.

Rob couldn't tell, because it had mostly been effaced. Great sheets of the plaster had somehow been broken from the wall, taking the paint with them. Parts had been chipped with spears or farm implements, or smeared with the Hordelings' favorite medium, their own shit.

But what had the normally dark and hale-looking *jinete* captain pallid green and visibly working his jaws to hold in puke was the gouges in the plasters in the unmistakable pattern of human fingernails—that turned to five tracks of blood.

"When I was Voyvod of Misty March," said Karyl, standing at midroom, "I tried my best to discourage arts, music, dance, and pleasure itself as conducive to destructive passions. And in any event frivolous."

He drew in a deep breath and sighed it out through pursed dark-bearded lips. Which always struck Rob as oddly sensuous for a man who looked like the craziest of self-denying Life-to-Come ascetics. Though he no longer dressed like one, in a simple hooded hemp-sack robe, the way he had when Rob first found him, busking, penniless, and sword handless, thousands of others' lives ago in the small village of Protector-de-Feu.

Instead, he dressed as he had since the Army of Providence that Rob had helped him raise first went to war with Crève Coeur: like Tristan, in typical light-rider's garb of light shirt beneath a light springer-skin jerkin, dark trousers, and high-topped boots, with a belt for knife and sword. He wore his hair as he often did, long grey-shot locks in back hanging free to his collar, the hair on his crown caught in a sort of topknot hanging over it. Rob had learned the curious style was favored among certain of the more barbarous Ovdan mounted-nomad tribes. Who were the man's own cousins, after all.

"Had I seen the likes of this," Karyl said, with an economical gesture that still somehow took in the whole scope of devastation, "I'd have rethought my policies. It's as if all these things were the purest expressions of humanness and put Raguel in a fury to eradicate them through his slaves."

"That's why I suggest burning it," the knight said in her heavily Spañol-inflected Francés.

At 178 centimeters, she towered over Karyl and had five centimeters on Rob, who liked to think of his as the height of the common man. Slender, with black hair that she wore cut to her earlobes, the Castañera had been part of the army with which Count Raúl invaded Providence to take advantage of its defenders' retreat from the eruption of the Grey Angel Crusade. Sadly for them, they found themselves facing not Karyl's Militia but the bulk of Raguel's Horde. Mora Selena de Árbolquebrada had been one of a handful of knights to escape.

Now she belonged to what Rob supposed he'd have to get used to calling the Army of the Borderlands. Though, more to the point, she seemed to have grafted herself straight onto Karyl's hip. Not that Rob could blame him for allowing it. He didn't exactly find her hard to look at, even if a tad small-breasted for his tastes, perhaps overfond of dressing in black and with a perpetual haunted look in her dark eyes.

He found it hard even to resent her rather cavalier suggestion for dealing with his own new house, though, as he looked around semi-surreptitiously for something to wipe his boot against. *Nothing like seeing the limbs wrenched off your liege lord, and the meat scooped out and devoured by eager Hordelings as if he was a giant screaming crawfish, to knock out all the foolishness about chivalry and glory reading the romances put in you.*

The skill and fury with which she fought the Horde won her quick acceptance in the Fugitive Legion, which was in no position to be overly choosy about its recruits' antecedents. Although Rob still considered Iris, her purple-and-gold sackbut, an assault on the eye.

"We may still have need of castles," Karyl said quietly. "The whole region's likely to be in the same state, more or less."

"Barely a castle." She sniffed. "The idiot owner tore down the walls and turned the keep into a fancy-house."

Melchor's erstwhile barony lay in Providence's west, with the Imperial High Road its northern boundary and the Laughing Water River, running west to south, serving as the border with Métairie Brulée. It had known comparative peace for a couple of generations, with the bulk of Providence between it and the mountain passes and the raiders they sometimes admitted; even as nominal allies of Guillaume, the Burnt-Farmers had stayed passive. Given those buffers, the fertility of its rolling hills and valleys, lumber and game from a small swath of Telar's Wood, and the commerce the High Road brought it, the little fief had grown as fat and complacent as its last Baron.

"Not that fancy," Karyl said, his bearded lips sketching a smile. "The manor itself is strongly built, of good stone, and the windows are narrow. It's still defensible enough."

"Not that walls kept out the Horde," Tristan said.

He ignored the look, half puzzlement, half glare, that Selena shot him. She hadn't yet gotten accustomed to the rough equality that prevailed in Karyl's army, where rank was based more on proven ability than on birth—and the mostly lowborn light riders' impertinent wildness had been not just allowed but actively cultivated, by Karyl himself and their nominal commander, his spy-master Rob.

Rob approved of young Tristan's impudence. He had no great regard for the privileges and pretensions of the nobility—though, alas, that was the very kind of animal he found himself to be now.

He heard a scuffling noise from somewhere in the wrecked study. Selena's longsword whispered from its scabbard, its slightly more than meter-long blade split-ting a cloud-filtered sunbeam into two silver streams. Rob didn't lift the meter-long oak haft of Wanda, his dinosaur master's axe, from his shoulder, but was glad he'd thought to uncase her head to investigate the manor.

"Relax," Karyl said. "It's a rat."

A brown furry shape streaked from a mound of rot-ting fabric to a smashed-down cabinet. Rob heard a dis-mal squeak. And out from behind the wreckage strutted a *compito,* Nuevaropa's smallest raptor, with the rat squirming in its mouth. The dinosaur tipped its red-crested head ceilingward, and the mammal disappeared headfirst down its gullet.

"And there," Rob said, with a mix of dismay and de-light as befit a dinosaur master, "you have a perfect meta-phor for life on Paradise."

Selena shouted, "Ha!" and with a loud stamp lunged her sword at the Compsognathus. The tiny dinosaur ut-tered a surprised squeak and gained the sill of a broken-out window nearby with a single astonishing leap, its wing-arms spread. It turned for a moment as if to mock the knight, then vanished into the half-wrecked and wholly overgrown formal garden outside.

"I hate those things," the Mora said, her olive cheeks turning a girlish pink under the others' stares. "They eat cats. I . . . miss my cats."

"That the *compitos* do not, lass," Rob said. "They're much too small. The wild ones might eat kittens, but so might a stray dog. As for your kitties, well, knowing the sly beasts as I do, they'll have eluded the mad things and now thrive in the woods. Or scrub, or croplands, or whatever's around your home castle. If you return, they'll probably come meowing back, to rub up against your shins in welcome."

"You really think so? Most people think cats are aloof and unloving."

"Aye, I do think. Trust a Traveler and dinosaur master to know his cats—and think against the grain."

Chapter 6

El Basileia de Trebizón, **The Empire of Trebizon**. . . .
—The greatest trading partner and rival of our own dear
Empire of Nuevaropa, Trebizon borders Great Turán to the
east. Its dominions follow the Black River south from the
Ovdan Plateau to the Aino Ocean. Though dominated by
its *Griego*-speaking capital, the vast, fabulously wealthy,
and exotic seaport city of Trebizon in the Black River
delta, it is a polyglot dominion, comprising *Ruso*-speaking
provinces and the fractious Taliano city-states, as well as
Parsos and *Turanes,* who are cousins to the inhabitants of
Turania. Its ruler is called the Basileus, which means "emperor" or "autocrator." His court is famed for its intrigues,
and Trebizonians carry a reputation for conspiracy and
conniving throughout Aphrodite, whether justly or not.
Trebizon's Navy is the largest and most powerful of Aphrodite Terra's whole southern coast, and wise boys and girls
will realize it is no disrespect to our own brave Sea Dragons to acknowledge such a truth, but rather wisdom.

> —A PRIMER TO PARADISE FOR THE IMPROVEMENT
> OF YOUNG MINDS

IMPERIAL CAMP, NEAR CANTERVILLE, FRANCIA

"This is intolerable," Duke Falk von Hornberg rasped in his deep baritone. "We must wage war on Trebizon and make them pay for their insolence."

Melodía declined to look at him, lest her father and lover glimpse her hate.

Then she smiled. *I don't need to look at him to contradict him,* she thought.

"We can't, Father," she said. "It's premature. We don't know anything yet."

"She's right," Jaume said.

She smiled at that, too. Then frowned, briefly, because he sounded a trifle surprised. *You were my best friend almost my whole life,* she thought, *before we ever thought of becoming lovers. Does it really surprise you I'm more than facile and clever?*

It was a coward's way of extracting satisfaction from her rapist and despoiler, gainsaying him. But it was the only way she could see, with him a Hero of the Hour, to stand alongside Karyl and Jaume himself. And Shiraa, she guessed, though it was just a dinosaur. Not as if the beast was a horse or anything.

And it did gratify her. She promised herself more of that. Much more.

She was watching her father, who looked thoughtful. On the one hand, that was a good thing—he could be impulsive; and once he made up his mind, he clung to that decision like a matador gnawing on a Thunder-titan thighbone. On the other, before he made up his mind, he was easily swayed.

At least his damned confessor's not here, she thought. Which was no surprise. Fray Jerónimo never took an active role in Felipe's councils—as far as she knew, not even her father had laid eyes on the man. But she did know he'd been key in planting and nurturing the seeds of the Providence folly in her father's mind.

Except, she wondered, *was it really folly after all?* Felipe had taken his Empire to war precisely because he came to fear that Providence's philosophical dabblings— the Garden of Beauty and Truth—would somehow provoke a Grey Angel Crusade.

As, of course, it had.

But not for the reasons everybody feared. Raguel had orchestrated things from an early stage—had played the Garden's leaders, Bogardus and Violette, like *vihuelas del arco.* But still—

"You're right, dear."

Melodía looked at Felipe, feeling her eyes widen. He adored his daughters—when he remembered he had them. But even when he did recall them, he tended to regard Melodía, scion though she was, as a child who was only a little older than poor, poor Montse. Instead of twice her age.

Now he was nodding, his pale amber eyes half obscured by his somewhat full eyelids—a family trait of Torre Ramírez, the Spañol royal line, and one she was glad not to have inherited from him. Like his tendency toward corpulence, which she knew had been lifelong.

"We'd be fools to take any action so major until we have a better idea what really happened," the Emperor said.

She could hear the pain in his words. It throbbed in resonance with the wound in her own soul.

"Besides, Falk, my boy," Felipe said, trying to force avuncular jocularity and failing brutally, "young Hotspur that you are—and I owe my life to that; I won't forget— you're not a naval lad. Well, no more am I, nor even Jaume. But—Trebizon's an empire as large as we are, and possibly more powerful. The Basileus prides himself that the south coast of this whole end of Aphrodite Terra is his personal bathing-porch. And the *hada* of the thing is: he's right. The Treb navy masters the Aino as completely as our Sea Dragons do the Channel."

"Is there anything more to the message, Father?" It was like turning a spear-blade in her belly to ask. She didn't really want to know. But she had to.

Felipe nodded again, as if surprised his baby could muster such an adult line of thought. *He should be surprised I'm not shrieking the question at him,* she thought grimly. Grim being an attitude she was clinging to as a shield from the gibbering demons who were trying to crowd inside her soul and rip it to pieces.

"There is, *mi querida.* Our host, Prince Heriberto, waxes rather voluble, in fact."

He raised the parchment, crumpled in his right hand and visibly stained with fresh sweat. He frowned as he read.

"There's little enough. The villains killed two servants. But some survived to tell the story—including one who shortly succumbed to her wounds. Montse was snatched as her minders took her to a morning session with her tutors. She managed to flee to the kitchens. They cornered her there. The kitchen servants fought back—one bravo was blinded by a pot of boiling stew flung in his face. That's where the second servant was mortally injured. But the kidnappers were professionals. They beat down the servants, recaptured poor Montse, and dragged her off still clutching her pet ferret. There's no doubt they were the Treb delegation: not only did the servants recognize several of them, one was actually caught alive. Sadly, he took poison before he could be questioned. The other prisoners, including the scalded man, were mere rompadores hired out of the waterfront dives. They told all they know before Heriberto hanged them. But it was little enough, it seems."

As if it were lead and he was bleeding out, Felipe let

the hand clutching the letter fall to a pale, lightly ginger-furred thigh. Her father had never had fat legs, Melodía thought irrelevantly, even when his paunch was bigger than weeks on campaign had made it currently.

He sighed. "Heriberto's well and truly pissed," he said. "The mortally wounded woman was his senior servant in the Firefly Palace. And he was already out of sorts with me over the whole decision to make war on Providence."

"Senior servant?" Melodía asked with a catch in her voice.

Felipe nodded. "He even mentions her name—on account of her valor, you see. A woman named Claudia. She was highly regarded by all. Even the Prince, it seems."

Falk made a guttural sound of disbelief. "A mere servant?"

Melodía gripped the steel scabbard of her *talwar* until the knuckles of her left hand felt ready to explode through the skin. Now she looked at Falk and made no attempt to conceal what she felt.

No matter who or what you've faced in battle, Corpsetearer, she thought at the young Alemán, *you've never been closer to death than you are now.*

She pivoted and walked out into the night.

Claudia, she thought, walking blindly in the space between the Emperor's grand pavilion and her own tent. *I've done it again. I've gotten someone who helped me killed. Oh, Mother Maia, help me!*

She wept. She had the presence of mind to cover her face with her hands—she was a Princesa Imperial, and more than that, a Delgao. But that was as much control as she could maintain.

Claudia. Another servant who had gone nameless for Melodía. For years, apparently. Until, of course, she risked not just her much-sought-after position as a senior member of Prince Heri's Palace staff but her very life. To rescue her.

Apparently her own prediction had been correct: her status as a servant, and Heriberto's keen regard for his own prerogatives as host-by-rental to Felipe and his Imperial court-away-from-court, had shielded her from serious punishment for substituting herself for the similarly built Princess. She had swapped the cowl and hood of a plague sufferer—a rarity in Nuevaropa, and an object of horror accordingly—and allowed Melodía to walk right out of her cell in a Palace tower.

Because she felt sorry for Melodía—a Princess. And because Melodía's sister had asked her to. Melodía had never been quite as scandalized as Montse's minders were by her baby sister's fascination with the servants—it was at least better than spending all her time watching the armorers at work in the smithies or, worse, hanging about the notoriously vulgar dinosaur grooms and their great ungainly beasts. And for her part, the younger Imperial sibling had become a special pet to the staff.

So special that Claudia had put herself in a potential death cell because Montse asked her to. And ultimately gave her life trying to do what the vaunted Scarlet Tyrant—the bastard Falk's boys!—had failed utterly to do: save a tiny, helpless child from abduction by brutes.

Poor Claudia, Melodía thought, sobbing. *Poor Pilar. And poor Montse! I failed you all!* She cried until it felt as if her guts would turn inside out.

"—can't blame yourself, Majesty," Falk was saying in his rolling-rock baritone when Melodía reentered the warmth and butter light of Felipe's tent.

"How could you ever have dreamed of bringing a child so young along on campaign? That would have been the unpardonable sin. You acted correctly, my Emperor. You left her in her home, with every sign of security. If anyone's to blame, it's Prince Heriberto himself."

He scowled. "And my own Scarlet Tyrants, who did nothing to save her. It pleases me that Capitán Moreno had the wit at least to fall on his sword for allowing such a thing."

Felipe waved that away. "You can't blame yourself either, my boy. But the fact that Harry can, and ought, is not going to sweeten his disposition."

Evidently there was more to the Prince's message than Melodía had heard. "What else do we know, Father?" she asked, with emphasis on *Padre*.

As desperately as she wanted—needed—to know more about her sister and her possible fate, Melodía was scarcely less in need of a distraction. Otherwise, she would obsess over the brutal fact: her rapist was here to stay. And there was not one thing she could hope to do about it—now. He was an even bigger Hero now, tighter with her father than ever.

She thought—but dispassionately enough now not to actually jump right in and do it—about stabbing him anyway and getting it over with.

But that would end her aspirations to matter—to play a role on the Imperial stage. She'd gotten a taste of consequence in Providence. Even during her impulsive embassy to Count Guillaume of Crève Coeur, a disaster literally she alone survived. And more when for the first time she won something purely on her own merits—first the regard of Rob Korrigan, whom she respected for his ability, scapegrace though he was, and, more important, of Karyl, whom she came near to worshipping. And then command, first of a troop and then of all the army's light riders.

Giving in to the urge—the burning need—to jam her *talwar* right through Falk's rock-muscled belly, right above his prudish Northern blue-silk trunks, would end those aspirations. At best, her father would cover the thing—call her mad and seal her away from the world in some convent forever. If that even would be better than a discreet execution, followed by an announcement of the Princess's death in a tragic accident. Which she doubted Felipe would ever do to her.

Such an act would dishonor La Familia, she thought. The thought had an unfamiliar taste, like biting into a foreign coin and finding pot metal. She was Daddy's daughter, Montse's sister. She wasn't accustomed to thinking of herself as part of the larger clan. Yet she did, at some level.

And then again, staging a coup, slaughtering family members and allies (annoying assholes though they were), judiciously murdering Father's best friend, forcing an important heiress into exile, and, oh yes, raping her in the ass—didn't that dishonor Torre Delgao too? Suddenly, nothing in all of Paradise was clear except the air.

And, in her thoughts, the impulse to action died.

"They got clean away from the Palace," his uncle was saying. "No one even noted that."

Jaume forced his thoughts to narrow from a cloud of anger, pain, and self-reproach and to extract meaning from Felipe's words. That, at least, was a clear duty.

Falk nodded. "To the waterfront, unquestionably," he declared, "to take ship back to Trebizon."

"No," Jaume said, without consciously willing himself to speak. Falk's eyes narrowed; the man didn't take well to contradiction.

But Jaume, though no mariner himself, as Felipe pointed out, knew he was right. "The main base for the Sea Dragons lies right across Destiny Bay from the Palace. Whatever sway the Trebs have in the Oceáno Aino, the

Dragons own every square centimeter of La Canal. Their war-dromons would run them down inside a day."

"But what if the goblins threatened to kill the girl if the Sea Dragons didn't let them go?" Falk asked.

Felipe said, very quietly, "The Torre does not negotiate with those who take its members hostage. We kill them. No matter what it costs."

Melodía sobbed. Jaume's heart tore. *She's shown so much more fortitude than even I ever suspected she had in her,* he thought.

She mustered a smile through blinked-back tears when he gripped her biceps to calm her. Brave girl. He let his hand slide down her arm. She took it as if she were drowning and it was the rope.

"My nephew's right, as usual," Felipe said in conversational tones. Jaume was glad he couldn't truly know what that cost him. "They were reliably reported heading inland up the road from the Palace, obviously intending to get away overland. Four men, one with a bandaged face—that servant woman marked him, it seems. They were escorting a small coach with blacked-out windows. Too long after the fact to be useful, sadly, though Heriberto sent riders in pursuit."

"But they'll take ship at some point, surely?" Falk asked.

"Yes," said Jaume, glad to find a point of agreement with his erstwhile enemy. That was long ago; they were comrades-in-arms now. And though Jaume himself was the first to admit he had little skill at intrigue, he disliked being at cross-purposes with comrades. Graciousness—whenever possible—was the Path of Beauty. And that he had consecrated his life to walking, to the glory and love of the Creator Bella, the Middle Daughter.

"Probably somewhere south; they'll know as well as we that the Dragons can and will stop and inspect every bottom that sails La Canal, from the top of the Tyrant's Brow to the bottom of his Chin. Even if it's a rowboat, and obviously leaking."

"So what can we do?" asked Melodía. She didn't wail the words. They trilled with the desire to do so.

"I still say war!" Falk said heartily. "This is intolerable! It must be punished!"

"We don't know whom to punish."

For a moment Falk looked completely blank. He knew the words: every Nuevaropan, of whatever caste, was supposed to read and understand Spañol; Falk was clearly reasonably well educated even for a *grande*. Yet it was as if he simply lost the entire tongue momentarily.

Perhaps it's the speaker, thought Jaume with a smile.

Falk found his words again: "Why—why it's the Basileia of Trebizon, of course! We know their emissaries committed this foul act. What uncertainty is there?"

"Plenty," Melodía said firmly. "If the Trebs are known for anything, it's their own palace intrigues—as intricate as anything the legends of the Byzantines has to offer."

"I do not know these," admitted Falk, beneath lowered brows like smears of charcoal dust in heavy oil. But it seemed a sheepish frown rather than an angry one.

"This may be a power play directed more against the throne of Trebizon than the Fangèd one," she said, ignoring the Alemán.

"Then what can we do?" Falk asked. He directed the question to Felipe; he seemed uncomfortable addressing Melodía on the subject.

For his part Jaume filled with warm, buttery pride in his beloved. *She's really growing up,* he thought.

"War's out, for now," Felipe said in a tone that told Jaume that his usually malleable mind was no longer so. "But what shall we do?"

"The only thing," Jaume said. "I'll take my Companions, go find Montse, and bring her back to you safe. And her pet ferret. We can ride tonight. Give us two hours. One."

And Felipe shook his head. "No," he said.

Chapter 7

Los Compañeros de Nuestra Señora del Spejo, The Companions of Our Lady of the Mirror—An Order Military made up of dinosaur knights sworn to serve the Creator Bella, which was founded by its Captain-General, Comte Jaume dels Flors, to serve beauty and justice and aid the oppressed. Their churchly charter restricts them to no more than twenty-four serving members, picked from the most heroic, virtuous, artistically accomplished, and beautiful young men of Nuevaropa and beyond, not all of noble birth. They are encouraged to form lasting romantic pairs among themselves to further cement their bonds. Nuevaropa's most renowned warriors, led by its foremost living philosopher and poet.

—A PRIMER TO PARADISE FOR THE IMPROVEMENT
OF YOUNG MINDS

The word struck Melodía like a falling anvil.

"No?" said every voice in the room but the Emperor's as one.

"I don't dare let you go, Jaume," Felipe said. "I have another daughter to worry about—my heir. Your betrothed, as soon as I get space to make the announcement in proper style. And how can we know we're not the next targets?"

Melodía and Jaume began talking at once. She had no idea what he even said. She barely heard the words that poured from her own mouth.

Falk rubbed his chin, feeling the reassuring crispness of his beard, and the solid jaw beneath.

What do I feel? he wondered. *What should I feel?*

For Jaume to go bouncing off in pursuit of the lost Infanta served his interests. Or at least his mother's: she it was who insisted the Imperial Champion was his chief rival, through her minion, the unwashed devil Bergdahl.

And thank Chián I'm shut of that terrible creature now, he thought. *And by my Mother's own design!*

And Felipe's desire for Jaume to stay and protect him and Melodía implied the Emperor lacked faith in the Scarlet Tyrants to do the job—hence, lacked faith in Falk.

For his part, Falk regretted the prompt suicide of the officer he'd left in charge of the rump detail remaining in the Palace. He'd have liked to look into the man's dark eyes—they had conspicuously long lashes, Falk had noticed—as he throttled the life from him. Or let Snowflake take his head for a morsel, as he had that of Felipe's Chief Minister, Mondragón.

But if he doubts, he doubts, he told himself. Whether or not he sends Jaume or keeps him.

And Falk felt a strong personal inclination to see Jaume let off the leash and well away. And his pretty boys, what the meat grinder of Raguel's Horde had left of them. The fact was, Jaume's presence made him uncomfortable. And not just because of his near conviction that the Catalan was the better man.

His eyes ran down Jaume's lean and sculpted

nakedness—thoughtless, as if unaware of the shame—
and then up again. Yes. His presence was . . . disturbing.

*And yet. And yet. Somehow I feel the urge to see his
desires thwarted,* he thought, *simply because he is still
the Emperor's favorite. And always seems to get his way.*

*As I never seem to get mine. Because no sooner do I
learn that Bergdahl's been removed from my neck than
that an even greater burden's about to land on it.*

He sighed. Surreptitiously—a thing he had long practice in doing. From earliest childhood, in fact, when the
old Duke his father was alive.

Especially then.

Mother wills it, he knew. *And Mother knows what's
best for me.*

Mother always knows best.

And he opened his mouth to add his own voice to those
of the Champion and his cinnamon-skinned strumpet,
urging Felipe to let Jaume go.

For a moment, Melodía actually wavered.

But what if? The thought whispered in her skull like
an unlooked-for traitor's voice.

*What if Daddy doesn't let Jaume go? He and I will be
together. Forever!*

A picture followed the words into her mind: the face
of her little sister, more gold than her own pink-olive,
round rather than oval, with a nose snubbed rather than
narrow (and somewhat long, in Melodía's self-critical
eye), grinning vastly, impishly framed by dreadlocks of
dark blond hair that seemed powdered in gold dust, and
the black-masked silver face of Silver Mistral peering with
loving and myopic mischief from right beneath her chin.

Montserrat. She was gone. Melodía wanted her back
more than anything. Ever. More than she had wanted to
flee the rotting beauty and horrible power of Raguel in

the Garden Hall. More than she wanted not to feel the toothed yellow muzzles of Count Guillaume's Horrors, already streaked with Pilar's blood, razoring into her flesh. More than she had wanted Falk's cock to stop plunging like a horrible giant iron turd into her bowels, there in the cell in which he had her thrown.

"Daddy!" she cried. She threw herself to her knees before his bare feet. "Please let Jaume bring her home!"

She felt his hand on her head, gentle yet surprisingly strong. The blisters left by swinging a longsword into Hordeling faces and necks had popped and not yet healed; they caught and tugged slightly at her hair.

"Sweetheart, sweetheart," he said, gazing into her eyes with his own, like pale green jade. And she felt a spring of hope: he's going to give in!

"I can't," he said. "I've let one of my girls down. I let you down, too, sweetest—I know that, too.

"And I'm not about to lose you again along with Montse."

She collapsed in a sobbing heap. She hated herself. She could not help herself.

She heard her father cluck in sorrow. "I know," he said. Then resolute, and sounding as if he had raised his head: "We'll get her back. Safe and sound. I swear to you all on my life and honor, as Emperador and as a Delgao. But I simply cannot let you go right now, Prince Jaume.

"I just can't risk it."

"Beloved Brothers," Jaume said to the dark forms who waited in the camp of his Companions. "There's something I must tell you. Quickly."

A figure stepped up to take him in a hug. He knew, from the silhouette with its hair like a kinky pyramid to his shoulders, who it was before he smelled his distinctive scent and felt his unmistakable embrace. Florian, the

Francés guttersnipe who had fought and painted his way into the most select Order in Nuevaropa. His closest friend, now, with beloved Pere gone down a sea-monster's terrible mouth. His right-hand man as well, with Manfredo left and Jacques dead.

He was also perhaps the most beautiful of all the Companions, themselves selected for physical beauty as well as the beauty of their natures, and for their multiple excellences, including battle. Feeling his smooth skin over his hard-packed, flat-muscled frame made Jaume regret more keenly than usual that Florian, alone among current Brothers-Companion, declined to make love to men.

He regretted it even more keenly when Florian, for the first time ever, kissed him briefly on the lips. Unworthy though Jaume knew it was when things stood as they did, Jaume felt a brief breath of arousal.

How I'll miss you, my Brother, my friend, he thought, fighting to hold in tears. *How I'll miss you all.*

Then Jaume felt his strong hands grasp both his own biceps hard and himself thrust back to arm's length.

"We know, Captain," Florian said.

Jaume blinked. "You know?"

"Our squires are like that with the Imperial servants," Florian said, grinning and holding up crossed, slim fingers. "We heard every word, scarcely after you did."

Jaume shook his head. Despite the fact his heart was so full of sorrow that he was surprised it wasn't leaking—out the very pores of his skin—he smiled back.

"Florian," he said, stroking the man's lean cheek. To his surprise, he felt not even the fine blond down that should've grown there by this time of night. Florian had shaved recently. "You never cease to surprise me."

"One thing," Florian said, uncharacteristically serious. "Are you sure about this, Captain? Even for the Imperial Champion and Constable of all the Empire's armies, it's a grave matter to disobey a direct order from the Emperor—your uncle. Maybe the worse, considering."

Jaume sucked a breath in sharply. "You knew that too? It's not as if I breathed a word of it to Felipe."

"We know you, Jaume," said Machtigern. As his eyes got used to the starlight and the faint shine of Eris at half phase, partially obscured by a dark patch of cloud, he could see the Alemán knight was fully dressed in traveling tunic, with his trademark war-hammer propped across scaffold-wide shoulders. "And allow me to contradict the Captain-General: we won't be ready to ride in an hour, less two. The beasts are ready now. We've amblers mounted to ride, and the hadrosaurs ready to follow on their leads."

"You're not going anywhere! The Emperor—"

"Has the Scarlet Tyrants to guard him, as usual," Florian said. "Plus the Brothers-Ordinary will stay and help. And the 3rd Nodosaurs, of course. Not to mention the rest of the Imperial Army, what hasn't already broken away back to their homes. Though they're mostly just bucketheads and peasant levies, granted."

"But the Princess—"

Florian laughed. "That *cacafuego*? I don't doubt she'd protect her father as well as Falk and all his gold and scarlet boys. You wouldn't believe the stories we've heard about her since the battle!"

"Yes," Jaume said. "I would."

Florian laughed and clapped his arm. "And so do we. The Nodosaurs saw her fight a dinosaur knight on a sackbut. And they'd rather eat their own boot-tacks than praise a noble, even the Emp's own daughter."

"She'd make a worthy Companion herself, Jaume," said Bernat, Jaume's blunt-faced blond fellow countryman and the group's chronicler.

"Why that look, Captain?" Florian asked in sudden concern.

Jaume shook his head. "Nothing. I—well, it's past now. And so is this. I love you all—more than ever before, if that's even possible. But no. You can't come with me. It's out of the question."

"Oh, nosehorn shit," Machtigern said.

Jaume stared at him as if he'd sprouted a massive horn from his own broad, well-broken nose.

"If you think you can ride away alone and leave the rest of us behind, you're a total fool," the Alemán said. "Since our vanity won't abide us believing we've followed a fool through Hell—through an entire Grey Angel Crusade, side to side, not once but twice—let's have an end to all this crazy talk."

"Shut your mouth and get ready to ride, Companion," said Florian, for once without his usual bantering tone.

He flung something against Jaume's bare chest. Jaume caught it. He knew what it was by feel and the smell of nosehorn leather before he glanced at it. It was his own baldric, on which he customarily carried Beauty's Mirror.

"We have a child to save," Florian said. He smiled. "That's what we do. We're fucking heroes."

Chapter 8

Cinco Amigos, **Five Friends . . . .**—We have five domestic mammals unlike any others in the world: the horse, the
goat, the dog, the cat, and the ferret. Because all are listed
in The Bestiary of Old Home, most believe that the Creators
brought them to Paradise to serve us.

**—A PRIMER TO PARADISE FOR THE IMPROVEMENT
OF YOUNG MINDS**

"**P**lease don't make me part from you, master."
Rob looked beseechingly at Karyl through a
curtain of water, both free-falling from angry
nighttime skies and falling like a curtain from the front
brim of his hat, sadly sagging.

*A body could wish for a slouch hat with less slouch to
it,* he thought, despite the pain he felt inside.

Rob and Karyl stood in front of the manor's door. It
was late afternoon or early evening, three days after their
arrival. Not that you could tell in this pissing rain. Helped
by hired local peasants, the party of volunteers Karyl had
brought with them from his chosen ducal seat at Séverin
Farm had worked wonders cleaning the foulness out of
the main house.

Behind Karyl Shiraa stood saddled, head down and

patient. Mora Selena sat her bay ambler ten meters from the huge predator. The horse still shifted its weight and rolled its eyes in agitation. *Selena's* hat-brim held up fine.

"I'm not your master," Karyl said. His head was bare. The water streamed down his hollow-cheeked face and soaked his cloak. "Please don't call me that."

"Ah, but see, now—the Emp has gone and said you are, my liege," Rob said.

"I'm still your friend."

"Yes. But you're going away, anyway. And making me stay."

"Yes. I need men and women I can trust to help me put this land back together. Just the way I needed you to serve as my eyes and ears before. Do you want a different fief? This seems like a decent enough place, or what Raguel's slaves left of it. Better off than most of the *Marca.*"

"True," Rob said.

The devastation they'd seen on the ride back east had shaken both men to the core. And they'd seen far too much of it happen, firsthand. The one, slight grace was that the Horde had seldom stayed still in one place for any length of time—no longer than it took to drive out, absorb, and kill the people who lived there.

If they'd been more persistent, they'd have left nothing but blank desolation behind, like a lava flow covering once-prosperous villages and farms.

"We'll only be thirty kilometers or so apart," Karyl said.

"It won't be the same," Rob said. "We work so well as a team, mast—Karyl."

"Yes. And we'll continue to. But my work is at the farm. I need you here."

"And that's where I—I'm lost," Rob said, shaking his head and trying to squeeze back tears with cheeks and eyelids. "I've no idea how to be a Baron."

"You've got your seneschal to help you," Karyl said. "He seems to be steady enough. And I'll help you and give you advice whenever you want."

"But—responsibility."

"You took on all kinds of responsibility when we built the army in Providence," Karyl said. "And later when we had to flee and fight for our lives against Raguel's Crusade. You did a fine job as spymaster and chief of scouts. Even quartermaster, until Gaétan enlisted his cousin Élodie to do the job."

"The job which I loathed and despised."

"Yet you did it. It's not so different from the work of a dinosaur master. Which you also performed excellently for us."

"But that was all spy games and dinosaurs," Rob said. Thunder rumbled off across the L'Eau Riant River. "Even the quartermaster stuff was little more than rounding up fodder and drink, just as I would for monsters under my care. As you yourself told me. But this is different. There's *people* in it."

"Well, at worst, you won't be the first lord to neglect your vassals, if you chose to do nothing more than sit in your castle all day and play the lute. Probably do less damage than most that way, in fact. Most of your real task is keeping the inevitable bandits off the people's backs as they do the necessary. The same as mine."

I can't! Rob thought. *I'm not meant to be a noble! It isn't* natural.

Karyl laid a dripping hand on Rob's bare shoulder. His palm felt hot after the rain's chill.

"You'll do fine, once you've picked a task and started on it," he said.

Rob didn't meet his eye.

Damn him, he thought. *Damn him for his certainty! He always knows just what to do.*

Where I . . . do not.

Karyl glanced around. The rain showed no sign of slacking. Though Mora Selena's face and eyes were indistinguishable in the gloom, the way they pointed and her attitude in the saddle told Rob she was gazing intently at Karyl. *Could that be why he's so eager to get shut of me, then? Am I an unwelcome distraction?*

Looking back to Rob, Karyl stuck out his hand. "I have to go. I will miss you, my friend."

Rob took and shook the proffered hand, then reeled Karyl in for a fervent hug. Karyl stayed as rigid as a plank but managed to bring himself to pat Rob's ribs vaguely.

Reluctantly, Rob let him go and stepped back onto the small stoop. "All right. I won't delay you anymore."

Karyl nodded. He turned about and walked back to the waiting Shiraa. She murmured her name to him. He scratched her snout in passing, said something Rob couldn't make out. She squatted into the mud of the yard, he climbed aboard, and she stood up again, with a smooth-muscled grace that took Rob's breath away. Even sunk in sorrow and despair, he couldn't fail to appreciate such beauty in a dinosaur.

Karyl nodded once, turned his matadora away, and set her off at a trot for the road. His companion raised a gloved hand in brief salute and followed. The rest of the party had headed back for the farm earlier.

The brim of Rob's hat collapsed, dumping a load of cold water on his shoulders. He stood watching as the rain swallowed the two riders and their mounts and then for a long time after, as tears mingled with the rain streaming down his face and into his beard.

SOMEWHERE IN SPAÑA

Montserrat Angelina Proserpina Telar de los Ángeles Delgao Llobregat, Infanta of Los Almendros and of the

Empire, Flower of the Realm, heard someone sniffling. It made her mad.

"Quit sniveling!" she ordered aloud. Quietly, but aloud. So she did.

The straw she lay on prickled the skin of her cheek through the thin felted-feather blanket she'd been given. Its smell and the condensation on cool stone of the storehouse walls filled her nostrils. In her arms, Silver Mistral stirred, a warm, pliant softness with a core of springy strength inside that soothed her. She knew the ferret got impatient if forced to hold still too long—and knew she was doing her best to do so to comfort Montse.

But even though the straw was fresh and clean and she had enough blankets to go on top of the hemp smock she had been wearing in the Palace when the bad men grabbed her to make sure she stayed warm, comfort wasn't going to be easy to come by.

She frowned. Then she caught a whisper of sound through the bolted and unfortunately quite solidly constructed oak door. Glad of something to concentrate on except simmering in her own internal broth of fear, sorrow, and helpless rage, she frowned hard to listen.

It was one of the shaven-headed men in the dark robes speaking in a language she didn't understand. She guessed it must be Griego, because that was what they spoke in Trebizon. He had a tendency to hiss. But he was making no effort to keep his voice down, and it turned strident as he kept talking.

A calm voice answered. Her scowl deepened until it actually pressed the lid against her right eye. That was the man who had stabbed Claudia. He was languid, tall, and lean, with neatly trimmed hair and beard the color of iron.

Montse's friend had fought like an angry vexer there in the Palace kitchen. She had clawed his face up pretty badly with just her fingernails before she fell. The times she'd glimpsed him since, he had had that whole side of his face bandaged, often showing rust-colored stains in the area of his left eye. So Montse hoped Claudia had taken his eye out.

Of course, she was probably dead now. Montse hoped she'd recovered—she knew that if wounds didn't kill you fairly soon, you generally did. But she had looked bad when the black cloth bag was dragged over Montse's head and she was picked up and carried away, kicking furiously and clutching Silver Mistral to her chest.

The first man started to talk back loudly. He was cut off by a third voice, definitive as a door slam: it was one of the two women. The one who shaved her narrow head and apparently even her eyebrows, which were then painted on over a pale base in a high-arched way that made her look like a frightening statue or terrible doll. She wasn't large, but the others deferred to her. Even though the hissing man was supposedly in charge.

The conversation grew heated. Montse managed to catch and comprehend one single word: Basileus. Which she knew was what the Trebizonés called their Emperor, *Basileo,* in Spañol.

The thought so flooded her with relief and joy that she bit the inside of her bottom lip hard enough to wince to keep from tumbling into the chaos of tears again. *I understand!* she thought joyously. *I finally can understand . . . something.*

It was a victory. But a minor one. Aside from catching the bearded man's name—Dragos—go by a couple of times, she might have been listening to a fountain bubble in one of the many gardens inside the Firefly Palace.

Bad thought. She had to suck in her deepest breath and frown real hard not to break down over that memory and the wave of homesickness it hit her with.

The conversation—argument—ended. She heard footsteps, at least one person stamping as hard as sandaled feet could. A door slammed.

Another woman's voice—less sibilant, softer, more . . . reasonable somehow. It spoke a language unmistakably different from the first.

Dragos answered. This conversation was quieter and calmer. Holding Mistral with one hand in a sort of furry hoop, Montse pressed her ear hard against the door, plucking at the front of her gown to let the sticky bits of straw that had gotten inside fall down and quit sticking her.

She couldn't follow this language, either. Yet—it seemed as if she almost could, somehow.

Some of the words sounded lots like Spañol, she thought. But their accent—it's like Slavo. She spoke none of that tongue—not even her sister did, so remote and lightly populated with the smallest Gente of her father's Empire. But there were still Slavos, mostly emissaries of their King, at her father's court. She knew what their accent sounded like—the rhythms of their speech, the way they pronounced their words.

She tried to focus on following the conversation. Whatever they were speaking, it offered more promise than Griego, which might as well have been the Heavenly Tongue for all the meaning she could wring from it. But despite her gift of intense concentration, another thought distracted her.

Dragos was not stupid. Unlike most of the adults she'd ever met, and all the children near her own age. He had also seemed inclined to treat her decently, discouraging the others when they handled her roughly or even carelessly.

Which would have won her trust by itself. If she hadn't watched him stab Claudia repeatedly in the belly and sides.

Suddenly she realized why her mind had wandered

down that path: it was a problem! One she could study
and work out.

The problem of Dragos. Not in command of her surprisingly large party of captors—she'd seen over a dozen
people while riding in the coach with covered windows
and during the brief intervals when they took her hood
off inside whatever new place they were keeping her. But
clearly important. And, she thought, smarter than his
nominal superiors.

Why does he treat me better? she wondered. She
thought the answer was key to helping her understand
him.

She didn't understand people. Not easily. She'd learned
many ways to get others to do what she wanted them
to. She'd had the habit when she became aware of herself, around her sixth birthday, and had cultivated it ever
since. But she still couldn't seem to grasp people's true
feelings and motivations. Not the way Melodía did.

It seemed to her that she might be getting an idea of
Dragos's strings—and how to pluck them to her advantage.

It wouldn't be easy. It would take time and effort.

"What else have I got, Mistral?" she whispered to her
ferret. Who stared at her with her eyes beadlike in her
pointed, masked face, keenly attentive, as she tended to
be. "What else do I have to do?"

Well, she could cry and whine and carry on. She actually snorted at that.

"I will learn," she promised. "I'll figure him out. I'll
figure out how to play him against the other bad people."

She slid down the door, suddenly weary. Released, Silver Mistral poked her pink, damp nose against Montse's
own. It was the ferret's best effort at a kiss, Montse had
long ago realized.

She smiled, unable now to hold back tears of love and
gratitude—completely. She picked her friend up again,

soothed by the warm softness of her fur—and the hint of wiry strength in the long, narrow body within.

"We'll get out of this," she promised. And the tears came in a hot curtain. But now they were fierce. "We'll beat them.

I will kill them all. Kill them hard. I won't torture them. Bad people do that. But when the time comes to kill them, I won't try real hard to make it easy on them!"

She put Mistral down on the beaten ground at her side. Instantly, the ferret arched her back and began to hop and beep. It was a common trick of hers that Montse thought of as the Ferret War Dance. It usually meant she was ready to play—or less frequently, fight.

And now, Montse realized, it meant both.

"Welcome, Baron," Rob's new seneschal said as he stepped inside, his rain-soaked hat and heart both heavy. The man was tall and built like a scarecrow, with a slat-thin torso and wide shoulders, and his face was homely enough, with its great blade of nose, to frighten horrors. "I've prepared a nice hot toddy for you."

"Thank you, Bergdahl," he said. "It's most kind of you."

Chapter 9

La Majestad, Majesty—Is the capital of Empire of Nuevaropa, located in the Sierra de Gloria in the midst of the
Meseta in Spaña. It is an autonomous city-state, admin-
istered by the Imperial Diet, which convenes there. The
first Emperor, Manuel Delgao, known as "The Great," built
the beautiful city atop a leveled-off hill called La Mesa de
Gloria. A drawbridge connects it to the Emperor's Palace,
El Corazón Imperial, which Manuel had built into the very
rock of Monte Gloria, the highest peak of the Glory Range.
Its residents call themselves Majestuosos, to reflect the Imperial capital's pride and dignity, of which they tend to be
ever conscious.

—A PRIMER TO PARADISE FOR THE IMPROVEMENT
OF YOUNG MINDS

Melodía woke up.

The clouds above were bright and nearly
blinding-white.

The land around was shades of yellow and brown.

The air smelled of dust, the warm silver hide and rich
sweat of her mare, Meravellosa. And the shit of a hundred other horses and grunting dray-dinosaurs.

For a moment it was as if she could remember nothing past that terrible night, the night they learned of her beloved sister's being cruelly snatched away from the Firefly Palace—and the servingwoman, Claudia, Melodía's savior and a friend she hardly knew—stabbed to death before Montserrat. The night her beloved Jaume, with whom she had so recently been reunited—and reconciled—ran away with his men to hunt down Montserrat's abductors and bring her back safely, in defiance of the Emperor's orders.

As Melodía had devoutly wished he would. Her father too, probably, she guessed. She didn't know why he'd forbidden Jaume, his established Champion, his kinsman and friend, to go after his daughter. She had no idea why he made a lot of his decisions. Fewer still these days.

But it wasn't true, she realized, as she came fully aware of her rocking in response to Meravellosa's upward pace and the swishing black tail of her father's bay right before her. It wasn't really that she'd slept that whole time. More dozed. There was only so long she could sleep, she recalled, before the dreams started.

Of a hundred possible horribles that might be befalling her sweet baby sister right now at the hands of the notoriously cruel Trebs. Of her friends, dying before her eyes. Of the horrors worked by the Grey Angel Horde. Of Falk and the rape. Of Raguel Himself—the first time he was revealed to her as the real guiding spirit of the Garden of Beauty and Truth. And later, when he presented himself openly to his followers and the world in the Garden villa's great hall and the memories he had stolen from her of their first encounter flooded back and the Grey Angel Crusade began.

She recalled a few things of the last two days, a scatter of incidents. Mostly her father dismissing her small retinue of *jinetes,* the light riders she'd commanded for Karyl, and Rob Korrigan his spymaster and friend. She remembered, or thought she did, his telling her with deep paternal concern that he didn't want their presence reminding her constantly of the horrors she had just lived through. She remembered feeling sad and also laughing, because it was so funny that her father or anyone could imagine she ever *stopped* thinking about the things she had seen and heard . . . and smelled. But at the same time the sadness and hilarity felt distant and removed, as if they were happening across a big room to someone she scarcely knew. Maybe she only laughed in her mind, before sinking into the clammy but somehow inviting depths of despair once more. . . .

It was morning and hot. A low, broad conical hat like the ones peasant farm-laborers wore, but made of silk and struts instead of woven out of straw like theirs, shielded her face from the sun, which, despite the constant clouds, was fierce, halfway up the eastern sky. A yoke of feathers, gold and red in the Imperial colors—and those of her family, Torre Delgao—protected her shoulders. A dun panorama of hills and scrub, slashed across by green lines of streams and *acequias* and patched with cultivated fields, spread out to her left.

Finally, she knew that they were approaching the top of the road that switched its way up the southwestern face of La Mesa de Gloria. Though they had approached from the northeast, they had to work their way around the whole of what was misleadingly called Sierra de Gloria, the Glory Mountains, but was really just different parts of a single looming mountain, to reach the road that led to the city and the palace of La Merced, capital of the Empire of Nuevaropa.

Last, she heard the excited buzz of voices, from their escorts ahead and from the long procession winding behind. She had particularly forced awareness of voices from her conscious mind, for fear she'd hear the one that terrified and sickened her most of all: that of Falk, Duke von Hornberg.

Pressed to the side of the road near the Plateau's rocky top were wagons piled high with bales of foodstuffs and kegs of water to provide for the hunger and thirst of city and palace. The draft animals, mostly nosehorns with a few other types of hornface thrown in, tossed their heads and bawled in annoyance—and in their own thirst and hunger. The Imperial Herald and a contingent of horseback-mounted Scarlet Tyrant escorts had ridden ahead to clear the way for the Imperial train. Which was now much reduced, with the departure of the peasant levies and most of the knightly contingents back to farms and fiefs, though the 3rd Tercio of the Brown Nodosaurs, the Imperial Will, which had accompanied His Majesty from La Merced, tramped stolidly in everybody else's dust in the column's rear to provide an escort only the rashest would care to tangle with.

Her enemy—she hated even to form the name in her mind—rode in a place of honor at the very head of the Imperial cavalcade. It had paused at the Plateau's base to allow beasts and humans to drink from the Raging River that curved around it while the dinosaur knights still accompanying Felipe had switched to their warmounts. Now Snowflake, the unique white Tyrannosaurus, led the marching Imperial bodyguard, the Scarlet Tyrants. Or the sorrowful remnant who were left after Canterville. She had seen their distinctive red and gold armor and plumes among the bodies strewn up the side of the round hill called Le Boule. So many bodies . . .

She had thought she'd seen great numbers of bodies left in the wake of the Horde. The dead of Canterville could have filled a whole great city with ghosts, had there been any such thing. Even after experiencing the mobs of La Merced, filling the streets and squares for festival and riots, two things they loved most in all the world, she had somehow never thought that that world held as many people as were dead on that field.

Or worse, so worse—not dead.

With her head raised from the perpetual nod it had occupied before, Melodía could see the Plateau level off before them and the beginnings of the yellow-brown walls of brick and stone and whitewashed mud that rose above the rim.

"La Majestad!" exclaimed a male voice behind her.

"At fucking last," a second said.

She twisted in the saddle and turned her head. Her neck creaked; having her head lolled forward on it for what was apparently a very long time had made the muscles stiff.

A quartet of Tyrants, their gilded breastplates bouncing off the highland sun in eye-hurting spears, their gold and red plumes gorgeous and nodding, rode horses not far behind her. Three chestnuts and a grey, she noticed.

"The Princess is awake!" the first one, a *sargento*, judging by the red-dyed sidewise crest on his golden helmet, growled. "Watch your fucking language."

The others stared at him, then laughed. He should have been commanding a *puño*, a fist of five men. Presumably three were all that survived.

"Way to go, Sarge," called the man to his left, whose voice Melodía recognized as the second speaker's.

The sergeant blushed to the grey roots of his black beard. A scar that ran diagonally across his face from left brow to right jaw shone stark white against it and the normal brown of his skin.

"I'm sorry, Highness," he stammered. "I spoke without thinking."

"'Sallright," she said, her words slurring as if she were drunk—or still half asleep. "I heard the word before. Said it. Fuck. There. See?"

The *sargento* looked at her with eyes like hard-boiled *compito* eggs. His three men crumpled up their faces to hold back laughter.

Melodía heard a voice cry ahead of her. "My dearest darling girl!"

She cranked her head painfully forward. Her father, wearing an outfit similar to hers, except that his feathered shoulder-protector was a red-and-gold cape that spilled halfway down his back, had turned in his saddle to see for himself. The look of relief and love in those pale-green eyes made her feel a pang of something like sadness.

Oh, Daddy, she thought. *I'm not back. I'm just . . . awake.*

She grew vaguely aware that he had been more attentive to her than he had been in the years since her mother, Marisol, died giving birth to Montse. A thing her father had never held against his second child. He had loved them both intensely . . . when he could be distracted long enough from the affairs of state to remember the fact.

Better late than never, I guess.

"Yes, Father," she said. Because she felt she had to say something.

"You had us all worried for a day or two, *mi corazón*."

"Really, I'm fine."

He nodded his ginger goatee into his second chin once vigorously. "Right." She could see awareness of her fall out from behind his slightly protuberant eyes even before he turned forward again.

"It figures," she said softly to herself. Given the clop and squeal of Meravellosa's hooves on the crushed pumice of the roadway, the jingle of harness, and the many noises of beasts and men and women, it barely reached her own ears.

In fairness, she thought, *he's probably quit worrying about me so he could go back to worrying about Montse.* She was mildly surprised at her acuity at figuring that out and felt briefly pleased with herself.

A brassy fanfare and a woman's voice boomed through

a speaking-trumpet, "All hail to His Majesty Felipe, Emperor of Nuevaropa, Defender of the Tyrant's Head, Jewel in the eyes of the Eight Creators! *¡Viva al Emperador! ¡Viva!* ¡Viva! ¡VIVA!"

And so the Emperor and his daughter returned in triumph and in sorrow to a city they had never loved.

They have provided me with paper, quills, and ink and are allowing me to keep a journal.

When I asked for one, of course they didn't want to. Though I have been treated well enough, except for being kidnapped and having a bag put over my head and stuff, they seem outraged at the idea of doing nice things for me. Luckily Count Dragos put in some words for me, the way he did at the outset when they didn't want to let me keep Misti—she's hopping and beeping at me now, trying to get me to play with her. Not now! When I'm done. This is important.

I hope.

Anyway, he said the same thing he did then: it will make me easier to deal with if I don't get bored. I know he's probably saying that because it's true, but I think I may hate him less than the others.

Also, he seems to think they're idiots. Which is right.

So the conversation ran like this:

Deep Voiced Boss Priest With Tall Hat: So, you want paper and pens, do you, little girl?

Me: I said so, didn't I? (My handlers back home say I am not patient enough with stupid people. If only there weren't so many of them!)

DVBPWTH: You want to draw pictures of funny animals, I expect? Like hippopotami and lions and cows? Little children like that, I understand.

Me: Actually, I'm designing a siege engine making use of a capstan—

DVBPWTH: Splendid, splendid. We shall see that you have those things.

(The evil noblewoman who stabbed my friend Claudia and wears too much kohl around her eyes said something in their mush-mouthed foreign gabble.)

DVBPWTH: What harm can it do us? Let her draw her little imaginary animals, as Count Dragos says.

At that point I tried to explain they were not imaginary at all, but are all clearly identified in the BESTIARY OF OLD HOME, but they had their big Spañol goons bundle me into a back room with their big goon hands. A little while later the door opened and the DVBPWTH, acting as if he were handing over the keys to the Basileus's personal commode, gave me a sheaf of paper, some horror feathers with tips cut for writing, a small pot of ink, and some sand to blot with. I asked for a small knife so I could sharpen my own quills, but they didn't fall for that.

They did let me have my own small metal spoon, however. I already see a way to use that.

But they're not completely stupid. And Dragos isn't stupid at all. I have to remember that if I am to get away.

Chapter 10

El Imperio de Nuevaropa, Empire of Nuevaropa. . . .
—Our own dear home, which occupies the land mass
at the western end of Aphrodite Terra and the island
kingdom of Anglaterra, which taken together are known
as the Tyrant's Head, because on the map they resemble
the skull of Aphrodite's largest and most fearful predator, Tyrannosaurus rex. It was founded at the end of the
High Holy War by the great hero Manuel Delgao, who
became its first Emperor. It has been ruled in relative
peace and growing prosperity ever since by Emperors
and Empresses chosen for the office by the eleven noble
Electors from Torre Delgao, from which Manuel I sprang.
It is sometimes referred to as the Empire of the Fangèd
Throne, after the gilded chair of state which Manuel is
said to have ordered made from the skull of a Tyrannosaurus imperator, a monster even larger and more dire than T.
rex, which he slew just before founding the Empire. Most
modern scholars consider T. imperator to be a myth, and
that story as well.
> —A PRIMER TO PARADISE FOR THE IMPROVEMENT
> OF YOUNG MINDS

"**M**y lords," the peasant youth said, "I know where you can find her."

Jaume froze with a spoonful of goat-cheese-and-mushroom soup—a specialty of the house, and quite delicious—halfway to his lips.

Neither he nor the other Companions gathered around the long table in the inn's otherwise unoccupied common room had to ask who he was.

"I'm Jaume," he replied, returning spoon to bowl. "Captain-General of the Companions of Our Lady of the Mirror."

"I know, *Señor.*"

"What's your name, friend?"

"Pablo."

They had stopped for an early lunch and to cast about for information at a big, three-story fieldstone structure located on an important crossroads south of the Imperial capital city, La Majestad. It was called the Lambent Lambeosaur, following a fad for naming inns and taverns not just according to Anglaterrano conventions but in actual Anglysh, which had inexplicably swept Francia and Spaña following the Imperial conquest and annexation of the island kingdom in the mid-fifth century AP. Its size and location made it an important gathering place, though here in the late morning the Companions found they had it mostly to themselves.

They had ridden hard from the vast Imperial Army encampment in Francia's southeast corner, near the border with the Kingdom of Spaña. So great had been Jaume's urgency to take up pursuit of his kidnapped young cousin that they had left their plate armor and war-dinosaurs behind, to be brought to them by their squires when the latter could catch up. They took only their personal weapons, light jacks of springer leather, bedrolls and such personal effects as could ride in their saddlebags, with a pair of extra coursers to carry water, food (which they'd have little leisure to forage for), as well as kettles to cook with.

The full Companions were accustomed to riding light when called for. The new potential Knights-Brother would learn to do so as well, if they hadn't already.

"Grzegorz?" Jaume asked one of the two new knights-aspirant they'd taken on in the wake of their losses at the slaughter-field of Canterville. "If you please, make room for Pablo at our table."

The Slavo raised a blond brow in question. "A commoner, Captain?"

"We serve the interests of the common folk," Jaume said. "Companions claim no nobility beyond ideals and actions."

That and the fact that, if his news proved true, Pablo was a gift from Lady Li Herself. The Companions had gotten numerous reports of possible sightings of the kidnappers, from commoners as well as their lords. The currently ruling installment of the Imperial Delgao family was widely if not universally popular; people were generally appalled at the abduction of a young girl by foreigners, and it was widely and correctly perceived that the Emperor Felipe would look with extreme favor on anyone who actually helped to get his younger daughter back.

Now they had outrun their information. Which was the primary reason for their halt.

The muscular young knight shrugged. "All right," he said. He removed Bieta, his spear and favored personal weapon, from a chair at the table's far end from Jaume.

"Join us," Jaume told Pablo. The young man was handsome, his sharply sculpted features almost pretty enough for him to be a Companion himself, fresh-faced, with gleaming straight black hair. He was of about average stature for southern Spaña, 168 centimeters or so, more sturdy than spare. He wore an outfit common here in La Meseta, the somewhat arid central plateau of Nuevaropa's southernmost *reino*: a short cape or yoke of thatched straw, woven tight like a basket, to keep the sun from stinging his shoulders; a battered vest of some thin dinosaur leather; a brown linen loincloth; and buskins.

"Drink. Eat, if you want to. You're our guest."

But Pablo shook his head. His eyes, sharp and so brown as to be almost black, would not meet Jaume's.

"Please, lords," he said, with a meaningful glance at the publican, who busied herself behind the counter stacking mugs freshly cleaned by young serving boys and girls who by their looks could be her sons and daughters. "Outside."

"As you wish." Jaume pushed his chair back with a scrape of stout legs on rough wood planking. He rose, lifting the baldric that held the Lady's Mirror from where it hung across the back of his chair and slinging it over his back so that the longsword's silvered pommel jutted up above his right shoulder. "Outside it is."

Felipe turned and, smiling, beckoned Melodía to ride up alongside him. She dutifully urged Meravellosa into a brief trot and obeyed. She felt pleased that he was acknowledging her as a father. And as Emperor—especially after she had been exiled from his court-away-from-court because of charges trumped up by none other than Duke Falk.

She also felt a corresponding stab of anger that she had been exiled from his court-away-from-court because of charges trumped up by none other than Duke Falk. *Is it good that I'm feeling something again? Even if I'm not much enjoying the things I feel.*

Unlike La Fuerza, the seat of the King of Spaña, La Majestad had always struck Melodía as beautiful. It even did today, to the extent that anything piercing the curious roiling blanket of anxiety and gloom that now enveloped her could be beautiful. Where the Spañol capital was narrow and crabbed and looked dark, somehow, even at high noon with thin cloud cover, La Majestad, with its confining, twisting lanes and squeezed-together buildings, all dark stone or brick, felt light and expansive. The ways were broad—at least the major ones, such as the road the Imperial procession was passing down now, which led from the Plateau's edge directly to the drawbridge to the Palace. The houses and shops were wider and not so tall, built of yellow and tan materials, or, for humbler structures, their adobe walls were washed with the local limestone-rich soil, mixed with some kind of fixative to resist the occasional rain.

Not to say that the Imperial crown city was a hotbed of gaiety; that was La Merced, and Majestuosos would be mightily offended at being compared to Mercedes, whom they considered boisterous and addicted to frivolity. But whereas the citizens of La Merced were associated with bourgeois cheer and the occasional outbreak of civic madness, and Fuerzanos with paranoid mistrust, Majestics cultivated dignified reserve.

Although Melodía doubted that had much to do with the curiously muted quality of the crowds that thronged La Via Imperial to receive their Emperor's return. There were cheers and shouts and the waving of banners and songs of thanksgiving to Felipe and the Creators for delivering them from deadly peril. But they had a strange, strained, wild-edged quality, as if the cheers might at any moment devolve into sobs and wails of fear and shrieks of outright madness.

Because, after all, the true and truly terrible threat from which the recent victory had saved them had come from none other than one of the Eight's appointed servitors on Paradise.

When Melodía rode past a man with hair and beard

like a wild bush and wearing nothing but a coat of ground-in-looking grime—full public nudity being a recognized display of formal protest and reproof—standing on a nail-keg and screaming denunciations of them all for heresy and blasphemy, it scarcely seemed out of place. Nor did it strike her odd that none of the Majestics tried to shut up his spewing sedition. It was as if he represented their own consciences, and the guilt they felt at celebrating the fact that they were not all at this very moment dying horribly.

La Majestad prized itself on its tradition of free speech anyway. *La Dieta* encouraged plain and open public speech, by way of the city government, which answered to the Diet. Although exceptions could sometimes be found when that speech proved too pointed or personal about the Diet or its members.

But though La Casa de la Dieta dominated the city from the Plateau's northeast quarter, with its soaring, reddish-brown sandstone walls, its flying buttresses and narrow pointed-top windows and spiky finials, it was overshadowed if not overborne by the enormous pointed bulk of Monte de Gloria—Mount Glory—into the near face of whose steep southwest-facing granite main peak the Imperial Palace itself was carved. It couldn't match the snow-clad cloud-rippers that dominated the Sierra Scudo that separated the Tyrant's Head from Ovda. But it still thrust up an imposing three hundred meters of bare rock from the top of the Plateau, itself nearly a hundred meters higher than the surrounding Meseta.

Despite its dominating presence, it had never felt oppressive to Melodía before. Now the sight caused her belly to flutter and her throat to constrict with a terrible sense of apprehension.

Then again, she thought, *what doesn't, these days? It feels as if the only thing I can be bothered to feel is fear.*

The Imperial Way took a strider-leg jog around the

flank of the great Temple of All Creators, in order to maximize the impact of the first close look at the Palacio Imperial itself. Which even now, despite everything, caught Melodía's breath briefly in her throat.

As always, her first impression was left by El Salto del Corazón, Heart's Leap, a white-frothing cascade of water from between the main mount and a lesser peak on the left, northwestern side. It came from the amount of rain, freakish for La Meseta, which fell on the substantial but lower mass of the Sierra that extended to the north and east, masked by the great peak. Though rather thin, it made a rushing sound audible even from here, a quarter kilometer away, as it splashed down the grey stone and then, a couple of stories above the level of the Plateau, leapt into space.

Beyond a wide, open plaza directly ahead, a stout drawbridge crossed the thirty-meter gap of Martina's Moat, a natural though improved crevasse that separated the city from a great flat ledge jutting from the hip of the mountain. A wall of yellow limestone block rose fifteen meters from the very rim. A few rooftops, of yellow or pinkish-red tiles, peeked over the top. Both the bridge and the gate that stood open in the *cortina* wall were ten meters across, to allow for easy access. The whole suggested openness of access—which could, however, snap tightly shut at very short notice.

Which was both intended and correct, she knew. The Empire, and its ruling Torre Delgao, invited approach— but had a stern, fast way of redressing violation. *As Jaume's about to teach the monsters who kidnapped my sister!*

Forty meters above the ledge a crack opened in the steep cliff face. Inside that, as it narrowed toward the bottom, rose the façade of El Palacio de la Corazón Imperial: Imperial Heart Palace, stronghold of the Emperor of Nuevaropa. Begun by the first Emperor, Manuel, com-

pleted by his daughter and successor, Juana the Wise—
Melodía's heroine growing up, both the first and last
hereditary Empress, and the first person Elected to the
Fangèd Throne—it outdid both the Dieta and the Gran
Templo in displaying the exuberant ostentation of Early
Imperial Gótico architecture. Its golden limestone and
granite lines were designed to draw the eye up and up.
Numerous windows pierced it, to allow in abundant nat-
ural light.

As the Imperial procession approached the near end
of the drawbridge—which was unguarded, because what
was the point?—a score of trumpets blew a strident fanfare. Falk's Tyrant Snowflake, which had been tossing its
huge albino head and snarling through a silver cage of a
muzzle at citizens both terrified and delighted by the
monster's ferocious display, faltered. It did not seem to
care for the idea of crossing the chasm. Falk must have
said something, or maybe just pressed more urgently with
his knees, because shortly the monster stepped onto the
wooden span, its tail swinging almost from rail to massive rail with the rhythm of its walk.

Her father turned in his saddle to look back at her. He
smiled.

*It's the first time in a couple of days he's seen me look
alert*, she realized. She smiled back, tentatively.

Though the noise of the crowds—cheering, mostly—
and the trumpets inside the castle yard made it impossible to hear, he mouthed something and beckoned her
alongside him with his hand.

The boots of the thirty or so Scarlet Tyrants who
marched behind their commander beat the planking like
drums as she nudged Meravellosa up next to her father
on his bay. Her heart swelled. She had seldom felt such a
closeness with her father, a kinship, since her mother had
died giving birth to Montserrat.

The two horses added the higher-pitched clop of their

hooves to the wood percussion. Meravellosa all but pranced across the bridge, holding her head up proudly and perking her ears forward, as if to reproach the huge meat-eating dinosaur for its timidity at the crossing.

Melodía glanced down and to the right. The chasm plunged a good fifty meters, to end in a splash of spray on jumbled rocks. Such of the cataract as remained; the municipality of La Majestad collected much of its water by means of a great bronze funnel built out from the Plateau's side, discreetly out of sight below the rim, for storage in the cisterns dug deeply into it.

She had often felt a fleeting urge to throw herself into the Moat when looking down it, or from any other great height. She never knew why.

Now she felt the impulse, stronger than ever before, and not so fleeting. And knew why.

She saw Falk raise a hand gauntleted in blue-enameled steel to acknowledge the cheers that pealed out from the courtiers, soldiers, and servants gathered inside the Palace to welcome home the Emperor, and a new feeling—at least, new in this present, deadened reality—suddenly blazed up with searing heat.

Rage. It enraged her that her rapist should be cheered by those sworn to the service of her own family. Of her own father. Yes, he had done amazing feats protecting her father's life and that hill and Canterville. She'd heard too many accounts from those she trusted—not least Jaume, who did not and could not and must not know anything of her violation by Falk—to doubt his heroism of that day.

But it doesn't make him not *a monster,* she thought. *It makes him a brave monster. Nobody should cheer a monster.*

Thoughts of leaping to her death evaporated like water drops on embers. *I will not let him win!*

Roused, at least for now, from whatever swamp she'd

been submerged in, Melodía held her own head high as she crossed into a place she'd lived in but would never call home, while the feet of a dozen war-hadrosaurs slapped the bridge's planks at her back.

The Heart's entryway looked vast enough to admit a dinosaur knight on her dinosaur. Great age-greened bronze valves seven meters high and five wide stood open to either side. Ranks of Defensores del Corazón, men and women in blue and silver livery, with badges of gold and red, stood with their round shields and three-meter thrusting-spears grounded beside their thick-soled buskins, flanking the broad steps to La Entrada. Its clever design of pointed arches progressively stepped inward made less apparent the fact that the real entry narrowed to where it could be closed by more reasonable doors, hidden well back in shade, to keep the weather out.

As she and her father rode side by side down the avenue to the carven steps, Melodía wrinkled her nose at the smell and tried not to wince at the fearful blare of the trumpeters who lined both sides. Behind them a whole town's or at least a respectable village's worth of buildings stood between the Palace and the curtain wall. Though the Palace was dug far back into Mount Glory, and its cellars extended deep below the Plateau level, there was a limit to the space it offered for storage and habitation. Especially for draft horses and dinosaurs and war-duckbills. Outbuildings from shacks to dormitories of a degree of elegance, with shops and warehouses in between, all of a variety of styles—some pitch-roofed, many flat—had sprung up over the centuries. Even at that, large open spaces remained for mustering yards and the like; the ledge was larger than it looked from outside.

Melodía's enemy—she hated to even think his name— turned his white tyrant just in front of the great door and led his Imperial bodyguards to take up position in the yard outside it. Felipe continued right up to the base of the steps. Melodía rode with him, trying not to show her relief at not having to look at that man anymore.

Having preceded the Imperial cavalcade to cry their progress—the party was limited to marching speed by the contingents on foot—the Palace's own Herald, a middle-aged woman with short iron-colored hair and a build like a nosehorn, took up position atop the short stairway. Raising her conical speaking-trumpet, she bellowed the arrival of His Imperial Majesty, Felipe the First, Emperor of Nuevaropa, Protector of the Faith, and so on and so forth. Palace grooms, young men and women dressed in feathery headdresses and red-trimmed yellow skirts, ran down to take the reins as Felipe, his older daughter, and his retinue dismounted.

They led the mounts offstage to the left, to where a lane ran to a less grand-appearing gate set into the cliff, which really was large enough to admit a dinosaur rider. Horses, hadrosaurs, and the handful of lesser riding-dinosaurs would go down a ramp to underground stables. Mostly, Melodía knew, the entrance was used for the constant stream of supply wagons necessary to keep the Heart beating. Which was presumably already in motion behind them and would start rolling through the gate the moment her father and company went inside.

Stewards materialized to remove the Emperor's dusty trail-cape and replace it with a giant cloak bristling with long reaper plumes, all yellow and red, of course, and to plant the ruby-inset gold Imperial crown upon the close-cropped ginger Imperial dome. Felipe smiled hugely. He was as amused by Imperial ostentation and ritual, which he found completely ridiculous, as he was enamored of it. Fortunately, Melodía was spared: she had never enjoyed that sort of thing, and had far less patience than her father—still less patience for it now, she was realizing, after having found purpose and validation as the

Short-Haired Horse Captain, leading the mounted scouts for Karyl's army.

And Montse has a lot less patience for folderol than I, she thought. It went like a javelin to her heart.

As Felipe Delgao Ramírez, Emperor of Nuevaropa, swept into his Palace for the first time in years—looking for all of Paradise like one of the fully feathered adult Tyrants rumored to stalk the planet's cold northern climes—Melodía followed a dutiful step behind. The entrance hall was imposingly large, large enough to accommodate a mounted war-duckbill, even if the actual door was not. Walls of living rock, polished smooth and washed a pale gold color to enhance the light that poured in from windows and cunningly constructed light shafts, soared high overhead before joining in groined vaults. The floor beneath their feet was yellow marble.

The space was dominated by a gilt bas-relief of Manuel Delgao astride a sackbut bull, delivering a *golpe de gracia* with a lance thrust downward between the colossal gaping jaws of a *Tyrannosaurus imperator*.

Pages led Felipe through the hall and on toward the throne room. The corridor walls were scattered with statue niches, gold-framed paintings, and feather tapestries, all showing scenes from the illustrious career of the founder of Torre Delgao and the Empire he had ruled—with special emphasis on his most notorious feats of derring-do, which were now widely, albeit tacitly, accepted, in-family at least, as being wildly exaggerated if not outright made up. Even in her sunken-in state, it struck Melodía after years of absence that, while far from tasteful, the leitmotif—which continued throughout the Palace—was undeniably effective in producing an impression of mythic might and indeed inevitability concerning the man, his family, and his Imperio. That too was intentional. Martina Delgao, sister to Juana I and architect of both El Corazón and the modern-day Empire, had known the value of inspiring awe.

At the entrance to the throne room, her father stopped flat.

Melodía stepped up beside him—the corridor was easily wide enough to allow her to do that without jostling him. Which would be unseemly, even for his elder daughter and heir. That Melodía felt impatient at best with Imperial courtly norms didn't mean she flouted them.

Usually.

She saw at once what had halted him.

At the far end of another tall, wide chamber stood the Fangèd Throne. It was what the name suggested: made apparently from the skull of a Tyrannosaurus, jaws agape, with a thick cushion on the lower jaw in lieu of a tongue and covered in gold paint. Except it was enormously larger than that of any King Tyrant. It belonged, so legend—and even the official histories—said, to an Imperial Tyrant, an oversize Tyrannosaur that had terrorized this part of Spaña before Manuel Delgao, a dinosaur knight returning home after heroic service in the Demon War, killed it single-handedly. Then rode the wave of renown that deed brought him to reuniting the shattered lands of the Tyrant's head into the Empire of Nuevaropa, and himself to a throne made out of its head.

Since then nobody had ever seen an Imperial Tyrant. Not just in the Empire Melodía's illustrious forebear had founded. Nowhere. In any part of Paradise. Rumors of sightings cropped up every now and then, but never any official confirmation, from the enormous rest of Aphrodite Terra or elsewhere. Melodía thought the Demon War—the supposed Last Battle in which the Creators, their Grey Angels, and their hosts of pious human devotees had finally defeated the attempt of la Hada, the Fae, to reconquer what they claimed as their home world—to be a myth: some kind of altogether human civil war, glossed into glowing propaganda after the fact to legitimize both the Empire and her family's rule of it. Similarly, she considered the Throne itself to be a gilded plaster fake.

Of course, her doubt of the ancient legends had been shaken, at the least, by her three encounters with an actual Grey Angel, first in the decaying guise of human flesh and then in whatever Raguel was really made out of. But they couldn't *all* be true, all those absurd old myths and legends. Could they?

But, real or not, what the Fangèd Throne was not was empty.

A woman sat at ease on the crimson velvet cushion-tongue.

"Ah, Your Highness," she said in Spañol thickly flavored with Alemán, "please forgive me. I arrived this morning and could not resist the temptation to warm the Throne for you."

She rose. Melodía stared at her in astonishment not unmarked by alarm. She was a startling apparition in a white silk gown, accented in black and midnight blue, whose hem swept the floor. She seemed fully as broad as the Palace Herald but, unlike her, tall enough to appear . . . well, less squat. Above an imposing bosom-bulwark rose a great square pink face, framed by astonishing braids, white as the everlasting snow that crowned La Guardiana, queen of the Shield peaks. Her eyes were the bright and merciless blue of a glimpse of daytime sky through a rare tear in the clouds.

Felipe blinked at her from beneath lowered brows.

"And who might you be, Señora?" he asked mildly. Melodía admired his restraint, though she personally suspected it was misplaced. *Your huge Alemana ass doesn't belong on the Fangèd Throne!* she thought, with a degree of outrage that surprised her. *Only Delgao asses should be planted in it.*

Falk came clanking up on Felipe's left in the full midnight-blue personal harness he wore, instead of the Scarlet Tyrant's red and gold. He stopped. Melodía refused to look at him directly. But from the corner of her eye she saw his face had gone even whiter than usual behind his midnight beard.

"Mother?"

Chapter 11

Morión, Morion. . . . —*Corythosaurus casuarius.* A high-
backed hadrosaur, 9 meters long, 3 meters high at shoulder, 3 tonnes. A favored Nuevaropan war-mount, named
for the resemblance between its round crest and that of a
morion helmet.

—THE BOOK OF TRUE NAMES

"So, *amigo*," said Manuel. "What've you got for
us today?"

The yard smelled of dust and the dung of
large herbivores—horses and nosehorns, penned in the
stables behind the three-story fieldstone *posada* where
they'd stopped to refresh themselves and, hopefully,
find information about their quarry. The latter was not
unpleasant to Jaume's nostrils, since he'd grown up with
it. Small green- and blue-feathered scratchers lived up
to their name among the furrows of the inn's truck garden. The oviraptors chuckled to one another as they
picked caterpillars and big grubs from the small still-
green tomatoes and the bean plants. Dusty hills peeked
over the shoulder-high adobe wall that enclosed the inn-
yard, crowned with grey-green scrub juniper and yellow
limestone outcrops. The sky was bright through the

clouds, now thin and almost eye-hurtingly white, that perpetually covered it by day.

A cat lay atop the wall with its forepaws tucked to its chest, watching with knowing yet disinterested yellow eyes. Its cream-and-ginger fur reminded Jaume of the coloration of his beloved Corythosaurus war-mount. Like all the Companions' war-hadrosaurs—and even their full plate armor—she had been left behind for her squire to bring her to, and hopefully catch up with, her master.

Ah, Camellia, Jaume thought. *How I miss you.* He missed her almost as keenly as he did his *novia* Melodía.

His heart quickened at the hope he might soon be reunited with both.

"They're in Tres Veces, my lord," Pablo said. "A village of some substance, with many stone buildings, in a river valley not ten kilometers away."

Manuel grinned. Like Florian, he was a commoner who had risen through the ranks of the Brothers-Ordinary, the Companions' mercenary heavy-cavalry auxiliaries, to knighthood and full Brother status. Born and raised poor on La Meseta himself, he even somewhat resembled the informant, though taller and wirier. He was the obvious choice to do most of the talking, since he spoke the same dialect and knew the words and mannerisms that would put a fellow *campesino* most at ease.

"'Three Times,' eh?" Manuel said. "Perhaps you can tell me the story behind that name someday. For now, though, I'm wondering how you found out about them?"

"I saw them with my own eyes, lord. They were entering the village in two carriages with blacked-out windows. The second had a wheel loose on its axle. A half dozen horsemen rode behind."

Manuel cocked a brow at Jaume. "Matches the reports we've had till now well enough," Jaume acknowledged.

Manuel knew that as well as any. He had carried some

of those reports, from La Merced and its environs, when he met them riding hard the other way on the Imperial High Road. Recently returned from a solo mission for his Order, he had missed the latest campaign and its climax, the desperate fight against Raguel and his Horde, which had gutted the Companions' already depleted ranks.

The keenest strategic mind of the group, as well as a master of portraiture, the *vihuela del arco* family of stringed instruments, and the longsword, Manuel had advised them to head south in hopes of intercepting Montse's abductors en route to Laventura. So Jaume had done, leading his men around the isolated Sierra del Poder and its lesser offshoot, La Sierra de La Gloria, in the midst of La Meseta, which housed the Spañol and Imperial capitals, respectively.

"Well," said Will Oakheart of Oakheart, "there's one thing that's helping us: the Trebs aren't near as subtle as they think they are."

"At least they're not traveling with half a dozen baggage wagons," Florian said. "Consider the sacrifice they must be making for this."

"Consider the sacrifice we will exact from them," Machtigern said. The Alemán knight smiled readily. But seldom with such a raptor edge.

"How long ago?" asked Jaume.

Pablo shrugged. "The sun was already well up, lord."

Jaume dug in his purse and produced a gold Trono. He tossed it to the informant.

Pablo snagged it deftly from the air. "¡*Muchas gracias, señores!* May the Creators bless you." The coin was worth several months' income for a peasant like Pablo, enough to buy him a trained riding horse or arming-sword, either of good quality.

"Bless you, Don Pablo. If you've helped us rescue the little princess, it'll be the least of your rewards."

He looked around at his Companions. White teeth

grinned in all their faces, dark and fair, bearded or shaved clean.

"¡*Montemos*! Let's ride."

"Mother," Falk said as soon as the door to her apartments, on the floor below the Imperial level, had shut behind him. "What are you doing here?"

"Isn't it obvious, Falki, *mein Schatz*?" she asked, shedding her gown so that it shimmered to the floor. Beneath, she wore short silken trunks and a tight band to support her breasts—which by itself would be common full dress here in scandalous Spaña—instead of mere undergarments. The skin of her back was very pale. A wispy servant, shorter than she was but still tall for one of these Southerners, with curly dark brown hair and a thin fussy line of moustache, scooped it up and put it away in the wardrobe. "Or are you just being too lazy to think, again? I'm here to look after my boy."

He hardly registered the verbal slap. Instead, he was staring around in disbelief at his surroundings. They were opulent, a riot of fat silk cushions and brightly colored screens, most depicting a startling variety of erotic scenes. The indirect afternoon sunlight through the window did little to mute the garishness.

He gestured around. "What's—all this?"

"A few trifles. Mere scraps of comfort. Why would I want to be surrounded by Delgao braggadocio in the form of tasteless art? Oh, I've heard all about their conceit in this absurd cave-dweller Palace of theirs. I came prepared."

She smiled. "You know your mother is always prepared."

She accepted a cup of wine from the servant, who wore a natural-colored linen tunic over a loincloth and was obviously a Palace appurtenance rather than one of her usual gaggle of body servants, and drank deeply. She was never the sort of person to sip.

"What on Paradise made you think sitting in the Fangèd Throne was a good idea?"

She laughed and held the gilt goblet out to be refilled. "I was curious how it felt, to occupy the literal seat of the Empire's power," she said. "And I thought it was time an ass other than a skinny Delgao one sat on that cushion."

She turned her back on Falk again and then set her cup down on a sideboard carven with extremely unlikely images of naked nymphs with wreaths in their hair coupling with nosehorn bulls. In real life, such a juxtaposition, if it could be achieved, would prove immediately fatal to the nymphs. The Dowager Duchess Margrethe's own tastes were themselves conspicuous in Alemania, where the very sort of dignified austerity the Imperial Heart went in for was the norm.

Raising her arms, she said, "Parsifal, help me get these off. Then you may retire."

The servant stepped up and began unfastening the breast-band. "Besides," his mother said airily, "His Majesty took no offense. He seemed quite charmed by me, I think."

"The rest of the court was pretty thoroughly scandalized, though, Mother," he said.

She shifted her feet to part her pale thighs slightly to allow Parsifal to skin the drawers off her ample hips and down. Her bare buttocks, large but well muscled, rippled to the motion.

"They don't matter," she said. "Only the Emperor matters."

"But you said our mission was to win influence at court!"

"As a means of gaining influence over His Majesty. Who's not a bad-looking man, really—probably the Alemán part of him."

She stepped out of the garment, which the servant picked up and put away.

"You yourself have gotten influence with His Nibs, in your own way—after your battlefield antics, you hardly need worry what all the sycophants and mendicant knights and terribly tedious Diet members who flutter around the Throne whisper about you. And I plan to gain direct influence myself, in my own indirect ways. Parsifal, you may leave us for now."

The thin-moustached servant bowed and vanished.

"Very well, Mother," Falk said. "You know, of course, I'm delighted to see you. And I'll leave you now, since my Snowflake had a tiring day, and I must see him properly housed in the Palace stables."

She turned, smiling, and spread her arms. Her breasts had only slightly begun to sag into middle age. They were large and wide, with pale pink aureoles contracting into points as he watched. Her pubic hair was a wisp of white that scarcely concealed the lips of her sex.

"Oh, leave your lout of a squire to tend to your little pet. He does little enough as it is. Now come here and kiss your mother hello properly."

Wearing the only armor they had with them, nosehorn-leather jacks, the Companions pelted into the prosperous-looking village of Tres Veces. It consisted of several score of structures, some made of stone, as Pablo had said. It seemed oddly devoid of inhabitants or visitors. The narrow streets were empty, the windows of the mostly one-story, flat-roofed buildings stoutly shuttered.

Then they came with a clatter of hooves into the central plaza and stopped.

A dozen strange dinosaur knights lined its far side, facing them. Each wore armor of overlapping steel plates, and open, peaked helmets. Each sat astride a war-hadrosaur as colorful and splendid as the Companions' own absent mounts. A red banner with a white rose hung lank from the standard that rose from each high saddle cantle.

Each held an Ovdan recurved bow of laminated Triceratops horn with white-fletched arrow nocked and ready. Round shield hung by their pommels.

"Cataphracts?" Machtigern said.

"Trebs," spat Ayaks.

"Hail, Captain-General!" the man in the central position called in accented but clear Spañol. He sat a glorious white morion with a pink face. Even from thirty meters away, Jaume could see his dark face was clean-shaven and beautiful, with huge dark eyes like a new-hatched duckbill's. "I greet you and your illustrious Companions with love and honor."

"Damned peculiar way you've got of showing it," Will Oakheart said.

"You have the advantage of me, Señor Montador," Jaume called back.

"I am Roshan of the Shining Mountain. It is my honor to be Knight Commander of the Knights of the Flower of the Middle Daughter. These are my Flower Knights: Bálint, Dariush, Gyözö, Jahangir, Mas'ud, Omid, Sher, Temür, Yilmaz, Yuliy, and Zakhar. All as accomplished and gallant as they are beautiful."

All but the last two named were as dark as Roshan himself. Yuliy was blond; Zakhar, brown-haired and fairer-skinned than most of his brethren. Jaume recognized their names as Ruso, like his own Companion Ayaks, himself an immigrant from Trebizon. The other names he recognized as mostly Parso or Turco. The Basileia contained large populations from both groups, although Roshan's Order Military—which the Flower Knights clearly were—might have attracted aspirants from Gran Turán. As had his own, although none currently survived among the Companions.

"I surely recognize most of you by your repute: Bernat, Florian, Ayaks, Manuel, Owain, Machtigern, Will Oakheart. Noble artists and heroes all. And, of course, the renowned poet and philosopher of Beauty, mightiest hero of the Empire of Nuevaropa, the Imperial Champion Jaume dels Flors. But I regret two of you gentle sirs are yet unknown to me."

"They're Mor Ramón and Mor Grzegorz, Brothers-Aspirant who accompany us in hopes of winning acceptance to full Companions on our quest." Jaume could see no reason not to tell him. "Which I'm guessing you're so conveniently placed here to hinder us on."

Roshan laughed. But his beautiful features clouded quickly as a dawn sky.

"Sadly so. As holy duty binds you to free the Infanta, it binds us to stop you."

"She's a child," Jaume said, his voice rougher than he liked with emotion. "Is that knightly? Is that Beauty, since you follow the same Lady as do we?"

Roshan dropped his gaze to the paving stones, worn smooth by wagon wheels, horses' hooves, the feet of men and heavy dinosaurs.

"It is a duty which overrides all else," he said. "Those trifles, our hearts. And even our own idiosyncratic conceptions of our religious vows. It is the inescapable burden of a knightly order. And one not unfamiliar to you, I believe."

Jaume felt his cheeks blush hot. That *shot* had struck home. But that was information he wasn't willing to divulge—if his traitor countenance hadn't done so already.

"Believe me, Mor Roshan," Florian said, "we don't have any such ambivalence."

"In that you have advantage over us, my friend."

The Francés knight with the long golden hair, green

eyes, and twisting smile was Jaume's closest living friend among his beloved brothers. He was renowned for wit as sharp as his rapier, which he used with equal skill. But not always equal judgment. For a heartbeat Jaume was afraid Florian would unsheathe his tongue over the invader's use of the word *amigo*.

That under the tactical circumstances twelve *catafractos* as skilled as Jaume took these to be could drop him and all his men in a single volley before they could dodge did not concern him. It was that, enemies or not, there was no call to be *rude*. Courtesy was beautiful.

"I take it it's no accident we find you here," Jaume said, "instead of our quarry."

"Which has long since flown," Manuel said. "If it was ever here."

"Alas, you are both correct in your suppositions."

"Set up," Florian said in disgust.

"Like skittles," agreed Machtigern.

"Did you send the fake informant to mislead us?" Jaume asked.

"Would you have used such a stratagem?"

"Of course."

Many of the Empire's secular knights, and even certain other Orders Military, disdained the Companions for their willingness to use sleights. Then again those same critics tended to consider the use of any tactics other than blundering straight ahead in a full-speed charge as cowardly. There were reasons the Companions called many of their noble warriors "bucketheads," and not just because of their helmets.

Roshan nodded, as if taking in new information. "We did not. That was our . . . masters."

That would be the actual kidnappers, of course. *If* the Flower Knight was to be believed. The Trebs were famous for their intricate and almost compulsive intrigues.

But if Roshan's dismay at what his duty compels him

to do is faked, Jaume thought, *then his excellence as an actor is unsurpassed.*

Florian shook back his long, kinky locks.

"So what's it to be, then? Wherever the child snatchers you work for have gone, we're going to run them down. And you stand in our road."

"Indeed, Mor Florian," Roshan said. "But as the noted strategist Manuel de Piedrablanca has observed, we have done our duty and covered their escape. Though you came close, they were never here; this was always a pure ambush."

Which we fell into as obligingly as a blind matador, Jaume thought ruefully.

"But now we must end this delightful encounter," Roshan said. He spoke a single crisp command.

Hornbows rose. Thumb-rings pulled white fletching to cheeks in the distinctive and exotic Ovdan draw.

"*Scatter!*" Jaume yelled.

He knew it was futile even as he turned his mare's head to his left and nudged her light-grey barrel with his heels. But the volley passed over their heads with the unmistakable fluttering hum of arrows in flight.

Once out of sight of the plaza behind a two-story counting house, Jaume turned right down a twisting lane and set the mare galloping. He drew the Lady's Mirror from its sheath across his back. He knew too much about the Ovdan archer skills employed by Trebs as well as Turanes to believe he and his men had a hope of catching the cataphracts before they had drawn again. But he knew from the basic tactical knowledge he instilled in every Brother before he was ever accepted to Companion status that both the men with him and the ones who had broken the other way were now closing in like pincers on the *catafractos'* flanks.

The square was empty. Blank, shuttered windows seemed to mock the Companions like blind eyes.

"Spread out and sweep the village," Jaume called. "They can't have gotten far." Big bipedal war-dinosaurs could outsprint horses, but horses ran faster longer.

Five minutes later, they rallied on the road. "Nothing, Captain," Florian reported in disgust. "And the road's too well metaled with busted pumice to take prints, especially from big duckbill feet."

"How could they have gotten away?" Ramón asked. "It's like magic."

"Be careful what you say," said Owain darkly. The strapping blond Galés seldom spoke, though he sang with a baritone beauty that brought tears to his Brothers' eyes.

"You don't really believe they used magic to get away from us, do you?" Machtigern asked.

"Magic walks the world, my friend. We've seen it with our own eyes."

"But Raguel's gone from the world, for better or worse," Jaume said. "Better, I have to think, Grey Angel or not, since we all saw what he did."

"But they do not die," Owain said. "And he has six friends."

"You don't really think we're up against an Angel here, do you?" Will asked in Anglysh, the native tongue of both men. Jaume could follow well enough. Like most noble Southerners, he was at least conversant in that language, Francés, and in Alemán, along with the Imperial common tongue, Spañol, while knowing next to nothing of Slavo, the speech of the fifth and final Torre Major of Nuevaropa.

"No," Owain replied in Spañol. "But there are other magics."

"The Fae?" Jaume shook his head. "Too much for me. That's passing beyond doctrine and on to superstition."

Owain looked grim and shook his head, but said no more.

"Forgive him, Captain," Will Oakheart said. "The

Welsh are a superstitious lot." The two Anglaterranos were best friends, though never lovers, so far as Jaume knew. As Jaume had become platonic best friends with Florian, after the sea-monster took his childhood friend and lover, Pere, during a fight with pirates in La Canal.

"We don't have to go piling on explanations," Machtigern said. "They got away somehow. They're clever bastards. We'd probably find a way, too, in their position."

"It was almost as if they were trying to imitate your brotherhood," Mor Grzegorz said. "Ours. Or is that presumptuous? Pardon, I do not know."

"You're already our Brother, Grzegorz," Florian said. "You and Ramón. Don't worry about the details."

"All I'm worried about now is that we've missed the Infanta's actual kidnappers. And whether or not Roshan told us the truth, we have no idea where to find them."

"They are heading to Laventura," Ayaks said. The brooding blond giant was brooding harder than usual. He had left his allegiance to the Basileia—something that wasn't always necessarily strong to start with among its lesser nationalities, such as los Rusos and los Talianos—behind when he came to Nuevaropa to seek and win acceptance as a Companion. But he took his nominal countrymen's betrayal of both hospitality and diplomatic law personally.

Jaume wondered how Manfredo, the former Taliano law student—and former Companion—would have felt. Probably even more outraged; it had been the fact that his heart lay more with Torre, the Youngest Son, the Creator associated with Order, than with Beauty and the Middle Daughter that led to his splitting with the Companions. Jaume wondered how he and the Brabantés knight Wouter de Jong had fared after leaving the Order, disgusted by the atrocities committed by the very Imperial Army they were on the verge of joining in its then Crusade against Providence.

He didn't wonder long. The present was more urgent for him at the best of times. Which these were not.

"So we know," Ayaks said, "they will head just east of south."

"Many roads lead from here to Laventura, *hermano*," Manuel said.

"So how do we proceed?" Jaume asked.

"Let's scour the area surrounding for information," Manuel said, "and return to the Lambent Lambeosaur for tonight. Our squires and our war-dinosaurs should catch up to us by morning."

Jaume's own arming-squire, Bartomeu, had kept in touch with the Companions by means of horseback messengers since his group had passed the eastern tip of the Mountains of Power. He was proving adept at organizing and getting things done. *Have to think about knighting the boy soon, I suspect,* Jaume thought. *He was blooded at Canterville against the Horde, and did well. I'll miss having him as squire, though.*

"Do we have time?" Ayaks asked. "Laventura isn't far."

"They can't travel as fast as they'd like," Manuel said. "Not with the whole countryside roused against them by now. Especially not now that they've met with a dozen dinosaur knights, who doubtless came from Laventura to meet them."

"And we need our dinosaurs, to deal with theirs," Jaume said.

"And how about their arrows?" Florian asked. "If they use chisel tips, they'll shoot through our plate. And I doubt they'll shoot to miss next time."

"Which begs the question of why they shot to miss this time," said Will. The two Angleses lived up to the common stereotype of their countrymen by being accomplished archers of the longbow, a weapon almost never used on continental Nuevaropa, where the short bow—far weaker and shorter-ranged than either longbow or hornbow—dominated. Their problem was that, unlike the recurved Ovdan bows the cataphracts used, the longbow was badly suited to being shot from horse- or dinosaur-back.

"That's evidence their leader was telling the truth when he said they didn't much care for what they have to do, anyway," Florian said.

"They seemed to give us a great deal of information," said Bernat. As chronicler of the Order, he had a keen appreciation of such matters. "Was that a slip, I wonder? Arrogance or guile?"

"You can trust a Treb for those things, if nothing else," Machtigern said. He gave Ayaks a glance. "Present company excepted, Brother."

"I am no Treb," Ayaks said. "I am a Rus, a Companion, and I serve the Fangèd Throne as well as the Lady."

"They're playing some game of their own, those knights," Florian said. "We can rely on that, if nothing else."

"Indeed," Manuel said thoughtfully. "But the question is—what is it?"

Chapter 12

Los Libros de la Ley, THE BOOKS OF THE LAW—The Creators' Own Law. Popularly attributed to Torrey, the Youngest Son, who stands for Order. They are largely filled with explanation and annotation, since the actual laws are few and simple: for example, establishing worship of the Creators as the worldwide faith, although allowing it to take many forms; enjoining people to actively enjoy life; abjuring eternal punishment; mandating proper hygiene; and forbidding slavery and torture.

—A PRIMER TO PARADISE FOR THE IMPROVEMENT
OF YOUNG MINDS

I did it! My plan worked! I hugged Silver Mistral extra-hard when I got back to the carriage!

(The less said about the smell where I am now, the better. It's a mostly empty storeroom in a tanner's yard we're staying in for the night. As always, the bad people are afraid of being spotted if we stay in the open. Why they don't travel at night, I don't know, but I'm not about to suggest it to them.)

When I ask to go relieve myself, they let me. They find a sidetrack where they can get off the main road, or anyway as main a road as they ever follow. (They're staying mostly off the major roads to cut down the chances of discovery. I got that much from what they say in Spañol.) Then they stop the carriages under the best cover they can find.

When I go, they always send along Diego or Elfego in case I try to run for it—they can both catch me, big lumbering lunks though they look like. They also send one of the two priestesses. I actually prefer Paraskeve, even though she's real mean, because she mostly just ignores me, other than to keep an eye on me so I don't bolt.

But today it was the other woman, Anastasia, whom they usually call Tasoula because I guess that's her nickname or something. I really really don't like her. She doesn't hurt me or anything. She hardly seems to notice I exist, most of the time. But she's *dirty*. She looks all grimy, even though the Creators (whom I do not believe in) say we're supposed to keep ourselves clean, and shouldn't one of Their priestesses, like, set a good example? But she stinks like a Life-to-Come sectary, so it's better walking outdoors with her than riding in one of those stuffy carriages with her, let me tell you. When we were walking, she kept rubbing dirt and twigs and leaves on her face and skin and hair and talking to herself, I guess, about "the voices of the wildwood" telling her scary things and giving her scary orders. That kind of scares me, especially since sometimes it seems she's not talking just to herself but is talking to them? Then she caught some beetles and crushed them and rubbed the juices and goo all over her arms, which are the only parts of her robes left bare aside from her face. They look hot, as well as being gross. That made me pretty nervous.

Today I found a path that led to a stream among a small stand of pine trees in a mostly open area. The Meseta isn't as flat as I always think it is—there's plenty of rolling hills and low ridges, it turns out. At first I mostly took it because I didn't want the nettles to scratch my legs.

They hurt, and itch something fierce at night, too. But when I got to the little stream, I noticed a sandal print in some bare mud by the bank, so it wasn't just a trail the springers or maybe wild nosehorns made going to drink. So I'll try to pick out spots like this in the future where I know people might come.

Because I did it! I dropped my first note!

I stopped to hunker down and get a drink and slipped the note into some weeds. Both crazy Tasoula and Diego, who was the Spañol brute they sent to escort us today, were standing ten or so meters away, so all I had to worry about was making sure it was hidden from them. Neither of them noticed anything! But I hope anybody who comes to let their livestock drink at the stream, or fill a water skin, will see it.

It was exciting. Like when I used to get away from my dueñas at the Firefly Palace and then go watch Maestro Rubbio in the Armory, or visit the dinosaur stables, or even go down the ramp into La Merced and wander around. If I get back home, I'll never do that again.

Okay. I probably will. But the thing is, the *getting away* part was always fun. It was almost more fun than whatever I went on to do after I gave them the slip. And this was fun the same kind of way.

I should probably become a spy. It sure seems to pay well for the ones the Trebs hire. Though for Nuevaropa, not against it. I'd never do anything to hurt my Daddy or *mi familia*. Not even La Madrota, who's, like, 2,000 years old and scary as a slayer. Then again I also want to be a master of siege warfare. Maybe you can do both? I need to look into that when I get home. Someday.

(I will!)

It wasn't very long. I mostly just said I was all right, and roughly where I was, that the Trebs were heading for Laventura, and that we were traveling all over the landscape rather than going right there because they're super afraid they'll be caught. Looks as if word's gone out that they kidnapped me.

I also warned Jaume to be real careful whom he trusts, because everywhere we go the Trebs seem to know they can find traitors and spies who will help them. This worries me a lot. And not just about what happens to me.

Anyway, I spent almost as much time writing the instruction on the outside of the sheet of paper when I folded it—that whoever found it should please please *please* try to find Don Jaume and the Companions and give it to them, and Jaume would give them a Trono. I hope that's enough?

I also hope whoever finds it can read it. I drew a little picture of the front of a Trono with my daddy's face on it to help. It doesn't look all that much like him. But neither does the gold piece. Anyway, the Mercedes say country people on La Meseta aren't always good about learning to read, even though the *Books of the Law* say everybody should know how. How they're supposed to know what the *Books* say if they can't read them, I don't know. Maybe the priests tell them that at Church?

Anyways, fingers crossed for luck.

I hope this works.

I don't really believe in the Creators, but—please? Can you help? Maybe I can believe in Bella, just a little— Lady Li, the one Jaume works for.

Lady—please? Get me and Silver Mistral away from these awful people and back home? I know my family is worried.

Later—Duh. Of course they'll know where I was if somebody finds the note and takes it to them. I don't always think, sometimes.

"Daddy?" she said.

Though it was late the night of their arrival, and Melodía felt as if she was about to drop from sheer exhaustion—of mind and spirit as well as body—her father was still up, sitting on the Fangèd Throne and reading a book by the pungent light of a pine-oil lamp. With no one around except for a few palace stewards lurking discreetly in the fringes of the throne room in case the Emperor needed something.

He looked around. "Ah, Melodía! *Querida mia*, you must be spent! Why aren't you in bed?"

"I'm on my way," she said. "But I wanted to ask your permission to have Fanny and Lupe and my other ladies-in-waiting join us here?" She mentioned those two in particular because her father seemed to favor them most. Princess Francis of Anglaterra was highly respectable, and while Melodía's cousin Princess Lupe . . . wasn't . . . she *was* a fairly close kinswoman, by way of Felipe's mother, who came from Torre Ramírez, the Kingdom of Spaña's royal family.

"Oh, that?" He shook his head and laid his book down on the throne's arm. She saw it was a favorite of his, the romance *Los Montadores de Tormenta—The Storm Knights*. Supposedly a relic of Old Home, it concerned feats of derring-do by great warriors who traveled a vast plain mounted on magical mechanical contrivances. Inspired silliness, perhaps, but silliness as far as she was concerned. *Still, he needs some relaxation, after the day he's had dealing with the Court and the backed-up business of Empire.*

And the days preceding.

"I found a message on that very subject awaiting me here this afternoon, when I finally had time to deal with such things. Prince Harry was actually pleading with me to call them here." Prince Heriberto of the Tyrant's Jaw was a noted lover of all things Anglés, to such an extent that he actually preferred being referred to by the Anglysh phrase. "Even his own daughter, Josefina Serena.

It seems they're quite demanding. And unrelenting. At least he doesn't seem miffed with me for marching off to war in Providence anymore, since he lost our beloved Montse and all."

Her heart jumped. "And?"

He shook his head. "I told him no, of course. Wise Fray Jerónimo pointed out the folly of exposing them to the dangers of the road, when there are threats abroad in our Empire and in this very Kingdom. We cannot risk the children of such powerful families, least of all in a crisis like this. They're far safer in Firefly Palace."

She felt as if her spine had fractured like porcelain and was collapsing inside her. "But that's where Montse was kidnapped from!"

Her father shrugged. "And it's the one place in all the *Imperio* we know the kidnappers are *not*. I hope Heriberto isn't being so extreme in his measures to secure his own Palace that We have to take official notice of it. Mercedes are sadly known for losing sight of the Creators' Law when serious injuries have been done to them."

She sagged. It took a positive exercise of will to keep from collapsing in a puddle on the gold-veined black marble floor of the throne room. An exercise she wasn't sure was even worth it.

She knew his tone, seeming casual and even jovial, all too well. *He's made up his mind*, she thought. *And I might as well try to argue a thirsty Thunder-titan into turning away from water as argue with him.*

She turned and fled. She'd cried enough in front of him the last few days. She wouldn't do so again.

She held out until she reached her apartment on an upper story of the Palace, the highest level with external windows. Dismissing her body-servants—strangers all—with a wave, she rushed to her bed, threw herself on the red-and-gold silk coverlet, and sank into a stormy sea of tears.

"I found someone," called Machtigern.

Jaume looked up and around. He stood barefoot and shin deep in a chuckling stream, in the shade of a small copse of broadleaf trees in a little valley like a saddle between two hills, savoring the coolness of the water as well as its smell, after the hot Meseta dust they'd been eating all day. Beside him Camellia had her big round-crested head down and her beak in the water, lapping noisily with her tongue. Upstream and down, his other Companions did the same—except for the Brother they had left on watch.

The Alemán knight stood in some scrub oak on the edge of the stand of trees. A woman stood beside him. She was middle-aged and weathered—clearly a peasant, by the rude woven-straw hat and shoulder-covering she wore. Otherwise, she wore nothing but loincloth and breast-band.

"Señores," she said. "I beg your pardon for disturbing you."

"How did you find us?" asked Florian in alarm. He was sitting in the water while his sackbut Here Comes Trouble drank. Leaves above dappled the duckbill's striking calico coloration in white, gold, black, and brown, creating a curious counterpoint.

"Why, the whole countryside is abuzz with it!" the woman exclaimed. "What else can one expect when Don Jaume himself and his noble Companions ride through on their great beasts?"

"What indeed?" Manuel asked. He stood in tall weeds by the bank, rubbing the bridge of his morion Consuelo's green-and-gold nose. "City boy."

Florian shrugged as the others laughed. What can I say? I'm an alley rat born and bred."

"What's your name, Señorita?" Jaume asked.

"Oh, Señora, my lord. Three times over."

"You are twice widowed?" Grzegorz asked. "How sad."

"Oh, no. I have three husbands. And I am Desideria."

"Evidently," murmured Will.

"What brings you to us, Señora Desideria?" Jaume asked.

"This." She held out a folded piece of paper. It had writing on it. He accepted it with a frown of curiosity.

"Praise the Lady!" he exclaimed after a glance. "It says it's from Montserrat! And it's definitely her handwriting."

"What?" Machtigern said. "How can that be?"

"It also says, if you will forgive my saying so, that you will give me one Trono if I deliver it to your hand," the woman said.

"It does indeed. A moment—"

"I've got it," Manuel said. He dug in the purse he wore on the sword-belt buckled around his bleached linen tunic. He tossed a coin at her in an arc that glittered sporadic yellow as it spun through alternating shadow and light.

She caught it, peered at it, then grinned around happily. "Thank you noble gentlemen so much!"

"My pleasure," Manuel said.

"And mine as well," Jaume said. "Now, if you'll excuse us—"

Desideria dipped a curtsy, then turned and took up off the slope like a springer with a horror pack in pursuit.

"She acts as if she's afraid we will think better of it," Ayaks said.

"It's a princely sum," said Machtigern. "She could buy a good sword for that much gold. I wonder if the child knows the value of money?"

"Probably," Jaume said, unfolding the paper. "Montse's a very practical child. Much given to poking and prying into how things are done."

Leaving their mounts—who were both too well trained and too attached to their riders to wander—the nine men crowded around their leader, gawking like schoolchildren.

"I can't read it," Ramón said. "It's not Spañol. It's *like* it. But it's not."

Blond Bernat laughed. "It's *català*," he said. "The language of Jaume's homeland and mine. And also the girl's late mother's. I didn't know she could write that!"

"Neither did I," Jaume said, reading. "It seems she's full of surprises. She says this is her third note. It's dated yesterday—morning, she says. She warns us to be careful whom we trust. The kidnappers spend each night in a house owned by a Treb spy or sympathizer."

"The Empire's that riddled with corruption?" asked Will.

"It can't be!" Ramón said.

"If it weren't for corruption in the Empire, we wouldn't have jobs rooting it out," Florian said. "But I have to admit this shocks me a little."

"She writes that she spent the last night nearby—she's not sure where, but she scratched her initials into the walls and on the table of the room where she and Mistral were kept."

"Mistral?" asked Ayaks.

"Her pet ferret. Clever little beast, loyal and most engaging. They're inseparable. As witnessed by the fact that her abductors didn't manage to separate them."

"If the householders suborned, won't anybody who finds the marks she leaves be as well?" Manuel asked. "Or at least too afraid of their master to say anything to the authorities?"

Jaume laughed. "She's smart beyond her years, and resourceful—clearly. But she's still only sixteen. Let's give her until at least puberty to develop a tactical genius to rival yours, my friend."

Manuel grinned back. "Fair enough. She might give me a run, at that."

"We'll have a way to do some of that corruption rooting-out, at least," Machtigern said. "All we need to do is look for her marks, and we'll know we've found a traitor."

"We'll leave that for whomever His Majesty sees fit to send to investigate," Jaume said. He folded the paper neatly back along the precise creases Montse had put in it, raised it to his lips for a quick kiss, and slipped it into his tunic. He'd transfer it to his panniers directly; it was valuable evidence. As well as a link to someone very dear to him—very dear.

"Now, my friends—we know we're on the right track. So we'd best be after it."

Chapter 13

Cazador Jorobado, Hunchbacked Hunter, *Jorobado,* Hunchback. . . . —*Concavenator corcovatus.* Medium-sized bipedal, carnivorous dinosaur; most notable for the dorsal fin which stands just in front of its hips, and long quills on the arms. Grows to 6 meters long, 1.7 meters at shoulder, 1200 kilograms. Fierce out of proportion to its modest size. Native to Ruybrasil; a popular import for Nuevaropan zoos, by reason of its exotic appearance.

—THE BOOK OF TRUE NAMES

*S*ometime later she came back to herself, raising her head from her arms and the sodden silk with a gasp like a drowning person breaking water.

She shook her head. Then, turning, she sat and poured water from a gilded flask placed on a small table by the bed and drank it, holding the cup with both hands. Her head was slumped. Her hair, which had grown out several centimeters from the severe bob she'd worn it in during her first days as captain of Karyl's light riders, clung to the sides of her face like a needy lover's arms.

Into the grey blankness of her mind spiked red. *Anger.*

"I'm alone," she said aloud. "All right. So I am. But I'm not *helpless*."

She let the anger fill her, suffuse her like the welcome warmth of a campfire when the winds blew chill down into Providence from the ice-sheathed peaks of the Shield Range.

"I've let myself feel helpless before. And that *made* me helpless. Well, fuck that!"

She ended head up and shouting at the walls of her plain chamber.

The first fury of anger subsided. But the warmth remained.

So warmed, her thoughts proceeded.

There are things I can do, she realized. *So I will. I'll fight this fight by myself if I have to.*

She thought of Pilar, the friend she had so long dismissed as just a servant, defying custom and the social order on the road to exile from La Merced to tell the Princesa Imperial that she had to brace up and stop feeling sorry for herself now, or all the risks and sacrifices by her sister and friends—even ones she didn't know she had—to smuggle her out of her cell and the Firefly Palace would be pissed away. Pilar, who had given her life for love of her. Claudia, who had died futilely trying to protect her sister. And Montserrat, kidnapped by cruel strangers as part of some incomprehensible game.

No, she thought. *They didn't do all that for me just so I can give up now. When, what? My little playmates can't come play?*

"Fuck that," she said again, but softly. Her new servants might be strangers, but they were also blameless. No point frightening them—or giving them fuel for gossip, either.

"I'm going to destroy you," she said to a person who wasn't there in the flesh, but never far, and whose name she didn't like to say. "I'm going to destroy you, and you and your great blond nosehorn-sow of a mother can't stop me. I don't care what it takes!"

Oh my, she thought. *I'm shouting again. Oh well. Fuck that too, while we're handing out fuckings.*

"I don't know how," she admitted out loud, calm once again. "Yet. But I'll think of something."

And without calling for an undoubtedly well-spooked serving maid to come turn down her bed for her—a ritual that seemed entirely pointless and silly, after spending weeks sleeping in forest and field on campaign—she slid beneath the coverlet and fell asleep with the lamp still lit.

She slept soundly through the night for the first time since the horrible news arrived.

"I see the carriages, Captain," Will Oakheart of Oakheart called over his shoulder to Jaume as he slithered back from the scrub-feathered ridgetop.

His white breastplate was smeared in yellow mud, obscuring the orange circle-and-cross of Lady's Mirror symbol, as well as his own ensign of an acorn proper, meaning brown, on a field of gold. The Companions, all in full harness like the Anglés and with arming-squires holding their dinosaurs downslope by a stream, clustered behind the rise. As anticipated, the squires, war-beasts, and harness had caught them up at the Lambent Lambeosaur a couple of days before. Now they were just a few days' ride from the great pelagic port of Laventura, descending from the dry central massif of the Kingdom of Spaña into the wet Aino littoral.

"Going to start raining again at any time," Grzegorz said, his bare, close-cropped blond head tipped to the thickening and greying sky. "It will turn slippery mud into sinking mud."

"The life of a campaigner," Florian said.

"I know. But I do not have to like it." He laughed.

"Our information's solid this time," Will said, collapsing his telescoping brass spyglass. "They're parked in the yard behind a three-story limestone mercantile house on the far side of the Plaza. They've tried to disguise themselves under canvas, but their shapes're still too distinctive."

"I trust the source," Jaume said with a grin.

"It's a good job we're about to take them," Machtigern said, rubbing condensation from the steel head of his long-hafted rider's hammer with a rag. It didn't do any actual good, since the day was so humid. But it gave his hands something to do. "The little princess's scheme is working almost too well. The nobles are complaining about the expense."

Montserrat's habit of dropping crumpled pieces of writing paper and scratching pleas for help into every available surface where they stopped had resulted in a flood of reports as to her abductors' progress. The promise of a gold Trono reward for carrying the message to the authorities was proving effective.

"You'd think the *grandes* would be pleased," Florian said, "given that we give them two *Tronos* back for every one they can prove they spent on rewards."

"I know," Machtigern said, leaving off his futile drying and taking up his other pet pre-battle tic of tipping back his war-hammer and tapping its steel shanks against the flared pauldron that protected his right shoulder. "But our reserves are running dry."

That got another general laugh.

"I thought we were insanely lucky the Trebs weren't going balls-out for the southern coast," Manuel said. "Now thanks to the girl we know they're taking a circuitous route from sanctuary to secret sanctuary, to avoid detection with the whole country roused against them."

"We are lucky none of their spies've told them about the girl's little billets-doux."

"It amazes me they haven't caught on to what she's doing," Machtigern said. "She managed to scratch a message on a table in a common room at the last inn they stopped at. On a table. How the Trebs missed it is beyond me."

Jaume thought of the latest communication they'd received. That very morning, almost as soon as they took the road, they'd run into a woman farmer mounted on a yearling nosehorn riding the other way. She'd been excited almost beyond coherent speech when she realized she had stumbled right into the presence of the Imperial Constable and his handpicked band of champions. Though once Jaume read the note, the five Tronos he'd given her from their rapidly dwindling supply had shocked her into silence.

"The Trebs are a peculiarly virulent strain of buckethead, it seems," Florian said. "Despite their reputation for mastery of intrigue, they seem like the sorts who don't deign to glance at tabletops. Nor commoners. Nor little girls, beyond making sure they don't slip away."

Jaume marveled at his cousin's keen intelligence as well as her resourcefulness. She'd even been learning Griego on the side from the least offensive among her abductors, a sardonic count called Dragos from the Rumano, one of whatever the Basileia called its Lesser Towers—minority groups. She'd overheard that because of problems with their carriages—real this time—they needed to risk stopping at a sympathizer's house in the substantial settlement of La Bajada for repairs.

"I am amazed by how many spies the Trebs have among us," Grzegorz said.

"I don't think any of us suspected it," Manuel said. "But I should have. We've been at peace with Gran Turán right over the mountains longer than any of us have been alive, leave aside the usual bandit raids. Even though Trebizon isn't our neighbor, we're their real maritime commercial rivals in western Terra Aphrodite. It's why they've been trying so hard to get the Emperor to marry Melodía off to their Crown Prince Mikael."

"Who weighs two hundred kilos and never bathes," said Ramón. "Or so I've heard." Younger than his Slavo fellow Aspirant, he was naturally far less serious in demeanor. But he mostly kept silent now, apparently afraid of embarrassing himself and ruining his chance at acclamation to full Brotherhood.

"The key thing is, they've money and motive aplenty to build a spy network inside the Empire, or at least Spaña. And a perfect *entrepôt* through Laventura."

"Trebizon's westernmost stronghold, as they say," Florian said.

"All the more reason to make this work now," Jaume said. "If they get into the city, they're better than halfway home. You all know the plan. The Lady's strength to us all."

"Found us!" screeched the wild-haired noblewoman the other Trebs usually called Tasoula. "The heretics are right outside the village!"

Montserrat's first reaction to the outburst was to jump halfway off the chair in the *sala* on the emporium's second floor, almost spilling a sleeping Mistral to the rich parquetry floor.

The second was elation. *If she's right, I'm as good as free!*

Their host, a cadaverous middle-aged Taliano émigré at least two meters tall despite a stoop, who had a great wing of grey hair sticking out like the fin on a *cazador jorobado* from either cheek, did stand bolt upright from his chair and stare wildly about in alarm with sunken eyes.

"Calm yourself, Señor Alessandro," said Dragos, sitting on the *banco* beneath the front windows with his legs crossed, sipping tea from a green glass cup. "I doubt Count Jaume and his pretty bullyboys are about to burst in on us this moment. Although it'd be quite diverting if they did."

Paraskeve shot him a hot-eyed look of hatred, which, Montse reflected, was nothing out of the ordinary for her.

"He is!" Montse took the opportunity to pipe. "He's coming to kill you all, you murderous loonies!"

"Calm yourself, child," Akakios said. He stood by a side table looking on with an air of authority that, as usual, did nothing to command the proceedings. It was a constant source of exasperated wonder to Montse how these Trebs got anything done.

Dragos doing most of it, I think is how.

Akakios swept what he clearly hoped was a calming gaze around the richly appointed room. "She doesn't know what she's saying."

"Yes I do! Jaume's going to pull your guts out through your nostrils and *I'm going to watch*—"

"What do your cards tell you, Tasoula?" asked the priest Charalampos, his thin, bearded face even more twisted with tension than usual.

"The voices in her crazy head, you mean?" Paraskeve said.

Anastasia jumped up from the small table where she sat and flipped it over, sending the Creator's Cards spread out on it flying everywhere. They could be used either to cast the *yijing* or, as she'd apparently been using them now, to tell Tarot.

"They're not my voices!" she shrieked. "I don't want them in my head! But the cards tell me the Companions are right outside town."

"Surely, now, they must be wrong," Akakios said, making patting-down motions with his hands.

"We must fly! *Fly!*"

"Do people actually say that where you come from?" asked Montse, intrigued despite herself.

"No," Charalampos said. "She's just crazy. She read too many romances before the voices started talking in her head."

"I don't like it any better than you do," Dragos said, setting his cup down on the bare whitewashed stone and standing up from the red, black, and grey imported *Tejano* feather-work blanket spread on the bench for a cushion. "But she's been right more often than she's been wrong. We can't afford to ignore this warning."

"She is undoubtedly correct," said the tall man who stood quietly by the back wall. He was very pretty, in a round-faced way, with clean-shaven pink cheeks and big liquid-brown eyes. He was the leader of the Order Military of dinosaur knights who had ridden out from Laventura to meet Montse's kidnappers in the southern Meseta. Montse knew they spent a lot of time painting and singing and other arty things, and in general they struck her as nothing but a cheap imitation of her cousin's Companions. "It was inevitable that they'd catch us, sooner or later."

"Which they wouldn't do if you'd done your job before and destroyed them in the ambush we set up for you," said the other male Treb, the small, thin priest called Vlasis. Though he never spoke loudly or directly seemed to threaten, he scared Montse more than any of the others. Even more than the murderous Paraskeve or the raving Tasoula.

"If the Companions were so easy to destroy, Raguel would have finished the job," Dragos said. "Instead of getting seen off by a disgraced nobleman's pet."

"Blasphemy!" shouted Paraskeve.

"Fact," Dragos countered, calm as always. "Meanwhile, if you want my advice, and I know you don't, you'll send out the *Mirza* and his knights and be quick about it. They probably won't destroy Jaume this time, either, but they're your only hope of forestalling him carrying out his young cousin's quite entertaining prophecy."

Roshan nodded. "We will prevent them from overtaking you, Arch-Priest," he said to Akakios. "But you have to follow the seeress's advice and run."

"But the carriages aren't fully fixed," protested Akakios. For once his smooth, deep voice spiked in alarm.

"No help for it," Dragos said. "Better to risk a wheel falling off on the road than the Companions getting to you here."

"But what do we do if one does?" asked Charalampos.

"Run," Dragos said.

Everyone was standing and looking agitated. Alessandro, their traitorous host, was wringing his hands as if anticipating the feel of the headsman's axe on the back of his neck once his role was discovered. But no one seemed to be *doing* anything.

Except Roshan, who strode forward with long legs, bare beneath the simple red-dyed linen smock of his Order. The sword hanging from his belt had a curved blade. Montse wondered if it was a *talwar*.

"How can you help them?" she asked him. "I'm a child. They're *kidnapping* me! How is that chivalrous?"

"It isn't," the knight said, his face troubled. "But duty overrides all."

As he passed Montse, he reached down to grip her shoulder. "Be strong, Princess. Your people have not forgotten you."

She slapped his hand away. "Don't you dare touch me, you—you dung beetle!"

The hurt in his eyes seemed genuine, to Montse's surprise.

He left. "Come, everyone," Akakios said. "We need to be moving as well. Take charge of her, Count Dragos."

"You slapped the wrong person," Dragos said to her sidelong as he came up to herd her after the others.

"I'll slap you too, if you'd like," she said.

Chapter 14

Sacabuche, **sackbut.** . . . —*Parasaurolophus walkeri.* One of the most popular war-hadrosaurs. Bipedal herbivore: 9.5 meters, 2.5 meters tall at shoulder, 3 tonnes. So named because its long, tubular head-crest produces a range of sounds like the sackbut, a trumpetlike musical instrument with a movable slide.

—THE BOOK OF TRUE NAMES

Despite a saddle especially constructed to cushion the impacts, and Jaume's decades of training and practice in maintaining a proper seat, each footfall of Camellia's fast trot through the streets of La Bajada threatened to jar his every sinew right off his skeleton. He could ignore the rain pelting his face beneath his sallet's open visor. But though his morion's powerful three-toed hind feet gave her excellent purchase on most surfaces, the water running over the cobblestones made them slick as fine glass.

He led Bernat, Ayaks, Will, and Grzegorz down the left-hand, or easterly, path through the town toward the large mercantile house. Florian led the rest—Owain, Manuel, Machtigern, and Ramón—right of the main road. He kept his neck turning. He was worried not only about surprise charges or, worse, arrow volleys from a side street or alley but also about the winding way, whose already claustrophobic narrowness was accentuated by the way the tall, narrow buildings on either side had been built out toward each other. They'd be ideal for snipers with crossbows to shoot from, or simply to toss heavy clay roofing tiles down on their heads from. Jaume doubted that ease of ambush was enough to make the Trebs comfortable entering a town this large, no matter how urgent their emergency. The most likely reason they'd gone to ground so close to the potential safety of the coast and crowded sprawl of Laventura was that Treb money had bought an alliance, or at least compliance.

Either way, a quarrel through the neck will make me just as dead, he thought.

From his dealings with Karyl Bogomirskiy, then Voyvod of the Misty March, during the war against the Princes' Party in the North, Jaume knew true Ovdan warbow strings wouldn't lose tension in the rain. The Companions' main hope for overcoming the advantage the cataphracts' bows gave them was that the twisty streets provided only short sightlines—and in a pinch Jaume and his dinosaur knights would have a chance to dodge down a byway if they encountered archers.

The buildings showed drab, colorless façades in the rain. Having looked from the ridge before the rain began, Jaume knew most really were that drab, covered in yellow-brown stucco. But close up he saw that each structure was different in height or frontage—this one closer to its cross-street neighbors, that one farther—in what seemed like a defiant attempt at individual distinction. He found the aesthetic oddly satisfying, even if not to his eye beautiful.

Twenty meters ahead of him, a dark sackbut skidded into view around the corner of a three-story brothel, identifiable by two red lamps burning in the gloom. Three more war-duckbills appeared in quick succession.

"Bowl them over and pass them by!" Jaume shouted to his men. He didn't feel the need to add, "if you can." It skirted the edge of insult to tell his Companions that much, even the candidate Ramón—he and Grzegorz had been tutored intensively by the full Brothers on the chase.

Jaume slammed the visor of his sallet shut over the bevor that protected his throat and lower face, leaving only a narrow slit to see and breathe through. He raised his escutcheon-style shield. He carried the Lady's Mirror in his right hand. He and his men had decided there was little point in bringing unwieldy long lances into the confined streets of La Bajada. He was minorly disappointed to see the Trebs—these Trebs, at least—had made the same decision.

It didn't matter terribly much. A dinosaur knight's real weapon was his three-ton duckbill. He was mostly there to steer, and do what he could as a secondary thing.

The lead enemy rider showed an extravagant sweeping moustache as he rode bent far over his Parasaurolophus's neck. He and his comrades wore the same open-face spired helmets they had when the Companions first encountered them in the curious ambush Pablo the traitor had steered them into. He held a *talwar* up behind him, the point of its curved blade to the sky. The cataphracts eschewed shields, as Ayaks had assured them they probably would.

With the pressure of his knee, Jaume veered Camellia slightly to his right. Well trained and a thoroughly experienced warrior, the morion raised her head high half a long step before impact to clear it from the path of the two big dinosaurs' collision.

She deflected right. The sackbut staggered, tossing its head, rolling its eyes, and opening its beak in distress.

The Treb knight struggled to keep his saddle against his mount's flailing. Jaume's cross-saddle overhand cut sent the Lady's Mirror slamming against the vambrace protecting the left arm the Flower Knight threw up to shield himself. Steel plate flexed. Jaume didn't know whether he'd broken the bone beneath, but the blow was enough to knock the off-balance man over the hadrosaur's side.

Twisting in his saddle, Jaume swung his longsword back clockwise at a bearded knight mounted on a morion. He deflected the blow high with his *talwar,* then tried a countercut. Jaume dropped his elbow and took it at the juncture of blade and cross-guard.

Then Ayaks, riding past the Flower Knight on the other side, rose high in the stirrups of his gold-and-cream morion, Bogdan, and, swinging his 180-centimeter *dos-manos* with both hands, hacked through the man's helmet and into the skull beneath.

Camellia, slowed by her glancing impact with the sackbut, ran breastbone to breastbone up against a morion that was a bright enough blue to show through the rain and gloom, with some dark marbling. Jaume guided her past to the left. The rider, who was fair and clean-shaven, took a vicious overhand swing with a long-hafted rider's axe. Jaume opened with his shield as the blow landed, causing the axe head to glance off. At the same time, he turned Camellia into the blue morion, thrusting overhand for the man's exposed face. The knight had presence of mind and was skilled; he hadn't overextended with the axe blow. Instead, he leaned fast back and to his own right. The powerfully driven longsword tip didn't hit his face, or even his steel gorget; it took him just under his left clavicle. The heavy steel scales of his hauberk didn't let the Lady's Mirror penetrate, but, backed by Camellia's three tons, turning the stroke was still enough to send him sprawling out of the saddle.

Never one to admire the effect of a sword stroke, Jaume

was already twisting his body and his mount clockwise. As he did he caught motion from the corner of his eye. It was Roshan, on his pink-faced white Corythosaurus, turned shades of grey by downpour and light.

The Mirror caught Roshan's overhand-swung *talwar* flat to flat and carried it down past Jaume to his right, glancing off Camellia's sodden caparison of heavy cloth. Too over-extended to counterstrike effectively with the longsword, Jaume used his clockwise momentum to drive the upper edge of his shield toward the Flower Knight's face.

But Roshan was already steering the morion to his own left. He was able to escape the blow by ducking low over the dinosaur's strong white neck.

Jaume recovered. He kept Camellia turning right while holding his shield up cross-body and his sword with tip above left shoulder—a precarious pose for anyone but a master dinosaur knight and swordsman. Fortunately for Jaume, he was both.

Less fortunately, Roshan clearly knew it. He wheeled his mount quickly, trying to catch Camellia in the throat with his own morion's massive tail. Jaume gave off trying to set up a cut and instead caused Camellia to pirou-ette in place, using her own tail as counterbalance. At the same time, he took his left foot from the stirrup and swung his leg up. The enemy tail-sweep took Camellia flat along her left flank—a hit that jarred Jaume's eyeballs in their sockets but did her no substantial damage. And did not break his leg, thanks to his quick action.

But the blow staggered Camellia all the same. She had to step to her right to keep from going down. While Jaume, brilliant rider though he was, had to focus on stay-ing in his saddle with his left leg in the air.

Before Camellia could recover, Roshan wheeled his duckbill around in front of her again. Jaume got his left leg back down and readied to receive the Treb's next sword cut.

It didn't come. Instead, all of Roshan did, flying at him from his saddle as they came nearly knee to knee.

He had dropped his long, curved sword to swing from a lanyard. Jaume tried to smash his sword pommel into Roshan's head, but its spired shape made the blow glance off Roshan's left pauldron. Roshan got inside Jaume's shield and tackled him right off Camellia's back.

Like any dinosaur knight who wanted to live, Jaume spent frequent painful hours practicing falling off his high-backed steed without taking damage—or, at least, while taking minimal damage. But not even his and his fellow Companions' cunning and resourceful minds had foreseen this particular course of events. Jaume himself had managed to scramble aboard the notoriously wicked robber baron Sándoval's sackbut and break the Baron's neck from behind, but that was only possible because the Baron, a buckethead among bucketheads, arrogantly assumed that his opponent's lack of armor and lowly horse meant that he could do nothing to harm a fully armored knight riding a war-dinosaur.

We'll have to account for this maneuver in future, Jaume had time to think in the interval between his saddle and the ground, *if the Lady wills I'm spared.*

Except, fast as he thought, the thought got broken off halfway through its final word as Paradise hit him full in the back—and the weight of the heavily armored Treb knight landed on his *front.*

The air burst out of him like the guts of a melon stepped on by a Thunder-titan. *At least if a duckbill steps on us he may cushion me*, Jaume thought as he tried to blink his eyes into focus behind his visor.

Without conscious intent, he tried to punch his antagonist with the hand that still clutched the Mirror's hilt. Better prepared for the outcome of the unexpected attack—after all, he launched it—Roshan obviously had kept more of his wits about him than Jaume. He easily intercepted the blow, catching Jaume's right wrist with his left hand. His skin felt soft, but his grip was steel-hard.

Is he laughing? Jaume wondered, his wits returning faster than his breath.

"I learned well from the master," said the Flower Knight, who was unquestionably laughing.

"'Uz—onna—*horse*," Jaume managed to wheeze.

His shield was gone. He launched a left-hand punch for the side of that beautiful brown laughing face. Roshan caught that wrist too and pinned both to the warm wet cobbles. He had taken a low mount position astride Jaume's plate-armored belly. At least the structural strength of his cuirass prevented the Treb's weight from interfering with Jaume's gradually recovering breathing.

Most dinosaur knights trained in grappling, since it was as integral a part of dismounted combat as sword or knife play. The Companions went even further, *taking training from* a teacher imported from Ruybrasil, whose masters of the arts were esteemed as highly as any in the world. *He's good*, Jaume thought. *Lady grant that his Order hasn't taken its emulation of ours that far.*

He cranked his head from side to side, sallet clattering on the stones, to emphasize his helplessness. Then he relaxed, all at once, trusting his opponent was skilled enough to notice Jaume no longer resisted his wrist-traps.

Jaume felt, or thought he felt, a complementary relaxation on Roshan's part. Jaume rolled his hips slightly clockwise, then violently back the other way. He managed to twist his hips beneath Roshan's weight. He bent his left knee and brought it hard toward his left side. Aided by the steel cuisses that protected both men's thighs being slick with rain, he broke the leg free. He swung it up to Roshan's waist, twisting right again. This let him free his right leg.

And suddenly he had both legs wrapped around Roshan's waist in the guard position.

Roshan laughed out loud. "So the master's still the master," he said.

Roshan let go of both Jaume's wrists at once. Winging his elbows out to stave off Jaume's reflexive double-handed grab for his throat, he reached down, grabbed Jaume's visor with both hands, and yanked it open.

Dropping his face to Jaume's, he kissed him full on the lips. Or as fully as the bevor that still covered Jaume's chin allowed.

The unexpectedness of the act shocked Jaume into immobility for a heartbeat. He was aware of the thunderous falls of hadrosaur feet booming dangerously close.

Roshan pushed off him. "I wish I could embrace you longer," he said.

He reached up. An armored arm came down, and the two gripped each other forearm to forearm. The Flower Knight pulled his captain, armor and all, right off Jaume, leaving the downed Companion with the rain falling on his face.

Jaume sat up. A small Treb had leaned improbably far down out of the saddle on his halberd's high back to grab Roshan. Clinging there like a spider, he rode several booming bipedal paces of his mount as Roshan grabbed his saddle skirts and scaled up behind the cantle. The rescuer pulled himself back into the saddle, and they were gone down the sloping street.

"Much as I love you, I'm not going to do that," Florian said, riding up on his white-and-yellow sackbut, Voici le Trouble. "Mainly because I can't."

Jaume saw that Camellia still stood patiently by him. Springing to his feet, he whistled and made a downward-patting gesture with his empty left hand. Obediently, the morion dropped her cream-colored belly to the pavement. Feeling more stiffness in his hips from the fall than he'd initially expected, Jaume put a foot in the stirrup and swung up into the saddle as if his full plate harness weighed nothing. It was highest quality, of course, its forty-plus kilos distributed so perfectly that it hardly felt like an encumbrance at all. At least not to a man who routinely practiced acrobatics while wearing it.

"Pulled your Baron Sándoval trick on you, did he?"

"I was riding a horse!"

"They're copying us—that's clear."

"What's going on?"

"They've pulled back to the south side of town. The kidnappers seem to be on the road again. We did a quick check of the mercantile house—a nest of snakes that'll need cleaning out, I'm pretty sure."

"Later," Jaume said. "And not our job."

"You may want your shield. They've started shooting at us with their hornbows for real. Nailed Grzegorz in the shoulder pretty well at close range."

"How is he?"

"Angry—more at us after Manuel told him he had to stand down and get seen to. Local healer's got his upper armor off and is looking him over. The squires have joined up; they'll keep the *víboras* from trying their chances with a lone, injured Brother. Though I think he'd handle them, bare-chested and one-armed though he is. Good kid; think both he and Rámon will do."

"Let's go," Jaume said. "You take half around the right. I'll go left. Try to flank them—at least get as close as possible before showing ourselves. The bows mean we can't just bypass them; they'll just shoot us in the back."

Florian nodded, spun his mount, and dashed off. Jaume hadn't needed to tell him whom to take in the rightward sweep. All the Companions had the initiative to grab whoever was most appropriately placed.

Jaume glanced longingly at his shield again, then dismissed it and nudged Camellia into a trot. He'd take his chances on using the cover of the buildings. As he rode past, he glanced down at the Flower Knight Ayaks had dropped, lying pathetically on his face in a rainwater pool as blood and doughy brains diffused into it from his cleft helmet and head. He felt a pang of pity.

At first he tried to suppress it—the man was abetting a child abduction, for the Eight's sakes. But then he saw the more beautiful path and allowed himself to feel.

They're serving evil out of some greater duty, he thought. *Pity's the feeling that suits them all best. Especially Prince Roshan.*

The two wings of dinosaur knights converged just south of the big mercantile house. The buildings gave brief way to a clear space, slightly marshy, perhaps thirty meters across, before continuing to straggle down the Laventura road for several hundred more meters. Jaume led his wing out into the open to find Roshan and his ten remaining Flower Knights awaiting them on patient wardinosaurs. They had bows in hand and arrows nocked but not drawn.

Another thirty meters separated the tip of Camellia's beak from a light-colored Lambeosaurus—forked, Jaume saw, by the slight, drooping-moustachioed knight who had rescued Roshan. Twenty or twenty-five separated the Trebs from Florian and his contingent, emerging on the far side.

Without hesitation, Jaume turned Camellia toward them. His followers did likewise, as did Florian his. *They'll kill some of us*, Jaume thought grimly, *but then we'll have them.*

Before his morion had finished taking her second step, a wall of flame shot up in front of her, higher by far than Jaume's head on her high-arched back and roaring like a pack of angry *matadores*.

Squealing in ear-imploding terror, Camellia stopped and shied away from the inexplicable inferno. Jaume could smell its sulfurous breath, feel its heat on his still-bared face.

His loyal, well-trained, battle-hardened mount did something she'd never done before: turned tail and fled, despite her rider's shouts and sawing on the reins. The other Companions' duckbills did likewise, stampeding back through the town with a sound like a terrified wind-instrument orchestra.

Chapter 15

Bestiario del Hogar Viejo, Un; Bestiary of Old Home, A. . . . —A late first-century book, which describes in words and pictures over a thousand creatures claimed to be native to Home, the world from which humans and their Five Friends (horses, goats, dogs, cats, and ferrets) came to Paradise. Though superstitious people believe it was directly inspired by our Creators, educated folk think that many of the animals in it are imaginary. It does provide a rich source for art and heraldry.

—A PRIMER TO PARADISE FOR THE IMPROVEMENT
OF YOUNG MINDS

Something funny happened this afternoon after we had to run away from La Bajada.

We didn't go straight to Laventura, even though I heard Diego and Elfego saying we could make it there on a straight run by nightfall. Instead, we stopped in this shallow arroyo that this local guide Elfego—he's the one with bangs—found. A bunch of ginkgo trees hid us there. They seem to always be able to find traitors to help them, although I think maybe this woman was just slow-witted and eager to make money.

Anyway, they had to argue, because that's what it

seems Trebs really do. Akakios seemed all scared about immediate pursuit—even with those Flower Knights to stand off Jaume and his men. Paraskeve wanted to go on. Charalampos, who's a nervous fat man who always acts like he's got a secret he's afraid you're about to find out (aren't all Trebs supposed to be that way?), wanted to hide the way Akakios did. Paraskeve got real mad, the way she always does, and shouted that they were just cowards. But Vlasis, the little skinny intense guy, said something to her in Griego, and she got real pissy but agreed to go to ground for the night.

So they found this manor a few kilometers off the main road in a kind of nice little river valley and hid out there. The owner, a small-time war-hadrosaur breeder, made enough money to buy a minor patent. He's fat and has greasy black hair and beards all down his chins. It's gross.

After dinner, which was a pretty good roast haunch of a young halberd that I guess didn't make the cut to be a war-mount and some beans and *ensalada*, we all wound up in the sitting room. And Akakios, the boss priest with the fanciest hat, started losing his mind in buckets.

They were talking a mix of both Spañol and Griego. I was sitting in a corner by a bookshelf. I was mad because they wouldn't let me read any, even though some were on raising and training duckbills for war and I really wanted to see them. But they did let me sit there and play with Mistral.

She's been real good. She mostly hopped and beeped and rolled over when I waved my finger around. I think she understands we're in trouble, and we need each other more than ever. Even though it's always been kind of us against the world. Or the adults, anyway. Most of them. A lot goes on in that little head. She has no common sense, but that's ferrets. She is pretty smart. Like me.

Dragos sat in a chair near me reading a book of poetry in some language I didn't recognize—I guess it's from the Basileia. They got a lot of different kingdoms there with different languages, just like we do. Although I think they call them something else.

But what he was mostly doing was quietly translating the parts I didn't get. I caught a few words, like "fire." He's been teaching me a bit of Griego, and I've been picking up a little on my own. Not much, but I think everything helps.

The others weren't paying any mind to either of us, as usual. I'm just a little girl to them, which makes me stupid. I'm used to that from adults. It can be real useful. People who underestimate you are easy to fool.

They ignore Dragos as much as they can because they never like what he has to say. He is pretty sarcastic about them, even to their faces. And they can't do anything about it, which really chafes their beards. I think there's more to it—like whoever they're really working for would do mean things to them if anything happened to him, and I guess the stories about the Trebs being really cruel and good at it too do have something to them. These ones are sure scared. But also when they need something practical done, it seems like Dragos is always the only one who can really do it. And they're at least smart enough to figure that out.

Oh—one thing I better put down here. It doesn't seem like they're working for Mikael. I mean, that's what I thought this whole thing was supposed to be about: that they were trying to get my father to promise them Melodía's hand in marriage to their Crown Prince, Mikael—that's really how they talk: they say things like "give her hand in marriage." Like my sister's hand is a nice piece of sculpture or an old painting or something. Melodía was never going to agree to any such thing, even if she didn't love Jaume and plan to marry him—they had a fight, I guess, before we had to help her escape, but I don't think that'll last. Also, Prince Mikael supposedly weighs 200 kilos and never bathes, so gross.

So Akakios was claiming that magic was used to keep the Companions from chasing after the Flower Knights. He seemed even more upset about that than the fact that one of the Flower Knights got killed—good!—but none of Jaume's Companions did. He said it'd damn all their souls.

(I don't really understand that part. I don't pay much attention to religion, but I have to sit through a lot of Church services, when I can't get away, because Daddy's the Emperor and really believes that stuff. But when they talk about you dying, they say you just get reborn, or if you're really good you can choose to become one with the Creators. Or maybe even something else. But it's supposed to be good. Anyway, these Trebs seem to think when you die you can get punished. How you get punished if you're all dead and don't have a body, I don't know. The Vida-se-Viene cult people say similar stuff, but we know they're crazy. Even if Daddy's pal, who was the Pope but died, was kind of one.)

Also, he seemed scared because it was magic. I don't believe in magic, because it's dumb. But—they were all awful positive.

Paraskeve kept telling him to calm down. Tasoula sat in the corner pulling strands of her dirty crazy hair away from her head with her fingers and staring at them as if she could, like, read something in them. She was muttering about the voices and the spirits. It's like she believes in Fae or something. But I really don't buy that fairy-tale garbage. It's silly superstition. Not important superstition, like the Church and Creators and all that.

Funny thing, there—it was like Don Alfonso, the traitor duckbill-breeder, only wanted to talk to her, for some reason. As if he could get any sense out of her. But he hung back by her the whole time as if he felt safer near her. Or at least less scared than the others.

Charalampos said that Akakios needed to calm down,

that their cause was righteous. He might have been more convincing if he wasn't sweating so heavily—it was actually pretty cool inside the *sala,* with a breeze blowing in from the sea, even, and smelling like the flowers in the garden on the patio outside. And if he didn't keep looking everywhere as if he expected a horror to jump out of a secret panel and eat his face.

That'd be sweet if that happened.

Akakios kept saying it was too dangerous to mess with magic. Finally Vlasis spoke up in that tight-assed, hissing way of his and said that clearly they had the Creators' favor. If Akakios, a High Priest and Megaduke (which sounds even fancier than a Grand Duke, but Dragos told me it just meant an equerry) doubted that he was worthy of the Creators' obvious intervention on his behalf, perhaps the Magistroi needed to have a word with him when they got back home. That caused all the color to drain out of Akakios's big square face, but it did shut him up.

Vlasis told the others that was clearly what was happening: the Creators were helping them in person. And They'd help even more, should the heretics (he meant my cousin Jaume and his friends who are trying to save me, the bastard!) catch up with them. Paraskeve actually got all pious and made the Sign of the Grand Harmonious Principle. So that ended that.

Except Anastasia just stared for a moment and then laughed and laughed. The host made some kind of quick weird finger gesture and went out.

After that Dragos took me to my cell for the night. It was just an unused pantry dug into the ground near the kitchen. But it was clean and cool and had a pretty decent straw mattress without too many *piojos* in it. As we went I asked him why he kept helping me.

He said, "You're a brave girl, and a very capable one. I approve of the former when it's coupled with the latter.

I hope you remember these talks when you get—out of this."

I didn't say anything. For a moment I got real excited because it was like he was implying I wouldn't just survive this awful mess but get home and see Melodía and my daddy again. Then I made myself calm down because maybe he's fooling me, just to keep me from making trouble. That's how he got the others to go along with giving me stuff to write with. And letting me keep Misti with me.

(Akakios has been complaining about the amount of money they spend getting me fresh papers, pens, and ink. He's really obsessed with how much silver this is all costing, and Paraskeve again told him not to be such a cheese-parer about it, to give me what I needed because it was a small price to keep me quiet, so he should be quiet. She might not feel quite that way if she knew I was using half the paper to write those notes I drop off every time I have to go off in the woods to take a poo.)

Or maybe Dragos is fooling the others. I guess I'm sure he's doing that. And don't know what he's really doing with me. Except trying to suck up. But that's kind of working, because he's the only one who even talks to me except to boss me around or scold me, much less treat me with respect. Maybe only Jaume ever treated me with more respect, like I was a real person instead of some kind of—I don't know, animated doll.

I don't know.

One thing I do know: he's sly.

But one other thing: so am I.

Though her instinctive terror of fire had overwhelmed her training and loyal courage—and Jaume didn't blame her—Camellia recovered her wits quickly. As did all the other Companions' duckbills. One of the requirements for candidacy to join Jaume's Order was to have a fine mount, fully trained for war—and treated almost as a son or daughter.

With quick shouts to one another, they rallied by the mercantile house, then rode back down the main Laventura road to where the flames still visibly billowed. They were not much shorter than the three-story stone house itself.

When Jaume could feel the heat beating on his bare cheeks and Camellia was beginning to toss her round-crested head and roll her eyes, he stopped. The others kept a likewise respectful distance.

"How'd they do that?" Will Oakheart asked. Like the rest, he'd opened his visor. "In this pissing rain, no less?"

"Whatever it is is still going up like a fire in a pine-oil distillery," Machtigern said.

"We might ride around it," Machtigern suggested. "We might still catch them."

"No," Jaume said, reluctantly. "They'll shoot us down on the road before we can get close. They're playing for real now, as Grzegorz found out."

"But if we can overtake them—" Ramón said.

"Cool your heels, hotspur," Manuel said. "The Captain's right. And it's even worse: they'll stop from time to time to set up an ambush and slaughter us with those hard-steel chisel-tip arrows if we gallop into it. *I'd* do that. And I reckon these damned *catafractos* know their art a lot better than I do."

Florian had dismounted, leaving Trouble on his white belly in the mud. He cautiously approached the flame.

"Careful—" Jaume said.

But this was Florian. Who stuck his steel-gauntleted hand into the orange flames.

"*Els Sants Vuit!*" Jaume exclaimed, reverting in shock to his birth-tongue Catalan to invoke the Holy Eight. Only his *compatriota* Bernat among the present company could understand him, but the others likely got the drift.

But Florian was only frowning.

"Nothing," he said.

"What do you mean?" Ayaks rumbled.

"I mean, nothing." Florian withdrew his hand and pulled the gauntlet off. Then he waved his bare hand back and forth through the furnace wall. "It's not hot. It's not anything. It doesn't even interrupt the rain falling, as far as I can tell."

"What the Old Hell?" Will said.

"That may be where it comes from," said Owen, making the circle-and-S gesture of the Holy Symbol to ward off evil.

Florian walked through the flames. "No, nothing," he called from the other side. I can see they form a horse-shoe shape, to screen the flanks, maybe ten meters at the widest."

He reappeared, his beautiful long, wavy golden hair sodden and crinkled—but not so much as scorched.

"Whatever it is, it's not fire."

"But the heat!" Ramón exclaimed. "And the sound. And even the smell!"

"It's all an illusion."

"How is that possible?" said Machtigern.

Florian shrugged.

"Nothing natural," Owain said.

"You can't seriously be suggesting it's actually magic," Manuel said. "Magic isn't real."

"You might not say that if you'd seen Raguel Himself, riding into battle on a giant King Tyrant conjured from the dust itself," Owain said.

"I always thought the Grey Angels were metaphors myself, until I saw one," Jaume said. "And I'm still reluctant to admit magic exists. Well, *other* magic."

"It must be a stage sleight," Manuel said.

Florian cocked a skeptical brow. "When you calculate a way to do that that's not less plausible than magic, let me know, my friend."

Manuel sighed gustily. "Fair enough. I can't, of course."

"You can blackball me from the Brotherhood for asking this," Ramón said, "if that's what it deserves. But I have to. This isn't the first time this has happened—the Flower Knights escaped as if by magic after their weird, halfhearted ambush in Tres Veces. These Flower Knights serve the Middle Daughter, just the same as we do. What if She's choosing to use Her powers for them, over us?"

He started when Machtigern, whose brown-stripes-on-buff morion, Tiger, happened to be standing next to his red-and-white sackbut, Luisa, clapped him on the shoulder.

"When a Brother needs to guard his tongue among Brothers," he said, "there is no brotherhood. Don't worry."

"It's a good question," Jaume said. "And a wise one. But I have an answer, I think. We're served the Lady and Beauty for twenty years, we Companions. We've lost more Brothers killed than our Charter allows to serve at any one time. I can't claim perfection for me or any of us. But I can't believe the Lady Li would spurn our sacrifices, of tears and blood and lives, to favor anyone over us. Especially not a newly minted Order."

"And especially not one that's guarding child abductors," Will said, "whatever excuse they have."

"Where does it come from, then, Captain?" asked Bernat.

Jaume could only shake his head.

"More to the point," Manuel said, "what do we do now?"

"We go collect the squires and see if Grzegorz is fit to ride. Then we follow at a deliberate pace, using squires on horseback to scout. We know where they're going."

"They should be in Laventura tomorrow evening at the latest, unless they break down again," Manuel said.

"We'll have to hope we can get a chance to stop the carriages before they get there," Jaume said. "We need to keep in mind the Flower Knights aren't our targets. Only obstacles."

"What about the merchant and his traitors?" Will asked.

"We'll leave them to the local authorities."

"Your resourceful little cousin has warned us that they're not always to be relied upon," said Florian. "And I'd say that's clearly the case here."

"You hold the High Justice, Jaume," Machtigern said. "You can try, condemn, and hang them if they're guilty."

"It would be appropriate," Jaume said, "though I don't like to do so." He seldom exercised that power, preferring to execute Imperial warrants. The first men he'd tried and ordered hanged in a long time were a pair of rapist knights with the Army of Correction marching on the Redlands.

The flames went out. It was as if they were a single candle, snuffed by giant fingers.

"Neat sleight," Florian said.

"Enough," Jaume said. Manuel could be a bit of a hothead, and Florian was no stranger to taking a joke too far. Even with his Brothers.

But the Francés knight shook his head. "No. I mean, whatever it was, that's a pretty good trick."

"So we admit it was magic?" said Machtigern, looking as if he'd just discovered he'd bitten into a dog turd by accident.

"As Brother Goldenhair says," Manuel said, "if you can come up with some other explanation, we'd all love to hear it."

The Alemán could only morosely shake his head.

"This is bad," Ayaks said.

"It is, Big Brother," said Jaume. "And there's a lot here which needs to be investigated in depth. Including how these Trebs have done the impossible to thwart us—once for sure, and likely twice."

"They'll have more such tricks awaiting us in Laventura," Owain said.

"Then we deal with them when we run into them. But for now, none of that matters in comparison to saving a little girl, before those monsters get her out of the country and onto the sea."

Chapter 16

Año Paraíso, AP—Literally, "Paradise Year." 192 days, each of twenty-four hours (reputedly longer than Home days). Divided into 8 months named for the Creators' domains: Cielo (Heaven), Viento (Wind), Agua (Water), Montaña (Mountain), Mundo (World), Trueno (Thunder), Fuego (Fire), and Lago (Lake). Each month consists of three weeks of eight days, each named for a Creator: Día del Rey (Kingsday), Día de Spada (Swordsday), Día de Torre (Towersday), Día de Adán (Adamsday), Día de Telar (Telarsday), Día de Bella (Bellesday), Día de Maia (Mayasday), and Día de Maris (Marisday).

—A PRIMER TO PARADISE FOR THE IMPROVEMENT
OF YOUNG MINDS

"That Duke Falk!" Mor Patricio said, languidly trailing his dark brown fingers through the cool water of the rooftop garden's pond. "He's getting tiresome, frankly."

Melodía looked up sharply. She sat on a rosy granite *banco* in the shade of a feather parasol near the pond. Though the apartment building stood in an especially desirable location near the northwestern side of the Bulwark, near its juncture with the cliff, the sound of Heart's

Leap was no more than a pleasant susurration, like the buzzing of the thumb-size bees dancing around the flowers.

"He's always been tiresome," Doña Sonia said. She wore her dark brown hair cut in a sort of cap. She sat with a thin red-and-gold silk cushion protecting the bare olive skin of her behind from the sun-hot flagstones that rimmed the pond. Days were relatively cool up here on Mount Glory, and the daytime clouds were as constant as they were everywhere on Paradise, but the sun was intense. Though it was midmorning, the sandstone slabs that paved this section of the rooftop garden in the outer palace grounds would scorch unprotected soles. Which was why Melodía and the other three wore sandals, if nothing else.

"He's gotten more tiresome now that his great Alemana duckbill-sow of a mother's arrived," Mor Patricio said. Unlike the other two, he was a newcomer to the Imperial City and Palace.

"He's a fucking rebel," Don Máximo said heatedly. He was already pacing beside the pond. "I don't know why the Emperor coddles him the way he does."

"Well, he *did* save the Emperor's life at Canterville," Sonia said dryly. "That might have earned him a little indulgence."

"He's a traitor," Máximo persisted. "All that heroic shit he did in the recent battle should bring him no more than to zero, I say."

"I'm not quite that blithe about dismissing heroism," Patricio growled. Also unlike the other two, he was a veteran fighter, who had earned his knighthood in border skirmishes with rival *grandes* and bandit hunting in his home county southwest of La Majestad. Almost all the horde of hangers-on, minor nobles, and influence seekers who infested the court here far more thickly than they ever had in La Merced—Melodía had no idea who most of these fucking people were—claimed they had wanted nothing more than to join the Emperor in his recent great Crusade. As far as she could tell, though, Patricio was telling the truth: his liege had taken her time releasing him to join the Imperial Army on the march. He'd barely gotten past La Majestad when he learned of the Emperor's victory—and that the Emperor had dismissed most of his Army and headed back to the capital. So Mor Patricio had come here to wait.

Don Máximo held up placating hands. He was handsome enough, too, though pale for a Spañol—and a trifle pudgy to boot. "No offense, brother. I respect you knights. Someday I'll win my belt and spurs as well. I just—"

"This is beginning to bore me," Doña Sonia said, putting her sandals on and gracefully rising to her full lean height, a good five centimeters taller than Melodía's own 176. She stretched languidly, making her small dark-nippled breasts rise up her rib cage. Then she dropped her arms and scratched absently at the dense black bush between her thighs.

The casualness with which she did so reaffirmed Melodía's suspicion she was actually nobly born—a jumped-up commoner would at the least have turned away in embarrassment. Melodía knew the woman held a manor and estate of some description near La Barbilla, the Chin, at the extreme southwestern tip of Spaña—and, by extension, the Tyrant's Head. She was attractive enough for an old woman, if you went for those above sixty. She was certainly well preserved, and kept herself in top fitness through her love of a variety of vigorous pastimes, including dance and combat arts. Particularly grappling, so Melodía heard—of both the martial and erotic varieties.

"His Grace, though that term seems extreme in connection with such unwieldy Alemán bulk, is certainly in demand among the ladies of the court, I understand."

Melodía's stomach knotted with nausea. She clamped her jaw firmly shut. *I'm not going to puke*, she commanded herself. *It would only detract from my chances.*

Patricio cocked a brow. "You?"

She laughed. "Not my type. I prefer my men smaller, younger, and far less full of themselves. Anyway, the ladies of my acquaintance who have made his claim that, while he might have a nosehorn's size and strength, he lacks their endurance at pulling the cart."

"The boys all want him, too," Máximo said. "He just rebuffs . . . them." He, as well as Melodía's other two male companions of the moment, was openly bisexual. It was fashionable this season. He had also made a few attempts at gallantries with her, with the same result he'd obviously gotten from her nemesis.

"So," Melodía said, in a tone she hoped didn't sound as sly as she was trying to be, "he's resented, is he?"

"*I* resent him," Patricio said, sipping wine from a gilded goblet. "Even I'll admit he's been jumped up too far too fast—for, yes, a recent rebel. And he's overbearing."

"So there are cracks in his edifice?" she asked. "People might be willing to listen to some . . . unpleasant things about him?"

The others all stared at her. *I overplayed my hand*, she thought with a sinking feeling. She almost threw up all over again.

"By you?" Sonia laughed, musically but not seeming to be malicious. "Highness, you're not in a good position to go attacking war heroes."

"Not one who was heroically defending the Emperor from the ravening Horde while you were . . . notably absent," Máximo said, his full lips quivering on the edge of an all-out sneer.

"What the Old Hell do you mean?" She managed not to scream the words. "I was fighting the fucking Horde long before the Imp—*perials* knew they even existed!"

She had barely caught herself on the cusp of blurting "Impies." Which she'd realized at the last moment was not the most diplomatic thing for the Emperor's daughter and heir to say. Although she couldn't inherit the Throne any more than anyone else could: it was Electoral, not hereditary, though always occupied by a member of Torre Delgao.

"'Fighting'?" Máximo said with a toss of his long brown hair. "Alongside mere light cavalry? Slumming with the peasants is more like it. It may be dramatic charging around on a horse with rabble who oughtn't be permitted the nobility of riding. But it's hardly *fighting.*"

"I've run into a few of these light horse and dinosaur riders before." Patricio drained his cup. "Or *over* them, to be more precise. They're not real warriors, any more than peasant rabble afoot with pointed sticks they think are pikes are. Just rabble who get in the way of the real fighters. And not even that for long."

"And at that," Máximo said, clearly relishing this all too much, "His Grace was marching to war against the very place you'd bolted off to like a frightened bouncer—the place where all this recent trouble started!"

"I myself am not so sure your accomplishments can be so easily dismissed, Alteza," Sonia said. "But the majority of the *grandes* at court don't seem to share my doubt. Sorry."

She didn't seem to be trying to ingratiate herself, Melodía thought—she was clutching at such scraps of controlled thinking as she could muster, in an attempt to prevent herself being swept down by a maelstrom of betrayal and despair. She seemed to be one of the few hangers-on at the Imperial Court who weren't angling for influence and advancement. She seemed simply to enjoy the atmosphere, the quality of life, and the attentions of the beautiful young men and women who flocked there.

Mor Patricio shook his head. "You'll make yourself a laughingstock if you try impugning Duke Falk in public, Emperor's daughter or not. Huh. We seem to be out of wine. Where's that steward lazing off?"

"You—will excuse—me," Melodía said through gritted teeth, sounding to herself as mechanical as a windup doll.

She turned and practically ran off through the flowering lilac bushes that separated the pond and the decorative part of the garden from the part that grew vegetables for the Palace tables.

She just made it to a point where she dared hope they couldn't hear her and vomited violently between some square-framed containers of half-grown bean plants.

Sunlight streaming in the wide, tall window of Melodía's bedchamber wakened her like a lover's soft kiss on her cheek.

She sat up in bed and stretched. Her room was spare—just the bed, a small table beside it, a large wardrobe of oak whose front was carved with a battle between knights on sackbut back, a writing desk, and three chairs beneath the window. The walls lacked paintings, tapestries, or embroidery to relieve the yellow-grey, slightly rough stone. But what was there was luxurious and fine, like the scratcher-feather bed and cushions and the satin-covered upholstery on the chairs. The lack of ostentation was itself almost ostentatious, but comfort was key.

She padded to the attached water closet, a privilege of the Imperial apartments of which this was one. When she was done, she rang a gilded bell from the bedside table—they could maybe have shown a bit more restraint with the *dorado* everything while they were avoiding overt show, even though it was one of the colors of both Empire and La Familia—for her servants and requested a small breakfast and writing material.

The first whiff of bread freshly baked in the Palace kitchens awoke her appetite. It had lain dormant since the . . . news about Montserrat broke. She wouldn't let herself think about that too directly, as it would only interfere with doing what she had to do. Once awakened, her appetite proved a ravenous matadora indeed, and she made short, savage work of the plate (gilded, of course) of fruit, bread, sausage, and cheese that was brought.

Then, sipping a cup—by the current fad, heavy ceramic of blue-and-green-washed ceramic, thankfully, without a hint of gold—of still-hot *xocolatl* imported from far Tejas, its bitterness cut and richness enhanced by a healthy dollop of honey, she took up a strider-feather quill pen, dipped its tip in the inkpot, and began to write.

My beloved friends . . .

She paused. *Should I write each of them individually?* she wondered. To ask herself the question was almost to answer it. Her ladies-in-waiting got on remarkably well with one another. They teased and squabbled, of course, but there was none of the nasty gossiping and backbiting Melodía found so prevalent and distancing in other *grande* circles, male and female alike. Well, gossiping, sure—but about outsiders. Because they were nominally hostages, and Melodía's father treated her basically like a precious *objeto de arte*, taken out occasionally to be admired and adored, then stashed back out of sight and ignored, they had formed a sort of us-against-the-world common bond.

Whose depth and strength had surprised her—as did her ladies'—when they hastily banded together to co-conspire with Montse and a cadre of Firefly Palace servants to liberate her after she was falsely accused and imprisoned. By Falk, of course.

The problem was that certain of them did have a predisposition to paranoia. Mostly that was Lupe and Llurdis, incorrigibly overdramatic lovers and enemies who both fought and fucked with equal abandon, not to mention unpredictably and with lack of concern for bystanders. And they mostly liked to accuse each of plotting against the other, as part of their drama.

But Melodía reposed faith particularly in the ability of one of her friends to help her, and the problem was, this person wasn't only a known intriguer, she was a well-trained expert at it, despite her tender years—she was only a year older than Melodía herself, though that made her the oldest among their circle. Which was hardly surprising, because Abigail Thélème was the daughter of Arch-Duke Roger of Sansamour, a principality and Electorate nominally tributary to the crown of Francia. Though rumor had it that the truth was closer to the other way round. Roger rejoiced—literally, or so Abi said—in the soubriquet "the Spider," for weaving webs of intrigue whose intricacy and deadliness rivaled those for which Trebizon was so notorious. Abi was surprisingly frank about her father carefully training his heir to succeed him in every way. But then again, public knowledge of the fact seemed only to sharpen the fangs of her intrigues, like Roger's, rather than dull them.

If there was anyone among her friends who could carry out the task she was about to request her friends to carry out for her back in La Merced and El Palacio de las Luciérnagas, it was the tall, lean, coolly blond Sansamora, who bore the title Countess Silvertree in her own right.

If there was anyone among her friends whom the others would automatically view with suspicion if they all got letters individually requesting them to do Secret Things, it was Abi.

"No," she said aloud. "I don't want to tempt Fortuna here any more than I have to."

And so she wrote:

My beloved friends,

I have an important favor to ask of you all. I know that it may seem vain and frivolous to pursue my own concerns in the wake of my sister's kidnapping. And perhaps it is. But to my sorrow and anger the matter lies as far beyond my grasp as the Moon Invisible.

Though I already owe you, and others, a debt I can never repay, I nonetheless beg you, once again, to help me . . .

Chapter 17

Creadores, Los, The Creators, Los Ocho, The Eight. . . .
—The gods who made Paradise, and all things that live upon it: Chián, Father Sky or the King; Maia, the Mother Land or Queen; Adán, the Oldest Son; Telar, the Oldest Daughter; Spada, the Middle Son; Bella, the Middle Daughter; Torre, the Youngest Son; and Maris, the Youngest Daughter. Each has a standard appearance and attributes, yet also has manifestations of the opposite gender—and opposite attributes. Each has a Trigram, three solid or broken lines drawn one above the other, which together comprise what is called Bagua in the Creators' own speech, the Heavenly Language. Served by seven Grey Angels of nearly divine power and often terrifying aspect. Our faith tells us that They once walked Paradise Themselves, and even waged the High Holy War, vulgarly called the Demon War, against their arch-enemies, the Fae. Since no one has seen one for centuries, many now believe that's mere myth. Some believe the Creators are too. But quietly, for belief in and worship of the Eight is the universal law of Paradise.
   —**A PRIMER TO PARADISE FOR THE IMPROVEMENT OF YOUNG MINDS**

E ven as his eyes snapped open to his tent's darkness, Jaume knew something was wrong. Dagger in hand, he rolled off his pallet to the right—away from the tent entrance and toward the Lady's Mirror in her scabbard.

"I'm not a threat," a soft voice said.

"Roshan?" Jaume felt far more curious than afraid. Curiosity formed a far greater component of his nature than fearfulness. Also, he felt confident of his chances in a fight, even against a fighter as skilled as the Flower Knight Captain-General had proved to be, no matter how his opponent might be armed.

"Yes. Don't make a light, please. I'm not armed."

He opened the tent flap to allow the wan light of Eris to spill in between the branches of the cypress trees that surrounded the Companion encampment. It silvered his long, unbound hair and the bare skin of his right side.

"What are you doing here?" Jaume asked. He rose. He wasn't prepared to trust any uninvited midnight intruder to his tent, much less the chief of his enemies' fighting force. Still, his heart and gut told him he could.

He was a man who trusted both. But he had learned long ago not to trust them with unfettered control. He would heed his reasoning mind and reserve judgment. Until the time came to strike. Or—whatever else.

He struck spark to the wick of a pine-oil lantern. The tent filled with mellow gold light. Roshan's body was well muscled, with a little layer of softness about the middle. His straight black hair hung past his shoulders. His cock was small yet shapely.

"I took a liberty with you today, Don Jaume. I want to make amends. And to offer a warning."

"You did," Jaume said. He was still surprised and somewhat puzzled by how strongly unsettled he felt about Roshan's unasked kiss. Not the kiss itself: that it was done without his permission. There was a trail of those who had taken liberties with the Conde dels Flors in the past, or tried to. There was also an unbroken trail of their graves.

"The warning first, then."

"You will come upon our . . . masters . . . in Laventura tomorrow. Even if we wanted to try to stop you on your way, they have forbidden us. They want us protecting them until they depart."

"You defied their orders to come here?"

Roshan let the tent flap fall. Enough moon and star shine filtered in through the tent—workmanlike water-proofed canvas, not silk—for Jaume to see his teeth show in a smile.

"Not strictly speaking," he said. "The rest of my knights attend them. And none of them know I've even gone, much less where."

"And?"

Roshan's smile vanished, and the tips of his hair brushed his broad shoulders as he shook his head. "We cannot in honor hold back any longer. When we meet you, we must try our best to kill you."

"Fair enough," Jaume said. "Was that all you came for?"

Roshan smiled in a way that stirred Jaume strangely. "Not at all."

He approached. Jaume kept himself relaxed. He doubted his nocturnal visitor meant him any harm. But if he did, tension in the muscles slowed one's responses.

Roshan padded to within an arm's reach of him, held out his hand. Jaume, uncertain, put out his own. Roshan took it, gently, and raised it to his lips.

"I told you, my lord," he said, and kissed the back of the hand and then the fingertips, lightly, "I came here to make amends. With your permission?"

Without being certain what he was assenting to—beyond that it wasn't going to compromise his men or mission—Jaume said, "Yes, but I thought your warning would be enough of—"

Releasing Jaume's hand, Roshan dropped to his knees and took Jaume's cock in his hand. That startled Jaume into immobility. He barely had time to register that he was already halfway erect when Roshan leaned forward and closed his lips behind the head.

He began to suck, gently at first, then more intently. Jaume drew in a deep breath. He became intensely aware of his surroundings as pleasure flowed out of his groin to suffuse his body: the strong sharp smell of pine oil burning, and the scent of the sweat of light exertion on a recently bathed male body from Roshan, overlaid by a hint of rose-attar; the trilling of crickets and the croak of some big night-hunting flier; the subtly shifting balance between light and shadow inside his small, plain tent. The expert play of Roshan's moist, strong tongue on the underside of his cock.

He grasped the sides of Roshan's head as it began to work back and forth. He tensed as he felt an electric tension at the base of his penis.

It had been several days for Jaume since the last bout of lovemaking with Melodía in the wake of the Canterville battle. He had no lovers among the Companions anymore, since his adored Pere had been swept into the depths by a *bocaterrible* sea-monster in the Channel the year before. Nor would he again, given the Order's rule that Companions could only take lovers of equal status—and while all Brothers-Companion were equal, he was the Captain-General. He exerted power over his fellow Knights-Brother because they acceded to it, not because both Church and Empire accorded him a high degree of it; but there it was.

Which is to say, he came hard and fast. And copiously.

Roshan drank it all down eagerly. He continued to suck until Jaume's balls ran dry.

"You're skilled in many crafts, it seems," Jaume said, stroking Roshan's glossy hair and delighting in the feel. "Such as how you got past both our squires and the Brother on sentry duty. Bernat, I believe. I'll have to have a word with him."

Roshan smiled up at him, his eyes glistening with moisture. "Don't judge them harshly, my lord. As you've guessed, we emulate your Order in every way we can, because it's held in the highest esteem even in Trebizon. There are no others like you in western Aphrodite—and we wanted to come as close to your magnificence as we could. And we know you are adroit at the arts of stealth."

Jaume stroked his cheek. "And how may I—"

Roshan shook his head, making his hair rustle faintly on the smooth skin of his back. "No. Please. I told you, I was here to make amends for taking a liberty with you today, and kissing you without permission."

"I admit, I'm still not sure how I feel about it. It wasn't unpleasurable, I can tell you."

"But it was still a violation. I know. I couldn't help myself—chose not to, given what soon must be. I know what I did doesn't atone for it. But consider it a fine of sorts—though I did enjoy paying it."

He looked up to show a shy smile.

Jaume took him by the shoulders and urged him to his feet. The man was shorter by a centimeter or two than his hundred and eighty. He kissed him on the lips—then more deeply when they opened to his. He savored the salty sweetness of his own come.

Then, "Sit with me, at least," he said, seating himself on his straw-stuffed linen mattress.

Roshan did. He put his arm around Jaume's waist and laid his head on his shoulder.

"You travel in such spare style," he said. "Your tent's without ornamentation of any sort. We try to do the same, though we come from—different traditions than you."

"We've had Brothers from many traditions—including *Parsos*. One of us is *Ruso*, as I suspect several of your knights are, and we lost another in our most recent battle. And believe me—ostentation and weighing oneself down with tons of useless baggage on campaign are far from alien to the Nuevaropan *grande* nature, more's the pity."

Roshan laughed softly.

"I cannot stay long," he said. "I have to get back before our masters miss me. If they suspected where I've gone, my family would suffer."

Jaume clamped his teeth together in dismay. He knew that the Basileus, or ruler of Trebizon—or his underlings, or her, depending—had a reputation for a casual attitude toward the Creators' proscription of torture in their *Books of the Law*.

"I suspected that was the whip held over you."

"It's not the only one," Roshan said. "They use magic, these priests. Some of it quite—unnerving."

Jaume forced a small laugh. "So we were forced to conclude," he said. "Reluctantly."

"Believe me, we felt the same. When we could no longer deny the evidence of our own eyes."

"My question is, *whose* magic? Not the Lady's, surely."

"Oh, no. If anything, she would intervene against us, on your behalf. We don't know. We know they've used it directly against you, twice—once to cover our escape from Tres Veces, and once today, of a more potent kind. Also, they received some kind of magical warning of your approach this afternoon. Otherwise you'd have taken us unaware and . . . ended this sorry tale. For what we both know would've been the best."

"I won't deny it."

"We cannot hold back any longer when we face you tomorrow in Laventura, as we must. We'll have to try our best to kill you. At that point, honor will require it of us, as well as the other—penalties our masters hold over our heads."

"I'm amazed you did so for so long. Even when we killed one of your brothers. Whom I know you must have loved as deeply as I do mine." He didn't dishonor Roshan by pointing out that had been a necessity. Nor that the killing was, by any accounting, justified. That would be unkind; and Jaume doubted unkindness was beautiful in the Lady's eyes.

Roshan hugged him tightly. "Don't grieve, my Lord," he said. "We don't. You did dear Omid a favor: releasing him with honor from the curse his life had become. You gave him a beautiful death, and we are deeply grateful on his behalf."

I don't know how beautiful *it is, shitting your brains into the street from your broken head*, Jaume couldn't help thinking. But Roshan *sounded* sincere—joyously sincere. *Am I naive that I believe he is? I'm no intriguer, that's for sure.*

He knew he couldn't always trust his heart; a man that cold, as to be able always to do so, would probably never seek to become a Companion. Even Manfredo hadn't done so because he was cold: he had broken with the Order rather than rejoin the Imperial Army as commanded by the Emperor, after witnessing the horrors that army had committed on its march. He had chosen then and there to give up his service to Lady Li of Fire's Beauty and transfer it to Gen of the Mountain's Order—to the Creator most men called Torre, or whatever their word for *Tower* was. It was the very intensity of his compassion—his *passion*—that led him to break their fellowship and take Mor Wouter with him. As it was Jaume's passion for loyalty, not just to the Fangèd Throne but to his kinsman and friend who sat upon it, which had led him to proceed despite his own soul-blackening horror at what the Emperor had permitted to be done in his name.

But Jaume was not without judgment. His gut told him Roshan was honest. And he had long since learned to trust that.

"We can't hold back either," he said.

"I know."

Roshan stood up quickly, turned, and bent to kiss Jaume lightly on the lips. "One last time. I've got to go."

Thank you for doing me the courtesy of not asking if I'd try to restrain you, Jaume thought. From what Roshan had said, and what he and his Companions had seen, it would confer slight advantage, if any, in the upcoming fight—and bring a hideous fate to Roshan's loved ones. Such an act on Jaume's part would not be beautiful.

Although if forced to it, he would choose his duty, Montserrat and the Empire, over beauty. As Manfredo had learned, and could not in the end accept.

"You look so stern," Roshan said with another laugh. "Don't.

"What you must do is kill us all, Captain, my love. And then you must prevent this crime. For the sake of mighty empires and tens of thousands of innocent lives. But mostly for the sake of one innocent young girl."

Chapter 18

Laventura Grandísima de la Creación, Creation's Thrice *Grandest* Venture, Laventura—The Empire's most populous city and largest seaport, located on the Océano Aino on the southern coast of the Tyrant's Head. As such, it is the main focus of the fabulously lucrative trade with Trebizon, Vareta, and Chánguo. Bitter rival to the Channel port of La Merced, Laventura is an autonomous city-state, by a coterie of contentious nobles who act like bandits, and gang leaders who act like nobles. Its populace is heavily politicized as well as factionalized, and prone to civil strife and insurrection, of a much more violent nature than La Merced's frequent riots. Trebizonian spies and intrigues are common here, as well as troublemakers from much farther away.

—A PRIMER TO PARADISE FOR THE IMPROVEMENT
OF YOUNG MINDS

"They're at the wharf our info said they'd be, right enough."

It was early morning in the busy waterfront district. Jaume had dismounted in a narrow side street to stand beside Capitán Herrera, in command of the hundred-twenty-strong *manípulo* that had been all that the huge Sea Dragon base beside Laventura had been able to deploy on such crash notice. Bartomeu held the reins of the ever-patient Camellia—more patient by far than her master, whose heart was hammering as if it meant to break out through ribs and steel breastplate alike. The other Companions sat on their war-dinosaurs behind.

"The Treb priests seem to be arguing with the Treb ship's captain." The speaker was a young woman wearing a simple loincloth, a tight breast-band, and mostly sweat-streaked grime in the heat. Her square build and enormous shoulders would've fit the dockwalloper she seemed to be but came from pulling an oar in a powerful oceanic galleass. The local Sea Dragons, well acquainted with the Trebizon-style intrigue that apparently suffused the giant port, had sent in spies to scout ahead.

"Any sign of the Princess?" Jaume asked anxiously. He feared this would be a Treb ruse—a feint to draw off the rescuers while Montse's real abductors smuggled her out some other way.

The Marine spy shook her head. Her short hair wasn't anything unusual down here by the docks, Jaume had observed. "No. But—there are two women in uncomfortable-looking black priestly robes and those funny high hats important Trebs all wear. One of them's doing most of the arguing for their side, or at least screeching. They have a much shorter acolyte with them who's even more swaddled up. She looks like she's holding a little animal of some kind."

Relief almost turned the ligaments of his knees to boiled noodles. "That's her!" he exclaimed.

He turned to wave acknowledgment at his waiting men while Herrera bellowed at his own: "Light 'em up, boys and girls!"

Exchanging messages with the Naval base's comandante by galloper as he pushed his men down the road toward the city at a faster pace than was good for duckbills to sustain, he had managed to make sure certain preparations were made in time. Fortunately, Felipe had not seen fit to revoke Jaume's status as *Condestable*—supreme commander of all the Empire's war forces. Even more helpful, perhaps, was the fact that the Laventura Sea Dragons' Channel Squadron brothers and sisters had passed glowing reports of the balls and fighting prowess of Jaume and his Order across the grapevine.

Fully armored Marines tossed torches into the three cargo carts jammed axle to axle in the side street. Aided by some dry tinder beneath, the damp rags and scrap lumber, well doused in pine oil, instantly took flickering blue flame. And a beat of Jaume's racing heart later began to puke great aromatic gouts of dirty-white smoke toward the storm clouds quickly gathering low above the harbor. While a Dragon chanted a rowing cadence, they began to push each forward around the corner, a dozen Marines each pushing on the box and the two beams a nosehorn would normally be hitched between to pull it.

Bartomeu brought Camellia to her knees. Jaume almost vaulted aboard her. As she rose with a grunt to her big three-toed feet, he yanked free the loose knot that held his shield to his saddle, threaded his left arm through the band of his shield, and seized the grip. Drawing the Mirror from across his back, he twisted in the saddle and brandished the longsword.

"For Beauty and the Lady!" he cried.

"For Empire and the Infanta!" his Companions roared back.

Slamming his visor shut, he urged Camellia to follow the smoke-belching dinosaur carts toward the docks.

Just when Montse wasn't sure whether she'd first suffocate inside the cowl of the heavy black hemp acolyte robe her abductors had swaddled her up in to mask her distinctive dark-blond dreadlocks or expire from boredom at the sudden last-minute haggling about their passage, Paraskeve broke off shrieking *Griego* imprecations at the captain of the cog *Karagiorgos* and screamed, even louder, "They're coming!"

The priestess never eased her raptor-claw grip on Montse's left arm, though.

A nosehorn began to bray in panic from somewhere on the wharf nearby. Montse smelled smoke. She wondered if a street vendor's brazier had spilled and ignited some of the goods piled high on the dockside, causing the dinosaur's alarm.

Because there was only one "they" whose coming Montse could imagine the Trebs reacting so strongly to, her heart almost burst with joy. She wheeled around, fumbling at the hood with the hand that wasn't holding a quiescent Mistral in order to clear her vision as well as her airway. And immediately wondered how the awful woman could tell.

The smoke wasn't coming from a burning kiosk or a crate of fine Spañol fabrics bound for far ports. Instead, it boiled up from the beds of three carts that had appeared down the street that led to the docks. She could just see them moving closer, over the black-leather-capped heads of a brute squad of the *Guardia Civil*'s Shore Patrol and between the great war-hadrosaurs of the Flower Knights arrayed in a protective semicircle in front of them.

As if he read her mind, Dragos murmured, "Who else could it be?"

She cried out in fear as the Flower Knights loosed their bows. Smoke swallowed the arrows.

"They're shooting blind," Dragos said, slightly tightening his reassuring grip on her shoulder. "Also high, or I miss my estimation."

The ship captain turned and scuttled up the ramp,

bawling instructions. Montse had spent enough time hanging around the La Merced docks to realize from the way the sailors on board began untying lines that he meant to cast off as quickly as possible. He gobbled something down his beard at the others that Montse couldn't understand.

Is he going to abandon us here? she wondered. *I hope!*

His come-forward hand waving broke that hope. Akakios shouted out, "We're boarding!" in his booming bass voice. Evidently whatever point they'd been haggling about was pretty moot now.

Paraskeve was now yelling at Anastasia to do something. The wild-haired junior priestess turned and dashed straight up the ramp, tearing off her swaddling clothes. Since she'd seen that the Trebs were, if anything, more averse to nudity around others than a bunch of stuffy *Alemanes*, her behavior baffled Montse even more than usual.

Tasoula's madness seemed purposeful somehow, and that worried Montse. But at least Paraskeve let her go.

She and Akakios hustled up the ramp as Tasoula vanished from Montse's view. Their Spañol minions and Treb servants followed. So did the small, scary Vlasis, at a more deliberate pace. Chubby Charalampos stayed on the flagstones by the base of the ramp, shifting nervously from foot to sandaled foot. His eyes rolled left and right like a frightened horse's.

"Aren't you going to drag me aboard?" Montse asked the debonair Count Balaur, who still held her by the shoulder.

"Wait a moment," he told her. "And be ready."

Two of the carts swerved left and right to the sides of the wide, abruptly deserted avenue. Through the smoke around the one that stalled in the middle appeared the colossal, lurching forms of hadrosaurs with armored knights on their backs. Their harness was enameled white, and a red Lady's Mirror shone on the left side of every one.

The Companions! They really are here! Montse's heart almost burst from a passion more violent than joy. She jumped up and down, cheering and waving poor Mistral around in her hand.

It barely registered when two of the Treb knights, still meters away from the charging Nuevaropans, fell off their duckbills with a clatter of their armor scales.

The two lines collided like a wave and a rock of flesh and steel.

"They're drawing!" Will Oakheart of Oakheart heard Owain de Galés call in Anglysh.

The two Anglaterranos crouched between chimney pots on the steeply peaked roof of a tall building of yellow brick. The treacherous Trebizon emissaries were clumped at the foot of a ramp running up to a fat three-master carrack a hair over a hundred meters away, already riding low in the water with a full hold of cargo and supplies. They seemed to be embroiled in a heated dispute with the ship's master.

Will was aware of them, but his whole attention was focused on the eleven cataphracts who sat on war-duckbills arranged in a semicircle on the wharf to deny access to the ramp and the ship beyond. They had initially reacted with apparent confusion over the appearance of three carts smoking like self-ignited dung heaps that had suddenly rounded the corner and were bearing down on them along the broad thoroughfare, looking at each other and shouting words the pair likely wouldn't have been able to understand had they been able to hear them. But their leader came to a sudden decision. At his command, thumb-rings drew nocked arrows smoothly back to ears as the deceptively heavy-looking recurved bows of laminated Triceratops horn came up.

Shooting blind, Will thought. And why wouldn't they? Their arrows would do them no good in their quivers.

He and his partner were already drawing their longbows of stout Anglysh yew and sighting along their arrows, each fletched with two white feathers and one red, in the Companions' colors. Like the Ovdan war bows their enemies were preparing to loose, each required enormous strength and skill to use properly, and thus a lifetime's training. And like the hornbows, they were within easy range for archers as masterful as Will reckoned his enemies to be—and for him and Owain as well.

Will the chisel tip pierce those overlapping scales? he wondered as he drew a deep breath, let half go, and held the rest. *We're about to find out.*

He shot. A finger-snap later he heard the plangent note of Owain's more powerful bow. Though shorter by a hand than Will, the Welshmuhn was stronger.

His shot struck a clean-shaven blond knight on a redmarbled blue morion through the gorget. He loosed his bow into one of the flaming wagons, clutched the shaft with one hand, which was quickly sprayed with blood, and fell. He saw a dark-bearded Flower Knight go down as well.

The rest loosed their bows. Even at this distance, Will heard the deep music of the chord they produced and savored its curious Beauty. *The Lady and the Eight keep my Brothers*, he thought, and reached for another arrow in the quiver slung by his side.

A flight of arrows flashed through the astringent smoke and whuffled no more than a meter over Jaume's head.

"Go low!" he shouted. "They're shooting blind."

If they were going to do that, there was no more point in choking on dense smoke. They had eaten up almost half of the distance to the dock and cost the enemy a wasted volley. *It'll have to do.* He opened his visor with his sword hand just long enough to cry, "Sea Dragons, clear the way!"

Still cheering lustily, the Marines on the left and right shoved their carts to the side of the narrow street, upsetting kiosks of fresh fish and fried hornface-flesh strips abandoned by their proprietors when trouble broke. Even for the Laventura waterfront, a notoriously violent place, this was an extreme level of combat.

By oversight the third cart got left in the middle of the street. Jaume and his nine Companions, on their duckbills at a rolling four-footed lope, flowed about it like a stream around a stone. He rode bent down along Camellia's neck with his shield rim held up to his visor slot to present as small a target as possible to the expert Trebizon archers. He had to trust in Camellia's steel chamfron to protect his beloved mount's face and eyes.

The Flower Knights stood to receive their charge in a half-circular formation a mere thirty meters ahead. Behind them stood a phalanx of burly bravos in black-enameled boiled nosehorn-leather breasts and backs and leather caps, armed with shields, crude but deadly lead-head maces, and a few spears and halberds. Jaume recognized the Laventura *Guardia Civil*'s Shore Patrol, even more notorious for their wanton brutality than their corruption, which Herrera had warned they might find opposing them.

As the Flower Knights began drawing their bows for a second volley aimed at their now clearly visible foes, more urgent was the fact that Roshan hadn't told him the entire truth. He and his men *weren't* doing everything possible to thwart Montserrat's rescue after all. By standing to receive a charge by enemy dinosaur knights, they were putting themselves at a terrific disadvantage—one their priestly masters would be unlikely to deign to recognize. They had set themselves up to die—and lose—with honor intact.

They loosed their arrows.

Jaume felt an impact slam, first to the left side of his shield, then his visor, and then the cheekbone behind. His eyes watered at the jolt and sudden sting. He blinked to clear them. He saw young Ramón, the Brother-Aspirant, slump from the saddle of his brown-and-white sackbut bull with an arrow jutting from just in front of the crown of his horror-skull basinet helmet.

With his sword hand he reached for the arrow's red shaft. A squeal that threatened to shatter his eardrums through his helmet made him turn his head to the right. He saw Ayaks's morion Bogdan falling onto his golden side with an arrow sticking out of the left eye hole of his chamfron. The giant blond Ruso timed his beloved mount's fall expertly, leaping clear at the last heartbeat so that he landed on his feet and running with his greatsword held over his head with both hands.

With the first two fingers of his gauntleted right hand, Jaume gripped the arrow against the Mirror's hilt, snapping the arrow off with a decisive twist of his arm. The visor held the remaining section of shaft firmly enough that it didn't torque the head badly and expand the wound. But the action still sent a blinding-white sheet of agony smashing back through the left side of Jaume's skull like a heated axe blade.

His eyes streaming tears of intense agony as much as grief for young Ramón and the brave and beautiful Bogdan, Jaume let go the broken arrow and firmed his grip on his longsword. He thrust it out straight before him.

A beautiful green Lambeosaurus with white mottling reared up in front of Camellia, panicked at her charge. Even the best-trained war-dinosaur might break at any unexpected threat, as Camellia and all the rest had done in the face of the phantom fire in La Bajada. Jaume let Camellia knock the halberd right on its ass, expertly putting her shoulder in to deliver maximum force while suffering the least ill effect from it. Barely slowed beyond being forced to raise up slightly herself and tuck in her hoof-like forefeet, she kept running forward on her hind legs.

Before she had finished a fresh pace, the Lady's Mirror took a Flower Knight with an imposing plaited black beard right through his yelling mouth as the man, his bow abandoned, struggled to draw a *talwar* in time. The sword-tip smashed right out the back of his skull to tear his helmet from his head by the mail aventail behind.

As he delivered the killing blow, Jaume saw Ayaks, running with great bounding strides reminiscent of the duckbills and seemingly not much slower, deliver a screaming overhand cut of his *dosmanos* to a Flower Knight on an orange-and-yellow sackbut. The long blade hacked through the plate cuisse that protected the front of the Treb's thigh and chopped it to bone. The answering sheet of red that sprayed out told Jaume, as he ripped his own weapon free of the sagging corpse it had made of a lovely and valiant young knight, that the Companion would have no need of a follow-up blow. He had severed the great artery of his enemy's leg. The man would bleed to death in a few beats of his battle-accelerated heart.

Jaume started to twist back counterclockwise—and, letting go of the grip, threw the shield right at Roshan's unprotected face.

The Flower Knights were already overmanned—thanks in part to the rooftop sniping of the *Angloterranos*. But the street was now clogged by a seething scrum of war-dinosaurs, ridden and riderless. Jaume urged Camellia straight ahead.

"Make us a path, baby," he told her.

Almost at once a great pale shape barred their way: Gulrukh, his rose-faced white Corythosaurus. "Now you must fight me, my lord!" cried Roshan from her back.

But through the riot of dinosaurs and their-all-but-inconsequential human excrescences, beyond an increasingly uneasy wall of black-leathered *Guardias*, Jaume could see that the Trebs had concluded their disagreement with their getaway-ship captain, or at least wisely chosen to take it aboard, and were hustling up the ramp.

The small one hung back and swept her cowl from her head with a hand still holding a rather nonchalant-looking silver-and-black ferret. The hood fell back to reveal a familiar mass of dark-golden dreadlocks.

Montserrat! Jaume's heart soared at mere sight of her.

"No time!" he shouted at Roshan as a priestess in a tall silver-chased black hat yanked the Princess rudely up the ramp.

As they came knee to knee, the Flower Knight aimed an overhand cut at Jaume's head. Jaume leaned into it, bringing his shield up over his head from the left. The long curved blade glanced off with a scraping sound.

The Flower Knight swung his sword and managed to send the shield flipping end over end past him with a clang. And Jaume caught him with a forehand cut right under his left armpit.

The scales' overlap and inertia absorbed most of the blow's force. Jaume doubted he'd so much as cracked a rib. But the stroke was powerful enough to unbalance Roshan ever so slightly in his saddle.

Twisting his body right, Jaume withdrew the sword, then plunged it in a thrust to the left side of Roshan's chest. Delivered mostly with Jaume's upper body and arms, the longsword's point didn't come any closer to penetrating Roshan's coat of steel scales than the edge had. But it delivered enough of a shock to knock Roshan over his mount's left side.

Jaume yanked his left leg free of the stirrup and, pushing up from the saddle with his right, braced the sole of his left sabaton on the saddle pommel. Then he used his leg to launch himself right across Roshan's just-vacated saddle.

He landed in a graceless sprawl, facedown across the saddle. Bracing with his left hand on the pommel, he got his feet beneath him and threw himself from Gulrukh's high back toward her master, who had just landed on his back on the dockside pavement with a splash of latent muck.

As Jaume plummeted, he reversed his grasp on the Mirror's long hilt with his right hand, and seized it with his left as well. Using the full weight and momentum of his armored body, he drove the longsword straight through the center of Roshan's chest.

The Flower Knight's body arched as if to receive the blade as it punched through his scales, ribs, and heart.

Jaume let go the hilt and landed hard atop the fallen Flower Knight. This time, he'd been prepared for the drop and hadn't had the breath knocked out of him. Which wasn't to say the battle bruises wouldn't hurt more than usual tomorrow.

If he lived that long.

Roshan's smile was somehow sweet and horrific for being full of blood that was bright even in the near-storm light.

"They have more magic, and worse," he said. "Kiss me, my love."

Despite the gore, Jaume pressed his lips quickly to Roshan's. The Flower Knight sighed his final breath into Jaume's nostril. It smelled of rose pastille and fresh blood.

Jaume sprang to his feet. Most of the Flower Knights

were down. He slapped up his visor and whistled. From where she stood a few paces away, Camellia, warily watchful, trotted toward him.

Taking a page from Roshan's book, Jaume sheathed the Mirror, then grabbed his stirrup and used it and the rigging straps to haul himself and his twenty-plus kilos of armor right up her flank onto her high back. He took a moment to feel pleasure at the accomplishment—he'd practiced plenty of acrobatic maneuvers in full harness, but never that one—and then once more urged Camellia through the melee as the Companions powered down a last trio of Flower Knights.

He heard a scream: a keening, ear-stabbing warble of syllables in an unknown tongue. He had time to look up and see a naked woman with wild dark hair perched on the caravel's rail, gesticulating frantically with dirty-looking arms.

Then, like an ocean wave, cobblestones and the reeking soil of the dock itself rose up to wash over the combatants and him.

Chapter 19

Raptor irritante, Irritante, vexer. . . . —*Velociraptor mongoliensis.* Nuevaropan raptor, 2 meters long, 50 centimeters high, 15 kilograms. Commonly kept as a pet, though prone to be quarrelsome. Wild vexer-packs are often pests but pose little threat to humans.

—THE BOOK OF TRUE NAMES

"The woman," Will said to Owain. "Shoot her."

He was out of sorts because his most recent shot, at a small Flower Knight riding a dun halberd, had missed. He was reaching for another arrow, but the few remaining enemies were too intermingled with the Companions for even him to risk a shot.

"I don't like to. She's crazy."

The capering woman raised her eyes and her hands and gestured at the building closest to that particular dock, which showed the three round lanterns of a pawnshop. A dull orange tile arrowed off its steeply pitched roof and struck Bernat in the back. He toppled right off the back of his cream-and-brown sackbut, Jordi, as if it had killed him. Which, given that it might weigh thirty kilos, it well might have.

Without another word, Owain pulled back his already nocked arrow and loosed.

"But, Mother," Falk said urgently. "I have to talk to you."

"You are talking, my son. And I am listening. I don't have anything better to do right now, since you've interrupted my massage."

He frowned and swallowed. The operation was in fact continuing quite smoothly as two short men dressed in immaculate white cotton loincloths, their squatly muscled tan torsos twined with elaborate tattoos of giant serpents, fliers, and flowers, pummeled her bare back and buttocks with the blades of their stiffened hands as she lay with her face turned from him and resting on a plush, folded towel. They paid him no mind. Blind master masseurs of legendary skill from Zipangu, off the far end of Aphrodite Terra, they were said to find their services in demand all over the world. And to be accordingly well compensated. In this case, Falk's and his mother's hosts were footing the bill for his mother's indulgence. Rather than, as usual, the long-suffering peasants of Hornberg back home.

A pair of pet vexers, bred for plumage in the Imperial colors, dozed on the far side of a small pool beyond the marble table on which the Dowager Duchess lay. They were quite tame. Felipe, a great lover of the hunt, kept a pack of them for chasing small game in the scrublands around Glory Plateau. Savage though they were to prey, they were quite gentle and attached to humans, like cats. They had the run of the Palace, also like cats.

Falk felt an odd sensation in the pit of his stomach as the foreign pair, their hair glossy black and wrapped into tight topknots, each began to knead one of the Dowager Duchess's thighs, their fingers digging deeply into white skin. She made a soft growl low in her throat and fidgeted her butt. He moistened his lips with his tongue.

I wish I were more fully dressed, he thought, *even though it's hot and humid as a Black River swamp down here*.

"As you no doubt know"—because of course his mother still had spies watching her son's every move, even though his longtime servant and nemesis, Bergdahl, was temporarily dispatched to different duty in Karyl's new Duchy of the Borderlands—"I've followed your instructions quite scrupulously to diminish and disparage the Imperial Princess's reputation. Both to weaken the force of her inexplicable opposition to waging war on Trebizon to avenge the kidnapping of her own sister and, in case she's inclined to make use of her position as the Emperor's only remaining daughter, to level . . . certain potentially damaging allegations."

"Not yourself, though? I mean, I've been trusting you, but I know you sometimes fall short of justifying that."

If by trusting *you meant having that wretched asshole Bergdahl ride my neck like a giant leech the whole time I've been in the South*, he thought.

"Of course not." He caught himself, thank the Eight, before asking if she thought he was stupid. He knew too well what *that* answer was. Even if she'd be quick, as she always was, to assure him he wasn't *really* stupid, she knew, and that was why she was so disappointed. "I've spoke nothing but praise for Her Highness's service in fighting for the throne. I pay others to spread the rumor that she was merely slumming with useless peasant residue, along with a surcharge for appropriate snickering."

"And you have quite frustrated her efforts to build a base of her own from which to undermine your reputation," she said. He didn't bother asking how she knew that. He *wasn't* stupid. "You've done quite well in that regard, left to your own devices. For once."

He uttered a small, soft grunt, as if she had punched him in the stomach with her powerful right fist. She had seldom struck him as he was growing up—his father had more than made up that deficit, until Falk pushed him down the stairs one late night when the man was shitting-himself drunk—but Falk knew she could hit like a *Griego* pankratist.

"But that's all changing," he said, "despite the best efforts of my bribed courtiers. And I don't dare push them harder. Veterans of Karyl's campaigns have begun arriving at Court and telling far different tales of our pretty Princess's contributions in battle. Knights and *grandes* of immaculate birth and reputation."

She turned to give him a cool blue gaze. "Aside from having recently been placed under the Emperor's own ban and declared outlaws, you mean?"

"And personally pardoned by His Majesty immediately following the battle. He said, approximately, that he either had to pardon and ennoble everybody who'd fought on his side or hang them all for impiousness, himself included. And he started by making erstwhile arch-outlaw Karyl Bogomirskiy a Duke and giving him half of Duke Eric's lands for a fief."

She sighed gustily as the masseurs applied themselves to her feet. "One of Bergdahl's few total failures. It doesn't surprise me that you failed to kill him, even given a clean shot at his back. But it's unlike Bergdahl to leave his mark alive. Ah, well. Proceed with your complaint, dear boy."

"Some who originally marched with the Empire on Crusade against Providence also have arrived bearing witness to her actions. Specifically, she apparently faced the arch-heresiarch Bogardus himself, who founded the Garden and served as lieutenant to—to the Grey Angel

Himself. He had been a dinosaur knight, before he became a priest, it seems. He rode a war-hadrosaur and wore full armor, while the Princess fought him from the back of that pampered pony of hers, in only light leather and armed with javelins. And won."

"Impressive," Margrethe murmured.

"You see my problem."

She laughed. "Enough, boys," she told the blind men. They bowed and withdrew. She rose and stretched.

"Ah, they are good at that. And you have nothing to worry about."

"But our efforts—"

"Served their purpose."

She padded naked up to him. She was not much shorter than he was. He could smell the musk of light, clean sweat on her skin. Her nipples almost brushed his own bare chest.

"And now our dear Princesa is about to find her own efforts dashed," she said, smiling at her son. "Along with more than a measure of her hopes."

"How do you know that?"

She laughed. "Come now. You know I have my ways. I always have my ways."

She reached up and stroked his bearded cheek.

"So set your mind at ease. Nothing she says will matter soon. Against you or our lovely war."

She withdrew her hand slightly and gave him a slap across the cheek that rocked his head around on his nose-horn neck.

"Ow!" he said, rubbing his face. "What did you do that for?"

"For being a fool and running your fool tongue in front of servants. Did you learn nothing from your time with Bergdahl? Even when he was employed as a servant in the Firefly Palace?"

"But—they're outlanders. And they're *blind*."

"They aren't deaf, boy. Not mute, either. Luckily, I tip them handily, even measured against their usual expectations. They'll stay discreet."

That was another not-exactly-Alemana trait of Falk's mother's: she was always open-handed. Where her own pleasures were concerned, at least. And also her intrigues.

"And if not—" she shrugged a powerful shoulder. "I'll have them garroted and cast down the Moat for the rag-pickers to find. That's an expense service around here, too. But also well worth it, when it's called for."

"But they're the Emperor's own servants! Hired directly from their island kingdom at truly Brontosaurian expense, or so it's said."

"And he can afford to hire more. They're outlanders, and you know *they* aren't in good color here at court."

"Zipangu is a good deal farther from the Basileia than Trebizon is from here."

"And who knows or cares, when the Emperor's own baby daughter has been stolen away from her home by wicked foreigners? In any event, such an act is vanishingly likely to become necessary. And even less so to be connected with me. As you should know more than anybody."

He stood rubbing his beard lightly with his fingertips. As always under such circumstances, he felt an inextricable tangle of emotions, of which frustration, resentment, and adoration were large parts.

"You know I only do what I do out of love for you, Falki," she said. "Now run along, and stop endangering your mother's dearly bought relaxation with your groundless worrying."

She turned, walked to the pool, and dove in. The velociraptors jumped up when the ensuing wave washed over them, shook and ruffled suddenly soaked feathers whose gorgeous red-and-yellow colors had temporarily turned brown, and ran off with mincing steps of their hind legs, killing claws discreetly held above the smooth marble floor, chittering their outrage at each other.

From behind his right shoulder, Will Oakheart heard a squelching sound, a soft, sad gurgle of a sigh, and knew Owain was lost.

He continued his smooth draw without a hitch, sighting down the pale wooden shaft at the scrum developing by the ramp to the Treb cog. He noted that the wild-haired, capering nude woman had disappeared, and so had the wave of uprooted soil and paving stones. The nearby roof tiles now remained calmly in place.

But he found no targets. He trusted his aim—as did Jaume and the Brothers-Companion clearly overwhelming the last Flower Knights below. He saw Machtigern crush the skull of the small cataphract who had clearly just shot the shaft that had struck Owain. But what he did not trust was the random surge and weave of human and dinosaurian bodies in battle. The ultrahard chisel-shaped arrowheads he and Owain were shooting were the finest quality available on the Tyrant's head, made specially and at great price by the wandering smiths and tinkers of La Familia Herrera—or the Smyth Famuhly, as he'd say in his own tongue. If they'd punch through Trebizon scale, they'd punch through the backs of Companion cuirasses at least as readily.

Reluctantly, he relaxed his draw. Removing the arrow and returning it to his quiver, he glanced aside.

Owain lay on his back, his pretty lips slightly parted, his eyes mostly closed. There was no sign of the arrow that had struck him. Almost certainly chisel-tipped as well, it had passed through his torso side to side, on an upward course from lower left rib cage almost to the right armpit. A pool of blood had spread wide around him already on the burnt-umber-colored tiles, running in rivulets down toward the alley below. The sky, its clouds suddenly as thick and black as boiling blood pudding above, robbed his blood of its lustrous red hue.

It seems so unfair, he thought, as he laid his longbow carefully aside and knelt to cradle Owain's head. Owain opened his green eyes, so pure and bright, and with obvious effort turned his head aside to kiss the hand that caressed his beardless cheek.

"Don't stir," Will told him. He didn't mutter reassurances. They were both Companions, and of all of them Owain—and Will himself—would know best that the small, spurting holes on either side of his torso were plain signs of a mortal wound.

Owain smiled at him. His teeth were ghastly with blood.

"That was a . . . true shot," he croaked, and his head lolled to the side as the light left his eyes.

Will sat there for a time, feeling the dead weight of his friend and sometime lover's head on his bare thigh. He heard without registering the sounds and trumpeting and clangor of combat from the waterfront below. He wasn't sure how he felt. He had lost dear friends before—he had been one of Jaume's select Order for years, and that was part of their service as Companions of the Lady. But never had someone he had been lovers with die in his arms before.

Empty, he decided. *It's all I can let myself feel now.*

He disentangled himself from Owain's now-lifeless body. Gently, as if it mattered. He settled Owain's blond head on the tiles. Then he picked up his bow and rose.

A wall of fire roared alight between the Companions on their dinosaurs and the cog. From the savage heat Will felt even on his perch and the shrieks of the human-like shapes visible inside the inferno, he knew this was no illusion.

I've done what I can here, he thought. *Farewell, my friend, my love. We'll be back for you.*

He turned away and began looking for the fastest way down to street level.

Chapter 20

Dragones de la Mar, Sea Dragons (singular *Dragón de la Mar*, Sea Dragon)—Nuevaropa's Imperial Navy, named after the common name for large—and well-feared—carnivorous marine reptiles. Colors are blue, green, and silver. Their dromons, rowed war-galleys, patrol La Canal for pirates; larger sailing ships cruise the high seas and wage naval warfare. Every Sea Dragon serves as both sailor or rower and fighter. They also fight in boarding and shore actions as marines.

—A PRIMER TO PARADISE FOR THE IMPROVEMENT
OF YOUNG MINDS

I don't believe it, Montse thought, seeing the flagstones of the wharf and the very ground below it rise up to pelt the victorious Companions, in apparent response to Lady Anastasia's naked capering on the rail.

Montse made sure to stand well on the other side of the ramp from her—the breeze was blowing from the shore, picking up strength, which struck the girl since there were so many tall buildings to block it. But it meant she could barely smell Tasoula. The priestess's bodily hygiene left visibly more to be desired nude than clothed.

More than scared, Montse felt angry. *I don't like things that don't make sense!*

The only answer as to how the stone and soil fountain was taking place that made near sense was magic. And even after all that had happened, that she had seen, Montse hated to admit it was real.

Despite the unnatural interference, the Sea Dragons continued to battle with the Shore Patrol ruffians who backed the now mostly fallen Flower Knights. The mad priestess raised her attention to the pitched roofs beyond the docks, made gestures of pulling. Massive clay tiles began to detach and hurl themselves at the Companions. To her horror, she saw one fall. His visor was down; she only knew it was not Jaume, because Camellia was her old friend, too.

Tasoula's ululations ended in a strangled squawk. She collapsed on the deck. Montse had no idea why until she noticed the arrow sticking up at an angle from the planks. Gore dripped from its whole visible length, especially the feathers.

"No!" shrieked Charalampos, his pitch higher than the sorceress's had been. "Even Fae magic won't stop them!"

That word—*hada,* for he had screamed in Spañol—chilled Montse as none of the terrible things she had experienced or seen so far had. She was agnostic about the Creators. She was still reluctant to believe in magic, although she was grudgingly coming to accept that, rationally, it *did* exist. But she most powerfully did not want to believe in the Creators' ancient enemies, against whom they had supposedly fought the Demon War that gave birth to the Empire. A conflict that everybody she knew, including Jaume, who was so devout he was technically a cardinal, had always assumed was a normal human one around which a fantasy castle of legends had been built, largely by her own Torre Delgao as propaganda. Even here, trembling so close to freedom's brink, she hardly dared to breathe for fear of upsetting the outcome. Montse knew the ramifications of the Fae's existence would be terrifying indeed.

The plump priest hiked up his skirts and dashed down the ramp even as crew folk struggled to raise it. Jumping to the stone dock he turned right, and bolted along the waterfront, behind the ranks of men battling on foot.

Vlasis stepped up, raising his arms. "You must not speak the name!" he shouted.

At his gesture, a wall of flame blazed up, right at the water's edge. Montse smelled roasting meat, and, seeing the thrashing forms inside the mast-high fire and hearing the inhuman screams issuing from it, realized it was the smell of people burning. Among the doomed and desperately struggling shapes was that of Charalampos.

Dragos's grip tightened on her shoulder, then relaxed. "So," he said. "We don't dare risk it. I'm truly sorry, Princess."

The gap between rail and shore was visibly increasing anyway. She knew they couldn't have made it. *Well, I can swim and so can Mistral!*

She tensed to dash forward and throw herself overboard. A hand seized one arm from behind. She knew the touch of Paraskeve's hated claw. Tears of frustration scalded her eyes.

Through the wall of flame leapt a figure all in armor of steel plate, whose white enamel and red Mirror were scorched by the horrid heat. Its armored fingers caught the rail and clung.

Jaume! Montse knew. *I'm saved!*

The wave of dirt and stones dropped suddenly to the ground. Jaume saw the wild-haired woman toppling backward off the ship's rail. He caught a glimpse of the white-and-red fletching that was all that was visible of the arrow that had buried itself in her sternum.

As the air cleared, he saw a small Flower Knight, one of the last two remaining mounted, holding an empty bow and reaching for an arrow from his quiver. Machtigern appeared beside him on Tiger, his black-striped gold morion bull, and struck a blow with his long-handled warhammer that knocked the knight's spired helmet askew and crushed his skull.

Camellia was sidestepping and tossing her head violently on her powerful neck, rolling her eyes in alarm. Jaume patted her neck and spoke quick, soothing words, and she calmed down.

The last Flower Knight, a man almost as big as Ayaks with dark moustaches that swept straight out to either side of his dark face, was standing off three Companions with a straight-bladed arming-sword from the back of what Jaume thought was a deep purple Parasaurolophus. It looked black as brutal black storm clouds gathered like an angry mob, seemingly just above the ship's mastheads, and blotted out the sun. The rider didn't concern Jaume. He wasn't the target.

"Make way!" he yelled at the Sea Dragons, who had closed in on the Shore Patrol when the stone-and-soil rain subsided. What seemed the gleeful fury with which the Marines engaged them confirmed the hatred in Herrera's voice when he'd said they might well have to fight some. It wasn't just rivalry between the Imperial elite and city guards, either; the Shore Patrol were notorious, even among Laventura's notorious Guardia Civil, for corruption and brutality.

"They don't even stay bribed," Herrera had said, in a tone suggesting that was ultimate condemnation. And perhaps it was.

The Treb sailors, men and women more heavily

dressed than the nearly nude Laventura dockers, were hastily trying to cast off and get their big vessel under way. Jaume could see that a many-oared harbor tug was already roped to them and waiting to pull it away from the dock. The Sea Dragons had sent patrol boats into the harbor in hopes of interdicting the Trebs should they get away from land. Even as they prepared to light the smoke-carts for the final push, Herrera had informed Jaume that the boats—small galleys like the one that had brought him and his companions on their fateful voyage south after the Princes' War—were having trouble negotiating what seemed unusually heavy traffic of medium and small craft, even for the ever-busy harbor.

Herrera had grimly said they couldn't count on the patrol catching them before they got the day's seaward breeze—imperceptible from the waterfront, but Jaume believed that it was blowing today—in their sails and simply outran the rowed dromons.

So Jaume was fully prepared to ride down Sea Dragons as well as Shore Patrolmen, and pay pensions to the wounded or the estates of any he killed from his own pocket. He urged Camellia to get her bulk moving.

A new figure appeared in the gap at the top of the ramp: a Treb priest, visibly slight despite his plain black robes and a black cylindrical hat that was unusually tall even for the Treb clergy. He held his palms out before him.

He rapped out sharp commands. Jaume knew only a few words of Griego, learned from Timaeos, another Companion lost at Canterville. He did recognize *phōtiá*—fire.

"That trick won't work twice on us!" Jaume yelled as Camellia neared the shouting, flailing scrum. It pleased him to see the Marines had responded to his warning and were trying to move to both sides.

A sheet of flame roared up from the bare mud from

which the crazy magic woman had chucked the paving stones at them. As before, they reached to twice Camellia's height or more, with the heat and stink of a live lava flow. As before, Camellia shied.

He saw that a number of Sea Dragons and Civil Guards were caught within the wall of fire. And realized that the screaming wasn't mere fear.

"It's real, Jaume!" Florian shouted, as the last Flower Knight went down. "Get back!"

Instead, Jaume turned Camellia and walked the skittish dinosaur several paces back away from the horrifically real flame barrier. The Sea Dragons who weren't shrieking and flapping their limbs like fire wings as they burned had pulled back; the Shore Patrol who hadn't been caught fled, some throwing themselves into the reeking harbor water in their terror.

Jaume dropped Camellia to her belly on the quay, where the paving stones still lay undisturbed by unaccountable magic. Sheathing the Lady's Mirror, he dropped to the ground.

And sprinted straight for the bellowing furnace.

Alarmed cries from his Companions, Sea Dragons, and even onlookers followed him. He ignored them. Instead, he crossed his armored forearms before his eyes and sprang forward through the flames.

The metal seemed to flash heat to a forging point in an instant. The pain was intense. Jaume smelled his own hair smoldering within his sallet.

Then he was through. He felt scalded all over, and he could feel the heat beating inward from the curved steel of his visor. But he still could move.

He still could *run*. He did, right up the ramp, as the crew pushed the carrack vigorously off from the dock with long poles, and the rowers on the tugs began to bend their backs, and the sails rippled down from the yards.

Jaume flung himself forward off the ramp's end. Three

meters of green-brown water, whipped up into grey froth-crowned chop as if by a coming gale, passed below him. Then his stinging forearms slapped the ship's rail and gauntleted fingers hooked over the stout wood.

For a moment he hung there. He kicked the pointy tips of his steel shoes hard against the creaking, shifting planks of the hull for purchase and heaved himself up and over onto the deck.

Just like when Pere and I stormed the pirate cog by ourselves in the Channel, he thought. He refused to think how that adventure ended.

He reached over his right shoulder for his longsword's hilt. The small priest stepped up to confront him.

"Not so fast, my young friend," he said in accented but excellent Spañol. His blade-thin features reminded Jaume unpleasantly of the late Papal Legate, then Cardinal, Tavares, whose uncompromising and unwashed fanaticism had cost him so dearly on the march to Providence. So did the obsidian fire in his eyes.

"The Fae send their regards," he said softly as Jaume's steel began to slide upward from its scabbard. He held an open palm toward Jaume.

A fat spark cracked across four fingers of bare air from Jaume's palm to his white-enameled breastplate.

Agony worse than anything he had ever known or even conceived seized his limbs and his entire body. It was worse even than the searing flash of pain from the magical inferno. It seemed as if his muscles could do nothing but wind themselves tighter and tighter in pain. He couldn't move.

"You lose," the priest said. He put his palm against Jaume's cuirass and pushed.

Helpless, Jaume fell back over the rail and straight down into the bay.

The terror paralysis ended with the sudden splash and envelopment by cool water. Jaume's own wiry weight of bone and muscle, and his kilograms of plate, plunged him down and down. Water shot in through the eye slit of his helmet.

He began to kick and beat his arms powerfully. He didn't have much experience with ships or sailing, but, like all his Companions, he was a strong swimmer.

Somehow, between the air in his lungs and that trapped in his suit of armor and his own strong, not quite frantic efforts, Jaume managed to bob his head clear of the rank, greasy surface.

Exhaling explosively, he tore open his visor. In time to lock eyes with Montse, who stood in the high stern-castle of the Treb carrack, a priestess's hand clutching her arm and a tall, grey-bearded man's holding her shoulder. Cradling Silver Mistral against her chest, Montse stared hopelessly back as home and freedom receded.

A squall of such sudden savagery as to not seem natural swallowed the lumbering three-master. Lightning lashed the water and the docks with a monstrous rippling crack.

His strength draining suddenly from him, Jaume sank almost gratefully back beneath the increasing violent waves of Golden Venture Bay.

Chapter 21

Guerra Altasanta, La; High Holy War, The, La Guerra de Demonios, Demon War. . . . —177 to 210 AP. A global war waged between the Creators, their servitors the Grey Angels, and their human faithful against their archenemies, the *hada*—or Fae—and their allies. It culminated in Nueva-ropa's last Grey Angel Crusade to extirpate Fae-worship. Now widely considered to be a mythic account of the Years of Trouble, from the dawn of human civilization on Paradise in Year Zero to 210 AP, which led to the formation of the Nuevaropan Empire.

—LA GRAN HISTORIA DEL IMPERIO DEL TRONO
COLMILLADO

"And so—Majesty, Highness—we were defeated in our attempts to rescue the Princess Montser-rat."

As a multiply-throated gasp ran around the walls of the Throne Room, which was crowded with seemingly every courtier in La Majestad if not the entire Empire, Jaume dropped to one knee on the cold marble floor before the Fangèd Throne.

"I failed. I can only beg you both to please forgive me."
Though his head was lowered, he looked up from

beneath his brows. His Emperor only stroked his brief red beard and looked extremely grave, though Jaume could see the agony in his liege and kinsman's eyes. Melodía—

He had watched the color fade from his beloved's face by slow degrees as he had offered his account of the pursuit, the battles, and the Treb kidnappers' eventual escape with Montse, until her normal lovely cinnamon skin had gone the color of parchment. Now her features reddened in fury and tears began to leak from glaring dark-amber eyes.

"'Magic'?" a voice asked incredulously from behind his bowed bare back; he had presented himself before his Emperor ritually nude, to emphasize not reproof but abject submission.

He recognized the voice of María, Condesa Montañazul, widow of a man whom Jaume had bested in a joust for command of the Army of Correction, who had been a consistent thorn in his side on the following campaign and who had died upon defecting with the then Cardinal Tavares to Raguel's Horde at the Battle of Canterville. It rang with delightful silver contempt.

"He says he failed because of *magic*?"

She laughed. And one by one, voice by voice, a hundred other courtiers joined in.

"Your Highness! Wait!"

She stopped and spun back. She had been so crushed—and angry—that she had stamped out of the throne room without asking permission. A severe breach of protocol, but she suspected the Emperor would forgive her. *Not that it matters that much now*, she thought. *My sister's lost and my status is shit*.

Jaume strode toward her down the lesser passageway that led to the back stairs and the Imperial apartments.

A gaggle of courtiers fluttered behind the naked Champion, twittering like gaudy birds.

She pointed past him. "You," she told the gaudy hangers-on. "Leave."

They left. Much as they might disparage, or pretend to doubt, her fighting contribution to victory over Raguel's Horde, none of them felt like pressing their luck.

She glared around. The Palace servants who had been busy bustling up and down the corridor were nowhere to be seen.

"Melodía—" Jaume said, stopping a polite distance away.

"How *dare* you come back without my sister?" she raged at him before she could help herself. "Then tell some—some *fairy story* about magic."

"I wish I had a choice. I have spent at least half my moments, since the Sea Dragons and Will Oakheart fished me out of that filthy harbor, wishing they had never done so. And yes, I felt the same way about magic at first, too. And the Fae."

The word made her go cold. She recalled Pilar's last words, before Count Guillaume of Crève Coeur's pet horrors took her: *"The Fae sent me to watch over you, Princess. I've failed. May they protect you now."*

Could there be something other than mere excuse behind Jaume's words? she wondered.

"Have I ever made excuses for failure before?"

"Have you ever failed before? On this scale, I mean."

His long turquoise eyes looked devastated. "No. Not since I went out bandit hunting as a boy."

She felt a touch of pity for him. It quickly died. *I'm not interested in being placated just right now. I'm being mad.*

"But let me put it to you this way, my love—and still my love, regardless. You know I loved Montse, as your sister and my friend."

She nodded tautly. "You did. She always said you were the only person who treated her as an equal. An adult."

"And she loved and trusted me, as you and your father did. My Companions to a man followed me to save her despite the Emperor's forbidding it. Two of them died fighting to get your sister back. Do you think I or any of us would have come back without Montse had it not been impossible to rescue her?"

"I don't understand why the Sea Dragons didn't stop the ship," she said, aware that she was weakening her own grievance against Jaume by pointing out that at least he hadn't failed alone. Though he was still *El Condestable Imperial* and nominally responsible for lapses of those under his command. "Why their patrol boats couldn't stop it in the harbor. Or their galleys intercept it before it got too far from port."

"The Sea Dragons did send boats. They found their way blocked by hordes of uncooperative small craft—fishing vessels, dories, and the like. That sort of thing is far from uncommon. But not usually as pervasive as it was. The local commander suspects Trebizon sympathizers—and Trebizon gold. But neither aspect is practical to pursue. Golden Venture Bay is choked with traffic at the best of times. There's no identifying who was out on the water at that time, much less which weren't honest and merely in the way."

He pressed his lips together and frowned as if to muster his thoughts.

"If you don't believe in magic, then let's say the kidnappers had the Creators' own luck in the sudden strong wind blowing offshore—and the surprisingly violent squall which swallowed the fleeing cog from view almost at once. And when larger naval vessels—biremes—reached the area, they found a strong squadron of Trebizon Navy galleasses cruising back and just outside the harbor's mouth. The Sea Dragon squadron commander sent back for instructions; the Admiral replied that they were not to risk war by running afoul of a Trebizonés fleet. And I, as Constable of the Empire's forces, backed him in that. And still do."

The Sea Dragons would probably have lost had they tangled with the Trebs, anyway, Melodía knew. She was an avid student of Imperial history, especially its warfare. The Imperial navy was elite and proud—but the Treb navy was universally reckoned the best of all Aphrodite Terra, and possibly the world. The Sea Dragons were excellent. The Trebs were better. It wouldn't have stopped the Sea Dragons from taking them on, she knew. But— their admiral, and Jaume, were right. *Much as I hate to admit it to myself.*

Her eyes abruptly filled with tears. At the loss of her sister. At the loss of faith in her lover—her hero. At the unjustness of it all. "But don't you see? Your coming back with empty hands, and this, this ridiculous tale—it sounds that way, think of how it sounds, never mind what did or didn't happen. That destroys your credibility at court. And because I'm your betrothed, in all but name, it destroys mine."

"You're the Emperor's daughter!"

"Do you think the court's impressed with mere Imperial royalty? Many of them have seen Emperors and Empresses come and go. How much of what prestige my father even has with them rubs off on me? I can't even inherit the Throne; you know it doesn't work that way. And so I have to scratch and claw to get anyone to listen to me about—"

She stopped. It was as if she'd fallen out of a warm bed into a frigid Shield Mountains foothill stream. *I can't tell him no one will listen to me about Falk. He doesn't know what Falk did to me, either.*

And I can't tell him. He might challenge Falk on the

spot, and that—that would make my father look bad,
whatever happens. Worse than he does already.

Or, worst of all—he might not believe me, either.

I. Just. Can't.

"About stopping the war," she all but stammered. "This
war everybody—Falk and his frightful matadora
mother—keeps trying to talk my father into. Against
Trebizon, for my sister's kidnapping."

"I am so sorry, Melodía. That war must never happen.
I can't believe the Basileus is behind this crime, nor even
his son and heir, on whose behalf it was supposedly committed. The Trebs are famous for their plots, and that's
not wrong. And I think the Basileus is as much a target
of this one as Montse—or your father."

That made more sense to her than she cared for at the
moment. "Evidence?" she asked.

"None I can act upon, much less present before your
father." He shook his head, and she saw something in his
eyes and face she had never seen before, or ever thought
to. And now wished she never had: desperation.

"It might be better if I went away from Court for a
time," he said. "This war must be stopped. It would be a
disaster for the Empire, and for your father. And we've
just suffered one, and averted a worse. I'm afraid I'd do
more harm to your cause of trying to head it off by staying than help you."

She nodded. "You should go, in any event. And as for
my cause of stopping the war—right now, after what the
Trebs have done to my sister, I'm not even sure I want to!"

And she turned and walked quickly away before she
said another word.

PART Three

Malicious Intents

Chapter 22

Ángeles Grises, Los; Grey Angels, The; _Los Siete_, the Seven. . . . —The Creators' supernatural servitors: Michael, Gabriel, Raphael, Uriel, Remiel, Zerachiel, and Raguel, who are charged with maintaining sacred Equilibrium on Paradise. They possess remarkable powers and mystic weapons, and when they walk out in the world, they often take on a terrifying appearance. They are not humane, and regard all things as straw dogs.

—A PRIMER TO PARADISE FOR THE IMPROVEMENT OF YOUNG MINDS

here are alcoves inside the Imperial Heart, and then there are alcoves, thought Margrethe, Dowager Duchess von Hornberg, as she made her quiet and lonely way through the Imperial apartments in the milky afternoon light that spilled through the tall windows. *And this looks to be the right one.*

It was a plain oak door that might have led to an adjoining apartment or to a back passageway. The whole place was depressingly plain, as she had feared: a few feather tapestries showing hunts and battles, a few books, a desk with writing materials. The bed looked appropriately lavish in comfort, at least, being duly large and well stacked with fat satin cushions.

The key to open the plain door had cost her as much as a few minutes' unhindered access to the chambers. But it was only silver, of which she had much, and knew where to get more. It was expensive to buy a place in a game for these stakes; she well knew that.

But after the way of alcoves, it was neither wide nor deep. Yet the spillover light as she opened the door barely sufficed to reveal the outline of a figure sitting stooped on a stool with its back toward her and its hooded head slumped toward its chest.

For a moment, nothing happened. She waited. The figure started then. And rose—and rose. When it stood upright, the peak of its cowl almost brushed the three-meter-high ceiling.

It turned. "You do not belong here," it announced, in a voice both deep and doomful. Margrethe felt resolutely undoomed. "What do you think you are doing?"

"Well, the Emperor hasn't invited me here yet," she said. "But that's an oversight I'm pretty sure will soon be corrected. In the meantime, you might say I'm looking over the lay of the land. But mostly—I'm looking for you."

"This is a forbidden place. To enter is to die."

"One of many rules that do not apply to me." She squinted up at it. But it was no more than shadow within shadow. "Which one are you?"

"You have been warned." It raised its right arm.

She skipped back with an alacrity she knew belied her size. She liked being deceptively fast. She liked being deceptive.

"Here, now, lad. None of your Angel games."

The arm froze while still angled down. The sleeves of the hempen monk's robe were long and concealed the hands.

"Ah, I've got your attention, now, don't I? You're not Michael, certainly; he's too powerful and aloof, or likes to play that way. I know that much. You've played your part too long to be Raguel. Raphael? Come on, play along. Don't make me chant all seven of your names like a child's catechism."

"I am Uriel."

"Well met, Fire of God."

"How do you know these things?"

"The same way I got here. By knowing whom to ask, and what to ask—and perhaps most important, *how* to ask. Some questions are best tipped with silver, and others with steel. And others with things that I suspect you can't touch any more than I. *Fear*, for one.

"I know many things, and how to find out many more. I'm useful that way. And many more."

It lowered its head and seemed to study her. "You have an Artifact," it announced at last.

"I do." He meant the many-faceted jewel she wore on a chain inside her cream silk gown that appeared to be carved from nothing more noble than a lump of polished hematite. "Did you try some kind of mind-control trick on me? I reckoned you would."

"You have no conception of what that really is which you wear. It was originally crafted long ago, in a place you could not conceive."

"True."

"Where did a creature like you obtain such an item?"

"I know how to get people—and others—what they want. Or what they most desperately do not, depending on circumstances and, often enough, my whim. Mere *trade* is a vile and vulgar thing. But we more elevated souls still have needs and desires and, accordingly, may make exchanges. Which is another way of telling you that I'm not going to tell you."

"What do you want?"

"I told you—and, indeed, I've shown you. I am useful. You are powerful beyond imagining, and so on and so forth. We can help each other. I have . . . served the Grey Angels before. And they have helped me."

"How do I know I can trust you?"

"I can't hurt you in any way except to expose your masquerade, carefully built up and maintained for these many months. And as for that, who has more to offer me than you do?"

"Are you trying to blackmail me, woman?"

"That's such an ugly word. Let us say—truthfully, even—that I seek to come to terms whereby we cooperate to our mutual advantage. And given that I'm sure we can, your secret is safe with me, Fray Jerónimo."

"I consider this project a failure," Karyl said to the man he had made Count of Crève Coeur.

"How d'you reckon that?" Laurent, former Knight of Bois de Chanson, slouched at ease on a purple velvet cushion on his gaudy and improbable throne, its gilt flaking in spots to reveal bare wood, well set with red, green, blue, and clear gemstones, all probably paste. In his countly gown of blue, green, and silver silk, he seemed a perfect picture of decadence. But the hand that held a gilded goblet was hard and square, as was the scarred face beneath square-cut, dark-blond bangs. He looked more like a man of action than the sort of self-infatuated *grande* the place had been designed for.

As he was. With Laurent's former liege defeated and killed by what was then Karyl's Army of Providence at the Battle of Hidden Marsh, the new Countess that Karyl had installed in the unlamented Count Guillaume's place, and pretty much the county's entire aristocracy swept away by Raguel's Crusade, Duke Karyl had decided he was the best man available for the job.

"I was hired to spare Providence the horrors of war," Karyl said. He sat in a smaller, less pretentious chair set facing the Count on his dais in the domed, octagonal throne room. He wore a plain white linen blouse with black trousers and black jackboots with rolled tops. His sword-belt and scabbarded arming-sword he'd hung over its back. "As I hoped I'd done, on the battlefield and in securing the subsequent peace."

"On terms highly favorable to your employers, the Garden," said Laurent. Karyl did not feel he read people well—that was another thing he missed about Rob, having him serve as translator of sorts for what other people were feeling—but it seemed clear to him even so that Laurent was amused at the fact, not disapproving.

He shrugged. "They were, as you say, my employers. But I also hoped to spare the people of Crève Coeur a civil war, having seen off most of Guillaume's viable successors as well as Guillaume. I've seen too much devastation—wreaked too much myself—to want it visited on anyone unnecessarily. And yet—"

He shook his head. "Here we sit, with most of the city and much of the countryside lying in rubble, the fields stripped bare, and homes and shops leveled, regardless."

"Not even you could have known your employers were harboring an actual Grey Angel. Nor that he was grooming them to serve as the spear point for a Grey Angel Crusade. Not even Guilli suspected such a thing, and he was a man both wary as a cat at a Deinonychus synod and long-headed in intrigue, as the Northmen say." He tipped up his gilded goblet and tossed off the contents. "Even if he didn't know the difference between his ass and a posthole, in many ways."

"The Palace seems not to have suffered a lot of the Horde's insane vandalism," said Mora Selena, from the wall by the entryway. She wore a black springer-leather jerkin over a purple silk blouse with black trousers and boots like Karyl's. Her longsword, Tristeza, rode across her back with its hilt jutting above her right shoulder. Her garments were almost dark enough to let her blend almost completely into the shadows by the wall, except for her olive face, pale despite her nearness to the lamps set flanking the audience-chamber door. "Most places they looted bare of what they needed, and they destroyed the rest for the sheer exhilaration of it, or so it seemed."

"When Raguel appeared here," Laurent said, "just before He revealed himself in Providence, Countess Mara and her brave, noble retinue promptly fled. The castellan and servants she left behind bolted the Palace doors and took to the upper stories with crossbows. My former master may have tricked the place out like a whorehouse, but it was still well built to withstand attack. The Hordelings weren't big on siegecraft, even of a minor kind, and less on patience. They were easily discouraged by stout locked doors and a few quarrels through their pates and went off in search of victims easier to torture and dismember. Like the Countess and company, sadly."

He drained his cup and tossed it to a servant, who caught it cleanly, refilled it from a cut-glass decanter on a sideboard, and brought it back to the Count with a secret smile. Laurent thanked the woman with a nod.

"I don't blame her, at least," Karyl said. Mara had just come into Ladyship of a manor, when the consortium of merchants who'd won when Karyl auctioned off the countship left vacant by Guillaume's winding up with a steel-shod Triceratops horn poked through his belly had selected her to front for them. An amiable woman with the build and the placid demeanor of a barnyard Fatty, she had been selected because she had the most available pretense of birth to go with her complaisant nature. She had managed to enjoy the perquisites of figurehead reign for a matter of mere days before the Grey Angel Crusade flamed up to engulf her and her retainers before they reached the city walls.

"What happened to the wall hangings and paintings, if the Horde didn't ransack the Palace?" asked Selena. She gestured around the chamber. It was spacious, well supplied with tall, broad, round-topped windows, currently night-black. The marble walls between them and the eight half columns around the dome's base, though, remained conspicuously blank.

"Guillaume had a taste for pictures of Horrors hunting humans," Laurent said. "His favorite sport. Also pictures of Deinonychus and other dinosaurs fucking both men and women and not by their consent. For whatever reason, his successor never saw fit to remove them during her brief occupation. But while I'm no soft man, the damned things put me off my food. So I had them stored in the basement. Probably, I'll auction them off to whoever has the most debased tastes and exalted purse."

Karyl accepted a cup of pale local wine from a servant in blue-and-green tabard. It wetted his mouth and didn't taste conspicuously nasty. Which fulfilled his requirements for wine.

Selena pointed upward.

The Count's laughter followed her gesture and her gaze up the round vault of the ceiling above the throne. It was painted with a likeness of the late Count Guilli, naked except for glory, being borne up into the eternal daytime clouds, presumably to the abode of the Creators Themselves in the Moon Invisible, by a gaggle of winged pink babies, likewise nude. They were creatures that featured nowhere in Church canon yet frequently found their way into religious art. No doubt because they looked a great deal more appealing than Grey Angels in their natural Paradisiacal guise of tall grey corpses dried out midrot—as Karyl had seen for himself at the closest possible range.

"Oh," Laurent said. "That. It amuses me. Especially since the erstwhile Count's cock is substantially larger up there than eyewitness accounts by his playmates made it."

"I wouldn't want it dangling over *my* head," said Selena. She spoke flatly. Laurent cocked his brow quizzically at her. Karyl thought she had a sense of humor but was never sure when she might be showing it.

"You wonder why I haven't had it painted over?" Laurent said. "I do admire the art of it. And I'm thinking of having my own mug painted in place of Guilli's."

"You don't seem a man for that kind of vanity," Karyl said.

Laurent grinned. "You don't think you're the only one who's full of surprises, do you?" He gulped more wine. "Ah, well. To business, then. As to how things go here, I have news both good and bad."

"The good, then," Karyl said.

"So far dealing with refugees isn't much of a problem. Especially since news came that the promised Imperial food-aid trains have been dispatched. Meantime, woodsrunners from Telar's Wood in the eastern part of the province have been sharing their provisions with us. Raguel didn't have much luck recruiting the Free Folk, I gather, and his Horde preferred open fields to dense forests of hardwood and pine, where they could be subjected to the sort of unremitting rolling ambush the foresters specialize in."

Laurent shook his head. "I never expected to live to see the woods-rats and the farmers and townsfolk acting in perfect harmony. I'm glad I never indulged in Guillaume's passion for hunting them like bouncers."

The fact that Laurent hadn't joined in commiting atrocities against the woods-runners was a significant reason he'd made it home to Crève Coeur alive after

Karyl released him on parole. Which he knew as well as Karyl did.

"That is good. And the bad?"

Laurent sighed. "The *reason* we don't have a vast number of refugees to deal with. The fact is, the loss of life here was far greater than anybody even feared. It was truly terrible. We find skeletons everywhere we turn, it seems."

Though corpses didn't decompose as quickly in the relatively cool and arid foothills of the great Shield Range as they did in the coastal swamps and rain forests, the foraging wildlife—the insects, small mammals, fliers, and dinosaurs—were no less rapacious here.

"It's as bad everywhere we know of that the Crusade overran," Karyl said. "Worse, in the eastern sector of Providence. There we can't find evidence of a single living human soul."

"In Castaña the Horde carried the dismembered bodies of its victims as provisions and ate from them until the meat rotted from the bones," Selena said in a hollow voice. "I don't even know why they bothered. They always had new victims."

An uncomfortable pause ensued.

"Ah. Aren't you a cheerful sort, Lady?" Laurent said. "It's a good thing you're decorative."

"She's deft with that longsword, as well," Karyl said.

Laurent pulled a mouth beneath his moustache and nodded. "High praise indeed, from the Master who fought a Grey Angel."

"And lost," Karyl said.

"But not at once. And that's more than even any hero out of legend has been able to boast."

Karyl nodded briskly. Such lines of talk made him uncomfortable. They also struck him as unproductive.

"Another complication," said Laurent, "is that many of

our refugees, whether returnees or folk displaced from elsewhere, are former members of the Horde itself. Perhaps most of them."

"That's not causing us too great a problem in Providence," Karyl said. "The ones who were maddened by the touch of Raguel's mind suffer mostly some degree of disorientation, but seem to be recovering."

"Ah, but we find a certain number of ours fall first into confusion, and then into a lassitude in which they display similar indifference to hunger, thirst, or pain to what they did when they ran with the Crusade. Fortunately, instead of resuming their frenzied killing ways they simply decline and die in a matter of days. Sometimes hours."

"Our investigations indicate that such victims tend to be the ones who required the least compulsion to join Raguel," Karyl said. "Or none at all."

The Emperor had decreed that all those survivors of the Horde who could not be demonstrated to have joined of their own free will should receive full pardon, with more than a little latitude allowed for the fact that many had been faced with a choice of, *Join or be eaten alive or torn limb from limb.* Karyl had concurred in Felipe's amnesty. He despised unnecessary slaughter almost as much as he did cruelty.

Those who had joined voluntarily and without coercion—and there were more than a few, disproportionately noble *grandes*—the Emperor had placed under attainder, with all property and rights forfeit—including the right to life. Any man or woman could kill one such without penalty. For himself, Karyl did not consider slaughtering them unnecessary at all. Merely not top priority.

Laurent nodded. "Small loss. I'm not most comforted by the fact of what these people were up to last month, but we make shift with what we've got. A greater problem, now, is the marauders. It seems a lot of Raguel's surviving knights House-shields find it hard to let go of broadcast pillage and murder. We—"

The color drained from his face, and his green eyes grew wide. His features continued to grow paler, and it took Karyl a moment to register that was because they were lit by a harsh blue-white radiance from somewhere behind Karyl, growing like the light of an approaching forest fire.

The empty goblet fell from Laurent's fingers. He pointed past Karyl's left shoulder and began to gibber in mindless horror.

Chapter 23

Horror, Chaser. . . . —*Deinonychus antirrhopus.* Nuevaropa's largest pack-hunting raptor: 3 meters, 70 kilograms.
Plumage distinguishes different breeds: scarlet, blue,
green, and similar horrors. Smart and wicked, as favored
as domestic beasts for hunting and war as wild ones are
feared. Some say a *deinonychus* pack is deadlier than a
full-grown *Allosaurus.*

—THE BOOK OF TRUE NAMES

y dearest darling Melodía, she read in Princess Fanny of Anglaterra's fussily precise
hand by the white light of a pine-oil lamp. She
preferred those to the sea-monster oil or Trebizon ground-
oil burners more prevalent in La Merced. All three were
fragrant; the pine oil at least smelled nice.

It was late night in her apartment high in the Imperial
heart. She sat at the small writing desk beneath the open
window. The large courtyard, really a village unto itself,
was alive with orange lantern glow and the sounds of
music, laughter, and conversation. She knew some occupants of the Palace proper found that to be a disturbance and an affront. But it all reassured her, somehow.

It gives me the comforting illusion I'm not isolated and all alone here in this eerie old aerie.

Even though I am.

She had written to Fanny asking after her absent friends. She had gotten the reply this morning. She'd put off opening it until now. In part, because she felt obligated to stay by her father's side as much as possible as he continued to struggle, politically as well as personally, with Montse's abduction. In part, in the hope of restoring her spirit after another day of behind-hand sniggering and condescending looks at Court.

Belatedly, it occurred to her the news from the Firefly Palace might not exactly raise her morale. But she reminded herself of the warm feeling even surrogate contact with her best friend gave her.

We all think it's outrageous that anyone doubts either your courage or your contributions to the war against the Crusade. We all knew you had a strong, fierce spirit, waiting to be set free. It still saddens us that you had to undergo such awful things to get a chance to show it.

We've even heard accounts, which only Fina really credits, that you fought and defeated a dinosaur knight in single combat, mounted on your dear Meravellosa. For my part, I hope that's not true. I know it was war, and war's a risky business—to sound even more obtuse than I am. But that would have been desperate indeed.

Melodía had to pause to blink back tears. It was true—all of it. Of course, the dinosaur knight in question had been desperately unwilling to fight—above all, against her. He had been her father, her mentor, her lover, and eventually her betrayer when she sought shelter from her cruel exile at the Garden of Beauty and Truth in Providence. But he had suffered punishment enough to suit even her no-longer-very-forgiving nature after his secret master, Raguel, betrayed *him*—publicly breaking him to the Grey Angel's control and degrading him before compelling his body to commit horrid crimes even as his mind rebelled.

Bogardus had managed, at the cost of enormous pain, to open his visor to the cast of Melodía's last javelin— and had received absolution and mercy in the form of death at her hand. But before that his remotely operated husk and the sackbut they rode had tried with purpose and skill to kill her. She had come closer to death then than even when she faced Count Guillaume's pet Horror pack, who had hunted down and dismembered the peace delegation she led from the Garden, and murdered her maidservant and friend Pilar before her eyes.

Your example has actually inspired Lupe and Llurdis to enter training to be dinosaur knights.

Melodía shook her head at that. Jaume and her baby sister Montse both adored dinosaurs; she felt nothing but disdain for the great, ungainly, smelly beasts. Give her a fine horse any day—and there were none finer than her mare Meravellosa. As for becoming a dinosaur knight, Melodía would rather strap on three-quarter armor and push a pike in the line—as her father had done in his youth in Alemania.

Josefina Serena badly wants to train as one as well, but her father remains obdurate against it. Prince Harry dotes on her, and that might be the poor child's problem. His love scarcely lets her breathe.

And speaking of Fina Serenita returns me to your questions: we have found tantalizing hints about Falk's conduct here, but as yet nothing concrete. Abi has taken to the task like a hound to a fresh trail, predictably. And less predictably, Josefina Serena is proving as avid and not that much less effective as her assistant. Although I suppose the poor girl has always craved stimulation.

I've spoken to some of our allies on the Palace serving staff, who remain in shock and mourning for Claudia's dreadful murder. There is no question she died a heroic death trying to protect our beloved Montse. The Prince himself eulogized her courageous sacrifice at her funeral, though I suspect his desire to express his rage against the wicked Trebs for violating his hospitality in such a remarkably comprehensive manner played a part in his doing so. But we knew she was a heroine, did we not?

In any event, they report that a rather ill-favored northerner named Bergdahl found employment on the Palace staff soon after Falk's dramatic arrival at court here. He left when Falk did, and reports from some of the veterans who speak so glowingly of your own actions claim he was Falk's personal servant. He is not fondly remembered by the staff here. His temper matched his visage, it seems; and he had to be reproved repeatedly for attempting to make free with the female serving-maids. More alarmingly, Fina—of all people—has unearthed whispers from the dock district that he's suspected of murdering a prostitute who worked the streets there.

(It may be that we all have grievously underestimated our Little Serene One. I personally blame her propensity for falling into fits of disconsolate weeping at the drop of a hat, or at that selfsame hat's neglecting to drop. But I'm probably trying to deflect blame from my own shallowness.)

I find it disquieting to learn that the vile Duke von Hornberg's mother has appeared on the scene there *in La Majestad. We all warn you to guard yourself well against that one. Abigail Thélème's father in particular has sent warnings against her—both her cunning and what he terms, "rumored dark connections." As to what that latter bit means, I feel it might be impious, even by my scandalously unobservant standards, to speculate. But I think there's no question as to what Abi's father issuing that warning means.*

That reined Melodía in hard. Abi's father, Roger, was an Imperial Elector and ruler of Sansamour, an archduchy whose semiautonomous status was widely held to be euphemistic cover for functional independence from the Francés crown. Archduke Roger was the Empire's most notorious intriguer. Widely known as "Roger the Spider," he was even said to be able to beat the Trebs, reputed master intriguers of all Aphrodite Terra, at their own game. Although the clumsy brutality of their kidnapping of her baby sister made Melodía wonder if that reputation was based on anything but air.

But what can he mean about "darker connections"? Melodía wondered. It was whispered that Archduke Roger treated with the Fae—an act of treason against the Creators Themselves, and the only religious crime punishable by death, according to their *Books of the Law*. She did not want to think about what that might imply.

And speaking of such things, Fina—again—tells us that the whole Sea Dragon base here in La Merced is agog at reports from their comrades in Laventura. They claim it was magic that stopped the Count Jaume and his Companions from rescuing your sister on the waterfront there, and that nothing else could account for what the officers and marines who helped them witnessed. We don't know what to make of that—

other than that your dear one told the truth about why
he and his men failed, improbable as that may seem.

She put the letter on the table before her and drew a deep breath of the mountain night air, which seemed to be flowing down the face of the peak like a cool and invisible companion to El Salto, bringing the scents of sage and sun-warmed stone. The stories vindicating her role in the war, and Jaume's conduct in Laventura, had arrived at La Majestad as well, through equally unimpeachable messengers. To Melodía's sick frustration, it did no good. All anyone wanted to remember was the way everyone laughed at Jaume's story of magical intervention causing him to fail to rescue the Emperor's daughter.

Her tormentor's hand was in that, of course. Or his mother's. The warning from Archduke Roger chilled her blood. *What chance do I have against that kind of malice and skill? I don't know anything about intrigue. I proved that in La Merced—and Providence.*

Outside in the yard, a woman's voice sang a lament about her lover abandoning her. But it ended with a laugh at once bitter and joyous, and a verse about how she was better off free of the useless blot. It hit Melodía with a jolt to realize it was a song penned by Rob Korrigan himself. She wondered how he was doing as Baron. She suspected he wouldn't be happy.

It was better than thinking how her lover, Jaume, whom she had spurned after the others laughed at him, asked the Emperor's permission to withdraw from court for a time. Felipe had granted it; he had a forgiving nature for those who didn't do him intentional harm and, deep down, always trusted his nephew and Champion to be telling the truth of why he hadn't brought back Montse.

But I doubted him. And I wouldn't look him in the eye

before he turned and walked out of the audience chamber. Is he better off without me, too?

She took a sip of her still vaguely warm *yerba buena* tea to sooth her nerves and picked up Fanny's letter once more.

And what can we call improbable now that we know Grey Angel truly walked the world and took the field against the Empire—and was defeated? Many of the Life-to-Come zanies lament your father's victory there, but, as for me, I can't regret my life and the lives of everyone I cherish being saved, even if it took an act of defiance against the gods. And for his part, our new Pope, Leo Victor, has issued an encyclical to the effect that Raguel's Crusade (even now, I can hardly believe I'm writing such a fantastic phrase!) was meant as a trial of our Empire's continued right to survive and your father's right to lead it, and that apparently defeating a Grey Angel Crusade, far from an act of unimaginable blasphemy, displayed their worthiness and thus secured the Creators' divine favor. Which even I find more than a trifle dubious. But the alternative would be to excommunicate not just the Emperor but the entire Empire, so I suppose we should all simply heave a sigh of relief that his Holiness was able to concoct something even that plausible.

I run long, my dear friend. Apologies! I am pouring out my sorrow, all our sorrow, that we are still forbidden to join you there in that creepy old crack in the wall above La Majestad and that you have to face the calumnies of the Unspeakable Hornbergs and their minions alone. We only hope your father will repent and let us come to be with you.

I also am trying, I suppose, to make up for the paucity of real news of import. We all wish for nothing

more than to find the evidence that will at last allow
you to name and shame your attacker, hero of the
moment though he be.

   Please know that we will never stop until we find
something which can help you. And that we love you,
and miss you. And that I love you and miss you, and
long to be with you again, my Princess and friend.

Signed,
Frances Mary Martin, Princess of Anglaterra

And she appended three little hand-drawn heart sym-
bols, in her characteristic overly romantic and even child-
like way.

And that at last cracked Melodía's reserve. Tears
flooded her cheeks, so hard and fast she barely twitched
the paper aside in time to keep it from getting spotted.
Because she loved and missed her friends, Fanny in
particular, now more than ever. And because she had
underestimated them all, as she had Pilar—and because
she remembered too keenly how she had killed Pilar
with her own unthinking folly.

What disaster will I bring upon their loving, helpful,
innocent heads? And she recalled Karyl, paralyzed by
the scorpion sting of depression on the retreat before the
irresistible Grey Angel Horde, talking to her in his tent
about how his own actions seemed only to bring false triumph and the deaths of loved ones. And she wept like a
broken child.

Chapter 24

Montador, Montadora—To honor knights we give them the title of *Montador* or *Montadora*, meaning a man or woman who rides in battle, on horse or dinosaur. Usually we call them *Mor* or *Mora* for short.

—A PRIMER TO PARADISE FOR THE IMPROVEMENT OF YOUNG MINDS

Karyl spun.

Where behind him had been a blank wall a patch of dazzling blue-white light grew larger and larger. Its irregularity reminded him of lichen on a rock. He put up his right hand with fingers barely spread and peered between them to cut the glare.

The room filled with a sulfurous reek like a gas bubble bursting from a fumarole.

On the far side of the door from the terrible glow, Selena had drawn her longsword and held it ready in hands so taut they looked as if the bones would rip through the skin. Karyl felt terribly aware of the futility of the arming-sword whose hilt he was clutching with his left hand.

"No," he called sharply, as a shape began to warp and flow and resolve within the blaze. "You can't hurt it with that. Stand back!"

He saw her brow lower mutinously. But she stepped back, though she kept the sword up before her.

The seethe of not quite form within the radiance began to take fleeting shapes: A burning tree. A blade. A seven-pointed star. A featureless human-like head with bizarre heavy horns curling from either side.

And very suddenly, it became the face of a beautiful woman, her thin inhuman features molded intimately in fire. Hair danced about the face like silver flames. The eyes were canted narrow ovals of intolerable brilliance. It was almost as tall, he reckoned, as he was.

"Who are you?" he demanded. "What do you want?"

He keenly felt the absence of his staff-sword. He wore a sword when he traveled in official capacity, for the plain reason that a warrior-noble of his station—not to mention reputation—was expected to. To do otherwise would excite suspicion. Which he currently saw no reason to care about on its own merits, but the sword's absence was liable to put people on their guard or, at the least, make them difficult to deal with.

But then, while he knew that weapon could deal with otherworldly menaces, he wasn't sure it could deal with this one.

The figure opened its mouth. Its tongue was another blinding flame. "Why, Karyl," it said, "is that any way to greet your benefactor?"

"That's not what I'm seeing before me," he said.

"Oh, but it is."

The blue-fire face, which had appeared flat and flush with the wall, dissolved once more into a featureless glare and poured itself into the center of the room. In a flash it turned into a floor-to-dome flame pillar.

The fire went out. In its place stood what looked like a woman.

But not quite. The eyes remained white fire. The skin was unnaturally pale, ears and chin pointed. She was thin and nearly as tall as Raguel, over two meters, which made her look attenuated. Wisps of light, constantly moving and changing color, surrounded her. Her body, sporadically revealed beneath, was also like that of a human woman, and nude.

"You still haven't identified yourself," Karyl said.

"Haven't I? Who else would I be but Uma, the Faerie Queen?"

The name shot through Karyl like an ice-cold blade. *I've heard the name before. But was it ever from human lips?*

Selena took a step toward the apparition, though her whole body was visibly trembling so hard it seemed likely at any second to shake itself apart like a wooden toy knight.

"Tighten your dog's leash, Karyl," the creature who called herself Uma said. "You do not want me to."

"Selena," he said, using the tone not of a liege to a vassal knight but of master to pupil. Which he was; despite misgivings, for his last attempt had turned out poorly for his student, he had begun teaching her his own skill at arms. "Stand down. Now."

She shook herself one last time—like a wet dog for a fact—then stepped back from the blazing apparition and lowered her longsword.

Uma took a step toward Karyl. "You fear me?"

"With every fiber of my being."

"And yet you don't draw your own sword."

"It wouldn't do me any good."

She laughed. "You do have wisdom, for one so shortly lived and puny. And recently so helplessly dependent. Am I right?"

"I don't know." *I don't want to.*

"And now you need me more than ever, Karyl Vladevich, and I you. You look shocked. Does it surprise you that I know your patronymic?"

"You're a magical being who shouldn't even exist. I've no idea what you can and can't do. I'm lost here."

"You are! You don't know how lost. You're the one who shouldn't be. It's only I and my kind who belong on this world! We who existed before your precious Creators perverted our planet, our home, to make it an abode for their"—her voice rose in a contemptuous wave—"meat toys."

"I don't know anything about this. Take it up with the Creators, if you have a grievance with them."

"Oh, we have, Karyl dear. We have. Haven't you ever heard of the Demon War?"

"Of course. And of course I believed it to be a mere legend, to give a gloss of divine approval to entirely mundane political murder on a major scale. It feels as if it's becoming trite to say *I disbelieved this or that*, but there it is."

"And you also thought it ended? No. We suffered defeat, yes. But it was a mere setback in our struggle to reclaim our world. But we will win. We shall! However long it takes, we will have what is rightfully ours again."

"I'm hearing blasphemy," Selena croaked.

"We're all having a trying day, Mora," Karyl said. He glanced back over his shoulder. Laurent had his sandaled feet up on the seat cushion of the brummagem throne, both arms wrapped around his knees and the fingers of one hand in his mouth. His eyes were circles of nothing but terror.

He turned back to the glowing presence and wished he had the luxury of giving in to his own terror. Whose very origin he feared to contemplate.

"Your plan would necessarily seem to entail the destruction of all humankind," he said. "Myself included. Why should I help you?"

She smiled. "Because I am your only chance to keep

the humans from being wiped out immediately. And because you love me."

He opened his mouth. Yet somehow he could not deny it. Any more than he could deny the vein-bursting fear she inspired in him.

Uma spread her arms. "I leave you now to contemplate what I have said. Someday you shall embrace me as your mother and your lover. But now I shall make you wait."

She blazed into white light so intense he had to look away.

The hideous glare flicked out, leaving him blinking away great orange balls of light that seemed the only illumination in utter blackness.

"What was that?" Selena asked.

"In candor, your guess is as good as mine," said Karyl.

"But it was—it was a Faerie?"

"Yes. They're real. It seems everything is real, and nothing may be true. As to it being their Queen, I didn't think they were the sort to suffer such. But I could be wrong about that too."

"To traffic with the Fae is death."

He shrugged. "I've been under death sentence before."

I've died *before*, he thought. But for some reason feared to say as much, though he'd made light of it in the past. That was to Rob, with whom he felt more easy speaking his mind. But he doubted he'd make the same joke now, even to the closest thing he had to a best friend.

"You get used to it. But this"—he gestured at the spot where the thing had stood—"I'm not so sure about."

"Your Grace." The voice from behind quavered so much that he barely recognized it.

"Yes." He turned.

Laurent had his feet on the dais, at least, though his

face was still whiter than Karyl could readily credit it getting, and his eyes remained saucers.

"I . . . I resign my Countship. My cowardice there proved that I'm unworthy of my spurs, much less rule of a province. If you choose to take my life, I won't resist."

A corner of his moustache quirked up to a brief lopsided almost smile. His color was coming back, and it brought with it at least a shard of his usual insouciance.

"Not that it would do me any good."

Karyl shook his head once, briskly. "Impossible. Denied. I need you here."

"But my cowardice just now! I've shown I'm not fit to rule."

"As to whether anyone's fit for that, I have my doubts. In any event, you rule here, and I rule over you, and what I rule is that here you stay."

"But—"

Karyl raised his left hand slightly. "Enough. There's work here I need you to do, and fighting the Fae isn't any part of it."

Laurent bowed his head. "Why did you even appoint me, Your Grace? The first you saw of me, I was your enemy, and if your damned woods-runners and light riders hadn't caught me by surprise, I'd have helped to serve you so much dirt it might have choked you."

"You struck me as a capable man, and honorable for a man of your station. When it came time to pick someone to run Crève Coeur, Rob found no one who could offer eyewitness testimony that you had committed rape or murder, even under Guillaume. And by then I had the evidence of your ability and character from your service with my army."

Laurent raised his face enough to show Karyl an upraised brow. "You recognized me the first time you saw me, didn't you?"

"Of course. Blacking your hair, beard, and brow didn't

do anything to change your scar, nor your eyes." Rob had caught it too, within a day or so of Laurent's joining the Fugitive Legion in Métairie Brulée, right before their one-sided battle with the ill-advised—and ill-fated—Countess Célestine. Or rather Stéphanie the woods-runner had. She had been the one to bring the captive enemy knight before the Garden Council, as they sat in judgment on charges Rob and Karyl had betrayed the army to its defeat at Guillaume's hand at the Blueflowers battle. Her eye was at least as keen as Karyl's.

"You know everyone under your command, don't you?"

"Given time, and a sufficiently modest army. I still don't know everyone who had joined us by Canterville. Nowhere close. At the end that force was at least twice as great as any I've commanded."

"But I violated my parole," Laurent said. "I swore on my life and honor that if I ever returned to Providence, they both would be forfeit."

Laurent, Karyl had learned from him after Raguel's fall, had stayed out of Guillaume's fight at the *Marais Caché*, in accordance with the terms of his parole to Karyl. He had been in Crève Coeur town when Raguel's Cru-sade erupted and had barely escaped with his life. After several days of dodging the divinely crazed marauders, he had crossed the Lisette back into Providence, reason-ing that if he was arrested for violating his parole, Karyl would kill him far more quickly and cleanly than the Horde was going to. Hard a man as he was, he had seen things to leave him soul sick and shaken.

A *caballero,* a horse-mounted knight rather than a dinosaur rider, Laurent had enlisted anonymously with Karyl's now Fugitive Legion hours after it had crossed into Métairie Brulée. On the brink of battle with Count-ess Célestine's army, no one had been in a mood to ques-tion a prospective recruit with his own harness and war-horse and the build and well-scarred visage of a man who knew how to use them. Horse chivalry was reckoned of far less worth than dinosaur knights, anyway, although they played important parts in battle.

"I judged all such vows and warrants were voided by the Grey Angel Crusade," Karyl said. "Circumstances had changed. The *world* had changed."

He turned to Selena, who had put away her sword and was leaning against the wall as if she needed its help to stay standing.

"I've seen worse."

"The presence of the . . . uncanny unmans me," Laurent said. He heaved himself off the throne and tottered from the dais and across the marble floor to pour himself wine. If any servants had been around to witness the advent of Uma, they had fled. "Seeing Raguel in the flesh, or whatever he was made of, almost turned me to a eunuch then and there, and I never saw him closer than a thousand meters off."

"Fighting against the Fae is no part of your job," Karyl said.

Laurent held a goblet up to Karyl, who shook his head. Wine and herbs had long since proved false friends in dealing with the recurring pain of the dent in his skull Falk had given him at the Hassling or with the nightmares that periodically woke him screaming. Whose terrors seemed to cluster nearer to him now than ever before in waking life. Intoxicants did little to dull the edge of torments of body or mind but did erode the steel self-control he needed to keep himself from doing things not even he could live with.

Laurent proffered the cup to Selena. After a moment she caught Karyl's eye. He nodded. With an air of almost puppyish gratitude she walked briskly to Laurent, accepted the goblet, and drank.

"How did you face it so bloody calmly?" Laurent asked Karyl. "First, Raguel, now that—that *thing*?"

"With Raguel I saw little choice. He threatened my army—he threatened everybody. Someone had to act. So I did. But here—"

He shook his head.

"I have no idea."

"I knew you'd come," said Karyl, as soon as the door shut on the servants who had ushered him into his bedchamber for the night.

"And here I am," said Aphrodite, the sorceress and ageless Witness. And if he believed what she told him when she visited him after Raguel's fall, Paradise itself. Or at least its spirit.

"I'm tired," he said. "I know that the instant I close my eyes, the worst of the nightmares—the laughing inhuman faces, the ecstasy and pain, alike intolerable—will find me again. But still I need what sleep I can get after that. So please tell me what you can tell me, or will, and go."

She shook her head. She wore her usual cowl, but with the hood hanging behind her short hair.

"I wish you would stop treating me like an enemy, Karyl," she said. "I really am on your side."

"I accept that," he said, grudgingly. "But I don't know what you are. So I don't know why you're on my side. Nor what you want from me."

"It is simple: I need a champion. You, of all men and women here and now, have proven yourself best qualified."

"Really?" She was right that he didn't like asking questions for anything other than information. But the word was practically forced from his mouth by the pressure of his skepticism.

She waved a pale hand at him.

He sighed. "Point taken. I'm here. Very well: what was that creature?"

"What she said, amazingly enough. She is Uma, the Faerie Queen."

"But legend has it the Fae are hardly the sort to accept another's dominion. Or, really, even their own."

"That is true. But their behavior is truly unpredictable. She is one of the strongest among them. She also has the gift, almost unique for a Faerie, of possessing the capacity to form and follow a fixed purpose. She plans. That itself augments her power greatly."

"So those she can't overpower directly, she outplots."

"Precisely. Or at least that is the closest we can come to understanding their nature and their doings. They are truly and profoundly alien, no less to myself and the Grey Angels than to you."

"I thought you knew everything. And understood everything."

She laughed. It was so unexpected it came close to shocking Karyl. Even after everything he'd experienced in the past weeks and the past few minutes.

"I know much," she said, "and I understand much. But I am not omniscient by any means. And most of what I truly understand is involved with the business of keeping the world and those upon it, plants as well as animals, alive. That is why I spent so long observing human affairs, especially human conflict: to gain a measure of understanding of you. And in doing so, I have come to achieve a marked degree of affection for you."

"So what does she want from me?"

"I cannot say for certain. Or even make a good guess, given that 'certainty' and the Fae are incompatible. She no doubt is keenly aware that you and she share a common foe."

"The Grey Angels."

"Yes. For both them and the Fae, the Demon War never really ended. They just left—mostly—the physical plane of existence, and now battles are waged in the World Below."

"I take it that's a metaphor."

"In a way. In a way it is literal. Please do not ask me to expand."

"I won't. I have rather more urgent questions to ask. What do the Grey Angels plan to do to us?"

"For some, who call themselves the Purifications, to destroy you utterly. Raguel is one of them; and His attempt having been defeated by you and Shiraa—and do not deny your own part in the victory—it becomes the Preservationists' turn to try. They believe that it is only necessary to prune humanity back drastically to save what they conceive of as the Equilibrium of Paradise, rather than eradicate it of you."

"That's humane of them."

"Not in the slightest. You surely gathered from that that they still want to kill almost all of you?"

"I spoke sarcastically."

"Forgive me. I have little experience in dealing with humans, face-to-face."

"Except for doomed men and women, to whom you feel safe in revealing yourself as the Witness, since they'll never tell anybody." That was how they'd met, when Aphrodite had confronted Karyl as he fled naked and wounded from the aftermath of the Battle of Gunters Moll.

"Yes. The Grey Angels' nature might surprise you in its similarity to your own."

"That doesn't do much to comfort me."

"You are wise. But their interests are simply in no way congruent to your own. Concepts such as 'humane' or even 'inhuman' are as inapplicable to them as they are to the Fae."

"So you're thinking Uma wants me as an ally?"

"It seems likely."

"What good can I or any human do, much less for the likes of her? You tell me the Grey Angels will continue to try to wipe us out and cannot be killed."

"I did not say that."

"No. But you said the Fae had fought them for centuries. Have they succeeded in killing a Grey Angel."

She hesitated. "No."

"Then what can I or any of us do?"

"You have already thwarted a Grey Angel Crusade. That has never happened before. Not I, nor they, can truly predict what you might be able to do to them. You as a species—and you, Karyl, as an individual."

"Why didn't Raguel just wave his hand and make an end of all of us there on the battlefield? Or make an end of all of us, everywhere, if that was his intention?"

"Did Raguel display that kind of power on the field of Canterville?"

"No. And I've no idea why. He controlled the thoughts of tens of thousands of people."

"Over a hundred thousand. But he influenced their emotions, rather than controlled what they thought."

"Still, I cannot truly conceive of such power; I can only know that I witnessed it. Church canon tells us they are the Creators' own mystical avengers. What limits their power?"

"The same thing that limits mine. They, too, are subject to a geas. Even though they have warped the Creators' clear mandate to preserve the Equilibrium of Paradise to mean they must eliminate you, there are distinct limits which they dare not pass as to what actions they can take directly against you."

"I take it you mean 'dare not,' rather than 'cannot.'"

"You take my meaning correctly. There is a line for me. There is another line for them. For either of us to cross that line would mean our instant death. Our permanent extinction, not an inconvenience like the destruction of Raguel's avatar."

She stepped back and raised her hood to hide her features in shadow. "And now I have said all I dare for the moment. I cannot control your dreams, dear Karyl, but I can offer my true wish that they treat you kindly tonight."

She stepped back into shadow and was gone.

"They won't," he said, with a hand wave at the air. "But thanks for the thought."

Chapter 25

Titán trueno, Thunder-titan—*Apatosaurus louisae*. Giant quadrupedal plant-eating dinosaur, 23 meters long, 23 tonnes. Nuevaropan native. Placid and oblivious like all titans, Apatosaurus' sheer size renders it a danger to life and property, especially in herds.

—THE BOOK OF TRUE NAMES

"If you poke those bloody great beasts with those sticks," Rob shouted from Nell's back to the score of peasants of various ages who stood in the road holding long, pointy poles and gazing apprehensively at the Thunder-titan herd browsing on their crops half a kilometer away, "and they find out about it, you've thrown yourselves headfirst into a cesspit of trouble." A somewhat larger group of locals stood a safe distance back from the makeshift militia, watching from the sides of the road and irrigation ditches.

Tertre Herbeux was mostly flat, dotted with low round hillocks like the one the manor perched on, a little over a kilometer to the northeast, which gave the place its name. It was greener here than most of Providence, all of which in turn was greener than most of La Meseta. A trio of fliers flapped by to the west, big looking but not big enough to be called dragons, and hence a bother.

"Who's this lout?" demanded a stout, red-faced farm woman in a hemp smock, with a red rag tied about her head and some kind of long crimson feather sticking up out of it. "And on such an ungainly, ugly beast."

"My Lord," said Bergdahl, who rode alongside Rob on a great strider more villainous-looking than he, with blue body feathers, a yellow rough, and a tuft of oddly pink feathers sprouting from the top of its head. Its eyes seemed never to look in the same direction. "It is customary for a nobleman to have his House-soldiers whip any peasants who address him in such a disrespectful way. Before or after tearing their tongue out."

"But I don't have House-shields, or House-archers, either. Nor do I need any mailed mercenary bully-boys or girls to do my lout-thumping for me, should thumping be required."

The woman's hazel eyes narrowed, then widened considerably. "You're the new baron."

"Guilty," Rob said. "The very one you sent to have pulled out of his nice warm bed on a fine summer morning to save your homes and livelihoods, so. Those two there, in fact—they were the ones who fetched me." And he pointed to an adolescent boy and girl, familiar-looking despite the conical straw hats pulled low in front of their eyes. They were sidling off into the fields as if hoping to blend into the bean sprouts.

Though I don't look any too baronial, and that's a natural fact. He wore a springer-leather vest laced up the front, not so tightly as to hide the rusty fur on his chest, short breeches, and buskins, topping off the whole ensemble with a battered brown slouch hat to keep the sun from his eyes. The sun up here in the shadow of the Shields, clearly visible on the eastern horizon even here at the far end of Providence, seemed to sting more than it did in the lowlands, even though it was cooler here as a general rule. He wondered if the clouds, being closer, filtered less of the sun.

I'd regret not throwing a feather yoke over my shoulders before saddling up Nell, he thought, *but my head still throbs so hard from last night's merriment I'm ecstatic I can keep my saddle. I can hardly believe even I put away that much beer and Laventura sack.* Bergdahl knew an astonishing number of limericks in Anglés and Spañol, of equally astonishing obscenity. More surprising, he knew bawdy songs Rob had never heard, which he claimed came from Alemania and the isles of the Northmen beyond across the sea. Perhaps greatest wonder of all, he sang with a marvelous fine basso that Rob himself might envy.

"I see no need for thumpings, though," he said as he rode up to the farmers, who now seemed unsure which they should be alarmed of more, the mammoth dinosaurs lumbering toward their homes and livelihood or this outlandish new lord of the manor. "Anyone can make a mistake. I will even own that I've spoken in less than obsequious tones to gentle folk in my own time. But anyone who dares imply that Little Nell is a whit less noble than a sackbut fit for the Emperor Felipe himself— we're on speaking terms, you know—to ride to war shall answer to the fists of Rob Korrigan. Uh, Baron of Tertre Herbeux. Me."

And, reining Little Nell, he also scratched her neck in a way he knew would make her snort and toss her head, with its great odd, forward-hooking horn. *That* made the hayseeds jump back.

He swung a bare leg over his saddle and dropped to the road. The crushed pumice surface seemed threadbare, for a fact. Small surprise that verminous tub Melchor let his fief go to wrack and ruin, even before he scuttled off to Providence Town to join the very Grey Angel Horde that would soon lay it waste.

With all these poor people have to do to rebuild their lives, he thought, *Creators know when we'll get to setting things right.* At least most of them were original inhabitants of the barony—indeed, *most* of the original inhabitants. While the hapless inhabitants of the little manorial village of Sous-le-Tertre had been caught in their beds by the Horde's onslaught, the country folks' watch dogs and vexers had alerted them in time to bounce promptly away into the forest. There, throwing aside old enmities in the face of new and overwhelming danger, the woods-runners had taken them in. And ambushed the Hordelings who dared follow.

"Now, what have we here?" he asked. Nell stuck her beak in a green bush growing from the roadside and began munching happily.

"Uh—you did notice the herd of Thunder-titans, who are really, really close and getting closer?" asked a nervous, squint-eyed man with a prominent Adam's apple.

"Why, as it happens I did, bless your soul. And quite a handsome little family they are, too. A dozen adults and adolescents, is it, and four sprightly little calves the size of hay-wains. Five? Hard to tell, the way they gambol amongst the others. And that herd-cow—she's twenty-five meters long and thirty tons if she's a hand span. No, I'm taking stock of what I've got to work with here, not them."

Which for a fact wasn't promising. The colossal dinosaurs, with their little heads swaying at the ends of improbably long necks, their mound-shaped bodies, green-mottled on top, and a sort of yellowish khaki on the belly. They lacked the dorsal spikes that gave their lesser cousins, the spine-backed titans, their names but were perceptibly bulkier. He knew as well as the farming folk did that if they continued on their present course, they'd trample their just-sprouting crops into mud, and a number of their dwellings as well. And he knew, rather better than the farming folk were likely to, the futility of trying to fight them, even with arms considerably better than their crude and hastily sharpened pole-pikes and farm implements.

"It's the Angel's curse on us for defying him," an old woman called from up the road. "The behemoths have never been seen this side of the river before. It is His vengeance!"

"Enough of your noise, now, Becca," the stout red-faced woman who seemed to be in charge of the self-raised peasant levee said. "I notice you're still alive, and not long since eaten by the Horde and shat out their un-washed scabby asses."

"Blasphemy, Sandrine! What of your immortal soul?"

"It's still stuck firmly in my body, thank the Eight. Now piss off before I send a few of the gawkers to throw rocks at you. Or have done with your eye-harvester screeching, and you can watch the miracle our noble new overlord is surely about to pull out of his . . . ear."

Rob stood with fists on hips, appraising the onrushing herd. Well, onrushing by the standard of such unwieldy great beasts. Though the legs of the largest were longer than he was tall, he could easily outpace them by walk-ing briskly.

But the slowest of lava flows will destroy crops and villages in its path, too, he thought, *and no more surely than they.*

"Which of your fields lie fallow, now?" he called.

Sandrine pointed to a patch toward the green wall of Telar's Wood. It was naked yellow soil and looked un-cultivated to Rob's eye. But he had no more of a mind for growing stuff from the ground than these hayseeds had of teaching a war-hadrosaur to belly-down on com-mand. He nodded at the confirmation.

"Right." He rubbed his hands together. "Let's get to it, then. We've a job of work to do, and not more time than we need to do it."

"You already have a plan to deal with the monsters, lord?" asked the narrow-eyed man.

Rob laughed.

"I had that the moment I first heard of your little problem. In my prior life, before I was made noble for my sins, I was a dinosaur master. Meaning I still am, but now I get to put on airs and drink tea with extended pinky. If I drank tea, which thanks to the Lady Maris I do not. What I needed to know was how best to implement my cunning plan."

"What does that mean?" Sandrine asked.

"Watch and learn. Now, who's got rotted hay they'd like to get paid to dispose of? A nominal fee, to be sure, but—"

Though the self-constituted self-defense force stoutly refused to leave their posts between the Apatosaurus herd and the fields, Rob quickly got the onlookers chased off to hunt down the necessities of his plan. Which, fortunately, was simple and fairly easy to put in action—slow as they were, the monsters had halved the distance between the futile defenders and their tree-trunk legs.

"It's a month's supply of good pine oil for our lamps you're using up, there," complained Sandrine as a handful of the more reliable-looking peasants poured jugs of the fragrant stuff onto weeds growing by the ditch that crossed the dinosaurs' path. Which itself posed no barrier to them: the big ones could simply step across, while the notably more nimble young could leap it easily.

"I'll make it up to you," Rob promised. "We've casks upon casks of the stuff in the cellar beneath the manor. For reasons best known to his evil little toad mind, the former Baron Melchor put a stout lock upon the door, which was also stout. Patience was not a common virtue among the Hordelings, it seems; they moved on before doing more than clawing at the door a bit. Here now, Bergdahl, don't do that. *Bergdahl!*"

As any good dinosaur master must, Rob knew how to make his voice thunder. More to keep dinosaur grooms and apprentices from making disastrous mistakes with *grandes'* fabulously expensive war-dinos than for preservation of their own lives and limbs. Though plenty of dinosaur masters, like Morrison, reckoned the occasional fatality among their underlings an excellent lesson for the survivors, Rob had a soft spot in his heart and tried his best to keep casualties down among even the most thumb-fingered. And brained.

The lanky seneschal froze with his big fist cocked back by an ear to punch a peasant, who had apparently stumbled while helping shift a two-wheeled cart piled with straw and spilled some in the roadbed.

"None of that, now, there's a good fellow," Rob said. "It's a rush job. Mistakes happen, and nothing serious spilled."

Nothing but fucking hay, he thought. *What's wrong with the brute? Note: remember to have a good talk with Bergdahl about his ways of dealing with subordinates before hiring him on staff for the manor.*

With Sandrine's help, Rob chased the farmers, would-be warriors and onlookers alike, five or ten meters back of the line where the ditch crossed beneath the road. He had other helpers heap hay and such combustible trash as the nearby householders had been able to fetch on short notice and had the last of the pine oil spilled on it.

A breeze had come up, blowing out of the north. That meant the smell would only reach the dinosaurs when they were perilously close to the barrier. He had to hope the sight of what he was about to do was enough for the job at hand.

He had produced his key-wound spark-maker and poured a bit of tinder from a flask into a brass bowl on the road, behind the pine-smelling debris. Now he set it alight, blew on it, lit a splinter of kindling with a bit of oil on the end, and handed it ceremoniously to Sandrine.

"You do the honors, madam," he said grandly.

"You little beggars be respectful, now, and wait for your elders to begin," he added to the children and young folk who had eagerly started lighting their own splinters, first off the tinder-bowl, then from one another's torches. "Or thumping *will* be called for."

Amazingly, they held back, dancing with impatience behind Rob and the red-haired woman. She was looking from Rob to her own torch as if not sure what either was. He made urgent go-ahead gestures with his hands. The nearest, and also largest, Thunder-titans were less than thirty yards away; he could hear the muttering in their endless throats, even over the distant-thunder grumble of their bellies.

At last Sandrine shrugged and set fire to the hay and trash on the road. It flared up most satisfactorily, the flames pale blue and yellow in the cloud-filtered but bright morning sun.

The leading titan, the herd female, snorted loudly. Several others echoed her.

Smoke quickly billowed from the barrier across the road as the youngsters ran up and down the ditch, catcalling the behemoths and setting light to oil-spattered weeds. Which also commenced to smoke lustily, creating a most satisfactory if not entirely continuous line of flames and (mostly) smoke. Behind the ditch, which ran full with water today, a line of the farmers had assembled with buckets and ladles in case the fire got overambitious.

"Steady, there!" Rob called, as some of his youthful fire starters, job done, turned to dance toward the Apatosaurus herd, brandishing their firebrands and shouting taunts. "If you get one of those thing's attention, it can spin right round with surprising speed and whack you with its tail."

"What," Sandrine demanded skeptically, "one of those great fat wads?"

"Can break a bull Allosaurus' spine with a tail crack. I've seen it with my own eyes."

Well, no, he hadn't. His horrible drunken old Scocés dinosaur master, Morrison, to whom he'd been 'prenticed, had seen it with his eye—or maybe both, back when he still had the two. Or not; the foul-tempered old bugger was no more married to the truth than Rob himself was. Sod him in Hell; but he was a brilliant hand with dinosaurs.

With deliberation rather than alacrity, the lead dinosaur had turned southwest—back toward the forest, which here ran mostly to hardwoods, Telar be praised. The others turned to follow its example. Rob and his people wouldn't have to try herding the giants with torches and shouts until they wandered across one of the borders of the barony and became some other set of unfortunates' problem.

They liked the dense woods little better than the Hordelings had, though they faced little likelihood of woods-runner arrow-showers from covert. But by the locals' testimony they had crossed it to get here. Now it seemed they were willing to shoulder a path back, to get away from the flames.

The smallest of the juveniles, barely bigger than a yearling ambler, broke away from the herd to approach the fire-wall. Rob knew the beasts weren't powerfully bright; little call they had to be, given how much they could wring out of simply being *powerful*. Still, like any animal other than humans, they feared fire from birth. But this one let curiosity overpower instinct.

Rob had Wanda, his utility and sometime fighting axe, in hand; he'd used her to bust up some rotted planks from an old outbuilding to add fuel for his fire-wall. He ran toward the little dinosaur, waving the axe and shouting in Anglysh, "Away with you, you daft little bugger!

Shoo!" The baby titan blinked at him with large brown eyes and turned and cantered back toward its majestically retreating elders.

When Rob turned away, he noticed that Bergdahl seemed to have corralled several of the comelier local maidens, beyond the smoke and ditch. Rob hopped across and strode up to investigate.

"—ordered to present yourself at the manor at sunset," the seneschal was telling the three wide-eyed young women. "You must be prepared to serve your master the Baron's pleasures. It's the law, and your duty—and no more than his due, as a reward for saving your lowly crops and hovels."

"No, no, no. Wait, wait now!" Rob called. Not without regret, for the three—two black-haired lasses, one tall, one short, both slim, and a buxom blonde whose height was in between—were decidedly easy on his eyes. For all that they concealed their bodies beneath the sort of shapeless hemp or linen smocks people wore up here in the Sierra Scudo foothills, where it actually got cool at nights even in summer, when the wind blew down from among towering perpetually snow-sheathed peaks. "That's not right."

"Of course it is, my lord," Bergdahl said, turning. He sounded actively outraged.

"There's no such duty. It's forbidden by law to try to enforce it." *Not that I'm a man to stick closely to the law's letter, or any part of it*, he thought. *But in this case . . .*

"But your rights as lord of the manor—"

"You worked for the young hotspur Duke Falk himself, did you not? Now, surely he'd never contemplate such a thing, and him the big damn hero, and everything and such."

He noticed a down-drooping outer corner of one of his seneschal's eyes commence to twitch. *The man suffers tics, now, does he?* Perhaps he needed to engage more staff for the castle, to call it a *grand*er thing than it was, if the man was suffering so from overwork.

"And more to the point, my own Duke Karyl would hang me from a tree for doing it."

The wide shoulders shrugged. "Others do it, regardless of the law."

Don't I know it, Rob thought in rising anger.

"Ah, but that's the very kind of law His Grace is readiest to enforce. He hates such deeds with a fiery passion. And so do I."

Rob willed his fists to unball, restraining his urge to smash that beaked goblin face. *It's not his fault he's ill-favored as a reaper's ass*, he thought, *and a shame and a reproach to Ma Korrigan's boy to hold his homeliness against him.*

Actually, that was his second impulse. His first had been to split that round head with Wanda. But at least that one was easy to shrug off. Rob had never yet killed man or woman out of mere spite but had punched plenty of the Creators' own who pissed him off.

It's not your fault you don't know young bucketheads raped and killed my older sister for a lark, he thought. *But you don't need to know it, either. I don't know you, bucko. The Emp himself may vouch for you; but Himself has a bloody great Grey Angel for a confessor and is none the wiser, so.*

"Take the day off," he made himself say in an even tone—though he knew it would sound flat against his usual cheerful bantering nosehorn-shit.

"Oh, my Lord, I couldn't possibly—"

"What's this? A servant balking at time free from his chores? Truly, overwork has affected your mind, as well as causing that tic in your eye. Off with you, now."

He put a touch of steel in that last. He had plenty of experience bossing recalcitrant dinosaur grooms—and facing would-be tavern brawlers.

Bergdahl's shoulders slumped. He turned and shuffled back to his horse, whom he'd tied to the stout frame of a simple lever-style bucket hoist by the irrigation ditch that ran alongside the road. *Here, and it's in the sun,* Rob thought, annoyed that he'd missed the fact, *where it can't reach the water to drink! And a fine young plane tree stands just a few meters beyond to give the poor beast shade.* He added to his growing list of mental notes to talk to his seneschal about caring more for one's animals; the beast might not be a dinosaur, but not even Rob could hold that much against it. But not everybody had been brought up right in that regard, he knew, and would be better for proper instruction.

"So that's it?" Sandrine asked him, as they watched the Thunder-titans make their brisk—for twenty-ton behemoths—way toward Telar's Wood. They seemed to be heading to the road between the trees. Fifty meters or so on it crossed the L'Eau Riant by a bridge. Which, though clearly made of heavy hardwood timbers to support heavily laden wagons drawn by nosehorns, was never constructed to accommodate the weight of even one of the massive adult Apatosauruses. Rob was almost tempted to follow and see if they'd try to cross over it. For all their bulk they were surprisingly narrow, as dinosaurs tended to be; they might fit between the railings.

Or splinter them. The thought that he might have to bear the expense if they broke the bloody bridge doused his urge to spectate.

"Yes," he told her.

"That simple?"

"That simple."

She scowled. "Why didn't you just tell us? You could even have stayed in bed." *While common folk worked the fields,* she did not say, but he heard.

Her envy wasn't his problem. He'd slept as late as mortally possible when he was mere Rob Korrigan, even—

especially—when he was just scraping by as a minstrel, as he did between dinosaur-master jobs. Whose tenure was anything but secure, given the trickish ways of high-spirited war-dinosaurs. And high-spirited war *grandes*, who in general Rob found little brighter than his charges.

"Would you have believed me?" he asked. "That it was so simple and all?"

Her frown deepened, but seemed to soften its contours, becoming more a look of consternation than anger.

"No," she said. "Such huge things. Who'd have known?"

Anyone who remembered all things fear fire, he thought. But he used a skill he'd developed for the first time in his life while living and working closely with Karyl: holding his tongue. Which was a skill whose usefulness he'd quickly discovered. Although initially he picked up the knack in something of a hurry because he was terrified Karyl would kill him as casually as swatting a nosehornfly if Rob said something that angered him.

In this case, he might have need of such an ally as Sandrine, in this new and doubtful business of being a Baron. Something he sensed he'd made of her, despite her still-visible reticence. That was mostly show, he reckoned, for the saving of her face before the others. And welcome to it she was.

She looked at him now with just a V between her brows—appraising. "But now we know the sleight."

"I'd hope so."

"But you'd teach us to do something like this on our own? Protect ourselves?"

And how might I have accomplished the thing without your noticing that all it took was a little fire, well applied? I'm a dinosaur master and musician, not a conjurer.

"Why wouldn't I?"

She frowned again, this time in puzzlement—the

woman seemed to frown as her customary expression, but got a great many uses of it, the way Karyl's pet did with her lone cry of "Shiraa!"

"Because then we don't need you?"

I don't see what need you have of me ruling over you as a general thing, he thought. *But here we are. It is the Creators' Law, and I'm no man to argue with that. At least not now, with a thirst too powerful for water building within.*

"'Tis as you said," he told her. "The less need you have for me, the later I get to stay abed, *hein*?"

He hoped he used the last expression right, kind of grunting it out through his nose in the manner of this beastly Francés. He might have spoken Spañol with them, a language he was far more fluent in. As every subject of the Empire of Nuevaropa was supposed to be—and as everyone hereabouts was almost certain to be, given that Spaña lay a shortbow-shot away across the river. But Ma Korrigan had beaten courtesy into him with her large and rock-hard fists, along with many behaviors less widely esteemed.

The youths had joined their elders, with only a little foot-dragging and complaining, in dousing the fires they'd just had so much fun starting. They made shift by jumping in the ditch and splashing water on the flames by hand, laughing and hooting and splashing one another as often as burning vegetation. Which made no difference to Rob.

One especially large bush had apparently died for reasons it clearly found good and sufficient, and had begun to dry out. It burned stubbornly when all the other fires had been extinguished. Mounting Little Nell, Rob called the others off and rode up near the bush, where he turned and backed her up toward it, though she tossed her head and rolled her eyes in complaint—she knew full well what the crackle and the heat rising on her tail and broad backside meant.

Largely by accident, Rob had taught Nell to piss on command. That was how he doused the final flames: with a powerful backwards stream. Which smelled worse even than he'd anticipated, the pungent Einiosaurus wee going not at all well with burning weed and pine oil. Rob almost choked at the cloud of noisome brown smoke it raised.

But as he batted at it with his hands, and urged a relieved—in several senses—Little Nell away from the now-doused fire, he heard his audience of peasants burst into wild cheers, whistling, and handclapping. And he realized that by the neatly comic touch he had ensured that what had been, as Sandrine observed, a disappointingly normal and predictable turn of events would be remembered as a great and in some ways almost magical event.

So part of being a noble is being a good showman, he thought. *That, at least, I can do.*

And smiling and waving to the happy, foot-stomping crowd, he turned Nell and rode her back to the manor house. Where the waiting Bergdahl would undoubtedly try to get him drunk, again, though the sun was barely halfway up the western sky on its climb toward the zenith.

And to that proposition, he thought, *I shall make small argument indeed.*

Chapter 26

Dieta Imperial, La; **Imperial Diet, The**—The Empire's deliberative body, which sits in the People's Hall in La Majestad. Mandated by Imperial Charter, in the expectation, or anyway hope, that it would provide a check to autocratic tendencies on the parts of Emperors and Empresses. The Diet controls Imperial finances, although it is generally amenable to the Imperial will in that regard, and oversees the everyday administration of the Empire, as well as directly ruling La Majestad. It has three chambers: Superior, Central, and Lower. The Superior consists of the eleven Imperial Electors, who are almost always represented in the Diet by Deputies whom they appoint. The Central is made up of members of the nobility and clergy (or their Deputies). Members of the Lower are popularly elected, and include representatives from the odd free city, such as Laventura. Matters are first debated and voted on by the Lower Chamber. The outcome is then reviewed by the Central. Finally the Superior passes judgment, although it's considered pro forma, and in general it endorses the Central Chamber's vote. Their decision goes to the Emperor, who then does what he wants.

—LA GRAN HISTORIA DEL IMPERIO DEL TRONO
COLMILLADO

"What's the matter, Your Highness?" asked María, Condesa Montañazul from Melodía's left with carelessly feigned solicitude. "You've barely touched your salad."

Melodía realized she was staring at the jumble of fresh greens from the courtyard rooftop gardens—legumes, onions, and radishes—as if expecting to read a mystic augury there.

"If you don't want it, may I have it?" asked Don Silvio, the current Deputy for the Elector of the Lesser Tower, in the Diet's Upper Chamber. He was already hovering his fork perilously near her plate from his position across the table and to her right. Though he was tall and his dark-blue-velvet-clad torso was gaunt as a—she made herself think, *skeleton,* rather than the other thing, which she dreaded thinking about even more than the man who sat directly across from her—he ate ravenously, and apparently his appetite never gave him peace.

She successfully mastered the impulse to stab his long, languid, olive-skinned hand with her fork and instead sought to back him off with an icy glare. Which also succeeded.

"I'll get to it, Don Silvio," she said. He was a regular fixture at the semiformal state dinners Melodía and her father customarily attended in the Hall of Hospitality. Mainly because he hardly ever went away. Nuevaropa's tiny but vocal *Taliano* minority currently represented the Elector Menor in the Cámara Superior, and they were obsessed with pestering the Emperor to do something to "free" the Taliano city-states of Trebizon, allegedly held in vile servitude by the Basileia.

Since there were limited "somethings" one Empire could do to its rival, he had become a persistent voice for going to war over Montserrat's abduction. Which meant he caused considerable discomfort to Melodía—who, though her heart was divided, knew for a fact that such a war was almost certain to end in disaster for Nueva-ropa and her family. But since his three-year stint as Deputy for the Elector of the Lesser Tower had begun just a few months before, it was unlikely she'd be rid of him anytime soon.

She began to eat her *ensalada* without tasting it.

"Your daughter is looking peaked, Felipe," said a recently encountered and already thoroughly unwelcome voice from her father's right hand at the head of the table. The Dowager Duchess Margrethe, dressed as usual in a long silk gown—this one pale green—gazed at Melodía with a look of almost certainly feigned concern on her pink Northern features. Her long near-white blond hair was wound into buns at either side of her head. "Perhaps the girl is preoccupied by the lack of masculine companionship. Too long an abstinence can be bad for a young person."

She simpered, laid a hand on Felipe's arm, and winked at him. "Or old ones, too, for that matter. Right, Your Majesty?"

Felipe blinked slowly and looked grave. Which Melodía knew was generally a cover for being befuddled and not having any idea what to say.

Melodía took up a forkful of food, stuck it in her mouth, and dutifully champed at it. *Take your claws off my father!* she wanted to scream.

But of course she couldn't. And not just because decorum forbade it. Her father was a grown man, not her ward—often as she'd thought otherwise, when she was forced to take over managing their duchy of Los Almendros after her mother died giving birth to poor lost Montse, when Melodía was very little older than her sister was now. And, of course, he was the Emperor. Felipe had not stayed celibate after the loss of his beloved Marisol; no one expected that, least of all his adoring Catalana wife. But he had honored his lost love's memory by refraining from any true emotional romantic connection, instead periodically engaging the services of skilled and beautiful professionals from one of La Merced's highest class of brothels—located in the affluent hills of Los Altos, not in the tenements of El Abrazo, the dock district. It was all very regular and proper.

And now for this woman, of all people, to be clearly trying to entrap her father . . . and succeeding, at least to the extent he hadn't sent her packing . . . that was intolerable.

And what can I do? she thought. *As usual, nothing.*

"I'm sure the Princess can find suitable company among the courtiers," the Countess Bluemountain said. "The older ones, at least. Her time slumming among the peasants hasn't coarsened her that much."

Melodía declined to give the woman the satisfaction of glaring at her, though she shot her a quick sidelong glance, packed with as much malice as she could manage. Time had not exactly been kind to the Countess, whose dry skin seemed to be shriveling onto her hatchet features, and whose breasts sagged dispiritedly between the confection of strips of pale blue and white fabric she'd hung over her stooping shoulders. Or being married to the late Count, a thoroughgoing brute by all accounts.

"Surely you're joking, Gräfin María," Margrethe said. "The Highness is in the full bloom of young loveliness. Such more mature specimens as ourselves can only gaze in envy upon the smoothness of her face and the ripeness of her breasts."

Countess Bluemountain shot her the full-on glare of undiluted hate Melodía had been unwilling to visit upon her—upon either woman, truthfully. She almost felt sorry for the Spañola.

"I can only agree that she needs refreshing with the touch of a truly strong man," Margrethe continued. "And who better than my own son, Duke Falk, who so hero-ically defended her father our Emperor from the raven-ing Horde?"

Melodía put both hands on her bare thighs beneath the table and gripped them so hard her short nails almost pierced the skin.

Her placement halfway down the table was nothing un-usual, but a common family convention—to spread the wealth of the Imperial family, as it were. And to serve as something of a social consolation prize for those who weren't privileged to be positioned at either of the Em-peror's elbows. Or indeed close enough to get his ear without shouting in a most unseemly manner.

But it had pitfalls beyond exposing her to the short-range spite of Condesa Montañazul, or Don Silvio's greedy guts. Directly across from her, *he* sat: Margrethe's son. She could barely stand to think his name, and yet she had to let her eyes at least slide regularly over the space he occupied, or that would be snatched up by the avid eyes of the dozen or so courtiers and deputies sharing the Imperial dinner table.

"What a fine idea!" Countess María said. "Nothing like the touch of a real man to touch up the appetite."

"Count Jaume is a hero of the Empire as well, Dama Margrethe," Felipe said. "He remains my Champion—and my Constable. He enjoys my full faith. And he en-joys my daughter's favor."

"Despite losing your other daughter?" Countess Blue-mountain asked.

Felipe's face darkened. "Let's not speak of that," he said. "That wound's too recent, too great. And we know now that he told the truth of his defeat, after all."

"If you believe the words of mere peasants," Count-ess María said. But under her breath—although Melo-día heard her clearly.

And then again maybe she deserved a vile, violent

Horror like the dead Count Roberto, after all, Melodía thought. It struck her that the Countess had a certain interest in discounting accounts from veterans of recent actions. The Emperor had felt compelled to cover up the actions of certain of his highest-ranking clerics and *grandes* at Canterville, as part of his campaign to put as pleasant as possible a face on what remained arguably an act of outrageous blasphemy on his own part and on that of his whole army. But as word of Melodía's exploits had returned to the Imperial Heart, so inevitably had whispers of the Count's joining Cardinal Tavares in a shocking betrayal of his Empire, his Emperor, and his own kind.

"Here, now," Falk boomed. "Jaume is a hero, and I won't hear a word to the contrary! He proved himself a hundred times before the Battle of Canterville—in which we fought as comrades in arms. I might hope to prove as worthy."

Margrethe smiled. "Ah, my son. Ever so loyal and honorable! Still, you can't blame your old mother for putting a word in for her dear, downy chick, can you?"

"And after all, Melodía dear," her father said absently, "surely there's no harm in considering all options, is there?"

She slammed her hands on the table. The silver salad plate flipped and dumped its contents on the wooden surface. She shot to her feet.

"I'd think you of all people would remember how entertaining suits for my hand that were never going to be accepted turned out," she said, "for the Empire and our family, Father."

He blinked at her like a puzzled horse.

"I find myself fatigued," she snapped. "I'm going to bed."

She turned and marched out. But not before catching a glimpse of what she took for a glint of triumph in the blue eyes of the Dowager Duchess Margrethe.

In her apartment Melodía stood nude before the *espejo lucero*, holding a hank of her hair in her hand and gazing at her full-length image as if looking for an augury.

A warm night breeze through the open window brought the sounds of merriment and commerce from the great courtyard, as well as hints of song and a distinct aroma of baking bread from the city beyond the Moat. Unfortunately, it also brought the odor of the town dump.

But that suited her mood perfectly.

The finery she'd worn to dinner lay discarded by her feet: the discreet gold circlet buried by the gold and dark-green feather gorget and the brief emerald silk trunks with tea-green chiffon side panels, all crumpled upon her gilt sandals.

Look at yourself, she thought. She saw a tall young woman, trim, full-breasted, with hints of hard muscle underlying soft contours, especially in stomach and limbs. It was nothing extraordinary for a woman of her age and station; *grandes* of all sexes customarily trained in combat arts of various kinds. If anything, she was a trifle gaunt from the hardships of campaigning first with the Militia of Providence and then being hunted by both Horde and Empire as Karyl's Fugitive Legion. Although the life of ease—and despair—was filling her out and softening those wiry muscles.

My hair. She had cropped it to a brush when she and Meravellosa joined the army as a *jinete*, a light rider, scout, and skirmisher. When her abilities won her promotion, to command of a squadron and then all the *jinetes*, that had won her the nickname of Short-Haired Horse Captain.

Once Raguel revealed himself in His full beauty and horror at the Great Hall of the Garden villa—and the terrible memories of her first encounter with the Grey Angel, which He had stolen even as she fled in terror—and the Crusade struck the Militia camp at Séverin Farm like a volcano's glowing cloud, she had had no time to trim her hair. Or even pay attention to her appearance, when sheer survival was a full-time occupation.

And after the war was over, and the elation and exhaustion were replaced by the outrage and helplessness of the news of Montse's kidnapping—and with everything that had happened since—her dark red hair had continued to grow, as hair does, so that it now hung down to her jaw and neck. The body servants assigned her from the Palace staff—obsequious nonentities who seemed deliberately to evade her efforts to put names and characters to their faces—had kept her hair trimmed neatly, as impersonally and mechanically as they bathed her and laid out and put away her clothes. She wouldn't let them dress or undress her.

The Short-Haired Horse Captain. The first time I earned anything in my life. Except maybe opprobrium and scorn after my foolishness got my friends and my beloved Pilar torn to pieces by Count Guillaume's Horrors. Which I never received.

And now, look at yourself. The dashing Light Horse Captain, doer of daring and needful deeds, melts slowly back into Melodía Estrella Delgao Llobregat, Princesa Imperial y Marquesa del Duque Los Almendros: *ornamental, useless, and apparently helpless.*

I am once more becoming everything I fought not to be. It was all in vain.

And I don't know how to stop it.

She tugged savagely on her hair, feeling pain from the roots in her scalp.

"I could chop it all off again," she said out loud. "I could shave my head bald, like a nun from Chánguo."

She shook her head, feeling pain on her scalp all over again, and welcoming it as a sort of penance. Or maybe simply *stimulation*—a sign that she could feel anything but sinking, black, and cold despair.

"What good would that do? I'd still be here, and trapped, and helpless."

Tears flooded her vision. Strength abandoned her body. She collapsed like a discarded rag doll atop her discarded princess finery, and wept in defeated hopelessness.

The third time Melodía woke with a start as her chin almost reached her bare clavicle, she decided, *Enough!*

It was an unseasonably warm day for up here in the heights—enough for even Margrethe to doff her inevitable gown and go about clad the way the rest were, in a mere loincloth or trunks at most. Except for the courtiers, who had to swelter in overabundant court dress. *And serves them right*, she thought.

But she knew it wasn't the stifling heat in the throne room that was making her nod off. Or not only that.

"Father," she said, rising from her chair to the left of Felipe on his outsize golden Tyrant's Head throne. "I must ask leave to withdraw."

The Finance Minister, a curious little bread-loaf of a man whom she had interrupted in the midst of reading some list of Imperial expenses that stretched almost to the floor of the audience chamber, blinked his beady brown eyes through his round spectacles at her in molish outrage that she had interrupted him. *It's not as if I had a choice, you creepy little man*, she thought. *It's not as if you ever pause to take a breath.*

Margrethe poked her head around from her own lavishly becushioned stool on the far side of the Fangèd Throne. "Are you unwell, Your Highness?" she asked.

Yes, she wanted to say. *You make me sick. And your son's a rapist.* But she couldn't say the former thing any more than the latter. Especially since the Dowager Duchess of Hornberg seemed an irremovable fixture on her father's arm these days. Which contributed to her ever-growing burden of despair. But at least her vile son wasn't haunting the hall; he had no more appetite for boring minutiae of Imperial administration than she, and, unlike her, no reason at all to sit through recitations of them.

"I have a headache," she said. Which while technically not true was certainly going to come true if she stayed here a moment longer.

"Of course, Melodía, *mi corazón*," her father said, waggling his fingers at her. She curtsied and started to march out the door past the usual lines of favor seekers, bureaucrats, and idlers.

"Wait one moment, young woman!" a female voice called out, in a tone like knuckles rapping wood.

Melodía turned. Everybody turned. A tiny, incredibly wizened old woman—a thing rare enough to see in Nuevaropa, or anywhere on Paradise of which Melodía knew—had stepped out from behind the Fangèd Throne.

"Who is this wretched crone, who dares intrude in the Imperial Presence?" demanded Countess Bluemountain.

But Melodía thought to see a haunting familiarity in the strangely shriveled features. And she noted that the quartet of Scarlet Tyrants who stood flanking the throne and the door—who were trained to remain impassive and immobile for hours on end, seemed to have positively frozen.

Her father frowned. "¿*Abuelita*?" he said. "*Granny?*"

María de Montañazul's eyes went round and big as target shields, and her dark face turned the color of fine wood ash. Her tart words seemed to follow her color in headlong flight.

"Come, let me look at you, Pepito," the old lady said. Amid a lake of astonished faces, she walked right up to the Fangèd Throne on the side Melodía had just left, her gait showing no sign of a hobble, or her spine of stooping. She wore what might be taken for a mendicant nun's plain brown robes—until one noticed that they were made of finest silk.

She leaned in to kiss the Emperor's cheek. Which she then pinched between thumb and forefinger. Felipe winced.

"Ah, *mi niño*," she said, "being Emperor agrees with you, *¿qué no?* You've lost the slim figure of your boyhood, I'm afraid."

"I've never been slim, Grandmother," Felipe said aggrievedly. "I was a pudgy child. I was a pudgy youth, even as a pikeman in my uncle's army in Alemania. As a man I may have grown still pudgier, but . . ."

She let go his cheek and patted it. "Ah, forgive me, *nieto*. I forget these things in my dotage, you know."

"Horseshit," the Emperor said, evoking gasps from onlookers. Even Melodía felt surprise; her father seldom used vulgarity. "You haven't forgotten a thing in all your three hundred years, Granny."

"Here, now! Don't go aging me prematurely, boy. Two hundred fifty—well, *más o menos. Más*, to be truthful."

The Emperor was starting to look as if his pale-green eyes, always protuberant, were about to pop straight out of his face. She turned away from what was in fact her multiply great grandson. To fix her gaze upon the *Heralda Imperial* on duty. "Well? Aren't you going to announce me? You know who I am, don't you, girl?"

The herald, a short woman with short iron-grey hair and the build of a wine-tun, as befit a person of her profession, didn't pause to inhale before declaiming, "All rise to greet her Most Serene Excellency, Rosamaría Manuela Juana Martina—"

"Enough," the old woman said. Without raising her voice, she somehow shouted down the bellows-lunged herald. "I know my names, and no one else gives a pinch of dried nosehorn shit. The only ones that count anyway are my given name, and the name of my family. Everything else is dross. So wrap it up and put a bow on it, and let's get on with things."

"—Great Mother of La Familia Delgao," the herald finished. She may have been taken by complete surprise by the ancient woman's abrupt apparition in the throne room—everyone else was—but she was a dedicated artisan and had quickly recovered her professional aplomb. Melodía, who had acquired no little of Karyl's love of dedication to craft while serving under him, was impressed.

She was impressed by her forebear as well, although in a very different way. *I always expected the notorious and shadowy* La Madrota *to be a constant lurker in shadows, silent and subtle, a weaver of webs of intrigue and espionage. Our family equivalent of Abi's father, really.* Whom she knew was mentioned, always in whispers, as a frequent rival and ally both of the Imperial family's undying matriarch.

But here she's a blunt and foul-mouthed old lady— whom I'm pretty sure is sprier than she has any right to be. Though I can't be sure; I've never known many old people.

Nobody did. Hardly anyone got old enough to start looking elderly, which usually happened around the century mark. It was an axiom that everyone grew up with: "You could live forever here on Paradise, if nothing killed you first. But here on Paradise, something always does." Rosamaría was reputed to be the oldest living person in the world. She certainly was in the Empire.

"Now that I've formally appeared and made my obeisance to the Emperor, I'll withdraw now and cease interrupting your doubtlessly vital and gripping presentation, Don Armando," she told the Finance Minister. The little bread-loaf man bowed graciously. Which showed Melodía he had either more courtesy or active sense of self-preservation than she'd taken him for.

Turning to fix Melodía with eyes the color and hardness of obsidian, she said, "And I am taking your daughter with me."

"But shouldn't you ask His Majesty's leave to do that?" an Alemán voice asked with a ring like a servant-summoning bell. Margrethe of Hornberg leaned forward from her chair set altogether too close to Felipe's left hand. Her heavy white breasts swayed forward.

La Madrota turned her black eyes to the Dowager Duchess's light blue ones. It was a cliché out of the hoarier *novelas* that gazes clashed like flint and steel. But now Melodía could all but see the sparks fill the hot, heavy air between them.

"I have permission, Dama Montecuerno." She added something in fast Alemán, a language Melodía didn't understand—it always sounded to her like someone choking to death on roast scratcher bone—but which made her father, who did, blanch. Margrethe said nothing, but sat up with the arrogant dignity befitting a queen.

La Madrota grabbed Melodía's left upper arm with a strength the Princess, by this point, hardly found surprising.

"Let's go, girl," her multiply great grandmother said. "Try to keep up."

Chapter 27

Juana I Delgao—First Empress of Nuevaropa, and the first person Elected to the Fangèd Throne. Also called Juana *la Roja* ("the Red"), on account of her red hair, or Juana la Sabia ("the Wise"), on account of her rule. The older daughter of the first Emperor, Manuel Delgao, Juana was a brilliant, beautiful, and charismatic woman who succeeded her father after he died under unclear circumstances during the siege of his new capital of La Majestad by noble insurrectionists in 223 AP. She instituted the system whereby the Throne would not be hereditary, but rather eleven Electors (then nine, two more being added after the annexation of Anglaterra) would vote in each new Emperor or Empress out of her and Manuel's family, Torre Delgao. She subsequently abdicated the Fangèd Throne, to be promptly Elected Empress under her new system. From uncertain beginnings, Juana, in concert with her even more intelligent half-sister, Martina (called *la Negra*, "the Black," because of the color of her hair), built up both an Empire and an Imperial family which grew and prospered under her long reign, and which continue strong after half a millennium.

> —LA GRAN HISTORIA DEL IMPERIO DEL TRONO
> COLMILLADO

"Keep that pet monster of yours under better control!" Margrethe snapped at Falk. "He's frightening my poor horse."

His mother's mount of the day was a dun ambler mare lent from the Corazón riding stables, sturdy and serviceable, as was characteristic of her breed, but a bit flighty to Falk's eye.

She's annoying him with all her absurd prancing and fidgeting, he wanted to tell her. But what he said was, "Certainly, Mother."

Leaning forward, he scratched the smooth, white, pebble-shaped scales of Snowflake's neck and murmured, "There's a good boy. Calm, now. You can't eat her, however much we both want you to."

"What's that? What are you mumbling about?"

"Just trying to soothe my dinosaur. Just as you asked me to."

He wasn't altogether certain the beast wasn't catching the enormous parasol his mother was using to shade her fair skin on their morning ride over the scrubby foothills around the foot of Glory Plateau in the corner of her eye periodically, and spooking at that. Most likely it was both; a marchador was as well-trained as a war-horse, and just as expensively so. But unlike a courser or rare destrier, it was never trained to endure the nearness of a gigantic fearsome predatory dinosaur like Tyrannosaurus rex.

"Hrmph. Given that you're riding a King Tyrant who eats nothing but fresh meat and enough of that to beggar a Riqueza canton, what do you need with them?"

She jerked her head, wound about today in enormous white braids, back toward the quarter of Scarlet Tyrants who followed at a discreet distance of twenty meters or so on their horses, their red plumes and cloth capes bouncing to their trotting. The mountain air was still, which was rare. Falk himself wore a cap, a feather cape, and silken trunks, in his family colors of blue, silver, and black.

"Mostly to remind everyone that I command them," he said. A thought hit him. "And to make an impression. After all, only the Emperor and his daughters are normally entitled to such an escort by the Imperial bodyguard."

His mother chuckled. "Not bad. Sometimes you show promise you'll be worthy of the name I secured for you and the plans I've made for you and worked hard to bring to fruition. Briefly, at least. So why was it so urgent that you talk to me?"

"The old woman. The monster from the mountain. The one they call La Madrota—Great Mother of all the Delgao."

"What about her? She's well-preserved and spry, I'll give her that."

"But she's—she's here! She's rumored to be the secret true head of Torre Delgao."

"Rumored? I thought every blockhead knew it was true. But apparently not every blockhead. Do you have a point, or am I risking blistering the dainty skin of my ass, which I need to keep unblemished for the Imperial eye, for nothing?"

Falk physically shook himself to dispel the image that conjured up. "Why is she here?"

"I hope that's a rhetorical question and merely wasting my time right now, rather than serious, thereby showing I'm wasting my time overall."

"She's here to help Melodía against us, Mother. She has to be!"

"And?"

"I—I—she's very powerful. And she must be a great intriguer, to have kept her family in power for hundreds of years."

"It's a system that works," Margrethe said, "and for the most part smoothly. Until an ambitious sort like Felipe turns up to steer it down the rocky road to adventure. Which is the core of our opportunity. But certainly, she's *been* a master of intrigue. She's helped generations of unprepossessing Delgao whelps maintain their death grip on the Fangèd Throne, without a doubt. But still—I have my doubts about her, frankly."

"What do you mean? She didn't get that old by being slack at intrigue, Mother."

"Perhaps. Who even knows if she's real? I'm far from satisfied she's not a ringer—one of a succession of similar-looking crones to play the role of La Madrota. But if she is real, and centuries old: well, then sooner or later, she'll lose her edge. Perhaps that's happened already. And mine—mine is still busily being honed."

And she showed her son a smile that frankly discomforted him.

But he still didn't feel she'd answered his question. His fear of having it remain unresolved outweighed his fear of what she might say if he pressed.

"Well, be that as it may, what are we going to *do* about her?"

This time his mother laughed out loud: a deep, booming laugh, matching her large and powerful frame.

"*You* aren't going to do anything. You are going to strut about and play the great hero and cock slayer. Which role you perform admirably. You may not be overburdened with brains, but thank the King of the Creators and our strong blood that you're blessed with a stout frame and fast hands. The rest you are going to leave to your loving mother. You didn't think I came down here just to take the mountain air, did you? The aridity dries my complexion awfully."

They had almost completed their circuit and come back to where the road commenced to wind up the Plateau to La Majestad. Where a small stream gurgled through a dressed-stone culvert beneath the highway, hitch-bars and stone tables with benches had been erected in the shelter of a stand of young plane trees to provide a way station. Another trio of Scarlet Tyrants had chased the usual gaggle of hawkers fifty meters down the road. A two-wheeled carriage with a pair of bays in harness stood parked in the shade.

"You see, boy," Margrethe said as they rode toward the station, "now that Rosamaría Delgao has left her den tucked away high in the mountains above La Fuerza to come to the Imperial Palace, we know where she is. And here we can keep our eyes upon her."

"'Our'?"

The Dowager Duchess held up a hand. Commanded as if he were a mere servant, her son the Duke obeyed like one, halting Snowflake well short of the trees to allow her to ride her horse up to them in the brisk walk called an "amble."

Young male and female grooms in silk trunks of Imperial red and yellow swarmed out to meet her, taking over the reins and her parasol, even placing a red-and-gold-painted stool to ease her climb down from her horse's back. She could have vaulted off the beast, and back on, had she wanted; but she was where Falk had learned the desirability of making an impression, after all. The liveried grooms would return the mare to the Palace stables while Margrethe rode in comfort up the promontory in the conveyance.

A pair of figures stood apart beneath the trees. The taller, gawkier, clean-shaven one sidling uneasily from foot to foot was Albrecht, Falk's squire. The shorter was Parsifal, dressed in a scanty loincloth and buskins. He trotted forward and offered his arm.

"Oh, thank you, Parsifal," she said, taking it. "It's so good of you to wait upon me today. I understand you're being assigned to wait upon the Lady Rosamaría."

"It is indeed my great honor, Your Grace," he said. "As it was an honor to wait upon you, as well."

He turned and showed Falk a smirk. Falk had dismounted and stood with Snowflake, nuzzling him with his huge dagger-toothed head while he scratched him behind the nostrils and ear tympani and murmured endearments.

Margrethe likewise turned her head and gave her son a wink. "I do wish you wouldn't coddle that monster so," she sang out, as Parsifal led her to the waiting carriage, and Albrecht approached the duke and his Tyrant, reluctantly as always. "It's a disgusting display for a man of your age and station."

She climbed into the carriage. After helping her up, Parsifal went around and got in the other side. The coachwoman, who wore a headband with ridiculous, enormously tall gold-and-scarlet reaper plumes (to signify that she carried Imperial personages or, in this case, an honored guest) clucked up the bays and set off up the ramp.

As if to spite his mother, who doubtless wasn't looking, Falk said, "Who's a good boy? *You're* a good boy," as he scratched Snowflake beneath the chin. The Tyrannosaurus made a sort of deep purring sound and bobbed his head happily.

Falk handed his reins to his squire. The purr turned to a soft rumbling growl that Falk felt through his buskin soles. Albrecht, not swarthy by any means at the best of times, went as white beneath his curly black mop of hair as the albino meat eater. He began to quake.

Falk paid no mind; he never did. The lad had a sure yet gentle hand with Falk's beloved mount, though, and was a precise and dutiful arming-squire as well. Who never spoke back to his knightly master, much less subjected him to abuse the way the vile wretch Bergdahl did. Falk had no idea why his mother had chosen to detach her creature from Falk's back and visit him on Karyl's newly ennobled guttersnipe lieutenant, much less how she'd managed it in absentia, but he felt wonderfully relieved by the fact. He only hoped Rob, Baron Korrigan, was a horrible enough person to deserve him.

Instead, he laughed and patted Snowflake's cheek. "Here, boy. You know Albrecht. He's your friend."

The growl subsided. Albrecht did not look notably reassured.

"Come on, lad," Falk said to the squire, "buck up. Snowflake knows you. And he knows not to bite your head off until I tell him to."

And he laughed and laughed out loud at the look of utter horror on the young man's face. Really, it was a splendid joke, if he did say so himself.

"You need my help, granddaughter," La Madrota said as they walked side by side down the back passage that led to the upward stairs.

Though she was a head or more taller, and much longer in the legs, Melodía was finding she *did* have to hustle to keep up. For some unknown reason, that annoyed her more than La Madrota's high-handed way of simply marching in on her father's important, if boring, business and taking over.

"Do I?"

La Madrota snorted. "Don't try to bullshit a bullshitter, child."

Melodía shied away from her like a horse—well, one less mannerly and self-controlled than her beloved Meravellosa—shying away from a dry leaf skittering toward it across the cobblestones.

"Does language like that really befit the dignity of your age and position?" she asked, knowing the instant it came out how colossal a reaper that made her seem.

"I'm three fucking centuries old, girl. My fucking dignity is whatever the fuck I say it is. You were in Karyl's Fugitive Legion. You've heard such talk before. You've heard it from your ladies-in-waiting back at the Firefly Palace—whom your fool father should have summoned instantly to your side to aid and comfort you, not banned. Which is one of many matters whose bottom I intend to delve to.

"And speaking of bottoms, I saw the way that white-haired nosehorn cow of an Alemana has captured your father's eye, flaunting those great pale boobs and backside at him."

While she was no Rob Korrigan, Melodía was not a woman who found herself at a loss for words too often. Now was one of those times.

But La Madrota seemed willingly to go on supplying them. "I've been watching what went on in the Heart quite closely since you returned."

To her intense annoyance, Melodía actually gasped. "You've been here the whole time?"

"Oh, for Maia's sake girl, no! From the comfortable seclusion of my own sanctum. Through spies. I know you've no gift for it, but don't you know anything at all about intrigue?"

"I—well. No, I guess."

La Madrota patted her arm. Her skin was dry and felt like the finest strider-belly leather, like Francés gloves.

"There's a girl. You've wit at least to know what you don't know, when it belts you in the nose like a fool's blown-up bladder. And the courage to admit it. *That's* a thing less common than you think it is."

Trying to talk with her . . . ancestor . . . felt like trying to reason with a dust-*hada*. So Melodía said nothing to that.

"So," the old woman said, seeming to sense her surrender, "since we've gotten the nonsense out of the way—

once more: you need help. Specifically, you need *my* help."

Melodía sighed. "I do."

"Then prepare yourself. I am taking over your life as of now. Completely. You will attend my every word, unquestionably obey my every command. And most of all, listen and learn everything I have to tell you. Or everything I can. Because our need is great, and I very much fear our time is short indeed."

She stopped. "No."

A few steps short of the stairs up to the Imperial apartments Rosamaría stopped beside her and looked up. Melodía braced for a vicious verbal onslaught—perhaps even a physical slap, since there was no question who held the real power in La Torre Delgao—and accordingly, it was dawning upon her, in the Empire of Nuevaropa.

Instead, the old woman emitted a cackle of laughter like a delighted Deinonychus. "You still have the fire of spirit, flickering away among the ashes of despair. That's good; there's hope for you. Now don't let it flare in my direction again, for it's you they'll burn."

"What do you know of how I feel?" snapped Melodía, for the crone had summed it up perfectly.

"I've been there myself, of course. I know the signs. I don't even need spies on the servant staff to tell me you're mired deeply in despair. Though I have them, just to lay to rest any doubt."

"But how could you? I mean—you're the real head of the Imperial family!"

"And as the saying goes, I'm half as old as the Empire itself," La Madrota said. "At my age I've been *everything*. And believe me, the uttermost depths of despair are an all-too-familiar environment."

"Oh."

"Now." The old woman set off up the steps at the same age-belying pace she'd led to them. "Start by assuming that I know everything about you. I don't, but it's simpler than assuming the other way around."

Melodía stumbled on a riser and barely checked herself before toppling forward. "You know—"

"That that evil, bloated, black-bearded Horror falsely accused you of treason, imprisoned you, and forcibly fucked you in the ass before you escaped? Yes. Now breathe."

For a fact Melodía was having a hard time doing so. She finally managed a full inhale and nodded. They started climbing again.

"Your sister did a wizard job hatching the scheme to spring and bringing both the servants and your friends in with her. She's the brilliant one in your generation; you'll have to settle for being smart and beautiful. It was good enough for Juana *la Roja*; you should make shift well enough."

"The first Empress? You knew her?"

"Of course not. She died nearly two centuries before I was born. I'm her sister Martina *la Negra*'s several-times great-granddaughter, meaning you and Montse are too. A terrible shame about Claudia; her wits and courage were wasted as a mere servant."

"She was yours?"

"She was one who got away. Fiercely independent spirit, that one; resisted all attempts to recruit her. And I couldn't openly intervene to free you, obviously. That goes against the whole shadowy-power-behind-the-throne thing."

"Is that what you call what you did just now?"

"What do you mean?"

They were starting up the final flight of stairs to the Imperial level. Melodía hadn't by this point expected her ancestor to flag, so she wasn't surprised that she didn't. "I thought you'd be a master of subtlety. Yet the way appeared before the court . . ."

"What do *you* call my entrance?"

"Blunt and vulgar enough for a whole *tercio* of Brown Nodosaurs?"

"Reminds me you haven't had much actual experience of them, or you wouldn't underestimate them so. But, yes, close enough. So what do you think of that, now? Of me?"

"I . . . don't know what to think."

La Madrota patted her cheek. "Precisely. Now: the Trebs who kidnapped your sister are playing their own side false. I don't know the details, but I know that much—which is another reason war with the Basileia would be a disastrous mistake. As I know we're facing supernatural foes as well as all-too-fleshy ones."

"The Fae?" Despite herself, Melodía almost choked on the word. It still seemed too much like—like blasphemy, she supposed—to say it aloud.

"Them, too. I'm not sure in what capacity, but the little I know about them suggests they may not have any greater idea themselves. And yes, I'm fully aware it wasn't mere carelessness on your *novio*'s part that lost the poor child. I knew that from the outset."

"You mean you knew what stopped him?"

"Of course," she said. "But more than them, we have the Grey Angels to worry about."

"But we—I mean Karyl—I mean Shiraa killed—"

"Nothing and nobody but a few tens of thousands of hapless flesh puppets, and a few traitors to their kind. Raguel isn't dead. The slayer destroyed a throwaway corporeal form of an incorporeal being. Who's not happy about it. Whether from him, or others of his kind, we shall be hearing more soon, I fear."

To Melodía's surprise—*Why am I still even letting her do that to me?* she wondered—La Madrota sailed blithely past the doors to the suite she shared with her father, down the lamp-lit corridor to a blank wall. Which, after doing a few things with her hands she didn't let Melodía see, she slid open to reveal another passageway.

"Secret passages," Rosamaría said with almost child-like delight. "I have to love Abuela Martina and her sister: they schemed the whole thing out together, as they did everything—yes, including the Empire and our role as its perpetual rulers. If we can keep it. Which may prove a near-run thing. They kept alive both childhood fancies and the eyes to spot where they might come in handy. The bloody mountain is honeycombed with secret passages—and secret chambers."

She did another hidden thing, and another apparently blank section of barely smooth stone wall slid open to reveal a small but cozy and well-appointed apartment with a little but cushy-looking bed, a pair of chairs, a table—and a pair of irregularly shaped windows letting in afternoon sunlight from different heights on one wall.

"You even have windows? I've never seen them, nor openings that could be them."

"That's why they're called 'hidden,' my child. It's time you started learning the Heart's secret ways."

"Does my father know?"

"No." She pointed to a chair, plain wood though with a velvet cushion. "Sit. There's fresh, cool water in the ewer; pour and drink if you're thirsty."

Melodía found she was, so she did. It was cool. She thought about asking how it got refreshed, or who by, but thought better of it.

La Madrota plopped herself on the bed. "So: let's get to work. You've intrigue to learn, fighting skills to master, and we've got to head off a wicked mistress of intrigue before she sinks her fangs deeply enough in your father to place her son's broad Alemán rapist ass on the Fangèd Throne."

Melodía sucked in a sharp breath. "You can't be serious!"

"Of course I am. Of course she intends that. It's what *I'd* do.

"And there's lesson the first: never assume your enemy is less intelligent than you."

ChapteR 28

Gancho, hook-horn. . . . —*Einiosaurus procurvicornis*. A hornface (Ceratopsian dinosaur) of Anglaterra, where they are a popular dray beast: quadrupedal, herbivorous, 6 meters long, 2 meters high, 2 tonnes. Named for their massive forward-hooking nasal armament. Two longer, thinner horns project from the tops of their neck-frills. Placid unless provoked.

—THE BOOK OF TRUE NAMES

Riding Little Nell onto the grounds of Séverin Farm, a kilometer or two south and west of Providence Town, filled Rob with nostalgia. *Even though the last time we saw it, it was getting overrun by an army of demons in human form.* The sun-warmed dirt and the greenery around had their own distinctive smells, bringing on a nostalgic fit. And blessedly not a whiff of the unwashed, cannibalistic Horde remained. Though he felt a spiritual unease, knowing that they'd been here and what they'd done.

The first thing he saw were Melodía's successor as captain of the *jinetes*, a brown-haired young man named Tristan Épine, standing near the central stone house and talking with a light-rider squad leader named Simone, a

Slavia-born woods-runner named Dominika, and a male woods-runner he didn't recognize.

"Ho, my friends!" he called out as he came jouncing up toward them at the semivigorous lumber that served his hook-horn as a trot. "Looks as if we're to be back in the business of spying and slitting throats again!"

To his astonishment they glanced at him, then turned their backs. Frowning, he steered Little Nell toward a stone water trough in the shade of a barn, dismounted, and left her a bucket of grain and fresh-pulled fodder to keep her happy. Then he walked up to the small group.

"What's the matter? How'd I manage to offend you? Here I've been hoping some of you would visit me at my new digs. I don't think I was that odious a taskmaster, but I've been wrong before. Back in '29, I believe it was."

That didn't break out a smile. But the new light-rider boss sighed and turned back.

"They did," he said. "Your man turned them away."

Rob felt as if he'd been smacked in the face with a shovel. "The spalpeen did what, now?"

Dominika turned back to face him, shaking back her short dust-colored hair. "The ugly one. He told us you had no time for trash like us. That you were an important noble now, and not to be bothered."

"That's a steaming load of Slayer-shit if ever there was one." He didn't roar it, because the person the roar would've been directed at was several hours' ride away in Tertre Herbeux—and because he'd received a lifetime's worth of practicing restraining his urges since getting tangled with Karyl the year before.

"He insisted you'd instructed him personally to turn us away," Simone said.

"No, no, no," Rob said, shaking his head hard. "I said no such fucking thing. Nor would I. Come on, now; you all knew me. Well, except for our woods-runner friend here, whom I at least don't recognize. Does that sound like the merry, madcap Rob Korrigan you know?"

"No," Dominika said. "But this Baron Rob—him we don't know."

"Ah, but you do. The Emperor laid a burden on my shoulders, not a gift. And one I would've shrugged off if I could. I told my man no such fucking thing."

He stood a moment, considering. He knew his audiences, and this one was at least listening to him now.

"I'll host you to a banquet, when I get back to the manor house. All your old comrades and even new friends are welcome. As for Bergdahl—well, it's a different kind of noble he's used to serving. One born with blue blood, and not created on accident in the befuddlement that follows a battle. I shall set him straight. My word on that!"

"Your word," said Dominika, in a skeptical tone. "As a Traveler, and an *Irlandés*?"

"Indeed! And as a wandering minstrel, to boot! The word of a confirmed and lifelong rogue to a passel of spies and forest ambushers—so you know it's good!"

At that they laughed. He shook hands and clapped shoulders all around. "And where might I find Himself?"

"Around the house in the exercise yard, in the shade of the plane tree the monsters didn't chop down for the sheer joy of destruction," said Tristan, pointing. Rob nodded, thanked them all, and set off briskly.

Only to be stopped dead by what he saw. There was Karyl, a longsword practice-blunt in his hand—not his favorite weapon, but he could kill you with a wooden serving-spoon if that was what he had to hand, so it didn't seem to matter much. His chest was bare and pale above loose dark trousers.

Facing him was a nearly naked woman, a bit taller than he, her black hair tied at her nape and barely long enough to do it. Her olive skin gleamed with sweat. She held a longsword above her head, pointed at Karyl.

So that's the way it is, thought Rob, with a sort of crushing feeling inside. *It's sweaty play with the* Mora Brokentree *for His Grace Karyl, now. Small wonder he's no time for poor Rob Korrigan, once an honest scoundrel, and now a thief of a Baron.*

"Ahem," he said. He didn't clear his throat; he said the actual word, the one used by writers of the overwrought romances filled with ferocious dinosaurs and derring-do, which proved so enduringly popular with nobles and peasants alike. "If I'm interrupting an intimate moment, it's off I'll be, then . . ."

The woman turned, lowering her sword—but into a lower two-hand guard position, the tip of its meter-long blade now angling upward. She had appointed herself bodyguard to Karyl, as if he of all men alive ever needed such a thing. And for reasons of his own, Karyl chose not to send her packing.

And is this mere dutiful protectiveness I see before me now, Rob wondered, *or a matadora guarding her prey?*

He could understand Karyl's interest in her well enough. The body revealed by the silk band tightly wrapped around her small breasts and the wisp of a pair of trunks wrapped around her slim hips was that of the sort of dinosaur knight who trained rigorously for dismounted combat—not one who let herself go to seed because, when mounted, her real weapon was the giant war-dinosaur she bestrode, and she along for little more than guidance. Muscle rippled under every shiny square centimeter of her skin. A single lock of black hair had escaped her queue and lay plastered to her forehead in an almost fetching way.

Rob favored women a bit more padded, but there was no accounting for taste. He himself wouldn't kick this one out of bed, and only in part because he feared that if he did, she might just kill him.

But Karyl's face actually seemed to brighten when he heard and saw Rob, and his lips curved upwards. Which Rob knew served him the way a manic grin would a more . . . usual sort of person.

"Ah. You made it. Excellent." Karyl turned to the woman. "Enough for the day, Mora."

"Yes, Your Grace. And—thank you."

"It's always a pleasure to train an apt pupil."

She bowed and left with her practice sword. Karyl tipped his back over his shoulder.

"A curious young woman. Melancholy and . . . abstracted, unless she has a task to focus on. But she's an avid learner, indeed."

"No doubt mad avid for what you have to teach her," Rob said.

Karyl ladled water from a bucket and drank. He held the ladle out toward Rob. Rob raised his palm in polite refusal.

"Count Laurent sends word that strangers have been haranguing the folk of Crève Coeur," Karyl said, returning the ladle to its rightful place. "Even on the streets of his seat of *Languissant l'Amour*, to the effect that Laurent's a usurper, and that the rightful count is one Baron Eric."

"Should I know the wight?" asked Rob, intrigued despite himself. *And here's a fickle heart that can't even hold on to a case of the dudgeons*, he thought. *And isn't that an* Ayrishmuhn *all over, then*?

"I doubt it. All I know about him is that he's a widely reputed lackwit. And Duke Eric's nephew."

"Oh. So speaking of hearts broken and languishing, the Duc de Haut-Pays still pines for the dominions Raguel wrenched away from him with his filthy claw and Felipe saw fit to bestow upon you?"

"Such is Laurent's surmise."

"And so you've need of a spymaster once more, perhaps?" asked Rob, pulse quickening.

"It appears so, old friend. I've told the good Count to restrain his impulse to have them sworded, or at least publicly flogged, for their sedition."

"That seems downright forbearing, even for you—since crying down Count Laurent is the same as crying down the man who made him. But also the Emp, so?"

"Possibly. But it may muddle the case sufficiently for Eric to escape accusations of *lèse-majesté*, if it all can be made a matter of Julien's inheritance and the putative longing of the Brokenhearts for their rightful ruler."

"I'll never understand dynastic politics."

"That's two of us. But Laurent does, and thoroughly. Which is a reason I chose to put him where he is."

"So—you don't want him squashing these agitators, because you want 'em investigated and well shadowed, to see what devilry the jilted Duke Eric has in his black heart?"

"Precisely! If more . . . poetically phrased than I would." Karyl actually smiled and made as if to clap Rob on the shoulder. Then he stopped awkwardly and dropped his hand. Karyl seemed to have trouble laying his hand upon another unless to kill him; Rob knew and made allowances. "And I need to know how widely he's flung his net. Providence was his, as well."

Castaña, the third county of the new Borderlands, lay in Spaña and was never part of Eric's realm. Rather it had been held in vassalage to the Spañol throne. And if the King—Felipe's own cousin Telemarco—objected to having it removed from his ownership, he'd not peeped about it that Rob had heard. Not that he exactly kept current on court gossip from La Fuerza, despite his own fief lying right across the river from Castaña.

"So you'll be wanting me to shift back here to the good

old Farm," Rob said, mentally rubbing his hands in eagerness. "And then it's back to the good old days!"

But to his horror and sick dismay, Karyl shook his top-knotted head.

"I need you back in Tertre Herbeux," he said. "Especially if, as Laurent suspects, Eric's up to some perfidy here in Providence. I need you to stay on top of rebuilding your domain, as well as serving as my spymaster once more."

"But—"

"I am sorry, my friend. Truly. But you can do the job as well from there as here. And now let's get Little Nell tended to properly and you and I cleaned up. I want you to stay the night here, at least, and help me plot. Which I know is a pastime dear to your heart."

But I am not dear enough for you to keep next to yours, he thought. *Because you're so occupied with our Lady Brokentree that's it's no more time for our friendship you have?*

But he nodded and forced a smile. Because even cast aside, anything was better than brooding alone and drinking himself into eventual dissolution at Melchor's former lair. Which Bergdahl, with all his misplaced zeal, seemed bent on helping him do.

So once more I'll smile and do what he asks, against all my inclination, Rob thought. *And I thought I was the sharp dealer here?*

At the smell of roses and the shimmer of blue-white light on the far wall of the library, Karyl looked up from the book he was reading. It was a compact treatise on war strategy on sea and land by the famed sixth-century Trebizonian Grand Admiral Spyridon of Mykonos, which had been found in the wreckage of a home looted by the Horde in Providence Town and brought by his light-riders to add to his collection. As they did, unasked.

He laid the book on the table beside his chair and rose, picking up the blackwood staff that leaned against it and drawing the blade concealed within.

This time the intruder showed a form of human female size as well as shape, taller than Karyl, still, and attenuated but no longer monstrously tall. Her body was still as much revealed as concealed by shifting veils of light, her features were still beautiful if sharp, with pointed ears, and the smell of attar of roses was already growing overpowering in the room. And she still shone with a blue-white radiance.

"Is that any way to treat your savior, Karyl, dear?" she asked in a voice full of sweet music and malice.

"Is that what you are?"

"I'm Uma, if that's what you mean."

"In part." He had set down the staff-scabbard and held the sword before him with both hands on the long hilt, as if it were a longsword. He kept the tip of the single-edged weapon pointed at her face.

She approached without fear. "Surely you've heard the song of how the Queen of Fae caught you, when from the Eye you fell?"

He frowned. He had indeed heard snatches sung to that effect, during the flight from Raguel's Crusade. He had noticed that it seemed to infuriate his spymaster, Rob, in particular. Though the bard and dinosaur master was liable to take great offense at songs for no other reason than that they were sung badly.

"I have no ear for music. Anyway, it's just a song. Not even a rumor."

"It surely is the one, sweet Karyl," she said, coming close. The rose smell had grown so strong as to seem to fill his nostrils and his throat. "And most assuredly not the other. How did you think you survived falling off a three-hundred-meter precipice with blood spraying from the severed stump of your arm? Did you think you caught yourself with your remaining hand, perhaps on a convenient bush, like a hero from one of your romance tales? Even if you had, dear child, you would have quickly passed out and fallen the rest of your way to your death."

Horror rose like a tide inside him. He had wondered that, of course. He had largely suppressed the habit, arguing to himself that it was a mystery whose answer was unlikely to benefit him even if he solved it, and so not worth considering.

But he also knew the truth: that thinking too deeply about the question brought in waking bouts of the uncontrollable and unendurable horror that woke him screaming on so many nights. The same visions of laughing faces and exquisite pleasure and excruciating pain.

Faces not dissimilar from the one Uma chose to show him.

He felt as if part of his mind was hunting for escape, like a young *compito* cornered by a hungry Tröodon. He kept his will focused on keeping the blade in place. Such focus had held his sanity and soul together before. It would have to do so now.

"And where do you think you came by that bauble you hold?"

"I don't know," he said hoarsely.

"I did save you, Karyl. I took you in and healed you. And set you free again, on the roads of your world, not far from the Eye Cliffs where I caught you, with the sword to keep you safe."

"Why would you do such a thing?"

"Out of the goodness of my nature?" She laughed as if in girlish delight. "Why do you look so skeptical? Do you doubt my benevolence?"

"The Fae are notorious, but not for that."

"Do you think us all evil, then?"

"I think you are . . . other. As different from me and anyone I know as I am from one of the rocks that fall from the sky. And I believe that your motivations are unknowable."

"You're not wrong. I *am* that different from you—and from my fellow beings of lights. Especially that witch Aphrodite. And our common foe, the Grey Destroyers."

"Come no closer," he said. The feel of the blackwood sword-hilt in his hand was all that kept him from flying into a million pieces.

"Do you think that toy can hurt me?"

"Can it?"

She laughed. "I am no common Faerie. I could touch you. It would feel like the touch of a human woman. But immeasurably more pleasurable, of course."

"Or painful."

"That too."

"What do you want from me?"

"Would gratitude be too much to ask? Never mind. Your human thanks are as paltry as your lives. Rather, I want to offer you more."

"What?" *I didn't think I could feel any more frightened*, he noted with curious detachment. *I was wrong.*

"Alliance. I spoke of our common enemy. Do you think they'll rest, now that your pet has so summarily disposed of Raguel's Paradisiacal form and ended his Crusade in unprecedented humiliation? Do you think they like you better now?"

"No."

"Remember: I healed you."

"Except for my hand."

"You humans! You call us capricious. But I give you a miracle, and instead of showing gratitude, you cavil."

She extended a hand: long, slender, so long and tapering in the nails to remind him of a raptor claw, glowing gently blue-white.

"Join me, Karyl. I am your only hope."

With a raw caw of rage, he slashed at the hand. She exploded into glittering shards an instant before the blade touched her simulacrum flesh, like a lantern dashed on flagstones. They slashed the skin of his hands and face like tiny knives, stinging like hornets.

The pain transformed into near-orgasmic ecstasy. The tiny slashes healed, leaving droplets of blood. He slumped to the maroon tiled floor amid a dwindling smell of roses and a fading ghost of laughter.

Chapter 29

Torre, **Tower**—One of the ruling families of the five Kingdoms which make up the Empire of Nuevaropa, plus the
symbolic *Torre Menor*, or Lesser Tower, which represents
the recognized Nuevaropan minorities in the Diet, and
Torre Delgao, the family from which the Emperor or Empress is always Elected.

—A PRIMER TO PARADISE FOR THE IMPROVEMENT
OF YOUNG MINDS

azing down at her hands as she intertwined the
fingers on the writing-desk surface like nervous
snakes, Melodía sighed.

Glancing up to where La Madrota sat cross-legged on
her bed in the gloom of her hidden nighttime room, she
realized she was going to receive neither sympathy nor
slack from that quarter. No matter how brutal it had been
to tell the tale of the events leading up to her arrest, imprisonment, rape, and escape, in her own words, just now.

"I thought you knew everything," she said accusingly.

"I never said that," Rosamaría said. "I said that it would
save time and breath to presume I knew everything about
you. And to save the expostulation you're inhaling for,
the point of this inquisition is to examine your own

perceptions, then and now. Would you say your evaluations of events around you have been changed by what was done to you?"

She drew in a shuddering breath. "Oh, yes."

"Good. Would you say, for the better?"

"No!"

Would you say your assessments have grown more realistic?"

"Yes."

"Very well. Now I want you to describe, as best you can, the mistakes you made that allowed all of that to happen."

"You're not going to tell me it was my own fault, and not—not his?" Having spoken his name repeatedly, in a fashion so matter-of-fact as to surprise her while she was doing it, during her narrative, she now found herself unwilling to taste it in her mouth again. She felt afraid that La Madrota would take her to task for the sudden circumlocution.

"By no means. We are not instructing the Duke of Hornberg here today. Nor, sadly, dispensing him justice—and, young lady, let me assure you, as the lifelong keeper and guardian of the Torre's honor and welfare, only you on all of Paradise can possibly long for that reckoning more than I. He committed crimes. You did things, or did not do them, that rendered you vulnerable to his attacks. That doesn't make you culpable; it only makes you a doomed fool if you choose not to face them and learn from them."

"Very well. Do you want all of them?"

La Madrota laughed: a surprisingly hardy sound for one so seemingly shrunken.

"You are years from coming close to seeing most of them," she said. "It's almost certain you'll never see all. We aren't aiming at perfection here. That's not attainable by any of us mortals, walking the surface of this world.

And yes, I'm as mortal as you. I've merely managed to defer proving it beyond doubt. No. Sketch the picture as you see it, in a few broad strokes."

"Very well. I was . . . outspoken in my opposition to my father's idea of expanding his war upon his own subjects. That exposed me to the suspicions of others that I might prove disloyal in other ways. I suppose that I relied on my position as the Emperor's daughter and heir to his duchy to protect me. Instead, it made me a target, didn't it?"

"It did. Go on."

"I made no moves to secure my . . . safety? Is that the word? It'll have to do, I guess. Or my position. Because it never occurred to me I might need to."

An unease in her mind interrupted her flow of words. She glanced down at her hands, now still, and then up at the ancient woman.

"That was my real mistake, wasn't it? Never thinking I'd need to protect myself, in my longtime home, surrounded by my family, and, and friends?"

"Perceptive. You have learned."

But saying the word *familia* had undone her. "My family—my sister. Montse. She didn't do anything, did she? Not to help those evil monsters kidnap her?"

"Not except be born into the family at a time in which its foes needed a convenient target. For reasons which I am convinced we know little about."

Melodía ran her hands back through her hair. She saw tears puddling on the desktop, by the light of the turned-down lamp that rested nearby. She wasn't aware of having started crying.

Now that she was, she found herself overcome for several minutes, able to do nothing but repeat, "Montse, Montse, my poor darling sister," over and over.

In the gloom, the dark figure of her ancestor sat patiently.

Regaining some measure of control, Melodía looked up at her in desperation. "How do we get her back? Surely you have a plan. You've *got* to."

"I doubt that we can," Rosamaría Delgao said calmly. "She is lost to us. The best we can do now is hope and pray that she finds her way safely back to us on some day not too distant. The likelihood of which I deem to be high, for what that's worth. But her fate lies beyond our hands to control or even affect."

For a moment Melodía was too stunned to ask or even to breathe or blink.

"You can't mean that!" she said, when the need for air overcame her shock. "You can't be that cold-blooded. She's your granddaughter, however many times great. Your flesh. Your blood. How can you . . . let her go so casually?"

"It is not casually. I let her go because I must."

"I see," Melodía said in growing anger. "She's too distant from you, from your, your own offspring. Isn't she? You don't love her. She's not real to you!"

"I do love her. I love you. I love your father. I love myself, for that matter, despite so many of the things I've done; call it a vanity necessary to preserve myself to serve the family. And I would sacrifice any of us without hesitation to protect our family, or even enhance its position. Without hesitation. And unless it were myself, in which case neither would be germane, I'd eat heartily afterward and sleep soundly."

"You can't be serious!"

"I am, literally, deadly serious." She leaned forward, and her eyes caught points of pale blue light like obsidian facets. "Do you think it's anything I haven't done before? A hundred times? Do you think I haven't sacrificed the fruit of my own loins to keep the Tower standing and strengthen its foundations?"

Her vehemence struck Melodía like a slap in the face—the more so because she did not raise her soft, dry voice.

"I mourn each and every loss. The deaths I could not avert. The deaths I allowed. The deaths I *caused*. But none of them matter. Only the family matters."

Melodía felt as if she were choking, though the hidden windows were open to allow the cool, clean mountain air into the chamber.

"I can't imagine how lonely you are," she said at length.

The dark features, which for the most part might as well have belonged to an idol carved of blackwood, twitched briefly into something resembling a smile.

"You are learning, my daughter. My beloved daughter."

Melodía sat up, spear-shaft straight once more.

"Now. Continue your account of your missteps in La Merced. And then we'll move on to examining your experiences leading up to the outbreak of Raguel's Crusade in Providence."

Mostly by touch, and that befuddled by drink and, of course, mind-numbing terror, Rob tried making his way back through a mostly darkened farmhouse to his own quarters. Which were large; having had some experience of the insides of nobles' dwellings as a hireling dinosaur master, he knew that Séverin Farm was sparsely populated for a ducal palace, as well as underdecorated beyond what would be dictated by its being in the process of being reclaimed from an army of human soldier ants. His straw-in-a-linen-sack pallet on the bare wooden floor wasn't abundantly comfortable, but it called to him now as if it were already occupied by naked seductresses.

I need sleep, Rob thought. *And the forgetfulness it brings. If I can only drink enough to fall asleep. And avoid the nightmares, of course. There's that thing too.*

He found his quarters, fumbled inside, and shut the door. The lights of stars and Eris, the Moon Visible, shone through an open window. Rob had plenty of experience negotiating darkened bedchambers, never you mind how. He was glad the nights were mostly cool up here and not biting at this season. The smell of human shit had not yet been fully scrubbed out of the floor planks. And walls.

He flopped onto the bed, picked up a bottle from the floor beside it, and drank. Whether it started half-empty or half-full, in the tavern philosophers' noted conundrum, it was soon fully empty.

Did I see what I saw? he thought. And: *Is it now my fate to stumble upon hidden, secret horrors?*

And third: *What could Himself be thinking? Or did my imagination truly get the better of me.*

All he knew was that on his way outside to relieve his bladder in the weeds, he had chanced to pass by Karyl's bedchamber and seen an eerie blue light shining through a crack in an indifferently closed door. Which itself was Karyl all over: he didn't much care if some would-be assassin decided to try his or her luck while he was sleeping. The like had often happened, with the upshot that—well, here he was.

But Karyl seemed neither sleeping nor alone. Rob heard him mutter something in a tone like a sullen child—which was itself not totally unfamiliar to him, who'd dealt with Karyl's grumps and sulks and nightmares on the road to Providence—and away. But when he heard a soft, sibilant female purr in return, that tweaked his gland of curiosity far more than concern did the gland he assumed to be in charge of self-preservation. After all, he knew full well his friend had arrogant assurance in his skills and reflexes enough never to strike before he was sure his target was a foe.

Ah, now's my chance to confirm my suspicions as to why Karyl's got no time for me. Nor did the prospect of seeing the Mora Árbolquebrada nude— boyish figure, negligible teats, and all—fail to pique his interest. *I'm just a man, and such that cares for women, so.*

He crept to the door with an eye—and ear—to spy.

Then he realized the light's hue was like nothing his eye had ever seen—except lightning, perhaps. But lightning was gone almost before one had the chance to blink at its brilliance. This was a near-constant radiance, subtly shifting as if to movement. And the voice—Karyl's self-appointed bodyguard had never a voice like that. Nor any human Rob knew or could imagine. It went up through his scrotum and pierced his bowels with terror like an ice misericordia.

What could I do, he thought, eyeing the bottle, *but turn and flee? I'm a man who has kenned the uncanny more than he cares for, as you'd expect for a Traveler, one named* touched by the Fae, *to boot.*

Now he half wished he'd taken that final half step, had seen and known for sure. And half rejoiced that he hadn't.

What is it you're into, Karyl, me dear lad? Something less savory than that lady knight's putatively tender nethers, I'm thinking.

Maybe it was the witch, Aphrodite, who first had hired Rob to return to her the penniless—and tone-deaf—one-handed busker she insisted was none but one of his boyhood idols, Voyvod Karyl the great, whom he himself had seen struck down from behind and swept away by the muddy, bloody river Hassling. And then had hired them both to travel to Providence and train up an army of pacifists to resist their neighbor's depredations. Rob had doubted her earnest insistence that she was a witch at first, too, if not so bluntly as Karyl. So he was almost as nonplussed when Karyl's lost hand, which she'd claimed her magic would grow back over time . . . did.

He'd not seen her since. But even then she seemed to have her eye on Karyl. Maybe she'd come to visit him now that he'd succeeded in the mission she gave him—as well as much beyond.

I have to think that, he decided now, restless on his bed. *Otherwise, the best friend of my entire life is at this very moment in a room not a dozen meters away, committing what by all standards human and divine is a frightful crime.*

He upended the bottle again, just in case. A final droplet splatted bitterly on his tongue.

Through the window, the sound of distant singing in the military camp that was Karyl's seat came to him. Not terribly bad, to his own connoisseur's ear. The mustering forces, especially his erstwhile scouts, seemed to be making merry late themselves.

Fuck it, Rob thought. *If they're still wary of me because of my man Bergdahl's obtuseness, I can* sing *my way back into their graces, sure.*

And in turn perhaps they'll let me drink myself into the stupor I require. He threw the bottle out the window, rose, belched loudly, and teetered off in search of the best solace he knew.

And also a long-deferred piss, which, somewhat to his surprise, he hadn't already taken down his leg.

Chapter 30

El Imperio de Gran Turán, Great Turanian Empire, Turania, Ovdan Empire—Nearest neighbor by land to the Empire of Nuevaropa, east from it across the high Shield Range. Spanning Aphrodite Terra from north to south, Turania stretches east for over two thousand kilometers of desert, arid steppe, and, on the Aino coast, rich croplands, dense forest, and swamp. Historically alternates between hostility and uneasy friendship with both Nuevaropa and Trebizon on the east. Has currently enjoyed two generations of peace with Nuevaropa, and maintains an uneasy truce with the Basileia. Its dominant languages are *Turco* and *Parso.* It is ruled by the Padishah, or as we sometimes call him in Nuevaropa, the High King. The current Padishah is Ertuğrul, first of that name. Turania is famous for its archers, who use powerful recurved bows made of horn, whether they ride horses, spike-frill dinosaurs (also called *Styracosaurus*), or in fighting-castle on the backs of the mighty *Triceratops horridus.*

—A PRIMER TO PARADISE FOR THE IMPROVEMENT
OF YOUNG MINDS

"Oh, Karyl, I am so sorry."

The new female voice from behind him was more familiar than the last, if marginally less unwelcome.

"I wish I could have spared you that."

Karyl raised the head sunk to his clavicle as he slumped, graceless and all but boneless, on the library's tiled floor with his cane-sword across his thighs.

"Wishes are cheap," he said. "I wish I'd never met her. Or you."

"But because I hired you to come to Providence, you saved the Empire. And probably your whole world."

"There is that."

He looked at her. Unlike the Faerie Queen and her eerie glow, Aphrodite appeared as nothing more or less than an attractive human woman. He realized it was a matter of aesthetic choice above all, though he reckoned that choice revealed deeper truths about both beings.

I have enough trouble trying to parse the motives of my fellow humans that I do not need to torture myself additionally with trying to read what drives supernatural beings.

"For what it is worth, Duke Karyl, you should feel honored. Or at least impressed. It costs even a Faerie such as Uma immense expenditures of will and energy to maintain such a form on this plane, for any length of time."

"No more titles between us. I find them burdensome at the best of times. Besides, if I were unquestioned Emperor of the World, I would still dispose of some infinitesimal fraction of what you possess. While I'm willing to accept you don't mean to mock me by using worldly titles, it still seems an . . . uncomfortable absurdity."

"As you wish."

"You've acquired the habit of appearing to me directly

after I encounter the Fae. Since you've clearly come to tell me something, tell me this: did she tell me the truth?"

"Yes and no. She did save you. She did heal you. But that is not all. What she failed to tell you was that she and her . . . subjects tortured you in the Venusberg as well."

Where he earlier felt his head had turned to lead, now he felt his body turn to ice. His stomach bubbled with nausea.

"Why?"

"For their amusement."

He gazed down at his sword-hilt, clutched in both hands as if he were trying to squeeze blood from the blackwood. Its solidity, its familiarity, reassured him. But not enough.

And then he remembered where it came from.

He looked up at her, feeling a starker desperation than he remembered knowing. Even when he was naked and pursued by hounds and then Horrors, when he woke in the shallows of the Hassling two days after falling in the battle there. The first time he had met this creature, in her guise as the Witness. The time that ended in—

Terror. Sheer, unimaginable terror.

She stood almost over him, hand extended. He batted at it. His hand passed through her slender forearm without touching anything, as he knew it would.

"Stay back! Get away from me!"

She stepped back. "You know that it's true."

"The nightmares—the fragmentary memories—"

"All real. Or as real as anything which happens in the Venusberg."

"Is this how you think to comfort me?"

She shook her head. "I know I cannot do that. So I shall do what I can. What I came for. Warn you.

"The Angels are making ready to march against humanity again. They have set their aim on the Empire once more. They take Raguel's defeat by mere humans as a personal affront, regardless of whether they favor his faction or not."

"I knew as much," he said. He said it almost eagerly. Talking about coming to grips with a known threat raised him from the depths of terror and despair.

Here's where I am, he thought in a moment of terrible clarity. *Where the Grey Angels seem a comprehensible, almost comforting foe.*

"There is much sentiment at the Imperial Court for war with Trebizon, for their kidnapping of Melodía's sister."

"I can't blame them for feeling that way, though it's a truly stupid idea. They can't beat the Basileia at sea, and they'd have to cross a thousand kilometers of the Ovda Plateau to try to come to grips with them on land. Which would be a greater disaster even if the Turanians permitted it. Which I can't see them doing."

Please keep talking about worldly strategy, he wanted to beg her. But he kept enough self-control to stop himself from that degradation, anyway. If barely.

"It is worse even than that," Aphrodite said. "I have evidence that Montserrat's kidnappers were acting against the interests of the Basileus and his family. Including his son, the Crown Prince Mikael, on whose behalf they were supposedly seeking the Princess Melodía's hand."

"You have human spies?"

"Of course. A few."

"So the Grey Angels are seeking to exploit the Emperor's just outrage." *And his daughter's, no doubt.* "Melodía showed some knowledge of military history, as well as great flair for the art. I hope she's not letting her own anger overcome her better judgment in this."

"That remains to be seen. But there is more: the abductors used magic to thwart Jaume and his Companions in their last attempt to rescue the Infanta on the docks of Laventura in their very moment of victory."

"Magic is a thing mere humans can command?" he asked in disbelief.

"Not really. It was a Faerie. Or even several Fae acting together. Their magic injured one Companion severely and killed several other humans. That is an act which dwarfs even Uma's manifestation to you of moments ago."

"Was she involved in that?"

"I doubt it. Certainly not directly. It conceivably could have been her allies. Although it is also important to remember that while she may be the most powerful among the Fae, she is not the only powerful one. And while it's rare, several lesser but still potent Fae might have combined energies to achieve it."

"She has enemies, it appears."

"She does."

"Assuming that the old legends of the Demon War are true—"

"They are, barring a good many details."

"—then I cannot conceive of why any Faerie might aid their bitterest enemies, the Seven. Unless they've made peace with the Grey Angels since being banished from the surface world?"

"The opposite. Their war has continued in what we call the World Below. If anything it has increased in intensity."

"But helping Montserrat's kidnappers can only benefit the Grey Angels, if their aim is to goad the Empire into a suicidal war."

"Indeed. You spoke truer than you may have realized when you said you cannot conceive of what motivates a Faerie. You cannot. Nor can I, nor the Grey Angels, even the wise and knowing Michael, their lord. Even most Fae could not form the conception of their own motivation, unless, like Uma, they can actually form a conscious purpose and pursue it. Which is what makes her so rare and dangerous."

"So—" He shook his head. "What am I supposed to do now? Unless your intent was to add unlimited confusion to my already all-but-limitless terror, at the knowledge of . . . what touched me and what still entangles me."

He fought that terror down with all his power of self-control. His own capacity for fixed, indeed fanatical, purpose aided him in that. As had the many disciplines of meditation and self-command he had acquired in his wanderings in the eastern portion of the continent, whose namesake this creature had taken for herself.

"Because you needed all that knowledge, and one piece more. Because Uma did tell you one more truth."

He raised an eyebrow.

"You have no choice but to ally with her against the Grey Angels, Karyl. At a cost I can appreciate more than you, who was in Uma's power for months of your time."

"No."

She bowed her head.

"I feared you would say that."

"Yet here you are."

He had to admire the skill with which she crafted a human look of desperation upon her human-looking face.

"I had to try. I will keep trying. I must."

"Leave me."

"If you need any comfort—"

"It will not come from you, nor such as you, Lady. Leave me."

She vanished. Far less theatrically than Uma had, but no less finally.

He managed to force himself to rise, recover his black-wood cane, resheathe his sword, and lie down carefully on the cool, unyielding tile again before the fear and horror overtook him, and he huddled into a knee-clutching ball and wept in utter helplessness and despair.

Tired from a day profitably and pleasantly passed in angling for the Emperor's eye and continuing quietly to stir the pot of courtly opinion against Melodía, her outlandish interloper of an ancestress, and their schemes to thwart her, Margrethe sighed in pleasure at simple comforts as she lowered herself nude onto her canopied bed. Her chamber was filled with the complex and pleasantly palate-tickling aroma of burning *agarbathi*, incense sticks imported from Vareta, located almost at the other end of Aphrodite Terra. She felt a moment's regret at doing so alone, but for a fact she was fatigued. And she had no doubt she'd soon have all the bed companionship her heart desired—and all the benefits that, in time, it would bring.

Tamping down the erotic feelings the thought of all that lovely power brought to her nether regions, she smiled, turned down the bedside lamp to a mere bluish flicker, and slid beneath the silken coverlet. She needed sleep, and a little anticipation would only whet her appetite.

Her foot touched something unexpected, down amid the puffy cushions that lay strewn across the foot of the great bed.

She froze. She hated surprises. They were frequently lethal. And meant to be engineered by her for the . . . benefit of someone else.

The unexpected something was hard to the touch. But between her bare sole and that hardness lay a thin layer of something else soft. And it moved perceptibly as she yanked her foot back.

She tucked her legs quickly up, thinking of spring traps

and poison needles. She turned the oil lamp up to its full blue-white radiance so that its piney aroma clashed with the soothing smell of incense. Bracing herself, she flung aside the spread.

Well, was her first thought, *it's no place he hasn't been before.*

But then he had the rest of him there, along with his head.

Parsifal's dark brown eyes gazed unblinking at the juncture of her pale thighs. His tongue, whose touch she remembered well, lolled from slack jaws.

His severed head lay on the bed, placed on its side, carefully, where her cushions would prevent her noticing anything amiss.

For Parsifal himself she felt nothing but a sense of good riddance. She had set him an important task. One in which he'd clearly failed her.

But then the anger stabbed through her belly. Because she was the one who took. And now a thing had been taken from her.

"So that's how it is," she said. She laughed a harsh, hoarse laugh. "Well, then, we shall see how you like my next move, you shriveled old cunt!"

She stood up. The silken mattress cover was of course stained and ruined. There was quite the mess to clean up.

Fortunately, the late Parsifal was far from her only creature on the Palace staff. She rang for the attendant, and through a crack in the door gave quick orders for someone else to be summoned from bed.

Then she went and sat back down on the bed, gazing thoughtfully at the remnant of her spy.

They'd best be quick about getting this all seen to, she thought darkly. *If I'm not asleep in half an hour, his might not be the only body dumped down the Moat without its head tonight.*

Chapter 31

Chillador, Squaller, Great Strider. . . . —*Gallimimus bullatus.* Fast, bipedal, herbivorous dinosaurs with toothless beak. 6 meters long, 1.9 meters tall at the hips, 440 kilograms. Imported to Nuevaropa as a mount. Bred for varied plumage; distinguished by a flamboyant feather neck-ruff, usually light in color. Frequently ridden in battle by light riders, as well as occasionally by knights and nobles too poor to afford war-hadrosaurs. Extremely truculent, with lethal beaks and kicking hind-claws.

— THE BOOK OF TRUE NAMES

"No," Melodía said.

"Here, now," La Madrota said from the shadows of her peasant-style conical hat. Like a peasant's, it was made of plain straw, not silk and fancies like a *grandeza's.* Melodía wished she had one too. The clouds were thin, and day was hot down here in the scrubland around the *Mesa de Gloria.* "You said you'd do what I told you without question."

"I'm not questioning, *Abuela.* I'm refusing."

La Madrota raised her head far enough that Melodía could see her cock an imperiously questioning brow.

She waved at the large beast standing fifteen meters away grazing at low brown bunch-grass.

"It's a dinosaur."

"What did you expect? Today you begin your training as a dinosaur knight. It follows, logically, that there is a dinosaur involved."

Melodía strode up to the great, ungainly creature in question and gestured up at it grandly, as if she were a war-dinosaur breeder looking to make a sale. A not altogether inapt comparison, it occurred to her. Except to the extent it implied any degree of choice on her part.

Melodía didn't know much about war-hadrosaurs. She recognized this one as a Parasaurolophus; everyone knew a sackbut. They were the most popular war-mounts in Nuevaropa. Most of the Companions rode them. And of course when she fought Bogardus he'd been riding one.

La Madrota strode up to the dinosaur and produced a carrot. The dinosaur took it in its beak, then made it disappear amid crunching sounds into the great battery of teeth behind. As its jaw worked, it nuzzled its red-and-black head with its distinctive tubular back-reaching crest against the old woman. Who cooed to it and scratched beneath its jaw as if it were—well, a decent, loving, lovable horse. And not a monster.

"His name is Tormento, by the way. Melodía, Tormento. Tormento, Melodía. I'm sure you'll be great friends."

"It's named Storm?"

"He. He is named Storm. Yes."

"That's hardly reassuring."

"Spirited knight, spirited mount."

"I'm not a knight of any kind. And I am most particularly not a dinosaur knight."

"And that's what we are beginning to remedy this very moment."

"I leave that sort of thing to Jaume and others who go

in for it, thank you kindly. I ride horses." She gestured toward Meravellosa, who was cropping the greener weeds along the actual stream.

"Oh, you'll thank me, girl. When you're older. Once you get properly started here, though, you'll hate me far more than you do already."

"I don't—" The look she got made her stop. "All right. I do some, yes. But I told you, I'm not becoming a dinosaur knight. Today or any day. I don't like dinosaurs."

Tormento took that moment to raise his head, look at her, and bob his huge triangular head and snort dismissively.

"And they don't like me."

"Nobody's preferences are being consulted here. You're becoming a dinosaur knight, and he is becoming a dinosaur knight's dinosaur. It's just *duty* for both of you."

She sighed.

"Don't you see? You really have no choice. No matter how heroic and effective you were dashing about chucking javelins at cannibalistic mad things as the Short-Haired Horse Captain or aswording them smartly with that curved Ovdan saber Karyl's cousin gave you—close your mouth, there's a dear; I told you to assume I know everything about you. In any event: you made me proud, but to the perfumed dandies at the court it's all still nothing but playing at war with worthless peasants for playmates."

"But I—"

La Madrota held up a hand. "Do you think you need to persuade me? Really?"

"No."

"Good. Now: this is Auriana."

The woman who stepped forward from the doubtful shade of a scrub cedar was of medium height, midway between tall Melodía and tiny La Madrota, and medium build as well. She wore a brown springer-leather jerkin over a white linen blouse, loose black trousers, and boots, much as Karyl had in the field, or Melodía when she rode with the *jinetes*. Her square-cut hair was dark gold and apparently natural, like Montse's, though her skin was darker than Melodía's, and her eyes were so dark a brown as to approach Rosamaría's black ones.

"Hello, Melodía."

"No 'Princess' or 'Your Highness'?"

"I am Maestra Auriana. Or simply Maestra. You are Melodía, or whatever I choose to call you. Whether 'hey, you,' or something more evocative."

"So it's to be that way then."

Auriana gazed calmly at Melodía. The dark eyes never even flicked toward La Madrota. "It is."

"Fine."

The Maestra held out a square, scarred hand to shake. Melodía, whose always-strong grip had only gotten stronger in the field, was for some reason seized with an urge she'd never felt before: to play the knuckle-crushing game. She smiled broadly as she enfolded the smaller, darker hand in hers.

"Is this a piece of dinosaur shit pressing into my cheek?" she asked a moment later. "It's *damp*. And the grass is poking me kind of close to my eye."

A shadow fell across her where she knelt with her arm twisted up behind her and her face almost in the packed dirt of the yard. "Why, yes," La Madrota said, "I believe it is. Tormento has his bodily functions, like us all. Perfectly natural. You should beg la Maestra to let you up."

"So I should say, sorry?"

"Will that suffice, Maestra Auriana? Splendid. Yes, you should."

To make an apology was no small thing for a *grande* or *grandeza*, potentially compromising not just his or her individual honor but that of their *familia* as well. Given who was telling her to apologize, Melodía reckoned she was safe on that latter score, anyway. Along with her personal dignity, the honor of Torre Delgao was pretty much what Doña Rosamaría said it was.

Melodía drew a deep breath, squinting when she was afraid that made the straw endanger her left eye even more. "I apologize from the bottom of my heart, Master Auriana. And I won't try that again."

Auriana let go her wrist and stepped back. "A shame," she said with a laugh. "That was fun."

"You'll get your chance again," Rosamaría told her. "Mora Auriana isn't just a dinosaur knight and instructor in all the skills necessary to become a proper one but a full weapons-master. Not on a par with your old boss, Karyl; no such one exists on the Tyrant's Head that I'm aware. But she's as close as I've been able to discover. And as you should realize by now, smart girl as you—mostly—are, I have reasonably extensive resources. Now, quit wincing and rubbing your cheek; it's thoroughly dry, and plant-eating dinosaur turds aren't any more odious than horse apples. It's time to begin your lessons."

Still openly grinning, Auriana pivoted away from her victim and gestured sharply at Tormento. Having seen Jaume and his Companions often make the same signal to their own war-hadrosaurs, Melodía knew what to expect. The two-and-a-half-ton sackbut promptly lowered his russet belly to the dirt.

Melodía blinked up at his back, which started relatively low and climbed toward his rump—opposite to that of a Corythosaurus like Jaume's Camellia, which started high around the shoulder and tapered back. His shoulders were still dauntingly tall. And—

"But he's going to stand up," she said doubtfully. "With me on him."

"He is," Rosamaría said. "That's rather the point, you

know. You've ridden horses all your life; you already get
the basics."

"But I'm going to fall off!"

"Repeatedly," Rosamaría agreed. "So, best get to it!
And now I shall leave you children to your healthful exercise."

She turned and walked back toward her light two-
wheeled carriage with the fringe on top. She climbed
into the driver's box, picked up the skinny shaft of a
driving whip, and touched its tip to the long green-
feathered tail of the Gallimimus harnessed to it. The
six-meter bipedal dinosaur jumped in surprise and
squawked, bobbing its head and the ridiculous sun bonnet that shaded its head. Ignoring its display of outrage,
La Madrota took up the reins, clucked to it, popped the
lash above its rump, and set it trotting across the dry dirt
toward the long ramp of Glory Plateau, leaving her distant descendant to the tender mercies of the dark-gold-
haired knight.

Who smiled at her toothily, like a velociraptor spying
a mouse trapped in a corner.

"So it seems that the young Archduke Antoine gave a fair
summation of the reasons a naval war is madness," Rosamaría said. It was late at night in her secret apartment
in the cliff cleft high above the great courtyard of the
Imperial Heart. As always, Melodía was alone with the
Great Matriarch to report on the evening's doings at her
father's court.

"Yes. It was all pretty obvious stuff: the Basileia's navy
is bigger than ours, and the Sea Dragons themselves
frankly admit it's better. They're probably the greatest naval power in all of Aphrodite Terra."

"Indeed. But from your manner I gather he didn't
stop there."

"Oh, no. No, he most certainly did not." She drew a deep breath. "He went to advocate a land war instead."

Rosamaría raised a brow. It reminded Melodía of Karyl.

"He did what?"

"He said the only way to avenge the honor of the Empire and of our own family was to carry the war directly to Trebizon by land. Where they're strong but not unbeatable."

"Across the Shield Range, and thousands of kilometers of desert and steppe on the Ovdan Plateau?"

"Yes. He acknowledged those were difficulties. But he claimed that the Empire in its just righteousness could surmount them. He—he even invoked Jaume's name as the commander of just the genius necessary to pull it off."

"Well, if anyone could do so, it would probably be your boy. Given that Duke Karyl was unavailable."

"As I'm certain he would be. He'd see fallacies in the plan the Archduke of Lumière couldn't conceive of." Nor Jaume, she acknowledged to herself; her fiancé admitted he was not strong as a strategist. Karyl was; from all she could tell he was master of every phase and level of the combat arts. Though less a master of himself and his dark moods.

She felt at once aggrieved and relieved Jaume wasn't in the Heart. It would have been good to have his support. But, somehow, though his account of his defeat at Laventura had been vindicated, the taint on his reputation lingered. As did the blemish on her own for lowering herself to fight as a peasant.

I'm still pissed at him for losing Montse, she thought. *But like my fear and grief for her, that's just something I need to put aside to carry on.*

"Did that nitwit Antoine address the small issue of what the Padishah of Gran Turán might have to say about a full-scale invasion by his ancient enemy?"

"He said that High King Ertuğrul would naturally choose to aid us."

"Really?"

"He said that the Padishah would surely recognize the justice of our cause. After all, he said, Turán shares a far greater stretch of readily crossable frontier with Trebizon than it does with us, and while there's no current state of war, what prevails between them can't be called 'peace,' either. Finally, he claimed that the benefits of the peace which has existed between our Empires were as obvious to Ertuğrul as to us, and so naturally he'd opt to support us, in order to strengthen that peace."

"He made, then, in reverse order, a superficially persuasive argument, a sound one, and a load of fatuous titan shit. He didn't say anything about rescuing your sister, I take it?"

"He seemed to regard her as just as expendable as you do."

La Madrota let that pass by.

"And what did you say?"

"Nothing." Melodía blinked at sudden tears. "It's not as if I don't know blundering into Ovda would ruin us. I feel so useless here!"

"You are not," Rosamaría said, almost gently, "except when you've surrendered to self-pity. I advise you to get over that habit completely; it never did me a shrew shit of good. Did anyone rise to argue against him?"

"The Duque de Mandar did."

"As well he should." As a cousin of the king of Spaña, Duke Francisco was a somewhat more distant cousin to Felipe, hence to Melodía and her sister. Though friction frequently occurred between the families, in crisis Torre Ramírez was expected to stand with the Delgaos. And usually did.

"He made the obvious counters, as well as pointing out that even if all went as the Archduke proposed it would, our army would be one misunderstanding, honest or otherwise, away from war with our hosts. And then they got into the predictable wrangling about how even our Empire could muster an army sufficient to challenge the Basileus in his own realm, and the inordinate difficulties supplying it—even assuming the Padishah's help."

"And what was the outcome of all of this?"

"Sentiment ran in favor of Antoine and against us. It seemed to help Lumière's position that his wing beat the Horde knights at Canterville, though he attacked without permission, whereas Mandar was defeated, through no fault of his own, as he found his cavalry and dinosaurry outnumbered."

"And your father?"

"He looked grave—the face he gets when he's hearing things he doesn't like. And he had that witch the Dowager Duchess literally hanging on him and whispering her poison in his ear the whole time. But you know how he is when he's made up his mind. He still says no war."

La Madrota grunted.

"Shouldn't you have been in court, arguing the case yourself?" Melodía asked.

The ancient woman sighed theatrically. "If you contemplate long and hard, girl, you may one day see that playing the role of power behind the throne entails staying behind the throne. Pretty much by definition."

"But you made a splashy enough entrance when you arrived! Why did you come here, anyway, if you prefer to stay so far behind the scenes?"

"That's a fair question, at least. The answer is that there's a limit to how quickly information can come to me in my own lair. And limits on its quantity and quality, inevitably, no matter how finely tuned my network of spies and informers is. Things had clearly come to a crisis here. I needed to be able to monitor events as they happen.

"As for my openly arriving, this is your father's house and yours. But I am Torre Delgao, and I belong here as thoroughly as whichever of my offspring sits on the Fangèd Throne, and his or her close family. I wasn't going to sneak in like a burglar. Nor did I think as cunning a *bruja* as Margrethe would fail to discover I'd arrived. So I chose to make a noisy entrance. Anyway, it was fun. It's always enjoyable cussing in front of the courtiers, especially those noxious deputies from the Diet. They always look as if somebody's grabbed the stick up their asses and given it a good stir."

"Why do I only ever see you here?"

"Because this is the only place I chose to have you see me. Enough chatter. Tell me who supported the one, and who the other."

Dutifully, Melodía began to list them.

La Madrota promptly interrupted. "Wait a moment— did you just say *Condesa Estrella de Hierro* supported the new proposal to march on Trebizon overland?"

"Yes," Melodía said. "It surprised me too, frankly. I thought it was pretty bold of Countess Ironstar to turn up at La Majestad to bring a suit against . . . the Duke von Hornberg for killing her husband. Given that I heard Hornberg took off Count Desmondo's head for spreading defeatist talk in my father's own presence during the battle at Canterville. Which my father had given the Duke orders to do earlier, I'm told."

"Ah. Felipe seems to have cast his nets of amnesty wide. Not that I blame him, given what he found himself facing on the battlefield."

"Am I being too forward to suspect that the new ruler of County Ironstar has reached a . . . private settlement with the Hornberg family?"

"You'd be backward not to. As I am backward for not already knowing about it. Proceed."

Melodía did. The list of *grandes* and Deputies supporting Antoine's new war plan—or war by whatever means, since some were patriotically unready to concede Treb control of the sea—outnumbered those opposed by such a margin that each name felt like a new lead weight sinking to the bottom of Melodía's stomach.

"So many," Rosamaría said when she had done.

"Yes."

"I've gotten complacent. Lazy. I've assumed I still had control of strings that have been snipped." She shook her head. "I'm tired. Maybe I'm getting too old at last."

"It can't be an easy job running the Empire."

"Haven't you been paying attention? I don't run the Empire. I don't really run Torre Delgao, either, just do what I can to keep it together and planted firmly on the Throne. In fact, nobody runs the Empire. It's a sort of machine designed to run itself, put together out of interlocking self-interests. If it makes most people happy, from the highest to the lowest, there's little incentive to rebel."

"It's not a very peaceful place."

"We contain and channel the violence as best we can. We can't dispense with the martial nobility, even if Creators' Law allowed it. They're our last resort for keeping control, as well as protecting what we have against an envious world. That's what your father doesn't understand, the poor befuddled dear. In escalating violence from the center he risks destroying a delicate equilibrium. May even already have destroyed it."

"What about our duty to the people?"

"There's no such thing. We rule. My duty is to keep it that way. The Empire is set up to benefit enough people enough that they will by and large serve us willingly.

"In the abstract I wish it were otherwise. I'm like you: I love kittens and puppies and vexer chicks and wish everyone was happy and full and never sad. But rule is for the rulers, though most of them hide the fact to spread the comforting lie that they're the guardians of the people, rather than simply masters. The people of Nuevaropa are lucky that Juana and Martina chose to set things up that way rather than rely on simple despotism. Not like the Trebs, say. They don't practice simple despotism; nothing about the Basileia is simple. But they tread much closer to it than we do.

"But in the end, if I'd sacrifice my own flesh and blood—or myself—for the good of La Familia, how much compassion do you think I have to lavish on the common people?"

Melodía felt tears streaming down her face. *Do I have to become like you to survive?* she wanted to shout.

She didn't, not because she feared La Madrota's response to being asked the question. Because she feared her answer.

"I understand how you feel. Youthful idealism runs strong in our family and dies hard. Felipe is not the first among us to be butt-stubborn. His stubbornness is more pronounced than most. But in your father you can also see the consequences of choosing to cling to such ideals, even when they've been proved wrong.

"And now, since you're crying already, I'm afraid I have some bad news of my own to impart, my child."

Chapter 32

Rasguñador, **Scratcher**. . . . —Various small, domesticated (and feral) species of Oviraptor. Though some foreign wild types grow much larger, Nuevaropan Scratchers range from less than a meter to 1.5 meters long and 10 kilograms. True omnivorous dinosaurs, named for their habit of scratching with hindlegs in farmyards for insects, grubs, and seeds, they are distinguished by big, sharp, toothless beaks. Breeds vary widely in plumage and color. Prized worldwide for their egg-laying as well as their meat.

—THE BOOK OF TRUE NAMES

eneath an already clouded-over sky that still awaited the sun's arrival from the west, Rob sat on the low stoop of his Tertre Herbeux manor house, strumming his lute and composing aloud.

> *"He said, 'You won't!' to the Angel's will,*
> *Alone on the field of Canterville."*

He paused to wet his whistle with a long draft from a wine bottle. A Luciferian vintage—from Lumière, which they called *Lucero* in Spañol—to judge by the wood-block-printed label pasted to it. He hoped vaguely that

Bergdahl wasn't splurging too much silver on fancy tipple, when frankly almost any random slop from a village vintner's would suit his palate as well. And get him as drunk, more to the point.

Especially now.

"Well, that's some awful doggerel, Rob Korrigan," he said aloud to the predawn crickets. He raised the half-empty bottle in salute. "And here's to it! It's kept my meat on my bones, more often than not."

He wondered how well he could recast the wordplay into Spañol. Though he'd been raised to speak the universal Imperial tongue, *Irlandés* and Traveler or not, he still thought more readily in his native Anglysh. Which meant he wrote lyrics better in that tongue.

"It flows. It suits me. Fuck it." He strummed a minor chord.

"My lord."

Rob leaned back, then craned his head back farther. *My seneschal looks none the more appealing upside down, poor blighter*, he thought.

"Ah, Bergdahl. I trust I didn't rouse you with my singing. To give it a name it scarcely merits this fine morning."

"It's poor practice for a servant to eavesdrop on his master."

"I reckon it's poor practice for a Baron to sit on his porch before sunup, swilling wine and making up shit he calls a song, too, yet here we are. And please, if you must call me something other than my own name, don't call me your bloody *master*."

"Yes, my lord. I came to inquire whether something might be troubling you? It's not your practice to rise . . . so early."

"Before the crack of noon, you mean? Well, I never did get to sleep last night. There's the answer to your riddle."

"It wouldn't have anything to do with your recent trip to visit His Grace, would it?"

Rob sighed. He realized midgust that he was doing so far too emphatically to make any subsequent demurral believable.

"Well, yes. Can you keep a secret, Bergdahl?"

His seneschal stood up straight—he had a tendency to stoop—and raised his chin. Rob somehow managed to swallow his reflexive giggle. *He's just a poor* hada *trying to do his job, and a thankless one it is. Though not as thankless as shaving that face, unless he's mastered the trick of doing it without a mirror. But it's not his fault he was born with a mug not even his mother could love, even if she was like mine, and in no state to be particular.*

"I am the soul of discretion, my lord."

"Aye, I reckon Duke Falk gave you plenty to be discreet about. The man's a noted horn, if camp gossip's to be believed. Which it isn't, but why ruin a good story?"

"Whatever you say, my lord."

Rob's neck bones were beginning to complain, so he straightened and half turned on the cool stone instead. "I can, too, you see. Keep secrets. And now I learn I'm fated to encounter unseen horrors in unlooked-for places and ever after carry the burden of secrets I daren't share."

But you're coming close to the line as maybe now, boyo, he told himself. *And maybe racing 'cross it with your balls hanging out your loincloth, too.* It was the wine talking; he had enough experience channeling its voice—and that of ale and harder spirits as well—to know it when it came out of his mouth.

It had shaken his world and his soul when he peered into the Emperor's tent the evening of Canterville, all innocent—well, not so innocent, perhaps, but certainly unsuspecting—and learned that the long-held secret of

Felipe's mystery confessor was that Fray Jerónimo was a Grey Angel, in all his corroded majesty.

And if I saw and heard what I think I saw and heard in Karyl's study, night before last—it scares me that much to think what that might mean for my friend and for Ma Korrigan's favorite son. And maybe for the whole wide world beyond.

Karyl had looked surprised when, at another unwonted early hour of yesterday morning, Rob had appeared before the blazing hearth of the common room all dressed for the road and announced he had decided to head back to his own fief after all. It wasn't as if Rob had made any great secret of his disappointment that it was the thing Karyl asked him to do instead of staying by his side to serve him yet again as master of scouts and spies, as was only fitting. Yet here he was, saying his farewells in the cool piedmont dark before breakfast! Not that he'd often got to sleep later during his months of association with Karyl Bogomirskiy. But that was the curse of a man who chose to consort with a legendary hero.

"I have likewise seen many things, known many things, and lived through many things which even I found impolitic to talk about," Bergdahl said into his reverie.

"We've all seen uncanny things, the last few months. Were you at the Canterville field?"

"No, my lord. I was carrying out my duties as His Grace Duke Falk's manservant in his tent in the Imperial cantonment behind the hills. I was ready to defend his belongings against the Horde if necessary, but the Horde didn't penetrate to there."

"So you were spared the sight of Raguel?"

"I heard and felt things during the battle I never had before, my lord. And which I think no man should feel and hear."

"Aye, and that was the great beast himself. Creators' own Avenger he might be, but his purpose in visiting our land was fell, and I can only think of him as dire himself."

"If I may speak freely—"

"Ah, speak up, and boldly, my man! This is Liberty Hall, and you can spit on the mat and call the cat a bastard. Though, please, no spitting in fact; I've a surprisingly delicate stomach where the like's concerned. And I should get a cat. They're egg robbers after my own heart, who pick their friends and take no shit from any man. Though like myself, they don't always choose so wisely . . ."

"I have heard certain disquieting rumors," Bergdahl said, with force behind the words, still courteous and deferential, but as if to push his master back to the subject at hand, "concerning our liege, His Grace, Duke Karyl."

Rob felt his brow crumple in a frown. "Have you, now?"

"Rumors have reached my ears that on a recent visit to the newly installed Comte Laurent de Crève Coeur, a Faerie appeared in the Count's own throne room and accosted Karyl by name as if familiar with him, and that they briefly conversed."

Rob's head jerked up as if pulled by a noose. *Careful of that image, lest you make it so. Your mother often foretold that as your fate . . .*

"Laurent I know," he said. "Didn't I see him brought all trussed up like a Year End scratcher into the Great Hall of the Garden Villa by a woods-runner woman warrior in all her naked glory? Him having been caught by my own scouts, spying and meeting with traitors on behalf of his lord, the blessedly late Guilli? Karyl sat him on Guilli's own throne after the Crusade was put paid, largely because there weren't many halfway decent candidates yet. And for all of that, he struck me a fair choice."

He waved his hand again. "But I'm distracting myself.

I'm drunk, but not too drunk to notice. Say on: how did you hear that?"

Bergdahl looked reluctant. But only for a moment. *It seems I'm not the only one who fancies spilling secrets*, Rob thought.

"Servants' rumor. We are often overlooked. But our eyes still see, and our ears hear, despite our lowly birth and station. They spread like all other rumors—as fast as if blown on gale winds."

There was a time I'd have caught that rumor, Rob thought. *Or my scouts would catch it and bring it to me. Ah, well, it's good that I'll be doing that again, at least.*

"Frankly, I understand the palace servants were hesitant to speak of what they'd seen and heard," Bergdahl said. "The penalty for dealing with the Fae is death. As to whether it makes a difference whether the contact is desired or even accidental—well, I'm no student of law, but I understand that the matter's far from settled in the eyes of Church and Empire."

"And you're to say nothing of it," Rob said, "to anyone. Even speaking of the Fae is poor policy, if your head likes its resting place atop your neck. And spreading loose talk about Karyl is poorer still."

Bergdahl raised his hand bladewise, in a brief and placatory gesture. "I only thought that you should be aware. Do you think it possible that the Fae have . . . marked our good Duke somehow?"

Yes.

"Of course not!"

"After all he's been through, he might prove a tempting target for their seductions. And even . . . susceptible. I merely say this by way of service to my lord, who treats me fairly and has yet to beat me."

Rob produced a rumbling low in his throat, like a volcano freshly waked and feeling dyspeptic. Even he wasn't sure what it meant.

"Enough of this," he said pointedly. "Now, I've thought of another matter. I gather you've seen off certain parties who've recently turned up asking to visit me?"

"Scurrilous persons, of the lowest station and nature. Even woods-runners, who are known and notorious thieves and cutpurses."

"So are Travelers, of which I am one, though now the Emperor has granted me the license to do those things freely, if I will. Regardless. They are my friends, as it happens, I suppose I mean. And now they are once again my employees. So should anyone else seek audience with me, no matter the hour of day or night"—*And there's the bad side of being back in the saddle again*—"admit them promptly. Pour a bucket of water on my sleepy head if that's what it takes."

"Even the scurrilous—"

"The more scurrilous, the better. Now, please be a good lad and fetch me a bottle of our good Haut-Pays ale. Drinking before noon's a sin, I'm told, and it's one I sorely need to get back to wallowing in!"

Chapter 33

Nodosaurios Imperiales, **Imperial Nodosaurs, Infantería Imperial (Official), Imperial Infantry**—Elite armored infantry, backbone of the Empire of Nuevaropa. Their colors are brown, black, and silver. Their basic formation is the *tercio*, a phalanx of three thousand pikes supported by more lightly armored hamstringers, arbalesters, artillerists, and pioneers. *Tercios* have died in battle to the last man and woman, but never broken.

— A PRIMER TO PARADISE FOR THE IMPROVEMENT OF YOUNG MINDS

"It hurts."

"Did you break anything?" Auriana asked, leaning over Melodía where she lay on her back on the hard-packed dirt beside the wide bed of a small stream. The hard, hard-packed dirt. Which was hard.

"Would it do any good to say yes?"

Having shed her for the tenth time that day, Tormento had trotted to the shade of a cottonwood tree and stood at his ease, gazing at his victim in what seemed to be malicious satisfaction. Half a dozen dinosaur grooms peered warily at the scene from behind the wagon that had brought them and the gear down from the Mesa, drawn by a nosehorn that was currently unhitched and dozing beneath some scrub trees. When Tormento was feeling particularly high-spirited, he liked to give them a shoulder or a playful swat with his tall, narrow tail. Not enough to break anything of consequence. But enough to knock them on their asses. Or even flip them ass over eyeballs. So they refused to get near the sackbut unless duty—meaning the Maestra—demanded they do so.

"None," Auriana said. "Unless it's your back that's broken. And good luck trying to fake paralysis to your grandmother."

"It hurts a lot." As it did, despite the fact that Melodía wore a well-padded gambeson to absorb the impact. Mostly that seemed to have the effect of making her sweat profusely inside it in the afternoon heat. Its padding did absorb much of the perspiration, causing it to feel as if she were increasingly being laden down with felt blankets soaked in lukewarm water.

Auriana reached a hand down toward her. Sighing, Melodía took her forearm to forearm and was hauled straightaway to her feet as if she didn't outweigh the weapons-master by a fair margin. The dinosaur knight was clearly strong from her build, with wide shoulders, tapering upper torso, and no great narrowing at her waist. But it always shocked Melodía all over again when she demonstrated just how strong she was.

"I respect your accomplishments and proficiency as a fighter, Melodía," Maestra Auriana said. "You have experienced far more real combat in your brief time on campaign than many we call seasoned veterans. So you know that a warrior can't let being hurt stop her. You know too well that hurts that aren't of the body can stay with you longer and worse than physical wounds."

"But the physical ones still hurt."

"That's why we call it 'pain.' Now: you were trained in grappling previously, particularly at the Firefly Palace?"

"Yes."

"Excellent. I know Prince Harry's *maestra de las armas*, passingly. You were trained to fall properly. Also, you must've fallen off horses many times, learning to ride them."

"Well . . . yes. But not from the back of a ten-meter-tall dinosaur!"

"Nonsense. Tormento's just nine and a half meters long, beak to tail. Even when he stands, your saddle only rides two and a half meters off the ground. But the principle remains the same as in wrestling. Try to get a shoulder tucked and roll off the impact of landing. And above all, try not to land as flat as a plank of wood, like you did."

"Won't it still hurt?"

She shrugged. "Eventually, you'll come not to notice it. Until then, it will serve to remind you that the whole point of this particular drill is not to fall off."

A memory came to her that made her shoulders sag, more than the weight of the gambeson, growing evermore waterlogged with each passing moment, did.

"I've seen Jaume and his knights practice falling off their dinosaurs deliberately," she said glumly. "In their plate armor. For hours at a time."

"Of course. The ability to fall safely in full harness and then bounce back up is second only to the ability to stay on one's mount in the first place in staying alive. In a full battle between dinosaurry formations, to lie on the ground is to die."

"I know." She'd seen the consequences of being stepped on by a beast weighing upward of three tons, given its own bulk and that of its caparison or barding, its saddle, and its rider. The armor just served to direct where the soft parts and juices of you squirted out.

Still—"Shouldn't I have armor?"

"Armor?"

She indicated her body, which was contained in a white linen blouse, dark trousers, and thigh-high boots. "You know. Plate. Like Jaume and his Companions."

She'd been provided with a suit of armor, cobbled together from bits available in the capacious Palace armory. But it hung on a rack over by one low but sheer cutbank of the little valley. Because La Madrota wanted to keep her training a secret, she wouldn't actually get her own panoply ordered until after she got knighted.

"Absolutely not," Auriana said. "It's actually more dangerous to fall off a duckbill in full harness than normally dressed. Or in leather armor. Or naked, though that tends to scuff."

She sighed and wagged her head in theatrical despair. "To think, you spent so much time in the presence of the finest pure dinosaur knights in all of Nuevaropa, and you never bothered *to learn thing one about their craft.*"

"It didn't occur to me it was a skill I'd need. Like carpentry. Or forging the metal bits for siege engines."

She recalled how avid Montserrat always was to watch the blacksmiths, or Maestro Rubbio the armorer in the Palacio de las Luciérnagas, at their work. It gave her a multiple pang: of missing her adored baby sister; of fear for the lost child; and of something akin to jealousy at how much she would've learned already that Melodía hadn't in fourteen more years of life. The little monster loved dinosaurs, too.

She had often wished, in the endless hours and days and weeks since news of Montse's abduction, that she could have exchanged places with her younger sister. Never before for such selfish reasons, though.

"Besides," Melodía said, "what about Karyl? He's a dinosaur knight too, you know."

"Oh, to be sure. And a great master he clearly is, as

well. But riding a meat-eater?" She shook her head. "Hardly an orthodox technique. Which is why I specified *pure* dinosaur knight."

A mischievous impulse overcame Melodía. "Do you think you could take him? In single combat?"

"What? Who?"

"Karyl Bogomirskiy. Uh, Duke Karyl, I guess I need to call him now."

Auriana's brown face went pale. Her eyes rounded with cold fury.

"Don't mock me, Princess," she said in a deadly low voice.

"I wasn't! I—" Auriana's response shocked whatever explanation Melodía might have given for her jape right out of her head. She'd been trying to tease her teacher gently—but only now did it occur to her that could be construed as mockery—"I meant no harm."

The maestra turned away. "I am your master. And I know mine. I'm good; I'm reckoned one of the best. Karyl's skill stands as far above mine as mine does yours. It is transcendent."

She spun back to face the still-shaken Melodía. "I wish I could have been there, fought on the field of Canterville. I did not join the original Crusade against Providence, because I had no taste to step on the necks of some folk for their silly and probably harmless interpretation of Count Jaume's philosophy."

Melodía looked down at the sand that floored the arena. "It turned out not to be so harmless."

"True. Nonetheless the evidence wasn't there. I held back—and by the time I knew your father'd be facing a far different kind of Crusade, with everything at stake, it was too late. And I'd gladly have died there had I just lived to see Karyl Bogomirskiy lay blade on a Grey Angel. It was the act of a hero for the ages!"

She grinned, in that sometimes disarmingly girlish

way she had. *Almost* disarming. Melodía had learned better by now.

"But enough of my schoolgirl admiration. The key, I guess, is that being second to Karyl at the arts of combat is no bad thing at all. Like being second as poet-philosopher to Count Jaume . . ."

Melodía squinted at her in sudden suspicion. Was that a wistful hint in her voice, normally so businesslike? A dreamy look in those eyes, normally of the same softness as well as the hue of the steel breastplates that gave the Brown Nodosaurs their name?

My goddess Lady Li, she thought. *She wants him!*

That tempted her to crack a smile—something she also knew better than to do during her lessons. Why *wouldn't* she want him? What woman wouldn't want to take the beautiful and heroic Jaume into her bed and body, given that she liked men at all?

She'd find her master there, *quickly enough*, she thought with satisfaction.

She noticed that Auriana's eyes had narrowed. She had no way of knowing the exact nature of Melodía's thoughts. Melodía was pretty sure. But seasoned teacher that she was, she did know the signs of when a student was thinking rebellious thoughts . . .

"Good news," she said. "I think you're done with your dinosaur-riding lessons for today!"

"Wonderful!" Melodía almost went dizzy with delighted relief.

And then she came as close to blurting out, "Oh, fuck, you caught me again!" Because Maestra Auriana's raptor smile was back, as gleefully malicious as ever.

"Speaking of your spending hours in the presence of great masters of their craft, tell me again: you never did think to seek instruction in the martial arts from your commander, Karyl?"

Melodía looked down at the sparse grass and yellow

dirt. Which she knew she'd be visiting again shortly, and at speed. "No."

"Well, then! *Now* on with your plate, girl. It's time to practice longsword play. And to make you repent more fully the laxity of your former ways!"

"I do not know why you are willing to work with me," the Grey Angel who pretended to be Fray Jerónimo said in his darkened cubby off the Emperor's bedchamber. Margrethe still wondered what use it might conceivably ever have been intended for.

"We're both looking to work through the Emperor, aren't we? Perhaps we have similar aims. We both want him to go to war with Trebizon over his daughter's kidnapping, don't we?"

"True. But what if our aim is the destruction of your species?"

She laughed. "If that were easy, even for your kind, you'd have done it already. For whatever reasons, you need to work through humans. Well, I'm a human, willing to work with you. And as for the 'destruction' aspect—well, I suspect terms can be reached and accommodations made for those who prove sufficiently useful."

"That is not . . . irrational."

Not that I trust you, you great grey beast. But you're not the only power who thinks I'm its tool.

"I know Felipe's been a very good little boy indeed about doing what you tell him to," she said. "It must be frustrating, being unable to shift his mind on this."

"It has proven unexpectedly difficult."

"I can help you with that."

"You think he will listen to you in a matter where he no longer even heeds me, his confessor?"

"I find it funny that he thinks you speak for the Gods—

and would be scared into shitting himself if he knew how literally true that was."

"Grey Angels do not speak for the Creators, but only act on their behalf."

"Certainly, certainly. As for why he'll listen to me— well, give me time, and see."

"If you can do anything, be quick about it."

Just impatient, are you? That seems unlikely for someone who spends all his time sitting alone in a tiny dark compartment. So what could make a Grey Angel feel hurried?

"I shall do what I can. Say, don't you get bored always sitting here in the dark like this? Do you sleep all the time?"

"I do not get bored. Nor do I sleep."

"Different people have different pleasures. I suppose it's the same for supernatural beings."

"Despite your flippant tone, I do perceive possible uses for you, Dowager Duchess. So I will warn about the greatest threat to your plans."

"The doddering old husk they call the Great Mother? She's old and losing her touch. She's formidable. But I can still overcome her."

"No. Your greatest threat at this moment is the man called Karyl, Duke of the Borderlands."

"Him? That annoying little handroach? I know he's all the rage in Nuevaropa at the moment, having spoiled the party for your brother Raguel. Are you simply being vindictive?"

"Do not assume I am displeased at the failure of my brother's plan. He poses danger to you."

"He knows war, not intrigue. He lost his county to intrigue as a boy—and wandered the entire continent studying war instead. I don't propose to meet him on the battlefield. But I'm sure I can win if he faces me on mine."

"Others have underestimated him. Raguel, for instance."

"A hit! A palpable hit. Well, as it happens, I already have plans under way to neutralize him, just in case."

"Why that, if you believe he poses no threat to you?"

"Shall we say—loose ends?"

Chapter 34

Bicho-cazador, **Bichador**, **Bug-chaser**. . . . —*Anurognathus ammoni*. A nocturnal *Volador Chato*, Flat-nosed or Snub-nosed flier: a small pterosaur with a short muzzle instead of a beak, 50 centimeter wingspan, dark fur, needle teeth to catch insects.

—THE BOOK OF TRUE NAMES

"Now, what matter could bring such a fine and famous gentleman as yourself to visit the humble likes of me?" called Rob Korrigan as Jaume rode up to his manor on a sorrel courser mare.

The bard, dinosaur master, and now Baron stood before his front door, wearing loose brown trousers, a loose unbleached linen blouse, and no shoes. He smoked a clay pipe with a long, thin stem. Beside him stood a pair of young women with long braids and strung shortbows over their shoulders, obviously the so-called woods-runners who had served Rob and his master, Karyl, so well in the recently ended wars. They gazed at Jaume with curious eyes but neutral expressions.

A gaggle of peasant children stood in the road at a respectful distance behind his horse's swishing red tail as he reined her to a halt.

"I wish you good day, Baron Korrigan."

A look of what appeared to be genuine pain crossed Rob's face. "Please don't call me that," he said. "It's a thing I like even less than deserve. Especially coming from such a great lord and hero."

"I'm less of those things now than I was," Jaume said, as lightly as he could. "At least the latter, since His Majesty's seen fit to let me keep my ranks."

"Never less to those who know you and your deeds. Nor, if I may flatter myself, those who've heard the songs sung that I myself have written about you. Which are mostly even true, so far as I can ascertain."

Jaume laughed. "I've heard some of them," he said. "You do me great honor. You've a gift for words."

"You can't mean that—the Empire's greatest poet, praising my barroom doggerel?"

"Since you know so much about me, do you think I'd lie about such a thing?"

"No, never, Count Jaume! I most humbly beg your pardon." And the man began to kneel.

"No, no, what are you doing that for? It's me who's visiting your land—I hope by your leave."

"Always! And here's you not just a Count on your own account but here a Cardinal and Prince of the Church and all, hence of a dignity equal to a duke."

"True enough. Still no need to kneel. I fancy we're comrades of sorts, since we both faced the Horde at Canterville. And in any event, may I dismount?"

"Of course! And make yourself welcome at my humble house. Please come in, take a load off, and let me offer you aught to wash the trail dust from your throat."

"Thank you." Jaume dismounted. "And if someone might see to my mount, get her watered and into some shade, if you please?"

Rob cocked a finger at the peasant children. Jaume saw that they had edged closer.

"You, Livie. Take the Champion's horse round to the stable and let the grooms take care of her, there's a good lass."

He tossed a copper coin to the small girl who had trotted eagerly forward. Her short hair, face, eyes, and hemp smock were all exceedingly similar shades of brown. She caught it deftly as a snub-nosed flier, Anurognathus, capturing a moth at sunset.

"Are you really the Imperial Champion, Count Jaume dels Flors, *monsieur*?" she asked.

"Guilty as charged. Here you are." He handed off the reins. "Treat her gently and she'll be gentle with you. She's a good mount, for a horse."

"What's her name?"

"I've no idea." She wasn't a dinosaur, after all. Jaume was kind to all animals, as a matter of personal inclination and because of his religious obligation to act in accordance with Beauty. But in the end a horse was a mount, no more. Not a person like Camellia, or his men's lovely hadrosaurs.

"Off with you, girl," Rob said. She led the animal around the grey fieldstone hip of the manor. "She'll remember this day all her life. To what do I owe the honor, Mor Jaume?"

"Well, I knew—given what I heard from Melodía and others after Raguel went down—that I'd little hope of crossing into Providence without attracting your eye. As indeed I appear to've done. Good day, ladies."

He nodded to the woods-runner pair. The shorter, dark one grinned and nodded shyly. The taller, red-haired one just glared at him from her sun-brown, freckled face as if daring him to start something.

"I hope you take no offense, Count Jaume," Rob said. "The runners have little love for authority or noble birth, and less respect."

"I'm not thin-skinned in that regard."

Walking up to Rob, he bowed deeply to the woods-runners, then held out his hand to the Baron of the place. Rob gazed at it a moment as if uncertain what it was, then gripped him forearm to forearm in greeting.

"So I thought I'd make a virtue of necessity," Jaume said, "and turn a courtesy call upon the lord of this land into a plea for help, knight to knight."

"Help?" Rob stared at him with green-hazel eyes. He had a curiously handsome face behind his red-bronze beard. It went oddly with his long-armed, short-legged, powerfully bodied build. "What help could I ever give you, of all the people beneath the clouds?"

"I need to beg Duke Karyl for help in a vital mission," Jaume said. "I'd like you to keep him from killing me before I can state my case, if you would be so kind, Mor Korrigan."

"Where is that body servant you had, Doña Rosamaría?" Melodía asked when she arrived for her evening lesson. As usual, her body ached with the day's exertions. Even more than the bruises Auriana's play with grappling, wooden daggers, and longsword blunts—and, of course, falling off Tormento, deliberately and otherwise—would account for. Her muscles were protesting.

But less and less each day. She knew that meant progress.

"The one who was fluttering around you like a moth for a few days. Parsifal, I think his name was."

The dark figure on the simple bed nodded. "His employment was cut short. He met with an accident."

Melodía frowned. She'd heard nothing of that. Then again, she had made no personal connections with the servants who waited on her within the Corazón Imperial. With smooth, courteous indifference, they had initially simply ignored her efforts to get to know them. Then, later, La Madrota had advised her to be wary of any kind of intimacy with the staff, because Duchess Margrethe had certainly suborned some.

Speaking of which—

"He was a spy," she said. It was not a question, but a realization. "For Margrethe."

"Just so."

"You killed him."

"Not in person. But yes."

Melodía felt her face fold up in a frown. She *hated* puzzles.

"I don't understand," she said. "From the lessons you've taught me, wouldn't it be better to leave a known spy in place? Rather than risk a more efficient, or at least subtler one, being set on you?"

"In general. I had my reasons for acting so precipitously in this case. In part, I confess, because I was offended that the Dowager Duchess would try such a transparent trick on me. In *my* house. And in any event she certainly has a great many more spies on the staff. Even more than the ones my own spies have identified."

Melodía pondered that. "But didn't you also tell me it was useful to have your opponents underestimate you?"

"Indeed. There are limits to how much Margrethe will accept that I've fallen into my dotage and final decline. I decided it would be useful to show her that I had achieved neither my longevity nor my position—to say nothing of having maintained the family's position as Imperial Tower—by falling short of needful ruthlessness. Also, he annoyed me; I'm only human, after all."

"Why would she try something so obvious?"

Rosamaría's wizened face wrinkled deeper into frown. "I wish I knew. We all make mistakes; no one is perfectly cunning."

"Even Raguel made mistakes, it seems," said Melodía with a smile. The fact that they had beat Him, and she had played a role in that defeat, was sometimes all that kept her going through the uncertainty and despair, and constant worry for her baby sister.

"Even Him."

"Did you believe in the Grey Angels? Ah—before, I mean?"

"No," La Madrota said. "Any more than I 'believe' in air. I knew they were real, and not because of Church doctrine or our family's official histories. Which are as packed with self-serving fabrications as I believe you've always suspected them to be; it's just that not everything they claim is a fable. Even some of the more outrageous elements. I've never seen one, thank the Eight. But I've . . . seen their workings before."

That made Melodía regret bringing the subject up. Raguel had violated her mind, as Hornberg had violated her body. The Angels terrified her.

"And yet," Doña Rosamaría said, "this move of Margrethe's does seem painfully clumsy. Of course, it's a truism that it's dangerous to presume an enemy's actions are a mistake. But in the kind of war we're waging, it can be as fatal to judge a mistake as a cunning stratagem as vice versa. That's why no one wins forever. Not even me."

"I'm confused," Melodía said, shaking her head. "It seems she's outmaneuvered you on several occasions."

Even though by now she knew her ancestor better, part of her still quailed to utter such a criticism. But La Madrota nodded.

"She has. I find her . . . curious. She still holds the upper hand in our campaign, now that she has your father's ear on the same pillow with her, though he stills holds out against going to war with Trebizon, bless his stubbornness."

She actually laughed. Though small and soft, the sound jarred Melodía.

"Mother Maia knows I never expected to say *that*.

Still, despite her getting the better of me, I sometimes wonder if—like the Trebs—she's as clever as she thinks she is. Perhaps it's just my old woman's vanity, but I have to wonder if she's getting help of some kind."

"From where?"

"Where, indeed?" La Madrota asked, her black eyes particularly sharp in the low lamp light.

A thought struck Melodía that made her insides quiver.

"You don't mean the Grey Angels!"

"I do. Or others."

"But it can't be! We just finished standing off Raguel's Crusade!'

"You have firsthand experience with those who have bargained with Them for power and glory, I believe."

"Oh, yes," Melodía said. Quietly, as if she feared to hear the words. "And it ended in horror for them."

It came to her, briefly, to wonder what had driven Lady Violette to her compact with Raguel. She knew that Bogardus had allowed himself to be gulled by his belief that the Grey Angel he secretly served shared his beautiful vision of making all of not just Nuevaropa but Paradise into a garden of love and peace and calm, reflective beauty. His idealism betrayed him. But what pain moved his co-conspirator Violette to betray humankind, and ultimately herself?

Melodía wondered if the decisive snap of Shiraa's jaws had granted her merciful release. As her own javelin cast through the eye had given Bogardus.

Then she thought, *Fuck her. I don't care. Karyl's pet matadora gave her better than she deserved.*

"And for hundreds of thousands of others," Rosamaría said with some asperity. "The reports I received indicate that the Grey Angel Horde slaughtered scarcely imaginable numbers in the areas they overran. If it's true that Margrethe is being aided by one or more of the Seven, then I'm far less concerned with the possible dangers to her than I am the danger she poses to us, the Empire, and all of Paradise."

"But we can't know."

"No. Nor will it be easy to find out."

She sat a moment with her head sunk to her clavicle, swaddled as always in her plain black robes.

"It troubles me that after centuries of inactivity, the Grey Angels have taken action against us humans again," La Madrota said. "Why now? What's their end?"

"We're taught they act to correct imbalances in the Equilibrium of Paradise."

"But how did the Empire threaten to throw Equilibrium out of true? Or was that it at all?" Rosamaría shook her head. "Whatever They are, the Grey Angels are not human. Their motivations are not ours. Which makes it futile to speculate on them, as vital as it may be to learn what they are. And it makes it so much the harder to learn whether the Duchess Margrethe has made her own arrangement with more-than-human powers."

"How can we find out?"

"Be alert. I will delve, but quietly. We have to remember that neither you nor our new Duke Karyl, nor anyone else suspected Raguel's presence and influence in the Garden villa. Except for the plotters Bogardus, Violette, and that other Council member, the one Karyl caught in treason and killed."

"Longeau."

"And yet presuming supernatural influence exists where it does not can be as dangerous to us as refusing to accept the possibility that it does. The dance is intricate and difficult."

They sat awhile in silence.

"And my lesson for tonight?" Melodía asked at last. She was starting to nod off, in truth. She was sleeping better now, since her training with Auriana was at least giving her a passable counterfeit of the sensation of action and purpose. But her daily exertions also wore her out. And her mental training with Rosamaría drained her energies to a surprising extent.

"You have had it, my dear. Leave me. And . . . take care. More even than you've been. Matters approach some kind of head."

I didn't know you cared, Melodía thought.

"I told you before, child," La Madrota said. "I love and care for you, and all my descendants. It's just that I must sometimes act as if I do not care."

"You can read minds?"

Again, the smile—surprisingly warm and gentle, for one so harsh.

"No. I can read faces. They can be good guides to what's going on behind. Now go. And know that I do love you, Melodía Estrella."

A half dozen of Karyl's war-Triceratops lumbered about the broad bare yard of Séverin Farm when Rob rode jouncing up on Little Nell's back onto the grounds alongside Jaume on his red horse. The sun was falling to its early grave behind the Shield range, still many kilometers to the east and blue but showing silvery glints of the eternal snowcap topping the higher peaks.

Great mottled-grey-and-brown feet shuffled up great, prodigious clouds of dust as the three-horns trudged in circles, their huge frilled and horned heads lowered, murmuring cavernously at one another. Wood and wicker fighting castles were strapped to their high backs, though no one rode the ten-meter-long dinosaurs but their drivers. These were small dark men and women, Turco nomads from beyond the Scudo. Mercenaries of a sort, though combatant only when things went well and truly to worms, they sat astride the three-horns' necks on saddles with special wooden chocks to prevent the monsters from lifting their heads far enough past dead level to crush them with their bony neck-shields.

Best of all, there was Karyl standing bare-chested to one side with his hair caught up in a horsetail topknot and his blackwood staff in hand, nodding and talking to his head as he presided over the exercise.

Rob inhaled deeply and felt his face split in a grin. "Ah, dust and dinosaur farts!" he exclaimed. "It smells like old times."

His Einiosaurus wasn't fleet, though Jaume courteously kept his courser walking at her more . . . deliberate pace. But it had taken less than three hours' ride from that vile toad Melchor's former digs to what had been and was again Karyl's headquarters. Providence wasn't large. Their flight from the Horde outbreak, desperate though it had been, had taken much longer because they were still an army—Karyl kept them so, and so alive—and as such moved no faster than its slowest wagon.

Jaume smiled down at him. "You love it."

"I do. Ennoble me His Imperial Nibs might see fit to do, but three things I am first and foremost: an Ayrishmuhn, a minstrel, and a dinosaur master. And a rogue."

"Isn't that four things?"

"Did I claim to be a mathematician? That's one thing I'm not, Count of the Flowers. And some might consider the last item no more than a restatement of the first, so."

I love her less, though, he thought, looking again at the aide, now wrapped neck to booted toe in tight-fitting black, who nodded her short-haired head to whatever Karyl was telling her. *It's not that I grudge him a willing bedmate; he's been in dire need of such since long before I found him in that sulfurous little* Francés *village, and that's the fact. But I wish she didn't stand between us.*

Mora Selena glanced over her shoulder, and her dark eyes widened in surprise. Rob's apparition was no shock, though he granted his appearance might have been, to a lass of sensitive nature. But she knew the tall, orange-haired man who rode beside Karyl's spymaster.

Karyl turned deliberately. He had noticed newcomers riding up, and that openly, of course. But Rob saw his own left brow arch in an expression that served him as might another's shout of surprise.

"Rob," he said, nodding. "Captain-General dels Flors. To what do I owe this unexpected honor?"

Well, his manner's not effusively genial, Rob thought, *but that's just Him.* He still felt uneasy. He'd spent months hearing Karyl speak the name of Jaume dels Flors, and never as if it tasted like honey on his tongue.

To Rob's complete astonishment, Jaume nudged his mare a few paces out ahead of Nell's great hook-horned snout, halted her, dismounted, and dropped to his knee to show the orange queue at his nape to the Duke of the Borderlands.

"Your Grace," Jaume said, "I have come first to admit the great wrong I did you, your people, and your magnificent war-dinosaurs at the Battle of Gunters Moll, offer my heartfelt apologies, and beg your forgiveness. Or at least forbearance, because I have a much greater thing to ask of you.

"I led the attack on your rear that dealt the first, unjust defeat to your undefeated three-horn phalanx because His Majesty had received poor intelligence as to your own motives and actions. A fact I discovered, to my horror, as I spent the next half year restoring peace to Alemania before returning to La Merced. He gave orders based on that intelligence, and I followed them, as was and is my duty. But that excuses nothing, nor do I make excuse. I acted wrongly, and submit to your judgment. And vengeance, if you feel called upon to take it. But I ask one thing: that you at least hear my request, in hopes you will carry it out even if you take my life."

Rob had seldom seen his friend at any kind of a loss. It amused him to see Karyl stare down at the kneeling man in plain confusion.

But it didn't last. Karyl's face squeezed shut like a fist in what Rob recognized as a look of intense pain. Then he shook it once and raised it to gaze at Jaume with a calm, clear eye.

"I accept your apology," he said, only grinding out the words a touch. "You cost me a lot, that day. But then, it wasn't you who defeated me; it was the Baron, here, and his wild mace-tail herd. You merely delivered the killing stroke to my White River Legion. And I seem to have forgiven this rogue of an *Irlandés*, so in time I suppose I shall forgive you, too.

"In any event, to all intents the man to whom you did these things is dead. Twice over, though I am cursed to carry his memories, sorrows, and regrets. You are welcome, Count Jaume. Please, stand up. Will your Companions be joining us?"

"No, Your Grace," said Jaume, rising. "After I went into . . . voluntary exile, let's call it . . . from the Imperial Court, I decided to send them to the Mother House here in Francia. There they can rest, heal their bodies, minds, and souls, and most of all remain as remote, and hopefully safe, from intrigue as possible, under the auspices of Mor Jerome, our Master of Estates."

Karyl nodded. "Very well. I take it you have come for something else, as well."

"I have. I'm here to beg for help you and only you can provide, in hopes of saving the Empire from a catastrophe of hard-to-imagine proportions. Though you of all men will have the clearest vision of its potential scope."

"You've intrigued me, at least. Please come into my home, then, and give me the details."

He turned and walked toward the big house.

Jaume was a great, bold, dashing devil. And who knew

that better than Rob Korrigan, who so assiduously followed his and his Companions' every exploit? But still the Count held back, and his long turquoise eyes showed uncertainty as they flicked aside to Rob.

Who laughed. "D'you think Himself's the sort to make mere polite noises, my lord? If he still wanted you dead, you'd be bleeding out into the dust at this instant, not asked into his parlor. You can do as you will, but I'm going inside where it's cool and there's fine dark ale to wash the trail dust from my throat."

Chapter 35

Jinete, light rider. . . . —Skirmishers and scouts, often women, who ride horses and striders. They wear no armor, or at most a light nosehorn-leather jerkin, with sometimes a leather or metal cap. They use javelins or feathered twist-darts, and a sword. Some also carry a light lance and a buckler. A few shoot shortbows or light crossbows, but mounted archery is very difficult, and not much practiced in Nuevaropa.

—A PRIMER TO PARADISE FOR THE IMPROVEMENT
OF YOUNG MINDS

What does it mean? Melodía thought.

"You're learning, Princess," Auriana called down from her perch on the cutbank as Melodía rode her youthful sackbut, Tormento, in a placid circle on the flats by the little stream. It was late afternoon, and the heat had blessedly come off the day. The dirt and sand still smelled of it, though.

What does it mean for Montserrat? What does it mean for me?

Melodía knew she was improving. She had a fair degree of natural athleticism, and had been trained as a horsewoman most of her life, and taught combat on foot from an age not much greater than her poor lost sister, Montse, was now. Weeks of despair combined with the comforts and ease of life as a Princess of the Empire hadn't utterly robbed her of the physical edge acquired in prior weeks on campaign. Learning to ride the truculent Parasaurolophus had turned out in large part to mean adapting existing skills to unfamiliar uses.

It was another achievement. Another thing she'd done herself, not been granted by birth. And she couldn't even feel triumph in it. Instead, she felt sick and scared and angry.

What chance do we have, now that Rosamaría's told me my father's fucking the Duchess of Hornberg?

Melodía had slept fitfully after La Madrota gave her the news, late last night. She'd been sleeping better in the weeks since Auriana began training her—the brutally accelerated schedule Rosamaría had subjected Melodía to had the lucky effect of causing her to fall exhausted into bed each night, so tired that aching muscles couldn't even keep her awake. She hadn't even been experiencing that recently.

But the news had broken that cycle.

I'd be happy about it, if it was literally anybody else, she thought. *Except a Grey Angel.* She'd long outgrown hating and resenting the possibility that her father might take another woman into his life after her mother's death. Eventually, though, she'd come to understand that he'd adore his lost Marisol until his dying breath. For years Melodía had actively hoped Felipe would find someone to love. He had the occasional visit by a courtesan, well paid for her erotic skills as well as her discretion, to take care of his physical needs. That was only proper—and wiser than engaging in dalliances with women of his Court, like the older but still quite handsome Teresa de Rincón. Unusually wise, for a man she'd long since realized had an intellect that all but inevitably outpaced his judgment.

But to her disordered mind the real situation made the old saw about clasping a viper to one's bosom seem inadequate, if not outright preferable: a viper's bite could grant her father a quick death. Rosamaría seemed to foresee that the Duchess von Hornberg portended a lingering demise, not just for the Emperor but the whole of Torre Delgao.

And even she, the ageless master manipulator, seems at a loss as to what to do about it. That was the worst part of all to Melodía.

"You're not acting so damn self-conscious," Auriana called. "That may not be the best thing to remind you of. But it'll help you learn for the future: you already have the needed skills, from all your horseback riding. Stop worrying and let them take over."

She realized her *maestra* was right. Her mind was too preoccupied by a scarcely controlled seethe of thoughts and emotions to frantically overanalyze every twitch of her mount's smooth red-and-black-scaled hide. Instead, she let the muscle memory and subconscious alertness that allowed her to ride a horse without constant attention keep her aboard and in control.

It wasn't much consolation.

By now Melodía knew that La Madrota was using her spies and operatives among the Imperial Heart staff to keep the arena sealed off from intrusion during her lessons, even by other servants. The matriarch intended to keep Melodía's intensive dinosaur-combat training secret until it was time for her to be knighted by her father in a public ceremony. Even Auriana, who wasn't exactly paid to be effusive about her student's knightly achievements, freely admitted Melodía's solo fight against Bogardus, leather-armored on a mare versus a knight in full harness riding a sackbut, merited knighthood all by itself, as acts of prowess and daring go.

And coming to terms with the great unruly beast, of

course. By now the two had worked out a sort of wary truce between them, like an Imperial March and a Turanian Pashalik eyeing each other across a border stretch where the Shield Mountains offered little obstacle to crossing. Now she was persuading the monster to trot in the largest circle the yard offered a creature of his length, without his constantly dropping a shoulder or rearing up to dump her off. She already knew most of his maneuvers from horseback riding, though Meravellosa would never pull them on her. His were vastly more powerful, given that he weighed in at a slim 2,200 kilos, while her mare massed little more than a quarter-ton. His maneuvers were also slower, and the muscular preludes easier to read, by way of compensation.

She was just glad the high, humped structure of his back made it impossible for him to roll all the way over.

But it was hard to focus on any of that. Not even to take pleasure in her instructor's qualified praise. Which was another achievement she had earned, still a rare and precious commodity in her life.

No. What she thought was, *So my father is screwing the Duchess of Hornberg. The man who makes decisions based on the most persuasive voice he hears. How can it not be hers?*

How I miss war.

She nearly hated herself for the thought. But once it came, it was as if an incoming tide had met a dike of soft sand.

Even back when we were desperate fugitives, trapped between armies intent on destroying us, she thought, *I had clarity. I had action to take. We never knew who'd come back anytime we set out—never knew how long until time ran out on us all. But at least I could do something!*

So why not give in? Why not fight for my baby sister? Why not give war a chance?

Her mind tried to tell her that was crazy. But the black despair in her belly and the roaring in her ears as her heart raced out of control with fear for Montse drowned out reason.

We could do it! We could find a way! Maybe we could go overland through Ovda—the Padishah *doesn't have much love for Trebizon.*

And even if we failed, if we died—that would put an end to this feeling of helplessness. To the fact that I'm helpless—against the monster and his mother, against the hada *who stole my sister away.*

Sensing his rider had moved on to full distraction, Tormento stopped and tipped his body forward, lowering his beak to the bare, hard-packed sand as if to graze. The surprise motion sent Melodía flying feet-skyward over the saddle pommel and the sackbut's shoulder.

Because of the tipping, she didn't have far to fall. But he'd flipped her so that she landed flat on her back. Hard.

And even as her chest heaved to reinflate itself with lost air, she thought, *Would war really be worse than what I have now?*

"Thank you for coming, my friend," Karyl told Rob as he stood gazing down at the fire in the grate with his back to Rob. The wind blew chill from the Shields tonight. "And thank you for staying, as I asked."

As if I'd refuse your request, Rob thought. *Especially to spend more time acting like friends.*

"My pleasure," he said in a light tone. "Were you wanting to discuss the Count's proposal?"

"Jaume's? No. I'll do it. I saw the need for it as soon as he asked. Possibly more clearly than he does himself."

But you wouldn't tell him as much right away? Rob thought with a sly smile. *Is it that you wanted to let him stew in his juices, then?*

Or is it some deeper game you play? Knowing his friend as he did, he had to suspect the latter. Pettiness formed little part of Karyl's makeup that he'd seen, although he could get in peevish moods. Like anyone. Rob didn't want to ask him, didn't want to risk spoiling the moment. He was savoring the fact that Karyl would ask for his advice again on anything, even if no more than what wine to import for his cellar.

"So what is it you need?"

"The Grey Angels aren't done with us."

And don't I know that, thought Rob, *as I saw one playing the Emperor and all the Empire for prize fools in the tent that night?*

He was on the cusp of saying that when Karyl continued.

"They are going to try to use war with Trebizon over the little girl's abduction as a tool to get us to destroy ourselves. At which it would work well, at least for a start."

Rob swallowed hard. Karyl's words settled like lead pellets in his stomach. It had been terrifying enough listening to Jaume's oddly calm and factual account of their failed rescue of Melodía's sister and its reason: Fae magic, beyond doubt. That the Fae suddenly seemed more active in the world than ever before was unsettling enough to a man of Rob's background and experiences. Given what he'd seen in this very chamber a few weeks before, it was terrifying.

He didn't have to have Karyl's strategic genius to see that the man was surely right.

"Do you think they'll try another Crusade?"

"Not initially. As far as I know, no Grey Angel Crusade has ever failed before. At least not since the end of Demon War."

He paused, and a ripple of something like pain passed over his pale, gaunt, dark-bearded face. *Ah, Maris, his*

*old headaches from the dent Falk's axe made in his skull
aren't coming back now, are they?*

"This has the potential to light the fire of war across a
third of Aphrodite Terra. If they can embroil the three
empires that occupy this end of the continent, all battling
one another, that will provide abundant opportunity to
spread it. If their cunning matches their malice—which
I suspect isn't always so, but we can't afford to wager on
it—they can potentially carry it on to Vareta and the Central Kingdom and perhaps beyond."

Rob rubbed his chin. His beard, which he liked to keep
neatly done and trimmed to a point, was getting bushy.
He'd have to admonish his man Bergdahl for failing to
point that out for him. *Or maybe I need to instruct him
to do that? I'm used to playing servant, not being served.*

"At which point, with all nations—perhaps all men and
women—already battling one another, the time would be
ripe to start influencing the already battle-maddened people into a full Grey Horde, would it not? Perhaps turn
two against each other, and have them fight each other
with that crazy self-forgotten abandon that made them so
terrible to fight despite their lack of skill, or often weapons other than hands and teeth? They would rage and
slaughter until the last pair on Paradise died with their
own guts wrapped around them both like shrouds."

"That seems likely," Karyl said, nodding. "You dis-
claim any grasp of strategy, but you show a sound grasp
of the potential outcome."

Rob felt his cheeks heat up. "Sure, and I'd never pretend to know a thing about it, before such a master of the
art as yourself."

Karyl actually showed a flash of white teeth. "What
skill I have I've learned across a lifetime of single-minded
study. It's unkind to yourself to compare your own level
to mine—just as it was to compare my musical skill to
yours."

Rob laughed. "Aye, but your playing was that bad—still, I take your point. So, what do you need me to do? You haven't exactly filled me with confidence that Ma Korrigan's only son she didn't strangle before he got away can do much against such a world-spanning catastrophe. Which for a fact sounds as feasible as bailing out the Océano Guinevere with my hat."

"Let's remember that this is all possibility, not certainty. It's a possible lie to the future. Our task is to steer events in some different direction before they reach that land."

"You've the soul of a poet, despite yourself."

"No need to insult me."

But he smiled, slightly, once again. *His face'll ache for days from such unfamiliar exercise.* But Rob had to admire his self-control at being able to make even the mildest of jokes while pondering such matters. Or the complete cold-bloodedness. But Rob had spent enough time with the man to have his measure in some degree. Karyl's blood ran as hot as any beneath that calm and pallid surface.

"It still seems a mighty task," Rob said, "even for those who've done what some might call mighty deeds enough for a lifetime already."

"It is. And—I am beginning to wonder if we're up to it."

Rob felt cold. "Oh, no. Don't go saying that."

"The first time, Raguel's arrogance made Him overconfident. Not surprising, inasmuch as his technique had always worked before, in slaughtering human beings by the million. He didn't expect such a setback, any more than, frankly, I ever expected we could deal it to him."

"Yet you faced him. Alone. When no one else would."

Karyl sighed. "I was dead anyway—a state I'd be resigned to, if I could just achieve it and stay put. But I could not let myself simply die without fighting. It's what

I do. The only thing I saw to fear was not to face Raguel in battle, since I'd nothing more to lose."

"So the fierce pride of a master craftsman saved the Empire."

"And the jaws of my sweet, loyal, loving Shiraa." This time Karyl's smile was wide and prolonged.

How could I, a dinosaur master, not love a man who so loves a dinosaur? And such a fine girl she is, at that.

"But now," Karyl said, and the smile evaporated, "the Angels will come against us with greater force. They exist, in defiance of my lifetime of resolutely not believing in them, and they've demonstrated exactly the sort of vast magical powers the legends attribute to them. I—I don't really know how to respond to that."

"By fighting, of course," Rob said. "It's what you do."

"Indeed. But I am having a hard time seeing how we can defeat them without bringing some kind of force beyond the physical to bear."

"What about the witch who calls herself Aphrodite after the continent, then? Who hired us first to go and turn a sect of pacifists into an army? Which we did."

"She gave me back my hand. Raguel filled the minds and hearts of a hundred thousand with all-consuming rage. That's quite a disparity of power."

"Granted. And not even I know how to find her again. 'Twas her who sought me out. But at least we could try."

"Believe me," Karyl said, "she cannot help us. No. We are in a desperate strait, and against my own judgment— against my own terrors, against the nightmares that have tortured me for months—I begin to fear we have to contemplate allying ourselves with a different power. One which has no love of Angels."

And Rob knew.

First he went cold. *Bergdahl was right, all these weeks!* Despite the man's hail-fellow companionship, Rob somehow hated being forced to admit it. But he hated it even more because it meant—

His mind vanished in a roaring white flame of terror.

His heart broke. He fled—from Karyl's presence, from Séverin Farm, pausing only to reclaim and fumblingly saddle Little Nell before fleeing to the dubious sanctuary of his traitor's castle.

Karyl stood staring at the sudden vacancy of his study.

"I wonder what possessed Rob to take off like that," he said softly to himself. He had gone quite white behind his red-bronze beard.

He shook his head. He had other matters to concern himself with. Matters he desperately wanted not to have to confront, but he had no choice.

"I hope he hasn't suddenly taken sick," he said. "I'll send a healer in the morning to check on him. He's never been one to think about his own health."

He had hoped to get Rob's reassurance that an alliance with the Fae was, at least, a possible strategic option.

Or, to be honest with myself, that Rob would talk me out of the whole notion, somehow.

That easy escape now being closed to him, the foremost task he feared was getting sleep. The dreams were actually somewhat better, now that he knew what lay behind them.

And sometimes immeasurably worse, now that he knew. He put his friend's curious reaction from his mind, steeled himself, and marched off to his nightly battles against nightmare.

Chapter 36

Gordito, **Fatty**. . . . —*Protoceratops andrewsi.* A small Ceratopsian dinosaur: a frilled, plant-eating quadruped, 2.5 meters long, 400 kilograms, 1 meter high, with a powerful toothed beak. The only hornface to lack horns. A ubiquitous domestic herd beast, not found wild in Nuevaropa. Timid by nature.

—THE BOOK OF TRUE NAMES

"Have you ever been offered a proposition which horrified you too much to even think about taking it?"

Rob Korrigan slouched in a chair in the dining hall of his manor as if he'd melted onto it. Dawn light oozed from the window like pus from a wound. His beard scratched the skin above his collarbone, where his substantial rust-colored chest thatch failed to reach. A wine goblet stood on the table within ready reach. It was empty.

He wasn't sure which number it was.

"No, my lord," Bergdahl called from the kitchen, where he was chopping onions for Rob's breakfast omelets of scratcher eggs on a sturdy wooden table. A pan of fatty bacon sizzled and filled the air with a delicious aroma as it roasted in the fireplace. For such a strange-looking chap, Bergdahl was a startlingly good cook. "I can't say that I have."

"Ah. A downy scratcher chick you are, Bergdahl. Pray you stay that way."

"As you say, my lord."

After riding straight back from Séverin Farm to Tertre Herbeux as fast as Little Nell was willing to go, which wasn't very, Rob had thought his only interest was in getting drunk. Also as rapidly as possible. But the smells of his seneschal's cooking proved him wrong.

Now he wanted to eat *and* get drunk, both as fast as possible. He heaved himself up and, taking the empty goblet, padded into the kitchen with the blue-painted white tiles cool beneath his bare feet.

He spied the wine bottle on a side table. It was empty. Setting the goblet down beside it with a decisive *plonk!* of silver on knife-scarred hardwood, he went to the door to the underground pantry and opened it.

Just inside, down a ramp of hard-stamped dirt by a set of wooden shelves, he saw a heavy clay ale jug. If memory served, it was mostly full. He fetched it, came back to the short hallway that led to the kitchen, and pulled the cork out with his teeth. Then he set about seeing how fast he could make it go from full to empty.

He heard a loud knocking from the manor's front door. "If you can spare a moment from your cooking, Bergdahl," he called, annoyed, "go tell whoever the fuck that is to piss off promptly, there's a good fellow."

"At once, my lord."

After an indeterminate interval that Rob had spent, if not in bliss, at least blessedly oblivious in his single-minded focus on guzzling, he heard Bergdahl clear his throat from close at hand.

"What is it?" he grumbled, wiping his mouth with the back of his hand. He resented having his drinking interrupted, given that his seneschal didn't have the tone of a man announcing breakfast is served, and anyway Rob couldn't recollect hearing the promised omelets being cooked.

"It was a messenger from El Duque de La Marca, my lord."

"From Karyl?" asked Rob, who had completely forgotten the errand he sent Bergdahl on, and now felt even more befuddled.

"That Duke of the Borderlands, yes," Bergdahl said, with what Rob acknowledged to himself as laudably restrained sarcasm.

"What did he want?"

"She," Bergdahl said. "It seems that His Grace is worried about your health."

"What? Why?" He shook his head. The motion made his brain feel as if it were sloshing about in his skull. *Good*, he thought. *That means I'm getting properly drunk.*

He waved a hand. "Never mind. I trust you told her to piss off promptly?"

"As you commanded, lord."

"Well. Good. Carry on, then. I find myself craving that omelet. And a touch more to drink."

He upended the jug and let the amber liquid cascade, more into his mouth than down his beard to drip on his chest hairs, left bare by his open vest. The vessel's growing lightness weighted down his heart.

"So, my lord," called Bergdahl, back at the stove working his own arcane magic on his omelets. Or so Rob judged by the distance he sounded to be; he couldn't be arsed to look away from the all-important jug. Rob had no idea how he did the thing; his master Morrison had claimed Rob could burn water trying to boil it. But at least it meant he'd not had to add cooking to his endless list of 'prentice chores.

"Are you ready to face the truth?"

The words tolled like a great bronze temple bell in Rob's mind, suggesting it was still not sufficiently fogged. *It's all true*, he thought. *What I thought I saw in his library that night. What I heard. All true.*

"It may be sedition to say so," Bergdahl said, "but His Grace has clearly betrayed humanity and the Creators to the evil ones."

At that Rob wagged his head like a yearling three-horn brought to bay by a pack of juvenile tyrants.

"No," he said. "That I won't believe. I don't give a shit about him being a great lord again. It isn't that. Karyl's my friend. He wouldn't turn against his own kind. He fought for us."

"He also fought a Grey Angel—a servant of the Creators."

"When none other would. And your erstwhile master, the Duke of Hornberg, took the field against Raguel right along with the rest of us. No, I tell you. He's no renegade."

Not knowingly, he's not. But the Fae were notorious for their trickery. To Rob, that was more than myth or mere reputation.

"But why does he try to seduce you into dealing with the Fae, if he hasn't already turned?"

"Because he thinks it's right! He's obsessed with fear of another Grey Angel Crusade. Not that there's anything daft about that; I don't expect them to turn into docile little darlings now that one of them's been defeated for the first time in history."

Splendid job, Rob, m'lad, he thought. *You've reminded yourself of one more thing to be petrified of.* He drained the somewhat bitter dregs, tossed the heavy jug aside—sadly, it was stout enough to bounce on the flagstone of the hallway, not break satisfyingly—and went rooting for another.

"How can he possibly think dealing with the Fae's a good idea?" Bergdahl asked, scooping the omelets onto a silver platter. "Leave aside that it's a death sentence to do so under Creators' Law. The stories all suggest the Fae themselves will do worse to anyone who trusts them."

Don't I know it? Rob thought. He descended into the larder and found an unopened jug behind a sack of turnips. He hauled it out and took it back into the kitchen, where he began prying greedily at the green wax seal with a knife.

"Ah, there you go, you nosehorn's catamite! Got you."

He pried the cork out, upended the jug, and drank.

"I can't say what motivates the man. Unless he's that desperate. Or—"

He frowned and actually lowered the jug.

Wrapping a damp rag around his hand, Bergdahl pulled the bacon pan from the open cooking hearth by the wooden handle on its long metal tang. "The Fae are known for more than their tricks," he told Rob as he carried it spitting and hissing like a wet vexer to the main table. "They use magic too. It's said to be hard for them, but they have their ways as well as wiles."

"That's it!" Rob snapped his fingers. "The devils have ensorceled him!"

He waved the mostly full jug at Bergdahl. "Only one thing to do now," he said. "I see it plain as day."

"And what is that, my lord?" asked Bergdahl, back in the kitchen.

"I've got to"—he woke to the smells of dinosaur bacon and eggs cooking as to a lovely, naked mistress—"eat breakfast, then get drunk. *Priorities*, my man.

"And after I've slept that off, it's away to La Majestad I go to save my dear friend Karyl from his own enchanted self. And the world as well, I wouldn't doubt."

Chapter 37

La Vida se Viene, Life-to-Come—A radical sect of the
Church of Nuevaropa which preached self-denial, holding
that the Creators' mandates in *The Books of the Law* were
metaphorical, and sometimes even meant the opposite
of what they said. Despite its heterodoxy, which crossed
the line into heresy when some sectaries claimed that sin
could lead to eternal damnation, the Life-to-Come enjoyed
a substantial following in the early eighth century.

— LA GRAN HISTORIA DEL IMPERIO DEL TRONO
COLMILLADO

When Melodía entered the crowded throne room
pretending to support La Madrota's elbow—
the ancient got along as spryly as she herself
did, for all that she could tell, and better than Melodía
currently could with her body bruised and aching from
an early morning's training in the scrubland—she almost
stumbled when she saw who stood before her Fangèd
Throne.

Jaume was dressed in a red feather cape and white
trunks, leaving his heroic torso and long muscular legs
bare. He looked at Melodía. Her breath stumbled as her
feet almost had. She nodded once, slightly.

Yes, I forgive you. Yes, I was wrong to blame you. Again. Forgive me, my love.

She looked at Rosamaría critically, though, as they took their waiting places on the front row of the stands placed left and right of the doorway. "He's our secret weapon? But you can see—people are still snickering at him!"

"No. He's bringing our secret weapon."

The throne room was on the verge of stifling, more from the heat of the scores of bodies packed inside than from the heat of the day outside the Heart's thick stone skin. While Melodía wore little more than bangled loincloth and tiara, La Madrota was, as usual, swaddled like an infant, neck to soles in black robes.

As if to compensate, the matriarch held a lacy black fan before her lower face. "Subtle," Melodía said in disgust.

"Sometimes the direct means work best, child. Subtlety's just another tool on the bench. That's the lesson of Martina la Negra's whole life; you should study it again, and this time pay attention."

"Your Majesty, ladies and lords and Deputies of the Diet," Jaume declared, "please allow me to present the hero of the Battle of Canterville, Duque Imperial Karyl de la Marca."

It was an unusually warm day up here on the heights. Melodía, her father, and most of the Court had dressed lightly. Others, especially the Dieta Deputies and other officials, tended to affect the heavy black velvet currently fashionable for their breed, which Melodía gathered they thought enhanced their gravity and appearance of importance.

By contrast, Karyl strode in wearing the loose white shirt and black trousers tucked into the rolled-down tops of cavalry boots that she had grown used to seeing him wear during the Providence army's flight from Raguel's

Horde. He had only added a nosehorn-leather jack to face the Grey Angel Himself—and everybody knew it.

Whether on his own—and Melodía had decided he was a far shrewder motivator than he believed himself to be—or coached, he was clearly reminding the Emperor and all his court that he was first and foremost a peerless fighter. He strode in to thunderous applause, stopped at a respectful distance before the Fangèd Throne, and knelt.

"I thought he hated Jaume," Melodía said to Rosamaría as the tumult died.

"They seem to have come to terms."

"Rise, Duke Karyl," Felipe said. "Please. You honor us with your presence."

"Your Majesty is too kind." He stood up and took a step back.

"Your Majesty, Your Highness, Doña Rosamaría, ladies and gentlemen of the Court. I thank you for hearing me. What I have to say is urgent, and will be brief."

"Blasphemer!" a woman shouted.

"Bishop Charlotte," Rosamaría murmured to Melodía. "Deputy for Cardinal Beate to the College of Princes. She's a solid von Hornberg ally."

"He dared to cross swords with a Grey Angel!"

"Large crowd this evening," Melodía said.

"Having some idea what was going to happen, I made sure to rally our supporters. Margrethe in response rallied hers. So it goes."

The Duque de Mandar rose to his full enormous height, his gaunt, normally blue face red with fury. "Religion to the side, you're an idiot. You're impugning to his face a man who dared cross swords with a Grey Angel!"

Gasps greeted that observation—followed quickly by general laughter. "La Señora Obispa has also impugned me and whoever else fought against the Crusade, including His Majesty himself," Mandar added sternly.

Rolling her eyes like a frightened horse at Margrethe, who sat beside the Emperor with a curdled expression on her own square face, Charlotte melted back into the crowd with the look of one who wishes she could retract the past minute.

"*Grandes y grandezas*," Jaume said in a commanding voice that did not sound raised, "please. His Holiness, Leo Victor, has issued an Encyclical confirming the Emperor's proposition that in the Grey Angel Crusade, we faced not the punishment of the Creators, but a test imposed by Their servants for Their own reasons. A trial by combat, if you will."

"Excellent," La Madrota said. "Do you see what he did there?"

"No," Melodía admitted. "He seems to be prolonging irrelevant debate."

"No. He's ending it. Watch."

"But trial by combat's illegal," declared Hilario de Llanoalto, the realm's richest breeder of war-hadrosaurs, who towered above the other courtiers standing behind the front rank of seats for the most privileged. So dedicated was he to pressing his quest for ennoblement for his services—which really were substantial, Melodía knew—that he had followed the Court from La Merced here to the central Meseta highlands. Even if his dedication hadn't extended to accompanying the Army of Crusade Felipe had led off to Providence.

"For us," Jaume said. "Have you, my lord, reason to believe the Grey Angels do not follow their own set of Laws endowed by our Creators, as we follow the *Books*?"

A moment of silence ensued. Then the onlookers began to mutter to one another. Though Melodía couldn't make out the words, she could read their tone. She sighed.

"You're right," she said to her forebear and mentor. "As usual."

She was pleased to see on her own something shrewd

that her forsaken love had done: though as Captain-General of the Order of the Companions he enjoyed the ecclesiastical rank of a Cardinal, he hadn't used his own superior rank to bludgeon the bishop's objections, but the Pope's. And recourse to Leo Victor's finding carried with it a threat that Melodía realized, with a certain satisfaction, she'd never even have noticed before La Madrota started force-feeding her instruction in intrigue.

Rumors had arrived at Court—and Rosamaría confirmed them from her own far-flung net of sources—that His Holiness was carrying out a quiet but ruthlessly thorough purge of Vida-se-Viene sympathizers from the Church hierarchy, starting at the top and working down. At least four members of El Sacro Colegio had resigned from the Curia and their titular churches and left La Merced, along with a dozen Archbishops. While *The Books of the Law* recognized few categories of blasphemy or heresy, they specified condign punishments for willful twisting of their contents by priests and Church hierarchs. No one was eager to lose not just his red hat but the head beneath it to the Empire's first heresy trials in two hundred years—nor to the covert forms of execution said to have befallen certain individuals who'd been caught abusing high Church offices in particularly embarrassing ways.

Waiting for the low-voice conversation—which was still going his way—to dwindle, Jaume swept his hand toward Karyl, who stood at a respectful distance before the Fangèd Throne. "Your Grace, with His Majesty's permission."

Felipe nodded. "Please, Duke Karyl. I value your counsel highly."

"Look at Margrethe," murmured Rosamaría. "She looks as if she's gotten some spoiled tripes."

Melodía did, and had to restrain her own snicker.

"Thank you, Your Majesty, Count dels Flor," Karyl

said. His voice sounded dry and measured as grains of rye. "I commend the Court for having rejected out of hand the proposal for a naval war with the Basileia of Trebizon. It's an insane notion. I have come, in turn, to refute the notion that any manner of war in this case is a necessary, desirable, or anything but disastrous course of action."

"So you're willing to roll over and accept the Trebs' kidnapping of our Emperor's own dear daughter?" Margrethe burst out from her chair near the Emperor's left arm.

Melodía felt fists and guts knot. *At least she didn't defile Montse's name with her mouth.*

"Dowager Duchess," Karyl acknowledged. He had no patience for courtly formalities, Melodía knew, but as a noble born and raised, he knew his way around them. As he knew that flouting them would merely result in his arguments not being heard. "Please tell me, then, where the Infanta Montserrat can be found at this moment."

Margrethe blinked. "Why, why—she's on a ship, where her vile kidnappers took her. Of course. Every fool in the Empire knows that! Except one, perhaps?"

"Perhaps if we had a map brought in, you could point out to us her exact location," said Karyl in the same calm tone, refusing to acknowledge her insult with so much as a blink. Though if offered under other circumstances, to another noble, it could well lead to an affray on the spot and on the instant.

"Why—no point to that! I have no idea where she is."

Karyl nodded. "Thank you for your cooperation, Your Grace. If anyone can pinpoint the kidnapped child's present location, please tell us now."

That evoked a multitongued stammer of confusion. "We can't!" Llanoalto said. "How do we know where she is?"

"So tell me, please, Don Hilario, how you propose to rescue her, if you don't know where she is."

"Is he one of hers?" Melodía asked.

"Neutral, for now," Rosamaría said behind her fan. "Highplains is fishing for offers from the competing factions. He hasn't got a nibble yet from either of us. He may or may not, depending on what he says here."

"We know the Trebs have her!" It was young Archduke Antoine from Francia, rising from his front-rank seat across from Melodía and Rosamaría.

"And you know which Trebizonés, of course, Your Grace," said Karyl.

"Whatever do you mean?"

"Trebizon is a vast empire, almost as large and populous as our own. There are many Trebs."

"Why—the Basileus, of course! He ordered this frightful crime."

"The Trebs are known for treachery and intrigue. Please tell me whom you think they might practice on, if not one another. If you have evidence the kidnappers were loyal to the Basileus, rather than being traitors, we all await it."

It was the turn of the Francés king's nephew to go red, blink rapidly, and open and close his mouth like a fish in a glass bowl.

"Conspiracy twaddle!" bellowed Dowager Duchess Margrethe. Felipe murmured something to her. She paid him no mind.

"Why isn't . . . her son talking?" asked Melodía. He sat in the front rank nearest the Fangèd Throne, of course. Her eyes tended to slide past him unseeing, as her mind and mouth preferred to slide past his name.

"It would seem that she wants him to appear to remain aloof from this debate," Rosamaría said.

"So you necessarily believe," Karyl said, "that each of the Infanta's kidnappers arrived at the scheme of seizing her at the precise same time, entirely separately from one another."

"How preposterous! Of course not. Clearly, they carefully plotted together . . ."

Her words ran out. But Melodía saw it was already too late.

"In Spañol, the word for that is 'conspiracy,'" Karyl said. "As well as in all the other languages I've some conversance with—a dozen or so. Including Alemán."

"You had best watch yourself, little man."

"Indeed I shall. I'd hate to suffer a fatal fall down a darkened yet thoroughly familiar stairway, like the prior Duke von Hornberg. I won't offer you condolences, since as a fellow noble of the north, I know enough about your late husband to feel confident his mishap did a positive favor to you, your son, and the Empire as a whole. It'll no doubt relieve you to learn that I share few of his proclivities."

If it were possible for a human to shoot lightning bolts from her eyes, the Dowager Duchess would have crisped Karyl on the instant. Melodía had to fake a coughing fit to keep from laughing aloud. La Madrota turned to give her a reproving look, presumably for such an unsubtle ploy, and spoiled it with a wink.

"Your Grace," Felipe said, "the Dowager Duchess is my friend, and of a passionate yet sensitive disposition. Please, be gentle with her."

Karyl bowed. "Your Majesty. Dowager Duchess. Now, with your permission, I will continue my presentation. It's brief, never fear."

"Please do," Felipe said, before Margrethe had a chance to get out whatever she was opening her mouth to say.

"Who's that sitting next to . . . *him*?" Melodía asked Rosamaría, with a nod she hoped was perceptible only to her. "He must be a major crony, for the monster to use his position to get the Elector Menor's Deputy turfed out to give him a seat."

A pair of journeyman heralds had just spoken to Don Silvio, then rousted him from his chair. The tall and gaunt Taliano had been red-faced angry at first—heralds were, in their way, as callous in their disregard of persons and even rank as the Scarlet Tyrants were in their strict enforcement of rules of precedence only they actually understood. But Giustiniani had visibly become mollified as the heralds guided him to the entrance.

Perhaps they offered him a particularly sumptuous and plentiful dessert, Melodía thought. Heralds, especially ones as senior as these, also knew ways to defuse potentially disruptive reactions to their actions.

The man for whom the Diputado had been ejected was fully as huge and burly as the Alemán, black-bearded as well, though his skin and eyes were as dark as his companion's were pale. He wore a black velvet doublet and trunks over black leggings, all trimmed in silver, that must have been as uncomfortable as La Madrota's robes.

"Ahh, Count Vargas," Rosamaría said. "A thoroughgoing brute. He fought against the Empire in the Princes' War, which explains his connection with the Hornberg clan. A reputed torturer, slaver, rapist, and highway robber who's somehow managed to dance along the blade of Imperial justice. Though had your father's ill-advised Army of Correction continued on its original course, he might have enjoyed its full attention, eventually."

The two men finished a muttered and inaudible exchange. Then both looked right at Melodía. Vargas laughed.

Melodía went hot, then cold, and thoroughly sick inside. *Did the monster just brag to his creature about having his way with me, as he has to so many in the Court, in La Merced and here?*

She felt Rosamaría's hand grip and squeeze her arm, gently and briefly. She understood. Sucking down a deep, shuddering breath, she forced herself to stay calm and focus back on the proceedings.

"I still hope someone will tell me how an army attacking the Basileia by land proposes to locate a Princess abducted at sea," Karyl was saying to the Archiduc.

"We could force someone to tell us," Antoine said.

"We'd have to catch one who knew first, you young fool," Mandar said.

"We have no means of doing so, clearly," Felipe said. "Let us move on."

Another man stepped forward. He was of medium height, thin, though not in a cadaverous way like Francisco de Mandar or Deputy Giustiniani; rather, he looked to Melodía as if he'd been squeezed almost dry of juices somehow. His narrow features and grey hair cropped fussily close to the skull seemed to emphasize that appearance. He wore the brown robes of an Imperial Minister.

"Clearly, Your Majesty," he said, the accent of a Majestuoso born and bred, "compelling the Basileus to surrender your daughter would be a primary goal of our expedition. Along, of course, with punishing his Empire severely enough that it'll be another century before they think to try such an act again."

"Contreras," Rosamaría said quietly to Melodía. "Deputy Minister for Administration. A bureaucrat in charge of bureaucracy, as it were. You are keeping track, of course?"

"That is a valid strategic goal," Karyl said. "The first, I mean. You certainly understand that it will take a large army indeed to compel Basileus Nikephoros to do anything at all on his home ground."

"Don't you know already who's aligned with whom?" Melodía asked.

"The question is, do you?"

"Indeed I do, Your Grace!" Contreras said. "But I have

every confidence that the Empire of Nuevaropa can field such an army."

Melodía emitted a short, exasperated exhalation. La Madrota was always admonishing her to sharpen her awareness of intrigue: what games others might be playing. And what the stakes might be.

"Please outline for me your plan to feed such an army," said Karyl, in that same tone of calm, relentless reason. Melodía decided it must help to know with complete confidence that, with the possible exception of Jaume, you could kill anyone in the room without particular difficulty. "Men, women, and animals. And to provide them with water and the other necessities not just of war but of travel and life itself. Naturally, you have great experience at such undertakings."

"Well—not really. But there are those who do!"

"To be sure. I'm among them."

Contreras set his chin. "The Empire of Gran Turán can supply our needs."

Melodía gave a soft grunt. "Until he said that, he had me convinced he was sincere, not bought."

"Coerced," Rosamaría said. "But, yes. There is hope for you."

"Please share with us, Excellency, your plan to compel the High King to do so."

Contreras stepped back with haste surprising in one so professionally reserved. "We'll have an army in the heart of his ragged-assed nomad Empire," Antoine declared.

"Another way of putting that, Your Grace, is that we shall be at the end of an immensely long supply chain, in the midst of what we have suddenly made enemy territory, and all that enemy has to do is break a single link of that chain to kill our entire army of hunger and thirst. You naturally know how large the Empire of Grand Turán is."

Antoine, who had visibly been working his dudgeon

back to the point he felt confident speaking up again, broke into stammers: "I—well, I—it's large, of course. Every schoolchild knows that."

Karyl turned to Felipe. "Your Majesty, I shall happily offer more detailed critiques of the war proposals at your convenience, with the aid of maps—at some later time. No need to bore this august assembly with such details. Please accept that I stipulate to the Archduke's assertion that Turania is, indeed, large."

"A capital idea, Duke Karyl," the Emperor said amid general laughter. "I'm truly eager to share your vast knowledge and wisdom on war."

Karyl turned back to Antoine. "For now, Your Grace, let me ask, simply, what is the detailed plan to invade the Empire of Trebizon across two thousand kilometers of mostly arid steppe and desert? I've crossed High Ovda, in both directions. Much of it's not easy to traverse. And what is your contingency plan for waging a secondary—or, rather, at that point, primary—war against the Turanians? I'm truly eager to see it."

Antoine, who had the trained poise of an aristocrat but not much beyond, was blinking rapidly and swallowing.

"What difference does it make," bellowed a sturdy young knight. He wore his hair shaved on both sides, with only a black strip on top. Though Spañol by look and accent, he affected a full, black, Northern-style beard. A gold ring hung from his right earlobe. His tunic was gold on green. "One of our dinosaur knights is worth ten Trebs. And a hundred desert-wandering Ovdan scum!"

"Ugh," Melodía said to Rosamaría. "Baron Steban de Tresgarras. Untried and looking to make a name. Also to bed me. He may succeed at one of those."

"Nuevaropan dinosaur knights may well be the best on Aphrodite Terra," Karyl said. "But Ovdan and Treb warriors are also good, and substantially more numerous. I fear you may underestimate your foes, Mor Threeclaws. I've fought Trebizonian cataphracts and Turanian dinosaur knights, as well as nomad *guerrilleros*. And even if your assessment of relative worth is accurate, almost all of them carry recurved bows and can shoot through your finest breastplate at a hundred paces from the saddle, at full gallop of horse or dinosaur. So you'd be unlikely to get close enough to display your superior prowess."

Tresgarras got so agitated several of his companions had to physically restrain him from lunging at Karyl, who had come into the Imperial presence unarmed.

"I hope he gets loose," Melodía said. "I'd love to see how Karyl kills him."

A year ago you'd have found that cold-bloodedness reprehensible, Melodía thought. *Now you're genuinely eager. And I'm not sure the change is for the worse.*

She recalled the horrors that earnest girl's innocent idealism had visited on her and others—not the rape; that was purely Falk; but the fall that made it possible . . . and many, many deaths—and knew for sure.

But Margrethe held up a large white hand, as if acting the peacemaker—ironically, given the circumstances. The angry knight deflated back onto the bench as if she'd stuck a pin in him.

"Karyl claims he has no gift for intrigue or argument," she said to Rosamaría. There was little danger of being overheard in the sudden confused hubbub, which was turning to consternation, outrage, and outright laughter as it quickly became clear no one had any such plans. "But he seems to address every question or comment as if they were battlefield maneuvers. Or maybe as if he were playing a game of war, like chess or *weiqi*."

"You see why I considered him my secret weapon?" Rosamaría said with an undertone of undisguised glee.

"But how did you manage to get him here?"

"Why, through Jaume, of course. He's a dear lad, and you really need to stop flying off into a rage against him for every little thing. He truly loves you, loves your father—loves Montse, for that matter—and would die for any of you or for the Empire. He's quite brilliant in his way, really."

Melodía shook her head. She didn't feel like acknowledging her forebear was correct yet again.

"Your Majesty, I shall also be glad to discuss any plans for such an invasion with you in detail," Karyl said, as the commotion started to shift into bickering. Which shut off the instant he spoke.

Felipe nodded. "Thank you for that as well."

"So you're telling us you oppose this war, Duke Karyl." Though he'd clearly collected more wits than Melodía felt inclined to give him credit for possessing, Antoine seemed reluctant to say the title, given that Felipe had granted it at the expense of his uncle's vassal Duke Eric, and hence his uncle's. But court decorum left him no choice.

"That is most perceptive of you, Archduke. I am pleasantly surprised."

"Do you oppose all war, then?"

"Except for defensive purposes, yes. Otherwise, it isn't worth the cost."

"But surely you thought differently not so long ago, when you served the Empire as a mercenary captain? The rumors said you transformed your whole March into little more than a . . . a war plantation to keep your hireling army in the field!"

"He's having trouble remembering Margrethe's coaching," Rosamaría murmured behind her fan. "Odious little prick."

"I did," Karyl said. "I'm not proud of that now. But that

was a lifetime ago, Your Grace. I consider myself a different man than that one."

"So what do you have to say about your mysterious change of heart?"

"I neither denounce nor defend those earlier actions. My perspective has changed. Are you proposing to hire me to plan and carry out this expedition?"

Both catcalls and genuine approval greeted that. Melodía recoiled on her bench.

"What's he doing," she whispered urgently to La Madrota, "selling us out?"

Then she saw La Madrota grinning hugely behind her gold-and-scarlet Horror-feather fan.

Antoine looked around, then back to Karyl. "Why not? My money's in!"

"And mine!" Vargas boomed in a *matador* voice.

"And mine!" Margrethe added. "You talk big. Let's see how you deliver."

"Very well," Karyl said with a precise nod. "I decline. I make it a professional principle to accept no commission that has no chance of succeeding under any circumstances."

He bowed deeply to the Fangèd Throne.

"Your Majesty, I am done. I thank you for granting me the chance to speak. With your permission?"

Felipe's already prominent eyes were standing out of his head, and his face had gone blotchy and partly purple. Margrethe clutched his arm in alarm.

You don't really know him after all, you overstuffed Alemana *sausage*, Melodía thought with fierce delight. *That's the face my father makes when he's trying not to laugh out loud, and barely succeeding.*

Felipe made a shooing gesture. Karyl turned and marched out.

The audience chamber erupted in wild cheers and whistles, which quickly overwhelmed the few boos.

Rosamaría nodded, folded her fan, and put it away.

"We won that round," she said in Melodía's ear. "Let's go. I believe you have a reconciliation to attend to, my dear."

Chapter 38

Caracuerno, **Hornface**. . . . —Ceratopsian: a large, far-flung group of herbivorous quadrupedal dinosaurs, with toothed beaks and frilled, horned heads. (Although *Protoceratops*—the ubiquitous barnyard Fatty—lacks horns.) Mostly large, formidable herd-beasts, of which the largest and most formidable is the Ovdan Three-horn, *Triceratops horridus*. Nuevaropa's most common wild and domestic Hornface is the Nosehorn.

—THE BOOK OF TRUE NAMES

"Mother!" Falk almost wailed. "What are we going to *do*?"

"Sniveling isn't it."

In the hubbub following Karyl's surprise appearance before the Fangèd Throne they had retreated to Falk's apartment on the floor below the Imperial penthouse. The lamps were low on oil. Their light flickered orange, casting uneasy shadows across the feather tapestries depicting Manuel's epic fight on sackbut-back against the fabulous *Tyrannosaurus imperator*.

"But you heard him! You saw them! They lapped up everything he said, like hungry fatties when you pour maize-mush in their trough. Everything we've worked for—gone, just like that!"

"All is not as hopeless as your cowardice tells you," she said with icy calm. "We still have our adherents. And not all of them down to payments and threats—both of which remain in full effect."

Falk deflated in a gusty sigh.

"I just thought, now that you had finally gotten into Felipe's bed, that we could settle this once and for all."

She slapped his cheek. Though he had grown into a powerfully built man, with a neck like a hornface bull's, she could still rock his head around on it. He blinked at the sting of her palm.

"Never question my actions! Haven't you learned that by now?"

He put fingers to his bearded cheek and looked at her.

"You're not here to think. Why do you suppose I came to this arid wasteland? You are here to look big and beautiful and impressive and constantly remind these Southern weaklings what a real man and a real hero looks like."

"Yes, Mother."

Her face, which had gone bright red, softened and began to resume its normal complexion. She took his face in her hands.

"Oh, Falki, Falki, my little love. Haven't you learned yet that everything I do is for you?"

He couldn't meet her eye. "I know," he said, not loudly. "But I just don't see how we can—how we can rescue our plans now."

She smiled. "But I do." She pinched his cheek. "It all comes down to *Mutti* once more, doesn't it? Well, fortunately, Mutti is here to fix this. Honestly, *mein Schatz,* I don't know what you'd do without me."

Maybe be happy, at least some of the time? he wished he had the courage to flare back at her.

But the truth was, he wondered that as well.

"So you found your way to the apartments of Mor Patricio," Melodía said.

"With the help of the Palace servant you thoughtfully sent to fetch me, Highness," said Jaume with a small, lopsided smile. She could see flame highlights in his eyes, from the torches set around the corners of the small roof garden near the northern wall of the Palace ledge. "I know his family, somewhat. They have produced some distinguished playwrights."

"Mor Patricio aspires to more martial renown," she said, toying with a plate of grapes on the low stone-and-iron table beside the divan where she lay on her left side. "He wasn't able to join the Imperial Army in time for the Battle of Canterville. It still vexes him."

"He needs to talk to more of us who fought there," Jaume said somberly. "I'd call it an excellent thing to miss."

"He's not stupid, as such. But he does show me why you and your Companions are inclined to call your fellow knights bucketheads."

He stepped up beside the divan, took her free hand in his, and knelt with head deeply bowed.

"My deepest apologies for losing your sister, Melodía, my love," he said. "I pray that you can forgive my failure. Though I cannot."

She squeezed the hand tightly, then pressed it to her cheek.

"I forgive you—my love. You didn't lose her. You never had her. As for failing—you never had a chance, either. If you and your Companions couldn't rescue her, no mortal could. I see that now. I apologize to you for not seeing it then—when you first reported it to the Court."

"I knew it was an unlikely-sounding tale. But I owed your father, and you, the truth."

I knew it then, I think, she thought miserably. *I was just too childish and petulant to want to admit it*. She felt tears leave her eyes, blaze hot trails down her cheek to run down the back of his hand.

She turned her face and kissed his palm. "Get off your knee. The stone's hard. Come, sit down."

"Thank you."

He rose—only far enough to sit back down where he was on the red sandstone flags facing her. He pulled his knees up before him and encircled them with his arms.

"There are things called chairs, you," she said. "They're reputed to be quite comfortable. And look, there are two on either side of you!"

He grinned. "I'm fine here, Alteza."

Though he had appeared before the Fangèd Throne tonight wearing the cream-colored tabard with the Lady's Mirror in orange on the left breast over the white silk blouse and orange leggings that served his Order as a variety of formal attire, he had conceded to the night's unusual warmth by changing to a simple flapped loincloth and sandals—differing only in detail from what she wore. It left his muscle and scar-ribbed torso and long, exquisitely molded legs bare. *Does he mean to tantalize me?* she thought, eyeing the place where the flap met stone. *Because it's working.*

"One thing I have to ask," she said, because there were matters she felt even more keenly than missing him. "I never quite understood: why didn't the Sea Dragons pursue the Treb ship at sea?"

"I ordered such a pursuit. The company commander with me talked me out of it. There was a Treb war-squadron patrolling outside the harbor—out of sight across the horizon, to avoid giving provocation. But the patrol boats spotted them, of course, and were shadowing them. I didn't want to provoke a war right then and there—especially since even the Dragons candidly admitted they'd lose, at least with any force they could deploy in a timely way."

"But doesn't that prove the Basileus was behind Montse's kidnapping?"

Jaume shook his head. "Trebizon's bureaucracy shames an onion with its layers and an ant nest for its subterranean intricacy. The treason could have crept in at any of a dozen points, from the Court down to the squadron commander."

She sat up and wept freely for several minutes. He sat silent, comforting with his nearness.

"Which side of the line does Mor Patricio fall on?" he asked, when she cleared her eyes and raised her head.

"For war. He's really eager to recoup his lost chance at glory."

"A lot of young hotspurs who missed the fight are," Jaume said. "Plenty of not-so-young ones, too."

"Until tonight, that is."

"So Karyl's eloquence swayed him? It's what I hoped for. Though I hope it wasn't just him."

"You were there. I wasn't. Though I'd call what Karyl used more a calm confidence of knowledge and reason. That was what the audience found most persuasive, I believe."

"He is rather eloquent, though."

"He is. Though he won't believe the fact. He likes to think he has no skill dealing with people, though in fact he's good at it. It's a kind of negative vanity somehow."

"Sometimes that's the greatest vanity of all."

"Maybe." She tipped her head toward her right shoulder. "He didn't kill you, I see. Not that I'm not glad."

"No. Though I feared he would. He'd have had justice on his side."

"You, afraid?"

"There are few folk against whom I don't at least fancy my chances against in a fight. He's one. The only one I can call to mind, actually. And yes. I greatly feared he'd strike me down before at least hearing my plea."

He caught her eye with his and smiled. She felt a tingling beyond her belly.

"I gather I've got you to thank for that?"

She shrugged. "I told him what you told me after you came back to La Merced: how reluctant you were to attack your own ally, though you felt honor-bound to follow my father's orders regardless."

The last came out a bit tarter than she intended. *Do I still blame him for leading the Army of Correction against Terraroja, in spite of his misgivings?* She found that she did. But only slightly.

"I also told him how you'd investigated the charges laid against him that led my father to do what he did and found them baseless."

"So he believed you."

"Passably. You're alive, after all."

She paused a moment to think. "I know you are the most courageous man alive," she said, measuring each word carefully. "But I know you don't believe in throwing your life away, either. What made you take the risk?"

"I had destroyed my own credibility at court," he said. "And in the process yours, I fear. So I needed to recruit another voice to speak on the side of reason. Because if we don't stop the war with Trebizon, it will cost the Empire incalculable loss and suffering. It might destroy us. If I gave my life to stop that from happening—even trying and failing—I'd consider it a fair exchange."

She let out a long breath. "So it's that bad."

"You heard Karyl. You know. You know already. You knew before you ever experienced it firsthand that war's a thing to be undertaken only at the direst need."

"Yes. Although—"

She pressed her lips shut. *I don't want to confess this to the man I love*, she thought. But if I want to hope he still loves me, despite my faithlessness in casting him out, not once, but twice—if I want to earn that love, I need to tell him the truth.

"I've had my doubts. I almost hate myself for saying it. But—I miss my sister. It hurts so much to think of what she's going through. The fear, the growing sense of despair."

"Don't underestimate her. She's scared. She'd be foolish not to be. But she's resolute and resourceful—I told the Court how she smuggled messages to us, and gave us a lot of useful and even necessary information. She's the last person on Paradise to give in to despair. And is probably too busy scheming how to get loose and get back home to feel tempted by it."

She actually smiled. "Yes. That's Montse. But it wasn't just my desire to rescue my sister that made me wonder whether war was the answer. I had selfish reasons—selfish and weak."

She reached out and took one of his hands in both of hers.

"The Lady help me, I miss it! I miss the easy camaraderie of my *jinetes*. I miss the certainty and sense of power that war confers."

"Don't forget the doubt and uncertainty you also felt."

"You don't feel those things, surely?"

"I do. I'd be the crown prince of bucketheads if I didn't. And would have gotten myself and my men killed long since."

His face twisted in brief agony.

"Well—gotten more of them killed than I have."

"You didn't get them killed. You didn't waste their lives. They died fighting for the right. If they thought you were wasting their lives, they'd refuse to follow you, not flock from all over Nuevaropa and even Ovda and Trebizon to try to join you!"

"Well—I suppose I shouldn't underestimate them

either. They're none of them fools—not a buckethead among 'em."

"I do remember the uncertainty and doubt and all-consuming fear, as well," she said. She shrugged. "In my present surroundings, those seem . . . remote."

"I understand. You've been isolated here. Stymied. But you have Doña Rosamaría as an ally now."

"As an iron task mistress! You know her?"

"I certainly knew of her—I'm kin, after all. And you don't serve the Fangèd Throne the way I have without learning about the ageless La Madrota. We corresponded—she wanted to make sure I was approximately what your father thought I was."

"I hope she decided you were!"

"Adequately so, or so it would appear. After I took myself into exile, she wrote me to ask my help—another reason I decided to tug the tail of the King tyrant Karyl in his own den."

"Really?"

"Yes."

"She seems so stern and . . . self-sufficient."

"But she hasn't done what she's done without finding help when she thought she needed it. Keep that in mind. And that she loves you, very much."

"I guess so."

She lowered her face to the flagstone. But she looked at him sidelong.

Love. The word pricked her like a thorn.

Because I love you, Jaume Llobregat, she thought. *Do I dare hope you still love me, despite my faithlessness in casting you out not once, but twice?*

As scared as she had ever been in battle, Melodía chose to find out. She stood and held out her hands to him, smiling. *At least I've learned to keep fear off my face.*

"Come here, my love, and say hello properly."

He rose straightaway and crushed her to his bare, hard-muscled chest with his strong arms. He lowered his face to hers. They kissed, deeply and long.

She felt his hand kneading the left cheek of her rump. His cock behind silk felt hot and hard as an iron bar against the skin of her lower belly. She felt her nipples grow hard, pressed into her breasts flattened between them. Her knees grew loose with the need to take him inside her.

He broke away, raised his head to smile down at her. Torchlight glimmers played in his long, low-lidded eyes.

"Do we have privacy here?" he asked.

She grinned. "Yes. Mor Patricio assured me even servants will stay away unless we call for them."

"He'd do that for you, even though you're on opposite sides about the war? Or were until tonight."

"He fancies his chances with me, as Fanny would say. Not that he has many, since he's too callow and eager to prove himself. Mostly, I think he just likes the cachet of being known to be in with la Princesa Imperial. Even if she's not held in the best regard at Court."

Jaume shook his head. "Which is absurd. Well, enough of this—and fretting over the mystery of why such a doomed venture appeals to the ambitious Dowager Duchess, much less a knight as seasoned as her son Falk."

She went rigid. Desire died. Feeling died. She was left feeling clammy and empty.

Jaume instantly raised his hands to grasp her by the shoulder and moved a half step back.

"I've done something to hurt you," he said. "I apologize."

No, my love, she thought. *Not you. It was hearing the man I love—and fully intended to fuck until I couldn't anymore—say* that name.

She opened her mouth to tell him what Falk had done to her. And—couldn't. She could not force her lips to shape the words, nor her throat to pass the sounds.

Why can't I tell him? she asked herself. No answer came. It wasn't even the cold fact that Falk was still the hero who saved her father at Canterville, while Jaume remained barely rehabilitated, thus politically poison.

I just can't bring myself to tell him. Him, of all people. Because if I did, it would feel as if . . . that man violated me all over again.

It was a brutal choice between allowing her enemy to deny her the pleasure of full reconciliation with the man she'd loved so long—and defiling their lovemaking with his touch. But it was not a hard one to make.

She put a hand on his chest and pushed herself away, gently but definitely.

"I'm sorry, *mi amor*," she said. "I—I find I can't, much as I want to. I tried to rediscover my center in sex in Providence, and that didn't turn out well."

Which was true—as far as it went, which was only halfway. She knew, intellectually, that hadn't been the fault of the fucking, per se. It was that it had set her up for betrayal. Although in the end everyone was betrayed by those they trusted most, including Bogardus, whom Melodía mostly pitied now, and even the frightful Violette.

Jaume nodded and kissed her forehead. Which she realized was covered with sweat that the air had at last begun to cool.

"I understand. It's a partner dance, after all. And I can see why you still need time to recover. You've seen things that would have a veteran of years drinking constantly in the hope of driving away the waking memories and the dreams."

That reminded her of Karyl as they fled the Grey Angel Horde, waking himself and the Fugitive Legion night after night with his screams. *I can't compare myself to him*, she thought. *In any way.*

Besides, it seemed to her that it was somehow more

than Paradisiacal terrors that haunted his sleep. Especially given the almost relaxed disregard for personal danger he displayed when awake.

She laid her cheek on Jaume's clavicle. "Thank you," she said.

Her self-control broke into sobs that shook her entire body. She clung to him, her cheek pressed to the hard-muscled heat of his bare chest. Her tears slicked the skin between.

"But how will I get my sister back?" she wailed.

"When I know, my love," he murmured into her hair, "I'll be doing it. As I suspect you will. Until then, all we can do is hope, and pray—and try to keep from making her chances of coming home safe worse."

Chapter 39

Baraja de los Creadores, La; Creators' Cards, Creator's Deck. . . . —A deck of 72 cards: 8 Trigram cards, each representing one of the Eight Creators, and 64 Hexagram cards. They are commonplace throughout much of Paradise in a variety of designs of both faces and backs. The Creators' Deck is used for divination, in casting the Yijing, reading Tarot, or in other techniques; and, most often, for playing a wide variety of card games.

 —A PRIMER TO PARADISE FOR THE IMPROVEMENT
OF YOUNG MINDS

"I'm that glad you found me, Your Duchessness," Rob told the woman into whose imposing presence he had just been ushered by a solemn youth in a brown silk gown trimmed in silver thread. "It's my first time in La Majestad, sure and you see. I was a bit at sixes and sevens before your emissary found me and Little Nell. My hook-horn, she'd be."

When the young woman in gold-and-scarlet Imperial livery appeared at his knee and called him by name, he'd been gawking like a rube as he rode into the great city amid a profusion of pedestrians, random running urchins, nosehorns grunting and bleating, and the creaking wheels of the wagons they pulled. Even though he'd seen greater, for a fact. Lumière, for one, with its fabled million lights and mirrors. Although for all its reputation as a capital of the arts, he'd found it cold and unwelcoming. It turned out Lumièrois artists had a narrow definition of the word *art*, and it definitely did not include him, a mere pub-haunting hack of a minstrel, his playing and singing no closer to their music than the bowls of pickled *compito* eggs on a tavern counter came to their vaunted cuisine. La Merced, with its happy hedonism, appealed to him much the more, although he found the Mercedes' propensity for switching from "solid burghers" to "violent street rioters" at the drop of a feather mildly unnerving.

Still, the famous roof gardens of the Imperial capital, where even pitched roofs were often terraced to hold growing foodstuffs as well as herbs and flowers to fill their city with bright and never-ending colors and perfumes, had impressed him properly. As did the three-story building of polished dark granite not far from the main street to the Palace to which the woman had escorted him. The dash of color added by the orange trumpet-flowers that fairly dripped over its crenellations from its own roof garden seemed to emphasize its austere dignity rather than contradict it.

Perhaps most of all he was impressed by the large, handsome, painfully Alemana woman with the ice-white hair wound in a braid around her head who greeted him without rising from her dark-blue velvet divan in the third-story chamber to which the solemn household functionary he'd been handed off to had guided him.

"Your seneschal, Bergdahl, sent word ahead that we might expect a visit from you, Baron," the Dowager Duchess Margrethe von Hornberg said. She was a remarkably well-set-up older woman to Rob's eye, if a bit large in every dimension by his standards. Even reclining on one elbow, she looked to be a good half head taller than he. She was clearly a lady of mature years, though he couldn't tell if the hair was age-whitened, just that pale blond, or a combination of both. "As you may recall, it was my dear son, Duke Falk, who offered his personal manservant to help you adjust to the complexities of ruling a barony."

"And it's powerfully grateful I am to His Grace." In times of stress Rob often caught himself talking in a preposterous parody of an Ayrish brogue—even when he was speaking Spañol, as he was now. It was a habit long ingrained. It made him seem harmless to the great and powerful, who were in a position to have him drubbed or to make him disappear forever.

Despite his recent elevation, he felt little doubt that situation still applied. Even laying aside her rank or status as mother to the very hero who saved Felipe's Imperial arse at Canterville, she projected power. Which Rob's well-honed senses detected no sign of shyness about using.

A pale hand gestured him to a chair upholstered like the divan and placed next to it. A low, round table with a green-veined black marble top stood between them. Silver goblets and several decanters of fine Lumière glass, faceted like gems, rested on a silver tray. Like the decor and the structure itself, it all but screamed discretion, dignity—and wealth. He wondered if she owned the place.

"Sit, please. Refresh yourself. I've laid in wine and brandy to ease your thirst from traveling across this dreadful, dusty land—so different from the lush green landscape of home."

"Thank you." He sat and poured himself some dark red wine. The brandy sounded tempting, but he didn't want to dull his wits, at least until he had some idea what this affair was all about. He'd had not a drop of aught but water on the three days' ride here, and it had made him oddly conscious of how much drink Bergdahl had plied him with at home. The man was so confounded hale-fellow-well-met when the mood struck him that Rob found it hard to refuse when he offered. Not that Rob was in the habit of resisting overhard.

"Quite the setup you have here, Your, uh, Grace," Rob remarked, waving around at the rich but blatantly tasteful decor, all muted tones and earnestness. *If I can tell it's meant to be tasteful, the real word is likely "blatant."* "What is it, anyway? It has the air of a bank to it."

"Similar. It's a bourse."

"A *bolsa*?" He frowned. "A . . . bag? A purse?"

She smiled. She had a warm smile—he had to grant her that. Also one that tickled him along the bottom of his man parts. An impulse he stomped on hard; this one was dangerous to play with, if nothing else. And not in a tempting way.

Still, her white silk gown was cut so low in front that he was genuinely curious to see if she could manage to stand up without one of her substantial boobs popping out. He wondered what twist of Northern prudery demanded she wear the garment on the one hand, yet allowed it to conceal so little on the other. On an afternoon as warm as this, one of your Southern ladies would have thought nothing of welcoming to this clearly private parlor a visiting *grande* wearing just a loincloth or even nothing.

"It is a place where financial instruments are created, modified, and exchanged," she said.

"So, like pens and ink and ledger books and such?" He sniffed but smelled only whatever they applied to the wooden panels on the walls to make them so darkly shining and an unfamiliar hint of floral fragrance he took for her perfume.

"Something of the sort."

She sipped wine, holding his eyes with her pale blue

ones. "Bergdahl tells me that you have a problem, Baron Korrigan. How might I help you?"

It was as if his thick skull had turned to lead the way its sudden weight made his head fall forward. A trebuchet stone seemed to be settling in his gut at the same time.

So there it is, he thought. *Out in the open, then. Well, isn't that what I came for?*

He sighed. He supposed it was, indeed. *That's what you get for setting out in haste, sans plans, and utterly failing to hit upon a decent one the whole trip here. I may be a Baron all legal and proper now, but of fools I'm a veritable Prince.*

But his cunning, so ground in from earliest childhood as to be reflex, kicked in. "What have you heard, specifically? Uh, Your Grace?"

"Several weeks ago Bergdahl reported a rumor to me that a Faerie had appeared to Karyl during a visit to his newly installed count of Crève Coeur. He told me of your unnerving observation of what you suspected was Karyl directly trafficking with one in his ducal castle. And that he apparently asked you to approve his dealings with them. Did he report correctly?"

Managing, barely, to suppress a smirk at the sizable—but more stout than pretentious, like Little Nell—former farmhouse of Séverin being called a "castle," Rob considered his options. He liked the taste of none of them.

To be honest, for a change, I've always tended to ask myself, Why tell the truth when a charming lie will do? But for once he could find no lie that served him better.

"It's true enough," he said miserably. "All of it."

It occurred to him for the first time to wonder whom Bergdahl was really serving. *Well, he's been so confounded useful—and such a jolly companion—why should the question bother me unduly?*

She leaned forward. Distressed as he was, Rob did not

hold back from covertly eyeing her décolletage. Which burgeoned but did not burst, to his outright disappointment. He could use a bit of diversion here, as much as he knew he couldn't afford to stray from the terrible task at hand.

"Let me help you, Baron."

He felt his brow furrow.

"Why?"

"Duke Karyl has proven himself a great hero. The Empire always needs such men, and, in the current crisis, now needs them more than ever. For whatever reason, the Fae have caught his eye and led him astray. I feel it's my duty to the Throne to help you help him recover his path."

He sat and stewed in that. It didn't strike him as entirely likely.

"Please," she said. "Something tells me that you, of all men, know keenly just the kind of peril he's in."

He looked up sharply. *What, does everyone now know my great and awful family secret—that the very word "Korrigan" means "touched by the Fae," in a language so old it was never brought here from Old Home?*

But no. This bloody great Corythosaurus of an Ahlmayn duchess hasn't a mortal way of knowing that. Hard as it is to credit, there may be such a thing as too suspicious, even of bluebloods, Rob my lad.

And besides, it's still not as if I've any choice but to grasp at what straws are offered me.

"What do you propose, Your Grace?"

"To free him."

"And how exactly would you go about that?"

He saw a quick furrow to that milky brow that suggested the Dowager Duchess was none too accustomed to being questioned closely by her inferiors and little willing to learn the knack. But the hard look melted away as he watched.

"Enchantment by the Fae is a terrible and dangerous

thing. They have the means of influencing one's actions in a way so subtle that the victim never notices."

"So I've heard." *All my bloody life, haven't I? And don't I know from my own bad experiences?* "Can you cure him? Or free him from their power?"

"Yes. But we must work discreetly. It would be ruinous for the Empire if it got about that a man so renowned, so recently made Duke by the Emperor's own hand, had been trafficking with the Fae. And would likely cost your friend his life."

"And that means . . ." *What I fear I know already. But I still have to hear it. For penance, if naught else.*

"We must take him up and spirit him someplace where he can be isolated and treated. I have extensive contacts, even here. I can find experts who can free him."

He hung his head again. *Here's no good choice*, he thought miserably. *And I cannot doubt what the less-bad one is. Much as I fear to seal that fate.*

"How can I help you, then?"

This time her frown struck him as one of calculation. "It will take me time to make the arrangements. It will be a . . . delicate operation."

Before he could stop it, he laughed. She looked more shocked than angered.

"That's a bloody understatement, Duchess—and pardon my Francés. The man's a killing machine."

"What do you mean by that?"

"He's like a clockwork soldier, isn't he? Once you wind him up and let him go, you can only pray you live until he stops by himself."

"I see," Margrethe said. "Well, that's all the more reason I need your help so badly. You have to get him to a place where he can be taken up discreetly—and persuade him to give up without a fight."

"That's a tall task."

"Yet if anyone is up to it, it's you, his friend and trusted lieutenant."

Well, there it is, bald as an egg. Judas goat is not a role I thought I'd ever accept.

He remembered the peculiar nature of that blue glow from Karyl's room, like steady-shining lightning. And the dreadful, crackling sibilance of the voice he thought he'd heard whispering to Karyl.

"If needs must," he began, before realizing with a start that the rest of the chestnut ran *the Faerie Queen drives.*

"So you'll do it, Baron?"

For once his vaunted silver tongue—vaunted by himself, at any rate—failed him. He could only nod.

"Splendid," she said. "It is a very great service you are doing for your friend and for the Empire. As I said, it will take me a day or two to make the necessary arrangements. Maybe more. In the meantime, I think it best you not go to the Palace. We'll want to introduce you quietly when the time comes."

"Can you recommend an inn? Serviceable, but not too dear." *I'd think an Alemana would know good ale, but probably not the places that brewed it. So no point asking there.*

"By no means! You shall stay in a private apartment and enjoy all the amenities the capital has to offer: the best in food, drink, and smoking herbs. And women, if you like. Have you any preferences in the matter, Baron?"

"Well, clean is good."

She laughed. "Of course. Nothing but the finest. Discreet?"

"Not needed. I'm never that. Beautiful's a plus, though."

"Then beauty you shall have," Margrethe said. "The most beautiful—short of the Emperor's daughter, of course."

Rob went cold.

She saw it in his eye, that quick. "I have offended you," she said matter-of-factly, setting her wine goblet on the table with a clink. "I had no intention of doing so. Please tell me how I can make amends, Baron."

It's not just that Melodía's a friend, though I think I dare consider her such. She worked under me as captain of the scouts, and a bang-up job she did.

And under her worked Pilar, once. She loved me. Then she died.

He no longer blamed the Princess for that; she'd done enough of that. And likely hadn't stopped, nor ever would. He could not have said why the joke revolted him so completely. But it did.

"May I presume to remind you of the urgent duty you have to your friend and the Empire?" the Duchess asked. "I regret the necessity of bringing it up. But if my own inquiries confirm your fears, the matter's simply too great to allow other considerations to sway us."

He shook his head. "I'm with you, still. It brought up a bad memory, nothing more."

He put hands on bare thighs and rose.

"So, if that's the way it's to be, let's be about it!"

She raised her goblet in toast.

"Spoken like a man after my own heart. To a fruitful relationship, Baron Korrigan!"

Chapter 40

Iglesia Santísima de los Ocho Creadores, La; The Most Holy Church of the Eight Creators, Church of Nueva-ropa . . . . —Our Creators, in Their wisdom, gave us few commandments as to what or how to believe, other than that we all must believe in and worship Them. Our Nue-varopan branch of this worldwide faith is the Most Holy Church of the Eight Creators, also known as the Church of Nuevaropa. The Pope from La Casa de los Creadores (Creators' House) in La Merced. Sects and clergy can be dedicated either to all Eight, or to single Creators. So, of course, can individual persons. Among the rites offered by our holy Church is confession of our sins, to cleanse our souls of their burdens, and thus our minds, and to obtain spiritual and even practical guidance from one wiser than ourselves.

—A PRIMER TO PARADISE FOR THE IMPROVEMENT OF YOUNG MINDS

A curious stream began to run through Karyl's un-easy dream.

His life in the dream world took two main forms: horrific nightmares, and prosaically inscrutable dreams roiled by undercurrents of apprehension about when the terrifying visions and sounds and sensations would begin.

But now he felt something he seldom encountered in dreams or in the waking world: intense pleasure. He found himself in the midst of an erotic fantasy in which a beautiful woman's mouth gave skillful pleasure to his hard cock.

Awareness of how utterly unusual it was shocked him from sleep. He opened his eyes.

To see the blue-glowing figure of a creature like a woman but indescribably more beautiful, nude and straddling his bare legs, sucking on his penis with her dark-blue lips. Her hair was a dark-blue nimbus that moved as to a wind that was absent from his windowless chamber within the Corazón Imperial.

He yelled and kicked with his heels against the yielding mattress. The sensation as his cock slid out of the inhuman mouth was of pleasure excruciatingly delicious. He did not fail to feel a sting of regret.

But then he was crouched nude on this pillow with his staff-sword in his hands, also nude.

"Get away from me!" he snarled.

Uma, self-proclaimed Queen of the Fae, showed a look of surprise and hurt on her face. It was almost convincing. As was her very human allure.

Karyl knew better than to be fooled by either.

"Why, Karyl, my love," she said, "surely you know? You're not a virgin. We know; you have no secrets from us."

"I gave no permission."

She laughed. It was music, but also malice.

"When did any Faerie need to ask permission from a mortal? Much less the Queen of all."

"You're not the Queen of all the Fae."

"As far as you're concerned, I am. Or might as well be."

She stood up and ran her long, slender hands with their long, pointed nails down her naked counterfeit of a body. It was slender, muscles limned beneath silken skin. Her breasts were small, the aureoles a darker blue against the general silver-blue of her shining skin. The hair on her mound of Paradise was of similar color to her nipples. It looked as fine as vexer down.

"And as far as you're concerned, I am also a woman. I can give you the same pleasures as the most skilled courtesans, with the fervor of the most besotted." She smiled. Her canines looked unusually long and sharp. "As I have before. Don't you recall? The memories are as close as your dreams."

"You also gave me pains unimaginable, both in body and soul," he said. "I remember some of both, now, the pleasure and the pain. It makes the dreams easier to endure."

She laughed again. "Ah, your weather-witch told you, did she? We played with you in Venusberg. It's our right, after all. Especially with those whom we generously rescue, take in, and heal."

"What's your purpose in doing this?"

"Besides pleasuring myself? As I assure you I was doing. Your cock may be unexceptional by human standards, but the uniqueness of the rest of you gave it remarkable savor."

She wiped the back of her hand across her lips. "I wish to experience the tang of the actual semen of a man whom other mortals call a hero."

"Yes. Besides that."

"Why, did you not miss your pet when she strayed?"

"Not in this particular way, no."

"Still, you feel affection toward her, and sadness at the separation."

"I did. But we weren't separated voluntarily on either

of our parts, Shiraa and I. Whereas you dumped me on the road somewhere in southern Alemania, as devoid of wealth as of memory."

"But alive! And healed. Yes, yes, without your hand—no need to be tedious, and Aphrodite gave it back to you, so what's the difference? And with that most remarkable sword you're waving about in lieu of your now-shrunken cock. You may put it down, by the way. I won't approach closer without your permission. And don't be sure you won't grant it."

She cocked her hips back so as to flash a glimpse of the pale lips in the fine thatch where her legs met.

"I won't."

"Which? Put down your sword, or allow me to fuck you as you've never been fucked before?"

"Either. So the sword will harm you."

"Would I have entrusted you with an implement which could do me harm?"

"You're a Faerie; you'd do anything. And it already killed one of your kind. Much to my surprise, I grant."

"Of my kind in only the broadest terms. As far beneath me in power and status as a maggot is below yours."

"In the end, the maggots eat us all."

"Ha! Why, yes, I forgot how delightfully, disgustingly temporary your physical forms are."

He laid the weapon down on the bed, crosswise, and climbed off to the hilt side. Then he stood.

"Tell me why you really came." He realized his heart was racing and his breath coming short. He chastised himself mentally for poor discipline and began to draw in deep, slow breaths from his diaphragm. At once he felt his pulse settling toward normal.

"Well, one form of oral persuasion failed to convince you to give in to the inevitable. So I decided to try another. Because it pleasured me, of course. But also in hopes you would realize you had to make common cause with me."

"Now that I know what you've done, that will never happen."

She frowned, and purple lightnings seemed to run like bright serpents through her hair. Her eyes glowed.

"Do you imagine your pitiful world-witch can protect you? She's as powerless to harm the Grey Destroyers as they are against her. And she's no more like you than am I. What makes you think her thoughts and aims are any more comprehensible to your mortal mind, contained as it is in a wet, greasy lump inside your skull?"

"Nothing. But her malice, at least, is conjectural."

"You mean mine? You've seen nothing from me but mortal forbearance; hope you never see my malice. But don't forget the Seven. They have not forgotten you. They have already reckoned ways to overcome their built-in inhibitions against harming you outside of carefully prescribed limits. They will keep coming, and the power they bring to bear against you will grow greater. Until they win, and you and your kind are destroyed."

"What assurance do I have you won't do worse?"

She laughed again, her voice metal with anger. "None at all! But since you're so fond of the term, our bad intentions—mine, at least—remain conjectural. You know that theirs are real."

The look on her face softened—not to a frown but to one of puzzlement instead of near rage. She raised her head and her pupilless eyes seemed to lose focus.

As if she's listening to something I can't hear, Karyl thought.

"The trap is set," Margrethe told Uriel. "The bait is being dangled. We'll all be rid of that pest the Duke of the Borderlands in just a few more minutes."

"You had best pray the jaws break his neck properly

when they snap shut. He seems likely to be a little more forgiving of affront than we ourselves."

"Not just his, but that ale-sodden wretch of a jumped-up jongleur of his."

The false Fray Jerónimo raised two fingers in dismissal—a gesture all but wasted in the gloom of the tiny alcove. Then again, she knew it was pointless to curse the dark. It would hardly do to risk discovery, here in the Emperor's very bedchamber, even if he was lolling about the Fangèd Throne playing at affairs of state. As if any corrupt Southerner could truly understand power, much less wield it effectively.

"He is nothing. But do not underestimate your real prey. His is potent."

"More potent than thirty skilled assassins?"

There was no realistic way the Grey Angel's immobile features, which reminded Margrethe of a stripped skull completely covered in fat, petrified maggots, could express emotion. Nonetheless she somehow sensed the creature was surprised.

"Not the Kindred," he said. "They would never dispatch so many to a single task, whatever its importance. Nor will they soon risk operating within an Imperial residence again, having recently committed an indiscretion on that line and been . . . chastised."

"No. A more . . . secular contractor." Who whined mightily and demanded all sorts of unrealistic premiums for the effort of assembling such a large team of trained assassins in such a short time. Then tried to double it when they learned who the target was. Margrethe had acceded to the first demand but refused the second, on the principle that to fail to draw some line would suggest too much weakness to an organization professionally interested in exploiting such.

Not that the expense bothered her too much. She would soon be in a position to exact a full refund, should the shadowy proprietors of Acciones Aguanegro wish to continue breathing—much less enjoy the occasional odd bone of work she might choose to toss them. At a greatly reduced tariff, of course.

"It is good," Uriel said. "Others grow impatient. I wish to be ready to move soon."

"I believe I can deliver the opportunity to you. As I told you—"

"Wait."

The grisly head rose, like a Horror sniffing the air for prey.

"What is it?" she asked, trying to keep her alarm from her voice. *What could visibly upset* that? she wondered.

"I sense a presence," the Grey Angel said. "Something wicked. Something . . . unwelcome."

The dead, grey-marble eyes rolled as if to fix her with their gaze.

"I perceive that some powerful force, which I will not name, prepares to move against us and disrupt all our plans. You must act quickly, whatever the cost—

and you must not fail."

Uma looked at Karyl, and her eyes were wide. They blazed like lightning.

"I must go," she said. "But I won't be far. I'm watching over you, sweet Karyl."

"How reassuring," he said. His throat was dry.

"Expect betrayal."

She vanished. She went out like a snuffed candle flame. Or like a lightning stroke ended.

"I always do," he told the darkness.

For half a dozen deliberate breaths he stood in the blackness. He was waiting for Aphrodite to make her customary appearance.

The room stayed dark. He stayed alone, so far as his senses could tell him.

He padded to the sideboard and poured himself a mug of water from the ewer provided. He didn't need illumination to complete the operation. He reflexively memorized his surroundings before he surrendered himself to the trials of sleep. He knew where the room's few furnishings were, his clothes, and, of course, his sword and cane-sheath.

He heard a self-important patter of sandaled footsteps approaching down the stone floor of the corridor. He was already reaching for his plain robes when a rapping sounded from his chamber door.

Chapter 41

Spada, sword—The swords most commonly used in Nuevaropa are two-edged and used for cutting and thrusting: *spadacorta,* shortsword, to 60 centimeters long, half a kilogram, used one-handed; *spada,* or arming-sword, 100 centimeters, 1 kilogram, used one-handed; *spadón,* longsword, to 150 centimeters and 1.5 kilograms, used with one or both hands; *Spadataliana,* rapier, 120 centimeters, 1 kilogram, one-handed and used mostly for thrusting; *dosmanos,* greatsword, 180 centimeters, 2.5 kilograms, used with both hands.

—A PRIMER TO PARADISE FOR THE IMPROVEMENT
OF YOUNG MINDS

"Karyl," said Rob as Karyl approached at a confident near trot down the carven stone steps. The soles of his sandals made clopping noises like a horse's hooves. Each step's echo chased the others up the walls to the groined ceiling of the empty cistern deep in the bowels of the mountain, underneath the Imperial heart. Not that Rob favored thinking of "bowels" and "drinking water" at the same time.

At least he left his Castañera witch back home, to mind the Farm, he thought. *A small blessing, but where the likes of Karyl are concerned, I'll take what I can get and thank the Lady Maris for Her capricious favor.*

Rob wore his customary garments: vest, trunks, buskins. Karyl had forgone any concession to courtly garb and was instead dressed in his preferred manner, in loose white linen blouse and black trousers tucked into the rolled tops of riding boots. It lacked only a hornface-leather jack for armor and an open-faced helmet to be nearly identical to what the man was wearing when Rob first clapped eyes on him in person, mounted there astride Shiraa, wading to his doom across the blood-reddened Hassling. It was an outfit more typical of a light rider than a dinosaur knight.

It chilled Rob's core to see Karyl was carrying his staff-sword, an innocuous act, remarkable only in the incongruity of one of the Empire's most powerful noblemen bearing such a peasant item.

He knows! He can't know. How could he know?

"It's good to see you, my friend," Karyl said. *Twist the knife slowly in my heart.* "When did you arrive?"

Two days ago, Rob thought. He realized he didn't remember much of the time between then and now. *And here I thought Bergdahl had a knack for plying me with the booze.*

The Duchess's hospitality had so overwhelmed him with alcohol, herbs, and fucking that it was *that* great a marvel he was able to navigate, after a mere pair of hours to sober himself up.

"That's not important," he said as Karyl walked up to him. "There's something I've got to do—and I don't want to do it. You'll not credit this, but I do this from my love for you as a friend. You've been enchanted, and that's a fact. You need to be sequestered, for your own good, and that of the whole wide world. Please don't make this hard; just hand over that lethal secret you carry in your right hand, and I shall see that you are comfortable and safe until all this is resolved and you can walk free."

Karyl's brows lowered, and his dark eyes seemed to go obsidian-black. Rob swallowed hard and made ready to die.

Then his friend's face relaxed into a look of something akin to pity.

"You poor fool," Karyl said softly. "You don't know what you saw. Nor what's been done to you."

That prodded Rob's stubborn nature. "I do know what I saw and heard: you talking to a horrid Faerie. Do you deny it?"

"No."

"See?" Rob said, and then felt the fool his friend had just called him. *It's a poor time to be exulting in scoring easy points off your friend*, he thought. "But nothing's been done to me, I assure you. It's you. The demon's put you in her spell."

Karyl's face, which had gone impassive when his anger flashed, both sagged and twisted into lines and contours of such intense sorrow that it rocked Rob back more than his killing anger had.

"My carelessness brought this on," Karyl said, the words coming out as if they had been written on clay and broken apart—jagged, with uneven rhythm. "I always bring hurt on those I care about. Always."

He sighed, composed his face again, and stood upright, apparently calm and relaxed once more.

"Nothing for it, then. Let's be about it."

He swung the end of blackwood staff up toward Rob. Rob took firm hold and gently pulled, lest his friend think better of his easy acquiescence.

The blade hidden within slithered free with a serpent hiss of steel. *Ah, I seem to've overlooked that small detail*, Rob thought.

He found he welcomed the imminent kiss of death. Because some might see what he'd just done as betrayal of the best and one true friend he'd ever known but Little Nell—and he suspected he'd be among that "some," had he ever gotten the chance to reenact this little tableau in his mind. And because, well, he'd failed, and not even the Creators Themselves or their Angels could imagine what great evils a Fae-controlled Karyl Bogomirskiy might accomplish.

But, still, he didn't appreciate the sudden hard shin in the balls. Nor the way Karyl seized the hair atop his head and cruelly yanked when he bent forward.

Those struck him as plain gratuitous.

Pulling the doubled-over Rob past him to his right by his short brush of hair, Karyl thrust the staff-sword straight for the black-masked face that hung behind the spot where Rob had stood. It still had a black-gloved hand extended to encircle the bearded dinosaur master's throat. The eyes in the dark face above the black cloth that masked its lower half were black coins struck in the mint of sheer surprise.

The left eye looked even more surprised as the tip of Karyl's sword entered the right and struck through to the brain. The right was hidden in a rush of blood and aqueous humor.

He melted into a puddle on the tiled floor as Karyl pulled the blade free.

Karyl pivoted counterclockwise, stepping left as he did so. Had there been no assailants closing from that quarter he would have continued his turn to the one or ones he knew, without looking, were closing from behind. And if they weren't fouled by having Rob flung at their feet, his sudden sidestep should give them pause.

He felt no fear. If he died, he only hoped it would last this time. He felt *focus*. As he always did when he plied his craft.

The flat of his single-edged staff-sword clacked against the hardwood haft of a spear being thrust for his face, guiding its steel head past to the left. He took another quick step into the man, who like the first had his face obscured from nose bridge down by a black mask, though his skin was paler and his eyes were blue. Karyl turned his hips to drive power to the palm-heel blow he slammed into the swaddled chin.

He rotated his hips farther, sticking his right knee forward. His right hand slipped behind the now-stunned spearman's neck. Karyl stepped back and around with his left foot, tripping the assassin over his knee.

He slashed the man across the back of the neck as he went down. *Two dead.*

Another spearman rushed Karyl. Approaching from Karyl's right, the assassin hadn't been prepared for his target to slip away from him so rapidly. He'd been an eye blink slow in reacting. At the same time the man who had come in behind the one Karyl had dropped with an eye thrust before he could cut Rob's throat from behind was charging in with twin short swords.

That one held his left-hand blade out before him, angled up to guard against a body thrust. He swung the right-hand sword down. Karyl darted to his own left, slashing the assassin forehand behind the right—forward—knee in passing.

The black-clad man shrieked and went to his knees. He got his left hand down to keep himself from sprawling face-first onto stone, tried to keep the forty-five-centimeter blade in his right raised high enough to guard him. But his own momentum betrayed him.

Karyl's backhand slash took him across the face. He collapsed in a spray of blood, black by lamplight.

The other spearman was closing. He jabbed at Karyl's face. Karyl leaned right to slip the glittering head.

It was a feint. The assassin drew the spear back quickly, dropped the head, and rushed to stab Karyl through the body.

Karyl grabbed the spear haft behind the head with his right hand. He turned his hips clockwise to help him pull the wielder off-balance forward. Then rotated them quickly back to deliver, not the usual Zipangu-style draw-cut he favored with the staff-sword but a woodsman's axe cut to the throat.

The unnaturally keen blade parted skin, cartilage, muscle, and veins with almost no touch of resistance. Karyl felt a shock through the blackwood hilt as the edge struck the neck bone—and then more travel as it cut in.

He continued his twist to the left, pulling the sword free to the side. Taking the hilt with both hands, he came around to face toward the place he had flung his friend and betrayer Rob.

Rob got his forearms down in time to take the force of landing on the cistern floor with them, not his face. He left skin on stone, though.

Even as he was falling he saw a man dressed all in black, who must have come up right behind him without his noticing, leaping back and to his left to avoid being knocked down. Another stood behind him.

There was no way sneaking up behind Rob was part of the plan to take Karyl into protective custody. *I've been set up.*

Though he was having trouble forcing air back into his lungs, and the sensations from his groin didn't bear thinking about, the prospect of imminent murder focused his scattered wits wonderfully. No sooner had he barked his knees painfully on the floor than he got a booted foot beneath him and sprang forward and to his right.

The nearer man had his arming-sword and dagger still raised, as if still focused on his target—what else but Karyl's back?—and disregarded the bollock-kicked bard who'd been pitched unceremoniously at his feet like so much offal. He had no chance to lower either blade before Rob hit him right above the knees and slammed him over backward in a tackle.

Rob heard the air boom out of the man's lungs. He swarmed up him like a squirrel. He got his left forearm on the killer's right biceps, pinning sword-arm to stone, and grabbed the knife-wrist with his other hand right before his opponent could launch a proper attempt to stab him in the side. He saw the lower half of the man's face was covered in black cloth in the instant before he slammed his forehead hard into the masked nose.

He heard and felt cartilage break. The mask was instantly wet with snot or blood or both, and having neither on his face was to Rob's taste. But he'd had both there before and hadn't died, and that really was preoccupying him now—not dying.

He hurled his whole weight to his left. He kept his knees clamped about his stunned enemy's waist, and used his left arm as a handle to yank him right over with him.

To Rob's disappointment, the second would-be backstabber neither ran the man through nor slashed his back across. But he did stop dead, presumably looking for an opening to stab Rob past his comrade's thrashing body.

Rob drew his legs up and kicked the man he'd tackled at the second assassin with both feet. It was neither a clean nor a graceful shot, nor did he manage, with all the strength fear lent his short legs, to loft him far.

But it had the desired effect. The second killer had

recovered quickly enough to start an overhand cut at Rob with his arming-sword when his accomplice came flying and knocked his legs from beneath him. His sword and buckler clattered onto the stone as he caught himself only slightly more gracefully than Rob had a few racing heartbeats before.

Rob, meanwhile, had found his feet. He used the right one to deliver a mighty football kick to the second assailant's masked face, snapping his head up hard.

He had hopes of snapping his neck as well. Instead, the man kept wits enough to fall back and then roll hard away from Rob and his prone-crumpled partner.

If he gets back up, he'll have me, Rob knew. The killer hadn't lost his grip on either his sword-hilt or his small round shield. Once he managed to launch a proper attack with those, Rob's own ballad was at an end.

The corner of his eye snagged on a sliver of yellow light, shimmering on the floor. The man he'd tackled, head-butted, and flung about like a sack of grain *had* dropped his sword.

Rob stooped, snatched it, and then ran at the second assassin. The man in black sprang up as fast and fresh as if he'd only just commenced his daily exercise.

In time for Rob, clutching the arming-sword with both frantic hands, to punch its meter-long blade through his breastbone to the hilt. The man puked blood and collapsed.

Rob heard a scuffle from behind. He let go the sword and spun. The first man was swaying on his feet. As Rob came round to face him, he drew back the dagger in his left hand and lurched forward.

Rob kicked him heartily in the crotch. The man gasped and doubled over himself in a way Rob knew too well, from too-recent experience.

"You unfamilied bastard!" Rob yelled, and brought his right elbow down hard. He aimed for the nape of the neck but landed it on the shoulder blade just right of the spine instead. Given Rob's fury and barrel-shaped upper body, it was enough to drop the killer flat on his face.

Rob stepped round and jumped on the black-clad back. He grabbed the dark-haired head in both hands, raised it up until he felt his victim's neck bones creak, then slammed the masked face back down on the stone.

"Die, you fatty-fucker," he wheezed, as he raised the head again.

With savage glee he began to pound his would-be murderer's forehead against the cistern floor.

Chapter 42

Cofradía del Consuelo, La; Consolation, Kindred of—
Nuevaropa's most elite, effective, and exclusive company
of assassins, allegedly an official Sect consecrated to Maia,
Queen of the Creators. Most often acting alone, or in small
groups, Kindred are known to go to remarkable lengths to
reach their targets, whether by disguise, feats of stealth
and daring comparable to those of the legendary ninja of
Zipangu, or by infiltrating households, retinues, or other
institutions months or even years in advance, diligently
carrying out their ostensible duties while awaiting the order to strike. If they wish their involvement to be known,
they leave a dagger with a wavy blade, which they call
a Flame Knife, at the scene. They are known to refuse all
commissions against the Imperial family. It is even rumored
that sometimes they are used by the Grey Angels to perform covert acts of murder.

**—A PRIMER TO PARADISE FOR THE IMPROVEMENT
OF YOUNG MINDS**

"Y ou can stop, now," Rob heard Karyl say in an
astonishingly mild voice. "Once you see what
looks like clumps of uncooked dough there

amid the red on the rock, your enemy's not getting up again."

Rob let the assassin's head go. It fell forward with a sodden thump.

"I know that," he said. "The mushy feel of his head when I slammed it to the stone should've told me. Ah, well; I wish I could say this was the first man I'd beaten to death against a floor."

He stood up.

"So where are the oth—four? You killed four of them?"

"And you seem to have accounted for two. Well done."

"Well, all the years I spent learning to stay alive when I got knocked to the tavern floor served me in good stead. It turns out that pub bullies trying to stamp your head concave with bloody great boots don't differ greatly from masked bravos trying to stab at you with swords when you're down. Who were they, anyway?" Rob asked as Karyl reached a hand down to him. Which surprised him, though hardly more than the way he pulled him straightaway back onto his feet as if he were a child's rag doll.

"A kill team," Karyl said. "Sent to murder us both."

"They were *sicarios*? Actual professional murderers? I mean, I know, you—but why are we still alive?"

"*Because* they were assassins. They're killers, not fighters."

Rob wobbled on uncertain pins. He was uncomfortably aware of staring at Karyl with the wide-eyed incomprehension of a freshly hatched fatty.

"That strikes me as the sort of thing the advocates call a 'distinction without a difference.'"

"You mentioned tavern bullies. They're adept at hitting unsuspecting victims, but if their sudden blow or nosehorn bull rush fails—"

"They find themselves all at sea, facing a foe who's able to hit back. Aye, I've met my share. And several other peoples'. Numerous. A tavern minstrel attracts a certain amount of criticism. I take your point."

He learned, then, that there was an even scarier thought than that their attackers were *sicarios*, professional contract killers. Because he thought it.

"Were they Kindred of Consolation, do you think?"

"I'm not in with that Order, but I don't think so. The Kindred's style is far more covert—they prefer to use moles in place over the long term, or infiltration by small teams, or better, by individuals. This lot? I've seen better. They're clearly accustomed to hunting in packs, like Horrors. Perhaps your friend the Dowager Duchess decided to go cheap."

Rob's breath stuck briefly sideways in his gullet. "How did you know it was her?"

"Later. If we get a 'later.'"

"Well, it seems she's no friend of mine."

"That sort has no friends. Only conveniences. And her son." Karyl knelt to clean his blade on a dead enemy's black shirt before sheathing it.

"Somehow I don't envy the poor lout. Though he's doubtless in this to the lofty blue eyeballs, too."

He eyed the mess leaking out of the head of the second murderer he'd killed. "Remind me never to drink the water here. You don't think this was the lot of them, do you?"

"Not a chance," Karyl said. "Since Margrethe chose to rent killers in bulk, she's cunning enough to have rented more, in case we somehow got out of this tank alive."

Rob grunted. As usual, his friend's tactical assessment was immaculate.

He decided against salvaging a dirk, since he had no sheath for one and feared the blades were poisoned. After a moment's consideration he took up an arming-sword and a buckler, the weapons he was liable to be least clumsy with. *Parrying with the small steel round shield can't be that much different from parrying with a beer mug, can it, now?*

"I wouldn't plan on staying," Karyl said, rising. "You seem to have worn out your welcome as thoroughly as I."

"Sound counsel," Rob said. "Although it seems harsh, for I only came to the Palace tonight, and haven't gotten to see much of it yet. What now?"

"We get out of here as fast as we can. Alive, by preference. Then out of the Palace, out of La Majestad, and far, far away. Margrethe strikes me as having much in common with a Grey Angel: once she comes for you, she's not going to readily let you go. Is there another way out than the one I entered by?"

"There's a second set of steps at the far end of the cistern. It's purely for servants and the like; I came that way. Why they have a public entrance to a disused water storage tank is anybody's guess."

"I suspect the Imperial Heart has many unique features. Let's go out the back way."

"'Let's'? As in, me with you?"

"We've both been set up. We both have the same enemy. You fought by my side, like old times. Even though you were meant to be killed too, that buys you some grace."

Without another word, Karyl turned and started walking toward the second stairway. Rob hastened to follow, cursing every step of the short legs that meant he had to trot instead of stride.

"Aii!" Rob danced away, putting his back against the smooth stone wall, as a black-clad body tumbled down the stairwell, limbs flopping loosely as only dead limbs could. He managed to avoid the blood still fountaining from the severed neck, black in the low yellow light. *I think.*

"Way's clear," Karyl called down from the floor above. "For now. Come on."

Stepping carefully to avoid the great wetly gleaming blood splashes on the stairs—*Looks slick, and I don't want to take a nasty tumble, and me just spared!*—Rob obeyed. Only to find he had to clamber over a jumble of bodies in black to get into the corridor.

"Four?" he said. "Again? But that means we've killed a total of—"

He reckoned quickly in his mind—and then again on his fingers when his mind refused to accept its own sum.

"Ten? We killed ten of them? How many more can there be?"

"No way of knowing. But definitely more. These were probably set to guard the back way. I suspect the bulk of the team are securing the public exit and the ways that lead out of the Palace from it. So we'd best get as far as we can before they find out their quarry's slipped the snare."

"What if you're wrong?"

"We're likely to encounter more killers whichever way we go. So keep your guard up."

Rob flourished his arming-sword and buckler. "I'm right behind you!"

"No. This is where we part."

Rob's mad elation at having fought for his life and won—which increased wildly when he learned their foes were professional murderers, rather than common or garden alley bashers—turned instantly to densely compacted shit and thudded to the bottom of his belly. The strength flowed out of his limbs and into the stone floor.

So that's how it is, then, he thought. *It's cast aside you are, lad Rob. But what better could you expect? What you've earned of your friend is death.*

He wasn't sure that wouldn't be the kinder way to treat him.

"How will you get out?" he asked leadenly.

"I can find my way from here. If nothing else I can ask servants."

He started to turn away.

"When did you know?" Rob called, halting him. "Please. I have to know."

"The moment your summons arrived—with no prior notice you were here, or even coming."

"You're telling me you walked knowingly into a trap?"

"I don't know a better way to walk into a trap. I'd rather have my enemy strike at me at a time and place I know, in a way I can surmise in advance, than when I'm actually unawares. That gives me the advantage of knowing something the enemy does not: that his target is not an unsuspecting one."

He put his back to Rob and started walking at his usual pace when he was going somewhere in a hurry—moving rapidly without seeming to do so.

"You're wrong, you know," Rob called after him. "Margrethe isn't the only one here who bears you a grudge. There's another with an even greater grievance against you: a great Grey fucking Angel."

Karyl stopped once more and turned to face him fully.

"Surprised you, didn't I?" Rob crowed. Mad as it was to taunt the deadliest man in the world—as what other mortal could cross blades with a Grey Angel and live?—Rob couldn't stop himself from indulging. *Then again, given Himself hasn't killed me yet for betraying, a minor gloat's unlikely to set him off.* "It's true what they say: there's a first time for everything. And here's another: there's a bloody great Grey Angel in the Palace. Here."

Karyl stared at him.

Rob had a strong sense that, despite having just saved his life, Karyl would kill him if he thought he was lying to him about that; it would trample his trust for the final time. Rob felt greater danger from the man he'd betrayed than he had at any time that evening.

Meaning he was in greater danger than when six assassins attacked him.

"It's the Emp's mysterious confessor," he blurted. "Fray bloody Jerónimo, so called. I saw him with my own eyes, peeking through a hole in Felipe's tent, the night of the Battle of Canterville."

Karyl continued to stare a hole in Rob's soul for a score of increasingly frantic heartbeats.

"Fuck," Karyl said. "You didn't think anyone else would find that bit of information useful?"

"Sure, and I thought every living soul there is would do. But who the fuck could I tell? No one would've believed noted scapegrace and dinosaur master Rob Korrigan, not even you. And not a soul more would believe Baron Rob of Nowhere's Ass End, either. Plus, there's the small matter that telling tales out of school about the man—or monster—who has the Emperor's own ear seems a splendid bloody way for the recently elevated Rob to take an immediate fall—at the end of a much shorter rope."

Karyl looked at him a moment, then nodded. "Right. A word of advice: beware the Palace guards, and especially the Duke's Scarlet Tyrants. If they haven't been sent to arrest us on trumped-up charges, they soon will be."

"You think that witch Margrethe would dare?"

"I think there's little she hasn't dared already. This isn't the beginning of her skein of plots but rather somewhere in the middle."

He nodded, briskly but cordially enough given his nature. And then he was gone.

Though he knew his life depended on putting the Imperial Heart behind him as quickly as he could, Rob stared after his friend, his eyes slowly blurring with water, until Karyl vanished into another stairway.

Chapter 43

Nariz Cornuda, Nosehorn, One-horn. . . . —*Centrosaurus apertus*. Quadrupedal herbivore with a toothed beak and a single large nasal horn, 6 meters long, 1.8 meters tall, 3 tonnes. Nuevaropa's most common Ceratopsian (horn-face) dinosaur; predominant dray and meat-beast. Wild herds can be destructive and aggressive; popular (if extremely dangerous) to hunt.

—THE BOOK OF TRUE NAMES

R unning for his life, with a speed he was surprised his short, bowed legs could manage, Rob burst into a room filled with heat, steam and stray smoke, bustle, and surprisingly bright illumination.

He raced between aisles of kitchen servants in canvas aprons assiduously chopping vegetables and wheels of cheese and disjointing scratcher carcasses at work tables interspersed with stout cooking ovens with elaborate systems of funnel catchments and conduits to draw the smoke into the chimney from an immense fireplace. Other cook staff, mostly naked and pouring sweat, rotated an entire nose-horn, complete with gaping beak, on a stout roasting spit inside it, while others ladled olive oil over it to keep its skin from burning. The savory smell from a giant pot bubbling on a brick oven stirred hunger in Rob's belly, despite that belly being all in a ruction from the three *sicarios* following hot on his buskined heels.

The master cook, to judge by the traditional white mushroom hat stuck onto her big close-cropped head, her Little Nell–size body naked but for a loincloth and apron, never looked up from stirring her cauldron on its oven near the door with a meter-long wooden spoon as Rob raced by.

A tame vexer, streaked brown and cream in a pattern called *chaparral*, erected its black crest and screeched angrily at him from a chopping table as he passed.

"Stop, you!" a voice clanged from behind him.

He didn't know it was possible for his heart to sink lower than his sandal soles. *And I should've known they weren't to be deterred at this point from taking their prey.*

Inspiration, his inconstant blessing, struck him as he dodged between tables to another aisle. He did stop, to turn around and bellow—

"Assassins! They've come to kill the Emperor! Alarm, alarm! ¡Viva Felipe!"

That made everybody look. Specifically, everybody Rob could see in the vast kitchen stopped to stare, first at him and then, as if their heads were somehow joined together at the cheekbones, toward the three black-clad men who stood waving swords in the doorway. Except for the quartet tending the roasting nose-horn, who stuck single-mindedly to their task of not burning a Centrosaurus carcass bound for the Imperial table.

The *sicario* leader, the one who'd hollered after Rob, advanced. He swung his arming-sword left and right to menace the assembled workers.

"All right, you peasant scum," he declared as the other two took off running down the aisles flanking Rob to right and left to cut off his escape, "you'd better not interfere with us, or things will go badly for—"

Apparently for him, since the rest of the declamation was lost in demoniac shrieking as the huge chief cook wordlessly picked up the equally imposing kettle off the stove by its wooden handles and upended the boiling contents over the assassin's black-swathed head.

A blend of scratcher-meat, leeks, and garlic in goat-cream sauce, by the look and smell, thought Rob. *Tasty!*

The screams cut off when the chef reversed her grip on the black iron cauldron and smote him ringingly over the head with it. He fell down, his legs and hands twitching.

The vexer turned, skipped across the heavy cutting table, and, using the nominal lifting power of its outflung wing-arms, threw its ten or twelve kilos right into a *sicario*'s face. Its outsized hind claws began to rake at the man's black-cloth-covered faces as its teeth raked his exposed forehead. Its screeches were only marginally shriller than his.

All around Rob the kitchen staff had taken up whatever potentially damaging implements were at hand: large, scary knives; sharpening steels; stout metal ladles. The assassin moving down the aisle to what was Rob's right, now that Rob had turned back, slowed and brought up his arming-sword and buckler as a crowd of armed cooks barred his path. A tall youth loomed up behind him and buried a cleaver in his back with a mighty overhand swing.

The head cook turned to Rob. "You!" she said, waving the massive kettle at him with one hand. "Run and spread the alarm. Save His Majesty. We'll handle these monsters!"

Since all three *sicarios* had now vanished beneath mobs of yelling, red-faced, hacking, stabbing, and whacking cooks—and one still-infuriated vexer, now ripping at him with a red-stained muzzle—Rob wondered who was being more monstrous.

Not that the fuckers don't have it coming, he thought.

And, not failing to congratulate himself on his sudden bolt of genius, Rob turned to race on out the way he'd first come in. He only braked long enough to toss his purloined buckler clanging on the tiled floor, and pick up a stout cream pitcher in its place. It was mostly full, going by its heft.

"Now, this is a weapon I understand," he murmured. "Not quite a beer flagon. But close enough!"

He ran on out, hollering, "Murder! Assassins! They've come to kill the Emperor!" at the top of his well-trained lungs.

Five men in gold armor with scarlet plumes and capes suddenly appeared in the Emperor's candlelit private dining hall.

And here I thought the meal couldn't get more uncomfortable, Melodía thought, looking to her father and unavoidably noticing the white bulk of Margrethe von Hornberg at his side. Beside Melodía, Rosamaría calmly continued transferring to her mouth a spoonful of boiled scratcher-flesh in goat-cream sauce, with onions and a few green chilies imported from Tejas—the latest culinary fad to emanate from the great Western port of La Merced—to give it bite.

"Your Majesty," said the *sargento* in command of the Scarlet Tyrant *puño*. He had a complexion like a Spañol's, but like many Tyrants his accent was that of an Alemán-speaking Riquezo from a mountainous autonomous province in the north that was a nominal fief of Duke Roger of Sansamour. "The alarm has been raised. We got reports that assassins are inside the Corazón. And that they may be seeking to harm you. We're here to secure you."

Margrethe von Hornberg sat bolt upright. Her blue eyes were wide in alarm. It could have been for the safety of her lover and her Emperor. Or for something else.

Could you look more guilty? Melodía wondered, gazing surreptitiously at the Dowager Duchess's pale face. *But what does it matter? You know as well as I do that what my father thinks is the only thing that matters. And he sees no harm in anything you do, or you'd be out on your broad Alemana ass already!*

But the Duchess recovered quickly. "It's that Karyl behind it! It must be. I told you he was a snake, Felipe. You never should've pardoned his outlawry."

"He pardoned his daughter, too, Your Grace," Rosamaría said sharply. "And for the same reasons. Your son as well, for that matter, after the Princes' War. For reasons far less clear to me."

Felipe held up a hand. "Let it be, Grandmother. I doubt Karyl would turn on me. But I promise, I'm taking nothing for granted."

Rosamaría craned to put her lips near Melodía's ear. "Go, girl. Go and do what needs to be done."

"But my father—" she began out the side of her mouth. Her heart was racing so fast it almost tripped her words.

"Now she's fucking him, he's much more valuable to her alive than dead," Rosamaría said. "For now. ¡Vete!"

Melodía stood. "I'm going to see what's happening, Father."

Felipe's brow creased in concern. *At least he's been more aware of my existence since welcoming me back into the fold,* she thought. *Not that it's mattered. But it feels better, anyway.*

"Are you sure, daughter? These men and the Heart's Defenders are here to protect you, too."

"I've fought for you before. I'll do it now if I have to."

It clanged in her own ears as she said it like the pure bombast it was. Being her father, and part Alemán himself, Felipe ate it up. He showed his teeth in a proud and brilliant smile and nodded vigorously.

"Brave girl! Go. Whatever happens, you'll win more glory for La Torre Delgao."

Felipe stood. "Gentlemen, escort me to the throne room, if you please."

The sergeant's dark face went ashen. "Your Majesty, you're safe here. The throne room is the first place assassins would look for you!"

"And like this room, it has only two entrances," Felipe said. *That anyone knows about but us*, Melodía thought. "My good bodyguards can defend me there as readily as here, *¿qué no?*"

"*Sí*," the sergeant reluctantly replied.

"Splendid. If I am to die tonight, I prefer to do it defending the Fangèd Throne and my family's honor, not cowering in a refectory like a frightened child. Let's go."

He thrust his elbow at the Duchess. "Margrethe, my dear."

The Dowager Duchess stood up so hastily she knocked the well-cushioned chair over with her well-cushioned behind.

"Your Majesty, there's something urgent I must attend to," she said. "I'll join you as soon as I can."

She pecked him on the cheek and hustled out the front entryway with a speed that surprised Melodía.

Her father frowned in annoyance when, at a furious nod from their commander, the five Tyrants formed a diamond around the Emperor. Arming-sword drawn, the Riquezo sergeant unceremoniously led off out the servant's entrance. It was not his business to respect anybody's dignity in case of threats against the Imperial person. Least of all that of the man whose body he'd pledged his life to guard.

Melodía glanced at La Madrota. If this was not mere mad rumor but real and some scheme of Margrethe's—and Melodía knew her forebear didn't doubt that any more than she did—Rosamaría Delgao would seem the most logical target.

But the ancient woman nodded. Her thin and wrinkled lips were curved in what Melodía could only think of as the smile of a woman who knew *secrets*.

Which of course she did—a million more than Melodía could guess at. Either she didn't care if she lived or died now, which was unlikely, or she felt confident she could handle any threat. *Given how old she is . . .*

Without further thought for her mentor's welfare, Melodía went briskly out the back way as well, trailing by a dozen steps the extra Tyrant guarding her father. He was walking backward as a rear guard, with his own sword out. Since he knew the Princess posed no threat, his green eyes slid over her without seeing, as if she were a wandering house cat.

She was sure he didn't miss the fact that she ducked hastily down the first side passage that opened to her left. But that didn't matter.

Even as La Madrota had assumed—or more likely, deduced—she realized with sudden pride that she *did* know what to do now.

Several things, in fact.

Falk sat upright from between the comforting warmth of his bedmates as the door to his chamber slammed open.

"Get up, you great dunderheaded titan!" his mother commanded. "We've got a dire emergency."

"But, Mother, I thought you said you had it all taken care—"

"*Halt's Maul!*"

He obediently shut up.

"The serving-slut can go in the Moat with the other trash, easily enough," Dowager Duchess Margrethe continued in Alemán. She spoke as assuredly as if she knew neither of Falk's lovers of the evening spoke their native language. Knowing her, she did. "The Countess Rincón might prove a touch more difficult to dispose of. I trust she's here of her own free will, at least? Unlike the brainless chit you fucked by force in her father's own home last year, Teresa's got the intrigue skills to hurt you."

He nodded. "Both. They—they wanted to."

"Good. We don't need more complications right now. Things are going rapidly to shit as it is. Now quit fucking around and get your armor on. There's finally something useful for you to do!"

Chapter 44

Opening the door of the small mud-brick storage shed, Karyl peered into the courtyard of La Corazón Imperial. The immediate vicinity, here where the curtain wall surrounding the big ledge met the steep face of Monte de Gloria, was quiet and dark. Eris, the Moon Visible, had been up but had set already, he knew. The warm night breeze blew into his face from the arid land to the north.

He had no doubt he could find a way up and over the wall against which the shed was built and that formed one wall of it. He had a certain knack for escaping tight situations. He'd done it before. But he couldn't now.

Mostly because he couldn't bear to be parted from his lifelong companion, as he had ridden Shiraa to La Majestad. Jaume's ambler mare hadn't been best pleased, but her rider understood Karyl's reluctance to leave his matadora behind at Séverin Farm. The Conde dels Flors was famous for having a similarly close bond to his Corythosaurus war-mount, Camellia.

To keep Karyl's arrival before the Fangèd Throne a secret, a week ago, Jaume had needed to find accommodations for Shiraa. She couldn't be kept near duckbill war-mounts; though they were trained to face giant meat-eating dinosaurs, almost invariably marauding wild ones, they couldn't stand being in constant close proximity with a full-grown Allosaurus. Falk's Tyrannosaurus, Snowflake—small for a Tirán but bigger than Shiraa—had already been placed in solitary quarters in the Palace yard. As Shiraa's rage-fired breakout at Canterville had shown, she and the albino monster she regarded as her mortal enemy couldn't be stabled near each other, either.

But notwithstanding whatever shade under which Jaume had left the Court weeks before, he had returned as he left: still an Imperial Prince, still Marshal of the Armies and Condestable of all His Majesty's fighting forces, sea and land, and still the unofficial but universally recognized Imperial Champion. He had already made covert preparations for Shiraa to be safely, quietly, and well housed during her master's stay in the Imperial Heart.

Unfortunately, that safe, secure, quiet place lay at the Patio's far extent, across the main boulevard and the large open space before the Palace entrance. Though the rather random huddle of apartments and storage buildings blocked his view, he could hear great commotion from that direction, including the bleating of annoyed hadrosaurs.

Motion caught the corner of his eye. He saw a pair of black-clad and masked *sicarios,* arming-swords out, skulking down a passageway to his left, toward the Moat and the Plateau-top city beyond.

From the fuss out in front of the entrance, he knew the alarm had been raised in the Palace. He had to assume at least some of those responding were hunting him—either in good faith, because he also knew the Dowager Duchess was canny and quick enough to claim he was behind the threat to the very heart of the Empire, or because they were in on the plot. Or, likely, both.

Karyl stood in the deepest available shadow as a matter of habit. The assassins moved out of sight beyond a three-story dormitory with no sign of noticing him. He did not assume that meant they hadn't actually seen him. They were professional sneaks and tricksters.

They were also trained escapers. He was not. They'd be far more skilled than he was at running rooftops, for example.

So he looked for a narrow space between tall structures and ducked into it. Tucking his blackwood staff into the back of his belt, he stretched out his arms, satisfied he could exert sufficient pressure on both walls. Spreading both legs in a split, he put boot soles to brick and began to chimney-climb upwards.

He reached the top. To his left was a three-story warehouse, which, despite being made of humble bricks of stabilized local mud, sported a lush vegetable garden on its roof. On his right was the gutter of a pitched roof that had wooden planter boxes terraced up its steep slate sides.

"He's up there!" he heard from down the alley.

He latched on to the warehouse roof with his left hand, which was the master hand, and stronger—Aphrodite's insane magic had truly made it grow back as good as new. He yanked himself up onto its parapet and hauled himself over. It offered him a chance to increase separation from his immediate pursuers while he plotted an escape course. He could scramble up the terraced roof slope fairly quickly—but there it would pit the *sicarios'* presumed but likely roof-running skills against his paltry ones. Whereas he doubted they could *sprint* faster.

He did so, dodging around or vaulting the three-meter-square planting boxes. The cliff face of Mount Glory, and by extension its Patio, faced southwest. He had emerged from the underground passage in the far northeast. His destination lay at almost the farthest possible extent—by the point where the wall once again met the cliff face, three hundred meters northwest. His present course took him toward the great gate, almost due west. It was the direction his hunters would expect him to go, since it offered the fastest way out—through the gate, across the drawbridge, and into the huddle of La Majestad. Where even such as he stood a strong chance of eluding such as they.

For now, that suited him. During his chimney climb, he'd had time to think. That meant he had a plan.

Most of the Porch's pathways had grown up any which way over the centuries. Like La Majestad itself, and most of the Empire's other great cities, really. Only newer ones, or cities like La Merced that had been rebuilt after a thorough razing, showed anything resembling a neat grid. Here the only area to do so was that surrounding El Gran Patio, since those buildings' construction had been planned by the Heart's architect, Martina la Negra. And even during her lengthy lifetime, ancillary buildings such as equipment sheds and laborer's housing had begun to spring up wherever someone found it convenient to put them. For all her legendary foresight, Martina had never realized they'd mostly grow into larger, more permanent structures over time.

Ahead and to his left, Karyl saw that the end of a two-story building, the line of its peaked roof angled perpendicular to his route, butted almost against the roof he was on. Left of that, at its roofline's far end, stood another three-story building with a flat roof. He veered toward it, gained the nearer roof at a leap, ran along the peak without even looking down, and jumped to the next structure. He may not have had experience at scrambling over rooftops, but he had extremely good balance.

This building seemed to be an apartment, since the brick was finer, fired stuff, and blossoms fragrant despite being shut for the night seemed to be all around. Crickets sang here, as if to enhance the greater sense of luxury. He glanced back. The first two pursuers had just reached the top of the building he'd first climbed. But another pair came sliding toward him down the slope of building to his right. The glow of torchlight from the still-distant Patio skittered along the blades of the arming-swords in their hands.

Karyl turned his head wildly left and right, as if casting for a way to run. Just when he expected them to, the *sicarios* reached the gutter that ran along the pitched roof's bottom edge and gathered themselves to jump across a four-meter gap.

He darted toward them. He reached the parapet just before the black-clad man to his right landed on it. With his right hand he thrust the tip of his blackwood staff into the assassin's sternum. Knocked off-balance backward, the man hit the edge of the parapet with the soles of his felt boots. With a cry more of surprise than fear, he dropped from view toward the stone surface twelve meters below.

The second hit the roof's flagstones kneeling, with the buckler in his left hand dropped to them for support. He swung his sword in a vicious forehand cut for Karyl's advanced right.

Karyl stabbed the sheath-staff down against a limestone flag. The arming-sword clacked against it. Karyl thrust his own sword through the assassin's throat.

He pulled it free as he stepped back. He turned left at a right angle—southwest—and raced through the fragrant garden, then vaulted for the next roof, which lay at the same level and was also flat.

He jumped short. His boots missed the parapet. But he managed to fling his sword arm over it, catch himself, and clamber up and over to safety.

Relative safety. And temporary. He heard a whistle from his right. It was echoed at once by one from in front, from behind a higher peaked roof. Then a third came from behind and to his left. They came clearly audible over the rising clamor, especially from the open Great Courtyard right in front of the Entrada. Yet they'd remain meaningless to anyone who heard them who wasn't caught up in the deadly chase.

Neat trick, he thought. *I'll have to remember it.* He didn't bother adding any mental caveat about *if I live.* He never took the next second for granted, much less surviving an immediate threat. Of course, they were alerting him that at least three different groups were closing in on him. Clearly they preferred coordination over stealth. He presumed it a sound decision; he wasn't about to second-guess another artisan's craft.

That didn't mean he didn't intend to, in the vernacular of his long-ago youthful friendship with Smrdltska, back in Castle Mist, *fuck it right up.*

He was getting close, tantalizingly close, to the wall and the ten-meter-wide gate where the Via Imperial passed through. He raced toward it, to the far side of the new roof, another seeming dwelling place with more modest foliage, and jumped to the steep side of a roof with fired-clay tiles, scrambling up. The overlapped tiles gave decent purchase to his feet and even his hands, which were holding a sword-hilt and the sheath part of his staff. He quickly reached the top.

Two assassins were just cresting the ridge of the next

roof ahead. From his right he glimpsed a second pair racing across the garden of a three-story structure, right before they passed out of sight below the roof he was standing on. Both sets were sprinting flat-out as they closed on their kill.

Peripheral motion snapped his eyes left. A third pair were just clambering over the end of the roof he was standing on, not eight meters away. They were close enough he could see the triumph on their unmasked upper faces as each stood up and drew an arming-sword.

Without hesitation, Karyl rushed them. His habit, so deeply ingrained by training and experience as to be reflex, was to charge *into* an ambush. And no mistake: this was an ambush, albeit a rolling one.

The nearer one came right for him, swinging his sword overhand. The farther slid a couple of paces down the roof slope to Karyl's right—prudently flanking him away from his own sword hand. As expected, the man ran almost as fast on the steep pitch as he would on level ground, especially with the tiles' help.

With the flat of his single-edged blade, Karyl slapped the descending sword from the left, turning his hips to steer it past his body to the right. He dropped his right arm over the *sicario*'s, sticking the sheath—still held upward from his fist like a sword—against his right rib cage beneath the armpit. Pressing his left forearm against the killer's biceps, he locked his sword arm out.

Karyl now faced down the roof's side. The second assassin attacked from Karyl's right, arming-sword cocked over his left shoulder. Even by stars and backscatter lamplight, Karyl could see his pupils widen at the certainty of his kill.

The certainty was misplaced. Using unbearably painful pressure on his captive's elbow, Karyl swung the *sicario* into the path of his partner's powerful downward cut. The man howled and convulsed in Karyl's joint lock as the blade bit deep into his right shoulder and chest, almost at the base of his neck.

Karyl felt a strange looseness in the trapped arm. It told him the second swordsman had chopped the right side of his clavicle clean through—meaning the whole arm had just lost a major anchor point. Karyl might have lost the leverage needed to control him.

He didn't care. He raised his right arm as high as he could and gave the stricken *sicario* a hearty shove with his left, putting a clockwise hip rotation behind it.

The man's scream got louder as he plunged down the roof slope into the face of his companion, who was trying to yank his blade free of the man's body. The second attacker toppled over backward, and both rolled in an uncontrollable tumble of flailing limbs, down the pitched roof off to the street three stories below.

But now the other four had Karyl surrounded. They circled him with the deliberation of pure self-assurance. They held all the Creator cards now. As Karyl had reminded Rob, a lethally disadvantaged foe was the kind they were best equipped to fight.

Karyl circled and reversed, scanning his head left to right as he did so, as if trying to keep track of all four at once. He knew that was impossible. What he was really doing was swiveling his eyes to watch the faces of whichever two happened to be in front of him at a given instant.

He was reasonably confident they, whichever they were, wouldn't launch the final attack.

A bald man and a man with short red hair and unusually fair skin for the *sicarios* Karyl had seen tensed visibly. The bald one's dark eyes widened slightly.

Karyl spun counterclockwise, lashing out with his sword. The two assassins who'd been closing on him from behind leapt back.

His left boot slipped out from under him. He fell forward to his left.

Chapter 45

Uriel, *El Fuego de Dios*, **Fire of God**—One of the Grey
Angels, the Creators' Own Seven servitors and vindicators
of Their divine justice. A fire spirit, linked to the Oldest
Daughter, Telar, and imbued especially with Her Attributes
of both creation and impermanence. He is said to be allied
with Raphael the Healing-spirit, and Remiel the Merciful,
hence among the more approachable of the Seven. It is
wise to remember that such things are relative, since the
Angels' ministrations are seldom gentle.

—A PRIMER TO PARADISE FOR THE IMPROVEMENT
OF YOUNG MINDS

The assassin's arming-sword clanged against
Rob's silver pitcher, his parrying weapon of
choice. He stabbed furiously back with his own
sword. More by blind luck than anything else the *sicario*
didn't manage to bring his main-gauche dagger up in
time to stop four fingers of its tip from sliding neatly into
his gullet, just above the notch of his collarbone.

Well, now I'm only doubly fucked, Rob thought as he
averted his face to keep the answering blood jet from
catching him in the right eye. *That's what I get for trying to escape through a maze of a Palace whose innards*

I only clapped eyes on two hours ago. Having promptly gotten lost after fleeing the kitchen.

Well, and for trusting that blond Tyrannosaurus, Margrethe.

Until the last year or thereabouts, Rob Korrigan's experience at face-up fighting had entailed taverns and the consumption of copious amounts of booze. Though he was sadly about to die stone-sober, such brawls served him reasonably well in a fight like this, doomed as it was. By reflex he yanked his own arming-sword free of the assassin's neck and then flicked blood from it squarely into the eyes of the one rushing in with sword and buckler from his right. The man jumped back, blinking and dabbing at his eyes with the back of his sword hand.

Rob continued his spin in a rapid of not unduly graceful pirouettes. Only to see the third of the masked killers who'd surprised him by popping from a side corridor one floor up from the Palace kitchen. He had his right arm drawn back by his ribs and his arming-sword poised to deliver a thrust to an off-balance Rob, who had no Paradisiacal hope of preventing him from running him through.

The dark eyes went wide in bare surprise. The *sicario* went as rigid as if turned to stone by wild Faerie magic.

It was no accident. Karyl had faked a fall in order to roll at the feet of one of the pair of contract killers who'd attacked him from behind. The man jumped lithely up and let Karyl pass right under him.

Karyl let himself keep rolling. He heard his assailants cry out as they came mincing down the tiles with sideways feet, trying not to slip and join him.

When he neared the roof's lower edge, he flung out his right arm and leg, sprawling. Between that and the corrugations caused by the overlapping tiles themselves, he stopped himself short.

A *sicario* had changed course to come down almost on top of him, either to kill him if he caught himself or help him over the edge if he needed it. Instead, he trotted right into a forehand slash of Karyl's sword across the shins.

The man screeched and tripped over Karyl's prone body, showering the back of his shirt with hot blood. Using his staff to steady himself, Karyl rolled right and kicked the man off him. His yells got shriller as he rolled off the roof.

Karyl sat up. Before he could get a leg under him, he caught a blur in the corner of his right eye. He swung the staff-sheath over and back. By chance the blackwood deflected a sword-cut. He cracked the assassin with it smartly across the masked mouth in riposte and came up on his right knee. Another charged in from the left with his arming-sword pulled back two-handed for a thrust. Instead, he ran himself onto Karyl's blade.

Karyl pushed off with his right foot, driving his sword through the bald *sicario*'s stomach to the hilt. His sword-point was already past Karyl's left shoulder. He pushed himself past the assassin to his own left, spinning him by the sword that impaled him as if it were a handle.

He turned him clear around, put his right boot to the point between navel and balls and shoved him off the sword and at the *sicario* he'd hit in the face with his staff. The killer dodged and his stricken companion skidded, moaning, into space.

Karyl swung a blind stroke left with his sword, causing the opponent trying to close from that side to dance back. He got both feet beneath him. He was almost at the bottom edge of the roof now, the gutter mere centimeters below his left boot.

They charged him together. He spun clockwise, de-

flecting a sword slash from the man who had been behind him with the staff. He ran past, readying to hack
him across the back.

Instead, his foot slipped for real. He slid down. His feet
flew over the gutter and into air.

Melodía's friends and nominal subordinates the woods-
runners had taught her a lot about backstabbing. Not in
intrigue. The literal thing.

Although the first thing she'd learned on joining Rob
Korrigan's Providence Militia scouts as a simple *jinete*,
or light rider, had been that the woods-runners accepted
no one's dominion. But they would pay attention to those
they respected. Even their own "chieftains," like Emeric
and his scarred and vengeful sister Stéphanie, exerted no
control. Only influence. Which she was proud of having
won in her own right.

During the fights against border raiders, and then
the long fighting retreat culminating in the desperate
battle with Raguel's Crusaders, she'd had no opportunity to use that knowledge. The skirmishes with the
mostly Castañero marauders had all taken place on the
back of her mare, Meravellosa. And the Horde tended
to mindlessly attack anyone not part of it whom they laid
eyes on; they seldom presented their backs, especially
to a dagger thrust.

But she used that knowledge now with both calm determination and a savage glee. The pain of that first kid-
ney thrust momentarily paralyzed the *sicario*. But she
had also learned from her wandering teachers that you
could never count on a single body stab to incapacitate
your foe, much less kill him.

So as fast as she could she withdrew the dirk and
plunged it into the black-clad back again, half a dozen

times in rapid succession. Blood splashed her belly and thighs.

His knees buckled, and he dropped to his side. He instantly curled up into a ball of mewling agony. Overcoming a reflex stab of compassion at her heart, she leaned down, stuck the tip of her dagger into his neck just before the spine, and cut forward and up with a decisive twist.

She had even remembered to step back, so that the sudden fan of blood from the severed artery beneath his ear missed her completely. It showered Rob, though. He was already pretty much drenched in gore anyway.

"Behind you!" she shouted.

Rob dropped to his left knee, pivoting and bringing up the heavy pitcher he improbably held in his left fist. Even more improbably, yellowish goat-milk cream slopped out the top to join that already running down its sides.

The arming-sword the last remaining black-masked man had swung at the back of Rob's head glanced safely away from him. Rob hacked the man above his left knee. It gave way beneath him. He went down and struck it hard on the unforgiving stone floor.

Rob snapped up and kicked him under the chin. The killer's head snapped back, black hair flying. Melodía wondered if the kick had broken his neck as he folded backward with his right leg sprawling out at a clumsy angle.

Rob was taking nothing for granted. He tossed his pitcher aside, ringing it off the bare stone wall of the servants' passageway and decorating it with a hearty splash of cream. Reversing his sword in his right hand and folding his left over the plain steel pommel, he strode to the supine man and glared down at him.

The man was alive and conscious. Melodía saw his eyes standing out from his head and his mask. He opened his mouth.

"Fuck you," Rob said, and plunged the blade down through mask and open mouth so hard it punched out the back of the man's skull to screech against the stone. The assassin spasmed wildly, back arching, limbs failing. Then he went limp and empty of life.

Rob let go of the sword, which fell over, turning the man's head to one side. His open eyes gave the impression of staring in shock at the horrid mockery of his tongue.

Melodía was looking up and down the corridor. The dagger she'd drawn from her gem-bangled belt of gold-painted leather had rubies and topazes glittering in its hilt, but the blade was sturdy, keen, and true. As the blood dripping from it proved.

"Baron Korrigan," she said, "what are you doing here? I didn't even know you were in the Palace."

Her former boss stood bent over with his hands on his thighs, panting.

"Smuggled in . . . discreetly . . . this evening, Your Highness," he puffed.

"Melodía. Why were you smuggled in?" she asked.

"It's Karyl . . . He's . . . caught in a wicked web."

"That's histrionic."

"Muh trade . . . lass. The Duchess . . . lured me here, got me inside. I did . . . a terrible thing. And now her *sicarios* are hunting both me and Karyl!"

"*What?*"

He looked up and grinned through the blood, fresh and half-dried, which turned his face into a frightful demon mask.

"Is this how you go to battle, then, now you're a princess again?" he asked.

She looked down at herself. She had forgotten that aside from her slim belt she was dressed only in sandals, a jeweled loincloth, and a tiara. The green silk was stained beyond repair by gore.

"I was at dinner."

She'd been taking a shortcut to her apartments to grab more suitable clothes for what she had in mind. Armor was out of the question, given her need for haste, but she doubted it would matter for what she had in mind. The builders of the Imperial Heart had neglected to build a secret passageway from dining hall to penthouse. Or at least no one had ever revealed one's existence to her.

"Now, what the Old Hell's this shit about you and Karyl? I thought I was willing to believe anything evil of Margrethe, but this? I know she hates Karyl, but why would she set professional murderers on you? And how did all this happen?"

"She played on my fears," he said, painfully pushing himself upward and then straightening his barrel-shaped body as if by means of a crank and ratchet. "She and that *hada*-spawn Bergdahl, whose goblin looks don't lie as to his black nature."

Bergdahl. She remembered her apprehension when her father had announced that the man—her rapist's creature—would serve Rob as seneschal to teach him how to be a Baron. But the world-shattering news of Montse's abduction had driven the matter entirely out of her head. As it had so many things.

She frowned as the import of what he was saying hit home. "You didn't—"

"Ah, but I did, lass. I feared for his soul—that he'd be captured by the magic of the Fae. So I agreed to lead him where he might be taken into . . . protective custody. There to be exorcised of their evil influence."

He shook his head forlornly. "'Twas for his own good. So I told myself. And so the witch Margrethe assured me. And see where it led?"

"He was your best friend! *How could you betray him?*"

"How could you lead Pilar to her death?" he flared back.

She felt her eyes widen, felt cold fury fill her stomach. It was a terrible thing to say.

Because it was true. He had loved her childhood friend turned servant and then friend again. Melodía had watched her die, trying to help her escape from Count Guillaume of Crève Coeur's pet hunting horrors—where Melodía had led her and a number of Garden dignitaries on a misbegotten errand of peace. And Rob had seen what the Deinonychus pack had left of her, moments after Karyl and the light riders had appeared to kill the monsters and save her life.

Rob sighed and dropped his hazel eyes, now green with fury, from hers. He flapped both hands in a gesture of conciliation.

"Peace," he said. "I beg you—for Karyl's sake, and maybe your father's, if not for mine. I spoke out of turn. We both did what we thought was right and were fucking idiots to do it. I can't make it right, what I did or what I said, since two wrongs just make twice the wrongs. But can I hope that since we've both drawn heart's blood, honor's satisfied for both of us, at least?"

She had to smile. "It's hard to stay mad at you, Baron Rob."

"Ah, well. Get to know me better, it'll come more easily. But now we've places to be."

"Where's Karyl?"

"Away free and clear, that's my devout hope."

"Where are you bound?"

"The same general destination, if not specific. Himself is through with me, I fear, and no blame to him. If he did anything wrong it was likely refraining from killing me for what I did."

He was an expert performer, she knew. But if his grief and regret were anything but real, he was the greatest actor in the history of the world.

"How did you wind up here?"

"I led three of the devils through the kitchen, where Lady Maris herself must've inspired me to raise the alarm they were really here to kill the Emperor. Which, mind you, I don't know is even false. They dispatched the rogues and raised the alarm while I made off at speed. And got lost."

He gestured at the floor, and the huddles of black and crimson.

"Till they found me."

"You've got to get out of here." She gave him quick instructions on the fastest way to the Entrada.

"I'd be a poor fish if I didn't suspect that Margrethe was spreading word that Karyl and I are behind all these murderers and all this murdering, in an imagined plot against your father. If the Tyrants of Heart's Defenders come upon me, the kindest thing they're like to do is kill me out of hand."

She hesitated a moment. Time pressed like the whole weight of the thousands of tons of mountain stone above their heads. Then she untied her loincloth from about her waist.

"Please forgive the blood," she said as she tied it around his right biceps.

Rob raised an eyebrow. "That seems mighty informal dress, even for Spaña," he said. "Tiara notwithstanding."

"I'm the Princess. I could run around naked all the time if I chose."

"Fair enough. And while I don't mind the stains, given how you put them there, what's this for, actually?"

"My favor. The red and yellow jewels sewed in mean it belongs to a member of the Imperial family. Which means me, basically."

"But might they not think I killed you for it myself, what with the blood and all?"

She laughed. "I believe you used to like the phrase

'He'd gripe if you hanged him with a golden rope.' It's the best I can do. Now go!"

"What're you going to do?"

"Save both you poor fools," she said. "If I can."

Chapter 46

Volador, Flier, *Volado Peludo*, Furred Flier . . . .—*Pterosaur*: a flying reptile, covered in fine fur. Some have tails, some have crests, some have beaks, toothed or not. Not dinosaurian. Rivals to birds for the skies of Paradise and the offal of its streets. They range in size from tiny bug-chasers to the vast, majestic, and fearful Dragons.

—THE BOOK OF TRUE NAMES

etting go of his sheath, Karyl just managed to drop his right forearm in the bronze half-pipe of the gutter and clamp the lip between thumb and fingertips. His shoulder groaned as his falling weight hit it, and pain shot from his brutally torqued elbow. But he held on and didn't fall.

Yet.

The nearer assassin hacked down at him. He blocked the blade with the flat, at the cost of more agony to his shoulder and elbow. It was power against power, a thing he hated to get caught up in in a fight. But in spite of his superior position, the man had launched the attack hastily, in hopes of speeding Karyl to join the *sicarios* he'd sent tumbling to death or broken bones on the hard rock below, rather than from a set, strong position.

The man raised his arming-sword for another blow. Karyl sliced him across the right thigh. It was too high to cut the quadriceps tendon and too shallow to damage the big muscle, much less sever the femoral artery. But the man grunted and sat down hard, apparently to keep his knee from buckling and his possibly falling off the roof.

His blade dropped. Karyl's flashed in to lick across his face, left to right. Then back across his throat.

The blood geyser hit Karyl full in the left eye, temporarily blinding it as it covered his face in wet heat. His right eye saw the last assassin descending for it in a cut not even his viper reflexes could block.

He swung his legs and hips forward and let go.

He did not plummet to shatter his back and hips on the bare, unforgiving stone of the Porch. He did scrape his tailbone painfully on the inner edge of the planter on the railing of the balcony below. The pitched-roof buildings of the miniature city within the Palace wall were mostly or all dwellings. Most such had balconies, and every one that had a peaked roof had held growing containers. Karyl landed on his feet and took up a two-handed grip on his sword's blackwood hilt, blade aimed at the roof edge right above.

This *sicario* was cagey enough not to try dropping directly onto his prey. Instead, he swung down to land at the far end of the balcony from where Karyl had lighted.

They faced each other. Karyl kept his sword above his head but angled the tip down to the level of his opponent's face. Karyl's opponent was the red-haired man whose skin was a paler olive than most the assassins'. His dark eyes grinned.

The *sicario* advanced by half steps. He was armed with a single sword, which he tossed from hand to hand without glancing at it, as if to try to intimidate Karyl with his confidence and prowess—and hinted ambidexterity.

Karyl was unimpressed. He lowered the staff-sword to a conventional guard position, with the butt of the hilt a hand span above his advanced left knee. He kept his eyes at soft focus, directed toward the man's pelvis—he had long ago learned that, in combat, eyes and hands might lie but hips told the truth. *If he keeps up this juggling act,* he thought as his enemy drew within two meters, *he'll give me the opening I—*

The redhead darted his right hand into the planter and flung dirt into Karyl's eyes.

He managed to twitch his head to his left and shut his eyes. But he couldn't stop some dirt from getting in. As he blinked furiously to clear it, the *sicario* launched into a beautiful left-handed lunge.

Into air. Leaving his right hand gripping his sword-hilt by the end, Karyl put his left on the planter and vaulted himself to the balcony below. He inadvertently dislodged it. It banged off the planter on the level Karyl landed on and crashed into the street.

Though perhaps not consciously, Karyl had been half expecting such a move. Carrying various forms of powder, from ground pepper to lye, to throw in an opponent's eyes and blind him, temporarily or not, was a popular trick among the Vagabonds of Tianchao-guo, and their *shinobi* cousins from the island kingdom of Zipangu farther east. Karyl had gotten the impression early on that this gang was a pale imitation of the latter, also called *ninjas*, whose attributes and exploits were well, if not always accurately, known as in the romances so beloved in Nuevaropa. They might have picked up the ploy from reading adventure novels.

He's good, Karyl thought, moving back to the wall and taking up a two-handed guard stance again, facing outward. *He almost got me with it.* He managed to blink his eyes clear—clear enough.

But instead of jumping down to the second-floor balcony to attack Karyl once more, the assassin swung his legs down, dropped, caught himself on the planter without knocking it over, gave Karyl the finger of the hand holding his sword—still the left—and dropped to the street below.

He has style, Karyl acknowledged to himself. His insouciance reminded him of Rob, whom he hoped had at least managed to get away clear.

"So," a male voice called up from below. "Are you just going to cower up there and wait for my brothers to come help me get you?"

The *sicario*'s Spañol had a marked Catalan accent. Given that his hair was a lighter red than Melodía's—whose skin was darker—and darker than Jaume's—who was paler—his apparent origin didn't surprise Karyl.

"Such as you've left of us—you've hurt our fraternity badly, but we'll kill you quickly, once they're here. Or will you come down and play?"

"Neither," said Karyl, and pushed this balcony's plant container down on him.

He shifted left and followed it. He heard a crack from below, followed by a second, heavier crash. It sounded to him as if his opponent had tried to fend off the heavy trough, this one carven stone, and suffered a broken forearm for his trouble.

Karyl landed well enough, flexing his knees deeply into a crouch to take the impact. By chance he'd landed within reach of his fallen staff-sheath. He grabbed it as the assassin, his right hand flopping grotesquely from a new joint mid-forearm like a broken flier wing, rushed him with upraised sword.

He swung the staff up and cracked its tip underneath the Catalan's jaw. Dropping it again, he took a two-handed grip once more, raised his sword over his left shoulder, and chopped the *sicario*'s left hand off at the wrist as his opponent swung his arming-sword forehand and down.

Turning his hips, he let go with his right hand, rotated his pelvis the other way, and slashed his disarmed killer across the black-clad belly.

Doubling over his ruptured gut, pressing his spurting stump and extra-jointed arm against himself in a vain attempt to hold back the greasy dark-grey-looking loops of intestine, the assassin staggered back. He raised his face to Karyl.

"I suppose—mercy—would be too much—to ask?" he said, and for a wonder, kept the banter in his tone despite what had to be frightful pain.

Karyl answered with a thrust through his right eye.

"A quick death," he said quietly, as the assassin collapsed onto a pile of his own blood and guts, "is mercy of a sort."

He flipped the miraculously never-dulling blade to clear blood and sundry stray tissue from it. Scrupulously wiping it clean on the dead man's back, he recovered his sheath and returned the sword to it.

He heard what sounded like at least two sets of groans from the shadows. He ignored the wounded *sicarios*. They were no longer in his way. He'd given the red-haired man misericordia—the final blessing—as much because it was convenient to do so as for the fact he despised cruelty. But he felt no obligation to the rest of those who'd just failed in killing him.

And if they want to make a try at my back, despite their undoubtedly serious injuries, here on level ground, he thought, *well, let them*.

He walked on, no more watchful than usual, and no less.

As Karyl expected, the courtyard was filled with confusion. Ignoring the knights who sat their backs in states of dress from mostly full armor to mostly full nudity, nine or ten war-hadrosaurs were jostling in a courtyard their numbers and bulk managed to crowd despite its expansive size, then furiously blaring and pawing at one another. Retainers and servants darted about on foot trying not to get trampled or smashed to jelly by a tail swung in heedless anger. The humans all seemed to be bawling at the tops of their voices, too, though their efforts were feeble beside dinosaurian squealing and trumpeting.

He simply found the least well-lit stretch of the main thoroughfare from the courtyard and the Palace entrance to the curtain wall, where stout stone buildings choked it down to ten meters' width by design to funnel intruders who had made it this far and make it handier to murder them from above, and walked across with his usual purposeful, seemingly unhurried stride.

No one paid him any mind.

But once he was down the nearest alley on the far side, he ran toward the northwestern juncture of cliff and wall, leaving the gates and their promise of safety beckoning and open behind him. He had a greater goal than mere escape.

Melodía pressed her palms against her breasts even more firmly as she bounded up the stairs to the Imperial apartments. She'd been cupping them to keep them from bouncing as she ran. She knew that would be undignified, even if she were still dressed in anything but a belt and that ludicrous tiara. But they'd swung around enough to be uncomfortable when she was backstabbing the assassin as it was.

She almost ran facefirst into Jaume, striding down the hallway to the stairs from his own chambers next to hers. He still wore nothing but the sandals and loincloth he'd also worn to dinner. At least he was spared the tiara.

But he did hold the Lady's Mirror in one hand, and the longsword's sheath in the other.

"Princess," he said. His brow furrowed in puzzlement. "You wore more than that to dinner, I think."

A little breathlessly despite the endless hours of drilling with Auriana, Melodía filled him in on her encounter with Rob and the murderers—and a version of why edited to include only that Rob knew the Dowager Duchess von Hornberg had set the *sicarios* on both men.

He took it all in without raising a brow. "Where are you going?" he asked when she'd finished.

"To help them get away. Margrethe's no doubt told as many people as she could find that they're behind an attempt on my father's life. There'll be hanger-on knights turning out on their war-dinosaurs to stop them."

She hesitated. "I need to go out in the Courtyard. I need to be ready to fight if I have to. I'll need clothes for that. We can't let them get arrested."

Falsely, she thought. *As I was.* She burned with the need to tell him the story of her false accusation and imprisonment. And what happened next. But this wasn't the time.

It's never the time! She stilled the voice of the lost child within. Maybe the time would come—but this clearly wasn't.

Jaume shook his head.

"I'll go set things straight. Order the knights and the guards to stand down if I have to."

"No! You can't. You mustn't. Your position's still too precarious, and we can't throw away everything we've worked for." *That's part of the reason.* "I'll handle it."

"But if there's fighting—"

"I can handle it! You've got to trust me, my love."

"I do. But I don't want to send you into danger."

"I'm the Princesa Imperial," she said. "There won't be any danger." *Not deliberate, anyway.* Accidental *is an-*

other thing. "Now, go. Take care of my father. We can't assume he's safe!"

He nodded and kissed her quickly.

"What *are* you going to do?" he asked.

She smiled. "Your Princess is about to surprise a lot of people."

Including you, my love.

Here by the end of the Bulwark, El Salto*'s* noise was substantial, at the point of transition from splashing to roar. Karyl heard Shiraa trill a happy greeting even before he entered her temporary dinosaur barn, with his sword drawn and its sheath held in his right hand, ready to parry or strike. It was a warehouse built of fired-clay brick, long enough to allow all ten meters of the Allosaurus to stretch out, with room left over for dinosaur grooms to move safely around outside her makeshift stall; and she could curl up to sleep, as she sometimes did, without taking up even half its width.

When he and Jaume had arrived at the Imperial Heart, Karyl had been surprised to find the building emptied of whatever had been stored there in order to house his friend, given what he presumed was the relative premium on space on El Porche. Then again, the Imperial Champion and Condestable wasn't exactly without influence here himself. Also, Jaume appeared to be allied with Torre Delgao's ageless matriarch, Doña Rosamaría.

Now, by the light of lamps hung from the uprights, he saw that the spacious interior had been transformed again, from one pen to two. And that he and Shiraa were not alone.

"Rob," he said.

Shiraa's barn was cavernous enough to have an echo. It smelled of mice, and shorter-term occupancy by dinosaurs, and of fresh hay. From his daily daytime visits here, Karyl knew that scores of Anurognathus—small, furry, needle-toothed fliers called *chato* because of their short muzzles—had nests built among the stone-and-wood rafters. They'd be untenanted now; the snub-noses emerged at sunset to eat the insects that swarmed by night, even here in the dry uplands.

"You look like you had a rough night of it, Your Grace," Rob Korrigan said.

"You should see the other men."

Rob chuckled. "I've seen enough of what you leave of *sicarios* impudent enough to try to ply their trade on you tonight to last me. Oh, and I took the liberty of preparing your mount. As well as my own."

He slapped Shiraa on her smooth-scaled shoulder in a comradely way, just ahead of the foremost of the two girths holding Karyl's saddle on her back. She was gazing intently at Karyl with her two great scarlet eyes peering up past the twin bony flanges on her lowered snout. She stood half out of her opened enclosure. Behind her, he saw her toy still hanging from a stout rafter by a stout length of chain. It was a simple cycad log, fibrous, still green, and replaced as soon as it dried out by the Palace's nervous but dutiful dinosaur grooms. She could chew on it, worry it, tug on it, or amuse herself for hours by bumping it with her nose and watching it swing this way for that. Karyl's girl had simple tastes.

Thrusting his staff-sheath through his belt, Karyl went to her. He held his palm to her nostrils. She sniffed, then blew against it. Her breath was warm and moist.

He scratched the arched bridge of her nose and between the small horns. She bobbed her head and made slight chuckling sounds of pleasure.

The lower, dumpier dinosaur beside her blew emphatically through the nostrils of her own prodigiously horned nose. She had her saddle on as well, with a large pack behind and Rob's axe, Wanda, hung by the bow.

"Little Nell," Karyl said. "I should have expected to find you at the Palace, since your master's here. But why are you both *here*?"

"This was the only place they had to put her," Rob said, shifting to scratch her neck behind her frill, which had two long horns sticking up from its top. "And she got used to Shiraa's presence when we rode back to Providence together, you'll recall."

"I do," Karyl said. He had his right hand on his sheath, and while he held his sword in a relaxed position by his left leg, he still had it out. He kept his eyes scanning the shadows of the makeshift.

"As for me," Rob said, "I knew you'd not leave this good girl behind, any more than I'd leave Nell. So I thought it best to expedite our departure by making both ready. Sorry I don't have your own baggage. I was a bit discommoded to try fetching it from your chambers, what with bloody-handed murderers chasing me."

Karyl saw his trail blanket rolled and tied behind the saddle's high cantle. A dinosaur master to the bone, Rob had actually taken time to untie its ends and empty out the straw it had been filled with, to give Shiraa a vaguely man-shaped doll that smelled like her "mother" to comfort her as she slept. Karyl regretted that it wasn't feasible to sleep in the blanket himself, curled up with her here as he did on the road. But he appreciated the way his often careless friend could focus on details when it mattered.

He twitched the sword. "This is all that matters. But what's that on your arm?"

"Melodía's loincloth."

Karyl raised a brow.

"I ran into the Princess whilst blundering about the Palace, thoroughly lost. She saved my life, not to put too fine an edge on it. She gave me this as a sign I was under her protection, and not to be hindered on my way out the door."

Shiraa raised her head to stare hard at the partly open wooden door through which Karyl had slipped. She drew in a deep breath, whiffing notably through her nose. Then she uttered a low rumble of a growl.

"We've got company," Karyl said. He moved to the saddle and tapped its stout nosehorn-leather skirt with his fingertips. She promptly lowered her buff-colored belly to the bare stone to make it easier for him to mount. "We need to move. They won't be friends."

"Catch the door, there's a good fellow, Your Grace," said Rob jauntily as he swung up into his hook-horn's saddle and picked up the reins. "My lead, I think. If there's one thing Little Nell can do, it's clear the way!"

Karyl moved to the door. He heard a mutter of voices from outside, the slap of leather on stone. But he paused and looked back.

"Rob," he said, "thank you."

"You're welcome, Karyl. And also premature. If we get out of this alive, then's the time to thank me!"

Chapter 47

Saltador, Springer. . . .—*Orodromeus makelai.* Small, swift, bipedal herbivorous dinosaur with toothed beak, 2.5 meters long, 45 kilograms. Usually brown spotted white, with white bellies. Timid; adept at hiding. Flocks abound in Nuevaropa; common farm and crop pests. A highly favored quarry of hunters both human and dinosaurian.

—THE BOOK OF TRUE NAMES

He'll likely kill me in the morning, Rob thought as Karyl gathered himself and pulled the heavy door open on its rollers. *Should we live to see the sun rise.*

"Well, he's entitled," he said, pulling Wanda free of her straps. He left the leather case on her head. And clapping his boot heels against Little Nell's stout sides, screamed, *"Charge!"*

No Gallimimus as a sprinter, the hook-horn nonetheless had a powerful launch, with her squat build and mighty hindquarters—which the insensitive might call a "fat arse." She snorted eagerly and took off at a rolling gallop that was within a few paces of her top speed.

Karyl passed running the other way, toward Shiraa. Who was already screaming her name—the only thing she ever said, but for the odd gurgle chirp, or growl—in challenge.

Ahead he saw the cleared space in front of the warehouse was awash in flickering yellow torchlight. By the lights of those little fires he saw a dozen arms upholding them, left half bare by sagging mail sleeves, and faces male and female between the pointy-topped steel caps worn by Los Defensores del Corazón. Whose expressions turned from grim determination to bloodlust to a sudden unanimity of surprise—and fear.

It was well founded. The tough-looking female *sargento* leading the squad was knocked sprawling by the boss of Nell's gigantic forward-hooking nasal horn. She never had the chance to raise her round shield and spear.

The five squaddies behind her all carried, one-handed, the heaviest and most powerful kind of crossbows, already cocked by means of mechanical contrivances called cranequins and with bolts clamped in the slots and ready to shoot. At spitting range they'd shoot through any armor a human could walk around in and could drop even a smallish titan with a lucky shot to heart or brain. It was clear they had one aim: fast and brutal butchery of Shiraa and Little Nell, and their owners if the Creators smiled on them.

They got both monsters and riders, to be sure. And Rob thought the Gods of Paradise did indeed favor the Heart's Defenders squad when Little Nell merely knocked them sprawling. Even the one Rob felt squash-crack beneath Nell's off forefoot. His screams indicated that it didn't kill him at once. A mixed blessing at best, but blessing withal.

Little Nell bleated in glee. Though less immense, to say nothing of dramatic, than her cousins the Triceratops, she was still a nosehorn in good standing; and like most of that ilk, took almost as much joy in a good fight as any great meat-eater did.

Rob didn't look down any more than he regretted his beloved friend trampling someone. His heart was filled with righteous fury that they'd come with undeniable intent to harm Nell and Shiraa—bloody hero of the whole entire world that she was—much less him and Karyl. He swatted the ones who hadn't yet fled outside his arms' reach with his axe's leather-covered head and gusto.

The Defenders who didn't jump or get shouldered bodily out of the hook-horn's path were mostly overrun by those who had, but kept their feet. Then out from the barn's shadowy depths burst Shiraa, roaring her name in happy anticipation of biting off some faces.

For a moment Rob feared she'd miss her chance. The guards still standing threw away their torches and arbalests and ran away in all directions like a flock of springer who had, well, a raging matadora appear in their midst. Then he heard a shriek of wild terror from behind.

Since Little Nell was headed the right way, and more than canny enough not to run full tilt into a brick building no matter how happy she was to be trouncing louts, and he'd run out of foes in smiting range, Rob glanced over his right shoulder. A Defensor who'd been bulled to that side had lost his helmet but retained his crossbow. He had come up on one knee and was taking aim at Rob's back when Shiraa came thundering down on him on her powerful hind legs. He shrieked as her open jaws lunged toward his face.

The jaws clashed shut. The man's terrified outcries were cut off, along with his head.

Without breaking stride, Shiraa yanked up, freeing her prize of any stubborn bits of skin or sinew holding it to the rest of him. As the torso fell over, hosing blood from the surprisingly clean stump, she tossed the head aside. She was immaculately trained not to eat her kills without her mother's permission. Though Rob sussed that she mostly refrained not from dog-like obedience, but just to please her beloved human, the way a cat or ferret might.

His cheeks flushed hot as he turned forward again. *They'll not be welcoming us back here anytime soon*, he thought, *except to hang us. Well, it's not as if I've had that grand a time tonight.*

Little Nell was already loping between the dark angled masses of buildings. He steered her in what he hoped was the shortest route to the gate through the twisty maze of this part of the Porche, near the wall and far from La Entrada.

Then he got her nose turned down one of the more regular avenues near the Imperial Way. He had a straight sight line to the Patio, now awash in the orange light of dozens of torches and lanterns, as well as shouting men and rearing dinosaurs. At once he reined her to a haunch-dropping stop, waving Wanda frantically above his head in hopes of keeping Shiraa from plowing right into them.

The Allosaurus cried "Shiraa" somewhat peevishly. But Rob smelled no carnosaur breath, inevitably foul despite regular tooth cleanings, nor did he feel the impact of a couple of hurtling metric tons.

"I think it's your turn to take the lead," he said, twisting in the saddle. Little Nell was tossing her big head and blowing loudly through her nostrils in obvious agitation. At the smell and nearness of so many big, excited dinosaurs—and at one presence in particular.

Karyl had to lean left out of his saddle to see past Shiraa, who had her own large head raised and was staring keenly toward the Courtyard with torchlight gleaming in her scarlet eyes. Rob saw his own friend's eyes go wide. Then the lean, bearded face took on a look of the closest thing to pure pleasure Rob had seen that tortured soul express during all their months together.

"Yes," said Karyl, "I believe you're right." He raised his single-edged sword and nudged Shiraa in her ribs.

Rob pulled Little Nell to the limestone side of an apartment building to clear the way as the matadora bounded eagerly past.

"Knights!" Falk roared, rearing Snowflake and brandishing his knight's axe overhead in a gauntleted fist. The visor of the special black bascinet that his mother had brought from Hornberg, its "fatty-break" visor molded and painted to suggest a screaming toothed-falcon beak, was open to allow him to properly shout such orders. And display his manly bearded visage, of course. "Get ready! To escape, the traitors Bogomirskiy and Korrigan have to get through us!"

That was the story his mother had ordered him to spread: that the pair from Providence were behind an assassination attempt on the Emperor's life. *As if I didn't think of it myself before she even said it!* he thought. *She never gives me credit.*

Of seven war-hadrosaurs currently housed on El Porche, five had turned out to join him, including the green-and-gold striped Lambeosaurus, with Archduke Antoine on her back. Only Mandar, that old fart, held out, along with a mysterious blond woman who served the horrible old witch La Madrota as a retainer. Margrethe's best efforts to persuade Felipe to turf her sackbut out to house a dinosaur belonging to another of their loyalists had failed. Apparently, Rosamaría Delgao actually *owned* the Imperial Heart.

They had other dinosaur knights in their faction, of course. But their war-mounts were housed in La Majestad—as were several of the knights themselves, since accommodations were always at a premium inside the Wall. They were on their way.

But I'm not going to leave them the chance to do anything, Falk thought.

He kept Snowflake turning left and right to better spread the exhortations around. He heard a squawk of surprise and pain as her tail clipped someone on foot. He didn't so much as glance that way; whether foot soldier or servant, it was only a peasant.

He and his beloved white T. rex happened to be facing straight down the Via Imperial toward the gate when a single furious scream pealed from his right: "*Shiraa!*"

He grinned. "Time to finish what we started, eh, boy?" he cried to Snowflake as he spun the big dinosaur right to face his rival—and somewhat smaller—predator.

He saw a gape of red mouth, and teeth shimmering orange and gold in the torchlight, closing fast.

Too fast.

White rage filled Shiraa's consciousness and whole being like an all-consuming flame.

WHITE MONSTER! WHITE MONSTER! she thought.

HATE.

TEAR! KILL! EAT!

He turned to face her. Joy joined her fury as she clamped her jaws shut on his hated white snout. The blood that gushed hot into her mouth was the sweetest taste she'd ever known. Almost as sweet as the moment she'd first seen her mother's beloved form across the field of waiting food, after so many suns of separation.

I WIN!

The big albino meat-eater turned just in time for Shiraa to catch him by the snout with her jaws.

Snowflake whistled like a volcanic steam vent as Karyl sent his matadora running to her right, twisting the tyrant counterclockwise.

Clad in breast and back and helmet with its visor open, Falk turned toward him, mouth open, screaming something Karyl couldn't hear for the high-pitched bellowing of the two enormous flesh-eating dinosaurs. But in the blue eyes he saw a flash of pain—sympathetic pain for the hurt being done his war-mount and friend.

He was trying to swing his axe to cut down the unarmored Karyl. But Karyl had maneuvered Shiraa so Falk, who had no shield, still had to strike cross-body to hit him. Whereas Karyl's sword-arm was positioned to strike directly.

He thrust the tip into the bearded wide-open mouth. He felt the tip rake the top of the Duke von Hornberg's upper palate.

Such a stroke, if pushed to its fullest extent, would punch through the back of its recipient's mouth and pierce the brain stem, causing instant death.

Karyl did not press home the death blow. He drew back his never-dulling blade in a fountain of blood from Falk's ripped roof and cloven tongue. The Alemán fell away from him.

At the same time, his pressing knees sent Shiraa into a violent pirouette to her left. He sensed Snowflake's splayed white hind feet tangling. She overbalanced and went down.

Though already half unseated, Falk managed to fling himself away from his stricken mount before the animal fell and crushed his right leg between his two tons or more of bulk.

He really is a splendid dinosaur knight, thought Karyl. *And he loves his Snowflake.*

"Coming through!" Rob bellowed from behind. Karyl reared Shiraa back before she could try to rip out her fallen foe's snowy throat with her jaws. Karyl turned to see Little Nell thunder by just beyond Shiraa's left-curled tail to rudely shoulder Archiduc Antoine's halberd crest out of the way.

Karyl pulled the reins to turn Shiraa to follow. He felt her reluctance to abandon her fallen prey before finishing her kill. But she obeyed. She was the best of dinosaurs.

As she turned, he saw a massive blur in the corner of his eye. Swiveling his eyes, he saw a sight remarkable even for this chaotic, blood-drenched night: the Princess Melodía, clad only in a tight breast-band and cavalry trousers and boots, on the back of a Parasaurolophus bull that had blundered right into the midst of the Courtyard and Falk's assembled dinosaur knights.

Then he turned forward, as Shiraa followed Rob and the hook-horn out of the Patio and down the narrow Imperial Way to the open gates of La Bienvenida.

Chapter 48

Alabarda, Halberd, Halberd-Crest. . . . —*Lambeosaurus magnicristatus*. Bipedal herbivore, 9 meters, 3.5 tonnes. Prized in Nuevaropa as a war-hadrosaur for the showy, bladelike crest which gives it its name. Easily bred for striking coloration, like the more common *Corythosaurus* and *Parasaurolophus*; bulkier than either.

—THE BOOK OF TRUE NAMES

"Whoa!" Melodía yelled, as Tormento lurched across the crowded Courtyard at an angle.

The sackbut ran at good speed into the right haunch of Archiduc Antoine's blue-and-white halberd bull, Triomphe. Already off-balance from being struck hard, if glancingly, by Little Nell, disconcerted by the violent *paso a dos* between Snowflake and Shiraa, and the latter big predator's close passage, Triomphe all but toppled onto his beak. He managed to keep himself from going over onto his shoulder by dropping a hoof-like left forepaw to the Porche stone, but the unexpected impact and angle change in his mount pitched the young Archiduc right over the hadrosaur's left shoulder to slam upside down against a wall.

Serves you right, you insufferable prick, Melodía

thought savagely, *for advancing against Jaume's orders at Canterville. And for taking the side of the man who raped me!* She knew from servants' gossip passed on by Rosamaría that Antoine was all in a pet over a brisk letter he'd gotten from King Louis, telling him that going to war with Trebizon was an idiotic notion and that Antoine was to stop saying anything that gave the impression the Francés throne endorsed it. Yet he still stood willingly with the Alemán.

"I can't control it!" she shouted, sawing at Tormento's reins. Or miming it; she kept the reins just slack. In the dubious dance of light and shadows that filled the Patio, she hoped no one could tell they weren't straining taut.

She hoped to be able to squash Falk into red paste and agonized screams. Not even a full harness of plate armor could protect a knight on foot against being crushed by the weight of a full-grown war-duckbill, as Melodía had seen firsthand. But he stood off to one side of the open space holding Snowflake's reins as the Tyrannosaurus tossed his huge head, spraying blood liberally over both the rapist and several attendants trying in turn, to staunch the astonishing flow of blood from the Alemán's mouth. She was unwilling to risk crushing those who were possibly innocent, and her own mount wasn't about to go near the maddened meat-eater.

Instead, still doing her best to pretend her mount's actions were random, she turned Tormento back toward a pair of female knights riding their hadrosaurs side by side toward *La Bienvenida*. They were Mora Lindsay of Becca's Spring and Mora Ofelia de Ventoso, and first cousins, despite the one being from Anglaterra and fair, and the other a *Mesetera* with dark hair, eyes, and skin—even for Spaña. They were both in the Palace as paid bodyguards of hadrosaur breeder Don Hilario of Highplains. While their master played a dangerous game of neutral opportunism between the rival war and antiwar factions at Court, the women were merely turning out to answer an alarm, guilty of no more than no doubt hoping to curry Imperial favor. They were certainly no creatures of Margrethe's, nor her son's bedmates, especially Ofelia, who didn't like men.

As such, Melodía didn't bear them the ill will she did toward the Francés archduke. But that didn't stop her from seemingly getting control of her "rampaging" mount enough to turn him directly into their path. He reared up, trumpeting, and his tail tripped Lady Lindsay's halberd.

"Sorry!" Melodía cried, as the purple duckbill stumbled, forcing the Anglaterrana to jump off in case he fell.

She turned her sackbut back into Ofelia's female morion, who was blue with rather fetching pink spots—an unusual combination, meaning a chance for her employer to show off his prowess at breeding war-mounts for color. On his own, Tormento swatted the Corythosaurus with a nasty side swipe of his long-crested head, stunning her and causing her to reel off into the path of Mor Carlos de Ojosfrios, a young buck who had orbited Melodía's attacker from La Merced days on.

"*¡Disculpeme!*" Melodía called to Mora Ofelia.

She was thinking, *He did that on his own! He understands what I'm doing!*

It filled her with a warmth she never in all her born days imagined she would ever feel about a dinosaur, much less toward one. It was the sort of rapport she'd had with her adored Meravellosa for years. *He's smarter than I thought a dinosaur could be. Then again, Camellia and Shiraa are quite clever, too, so it needn't surprise me too much.*

"Good boy," she murmured to him, surreptitiously patting his neck. Then she caused him to career back across the Patio, still pretending to yank the reins and screaming "I can't control him!" at the top of her lungs.

"I'll save you, Princess!" It was the thoroughly odious Baron Steban de Tresgarras, wearing a cuirass like his idol the Duke von Hornberg, whose greatest toady he was. His head, with its odd Alemán-style strip of dark hair on top and full black beard, was bare.

He reached out a leather-gloved hand. To Melodía it was clear he was trying to snatch the rampaging Parasaurolophus's reins to help bring him under control. But she hoped no one else could see that in the bad light and utter confusion that filled the Courtyard.

"Get your hands off me, you *canalla*!" she screeched. "How dare you manhandle the Princesa Imperial?"

And she turned Tormento so that he viciously tail-swiped Threeclaws' green-and-yellow-striped sackbut's legs right out from under him. As several others had already, he dove out of the saddle, landed on his shoulder, rolled, and popped up gracefully, as a well-trained dinosaur knight should.

In time for Tormento, whom Melodía had kept spinning, to smack *him* with his broad tail. She had moderated his speed a bit. She had no reason to murder the young Baron, enemy partisan or not. Yet.

The blow did send him flying five meters to land in a sprawl almost on the steps of La Entrada. And at the sandaled feet of a five-man *puño* of Scarlet Tyrants.

"You dared lay hands on the Imperial Princess, you piece of fatty shit?" the sergeant in charge said to the prostrate and moaning knight. His blond Riquezo beard was split by a smile as he led his detachment in beating the shit out of the hapless Tresgarras for his presumption.

With the alert out for assassins on the loose in El Corazón Imperial, the Imperial bodyguards were not about to be separated from the Imperial body, even by their principal's direct command. But Melodía's breath still caught in her throat at the sight of the man who stood on the steps behind them.

"Daddy?" she said.

The bridge to the city was clear as Little Nell thundered onto it—except for a single half-armored knight on a Corythosaurus that showed what might be green-brindled grey. The knight wielded a longsword and a silver shield with a wide, jagged-looking green band running across the middle of it—what Rob thought the heralds back home called *fess dancetty*. Which mattered to him only if a song came out of this fiasco.

Which in turn would require him to survive. He couldn't tell the rider's sex, between a corrugated visor on an armet that appeared to be pierced with many holes to allow sight and ventilation and the plain breastplate and back clamped onto the upper torso. That mattered not at all to Rob: this was an enemy, who was set to do him down.

Rob slowed Little Nell, hoping Karyl would slow his own dinosaur in time—and knew, of course, that he would: Karyl was the master, and he and Shiraa were almost one single creature when he was aboard her. Rob pulled Nell's head up by the reins. She knew what that meant: menace the morion's lowered face with the tip of her wicked fat horn.

The big duckbill wasn't even wearing a heavy fabric caparison, much less a chamfron to protect her face. She shied up, carrying her rider out of sword's reach of Rob and Nell. Rob had the Einiosaurus lower her head and then drive with the boss against the Corythosaurus's exposed left belly.

Still swinging up, the hadrosaur was easy for Nell to topple over with an expert twist of her head. Squealing an ear-piercing alarm, the monster fell hard against the Bridge's rail. The stout wood palings held—and held her on her side on the bridge.

The knight was not so lucky. He or she plunged right over the rail into the Moat. The scream that faded downward to the Raging River was high-pitched, but Rob had heard men scream as shrilly.

He set Nell to a trot, swinging wide to the right rail to avoid the helplessly waving legs. He heard Shiraa's hind feet drum the thick planks behind.

But ahead he saw bad news. At least a score of the town watch, Majesty's Guards, had formed a phalanx of spears and shields across the great open Plaza on the Majestad side of the Moat and were advancing to block their exit from the Bridge. He uncased the head of his axe and hefted her in his right hand.

"Looks as if we've a job of work to do, you and I, Wanda," he said.

"What are you fools doing, standing around gawping?" Emperor Felipe roared. He had a surprisingly good roar for such a generally mild-mannered man. The footmen and women who filled the Courtyard—who had been far too busy hopping and darting about to avoid being smashed to rags by giant monsters to stand, much less gawp, stepped forward to the Princesa's aid. If a bit hesitantly.

Miraculously, the wild-acting Tormento calmed right down, even as the soldiers and servants took their first, desperately reluctant steps forward in obedience to the Imperial command. "Good boy," she told him under her breath.

He suffered his reins to be grabbed, and was even meekly compliant as many hands guided him back through the Courtyard and out of everybody else's way.

Others reached up—cautiously—toward Melodía. "Oh, thank you so much," she called, more loudly than was strictly necessary to be heard. She let them help her down without stopping her sackbut, much less lowering his belly to the ground. Which caused a final moment of low comedy as two male servants and somebody's female House-shield, badly underestimating how much a 176-centimeter-tall Princess who was exceedingly well if leanly muscled might weigh, collapsed beneath her.

"Thank you so much," she told them again, making a mental notation to see that all three got a financial reward later for cushioning her fall with their bodies. She knew as well as they did what a conspicuously bad idea it would be to just drop the Princesa Imperial on her ass on the bare stone of El Porche under the Emperor's own slightly protuberant pale-green eyes. But she still appreciated the gesture. And also not being dropped on her ass.

Her first thought was to go to her father, although with a swarm of a dozen Scarlet Tyrants surrounding him he was clearly in no real danger. To say nothing of the tall, dear form, equipped only with a loincloth and a long-sword, who stood at the Emperor's shoulder. She really wanted to run to him, but she heard a throat cleared from close at hand, and looked quickly around.

A compact female shape stood in the shadow of a narrow alley between a fancy stone apartment building and a scarcely less pretentious warehouse. Feeling guilty, Melodía walked to her.

"Did I disgrace you with that display, Maestra?" she asked softly, waving away the servants who tried to usher her back to her father and the Imperial Champion.

"That question might, Alteza." Melodía's cheeks burned at the words as if the smaller woman had slapped her. "Do you really think I'm not enough of a dinosaur master to recognize what you were doing?"

"I beg your pardon," Melodía said. She might be of the

highest rank, and Auriana a mere landless knight, but she meant it. She had come to respect her teacher as she did few others.

Auriana shook her dark-blond head. "That was a masterful display. You were a remarkable pupil. I suspect you have a natural aptitude for riding beasts of all descriptions, not just horses. You picked up in weeks what it takes most months to learn."

"Why didn't you tell me? I thought I was terribly slow."

"I didn't want to swell your head enough to shut your ears."

"So I don't have any more to learn?" Now she felt giddy. She realized part of it was reaction to the charge of excitement that had coursed through her veins during her performance on Tormento.

With Tormento.

Auriana scoffed. "Have you learned all there is to know about horseback riding?"

"What? No, of course not. The more I learn, the more I see I need to—oh."

"Yes."

"Will you tell my father?"

"I'll tell my employer. Duty binds me to that."

"So you will?"

"I don't work for your father, child. Remember?"

"Oh," she said again. *The woman has a talent for making me feel younger than Montse*, she thought. *And half as apt, though I suspect I'm that anyway.*

Auriana gave Melodía a quick squeeze on the biceps. "Go to your father. Hurry up; he's getting impatient. And don't think this gives you permission to be a second late for tomorrow's lesson, *chiquita*!"

With a somewhat wan smile—since she had a horrible premonition her teacher would now go much harder on her, instead of easing up—she turned back to her father.

"They're getting away!" she heard a familiar and hated voice roar. "What're you idiots doing? Mount up and get them!"

The words came out slurred and just on the edge of comprehensibility, though. Her attacker was still bleeding from the mouth, though he'd gotten his pet monster to calm down. The other dinosaur knights were mostly still trying to get their own agitated duckbills under control.

"Arbalesters," a second voice shouted from above. It was female, though scarcely less familiar or hated. Melodía turned and looked up to see Margrethe leaning out the window of her apartment in the Crack, on the floor below Melodía and her father's penthouse. "Shoot them down!"

Looking left and right, she saw Defensores del Corazón emerging from the doors that gave onto the top of the Wall where it met the cliff face at either end of the Porch. They carried heavy crossbows. Looking down the Via Imperial, she could see others already bringing the arbalests to bear from the ramparts to either side of the Welcome Gate.

But her father roared, "Everyone, stand down!" almost as loud as the Duchess's son had shouted.

Yet another voice screamed, "Fire!" What seemed like dozens of small but bright green glows glared alight atop the Wall.

Chapter 49

Blindaje, Armor . . . .—While many forms of armor are found in Nuevaropa, full plate armor is preferred by dinosaur knights, the lords and ladies of the modern battlefield. Its parts are as follows: the helmet protects the head; gorget the neck; pauldrons the shoulders; a breastplate and back, together often called a cuirass, the body; vambraces the forearm; steel gloves or gauntlets the hands; tassets the upper leg; poleyns the knees; greaves the lower legs, and the feet are encased in sabatons, which are armor shoes. The helmet usually has a visor to protect the face, which can be opened, and sometimes a bevor, which protects the lower face and also replaces the gorget. An average suit of war armor weighs around 20 kg and if properly made doesn't encumber the wearer, although it does limit his or her range of motion. Specialized jousting armor can weigh as much as 30 kg and does restrict movement, in the interests of safety. A complete suit of armor is also called a "harness."

—A PRIMER TO PARADISE FOR THE IMPROVEMENT
OF YOUNG MINDS

Holding up his hand to signal Karyl to stay back on Shiraa, Rob slowed Little Nell to a deliberate trot toward the Guardias de la Majestad, who had now closed off the end of the Bridge, two ranks deep. Heavy infantry with polearms were anathema to mounted troops. Horses and dinosaurs alike tended to refuse to impale themselves on masses of long, sharp sticks. Pikes scared them worse than a spear-and-shield bloc.

For Rob and Little Nell, though, a pike formation would have been nearly ideal. But the two of them could make do with Majesty's Guards as well.

He slowed Little Nell to a trot that was barely faster than his own short-legged fast walk. But it did make her feet thump the bridge's planking more authoritatively. He saw a certain shiftiness in the dark eyes peering at him from between steel-hat brims and brown round shields with a stylized picture of the city on its mesa painted on them in gold. He thought he saw the spear points begin to twitch.

He stopped with the tip of Nell's beaked snout a hand span from spear points that glittered yellow in the light from the pair of wind-blown torches at the Bridge's Majestad end. Before any bright lad or lass could get the idea of poking her with one, he urged her forward a tiny step.

She lowered her head and pushed her fat, forward-hooking horn right between the points. At a cluck from her master, she swung her head hard left, then right.

The spears, naturally, flew wide. Without needing his boot heels to thump her belly, the tubby dinosaur gathered herself and launched her 1500 kilograms of mass straight ahead.

The horn struck one shield dead center and knocked its wielder on his tailbone. That was unlucky for him. One of her forefeet came down on his shield, twisting it down to crush his gullet with its upper rim before her weight caved in his rib cage with a loud, multiple crackling. Rob judged that stopped his heart, because he stopped screeching as suddenly as he'd begun.

The man and woman to his left and right went flying in opposite directions as Nell's shoulders churned into them.

The Guards directly ahead of Nell in the rear rank promptly turned and ran away. They all had sense enough to wing off to the side. When she had her full speed built up, which she could do quite quickly, the hook-horn ran faster than they did.

Some of the others tried to jab dinosaur or rider with their spears. Rob knocked them away, laying about left and right with Wanda while frantically signaling Karyl to charge with his left hand.

He heard a happy "Shiraa!" from behind him. Then screams. And wet, crunching sounds.

He glanced back to see the Allosaurus swinging a Guardsman, the brim of whose steel hat the Allosaurus's jaws had crushed to his temples, by the head to bludgeon away the spear wielders to her left. *She seems to think the human head's just a convenient sort of handle*, Rob thought, as the rest of the knot of Guardias fled shrieking. *Curious beasts that way, slayers.*

What he saw when he looked ahead of him again made him slow Nell once more. The plaza had the shape of a hundred-meter-wide semicircle straddling the Via Imperial. From streets and alleys on both sides converged dozens more of the Majesty's Guards, most with spear and shield, some carrying halberds.

But not from the Way itself. From straight ahead approached a knot of knights riding hadrosaurs. At least six of the blighters.

"What now?" asked Rob, as Karyl pulled Shiraa up alongside Nell's left side.

"What do you prefer?"

Rob looked up at the man he still thought of as a friend, even though he himself had forfeited claim to even think the word. He brandished Wanda. "I'd rather die swinging free than chained."

Karyl had his sword tipped back over his shoulder, a gesture Rob had seen from Ovdan riders with their *talwars*, also single-edged, before.

"I do too," he said, and charged. Rob sent Nell following a heartbeat after.

The fight was as short and savage as it was doomed.

Rob saw Shiraa snap her jaws shut on the throat of a female Parasaurolophus who shied her head up away from the onrushing predator. The matadora jerked her head left, tearing away a great chunk of flesh and unleashing a flood of dark blood. The man astride the stricken animal tried to cut at her. Shiraa spat out the meat and grabbed his sword hand with her teeth instead. Rob saw her blood spurt as the sword edge dug into a corner of her mouth.

Meanwhile, Karyl ducked a sword stroke from a woman riding a morion on his left and severed her sword arm with his counter-cut. An eye blink later, Shiraa threw the rider of the duckbill whose throat she'd torn out clean over the tail of the Corythosaurus on her left.

Following as close as she could without getting whipped across the face by Shiraa's long tail, Little Nell rammed the morion with her left shoulder and sent him toppling to his right. Rob saw his knight jump from the saddle. A moment later, she screamed. The cry was cut short, and Rob could only imagine she'd jumped free of her falling mount only to get stepped on and crushed by another duckbill.

Ahead of him, Rob saw Karyl trading cuts with two more dinosaur knights, one on a sackbut directly in front of him, a morion rider to his right. Shiraa managed to rake the sackbut's face with her teeth. It fluted dismay and ran away.

A big dark Parasaurolophus rammed her from the left, throwing her hard down on her right side. Karyl was caught by surprise. With his cat's reflexes, he managed to avoid getting his leg caught and crushed beneath Shiraa. But he was slammed down and clearly had the breath knocked out of him, though he kept his grip on his sword.

Rob steered Nell right, hoping to interpose her between the Corythosaurus and his fallen friends. "Alive! They've got to be taken alive!" bellowed the knight who'd slammed Shiraa and Karyl down.

The morion rider turned away from Karyl and charged with bounds of the duckbill's big back legs at Nell. She raked her horn down his shoulder and flank, but he tucked in his forepaws and turned to plow into her with his breastbone. Bawling in fury, the Einiosaurus was slammed down on her left side,.

As she fell Rob put his left hand down and vaulted himself straight back. Fortunately, his own saddle cantle was low. He cleared it, landed straddling Nell's tail, then danced farther back to where she didn't break his legs as she thrashed it.

Majesty's Guards surrounded him. He split one man's steel hat with Wanda's blade, wrenched her free, and thrust the spike that tipped her haft into the face of a woman swinging a halberd at him.

He felt an impact and a stinging pain in his left shoulder. *Spear-thrust!* he thought. He tried to turn, and someone shield-bashed his right arm, striking the funny bone and momentarily paralyzing his arm.

Mouth streaming blood, Shiraa tried to get up. The bearded knight whose mount had knocked her down wheeled his sackbut to tail-whip her and put her down hard on her side again. She lay stunned.

Fists and spear-butts slammed Rob's head and ribs. He saw Karyl recover his wits enough to slash the legs from beneath a Guardia, but then he was swarmed and pinned to the ground.

Rob was knocked down too. The Guards began to kick and stomp him with their heavy hard-soled boots.

"What are you doing, Count Vargas?" he heard the Corythosaurus rider who'd felled Nell shout. "You told us, alive!"

The Guardias left off beating Rob bloody to pin his arms and legs to the limestone flags. He saw the big bearded man had ridden his sackbut almost up to Karyl's feet and sat grinning unpleasantly down at the captive.

"Alive, the Duchess said," he agreed. "But she didn't specify in what condition. You've caused us no end of trouble, Duque de la Marca, but that stops now. And I'm going to exact my own form of payment before letting Margrethe dispense hers."

Count Vargas reared his sackbut until the duckbill was propped by its own tail, then urged it forward. It started to step forward with its left foot, right onto Karyl's helpless body. Before it crushed his pelvis and thighs, Vargas rocked the beast back again.

"Will you beg for mercy, Duke Karyl? It won't help, but that usually doesn't stop anyone." He rocked the sackbut forward again.

The spearmen and women avoided Shiraa, though she lay still with her head on the flagstones, seemingly no more than semiconscious. Allosaurus had a reputation for cunning almost as great as for stealth. No one wanted to trust that the mighty carnivore was really out of action.

Instead, they surrounded Little Nell, who also lay helpless on her side, breathing heavily. One stabbed her in the shoulder with a spear, tentatively. Then another and another, with increasingly brutal force and glee.

"Leave her alone, you motherless shits!" Rob roared, despite the pain from cracked ribs—and the additional boots that got put in them. "Leave Karyl alone! May the Fae burn you all!"

A strange blue glare, the color of lightning, flooded the scene. Unlike lightning, it persisted.

Someone began to scream.

Rob smelled burning hair.

A remarkable figure appeared, hovering in the air a meter above the supine Rob. It was a tiny nude man, with wings too absurdly short to uphold even his presumed slight weight. Or would have been too small had he not seemed to be made of living blue fire. His glow illuminated eyes wide and mouths agape in disbelieving horror beneath steel helmet brims.

"As you wish, Master Korrigan," he said in a sibilant crackle that Rob knew all too well, "so shall it be."

He darted into the clean-shaven face of a spearman with a big black mole beside his nose. Blue sparks flickered from beneath his helmet. Smoke poured out. With a shriek the man knocked the steel hat from his head to slap at the blue flames dancing in his short, thick hair.

The tiny winged man darted from one Guardia beating Rob to another, kindling each one's hair in turn. They jumped up, letting Rob go to bat desperately at the stinking flames. Those with weapons in their hands flung them aside.

Rob looked to Little Nell. A swarm of small firefigures, some with human shape, some distinctly inhuman, some with no perceptible shape at all, had half her tormentors' hair alight as well. The rest had already run off screaming in mindless terror.

Rob realized the glare that lit the scene came from above, though; it didn't waver as it would if it were composed of dozens of discrete flame-creatures. He looked up.

Count Vargas had his sackbut rocked back with both feet on the ground. He was yelling at the Guardias to come back. And at his remaining fellow knights—Rob saw they had all run off as well.

But Rob realized the glare came from someplace *above* the Count.

Vargas's duckbill realized it too. It raised its triangular, tube-crested head and emitted the highest-pitched noise Rob in all his career had ever heard a dinosaur make. *It's a G7 at the very least*, he thought, not without a certain admiration. He had to clap his hands over his ears in hopes of keeping the drums from bursting.

Floating not three meters above the dinosaur's upturned beak was a thing of living blue-white flame. Its shape was roughly elliptical, narrow at top and bottom. Beyond that it was too eye-hurtingly bright for him to make out more than that whatever shape it had was constantly changing.

He felt heat from it on his face, like an open forge a meter away.

"*He is not yours to dispose of, mortal*," came a voice that both flowed like honey and sizzled like frying flesh strips on a hot stove. "*He is mine.*"

Rob's pulse spiked in terror. *It's the voice I heard whispering to Karyl! And that light's the same color!*

It's all true, then! And yet—I was still wrong.

That last scrap of self-knowledge strangely gave him something to cling to, to prevent him slipping away from sanity to drown in howling madness.

Count Vargas finally looked up. At first he simply gaped. The hell-glare descended toward him. He threw up his hands to shield his face from its heat.

Rob saw his leather gloves begin to smoke. Then they burst into flame as the fire-thing elongated and poured itself down on his face like molten iron. His beard caught fire, and the flesh began to melt and slough away.

But he screamed, more loudly than his still-fluting dinosaur.

He felt his mouth fill with vomit. But he couldn't force himself to look away.

The metal of Vargas's breastplate glowed red as the light seemed to pour itself down into his armor through the neck hole. The enamel blistered and burned away.

The awful glow shone out the armholes, then, and consumed Count Vargas's arms. The sackbut leaned forward over Karyl and snapped upright, shedding his burning master, and ran off.

What hit the plaza's yellow limestone pavement was already a shrunken black mummy of vaguely human shape. The cuirass flexed at the impact, then held that flattened shape, like wet clay thrown hard on a potter's table.

Vargas's shrieks continued for a dozen intolerable pounds of Rob Korrigan's heart. When they stopped, the glare went out.

The fires died away as well. Rob fought painfully to his feet. He started toward Karyl, but the man sat up and waved him away.

"Go, see to Nell," Karyl said. The sight of blood trickling from his mouth gave Rob a turn. But he saw it ran from Karyl's nose, bloodied by a spear-butt to the face.

As Rob lurched toward his wounded hook-horn, she rocked herself and then, getting a foot under her, fought her way to her feet. She shook her head. Dark drops flew from it. That almost stopped Rob's heart, but he saw the blood flowed from a pair of gashes to her frill and her snout. As with Karyl, nothing life-imperiling.

Nell stood panting, but let him gingerly run hands over her. She had at least a score of bleeding wounds, but none were deep.

"Will she carry you?" he heard Karyl call.

"I reckon she'll do," he said, turning. "There's a reason they make armor out of hornface hide, it seems."

He was about to ask after Shiraa. But she was already standing up with Karyl on her back. She looked none the worse for wear. Getting slammed to the flagstones by the sackbut had only knocked the wind from her, Rob judged.

"Shiraa and I are fit to flee," Karyl said, replacing his sword in the staff that served as concealment and scabbard. "Which we need to do at once, before reinforcements arrive, from city or Palace."

Rob glanced back across the bridge to the Wall. He saw great green fires blazing there, and lesser, yellow ones scattered about. He couldn't see what was burning to cause those. Given what he'd just witnessed, he was just as glad.

"They'll be a while chasing us from the Heart, at least," he said. He took Nell's reins, pressed down on the saddle with his hand. She flinched slightly, then seemed to stiffen, as if resolved. Which she probably was—she had a will of her own, did Nell, and it was no feebler than the rest of her.

He mounted. She swayed slightly, but held up under him.

"I agree as to the need for speed," he called to his friend. "Though Nell and I were never built for much of it, even when we're not both beat to shit."

"Then follow me." Karyl turned Shiraa and set off at an angle across the plaza, south, away from Via Imperial.

Nell needed surprisingly little urging to follow the big carnivore. She seemed as eager to put this ghastly place behind her as Rob was.

"Was that—" Rob said.

"The Fae," Karyl said without turning.

"They've torn it for us, good and proper. Whatever you were doing in the Palace—"

"Trying to prevent an unnecessary war with Trebizon. Which looked likely to escalate to an even more pointless and lethal one against High Ovda."

"Maia and Maris! Well, your friends have burned that to ash."

"Whatever they are, they're no friends of mine."

"Be that as it may, we're outlaws again for sure, the both of us. For good this time, most like."

"That much was guaranteed as soon as we escaped the Dowager Duchess's little deathtrap. Your friend Margrethe's got half the Palace believing it was all a plot by you and me to assassinate the Emperor by now, count on it."

"True enough. But whatever she is, she's no friend of mine."

"*Touché.*"

"Where are we going, then?" Rob asked. They were following a lane between dark, windowless buildings near the cliff. It was neither particularly broad nor particularly straight. "The guards are surely well alerted now. Singing merry songs as we ride blithely out the gates like a pair of drunken revelers isn't going to answer. Much as I wish I were a drunken reveler right now. Or at least drunk."

"We're going away from this place," said Karyl. "I know a way down."

"Really?" Rob cocked a brow, though Karyl couldn't have seen it here in the gloom even if he'd looked back. Which he didn't. "And how do you know that little thing, Your Grace, you who've been here less than a week?"

Karyl's answer was the same as it always was when he judged a question not worth answering: he kept on going with never a backward glance, leaving Rob and Nell to stay or follow as Rob chose.

"Well, it seems I've small choice but to trust the man and blindly follow," he muttered to Nell, patting her neck and wincing at the tacky half-dried blood that was left on his palm.

He sighed. Theatrically. He and Nell were always his best audience.

"*Again.*"

Chapter 50

Rank and Title—Social rank in the Empire of Nuevaropa roughly follows the shape of a pyramid, from the lone Emperor or Empress down to the mass of peasants. The ranks are: Emperor, Prince, Archduke, Duke, Count, Baron, Knight, and peasant. One of the eleven Electors is a prince, and called a Prince-Elector. Variations are many; for example, the count of a contested border province, or march, is sometimes known as a Margrave, Marquis, or Voyvod. All owe fealty: those below, service and obedience to those above; those above, protection and care of their lessers. As a rule, the higher the title, the larger the land-holding. However, the system as it has evolved has led to baronies the size of duchies, and archduchies as small as counties. Moreover, it is not unheard of for a count, for example, to hold a certain fief as a vassal to a baron. Needless to say, this complexity leads to resentment and friction, and hence, frequently, to conflict.

—A PRIMER TO PARADISE FOR THE IMPROVEMENT
OF YOUNG MINDS

"*The Fae! The Fae! Creators protect us, it's the Fae!*" The scream rose from half a dozen throats into the clouding-over night sky.

With a kind of horrified resignation, Melodía watched blazing shapes like T-cross meteors plunge downward into the Courtyard from the Wall. A Defensor del Corazón, hair ablaze, overbalanced and plunged downward to Melodía's left as she stood with Jaume, her arm about his waist, his around her shoulders, and her father among the protective block of Scarlet Tyrants on the Entrance steps.

She heard a softer murmur from nearby: "Faerie fire! It's just what the Champion described! He was telling the truth all along!"

Yes, you damned fools. Of course he was. Then she felt sicker, for remembering she'd been as big a fool as any—and only her father, it seemed, had faith in his Constable.

From the window high overhead Margrethe continued to bellow for the Defenders to shoot down the escaping pair. But even as her voice grew hoarse, it was obvious that none of them were obeying her.

What wasn't obvious to Melodía was that anybody *could* obey her. While some of the Palace guards were running away from the big, bright green fires that blazed up from apparently random points along the ramparts' top, some had their hair ablaze for true. And as far she could see, every arbalest on the wall was burning like a torch.

And her father the Emperor acted as if his mind was settled by emergency—as she'd been told he had, by those who witnessed him on La Boule during the battle with the Horde.

"Is that what you saw in Laventura, boy?" Felipe asked Jaume quietly.

She felt her lover nod. "Similar, at least. From what we saw, and learned from our investigation afterward, the green blazes may be illusion. But they can also set real fires, as well."

Felipe shook his head sadly. "I never believed in the Fae. Not before you told us what happened in Laventura that stopped you from saving my daughter. And even then—I found it hard to adjust my thoughts."

"All of us did, Father," Melodía said. It felt as if the words were blades, coming up through her throat.

Jaume hugged her tighter.

She turned to him and tapped his bare chest with her fingertip. He looked down. She nodded back toward the Entrada.

He nodded in return. It was clear there was no danger to them they'd be retreating from. And even more clear that there was utterly nothing they could do but watch.

"That's it, isn't it?" she said softly, when they'd drawn a few paces back. The cordoning Scarlet Tyrants had moved aside to let them pass with barely a glance at them. Though Melodía was a secondary object of their attention, their focus was on their Emperor. And being farther inside the walls of the Palace within a mountain behind them could hardly make her less secure. To say nothing of the tall, nearly nude man who had one arm around her and the other holding a totally naked longsword . . .

"It's the end of our peace faction."

"It's a nasty blow," Jaume said. "This ends Duke Karyl's influence, at any rate. I can't believe he's really dealing with the Fae."

"I don't believe it!" she said, with a protective fierceness she hadn't expected to feel toward her former commander. "He'd never betray us. The Empire and . . . everybody."

"You know him better than I do, *mi amor*. And I'm reluctant to believe it, given what he's done for the Empire and us all. But this is Faerie magic, and none of us can pretend it isn't anymore. We can't not believe anymore. I never believed in them, Prince of the Church or not, even though they're canon!"

"Do you think he had anything to do with the *demonios* preventing you from rescuing Montse?"

"I don't see how he could have. He might cut an enemy down in front of that enemy's family without a thought—and then protect that family with his own life. He wouldn't wage war on Montserrat, even if he were working with the Fae."

She nodded. "That's the man I served for months, yes. Don't you see what's happening? The Fae want this war! That's why they sabotaged you and your Companions in Laventura—and why they're sabotaging Karyl and Rob."

"You may be right, Princess. Now I ask you: who will ever *believe* us?"

She could only shake her head. And burst into tears.

"So naturally your escape route had to entail a sewer," Rob said, glancing back up and diagonally across the slope they were riding down at the yawning black mouth in the Plateau's sloped side and the noisome torrent gushing from it. He was trying to breathe shallowly, through his mouth. It wasn't helping.

The sky was rapidly growing more crowded with clouds. *I don't know whether to hope it doesn't rain*, he thought, *or that it does*.

"They frequently make good escape routes," Karyl said. "I doubt this was the first time you've used one for that."

Little Nell's wounds still trickled blood. But she seemed steady enough. His heart ached for her, as well as for Shiraa. But with the best will in Paradise there was nothing either man could do for either dinosaur until they were safely away from the city.

Then again, they couldn't do much for their own hurts, either.

"No," Rob said. "It was not. Which, strangely, makes me all the more reluctant to undergo the experience again! Why couldn't you have found us something more in a nice, clean storm drain?"

"Those are a separate system. They all lead to catchment tanks dug into the soil beneath the city. Similar to the cistern in which you set up our little appointment this evening."

Rob cringed at the reminder. But he was still supercharged with emotional and mental energy from the night's bizarre and horrifying adventures, despite the fatigue that weighed him down like a leaden cloak.

"And why would a sewer have an entrance large enough to lead a dinosaur down? I know why the main line would be big enough to pass a brontosaurus, but not that other thing."

"Maintenance, I suspect. A blockage or collapse could call for the application of substantial dinosaur muscle power."

"How do you know all these things?" he demanded.

"I asked questions, during my stay. Basic reconnaissance of possible engagement grounds. You're familiar with the concept, I believe."

Rob scowled. He'd served as master of scouts as well as spies for the Army of Providence, and the Fugitive Legion it was transformed into by the glowing-cloud advent of the Grey Angel Crusade. As Karyl well knew, since he'd given Rob the job.

"Then why doesn't the conduit extend all the way down, Lord Knowall?"

"Funding ran out, likely. The Diet is known for its arbitrary bouts of parsimony. Be thankful for their stinginess; otherwise, we'd still be struggling down a steep, wet pipe clear to the sewage farm. Not to mention that we'd end up in the middle of the sewage farm."

"The people who live above the outlet can't be best pleased."

"It's mostly a warehouse district. The tanners at the base of the hill are happy enough with the arrangement."

Rob snapped his fingers. "Wait. Wait, now. How to get dinosaurs out of a city with only one way in or out—that implies you can get them into it the same way. That's a smuggler's route, that is, and not another thing. You're a noble born. I'm a scoundrel, a Traveler and a minstrel, if that's not multiply redundant. I know how *I'd* know whom to ask and how to learn such clandestine things. But how did you?"

"You forget I spent years as a penniless wanderer, with nothing to sell but my own paltry skills at fighting—and the much more substantial skills of my mount. Not all the jobs I took on during that time were savory. You wrote songs on that very subject, I believe."

"That I did. Those Guardia dung beetles beat what poor wits I've got right out of me, I guess."

The two dinosaurs limped on for a spell, with no more noise than the crunch of dry vegetation and the odd piece of gravel underfoot, and their labored breathing.

"So I suppose we'll be parting ways, once we reach the bottom," Rob said at last.

"If you so choose."

"What? You mean you don't so choose?"

"No."

"Far be it from me to argue with what's still unquestionably the deadliest man on Paradise."

"It's never stopped you before."

"But why? Why wouldn't you want to see the last of me? I did a terrible thing, a terrible wrong. I *betrayed* you, Karyl. Sure, I did it for what I thought was your own good. And mine, and that of all the world. And I was that terrified of what you were dabbling in, that my suspicious nature never so much as twitched its nose hairs at the machination of that witch Margrethe."

He frowned. "Then again, she saw to it that I was drunk, drugged, and drowning in pussy my whole time in town, before tonight. And that goblin-visaged seneschal of mine, he's in it to the eyebrows, too! Why else did the Duke so kindly volunteer to lend the wretch to me? Great rogues, the lot of 'em! If Bergdahl knows what's good for him, he'll not be hanging about the manor house when I get home. Anyway—that still doesn't excuse what I did. I won't ask your forgiveness."

"Which is part of why I choose to give it to you," Karyl said. "I don't have enough friends to be eager to lose any of them. Any *more* of them. We've been through a lot together, you and I. You fought by my side tonight."

"As if I'd a choice, other than to let those masked heathens murder me!"

"You got Shiraa ready for me to ride out, when you could have gone on with a fair chance of getting away clean."

Rob sighed. "It's a fair cop. Very well. If you're too big a fool to discard me, the wretched Rob Korrigan, then I'll follow you to the ends of Paradise, Karyl. But there is one thing I have to say."

"I suspect I know what that is, too. The Fae."

"Aye," said Rob. "I told you so."

Chapter 51

Dragón Largovuelo, Long-Flying Dragon. . . . —*Quetzalcoatlus northropi*. The largest, mightiest, and farthest-ranging of the giant predatory pterosaurs called dragons or Azhdarchids. Up to 11 meters long, weighing as much as 250 kg, these majestic monsters get their names because they can cross the oceans of Paradise on wings which also span 11 meters. While it is a myth that Quetzalcoatlus or any dragon can fly away with a normal-sized adult human—reports exist of them carrying off small children, and they definitely make away with small livestock such as Fatties—they pose a very terrible danger to people and animals. Though unwieldy on land, they stand as tall as a reared-up *Tyrannosaurus rex*, and take their prey by stabbing it with two-meter beaks like spear-heads.

—THE BOOK OF TRUE NAMES

"The larger fires—the green ones—seem to have been illusory," Jaume said to Melodía and the Emperor. He'd just returned from making inquiries on the Majestad side of the Bridge, where acolytes of the various sects housed in the city's great temple, La Casa de Cielo y Terra, tended to the injured, while the mothers and fathers of the Church stood around in their fine ceremonial gowns of silk and feathers and looked important. "Like the first magical firewall we encountered in the village of La Bajada. The only real fires appear to have been set to things that catch light readily, like wooden-framed crossbows, or hair. The only deaths those caused were of people who panicked and fell into the Moat. It appears four Heart's Defenders died that way. Actual burns were mostly minor, I take it?"

"Yes," Melodía said.

She stood with her father, Jaume, and some key Palace personnel to one side of La Entrada. The Scarlet Tyrants and Heart's Defenders had tactfully but firmly kept the Emperor cooling his heels in the Patio while they scoured Palace and Porch. She'd spent most of the last hour helping tend to the injured. So far, they reported finding nothing but the corpses of a shocking number of *sicarios*, all dead of extreme violence.

If you go against Karyl, what else can you expect? Melodía thought. She herself was exhausted, but grateful her recent ministrations had given her something to do besides think of the shambles the night had made of all they'd worked for. And what the future might hold accordingly.

"The worst injuries we found were a few broken limbs from falling off the wall onto El Porche, and burns on Defensores' hands from trying to beat out the flames. A lot got some singeing on their scalps, but nothing terribly serious."

"Except for one," Jaume said, his beautiful face troubled. "Count Vargas was burned beyond recognition, and his breastplate and back were melted to his corpse, as if he'd been thrown in a smelting furnace."

"Similar to what happened on the dock in Laventura," Felipe said.

"Yes, Your Majesty."

"It seems as if it's hard for whoever it was who did

this—we might as well call them the Fae as anything—to work magic," Melodía said. "I mean, the wall of fire you ran into, and the bigger fires we saw on the wall tonight—those were just illusions. Almost all the real ones set fire to wood and hair but didn't burn anybody up."

"Living flesh is hard to kindle and keep alight," Jaume said. "It's too wet."

"Right." She swallowed. It wasn't a pleasant thing to know, really. "So in Laventura the real Faerie fire, the fatal kind, was saved for the key moment. As it was here, I take it?"

Jaume nodded. "Witnesses said the dinosaur knight had managed to knock Shiraa to the ground. The Majesty's Guards had Karyl pinned to the pavement. Vargas was toying with him, apparently preparing to have his sackbut step on him and crush him. Incinerating him saved the Duke of the Borderlands' life. Which the . . . entity who did it must have reckoned important enough to expend the effort to do."

Melodía shuddered. It was hard to think of anyone deserving so frightful a fate. Yet the Conde de Vargas had a reputation for cruelty to his serfs and others—just the sort of scofflaw *grande* her father might have sent Jaume and the Army of Correction off to sort out, if Raguel hadn't let word of his Emergence slip, so that the Pope declared Crusade against the Garden of Beauty and Truth in Providence. *But what he was trying to do to Karyl was no kinder,* she thought. *And that's one loud voice for war that's been silenced, anyway.*

Not that it would matter now, of course. She was half proud, half shaken to realize that La Madrota's way of thinking had taken root in her.

"What about the dinosaurs?" asked Felipe.

"There's a curious thing," Jaume said. "We couldn't find a single scorched scale on any of them. Shiraa killed Mor Francisco de Ávila's sackbut in the Majestad plaza and injured him severely. Mora Antonia López's morion, Redentora, had her shoulder broken when Little Nell slammed her against the Bridge's rail."

"Don Placido, our Palace dinosaur master, has sedated the animal with herbs and examined her," Felipe said. "He's a dinosaur chirurgeon of famous skill; he believes he'll be able to heal her, though right now he's trying to figure out a way to transport her safely into the city to treat her and clear the Bridge. Mora Antonia remains missing after her fall into the Moat. We have search parties down there now, but we can only surmise she drowned in the Río Rabioso, if the fall didn't kill her."

"I told you, Your Majesty," declared Dowager Duchess Margrethe loudly, as she emerged from the Entrada with her son in tow. "Karyl Bogomirskiy was never to be trusted. Now you can see I'm right. He maimed my poor son, who saved your life in battle, and his pet monster savagely scarred Snowflake's beautiful white face."

A light rain began to drizzle from the now-dense clouds above. *Appropriate*, Melodía thought, her stomach souring.

Though he still hulked over his already-large mother, the Duke von Hornberg looked oddly deflated, with his mouth stuffed full of bandages. *Poor baby*, Melodía exulted. *But why didn't Karyl kill you?*

Oh, well. We can't have everything. At least you're suffering.

"I for one don't pretend to have any idea what really happened here tonight," Felipe said.

"But it's plain as the peak above our heads, Your Majesty!" Margrethe exclaimed. "Karyl turned traitor, not just to yourself and the Fangèd Throne, but the whole human race! He colluded with the Evil Ones—I will not pollute my tongue with their name—"

At the word "tongue," her son squinted and made unhappy muffled noises.

"—as well as hired a band of murderers, in a blatantly obvious scheme to overthrow you!"

Felipe held up a hand. "Enough," he said, so forcefully the Dowager Duchess blinked.

You're not used to being spoken to that way, are you? Melodía thought. *Well, you may have snared my father with your* concha, *but he's still the Emperor, and you're still the back-country relict of a famously bad man.*

"I am far from satisfied as to what really happened here tonight," Felipe continued in a stern tone that was almost utterly unfamiliar to his elder daughter and heir. "Much less am I convinced that I played the total fool by elevating Karyl Bogomirskiy in rank. It could be so. But there's too much mystery here for me to conclude anything before a most thoroughgoing investigation is carried out. Which I shall supervise myself."

Margrethe's pale-blue eyes blazed briefly. Then she dropped them. "Yes, Your Majesty. I apologize if I gave offense."

"Oddly enough," Jaume said across the uncomfortable silence that ensued, "all the injuries to war-hadrosaurs in the Patio seem to have been a result of Her Highness's commendably zealous efforts to lead the pursuit of the fugitives."

He knows too! Melodía realized, from the way he smiled as he said it. As of course he would; he was still the most renowned dinosaur knight in all the Empire of Nuevaropa, because he was still the best.

Rosamaría stepped from the shadows into the light that spilled from inside the Heart. Which was such an utterly La Madrota thing to do that Melodía couldn't completely hide her smile. Melodía had noticed her ancestress and mentor standing silently by when she rejoined her father, in part, no doubt, because the ancient woman intended she should. But she had hung back, observing. As she had done for centuries.

"Felipe," she said. "Your daughter has learned the important skill of riding a war-dinosaur, if clearly still in somewhat . . . embryonic form. You will find, I think, that if it's not time to knight her, it will be soon."

She's thinking ahead, Melodía thought. *Past tonight's disaster to what she can do to undo or contain the damage.* Pride filled her at recognizing that—and then she had to blink away tears as pride at her own achievement overcame her. At her performance on Tormento, whose near-perfect success astonished her. At the equally astonishing rapport she'd felt with, yes, a war-dinosaur. He'd never supplant Meravellosa in her heart—no one and nothing could—but she now considered him a partner in a way she'd never conceived she could.

And she could never reveal what she'd really done. That she'd deliberately inflicted humiliation on so many important *grandes* would cause irreparable breaches within the Empire if it came out. But Auriana, Rosamaría, and Jaume knew. And that was almost enough.

To cover her sudden and probably disproportionate joy she flung her arms around her father's neck. "I've been training for weeks, Daddy! La Madrota arranged for it."

She began crying openly at seeing his eyes and face light up with sudden pleasure.

"In secret?" he asked, amused.

"It was supposed to be a surprise. But—I don't think it's anywhere near time to speak of knighthood." Saying that gave her an odd sense of relief. She rationalized it by thinking the way she thought La Madrota would: that to dub her so quickly would cause resentment that her father didn't need, now of all times.

The fact is, it scares me.

"Let me remind you, my boy," Rosamaría said, "that your daughter rode a hadrosaur in defense of you and the Fangèd Throne."

"Not very damned well," grumbled Archiduc Antoine, who was being helped into the Heart by several retainers. The Palace healer, a peasant-born woman called Maestra Inés, who shaved her head and whose age was unguessable, had smilingly browbeaten the fiery Francés noble into lying flat on his back for the whole last hour while she made certain he hadn't suffered injury to his spine. With luck, his body would ache for days from being chucked into a brick wall by a two-ton dinosaur.

His pride would ache considerably longer.

"Nonetheless," Rosamaría said. For her part, Melodía successfully resisted the impulse to give him *el dado*.

"If I might interject, Your Majesty," Jaume said, "the Princess Melodía amply demonstrated both her heroism and her skill in battle—ultimately, in service of the Throne—time and again in the fight against the Grey Angel Horde. As is more than amply attested to by numerous eyewitnesses, of noble birth as well as common."

Felipe beamed. "So you did, daughter my dear! And so it shall be. But—I think it's got to wait for a happier occasion."

"I agree," Melodía said, her heart in her throat from pride, trepidation, and relief at once. La Madrota nodded—openly, this time, though Melodía knew the gesture was aimed at her.

At least I'm spared for now. She couldn't really stay mad at Jaume for having thrust her to a place she really didn't want to be. But she did have an idea how she'd insist he make it up to her, later that night when they were alone . . .

"I so decree," Felipe said, looking around the now sizable group clustered outside the entrance to the Imperial Heart. His head was high and his gaze and voice were firm. Melodía saw that he was relishing acting altogether

Imperial and firm—something he seldom got to do. *Of course, the last time he did that, it ended in disaster,* she thought. *But he looks so happy in spite of everything that's happened that I don't have the heart to even try to bring his feet back down to Paradise.*

He's not the best Emperor, she thought. *He's not even the best father. But he's my father, and he loves me, and Montse, and we love him. Wherever my poor sister is now, may the Creators who I now know are real keep her safe! He's in his glory, and good for him.*

"Let's all go inside," the Emperor said, "enjoy some nice mulled wine or heated cider, and then sleep as soundly as we can. This *bodrio* probably won't look any prettier by morning light, but at least if we're well rested, cleaning it up won't seem quite as insurmountable."

"But Your Majesty!" exclaimed Centurión Lugo von Necker, the highest-ranked surviving Tyrant who wasn't their commander. "There may still be some intruders hiding in the Palace! It's the very nature of assassins to be stealthy."

"But it has never been my nature to hide, Centurión," Felipe said gently. "I trust the diligence of your men, as well as Los Defensores. Come inside with me, all of you. No point standing out here getting wet—"

"Look!" someone shouted. "Up above us!"

Melodía did. As did everybody else.

Through the clouds directly over their heads shone an intense golden light. As Melodía watched, it grew larger and more intense, until her eyes began to prickle and water, as if she stared too long into the sun.

A noise like a million trumpets blasting at once split the sky. Literally, or next to it: the dense clouds rippled away from the dazzling light like water from a thrown stone.

In the middle of the hole, in the middle of refulgence

intense as the heart of a lightning bolt, the figure of a woman hung in the sky, suspended by a pair of wings as vast as a Quetzalcoatlus's. In one hand she held a naked longsword; in the other, a huge, curled post-horn.

Chapter 52

Equilibrio Sagrado, **Sacred Equilibrium**—The Great Ultimate Principle of the Creators and their worldwide faith, called *taiji* in the Language of Heaven, which is spoken in Chánguo: dynamic balance among all things, characterized as opposing yet constantly interacting principles of feminine *yin* and masculine *yang.* Its symbol is the *taiji tu:* a circle containing a dark side and a light side separated by an S-curve.

   —A PRIMER TO PARADISE FOR THE IMPROVEMENT
OF YOUNG MINDS

"It's better than I dared hope," Rob said, squatting and gingerly examining the last spear wound he could find on Little Nell with a burning pine splinter in one hand and a wet rag in the other. "The deepest wounds only go into muscle, and those look as if they'll heal quick enough. No damage to her innards at all, so far as I can tell."

"Humans and dinosaurs have a lining around their stomach cavities," said Karyl, who was similarly engaged with Shiraa across the little fire they'd built on the side of the ridge they'd chosen to camp on. "It's tough to penetrate. Far tougher than most realize."

"Oh, aye," Rob said.

He straightened. The motion reminded him of his own cracked ribs. At least no jagged ends seemed to be poking him in the lungs; and aside from a stray finger or two and his nose, no bones broken. Nothing he hadn't had before. Especially the nose.

"How's your little darlin' doing?"

Karyl gently stroked Shiraa's side. She rested on her belly on a patch of low ferns, with her tail half curled around her "mother." It was an odd relationship, in which the giant meat-eating dinosaur both felt protected by and protective of her Karyl. But Rob of all men knew the strength of it.

They had ridden at a not very rapid but still punishing pace for an hour before Karyl called a halt. Though his every fiber cried out—and the aching ones, which were most, doubly loud—for them to keep fleeing until they were across the horizon and, better, across the Laughing Water and into Providence and the Duchy of the Borderlands, the dinosaur master in him wept inward tears for the pain their flight had put both their mounts through.

Neither dinosaur complained. They were seasoned campaigners, too. But by the end Little Nell was staggering and wheezing and clearly about to drop, and the matadora was in no better shape.

"I've checked her as best I can," Karyl said, turning to Rob, "and aside from some tenderness, which is to be expected, I can't find anything wrong with her. But I'd like you to run your expert eye across her too, if you will."

"Of course I will," Rob said. Of course Karyl was making a kind gesture for the man he, improbably, still held to be a friend. Karyl had been, to all practical purposes, a full dinosaur master far longer than ever Rob had. That was one of the reasons he'd been drawn to the man so strongly—that and the hero worship. Most fighting nobles who could afford war-dinosaurs loved them, as best they could. But they didn't understand thing one about caring for them. That was why the peasant dinosaur masters could continue to be highly paid and in demand. And why nobles were called bucketheads, so far as Rob was concerned. But Karyl was the exception.

As in so many things.

Rob began trudging the seven or eight meters around the fire toward Shiraa, feeling as if it were a mere eight-kilometer journey. But his steps faltered—more than they had already—when Karyl brought his head up and stared sharply at him. Then stopped when Rob realized his friend was looking *past* him.

"Karyl," a soft feminine voice said from behind Rob.

Rob spun about. A small female figure in a robe with a hood thrown back stood not four meters behind him, where the glow of the deliberately weak fire could touch her gold hair with fiery highlights.

"Aphrodite!" he exclaimed. "You gave me a turn, there, lass. How did you get here? And how did you find us, when we've barely found ourselves? It's uncanny, it is, and not another thing."

A brighter light shone on her face, illuminating a rapidly hardening expression. Rob's nut sack tightened as if trying to squeeze up into his belly. He'd seen a glow—a glare—of that peculiar, unsettling color and quality earlier tonight. And before.

"Shiraa," hissed the matadora, and rustled to her feet. Nell snorted and bobbed her head in agitation.

Rob smelled sulfur, lavender, and ozone. He heard Karyl's sword whisper free of its concealing staff.

"What are you doing here, monster?" Karyl said softly. It made the undercurrent of rage in his voice more chilling than histrionics would have been.

Soft female laughter answered. It sounded like that of a purely human woman, if spiteful. Almost. "Is that gratitude, to the one who saved your life? Again? To say nothing of your lackey's."

Fearing what he'd see, Rob spun back the other way, making himself dizzy in the process. Karyl had turned to face a tall woman whose slender naked body shone like blue lightning. "A Faerie!" Rob croaked.

He fell on his face and covered the back of his head with his hands. Terror tried to shake his mind to pieces.

"Not *a* Faerie, Rob Korrigan," said *that voice*. "The Queen of the Fae. Uma is the name I choose to be called."

"Rob," said Karyl, in a tone of well-strained patience, "you can't possibly believe the Faerie Queen is less likely to destroy you if you're lying with your beard in the dirt and your rump in the air."

"When I was a child," Rob said, in a voice so composed it almost frightened him, "I was taught that if I pulled my blanket over my head when I slept, the Fae couldn't get me."

"And how well did that work?"

"It didn't," Uma said, with an even more venomous laugh. "You should know that once you've been touched by the Fae, we never let you go—Korrigan."

Slowly Rob picked himself up. *I'm not scared anymore*, he thought, as he ruefully brushed bits of dirt from his beard. *This is all too unreal for me to be afraid.*

"You are persistent, I'll grant," Karyl said to the glowing woman-shaped creature. The icy anger had returned. "I was willing to die back there, if it would've averted this disastrous war. At least I'd be dying for something."

"I gave you back your life. It's mine now. As I told the Count, before I roasted him like a yam."

"Your interference destroyed everything I was trying to accomplish. Do you want war?"

"It was inevitable anyway."

"Do you mean because of the Grey Angel in the

Palace? The one who's masqueraded for years as the Emperor's confessor?"

"Oh, so you finally figured that out."

"His name is Uriel," said Aphrodite.

"But no," Uma said.

"Now we're outlaws," Karyl said, "thanks to you. Every word I said in opposition to the war can now be safely brushed aside by Margrethe and her allies."

"We were outlaws anyway, Karyl," Rob said. "And you might as well put away your sword. It'll do no good against the Fae."

"This one will," Karyl said. But he sheathed it and stuck the staff through his belt.

"I'm glad you're here too, Aphrodite," Rob said. "Witch or no, at least you're human flesh and blood like us. Perhaps there's strength in numbers, after all."

Karyl looked at her. "You tell him."

"I am sorry, Baron Korrigan. I am the Spirit of Paradise, and Caretaker of this world, and I am not here in physical form. I am also the one known in legend as the Witness. I am a sprite, more akin to Uma than to either of you. Although she hates me, and would love to destroy me."

"Of course I would, Aphrodite, dear," said Uma. "And I shall, someday. But not today."

"If you're really the world's Caretaker," Rob said to Aphrodite, deliberately, thinking his way through it as he went along, "wouldn't it destroy the world to destroy you?"

"Yes."

"So you aim to destroy Paradise itself?" he asked the glowing figure. *I can't believe I'm questioning the Faerie Queen*, he thought. *But is it that much more unlikely than encountering her face to face, then?*

She laughed. "Of course! We want our world to be the way it was before the self-proclaimed Creators came and polluted it with the likes of you."

Rob turned to Karyl. "She's been after you to ally with her against the Grey Angels, hasn't she? That's what this is all about."

"It is," said Karyl.

"And why would we ever agree to so daft a thing, if you want to destroy us too?"

"To live a little longer," Uma said sweetly. She approached Karyl with regal strides. Shiraa rumbled in her throat. "To enjoy however many more precious minutes of crawling through the muck you call the world may remain to you. I don't have the means to destroy you yet. Who knows? I may not for many of your years! But the Angels mean to kill you *now*. And will, without my help."

Shiraa roared, so loud and fierce Rob could scarcely make out that, as always, she spoke her own name.

"Ah, little one," Uma said to her, smiling. "Sweet child. You're the one I really should be allying with, perhaps, you who broke the physical form of the monster Raguel. A noble action, indeed, if sadly his essence survived."

The Allosaurus lowered her head almost to the ground, glaring at the Faerie from beneath her nasal flanges and rumbling deep in her throat. Uma wagged a finger at her.

"But don't think of trying the same trick on me. It would have a most different outcome. And one I would actually come close to regretting."

"Why would you help us, then?" Rob asked.

"It gives me pleasure to thwart the Angels."

"And you, Aphrodite—you've come to talk some sense into Himself, I trust? To tell him to spurn this frightful creature's offer?"

She shook her head sadly. "I have come to urge Karyl to accept Uma's offer of alliance."

"Even now," Karyl said. "After all the things she's done."

"Now more than ever."

"So what's it to be Karyl, my love? Tell me yes—or tell me yes?"

"No. I thought I might be able to trust you, at least so far as combating the Grey Angels was concerned. But one or more of the Angels are trying to bring war between Nuevaropa and Trebizon, if not Turania as well. And what you did back in La Majestad gave them everything they need to do it."

The laugh she gave to that, Rob thought, was fit to kill fliers in midflight.

"Do you really think you can spurn me? Do you think you have a choice?"

"Yes," said Karyl. "And yes."

Uma flung out her arm, pointing southwest—back toward La Majestad on its plateau and Mount Glory beyond, both hidden by the ridge crest.

"You're wrong!" she cried. "You've no choice left at all but to join with me. Look!"

As if in response to the word, a bright golden glow appeared in the clouds above La Mesa de Gloria. It grew brighter and brighter, as if the sun had decided to pay a visit to Paradise in the middle of the night. Then came a blast of sound so terrific that Rob had to press his hands to his ears for the second time that night. It exploded the clouds away from the light.

The brightness descended through the clouds, toward what Rob Korrigan somehow knew, in his dread and wonder-surfeited soul, was the Imperial Heart.

"What in the name of the Old Hell's that?" he yelled.

Aphrodite had turned to look, and her expression was thunder.

"Gabriel," she said.

PART FOUR

Arrival

Epilogue

Gabriel, *La Fuerza de Dios,* Strength of God.—One of the Seven Grey Angels, the Creators' Own Seven servitors and vindicators of Their divine justice. Alone among the Angels, She considers Herself female; her Aspect is that of a woman, inhumanly beautiful and tall, with pale skin, blue eyes, and red-gold hair. She serves Maia, Queen of the Creators, although it is also claimed that she frequently chooses to follow not Maia's Attribute as Mother but Her secondary, destructive and punitive side instead. Gabriel is associated with Raguel the God-Friend and Zerachiel, God's Command. Vulgar legend claims that during the High Holy War, She was captured, imprisoned, and tormented for a time by the demonios, or Fae. While we know little today of what, if any, supernatural component that great, global War might truly have had, that myth could certainly account for her reputation as perhaps the most capricious and dangerous of Grey Angels.

> —A PRIMER TO PARADISE FOR THE IMPROVEMENT
> OF YOUNG MINDS

Dearest Daddy and Melodía,
I'm free!
   Well, not yet, quite. But almost.

Yesterday sails appeared on the eastern horizon. As they got closer the lookout recognized them as a squadron of four triremes of the Imperial Trebizon Navy. As they came closer, my kidnappers began to get nervous. Tasoula was escorting me for my walk on deck with Mistral. I'd still rather have her do that than Paraskeve, even though she still smells bad, despite the sailors all complaining. I hate Paraskeve so much.

The sailors got excited, saying the squadron was moving to intercept us, and the Captain came on deck, trying to look important but mostly just looking as if he'd gotten some spoiled meat as well as being afraid.

Dragos came up to stand with me at the rail. I asked him why the Trebizonés would be so upset that ships from their own Navy were going to come talk to us? He said perhaps their consciences were bothering them.

They were standing a few meters away from me muttering to themselves. I could hear what they said. They still don't think I know any Griego. Did I mention I'm learning Griego? I can understand a lot of what people say now. Some.

It was enough. They were talking about magic. Tasoula was whimpering that the Creators had forsaken them. Vlasis said it was a matter of the mortal vessels regaining strength after expending so much to escape from the docks at Laventura. I guess he meant them? Anyway, for some reason they couldn't use magic now.

I didn't ask Dragos why they'd want to use magic against their own Navy. Even though he seems to know how to keep a secret, I didn't think it'd be a good idea to ask that question.

Especially since the only idea I could come up with was that they had kidnapped me and murdered Clau-

dia without the Basileus's permission. Maybe they even did it to hurt the Basileus somehow. Or Crown Prince Mikael.

One thing I knew for sure: they were terribly scared.

Anyway, the Trebizon Navy intercepted the ship. Their commodore and his captain came on board with some mean-looking Marines, and a big parchment sealed with what Dragos told me was the official seal of Crown Prince Mikael, shortly before making himself scarce. I don't know if they arrested the people who kidnapped me or what. They took them belowdecks to talk to them.

Next thing I know a pleasant and very young-looking Lieutenant, I think, Eleftherios had taken me under his wing. He spoke excellent Spañol, and seemed very concerned to make sure I hadn't been hurt or mistreated in any way. I said, except for being kidnapped from my own home and my friend Claudia murdered before my eyes, everything was fine. He said he was very sorry for that, and said he spoke for the Crown Prince in that, and that His Highness would do what he could to make it up to me, as well as to my family and the Empire.

Next thing I knew they'd moved me from the cramped little storeroom Mistral and I had been locked in to where I'm writing this, what they call a "stateroom," in the back of the ship.

She paused and set aside her pen, making sure to scatter some sand on the sheet of paper she'd been writing on to set the ink and keep it from smudging. She set the pen down on a pewter holder.

Mistral was on the desk beside her. Montse shooed her away from the writing paper. A ferret couldn't jump any higher than the arched-back hopping that constituted the animals' all-purpose dance, which could mean anything from anger to an invitation to play. Misti was a resourceful and determined climber, though, who could reach the most amazing places. Now she rolled over on her back, tucked her black forepaws to her silky silver-furred chest, and peered intently at Montse with obsidian-bead eyes.

I know what that means, Montse thought. "Yes, yes, I know you're cute," she said, and reached over to scratch her friend's belly.

She glanced out the window. Two triremes flanked the carrack's wake, easily pacing the bigger ship with breeze-bellied sails and long white oars sweeping in unison as they dipped into the white-frothed green waves. They were very beautifully made and functioning ships, and she hoped she could learn all about how they were built and how they worked. Montse could tell they must be extra-important vessels; where the Trebizonés Naval vessels she'd seen outside Laventura Harbor had plain white sails, these were painted gold, with the Trebizon arms of an octopus grappling a carrack in its tentacles painted on them in purple.

I never realized how ominous that insignia was before, she thought. Now that she saw it flying from a sleekly voracious blue-and-white warship, the implications became pretty obvious.

She put her hand around Mistral's belly, rolled her over, picked her up, and set her on the floor. The ferret hopped and beeped in mock-displeasure, then ran away under the bed to hide.

Like the rest of the stateroom, the bed was very much nicer than what she had in the musty-smelling little storeroom where they'd kept her before. It was even suspended in such a cunning way that it stayed mostly right side up when the waves rolled the ship, instead of tumbling her from wall to wall while her blanket pile tangled her up like the tentacles of Trebizon's heraldic octopus, the way she had when sleeping in the storeroom.

She wondered if the kidnappers would get locked in there now. *I hope so*, she thought. Vlasis got vilely seasick.

She took up the pen and wrote.

I'm locked in here, and there are a couple big Marines on guard. But Lieutenant Eleftherios assures me they're for my own protection. And I sort of believe him. After all, I was kidnapped, and the ship's crew were hired by the people who kidnapped me.

He said they're escorting the Karagiorgos to some fortified island a day or two's sail ahead, depending on how the wind blows. The Crown Prince is coming to meet us there. And see me on my way home to you!

I'm so happy, now that this will all be over soon. I miss you both very much and love you both very much. And please tell Cousin Jaume I love him too, and I know it wasn't his fault he and his Companions didn't rescue me. They would have, except nobody can fight against magic. I saw it.

I really hope it isn't true that Prince Mikael never bathes and smells bad. Because that would be gross.

See you soon!

Love,
Montse

Surrounded by her eyeball-scorching glory, the winged woman descended deliberately toward the Patio.

Melodía would not look away, though she had to hold up her hand and squint through barely parted fingers to stand the glare. She realized that the apparition maintained the same apparent size even as she got closer—a neat trick, although almost certainly an illusion.

All around her, Melodía heard shrieks of terror. She sensed people running away. She could hardly blame them, even though they were abandoning their Emperor to whatever fate this was.

I'm not scared, she realized, in added wonder. Even though she knew already there was only one kind of creature on Paradise the woman could be. And it was not a Faerie.

I guess at this point I'm just too curious as to what could possibly happen next.

The light winked out. The woman touched down, dropping to one knee on the bare rock of the great ledge and bowing her head. Her white-feathered wings enfolded her, then seemed to retract into her shoulders.

She stood, a full two and a half meters tall. She was dressed in white plate armor with the black-and-white *taijitu* emblem of Sacred Equilibrium on the breast. She had scabbarded the longsword at her waist, and allowed the golden post-horn to hang by a sling that appeared to be made of gilded leather.

She shook a cascade of long, kinky red-gold hair back over the flared pauldrons that guarded her shoulders.

"I am the Grey Angel Gabriel, Your Majesty," she said. "I have come to lead your army to destroy the evildoers who kidnapped your daughter."